Run Down the Wind

Laurence Eubank

WILD DOG PRESS

Copyright © 2013 by Laurence Eubank

All rights reserved. This book or any portion thereof may not be reproduced or used in any manner whatsoever without the express written permission of the publisher except for the use of brief quotations in a book review.

Printed in the United States of America

First Printing, 2013

ISBN 978-0-9894223-0-7

Wild Dog Press
www:http//rundownthewind.com
www:http//laurenceeubank.com

Dedication

To my mother and father
Dorothy Marie and Berton Eugene

Acknowledgments

A novel comes through a writer, but to my mind it is somehow the sum of all the people and experiences that came before, collected in the mysterious way a story appears. Without others' encouragement, attention, reactions, clarity, and editing chops, the journey would be far lonelier than it is. Notwithstanding all the other contributions, I extend great appreciation to these women and men, in some sort of calendar order:

Katherine Paul, for the very first edit, so precise and utterly invaluable.

Truette Stubbs – a native Georgian seer whose name I borrowed for one of my favorite characters.

Trissa Otto, for years of unflagging support and belief.

The Men, for their reading, questions, thoughtful considerations, delight, and bedrock constancy.

Dear son Louis – raising you got me thinking how boys became men when things were really tough.

Martha, for everything.

Anne, Dorothy, John – my siblings – all disassembled and recast in various pieces throughout.

Alan Rinzler – developmental editor – a pro's pro, one of the unanticipated sparkles.

Leslie Tilley – consummate copy editor (imagine an English teacher who makes you grin).

Laura Duffy – cover design – it looks this fabulous because of her.

Joel Friedlander – interior design and production – he's so good you don't notice.

John Swan – painter – I asked him to read the book and then create what he saw, and he did, magnificently.

Alin Wall, for providing the last loving vessel I needed to bring this home.

Also, to many, many readers along the way, whose comments – every single one – became part of this manuscript.

To all, thank you.

Author's Note

Many of the events in this novel happened (see History, at the back of the book); I needed only to sweep these characters into mid-19th century reality, and off we went. The origin of why is murkier – an idea takes hold and won't let you be – but three fascinations stood constant:

1. Clipper ships rose in their glory for nine years, give or take, from 1851 to 1860, truly stupendous achievements of construction and operation. The schematic detail of these vessels is jaw-dropping mastery. Then, when they were built – a 200-foot ship rising from keel to launch in three months – captains flung them around the world using a sextant, sun, moon, and the night sky to navigate immense and highly dangerous seas. I am in awe of the builders and sailors alike.
2. Sir Winston Churchill observed, "The American Civil War, which must upon the whole be considered the noblest and least avoidable of all the great mass conflicts of which till then there was record," though receding into history, still affects our daily lives.
3. Anticipating a boys-to-men adventure, I found introducing women made the novel more complex. Since I was raised in a family of iron-willed females, they naturally became the frames for the formidable heroines who wed our heroes, bear children, build the families, and stand among the strongest characters in the book.

Though largely scrupulous with real names, dates, and places, I do not claim complete accuracy. Please accept variances from actual fact with literary tolerance.

Any character's resemblance to people living may or may not be intended.

John Swan, my cover artist, said the only thing that annoyed him about my novel was that it ended. A sequel percolates, I assured him. Go forward a century, the southern side of the Tennessee River, around Muscle Shoals: Calhoun, Hatcher, Norton.

Thank you for considering my novel. Read on – I hope you enjoy. Please let me know.

Safe travels,

Laurence Eubank   Laurence@laurenceeubank.com
May 2013   www:http//laurenceeubank.com
Santa Monica, CA 90403   www:http//rundownthewind.com

Run Down the Wind

A SHIP'S SAILS.

INDEX OF REFERENCES

1 Fore topmast staysail
2 Jib
3 Flying Jib
4 Fore spencer
5 Main spencer
6 Spanker
7 Foresail
8 Fore topsail
9 Fore topgallant sail
10 Fore royal
11 Fore skysail
12 Mainsail
13 Main topsail
14 Main topgallant sail
15 Main royal
16 Main skysail
17 Mizen topsai

18 Mizen topgallant sail
19 Mizen royal
20 Mizen skysail
21 Lower studdingsail
21ª Lee ditto
22 Fore topmast studdingsail
22ª Lee ditto
23 Fore topgallant studdingsail
23ª Lee ditto
24 Fore royal studdingsail
24ª Lee ditto
25 Main topmast studdingsail
25ª Lee ditto
26 Main topgallant studdingsail
26ª Lee ditto
27 Main royal studdingsail
27ª Lee ditto

Chapter One

Cape Horn, June 1851

Lester fought for balance as the ship rolled and pitched in the cross-sea running a hundred feet below. Moments later, the big clipper breasted a wave and the boy inched away from the mast on a footrope no thicker than his thumb. Sleet struck like needles; the squall clawed at him. Dawn was three hours off.

Working blind in the rising wind, trying to swallow his fear, he leaned into the spar and grabbed fistfuls of canvas, wrestling the sail as it tugged and snapped. *Flying Cloud* lurched over another wave and a glob of snow smacked above his collar; moments later an icy trickle made him suck in his shoulder blades.

Groping for the rope gaskets that bundled the sail, Lester could smell the salt-beef breath of his shipmate an arm's length further outboard. Suddenly, a gust ripped the canvas from his grip, tearing a fingernail and flooding him with terror.

Jubal seized his shoulder. "Pull yerself in, Lester!"

Above the squall they heard a sharp command from aft. Captain Josiah Creesy had a voice that could make men wince.

"Strike the maincourse!"

"They're gonna lose it!" Jubal's high-pitched drawl sounded puny against the keening wind.

How his shipmate sensed anything on such a wild night was beyond Lester, though Jubal was as nimble in the rigging aloft as a squirrel running through treetops. Immense relief spun to embarrassment; Lester hated feeling inferior, particularly since his friend was likely younger, though he wasn't sure.

Cries chorused forward, immediately lost to a bedlam of canvas snapping like staccato cracks of gunfire. Lester shuddered, imagining the struggle high on the main mast, more than two hundred feet from deck to top, nearly as tall as *Flying Cloud* was long. After weeks at sea every sailor knew the ship intimately and never forgot that a wrong step or a misjudged handhold aloft meant death.

The wind had risen, its moan turning to wail, and the huge billowing sail—the largest aboard—threatened to overwhelm the ship's wheel. In a building sea, an overpowered clipper could careen down the swells like a canoe in rapids and twist sideways, to stumble and go under, vanishing without a trace.

Being the youngest crewmembers, Jubal and Lester handled the sails on the mizzen mast, aft, the smallest of the three masts rigging the ship, though it was the size and height of a mature fir tree. As they wrestled the sail into its gaskets, a sudden flash of lightning cracked overhead. In the instant, intense light, Lester saw thirty other men clinging aloft as the ship plunged into another trough of churning sea. In moments, the lightning snuffed like a doused candle, bringing some small comfort. Darkness was less frightening.

At the mast, he could barely discern his shipmate, a blacker mass against the night. As the ship rose and rolled to leeward, Jubal swung onto the wrist-thick shrouds and in one fluid motion sped down the net-like webbing of ratlines toward the deck. Lester paused and held tight as the ship heeled back to weather; the ratlines had iced, and losing footing on the weather roll would leave a man hanging above the sea.

On deck, the ship's bell rang. Eight bells, four in the morning, the end of the middle watch. He would have four hours to eat breakfast and sleep before the second mate rousted him for the forenoon watch. Two weeks earlier, when they were still above the equator, the first mate, Mr. Wainwright, had shown a rare flash of sympathy, growling it would get easier as he got older. Lester could only hope he'd become as accustomed to this routine as his shipmates, who seemed to regard four hours of wet sleep as normal.

Clinging to a lifeline, he hauled himself across the sloping deck. A knee-high wave swept under him but he groped toward the forecastle—the "forward castle" of medieval ships that over centuries had been spliced in syllables and lowered to a low-slung cabin housing the crew.

As Lester reached the forecastle door it flew open, nearly knocking him flat. A man snarled, slamming him aside with a forearm before two dozen sailors clambered past for the dawn watch. Lester struggled with the door as another wave washed the deck before staggering down the short steps into the crew's mess. Despite his oilskins, he was soaked.

Jubal had already wedged himself into the leeward bench, his face buried in a bowl. Nearby, a short, wizened black man labored over the long mess table balancing a steaming kettle. Cookie rode the ship's movement effortlessly, the whites of his eyes glowing out of a face the color and texture of a pitted prune.

Lester grabbed a bowl off the table and thrust it forward, watching carefully as Cookie ladled scouse, a rheumy sludge of porridge, lard, and molasses. A burly seaman thundered in and snatched Lester's full bowl from his hand, then slumped on the mess table bench, giving Jubal a careful berth. Another six men came through the doorway and took portions before Lester claimed his breakfast. A lamp rocked from a deck beam, throwing shadows across the ceiling. No one spoke.

Lester knew the seaman would have faced a knife had he tried to take Jubal's bowl. When Lester had come aboard the first night in New York, an older sailor also signed on and brought his duffel into the mess. Deciding he didn't like any of the remaining bunks, the man unceremoniously grabbed Jubal by the collar, yanked him out of his bunk and chucked Jubal's duffel onto the deck.

To the crew's utter astonishment, Jubal attacked the sailor. Quick as a cat he kneed him in the groin and had his knife tip on the man's eyelid. In the dead silence that followed, Lester, who'd never fought anyone but his younger brother, held his breath.

The message plain, Jubal calmly retrieved the meager duffel and climbed back in his empty bunk. No one had messed with the boy since.

"Soon as you stand up to one of 'em, Lester," Jubal had drawled later, "they'll stop treatin' you like a lubber."

Lester shoveled the hot, sweet porridge. "Bastardly weather," he tried to get the cadence just right, sneaking a glance. Men ate in silence, ignoring him.

Cookie grunted. "This'n barely a blow." Talking made his face pucker. He slid a ragged sleeve across his nose, taking a dribble of snot. "Horn'll show you weather. We 'bout there."

Cookie slopped scouse into two more bowls.

"Go t'ween decks," he ordered Jubal, "give to them buggerin' bastards."

Jubal bit his lip and stared at the deck for a moment before throwing his own bowl into a large washing tub. He snatched at the bowls, piling one onto the other, and reeled out of the forecastle. The door slammed.

Cookie spit onto the sodden deck. "Alabama, that boy," he observed with a dry, toothless snort. "Niggah on top riles 'im—gits all swelled up.

'Specially hauling slop for them Limeys."

Lester shuddered. One of the Liverpool sailors that now lay locked in irons had given him a look shortly after he boarded, something between a leer and the frank assessment of fresh meat. The men had signed on after being stranded in New York from a weekend leave neither could remember. While *Flying Cloud* ran down her easting into the mid-Atlantic, they'd surreptitiously bored holes under their bunks through the hull, hoping to force the Captain to England. Once the ship found the northeast trade winds she would turn south and be gone, heading on the long, downhill run past the bulge of Brazil on her way to Cape Horn.

Two feet of seawater sloshed in the hold before the ship's carpenter found their sabotage.

Lester scraped his second bowl clean as Jubal returned, swaying with fatigue, which made Lester feel better.

In the starboard forecastle, snores sawed from double bunks along the hull. The dank, dim room smelled of rancid whale oil, unwashed men, and wet wool. A small lamp swung from a deck beam, cutting the blue tobacco smoke of a man puffing his pipe. Lester staggered forward and waited for the roll; with a rough sea running, he could almost fall into his upper bunk.

As *Flying Cloud* sailed south from the equator, weather accelerated through the seasons. Approaching the bottom of South America a few days before the southern winter solstice, all aboard expected a hellish passage as the ship pushed west around Cape Horn, outbound to San Francisco. The risk was worth it—many crewmen were sure to jump ship, joining passengers headed for the Sierra Nevada foothills where gold had been discovered three years earlier.

Lester sucked the finger to salve the torn nail and keep his lip from quivering, finally tightening his eyes against welling tears. Aloft, the sudden clap of ripping canvas had sent shivers of memory coursing through him, a sound of fresh bed sheets snapping in the sunshine, of his mother hanging laundry along the Penobscot River in Maine on the day in late summer when she had asked for his help to feed the family.

The ship fell off a wave and heeled hard over. Lester let his body roll, and tucking his legs up, curled into the corner of his bunk. Tears mingled with the damp, moldy bedcovers until he finally fell asleep, still sucking his finger.

Chapter Two

"Turn to, starborlines! Do ye hear the news?"

Lester thought he was climbing out of a well. A rap on the chest startled him awake and he lay disoriented, wondering why they wouldn't let him sleep for more than a few minutes. Men shuffled and somewhere the ship's bell rang. With a groan, Lester realized the port watch was coming into the forecastle and he would be last of the starboard watch on deck again.

"Move your ass, Yank!"

"Damn you, Jubal!" Lester spit, but the boy was already out of the forecastle. A blast of snow blew the door open and swallowed a sharp command from on deck.

The wind had risen to a full gale. Under a gloomy dawn the sea churned, long tendrils of foam whipping off twenty-foot crests that marched at the ship in relentless procession. Lester stared at the slushy, phlegm-colored mixture of snow and seawater swirling on deck, knowing his oil-coated leather boots would be saturated in minutes.

"Norton!" Mr. Wainwright pointed to the shadowy lumps of men in the rigging on both sides of the ship, scrambling aloft or waiting for the roll as the ship bore through heavy seas. Lester grabbed the lifeline and slogged through a trail of slush, close on Jubal's heels. Climbing the icy ratlines, they both glanced eastward, judging the intermittent streak that looked like a long, mottled bruise on the horizon.

"T'will be a dirty day," Jubal drawled as they reached the mizzen topsail yard and waited on the roll.

"Ain't right a man should freeze in July," Lester griped. "A few months back, snow was waist deep in the woods, and here I am in winter again, soaked much as a damn cod! Now is high summer along the river, too, weather comin' fine." The thought made him misty. He could imagine the farmhouse on a rise above the Penobscot, apple blossoms littering the yard, corn and millet sprouting, little brother Johnny chasing a piglet around the barn while his sister Sally complained about something. "'Stead I'm hanging off a clipper in a damn snowstorm, like to spit at the ass end of South America!"

"Ain't home," Jubal agreed. "You'd likely bitch there jes' the same."

"Summer anywhere'd be right by me!"

"Come July, August, you'd melt in Alabama," replied Jubal, carefully. Occasionally his voice still broke. "Cotton greenin' along the bottomland—now that'd show you hot ..."

The boys sidled onto the yard and leaned together for warmth, waiting to gather sail when the mate slackened sheets from on deck.

"How come you get so crank with Cookie?" Lester asked.

Jubal bolted upright. "Ain't his place!" he snarled, moving along the yard. He stopped and pointed upward. Lester followed his gaze.

"There! The Cross—it's almost overhead."

"You can't see nothing!" Lester scoffed, annoyed at Jubal's abrupt change of subject to something he could brag about. Lester couldn't see a thing through the solid overcast; he hadn't been able to find the Southern Cross in a week.

"Bet capt'n will fall off, put her stern through and come onto the port tack."

Jubal's testiness had vanished but the nonchalance grated Lester.

"What for?" he challenged.

Jubal looked aft. "Figured."

Turning, Lester saw a small figure move across the quarterdeck to the windward rail and face the dawn. Against long, malevolent ranks of windblown seas, the silhouette seemed at once frail and majestic. Suddenly, the figure turned in one elegant movement and walked over to the wheelhouse. In the middle of the pirouette, a gust passed aboard, opening the unmistakable swirl of a woman's skirt like a delicate fan.

Two men faced the wheel. The helmsman had planted his feet wide to ride the roll as the ship rose and fell southward. Next to him a bearded man in oilskins sat in a high sea chair, his feet drawn up. Hesitant, white puffs from his cigar whisked away in the wind. He leaned to bend forward as the woman drew near. The boys watched as she took the bearded man's arm and steadied herself against the roll, his sea cap obscuring her face. A moment later she turned and paused, still holding the man's arm, while he covered her hand until the ship briefly steadied, then let her go. Sashaying with the roll, the woman swung around the wheelhouse and disappeared below.

At the wheel, the helmsman briskly nodded, turned to judge the swell, and then spun the big wheel one full turn. Slowly the clipper came ten degrees off the wind. A moment later the yard beneath the boys moved as deckhands trimmed the sail to run dead downwind into the morning.

"Another point to leeward," Jubal grumbled, "we'd have tacked."

Chapter Three

Eleanor Creesy paused at the top of the companionway stairs and waited until the seaway came dead astern. As a large swell lifted the ship she lightly descended and spun around the newel post and swept into the captain's cabin, closing the door behind her. With a soft chamois, she dabbed the salt spray off her sextant and nestled it into a mahogany case. Discarding her bulky oilskin jacket for a Kashmir woolen shawl, Eleanor moved over to the gimbaled teapot, and balanced against the roll, poured a shallow, steaming cupful. She savored a breath from the warm porcelain while mentally reworking her trigonometry.

Five days of overcast had obscured both sun and stars, preventing a solid position fix. Eleanor had gone on deck at dawn hoping for a glimpse of the waning moon to verify their position with a lunar sight. Although the captain trusted her navigation, Eleanor was uneasy approaching Cape San Diego and the Straits of Maire at ten knots. Before dawn, she had plotted their dead reckoning position two hundred miles north of Cape Horn and then worked backward, calculating the lunar angle that should correspond. Though she couldn't see the moon precisely, Eleanor thought they were several miles closer to the South American coast and made a mental note to include the current in her log notes.

"I think we've been set, Josiah," she had told her husband coming off the rail. "You need more sea room—a point will do now. Cape San Diego is about thirty miles; we should fetch it to starboard."

In the warmth of their cabin, Eleanor smiled, remembering her husband's reaction. Josiah had said nothing, but simply nodded and pressed her hand. A few moments later the ship had turned a point off the wind.

Still clutching the shawl close, she poured more tea. From a lacquered Chinese bowl, a heaping spoonful of sugar went into the cup, and she stirred, admiring the silver spoon's intricate Cyrillic lettering. After a pause she added a second teaspoon. Eleanor knew it would hurt the back tooth that needed pulling, but she shrugged, admitting it wasn't her only sweet tooth. The ship's supply of cream had curdled six weeks ago, eight days out of New York, which meant no more until San Francisco.

The tea tasted lovely and she spooned the last syrupy dregs. With a final, slow lick, she reached for the logbook and ink set before pulling a blank positioning worksheet out of the credenza and turning to her charts.

The captain's quarters were elegantly furnished with burnished mahogany paneling, leather settees, brocade curtains, and Persian rugs. Opposite the entry door, satinwood credenzas housing the sextant and other instruments flanked a rosewood table covered with nautical charts secured by movable brass rods. Above the table, slatted shelves held more charts and the ship's library, its titles dimly visible in the pewter dawn sky filtering through a leaded-glass skylight. For Eleanor, their cabin was sacrosanct, an oasis of comfort in the midst of a working ship.

She studied the charts and a newly published compendium of marine information she had insisted on bringing aboard. Seasonal conditions in every ocean, weather patterns, wind direction and speed, currents and tidal variations, monsoons, trade winds, tropical storm systems, and the shortest routes across the doldrums were distilled into two neat volumes. While many captains disdained the new material, preferring to command from their own experience, Eleanor regarded that attitude as obstinate and foolish.

"I don't believe we need this," Captain Creesy said to her when she first showed him the manuals, a week before their departure from New York.

"I do," she had replied. "I bought them this morning."

From a drawer, she withdrew a leather-bound book and briefly scanned entries over the past few days. Each was in the same, bold handwriting that flowed across the first page:

Log of Ship "Flying Cloud," J.S. Creesy Commander
Sailed from New York, June 2nd 1851 bound to San Francisco

On the position sheet, she noted their latitude and longitude, course, distance run in the last twenty-four hours, and wind direction. At noon, when her husband came below to share dinner, she would update the information, and he would make the log entry. As captain, Josiah Creesy was solely and utterly responsible to the ship's New York owners, Griswold and Sons, its two hundred tons of cargo bound for the California goldfields, and all souls aboard—sixty-eight crew, including himself and his wife, plus seventeen paying passengers.

Eleanor did the navigating; the log was his.

Three hours later, Lester stood high on the foremast crosstree, his arm linked through a line. Jubal's second lecture aboard had explained that each mast was in fact a three-piece, stacked assembly—a lower, top, and topgallant mast, each successively narrower, banded to the one below at a wooden ledge, the crosstree. Large enough for two or three men to sit comfortably, the crosstree also provided a lookout platform.

Memories of Jubal's first lecture, begun within five minutes of their meeting each other a month earlier at the wharves on South Street, still humiliated Lester. The mate had ordered Jubal to acquaint Lester with the ship since it was his first trip on a square-rigger.

"She's got three masts, fore, main, and mizzen, front to back," Jubal began, in a drawl so thick Lester wondered how anyone could understand.

"I know," Lester said. "Where you from? You talk like you're pouring cold molasses."

"Four sails to a mast," Jubal continued, "bottom to top: course, topsail, topgallant, 'n royal, each got its yard—them's the spars they hang from. End of it's called the yard-*arm*, 'cause that's where the stunsails git rigged when we're drivin'— they hang way the hell out there."

"I know," Lester lied. "Down South?"

"Lines. The standing rigging keeps the masts up? Them's shrouds. Halyards raise and lower the sails; sheets control on one tack or t'other. That's when the ship turns, puts the wind on the other side, starboard or port, right and left lookin' forward. Port tack, starboard tack … Git it?"

"I worked a schooner off Georges Bank," Lester declared, on safer footing, though his father's fishing boat wasn't much larger than the clipper's longboats. "I ain't no lubber. How old are you? Where you from?"

"Older 'n you."

"I'm near fifteen."

"Good fer you."

No way he's fifteen, Lester had often thought since, a conceit that comforted him as he hunched against the gale and tried to keep still. Now, a sodden woolen comforter chafed his neck but he stared ahead, mindful of the first mate's ferocious order to spot land while the ship had time to tack.

Below him, he felt the shrouds shiver; Jubal raced the ship's roll, ascending as if running up a ladder. Jubal cupped his hand to Lester's ear.

"Seen anything?" The Alabama drawl pulled his syllables apart.

"Snow," Lester grunted.

"Better 'n rain!"

Lester agreed. Snow was annoying but nothing could make a man miserable like freezing rain.

"Lord, let this easterly keep in," Jubal hollered against the wind. "We turn the corner, by God, capt'n'll drive her on!"

"What'll she carry?" Lester didn't like giving Jubal the opportunity to be an authority, but yelling took his mind off the cold, raw weather, and Jubal's voice might crack.

"Capt'n Creesy'll know!" Jubal ducked a blast of snow. "She's a Donald McKay ship. Ain't no man build finer, capt'n says."

Lester huddled closer. "Are we getting close to the cape? When do we hit it?"

"Don't. We run by it."

Lester ignored the jibe. He looked intently at the horizon, blurred by snow and overcast. Jubal spun, screaming to the deck below.

"Land ho!"

Lester ground his teeth.

"Where away?" Captain Creesy and Mr. Wainwright roared.

"A point to starboard!" Lester yelled, pointing ten compass degrees to the right off the bow.

Jubal had taken another look. "Dead ahead!"

Both boys stared forward. The coastline materialized out of the pewter morning like a sneer across the horizon.

"All hands! Prepare to tack!" Wainwright bellowed. Jubal was already off the crosstree onto the ratlines. As Lester waited for the roll he looked aft. Eleanor Creesy had come on the quarterdeck and was talking with the captain.

Chapter Four

Jubal licked his salt-beef gravy and noticed the untouched plate. Lester sat sound asleep. Quickly switching plates, Jubal shoveled the food, nearly choking, his cheeks bulging.

A resounding thump sounded off the forecastle ceiling. "Starborlines on deck!" Lester awoke with a start and stared incomprehensibly at the empty plate as the watch shuffled out. Jubal was already at the companionway, pulling a woolen cap low.

Lester caught him as they mustered in the ship's waist under gray, scudding clouds. "Bastard!" he hissed, "I wanted that slop!"

"You wanted sleep."

Lester bunched his fists but Jubal ignored him. Lester quivered, working himself to frothing, when a distant hail from the masthead spun his attention skyward.

"Land ho!"

"Where away?" Captain Creesy called from the quarterdeck, already moving to the starboard rail.

"That'd be Cape Stiff," Mr. Wainwright said, not even bothering to look. "I can't believe it, an easterly off the Horn in winter. By God, you tars be lucky! Aloft now, set all sail!"

Jubal ran for the starboard mizzen ratlines and scampered aloft, Lester close behind. They shook out the mizzen topsail while other seamen manned the fore and main masts. As *Flying Cloud* gathered speed her bow surged forward and the rhythmic *whoosh* of parting waves could be heard from high in the rigging.

"There she be," pointed Jubal. "The Horn."

Lester looked to starboard across the water. Five miles away a cliff rose, foreboding and bleak above a snow-covered shore. The entire visage was shades of sinister—black rock, ugly sea, a grim, leaden sky. For a moment Lester shuddered at the frailty of life aboard ship, tossing at the bottom of the earth.

Jubal turned to Lester. "You couldn't finish that slop. Wainwright would've boxed your ears, coming on deck tardy." He jumped onto the ratlines, grinning, then reached into a pocket and tossed something.

Instinctively, Lester snatched at it.

"Some joker," he muttered, fingering the piece of salt beef, his anger already sapped. Lester stuffed the junk in his cheek and made to follow, feeling whole again.

As they came off the rigging and set off forward to report to Mr. Wainwright, a feminine voice stopped them in their tracks.

"Boys!" Eleanor Creesy called from the quarterdeck. The captain's wife stood at the rail with her husband, holding a telescope in mittened hands.

Lester shot a glance at Jubal, who looked as if he'd been snared. The rest of the watch was scattered about the deck or still in the rigging.

"Lester Norton, Jubal Calhoun!" Mrs. Creesy called again, motioning. The captain regarded them without expression, his eyes shining from a face covered in beard.

Lester stood frozen until Jubal elbowed him.

"Us, m'am?" Lester croaked, pointing at Jubal.

Captain Creesy walked toward the wheel and checked their compass heading. Eleanor Creesy turned seaward and opened the telescope to study Cape Horn. The boys snuck another look at each other before slowly moving aft and up to the quarterdeck, feeling as if they were walking the plank.

"Yes, m'am?" Jubal doffed his cap.

Eleanor Creesy studied the landmass a moment longer then collapsed the telescope deliberately, almost delicately, until it closed with a soft, metallic snap.

"Jubal," she said, "you're from where?"

"Alabama, m'am."

"Mobile, isn't it?"

"Near 'nough, m'am," he answered, after a pause that registered in Eleanor Creesy's eyes. "A ways inland, though I sort of call Mobile home."

She regarded him briefly, before turning. "Lester, you're a New Englander, correct?"

Lester cleared his throat. Mrs. Creesy was being disingenuous; he had arrived in New York with a letter addressed to her from his Aunt Dorcus. Upon his delivering it to the ship, Mrs. Creesy had read the letter and immediately ordered the mate to show Lester a berth below.

Now, he didn't know why he felt terrified, especially when Jubal seemed calm. "That's right, Mrs. Creesy, m'am ... Maine," he blurted. "South Orrington. Below Bangor, across the river."

"Downeast," Mrs. Creesy smiled, remembering. "Penobscot Bay's a lovely place. I used the Camden Hills and Mount Desert to triangulate."

The boys looked at her blankly. She smiled, and then laughed outright. "My father ran a coastal schooner out of Marblehead," she explained. "That's where I learned to navigate. He taught me."

The boys stood waiting; Lester swallowed, frozen in place.

"And," Mrs. Creesy continued, "now that we're turning the corner"—she nodded toward Cape Horn—"I'm going to teach you. Oh, don't worry," she said, catching their looks of alarm. "The captain approves, isn't that so, Perk?" She seemed to be enjoying herself.

Captain Creesy came over from the wheel. "Put your cap on," he ordered Jubal. Snowflakes fluttered through the morning air. "You boys stand your watches like the rest of the crew. When you're off watch, you can learn your numbers."

"I'll expect you here on the quarterdeck every day, at noon," Mrs. Creesy declared. "Today I'll give you some books to share. By San Francisco, we'll have two more navigators in case I decide to stay ashore." The Captain looked sideways and she laughed gaily. "Oh all right, Perk; I'll take you to China."

Later, while the boys huddled in the forecastle lee waiting out another snow squall, they talked about the turn of events.

"Why'd she do that?" Jubal asked.

"By Jesus, how should I know?" moaned Lester. He wanted to learn navigation, but not at the expense of sleep. "I'll be a walking moron by the Golden Gate."

"You got a headstart."

"Shut up. Why does she call him Perk?"

"Perkins his middle name. I heard other captains call him that, though I wouldn't consider it, I was you."

"Are you numb?" The idea of calling the captain Perk made Lester shudder. "Why do you suppose she ...?"

~

That night in their cabin, Eleanor was eager to talk about her intentions for Lester and Jubal.

Captain Creesy tried to head off the inevitable as they readied for bed. "My dear, these boys are young men, signed on as crew. I can't have you playing favorites now, it won't do for the temper of the ship."

"You mean Mr. Wainwright? I'll speak with him."

Captain Creesy backtracked at the alarming prospect. "No need of that, I just think it would better for the crew's morale if you didn't try to …"

Eleanor stood in the cabin, her face etched with all the hurt and sorrow of a woman who would never be a mother. To her everlasting sadness, Eleanor had been barren, or he had.

Josiah Creesy stopped and came to his wife. With no children of their own he couldn't begrudge her, though he would have to mollify his first mate.

Without another word, he took his wife in his arms and held her, then pulled away enough to look. Eleanor's eyes were moist. He stroked his wife's hair, then kissed her forehead and let her be.

Chapter Five

Miraculously, the easterly wind held as Cape Horn sank below the horizon astern. In a season when ferocious storms blew out of the west for weeks, piling waves that could dwarf the largest clippers, ships often spent a month or more making the distance from fifty degrees south latitude in the Atlantic to fifty degrees south in the Pacific. *Flying Cloud* rounded in a week.

Under a press of sail, Josiah Creesy drove his ship northward relentlessly, making clear he intended a record passage. Decks were often underwater as the ship, sometimes making eighteen knots in the sharp squalls—faster than the oldest sailor aboard had ever seen—slashed through seas that came at them like rows of moving hills.

In early August, *Flying Cloud* crossed the equator, having left the bitter winter seas far to the south. Captain Creesy ordered all sail before the steady trade winds that drove them north more than two hundred miles a day. With forty sails spreading ten thousand square feet of canvas, the ship resembled an immense swan with a small hull attached to her feet, flung astride a vast air current to ride up the Pacific Ocean.

For Lester and Jubal, these were idyllic weeks. Though Wainwright kept the crew scrubbing and polishing, and *Flying Cloud* needed constant tuning as her manila and hemp rigging stretched, only minor sail trimming was necessary, making watches generally free of arduous labor.

Each day in good weather, Mrs. Creesy tutored the boys, who quickly understood she wouldn't brook slackers or tolerate sloppiness. Lester had more schooling and was the better reader but Jubal had a natural gift for numbers. Mrs. Creesy seemed clairvoyant, making Jubal focus on reading while directing Lester to concentrate on arithmetic. The boys were diligent, though different in their learning styles. Lester was always inquisitive, while Jubal hated to ask, though he showed natural intelligence that bordered on exceptional.

"You're mule stubborn, Jubal," Lester chided him after one lesson on the quarterdeck. "Why don't you just tell her you don't got it?" Jubal had miscalculated the ship's position and Mrs. Creesy was unmerciful.

"Your figuring is just about right, Jubal," she had said. "Though not quite. You're on the wrong side of the Pacific—our position is not off the coast of Luzon. We're closer to California." Jubal turned scarlet, realizing he'd added rather than subtracted from Greenwich time.

"Was up to you," Jubal snapped at his friend's teasing, "we'd be near Greenland." He had only gone to the one-room school for two years but wasn't going to tell that to Lester. "Why you s'pose she bothers with us? I don't recall asking to learn celestial navigation."

"Cookie say's 'cause she'd knew we was bright."

"Hard put for a dim man, knowin' what 'bright' is!"

Lester grinned; Jubal was still smarting from Mrs. Creesy's correction. "That thin skin of yours ain't a friend, Jubal."

Since leaving the high latitudes, passengers appeared on deck, where frequent card games, singing, and storytelling occupied many of the gold seekers. Most were men, so the handful of single women aboard could stroll under their parasols and enjoy a school of suitors following like minnows, eager for any scrap of interest.

Jubal and Lester often enjoyed the spectacle from aloft and made up stories to fit the scenes below.

"See that one there," Jubal said one afternoon, pointing to the ship's waist. "The feller shaped like a pear, following that corset? She could do some crushing, by God, with them hams. 'Course, she'd have to work to find it. Man that round gots to be having a mighty small pecker."

Lester laughed so hard he hugged a shroud to stay seated. "See his hand, always in his pocket, knotted right up?"

"How many times you done it?"

"Ah ..." Lester stroked his chin fuzz. "Well ..."

"Not includin' pigs or sheep."

Lester tried to punch him but Jubal scrambled out of reach.

"How'd you keep a mouthful of teeth, Jubal? I'm stumped you got any left—just be a matter of time."

"Yeah, well it won't be you." Jubal's tongue poked out his cheek. "How many times ...?"

"Truth is, I ain't done her yet." Lester looked sideways at Jubal, ready to charge any insult. "You?"

"Almost," Jubal replied.

"Almost? What? How can you 'almost'?" A sudden alarm seized him; he might be ignorant of something any man knows. "You either do it or you don't, right?"

"Coulda had me a little niggah girl," Jubal said. "Uncle told me was all right, thought I were ready."

"What happened?"

"T'were in the baling shed," Jubal's voice lowered, and his face went far away. "I come on hot, and she laying there kind of waitin' like."

"Yeah?"

Jubal shook his head. "She jes' stared to me. Then turned 'way, look a disgust I never did see. Throw'd my bacon right in the dirt."

"Just because she looked at you? What ...? Was she experienced?"

"Doubtful ... She weren't but ten. Lordy ... that look ..."

"Jeez. Your uncle said it was all right?"

Jubal shrugged. "She be his." He looked away. "Woulda been a poor go ..."

The boys were silent for a moment. Lester stared at the horizon. "When was that?"

"Better 'n a year ago," Jubal replied. "Near two ..."

"What was her name?"

The faint sound of the ship's bell rang from below. Jubal swung onto the shrouds. "C'mon, our watch is done."

Lester grabbed Jubal's shirt, suddenly desperate to know. "Dammit, man, can't you answer a simple enough question?"

Jubal yanked himself free. "Yank, you kin ask a week's worth of questions in five minutes!" He started down but stopped after a few steps. "Cora."

The boy danced down the ratlines.

Chapter Six

Captain Creesy grew terse as the ship sailed north, rarely speaking except to give orders. He seemed to live on deck and was noticeably thinner. Dinners with first-class passengers, where he had been an affable host, were a memory left in the Atlantic. Mrs. Creesy continued to extend the hospitality wealthier passengers expected, though by late August the entire ship's complement chafed to raise the Golden Gate. A record passage was possible; with good weather *Flying Cloud* could beat the standing record of ninety-six days from New York. For impatient passengers, every day at sea delayed their opportunity for adventure and wealth.

The crew was also anxious. Lester, who'd signed ship's articles for service until *Flying Cloud* returned to New York, gradually realized that many seamen intended to jump ship and head for the goldfields. He mentioned it to Jubal one evening, close on sunset. The ship had tacked six times as Captain Creesy clawed his way north through rainsqualls that kept hammering them with short, violent downpours.

"You know about Dandy?" Lester asked. The boys were catching their breath after wrestling sail, holding on as the ship labored in cross-seas against a biblical evening sky. High on the mast, they swung in long arcs that would have made Lester sick a few months earlier.

Dandy was the most vocal sailor in the forecastle, frequently anticipating the pleasures of his favorite San Franciscan whore, Carmelita. "That Chileano sweetie," Dandy had crowed, "be knockin' boots in no time!"

"He's jumping ship," Lester continued. "I heard him say the very same! Others, too!"

"They ain't the only ones," Jubal replied. "We'll be going ourselves."

Lester's mouth went slack. "We signed on! Gave our words!"

"You think Perk's going to follow a couple sailors up the Sacramento River?" Jubal scoffed. "I'm sick a being poor. Been poor all my life, and I'm done with it. Shit, we just dig in the river, be rich."

"You're crazy, Jubal Calhoun!"

"I'm poor," Jubal declared, "'n had my fill of it, every live-long day." Suddenly, he pointed forward. "I'm also getting the hell off this mast, see that there squall?"

Lester followed down the shrouds as the squall roared in, turning the twilight into gloom and blowing so hard he couldn't think. Rain chilled him and he felt deeply unsettled. The idea that Jubal had dreamed up some wild scheme alone was strange and uncomfortable. Lester could understand the allure of the goldfields, but after signing ship's articles, he knew the captain expected him to honor his word, and hated to think what Eleanor Creesy would say.

As they came closer to California, the weather became erratic, with light breezes broken by rainsqualls, leaving the sea glassy one day and lumpy the next. Captain Creesy was taut as a wire and almost as thin.

At two a.m. on August 31, *Flying Cloud* raised the lighthouse on South Farallon Island and by seven that morning a harbor pilot had boarded to take the ship into San Francisco Bay. The captain and his wife stood to windward on the quarterdeck as they came through the Golden Gate. In the ship's waist every passenger jammed the rail, and the entire crew was either on deck or aloft. Captain Creesy checked the time again and his wife smiled.

"Josiah, you've done it," Eleanor said. "We'll be anchored before noon. That makes us eighty-nine days and twenty-one hours out of New York." She put an arm through his and leaned against him. Eleanor could feel her husband's ribs and knew he was exhausted.

Josiah Creesy nodded, feeling the quiet knot of pride in his belly. He'd commanded slow ships for a decade in the China trade and had used every measure of persuasion before the toughest ship owner in New York, Nat Griswold, gave him command of *Flying Cloud*. Griswold expected a record passage, and Creesy had delivered.

"We're going to be the talk of the town, Perk!" Eleanor laughed gaily. "And I'm going to dress up." For the first time in two months, her husband cracked a smile.

High above the ship, Lester and Jubal stood on a yard taking in the panorama of San Francisco. Hundreds of ships clogged the harbor, a virtual forest of masts and rigging jammed so together a man could walk from one end of the waterfront to the other and never touch the wharves. As *Flying Cloud* drew closer, they could see several ships, then dozens, looking ragged and derelict. Some were sinking while others lay canted to one side, already in the mud. Most were ghost ships abandoned by passengers, officers, and crew, but a few carried the fluttering, ragged laundry and makeshift stovepipes of flophouses.

Behind the wharves, the town spilled over hills in a jumble of buildings and muddy streets. City sounds jangled across the water, a raucous mélange of shouts, cries, laughter, banging hammers, and braying animals that left Jubal and Lester gawking at the spectacle until their reverie was interrupted by a shout. Wainwright motioned them down.

The boys raced to the deck but the mate hadn't waited. A seething babble of passengers argued, yelled, and fought for positions along the rail. The ship's company, which had become a contained, intimate world over three months, disintegrated before their eyes. Lester and Jubal stood, uncertain what to do, until the mate hollered.

"Norton, Calhoun!" Wainwright was at the bow, readying to drop anchor. The boys started forward but he stopped them with a shout. "Go aft!" he pointed. "Captain wants you!"

Chapter Seven

*F*lying Cloud glided toward its anchorage as the boys climbed to the quarterdeck. Captain Creesy stood taut as a cocked pistol, surveying for anything that might be danger. Lester and Jubal stopped a short distance away, waiting.

The captain turned and pointed a gnarled finger at them. "You listen, boys! These," he waved a dismissal at the ghost fleet, his eyes darting back to the approach, "were manned when they arrived and everybody jumped ship for the goldfields. For every man that struck pay dirt, a hundred went bust and thirty died. You signed on until this ship returns to New York City and each of you gave an oath to obey my orders." The captain abruptly turned and stared at them, his face severe. "This is my order: *Stay on the ship until you're given temporary leave, and then get back here!* Now go forward and make yourselves useful."

Stunned at the captain's vehemence, the boys meekly turned away.

"Lester, Jubal," Eleanor Creesy motioned to them from the rail. In her black, full-length dress and tight bun, Mrs. Creesy was a feminine reflection of the captain's severity.

"This place combines the best and worst of humanity," she said, as they stood before her, holding their sea caps like schoolyard scamps. "When we were here last year the place was lawless—a hundred murders in two months, not one conviction. Maybe the law is stronger now, but I doubt it. You're not ready for this city and your mothers don't want you dead!"

Neither Lester nor Jubal moved. Behind them they could hear passengers elbowing for position against the gathering noise of the city. Eleanor Creesy stared, her mouth set in a hard line. She too, raised a weathered finger and pointed at them.

"*You shall not jump ship,*" she declared. "I require your word."

Lester swallowed hard, his mouth dry. He didn't know what Jubal's mother was like—his friend had not mentioned her once in the entire passage—but Eleanor Creesy and his mother Jane Norton were cut from the same cloth. "Yes m'am," he said.

"Jubal," Mrs. Creesy pressed, her eyebrows arching, "your word as a gentleman."

The word lanced Jubal. A sudden vision flashed of plantations along the Alabama River—of gentility he'd seen from a distance, a Southern gentleman riding through cotton fields in the sultry heat, going to Sunday church under a canopy of moss-covered, live oak trees, a world that had been so close but impossible to reach.

Jubal knew he was trapped and hated knowing. He nodded.

"Say it, Jubal," Eleanor Creesy said.

Jubal shifted his feet like an ornery mule. "I give my word," he said, finally, the drawl thick with tension.

As *Flying Cloud* dropped anchor, a flotilla of small boats rowed out to meet her. Crimps and touts jockeyed for position near the big ship, throwing whiskey aboard and loudly promising the finest accommodations north of Cape Horn with the best food and entertainment in San Francisco. Within an hour some sailors were so drunk they fell off the ship directly into the boats. When passengers realized the ship had to wait for longshoremen to warp her dockside for unloading, anxiety and complaint grew until the crowd sounded like a herd of cows that had missed a milking.

In late afternoon, Lester and Jubal watched from the foredeck as *Flying Cloud* came to her berth at the Pacific Street wharf. Passengers jostled in the ship's waist, jamming the gangway entrance and threatening to turn disembarkation into a riot. Stevedores and longshoremen crowded the wharf ready to begin unloading cargo, while behind them teamsters, livery cabbies, porters, hawkers, and pickpockets waited like vultures. Within minutes dockside was complete pandemonium.

"Damn!" Jubal said, for the fifth time. The boys could only stand and watch.

Lester was relieved, though he tried not to show it. New York had been a shock when he first arrived on a coasting schooner, but even amidst all the seaport activity it had a feeling of order. San Francisco teetered at the edge of anarchy, more dangerous than exciting. Lester thought that if Mrs. Creesy had meant to scare them, she'd succeeded.

"What the hell got into you, captain's wife and all?" Lester poked, amused his friend got so touchy.

"Shut your mouth, Lester," Jubal glared at him. "You got no idea."

Wainwright cut short Lester's retort. "Calhoun, Norton! Get them hatch covers off! Got us a ship to unload!"

Chapter Eight

While Captain and Mrs. Creesy took up residence at the Oriental Hotel, the finest in the new city, the first mate kept the boys busy aboard ship. Within a week, crewmen began straggling back aboard, crawling into their bunks as if they'd found a safe cave after surviving an ambush. The men returned disheveled, destitute, nearly poisoned by rotgut whiskey, with missing teeth, black eyes, and several broken bones among them. Two sailors carried back a delirious, buck-naked shipmate who thought he was in Valparaiso. Dandy had managed to find the ship by reeling down to the wharf and falling into the harbor alongside *Flying Cloud*. Lester and Jubal fished him out like a half-drowned cat.

"How was Carmelita?" Lester asked as they carried him to his berth.

"Who?" Dandy mumbled between retches of seawater, before passing out. Three days later he staggered on deck looking like he'd been dragged behind a wagon. He blinked in the sunlight and retreated to his bunk.

Lester and Jubal spent their days deep in the ship's hold, alternately shivering and sweating in the dank fog or midday heat. Each evening they sat high in the rigging, scanning the city with telescopes. Though neither would admit it, their vigils made the ship feel safe. Substantial two- and three-story wood-framed buildings faced San Francisco Bay, but inland the city became a slum of shacks, tents, and campfires. From high aloft the boys witnessed several brawls, a gunfight, and the hanging of a man who started a fire and was summarily strung up by vigilantes.

Finally, on a fine September morning eight days after their arrival, Mr. Wainwright issued each boy ten dollars and released them to the city, demanding their return by nightfall. After they dressed in faded cotton shirts and patched dungarees, Jubal pulled a kerchief from his kit, tying it around his throat, before heading on deck.

"Well, ain't you the rake," Lester remarked. A familiar feeling of inadequacy stung him; he always seemed to be following the younger boy. When they hit the gangway, however, he couldn't help his rising excitement. As they broke into a run a voice rang from the foredeck.

"You boys!" Mr. Wainwright yelled. "Don't bring back anything you don't want to keep!"

"What's he talking about?" Lester asked, as they made their way onto the boardwalk.

Jubal looked at him like he was an idiot. "What the hell you think? Pecker rot!"

"Oh," Lester blushed.

The insecurity gnawed at him as they spent the morning walking downtown. Jubal strolled casually, like a young man born to the city, but Lester couldn't help craning his neck at the strange collection of sailors, gold diggers, Mexican vaqueros, Chinese laborers, sailors, businessmen, shopkeepers, and the occasional rouged woman in a low-cut dress that accentuated her tightly corseted waist.

Finally, after they had looked in most every shop near the waterfront, Jubal stopped in front of a small haberdashery. Men's clothing and hats occupied the small window display.

"Here's what I'm looking for," he declared.

"You going to buy a suit with ten bucks?" Lester asked. "Which part of it?"

"Nope," Jubal refused the bait. "I want me that hat."

"Tag says sixteen dollars. Thought you were broke."

"Ain't bought a thing in a year 'cept some food." Jubal headed into the store. "Wait here."

Lester turned on his heel, damned if he'd watch. Twenty minutes later he was still stewing when Jubal came out wearing a fine beaver-skin derby.

"I suppose you're thinking of visitin' one them fandangos?" Lester scoffed, feeling like a bumpkin.

"Damn right!" Jubal had grown some in the passage and was now almost Lester's height, though heavier, and his voice had settled lower, seldom cracking anymore.

"You're a pretty good show, Jubal." Lester made no effort to hide the sarcasm. "What you aim to do with them Chileano whores?"

"All kind of mischief you wouldn't understand," Jubal drawled. "C'mon, best follow 'long."

Lester struggled to keep from tripping him as he walked past. A city block later, Jubal politely tipped his hat to a young woman sweeping the steps in front of a hairdressing salon. That did it.

"Sure is nice walking with a real 'gentleman'."

Jubal stopped on the rough boardwalk, hands to his hips. "Lester, we're shipmates sure enough, but I swear you mention that again and I'll kick your ass right here in the street, so help me."

Though he'd gone for a nerve, Lester was taken aback. The boys had bickered endlessly since New York, but a fight on land after three months at sea seemed stupid. Lester didn't relish being alone in San Francisco if Jubal got angry and stormed off.

"You take yourself some serious," he bluffed.

"I mean it, Lester!"

"Stand there like a goddam bulldog then," Lester retorted, setting out. "I'm gonna see me San Francisco."

Jubal said nothing, but followed. Though Lester didn't know where he was going, his determination marched them deeper into the city. Each boy nursed his grudge, even as the streets grew narrower.

Lester stopped so suddenly Jubal bumped into him. "Let's get some whiskey!"

Across the street, a saloon door opened in a ramshackle wooden building. A hand-painted sign in the filthy, cracked window advertised Casa Carmelita.

The saloon was empty save for a man folded face down on one of the tables. A bar ran along the inside wall to the far corner, where stairs rose to a railed, second-floor walkway that lead to several doors.

From behind the bar, a woman regarded the boys. Jet-black hair, going to gray, hung below her shoulders, framing the high forehead and nut-brown complexion of an Andean woman. She kept her eyes on them as they entered but pulled a bottle from under the bar and poured two glasses, pushing them forward as the boys approached.

Jubal sniffed carefully, then threw back his head and downed the entire glass in one quick gulp. Lester did the same, and though the liquor raked his throat like granite dust he managed to keep it down. The barkeeper poured again, expressionless, while Jubal looked at Lester and shrugged. Each drained the glass again, this time in two swallows. Lester hadn't taken a breath before she refilled the glasses. He stared and gulped, then emptied the glass, hoping it would be his last.

"Isabelle!" the woman called. In the long silence, a door opened upstairs, all eyes following the sound. A young woman slowly walked from the room and came to the balcony railing. She was young, the color of polished brass, with black hair twirled high like a headdress. Lester stood transfixed as he gazed upward and realized she wore a short, white skirt, and nothing else. And she was smoking a cigar.

The woman at the bar pointed to Jubal, who looked frozen, then curled her finger at Lester and strolled toward the stairway.

Three hours later Lester awoke, his tongue feeling as though he'd been grazing in the street. Despite a splitting headache he managed to sit upright on the bed, though the room felt like the forecastle in rough weather. Lester looked down, relieved to see that although shriveled, he recognized himself. Moving carefully, he found most of his clothes and was half-dressed when the door flung open. A miner tromped in, smelling of mules. The bartender stood behind him, her face glistening in the uneven light.

"Git!" The man hawked tobacco juice toward the corner spittoon but missed, splattering the wall. Dribble glistened off his greasy beard.

Lester fled, holding his boots while fumbling with shirt buttons as he reeled to the room where he'd seen Jubal go in with Isabelle. The saloon downstairs was full and he heard several loud guffaws but couldn't look below at the men mocking him. He tucked his shirt in, pulled on the boots, and stared at the door, before knocking tentatively. Nothing. He rapped louder.

As laughter below turn to howls, Lester carefully pushed the door open and peeked.

Isabelle lay on the bed, leaning against the headboard with her legs crossed, stark naked, smoking a cigar. Jubal's naked legs were on the bed, though the rest of him was out of sight.

"'Lo," Lester mumbled, stepping into the room.

Isabelle took a puff of her cigar and blew it at him, then opened her legs. Lester gulped and he could feel himself stir. The girl took his breath away. He turned his pockets inside out and she studied him, then took another big puff and languorously crossed her legs.

Lester stood flat-footed at the foot of the bed before shaking himself into motion and making his way to stand above Jubal. The boy lay flat on his back, a sheet covering crumpled over his trunk, snoring lightly. Lester nudged him with a foot and yanked the cover. When Jubal stirred, Lester tossed his legs on the floor and hauled him upright.

"It's dark," Lester hissed. "We got to get back!"

Jubal's face scrunched as he tried his eyes. The boy reeked of sour tequila.

"Get dressed!" Lester urged. "The mate'll throw us in the hold!"

Jubal wobbled and Lester grabbed his clothes to help dress him. "Here, get your boots on. Oh, for Christly sakes! Jubal, gimme your foot!" Jubal's pants were still open and Lester felt the empty pockets, then checked his own. Between them they didn't have a cent.

"Button up!" Lester groaned. "Jesus Christ, looks like you been stomped! C'mon!"

Jubal struggled into his shirt as Lester shoved him toward the door. "My hat," Jubal moaned, buttoning his shirt cockeyed. Lester started to ask Isabelle but she opened her legs slightly. He spun around, frantically looking until he got on his knees and pulled Jubal's hat from under the bed.

"Bye," he said, pushing Jubal onto the balcony. Isabelle took another puff of her cigar and blew a smoke ring at him as he closed the door.

Chapter Nine

Nearly half the crew had deserted for the goldfields but Captain Creesy managed to find a few stranded men, and three weeks later *Flying Cloud* cleared the Golden Gate, heading southwest. The second mate, Mr. Hare, took over from Wainwright, who had been left in a San Francisco hospital after his temper tangled with another sailor's knife in a waterfront brawl. Mr. Hare, quiet as he was competent, had gained the respect of the crew on the passage from New York simply by doing his job without bullying.

After the ship picked up the northeast trade winds and settled into her long ride across the Pacific, Lester and Jubal spent hours aloft maintaining the miles of rigging that kept the clipper in trim. As they sailed over brilliant tropical seas with a fresh, constant wind off the aft quarter, the boys continued to take celestial sights each day, and Mrs. Creesy supervised what amounted to their education. Jubal grumbled about the attention, yet he thrived as his penmanship improved from scratches to a flowing cursive that he regarded with quiet pride. Lester was equally diligent, appreciating the opportunity to read and write.

"Otherwise," he pointed out to Jubal on an afternoon while they were copying in their navigation journals, "we sure to be like the rest of these fools who wouldn't know which side a newspaper's up."

When he concentrated on writing, Jubal often chewed his lip. "You look like a goddam beaver," Lester teased. Jubal didn't even grunt, but silence left Lester uneasy and he'd talk to hear something besides the constant wind. Other than a skeleton crew, the ship was empty—neither passengers nor cargo came to China.

On the day *Flying Cloud* crossed the date line and the boys' log entries went from one hundred eighty degrees west to one hundred eighty degrees east longitude, Mrs. Creesy gave them an assignment to complete before the ship returned to New York.

"The whole thing?" Lester wondered, when Mrs. Creesy called for the boys in the captain's cabin. Jubal looked like he wanted to run, and Lester could barely talk, nearly petrified that Captain Creesy would walk in.

"Yes," Mrs. Creesy ordered, handing them blank, leather-bound books. "Here's your new journals, you both make copies. Lester, you help Jubal with the reading, Jubal you help Lester draw the charts. Done by New York. In exceptional weather, with my permission, you may take these volumes, *one at a time*, on deck, but if you should lose one overboard I imagine the captain will throw you after it."

Eleanor Creesy picked up the marine compendium she had bought in New York. "For two hours every day, during the afternoon watch. In weather, use the third mate's cabin, it's empty. Every few days I'll check your progress." Captain Creesy came in then and gave the boys a look that sent them fleeing like hunted chickens.

"Jubal, how can you write so pretty?" Lester asked the next day. Initially, Jubal tensed, but Lester's honesty encouraged him to practice with the charts until his drawings almost became pictures. Lester grew fascinated with the play of currents, seasons, and trade routes.

"No wonder!" he exclaimed one afternoon, as they sat under the windward rail in the ship's waist.

"What?" Jubal rasped, annoyed at another interruption.

"Cape St. Roque, 'member? We was in sight of land all day, coming round the cape where it bulges out from Brazil."

"So what? Captain was like a horse with a tick on his balls."

"Because it was shoaling down to sixteen, seventeen fathom," Lester pointed at the drawing, "ol' Perk nearly beside hisself. But the missus insisted she was right where we supposed to be to pick up them inshore currents and a breeze off the land. She knew because it's in here!" Lester thumped the volume. "That woman is something smart."

Jubal picked at his tooth with a fingernail. "Capt'n," he allowed, "does listen to her."

⁓

Lester's curiosity finally impelled him to ask the second mate why Mrs. Creesy allowed them time to learn. The conversation came at night in the middle watch with the ship under full sail a thousand miles south of Hawaii. Trade winds had eased after dark, and the full moon hung like a lantern in the sky, so bright Lester could read a book. Although Mr. Hare commanded the quarterdeck, Captain Creesy usually appeared once or twice to look around, though he spent most nights with his wife in their cabin.

"I wondered the same thing," the mate answered. "Not fair to the other crew, except your pay don't match on account you're green. So I asked the captain."

"What'd Perk have to say?" Lester asked.

"Don't forget your place, boy!" Mr. Hare answered, warmth suddenly gone from the evening.

"Sorry, sir!" Lester winced, his innards twisting. "Won't happen again."

A long silence followed, but the sibilant rush and undulating sea rhythms lulled them and the night was too beautiful for Mr. Hare to stay offended. Far forward, Lester could see the flashing, iridescent shapes of dolphins riding the bow wave. Astern, *Flying Cloud* left a phosphorescent wake straight as a rod; occasionally, he turned to feel the thrill of competence at steering a dead true course.

"Captain Creesy said you might come on right. I take it you're some relation to a mate he shipped with twenty years back, now also a captain, and the wives are friends." Mr. Hare's voice came quiet out of the night. "Though, you ask me, it's likely 'cause the missus never had a son and you lost your father."

Lester's mind went blank.

The mate stiffened. "You're falling off ... bring her back, Norton!"

Lester shook himself and corrected course, looking forward to put the bright, blinking star Sirius midway between the port foremast shrouds and the flying jib. The breeze came off the back of his head until he could feel it on his ear again and he knew he'd almost gone under the wind. He did not want to face Captain Creesy after inadvertently tacking ship.

Lester checked the compass, his heart pounding. "West by nor'west, sir," he said.

"Very good," Hare answered as the door opened from the quarterdeck companionway.

"Wind shift, Mr. Hare?" Captain Creesy was barefoot, wearing light silk pajamas.

"No sir," Lester replied. He swallowed hard but didn't want the mate to be blamed.

"Mr. Hare?" the captain growled. Lester was afraid to look.

"Begging your pardon, sir," Mr. Hare said. "Won't happen again."

Captain Creesy stood on the quarterdeck a few moments longer, looked aloft, then turned and left without a word.

Lester clung to the wheel, trying to stand stolid against a jumble of emotion. He knew his father had been a sailor on the big ships before he started fishing. Lester's fondest memories were of snowy evenings around the fireplace in the Penobscot farmhouse, six miles upriver from the bay. In winter, John Norton hauled their small schooner for the season and stayed busy mending nets and repairing dories and gear. At night, he'd gather the children and tell stories of his voyages on the oceans, a world of strange-sounding names, exotic ports, and furious storms.

John Norton had died in 1845 when his fishing boat vanished in an October gale. Twenty-one vessels had foundered on the Sable Island shoals south of Nova Scotia and bodies of fishermen washed ashore for a week after the storm. Lester had turned nine while his father was away, on that last trip to the Grand Banks.

Lester stared at the compass, almost in a trance. For several minutes he willed himself to concentrate on steering, though his stomach churned. A gentle push confused him for a moment.

"Permission to relieve Norton, Mr. Hare?" Jubal asked. Lester realized his friend had come off the mizzen doublings, where the lower mast held the topgallant mast above. Jubal must have heard the conversation, carried by the soft breeze.

"Aye, steady as she goes, Calhoun," Mr. Hare answered. "West by nor'west,"

"I'll take her, Lester," Jubal whispered.

Lester stepped away from the wheel and placed a hand softly in Jubal's back as his friend took over. Taking a deep breath of night, he went over to the mizzen shrouds and slowly climbed to the doublings.

Lester had never cried over his father's death. When remnants of the fishing fleet returned there was so much grief around the bay that he retreated into stoicism. As the eldest son, he became man of the house. Now, in the brilliant Pacific night, sitting in the rigging, his legs dangling above *Flying Cloud,* he suddenly understood the wistful cast to his father's voice on those winter evenings.

In the farmhouse, Lester always wondered why his father wasn't the captain of a big ship, like the fathers of some boys he knew at the school in Eastport down the bay, who lived in large houses with widow's walks. On the mizzen doublings of *Flying Cloud,* a sudden flash of understanding closed Lester's eyes and he imagined the white heat of his mother, struggling on a saltwater farm with three small mouths to feed while her husband was away for years at a time. When Lester was about four—he couldn't remember exactly—his father had left the deep sea, sort of, and become a fisherman, first as crew and then later on his own small boat. Then he was gone only a month at a time, not years.

On deck, the ship's bell rang off the middle watch. To Lester, it sounded as if the bell tolled for his childhood. A vision of his father filled him, that of a young man aloft on a brig in the South Seas finishing the middle watch. A tear formed at the corner of Lester's eye and he could taste the salty anguish of his mother, whom he had tried so hard to console when they'd learned. She had pleaded with her man to leave the deep, and he had. Still the sea took him.

The shrouds vibrated and moments later, Jubal came onto the doublings. He looked closely and sat beside his shipmate. Their shoulders touching, they watched the tropical night surrender to vivid dawn as the moonlit sheen off Lester's glistening face slowly gave way to tiny salt speckles that blew away, one by one, in the early morning breeze.

Chapter Ten

China, December 1851

Jubal yawned, hoping this would be his last turn around the quarterdeck, and glanced again toward the low shadow of Whampoa Island. The night was pleasantly warm and moist, with zephyrs of a dying sea breeze ruffling through the ship's rigging. *Flying Cloud* lay anchored in the Pearl River a dozen miles below Canton, bow to a sluggish current spilling off the Chinese mainland.

Moments later, Mr. Hare came to the ship's bell. Jubal counted silently as eight bells struck, signaling midnight. Most of the crew slept; only Lester at the masthead and a sailor near the bow manned the anchor watch. The forecastle door closed and moments later a silhouette climbed into the rigging and disappeared aloft as another man approached the quarterdeck. With a soft thump, Lester came off the shrouds and landed on deck, nodding at Jubal.

"All's well, Mr. Hare," Jubal reported softly. The night hush was infectious.

"Very well, Calhoun. You and Norton are relieved." The formality left the mate's voice. "Merry Christmas, lads. Make ready for 1852—t'will be men's work."

"Will be?" Jubal whispered a few moments later, hoisting himself onto the forecastle roof to sleep in the lullaby breeze. "What we been doing this year if it ain't been men's work?"

"Means we're going to have more 'n one woman," Lester hoped.

Jubal snorted, tucked an arm under his head, and was asleep in seconds.

Later that morning, Dandy steered the longboat as the boys rowed the captain and Mrs. Creesy upstream with the tide, maneuvering through scores of sampans and coastal junks clustered around teak wharves jutting from warehouses that lined the Canton waterfront. Chinese merchants and foreign shipping agents milled about the two-story hongs and godowns crammed with tea, silks, and porcelains. While the captain completed his cargo negotiations, Eleanor Creesy let the boys roam ashore, admonishing them to stay within hailing distance.

"Some strange, this place," Jubal remarked, looking into an open hong. Boxes of tea piled high on both sides of a long aisle that ran the building's length gave off a musty scent that made him rub his nose. Whenever he became annoyed, Jubal's drawl grew more pronounced, and Lester could hear it now.

"Who these Chinamen think they are?" Jubal demanded, "saying we can't go into Canton?" Through the far end of the building two Chinese guards stood at a door built into a high wall separating the foreign zone from the city.

"Their country," observed Lester. "What'd you say if some Chinese sailor went sauntering round Mobile?"

"That's the point! Chinaman could, even if they got their ass kicked. But here, you telling me I can't? Riles me."

"Go head. Poleax them two guards and walk right through that door."

Jubal shook his head. "Sometimes you're useless to talk to."

Captain Creesy emerged from one of the hongs with two other men who appeared to be bidding him farewell. A gowned Chinese mandarin bowed, his pigtail straight as a black needle; next to him a European trader in waistcoat and broad-brimmed hat shook the captain's hand.

A piercing whistle reached ashore and the boys bolted back to the longboat. Dandy waited aboard with Mrs. Creesy, who sat under a stern awning facing an easel.

"You should be drawing this, Jubal," she remarked. "You're a better artist than I am."

Jubal shuffled, embarrassed.

"He's grumpy, ma'am," Lester volunteered, "'cause he can't go into the city."

"Jezus," Jubal muttered.

"Jubal Calhoun, are you British?" Mrs. Creesy asked. "Your ancestry?"

The question took Jubal by surprise. "I don't know, precisely," he allowed, "though I believe my grandfather were from Scotland."

"So that's the trace of red in your hair?"

Jubal blushed.

Mrs. Creesy studied the hongs. "I surely wish Harriett Low were here."

The boys looked blankly at her.

"Harriett lived here in the early forties with her aunt and uncle," Eleanor Creesy laughed, "when these waters opened to American ships after

Nanking. The Chinese forbid women to be in this settlement—they're picky about everything—so she dressed like a man and snuck in."

"You could do the same Jubal," Lester offered. "Dress like a coolie pulling a wagon."

Jubal ignored him. "How come they're so …?"

"Mud," Mrs. Creesy replied. "That's what the Chinese call opium. Ten years ago the British forced them to take it in exchange for tea, rather than gold, which the Chinese wanted. The British Navy slaughtered a few thousand Chinese sailors before forcing a treaty on the emperor—they signed it in Nanking—that gave the Brits Hong Kong for a hundred and fifty years. There you have it, the makings of hatred. The Chinese detest us, but we buy their tea. If you don't like them, believe me, it's nothing to what they think of us."

"We're not Brits," Jubal protested.

"Same difference to the Chinese, except for the hong merchants," Mrs. Creesy replied, spotting her husband striding onto the wharf. "There's Perk!" The excitement built in her voice. "I can see by the way he walks we're leaving! Prepare to cast off!"

In mid-afternoon, as *Flying Cloud* tacked down the Pearl River, Eleanor Creesy visited the quarterdeck several times. The boys knew she constantly plotted their position, triangulating off islands and headlands. Jubal had consulted the marine volumes while they lay anchored and learned that the river mouth was a welter of uncharted reefs, shifting sandbars, and dangerous cross- currents. Near the coast, erratic winds wafted through a maze of islands in the broad estuary where the river finally yawned open to the South China Sea. As the afternoon gave way to twilight, the breeze died and a misty overcast cloaked the ship until she was ghosting along with the outgoing tide. When the watch turned, the captain ordered Mr. Hare to ready the anchor. Mrs. Creesy called the boys to her cabin.

"This is the estuary," Eleanor Creesy said, pointing at the chart. "Right now we're heading"—she checked a small compass, oriented to the ship's keel—"a little east of north. Hong Kong is to the northeast; Macao's east, southeast. Like guardians at the gates, aren't they, of the Pearl River? British on one side, Portuguese on the other, both islands stolen from the Chinese."

Mrs. Creesy tapped the chart with a pencil. "Imagine the approaches to Boston Harbor," she said, a note of disbelief in her voice. "The Chinese seize Spectacle Island, the Siamese grab Marblehead. Talk about a tea party …"

Lester lost the reserve he always felt anywhere below deck aft of the mast and leaned forward. "This is the only thin sliver of a window into an enormous, three thousand-year-old country," she said, "and I don't blame them a damn bit. Mud!"

Mrs. Creesy looked away from the chart and suddenly wheeled on the boys, pointing her pencil. "Don't ever do something you'll be ashamed of the rest of your life, just for profit!" Mrs. Creesy looked so fierce Lester stepped back. She glared from him to Jubal, before abruptly turning back to the chart table.

"Josiah says this mist will probably stay with us until it burns off in the morning, unless we get a breeze that pushes it out. So I need you both to climb the main royal, see if you can get high enough and check our position. The water shoals rapidly here," her forefinger traced the chart and Jubal noticed the hand looked wrinkled and older than the woman. "The tide is about to turn, so we'll anchor because the flood comes through these islands here, and that'll turn our head some, more toward east-northeast, and we might not have enough steerage to make it through. See these islands? Triangulate them when you get aloft. It doesn't matter which way the ship moves on her anchor, they shouldn't move relative to each other. If they do, holler down because we mustn't drag!"

An hour later, nearly two hundred feet off the deck, the two boys settled onto either side of the royal crosstree and examined the darkness. Though Lester felt like he was looking into ink, Jubal quickly identified the islands. Lester tried to keep the relief from his voice.

"Best not disappoint that woman," he said. "'Reminds me of my mother. You too? Yours?"

A long silence seemed to make the night blacker, before Jubal murmured, his voice a tight snap. "Nope."

Chapter Eleven

Flying Cloud, now laden with its cargo of tea and silks, cleared the Indonesia archipelago through Sunda Strait in the middle of January to ride trade winds across the Indian Ocean on a course that never wavered more than five degrees.

In addition to the navigation lessons, Eleanor Creesy ordered the boys to read to her from *Leatherstocking*, by James Fenimore Cooper, a new book she had purchased in New York. Mrs. Creesy sat between them, forcing Jubal and Lester to sound out difficult words as each read a few pages and then passed the book to the other. Lester could read passably well, but Jubal was so self-consciously shy during the readings it almost hurt to watch.

Jubal quickly decided he'd rather suffer the humiliation of practicing with Lester than appear stupid in front of Mrs. Creesy, so he asked to borrow the book and began reading in the forecastle. Most of the men ignored him, but Dandy was illiterate, loved stories, and insisted on listening. Consequently, Jubal read *Leatherstocking* twice. Determined to hold his advantage, Lester did the same. By the Cape of Good Hope, both boys read better than they had ever expected to in their lives, a fact Mrs. Creesy hammered home more than once.

"You've learned new words, each of you," she'd wag a finger, "and your vocabularies have greatly improved. Now use those words! And no teasing the other; I won't have it."

Flying Cloud rounded Africa and made the turn northwest, barreling up the South Atlantic on her last leg home. Captain Creesy pressed the ship, using the southeast trades to drive her hard toward New York. With a blustery trade wind dead astern, the captain flew every sail *Flying Cloud* could carry, so two men usually stood the wheel, wrestling it to hold course. Mr. Hare often looked aloft with a glint of fear, waiting for something to break. The captain, however, stood on the quarterdeck hour after hour with arms folded and eyes constantly moving in a ceaseless vigil, from sail to line to shroud.

Sometimes Eleanor came to join him, wordlessly locking an arm in his and enjoying the thrilling spectacle. On one of those afternoons, she spied Jubal and Lester peeking at them and promptly motioned the boys aft.

"What do you think of the music?" Mrs. Creesy cried. Her hair, usually in a bun, flew free in the wind.

Lester and Jubal stood sheepishly, eyes darting at each other.

"Well, don't stand there like stumps! *Feel* the ship. What is she saying to you?"

The boys had no idea what she was talking about.

"Come here," she urged, taking them to the quarterdeck rail. Captain Creesy watched and Lester almost looked at him twice, wondering if the captain actually had cracked a bemused smile.

"Look down the hull," Mrs. Creesy directed. "A clipper at sea is a mercurial, moody instrument. She's either stretched to the point of snapping or sagging out of tune. Look aloft," she pointed. "The ship is counterbalanced; it must constantly battle opposing, wrenching effects of wind, masts, and hull, like a hammer trying to pull nails from a plank." Mrs. Creesy's voice grew animated and her face glowed. "Run your eye along the rail. She's fair in the bow and stern, widens amidships, right? And feel this huge wave surging underneath us! Every day, every hour, disproportionate buoyancy—her belly on a wave, the ends hanging off—stretches the keel into an arched backbone, like you'd snap a long stick for firewood. Now watch! We're sluicing through and the wave is twisting us, racking the hull as if a gigantic hand was wringing a washrag! Imagine the forces at work!"

Mrs. Creesy gave a joyous, full-throated laugh. "Josiah, this ship is a masterpiece!"

The captain grunted agreement, briefly glancing at the boys. "As you were!"

Jubal and Lester fled.

The trade winds sputtered out as *Flying Cloud* approached the southern doldrums, rolling on glassy seas under a merciless sun. Occasional, violent thunderstorms pummeled the ship and then left it wallowing as the squall line passed. Breezes became fluky, and the entire crew, anticipating New York's pleasures not three weeks away, grew restless and irritable as the ship crawled toward the equator.

On a sultry afternoon in late March, the boys were aloft with Dandy splicing a repair to the rigging when Lester, standing at the masthead, suddenly cupped his hand and hollered down, "Sail ho!"

Jubal and Dandy, straddling the yard, both looked out to the horizon where a small speck of canvas showed briefly against the wall of an approaching thunderstorm. Already they could feel a fitful breeze. Dandy took off the red bandana he habitually wore, wiped his eyes and forehead, and took a long look at the distant vessel, still hull down below the horizon. Sniffing the air like a hound dog, he retied his bandana. Satisfied, he turned to his work but stopped at Lester's perplexed expression.

"Too far to tell, but likely a trader," Dandy explained. "She were a slaver, this breeze we'd get a whiff. Close on her, t'would bend yer nose strong as a privy!"

Lester glanced at the sail again. "Damnable abomination, you ask me!" Lester remembered the phrase from a sermon he'd heard a traveling preacher make on a summer Sunday when his mother had dragged him to the small church in Orrington.

Jubal's head whipped around. "Nobody fuckin' asked you, Lester!"

Lester's eyes bulged and he stared at his friend, dumbfounded. He had never seen such a rage in Jubal's face, blooming as if from nothing. The flutter of a sail sounded loud in the stillness.

"Man's entitled to an opinion," Dandy remarked, as startled as Lester. But Jubal looked ready to charge and Dandy had no intention of breaking up a melee so high in the rigging.

Jubal bared his teeth. "The opinion of someone born in lily-white Maine couldn't hold a cup of cold piss!"

Lester's face burned beneath the coconut tan. "Well, sir ...!"

Jubal chucked the tattered piece of line Dandy had cut out of his repair. "Best work at something you can understand, Lester, before your mouth overloads your ass!"

Before Lester could reply, a sudden flash of lightning snapped their attention. The violent clap of thunder followed a few seconds later.

"Whatever's comin' don't look good!" Dandy exclaimed. He bellowed a warning to the deck and gathered his splicing tools. "Quit your bawlin', take in sail!"

"Get those stun'sles in!" Mr. Hare cried from below, running for the rail. "Captain!"

Captain Creesy had ordered all sails set, intent on crossing the belt of doldrums either side of the equator as quickly as possible. The studding sails—stunsails—hung out beyond the sides of the ship like giant tablecloths, providing extra canvas in light airs, but they were clumsy to rig and could be carried away if the wind rose from any direction but astern.

"All hands aloft!" Captain Creesy roared, moments later. He had been below deck, taking a late lunch with his wife in their quarters. Hearing Mr. Hare, he'd quickly come up the companionway, followed by Mrs. Creesy. The captain took one look at the horizon. "We're in for it," he said to his wife.

Men poured out of the forecastle and looked around quickly. The squall line was changing before their eyes, going from a vague clot of bluish gray to inky mud, then pitch black, in two minutes. A jagged flash of lightning hit the sea and a split second later the thunderclap slammed them, smelling of singe. Captain Creesy raced down the quarterdeck stairs into the waist, yelling behind him to drop the triangular sail above the wheelhouse.

Lester gulped, still stunned by Jubal's inexplicable explosion. Another look at the horizon jolted him into action.

"Gawd, that looks some dreadful," he murmured before scrambling to pull in the moonraker and the main royal, the highest sails on the ship and small enough to handle alone. The distant sail had disappeared into the cloud wall.

The wind died, and for a moment the ship lay becalmed on a glassy sea, men crawling over the rigging like insects. Eleanor Creesy ordered the helmsman to help forward, then took the wheel. Lester frantically swept folds of sail in his arms as the squall came on, spitting lightning. Captain Creesy ran from one mast to another, releasing halyards and dropping the triangular staysails that hung like angled tall half-napkins between the masts.

The fastidious, ordered routine of the ship disintegrated as every man struck any sail he could reach. Aloft, sails were lashed haphazardly as the squall closed on the ship. In the deathly stillness that followed deafening thunder, they could see the ocean begin to seethe.

Lester secured the two sails and dropped down to help Jubal and Dandy on the topgallant yard. Hearing Mr. Hare's hail, Jubal, agile as a monkey, made for the weather end of the yard to release that stunsail, so Lester headed for the other side as the mate made ready to haul both sails to the deck. Between them, Dandy wrestled the topgallant alone, more than one man could handle himself, but it couldn't be helped.

Though Eleanor Creesy tried to steer away, with little momentum *Flying Cloud* lay nearly broadside to the wind wall when it hit with the force of a locomotive. The ship staggered as though she had run onto a reef and buckled over.

Lester let go the sail and hugged the yard as the ship rolled until he was almost parallel to the ocean far below. On the other side of the mast, now almost forty feet directly above him, Jubal couldn't release the sail before it ballooned and shredded. A line belaying the stunsail whipped taut, snapping the boom like a twig. Jubal instinctively threw up an arm to protect his face but the broken boom slammed his forearm so hard he lost hold and toppled backward, falling fifteen feet into Dandy below him.

Lester watched in horror as *Flying Cloud* lay over on her beam. A red bandana flashed by with a shriek and then Jubal's body, his fall broken by Dandy, smashed into Lester. As they both fell, Lester snatched at his friend's wrist.

Lester struck his head on the boom and was clotheslined when his chin caught the footrope, but it checked him for an instant and he clawed a grip as *Flying Cloud*'s rail plunged into the sea.

As her bow came round, the ship lay suspended for a moment, as if debating whether to lie down forever. Hanging to the footrope by one fist and holding Jubal in the other, Lester dangled thirty feet above the waves, nose gushing blood, fearing his shoulders would tear apart. Below Jubal, the main yard end speared twenty feet into the sea. A broad swath of slimy coppered hull lay exposed.

Lester begged *Flying Cloud* to get up. For several long seconds the ship hovered, and then through his prayers he felt her pull loose and recover. To his horror, Lester realized they would go shooting skyward as the ship rolled back like a pendulum. He yelled at Jubal, but his friend's eyes lolled as the rain wall swept over them.

The deluge seemed to drown the wind's full fury, and *Flying Cloud* righted herself, the yard rising slowly before the ship's rail ripped out in gush of foam as she sprung upright. Lester used the accelerating momentum to scissor his legs under Jubal's shoulders, freeing his grip to grab the footrope with both hands. The mast swung upward through its arc as Lester hung on for dear life.

Rain came in torrents. Lester tried to move but could only hang on or fall. Jubal was barely conscious and one arm hung limp like a broken wing, the forearm bent at a weird angle and watery blood dripping off his fingers. Lester sputtered and gasped for breath as if he were drowning, his shoulder sockets feeling molten.

Far below, the cry sounded twice, "Man overboard!"

Sickened by the terrible thought of Dandy plummeting into the sea—he knew it must have been him—and nearly passing out from the agony in his shoulders, Lester could only close his eyes, lock his legs around Jubal, and hold on.

Somehow, Mr. Hare climbed the rigging and leaned out from the mast to get an arm around Jubal's knees. "Swing him over t' me, lad!" With the last of his strength, Lester kicked out as Mr. Hare ducked. Lester opened his legs and Jubal flopped over the mate's shoulder.

Lester hung from the footrope knowing he didn't have enough strength to pull himself back to the mast and Mr. Hare couldn't help, already trying to hold himself and Jubal secure. The ship scudded off under bare poles. Any sail left flying was now in tatters, but torrential rain had knocked the wind down. Lester nearly let go, almost delirious with pain, when a stupendous lightning flash shattered the rainstorm. Terrified, he lurched for the mast and with the last of his reserves, climbed down into the doublings to collapse against the shrouds.

The squall passed in minutes, leaving *Flying Cloud* wallowing in shock on a diminishing sea under the blazing tropical sun. The deck steamed from evaporating rainwater and sails hung limp, many in shreds. Others were knotted around the rigging in a snarl of canvas and line. The entire crew stood motionless, as if they had somehow survived an explosion.

Lester trembled on the doublings in a dreamlike trance that barely registered the captain's call to lower a boat. Mr. Hare yelled down for help but had to wait before men could rig up a line to lower Jubal. Lester recovered enough to help and then climb down himself. He staggered onto the deck, wiping his bloody nose, watching the longboat slowly scour the sea.

Captain Creesy, walking the deck to inventory damage, took one look at Jubal's arm and called to his wife. Between the elbow and wrist, Jubal's forearm took an abrupt, oblique-angled turn. The boy stared numbly at the splintered bone protruding from his skin. Eleanor Creesy came bustling up, looking slightly disheveled. In the tempest her bun had partially collapsed, releasing a tress of long, brunette hair so incongruous the men gaped.

"Mother of God!" Mrs. Creesy breathed, praying the boy wouldn't become her first amputation. "Mr. Hare, please carry him to the third mate's cabin, my things are there. Lester, bring hot water!" As Mrs. Creesy carefully held Jubal's arm, Mr. Hare laid the boy gently over his shoulder, where he hung like a rag doll. Waves of nausea overcame Lester and he couldn't move, his feet like granite.

"Norton, get the water!" the captain barked, yanking Lester from his shock. ""Cookie may need a hand," he added, a note of resignation to his voice. The captain sighed, scanning the horizon. "Well, we lost that skirmish," he said, to no one in particular. He went to the rail and looked out to the longboat. The man at the tiller silently shook his head. There was no sign of Dandy.

Cookie was on his knees in the galley, shoveling stew he had prepared for supper off the deck into his large cooking pots. Lester stood in the doorway, taken aback by the carnage. The galley floor was a chaotic mess of salt beef, gravy, vegetables, pans, wood ash and coal, pieces of bread, and coffee grounds. A small barrel of flour lay lopsided and half-smashed on deck.

"Be taken 'while," Cookie replied to Lester's request. "Close to cuttin' us a somersault, we did. Tell Capt'n water be hot, by and by. Put some sea water on that nose." The cook started humming a tune.

As Lester went aft looking for Captain Creesy, Mr. Hare shouted orders to the entire crew, who had spread into the rigging. The courses and topsails had been set again and men were on the topgallant yards. Amidships, the carpenter examined broken spars and blocks while the sailmaker looked over remains of canvas. Captain Creesy was nowhere to be seen.

Lester poked his head into the doorway that led from the ship's waist into the aft quarters and timidly called out to the captain, but got no response. He hated going into the officer's companionway even at Mrs. Creesy's insistence. Lester swallowed and was about to call again when Captain Creesy came from his cabin and walked forward holding a pint bottle. He stopped at the third mate's door and Eleanor Creesy's outstretched arm appeared.

"Capt'n, Cookie's rebuilding the fire," Lester reported.

The captain nodded, giving his wife the bottle.

"Tell him it has to boil," Mrs. Creesy's voice ordered.

A half-hour later Lester was forward, untangling the mess left by the shattered jib when Cookie called to him. Lester ran to the galley and found him back at his counter, elbow deep in flour, making bread. Another pot of salt beef stewed on the cookstove.

"Good Lord, Cookie!" Lester exclaimed, "looks like nothing happened!"

"Oh, ship she jes' sneeze, dat's all," Cookie laughed, nodding toward the stove. "Water a'boilin'. Who it for?"

"Jubal," Lester replied. He sagged suddenly to his haunches as Cookie brought a steaming kettle to him. The black man stood over Lester for several seconds, and then nudged him with a foot.

"Wha'sa matter, boy?" he asked gently.

Lester fought back tears, overcome by thoughts of Dandy sinking forever while the best friend he ever had was about to lose his arm.

"If ... if only I hadn't started that fight with him, none of this would have happened."

"Oh, no son," Cookie said, after coaxing a brief, halting description of the clash from Lester, "nothin' be 'shamed of. The sea's a chancy business. Dandy knew that, seen many men go afore him. And Jubal ... well, a boy born in cotton, learnin' to whip before he could talk's gonna have fight to 'im."

Cookie reached into a cupboard and pulled out a jug. Uncorking it, he handed it to Lester. "Swig this. Bestest rum molasses you'll ever swaller, made meself."

The sweet, biting syrup steadied Lester, and wiping his eyes with a bloody sleeve, he nodded gratefully, straightened, and headed aft with the steaming kettle.

Above, the ship was fully clothed again, sails hanging limp in the dead quiet. The squall seemed to have smashed the trade wind south, leaving a weather hole above the calming sea. Lester caught sight of the captain, whose iron mask broke only in brief moments of disgust. Captain Creesy exhibited no patience in the doldrums, much preferring Cape Horn to the sweltering, unpredictable weather on either side of the equator. And now he had lost a man.

Lester went to the third mate's door, knocked softly, and swallowed hard. Eleanor Creesy said something unintelligible, so Lester nudged the door open. She had lashed Jubal to the bunk; the boy was semi-conscious and babbling. Lester could catch some words but mostly the sounds were nonsensical.

Mrs. Creesy pointed at two porcelain bowls on the small corner table. "Strip off your shirt and fill those bowls, then scrub your arms and hands until they hurt," she ordered. "Did they find Dandy?"

Lester hung his head; he couldn't look at her.

"God rest his soul," Mrs. Creesy said softly. Her voice hardened. "Now, we're going to save this arm."

Clean towels, a pitcher, and a small dish of lye soap lay at the back of the table. Beside Jubal's bunk she arranged a small chest and stool, opened a leather satchel and laid out small fleecing knives, pliers, spoons, needles, and a metal pan. She reached for the kettle and filled the pan, then carefully placed the instruments in steaming water.

Lester tried the water, but even his tough hands couldn't tolerate the heat. He wordlessly pleaded with it to cool until Mrs. Creesy came over, splashed some water from the pitcher into the bowl and plunged her hands in. "Hotter the better," she said, vigorously scrubbing. Lester followed her lead, wincing as he slopped the scalding water over his calloused fingers. He noticed the blackened fingernail had almost grown out.

Suddenly, Jubal slurred, "Hey, Lester, yew gonna fix my arm?" Lester had never heard his friend use the slow, singsong drawl, a cadence that sounded like Cookie. "So I kin hold on that lil' Chileano …" A drunken chuckle petered into silence.

Lester froze, appalled. "Jubal!" he hissed.

Mrs. Creesy paid no attention. "He's drunk, and I mixed in some laudanum."

Lester stared at her.

"The captain has some Kentucky whiskey. Laudanum comes from the opium and will help the pain. I hoped he would be unconscious, but I'm afraid of giving him any more." Mrs. Creesy gestured to the pint bottle. "Half of that would knock me out for two days." She looked at Jubal, her expression turning pensive.

"Now then," she turned briskly to the table and reached for a knife, "here's what we have to do."

For an hour, Mrs. Creesy worked carefully, establishing the extent of Jubal's injury and describing to Lester how she planned to reset the break. With a razor-sharp knife she opened the wound enough to probe for and remove a shattered bone splinter. Lester initially quailed when she made an incision, but he surprised himself. Curiosity, and her confidence, soon grew compelling. Once the initial shock subsided Lester watched open-mouthed, listening to Mrs. Creesy explain what she was doing and why. He was totally unprepared, when in the midst of cleansing the wound before setting the bone, she asked him a question.

"The Chileano … a friend of the family?"

Lester's comfort vanished. "Well, ah … sort of," he stammered. "Why yes, m'am, suppose you could say that."

"You know about Jubal's family?"

"Well, yes m'am ... I mean, well ... no, not very," Lester dearly wished Jubal were awake and suffering. "Not too much," he finished, lamely.

"Enough to know the Chileano, though?"

"I think she's a friend. Certainly of Jubal's," Lester replied, closing his eyes at the stupidity. He dreaded another question, but Mrs. Creesy seemed satisfied.

When they finally took hold of Jubal's arm, Lester at his shoulder and Mrs. Creesy pulling at the wrist, the splintered bone slipped back under the skin with a little slurp that made Lester queasy. Working with one hand on the break and the other carefully maneuvering Jubal's wrist, she aligned the bones.

Jubal's stirred. "I'm sorry ..." he croaked, barely audible. Eleanor Creesy stopped, and both she and Lester waited. Jubal went silent, however, a dreamy, faintly troubled look to his face.

Mrs. Creesy glanced at Lester, then strapped a splint to Jubal's arm, and stitched the wound before wrapping arm and splint. Daylight softened through the skylight, afternoon approaching tropical sunset as Eleanor carefully finished the surgery. Mostly Jubal stayed silent, occasionally mumbling in a garbled drawl, gazing at the ceiling with glazed eyes and a beatific smile.

Finally satisfied, Mrs. Creesy ordered Lester to refill the bowl with fresh water. She washed her hands before covering Jubal with a blanket, looking at the young, unlined face with unabashed affection. She gently stoked his cheek.

"Ohh ..." Jubal sighed, "Cora ..."

Lester looked at his shipmate. Mrs. Creesy watched Jubal, and then turned. "Who's Cora?"

"No idea, m'am," Lester dodged.

Eleanor Creesy regarded Jubal in silence, reaching for the wash towel. "He mentioned her earlier, after the whiskey and laudanum," Mrs. Creesy murmured, wiping her hands. "Something about 'Cora'," she continued, carefully tucking the blanket under his chin. "And 'Momma'."

Chapter Twelve

For a week after the operation, Jubal only moved from the third mate's bunk to relieve himself. The first tries were embarrassing, but Lester held him at the chamber pot, prompted by Mrs. Creesy. "Some things will be difficult at first," she said to Lester a day after they'd set the bone. He looked puzzled for a moment and then reddened. "Please keep an eye on him. Though," she added dryly, "I wouldn't expect gratitude."

Jubal didn't disappoint, reacting with indignation when Lester offered to steady him, even though unable to do his business without assistance.

Eleanor gave Jubal one book after another. To Lester's surprise, Jubal accepted without complaint and spent long hours reading. Stories were a distraction from doubt and temporarily quieted the insidious terror that his injury might leave him a cripple. Otherwise Jubal said little, even when Lester tried to draw him out. The young man had entered a hall of silence, but there was an edge to him, as if he'd been drawn unwilling to a place better left alone. Mrs. Creesy's books provided a refuge.

The splint stayed until *Flying Cloud* closed the American coast. Shortly after sunrise on a cool day in early April, Mrs. Creesy called both boys aft. The weather had turned gray, with a raw wind out of the northeast.

"Looks like we'll have to beat up to Sandy Hook," she shivered, bundled in a heavy, woolen sea coat. "Leave the Gulf Stream and the temperature drops like a stone!" The sudden shift from tropical weather had chilled the entire ship. "You'll be needing a coat, Jubal," she continued, "so I'm going to trade that splint for a sling. I want you wear it for a month. One month, no less. Promise."

"Yes, m'am."

"Good. If that arm breaks again before it's healed properly, you might as well cut it off."

With his arm in a sling, Jubal watched from the bow as *Flying Cloud* made Sandy Hook by late afternoon and charged up the Narrows toward New York Harbor, wheeling into the wind off Governor's Island at sunset. On both the Hudson and East rivers, dozens of small craft skipped or plowed along in every direction. A fully laden clipper passed outbound, towed by a small steam tug belching black smoke into the gray twilight. Men scrambled through her tops, dropping the large canvas sign advertising California.

A tug, alerted by the signal station at Sandy Hook, waited for *Flying Cloud*. Lester finished furling the mizzen topgallant for the last time while sailors secured lines to the tug. All over the rigging, men readied their ship for port as carefully as if they were tucking her into bed. A sloop came alongside to take a copy of the manifest from Captain Creesy and pass up newspapers and mail before immediately peeling off for Battery Landing, where shipping agents from the Broad Street Exchange and South Street waited. With fortunate timing, the cargo could be largely sold before *Flying Cloud* came to her berth, where stevedores and longshoremen would be ready to unload.

"Poor bastards," Jubal said, nodding to the sailors working in the outbound clipper's rigging. A faint chantey began, and the ship's main course dropped and filled. Men cheered and another course fluttered before billowing full with a loud snap.

As they cleared Governor's Island, New York's noise and bustle turned them landward. Masts and rigging clogged the East River wharves like spiderwebs spun through a forest. Hundreds of street lanterns twinkled, and the city beckoned, humming with energy.

"By God, Jubal," Lester breathed, "we done been 'round the world."

"The world's a safer place than this town," Jubal remarked. Lester looked at his friend, surprised to see a trace of fear. The boys hadn't discussed any plans; neither knew what the other would do when they left ship.

"Where you going?" Jubal asked, as the ship bumped once against the wharf and lay still.

"Well …" Lester fidgeted, a little embarrassed, "I don't rightly know. Ain't really thought about it, strange as that seems. When do you suppose we get paid?"

Before Jubal answered a familiar feminine voice called from the quarterdeck.

"Now what does that woman want?" Jubal muttered. They came aft and nearly got run down by three seamen who burst out of the forecastle with their duffels and raced for the rail. The men waved and wished the boys "good thrustin" before taking the gangway in long, loping strides. In moments they vanished into the teeming dockyards.

Eleanor Creesy was ready for the city, dressed in a hooped dress, lace shawl, new shoes, and a fine, beribboned hat. "Do you have a place to stay?" the captain's wife asked.

Neither boy spoke.

"Yes, I'm not surprised," she continued. "Most of the men will end up in ... well, we know." She looked at Jubal closely. "You've got to protect that arm, so I've instructed Mr. Hare to let you stay on the ship for a few days. You can go into the city, but ..."

The captain's wife regarded them for a few moments longer and began to smile. "We will stay at the Astor House," she said, pulling beige kid gloves from her handbag. "Broadway, near Water Street. If you need anything you can find us there. Now then, Lester, be so kind as to go below and help the captain with our overnight bags. Mr. Hare will get the rest of our luggage to the hotel."

Lester knocked softly at the captain's quarters. Captain Creesy grunted, and as the door swung open, Lester swallowed and tried to hide his astonishment. Josiah Creesy stood resplendent in a charcoal gray suit of fine English wool and custom-made boots. A white shirt and black cravat, both Chinese silk, shone in the soft lamplight of the cabin. The captain cradled a beaver hat under one arm and held a small maroon calfskin satchel.

Lester swiped off his sea cap. "Your bags, sir?"

"In a moment," Captain Creesy replied, motioning him in. He reached into his coat and brought out two small leather purses with brass clasps. "Mrs. Creesy says Calhoun's arm will need at least another month, and I'd mark it June before he's ready for the rigging. We'll be gone by then. I've informed Mr. Hare that you may stay aboard until she's smoked. Make other arrangements before Friday."

Lester knew that deep in the hold rats had grown to the size of cats. Once the cargo was unloaded and the ship completely empty, every hatch and opening would be sealed and a smoldering fire ignited in an iron barrel resting on the keel. Twenty-four hours later, the ship would be opened and several hundred suffocated rats tossed into the East River, unless some enterprising merchant had already arranged their purchase for meat to sell to impoverished immigrants.

"I advise you leave this port," the captain continued. "Your wages won't last long, even under the best of circumstances." Lester had always wondered if the captain knew about their escapades in San Francisco. He remembered Cookie's comment—"Capt'n know everythin' 'bout ever'body"—and realized it was likely true.

"Here's your wages; give Calhoun his." Captain Creesy handed Lester the purses.

Lester suddenly felt stricken and began to stammer thanks, but the captain waved him off. "You're good sailors and welcome aboard my ship again if our courses cross. Now, one other thing, then take our bags to the wharf, there's a coach waiting." Captain Creesy pulled an ivory colored envelope from his inside pocket. "Here, when you're ready, give this to Donald McKay, East Boston." The captain slipped the envelope inside the satchel and gave it to Lester. He'll use you right."

"Thank you, sir. The shipbuilder?" Lester asked. Sailors endlessly discussed the qualities of their ships, and he knew *Flying Cloud* was McKay-built.

The captain nodded. "A good man," he said, carefully adjusting his hat. Lester tucked the satchel under his arm and followed Captain Creesy out, a bag in each hand.

At the coach, Mrs. Creesy turned to the boys. The schoolmarm had vanished. In her place stood an attractive woman whose stylish dress and regal bearing verged on elegance, all enhanced by the incongruity of a lined and deeply tanned face. "Thank you for your service," she said, her eyes sparkling. Mrs. Creesy looked from one boy to the other. "You've got wonderful minds," she murmured, "both of you. *Use them.* And write me!"

The captain helped his wife into the coach and then turned and shook hands with Lester. "Your father would be proud of you," he said softly. Then, without letting go, he offered his left hand to Jubal. Jubal's right arm was in a sling so the captain connected them all in an odd but touching way. "Good luck, men," he said in a voice so low only they could hear. "Read as much as you can. And keep your knives sharp."

Lester was too stunned to say anything. He stood mesmerized, watching the carriage disappear into city traffic. Finally, stroking the supple leather satchel, he pulled the letter free.

"We reduced to delivering mail?" Jubal sniped, taking the letter from Lester's limp hand. Flowing script graced the cotton envelope—*Donald McKay, East Boston.*

"'E gods, Jubal, ya carry an attitude," Lester said. "I'll deliver the letter, you can do anything you damn well please." He snatched the envelope and walked back up the gangway, anxious to be aboard ship.

"Lester, wait for me!"

Lester turned, waiting for another sarcastic comment. "What now?"

"They just act like some emperor and whatever you'd call his wife!"

"Empress. The very one who saved your life!"

"I was grateful. I did my duty!" Jubal looked spent. "Lester, people been telling me what to do forever. Don't you ever get tired of it?"

"You feeling like a slave?" Lester snapped.

Jubal sucked a breath. "Just what do you mean by that?"

"Prob'ly jes' what I said," Lester drawled. He could neither stop himself nor understand why he felt so raw.

For several moments the boys stared at each other, oblivious to the gathering night.

"C'mon, Lester," Jubal finally whispered. "We're shipmates."

Lester felt the bile wash from him. He was close to tears. Before him, Jubal stood silent, his good arm guarding the protective cradle of his sling.

Lester wearily turned toward the forecastle. "Let's get some sleep and we'll go in the morning."

"Go where?" Jubal's surprise cracked his voice.

"Best get you home. Maine."

Darkness had lowered as the boys went below, leaving the city streets alive in lights and sounds.

Chapter Thirteen

Four days after arriving in New York, Lester and Jubal sat on short barrels of molasses strapped aboard the coasting schooner *Mattie Mae* as a crisp, brilliant spring day dawned over Maine.

Penobscot Bay lay open to the north like a basin, speckled with islands and bordered on either side by the Camden Hills and Isle au Haut's rugged upland. As sunrise gave way to morning, the brooding evergreen forest clothing the islands softened into austere emerald, a reminder that warmth was but a visitor. Spruce and fir trees marched to the shore like sentinels, embracing flanks of monolithic granite. The texture of land leached seaward, giving the ocean a deep green, almost ominous hue. Low, glancing shafts of sunlight mottled the landscape from sparkle to deep shadow, its pristine severity relieved by an occasional steeple rising above the trees or a tiny, white clapboard house nestled at the head of a cove.

Mattie Mae was one of hundreds of schooners that plied the coast from Canada to the Rio Grande. Clyde Pingree and his son routinely made the run from Bangor, usually loaded with lumber destined for the insatiable New York shipyards that provided good prices for white pine, oak, and hackmatack. Sometimes Pingree would bring Hurricane Island cobblestones, apples, or ice blocks in summer, returning home with products ordered by storekeepers along the coast.

"How come you always say '*down* east'?" Jubal asked, huddling in his coat. "We're going more north."

"Downwind," Lester replied. "More'n likely, the wind's out the sou'west. From New York or Boston, you lay over on a broad reach. Coast makes out easterly, too." Their coats were buttoned to the throats, an object of merriment for Clyde Pingree, who wore a flannel shirt and proclaimed the morning "balmy" in an accent thick as a clamflat.

"I kin barely understand the man," Jubal muttered.

Lester grinned. "We been in the tropics, Clyde!" he called back to the elder Pingree. He laughed, a joyous, infectious sound that even Jubal couldn't ignore. "Jubal here," Lester crowed, "he ain't used to icicles on his mustache."

Jubal glanced at him, the trace of a smile gone. He was sensitive about his mustache, a scrawny upper lip that looked like a tabby cat's tail "with mange," as Lester put it.

Lester grinned wider, in high spirits. "Goddamn, Jubal," he said, "fine to be taking you home! Ma will be some tickled!" Thoughts of homecoming made him misty. With a fresh morning breeze the schooner moved along nicely a few miles off the coast. Lester had been on deck since dawn as they sailed past islands and headlands as if they were steps on a stairway to his boyhood room.

Jubal stayed silent as Lester chattered on. He reached into his jacket with the good arm and brought out a pipe and tobacco pouch, a new habit that took his mind off being handicapped. Showing a dexterity that Lester regarded with equal parts admiration and annoyance, Jubal filled the pipe bowl, replaced the pouch in his pocket, and then struck a stick match against the deck. Lester cupped his hands until the pipe was drawing well and Jubal nodded, flicking the match to leeward.

As the schooner sailed northward, Lester's conversation dwindled. He stood erect, aware that he had grown, and though his deep brown hair still had a rich luster to it, his face was tough as leather. After nearly a year aboard *Flying Cloud*, he felt like a young man.

"You boys want some biscuits?" Clyde Pingree called forward. "Won't be a one left when Cub hits 'em." Clyde Jr., or Cub, as everyone called him, had steered the schooner on the dawn watch while his father made coffee and biscuits in the tiny cutty. Then the twelve-year-old curled in a ball beside the cabin roof and fell sound asleep in the warming sunlight.

Lester rose without a word, grateful for the interruption. Coming home wasn't supposed to be more of the same confusion he'd felt since glimpsing Manhattan. After sailing three oceans, Lester thought he would return something of a hero, but he didn't feel heroic, just bewildered. He wanted to see his family, though the closer he got to Maine the uneasier he felt. Lester often talked to cover an inchoate feeling of dread, which made no sense to him because he was safe, surrounded by familiar landmarks, approaching a place that held most of the good memories of his life. Yet as *Mattie Mae* passed Owl's Head and entered Penobscot Bay, Lester would have been more comfortable reefing the main topgallant sail of *Flying Cloud* in South Atlantic sleet than bringing warm biscuits and a coffee pot forward on the sloop.

Jubal watched Lester arrange the fixings on a molasses barrel.

"Warming some, isn't it?" Jubal observed. "Be a good day, little on the cool side."

Lester grunted, aware that Jubal was making small talk, which he did about as often as sneezing.

"What's eating at you, Lester?" Jubal asked, carefully breaking off a piece of biscuit.

Lester pondered, chewing his biscuit thoroughly. "I don't rightly know, Jubal," he replied at length, taking a gulp of coffee. "I kind of feel like I grew up, and didn't know it. Now, I'm coming back, and ... well, don't get me wrong, I want to see Ma, I know she misses me awful. Johnny, 'n Sal too. But I don't rightly know what it is I'm coming back to. Or for ... except family." Lester took another swallow of coffee, then looked at his friend. "When's the last time you were home?"

Jubal thought for a moment. "Coming on three years since I left Gee's Bend. That's where I were raised, though it don't feel much to home."

Lester regarded him quizzically.

"Can't hardly say," Jubal continued, "but maybe ... Well, thing is Lester, I don't know but that home ain't a place anymore, just something we hold to in our mind. We're not exactly adrift, but we went to sea. Speaking of myself, I'm still sort of there."

Lester finished his biscuit, considering. Sunshine gathered on the hills and began to seep into the valleys, bathing the morning in light so clear the day almost crackled. The bay sparkled like a field of diamonds, intermittently crossed by fleets of cormorants zipping a foot above the glitter, and the boys sat quietly, absorbing the benign, peaceful pace that was so different from a working clipper ship.

"Reckon we done the tide good," Cub Pingree said in early afternoon, sounding as old as possible. He'd thought for two hours about what he could say to the blue-water sailors who looked impossibly exotic and capable. "Shore breeze comin' in good shape; we be at the mouth afta suppa. P'nobscot comes on a freshet with the melt, but tide turns her. Bangor near midnight, reckon. Ayuh."

The last syllable sounded like a gasp that got swallowed. Jubal glanced at Lester, who said nothing and didn't let the smile in his eyes reach his mouth.

Chapter Fourteen

Betty, the big ten-year-old milk cow, heard them first. She started fidgeting, uneasy about the strange smells coming out of the dawn so soon after she had calved.

"Stay still, for criminy sakes," Sally Norton snapped. "You too, Arthur! Wait your turn!" The calf strained at his rope, slobbering, and let out a half-strangled bay. Sally doggedly pulled at Betty's long teats, hoping to fill the milk bucket before Arthur's racket riled his mother. Sally leaned into the cow's flank—she had learned to doze against the warm blanket of Betty's hide while continuing to milk—and tried to resume her dream when Betty shifted so abruptly that Sally nearly fell into the milk pail. She jumped back and whacked Betty on the rump.

"What's got into you!" she cried, both peeved and perplexed, since milking Betty was usually about as exciting as watching rain. Then Sally heard the scraping sound of the shed door.

A young man stood in the doorway, his features shadowed from the faint light spilling from the lantern she had hung on a post between the door and milking stall. They stared at each other until another man came out from behind the door and stepped into the shed. Sally regarded them for a few seconds, her head cocked like a puppy.

"Lester!" Sally's scream shook the shed. She flew into her brother's arms with a thud that made Jubal step back. Sally squealed, jumping up and down, yelling so loud both Betty and Arthur started lowing.

"'E gods, Sally!" Lester laughed, "you're gonna wake all of Bangor!" He tried to give his sister a decent hug but she was all over him.

Jubal heard a door slam and the brief clatter on steps. A shape materialized out of the darkness and he stepped farther back as Jane Norton hurried to the shed. Lester turned, one arm still around his sister, to see his mother pause and a hand come to her mouth before she whimpered and threw her arms around her son. She clutched him, sobbing soundlessly, her body heaving in great, silent spasms. Jubal bit his lip and turned away to stare at the crimson-edged hills.

"Yeah, Momma, I missed you so much," Lester whispered, burying his head in her shoulder. They silently held each other so long Sally tired of waiting.

"You come with Lester?" she asked.

Jubal turned, trying to hide a smile.

"No," Lester said, still holding his mother, "he's under arrest, caught him about to steal Betty."

"Stop it, Lester!" Sally wailed, "You're teasing already and you ain't been home a minute!" She looked right at Jubal. "I'm Sally and I'm twelve. Thirteen this summer, in three months."

"She's shy, too," Lester added.

Jubal looked from one to the other, not quite sure what to make of the banter. "My pleasure, miss," he drawled, and tipped his hat.

Sally stared at him, awestruck. "Where you from?" she managed.

"I'm from Alabama, miss. Your brother Lester and I were shipmates." Jubal thought to be helpful since he had no idea what lies Lester would dream up next. "I weren't about to steal your cow, either ... Lester, he tends to exaggerate some. I expect y'all know about that."

Lester looked at his sister. "You're special Sal. Four, five sentences, took me a month to get that much out of Jubal. We are shipmates, but he's not what you'd call a talker."

"But I expect you eat," Jane Norton said, wiping her glistening face. She was short and solid, largely hidden under a long shawl that draped to her knees. A faded kerchief covered graying hair. Large, luminous eyes, and a strong nose dominated her features, seeming to pinch her mouth in a short, tight smile. "Come inside," she directed, "I'll make breakfast. Lester, you have to tell us everything."

"Sure will," Lester agreed. "We ain't had much but biscuits 'n beans these last few days. Now where's Johnny? He sleeping late, not doing chores?"

The light, barely coming into the sky, suddenly seemed snuffed out. There was an awful pause and Sally looked down.

"We wrote ..." Jane Norton replied, in a ghost of a voice.

Lester looked from his mother to Sally and back. "Haven't heard nary a word since I left. We always outrun the mail, I guess ..." He waited, his stomach knotting.

"Johnny's with your father," Jane Norton said in a cadence so flat and bitter the morning seemed to die right there.

Lester felt as if he'd fallen in the spring runoff of the Penobscot River. He tried to gather a breath but couldn't.

"Measles," his mother said, her face expressionless, looking drawn and hollow. "Last August. Two days after his birthday. He wanted to make his birthday."

Lester reached for a post. He massaged his forehead, letting out a strangled sigh. No one spoke until Sally looked up at Jubal.

"What'd you do to your arm?" She was so tired of grieving for her brother. Nothing ever brought him back, but now Lester was here.

"Sally!" her mother admonished.

"I'm curious Ma, that's all. Don't mean nothing by it."

"Got broke," Jubal replied, quietly. "Hit us a squall, south of the equator. Lester helped doctor it."

A long silence followed until Lester looked up. "Did he suffer awful?"

"Come in for breakfast," Lester's mother said, gently pulling her son from the barn. "It's chilly. Come in now."

"Here," Sally said, handing the milk bucket to Jubal, "use your good arm. I got to reach an understanding with Betty and that dumb calf of hers, Arthur. He'll make good steak, he lasts that long." Johnny's death had just about taken the life out of her mother, but Sally was determined to bring laughter back in the house. She couldn't bear living in a tomb.

Lester walked to the house with an arm around his mother, feeling almost in a dream. He couldn't believe Johnny was gone forever, and tried picturing the tousle-haired, mischievous kid, running through the field two steps ahead of his sister after he'd hit her with a rotten apple. Lester was too stunned to grieve and everything felt overwhelming again until he entered the house and smelled baking bread.

Jane Norton expected young men to have appetites, but she was amazed at how much food Lester and Jubal consumed. Eggs, flapjacks, baked apples, smoked bacon, all of Betty's milk and, finally, a large pot of tea disappeared.

"No coffee's a catastrophe," Lester belched, midway through his stack. "Have to fix that." Otherwise, he said very little at breakfast.

Sally watched the boys. Her brother had grown several inches taller, and was lean and dark-haired, with a lanky, loose-limbed ease. Jubal stood shorter and thicker, with powerful hands, a square face, and a mop of sandy hair that shone in the morning light. Sally felt latent strength and an element of danger. She could read Lester like an open book, but Jubal was bound shut. Sally immediately decided to explore; she loved secrets.

"What are your plans?" Jane Norton asked, shoving the thoughts of her youngest child away to a private hurting place. Both the boys sat immobile before plates they had wiped clean. For such an assault on her pantry, the table looked remarkably ordered.

"Don't got but one," Lester groaned, "crawl upstairs to bed."

"Had enough?" Sally wondered. "Dinner's next week."

"For now," nodded Lester. "Sure beats Cookie's efforts."

"Maybe you can tell us," Sally said, turning to Jubal, "while Lester licks his plate."

Jubal's grin captivated both mother and daughter. "A man leaves food in the forecastle mess, next time he'll git less. And you never know when you might eat again." Jubal nodded at Sally's mother. "Mrs. Norton, m'am, I don't remember when I last had such a marvelous meal. I hope to tell you it was fine."

"So's your plan to eat here till you drop or we starve?" Sally asked. At the rate her brother and Jubal consumed food, the pantry, root cellar, and small smokehouse would be empty in two weeks.

"That will do, Sally," her mother directed, pleased the boys had eaten so well.

"Plain fact is we been short of plans since … when, Lester?" Jubal asked, stifling a yawn. "China, I guess."

Lester glanced at Jubal, aware again there were unfathomable parts to his friend. Observing him interact with his mother and sister was like watching another unknown color appear as a prism turned in the light.

"Well, Ma," Lester said, "depends on Jubal's arm. Mrs. Creesy …" he paused, regarding his mother with a look that said there was an untold story now ready for the telling. She held his gaze. "Eleanor Creesy," Lester continued, "said it's got to be in that sling for another month. Been broke about three, four weeks now, right Jubal? How's she feeling?"

"Aches a bit in the damp," Jubal replied, "but the skin's healed and I plan to take off the sling soon."

"Please don't rush," Mrs. Norton warned. "I expect you to stay until it's fully healed. A month will go by quickly."

"And Lester," Sally chimed in, "we need 'bout twenty cord a wood for next winter, beans and corn'll go in by a month, shed's ready to collapse, the roof leaks above my bedroom, and there's a skunk living under the house that I ain't dealin' with."

Lester yawned, the cookstove heat closing his lights sure as a shade. "Bossy as ever."

"You two get some rest," Mrs. Norton directed. "We'll talk later. Jubal there's an extra bed in the boys' room ..."

The kitchen went quiet. Lester got to his feet with the slump of an old man.

"Welcome home, son." Jane Norton said, her eyes tearing. "And thank you for coming, Jubal."

―

The next day it snowed half a foot. Lester stayed in bed but Jubal was up before dawn, ready to start the fires, help Sally with the milking, collect any eggs from the dozen chickens in their pen, lug in a few chunks of wood, and anything else he could do that wouldn't take more than one arm.

Sally thought he was a little crazy. "Jubal," she said, milking Betty, "I appreciate the company, but don't you want to sleep a little? Lester said you only slept four hours at a time? That'd make me throw up."

"Lester does likes his sleep," Jubal agreed. "Probably thinks to get it while he can."

On first sight, Jubal thought Maine looked pretty but he couldn't understand why someone would choose to live in a place where it snowed at the end of April. Jubal hated the cold, which meant anywhere above or below the subtropics.

"Can I do something?" Jubal asked, feeling useless. He had already decided that if he ever lost an arm by accident or in a fight he'd shoot himself.

"Get that pot over there, top the bench," Sally directed, her curly auburn hair planted in Betty's flank. "Slosh some water 'round it, there's a bucket by the door, bring it here. I'll pour some for Arthur. You'll probably have to stick your finger in his mouth to suck, he's too stupid to drink on his own yet but once he gets going, he'll figure it out. If he don't, have a drink of warm milk yourself."

Sally kept to her milking but her attention was on Jubal. She could hear him, then saw his legs disappear behind Betty's big belly. A moment later she heard a thud as Arthur, smelling the milk, butted Jubal. Sally giggled and listened for a moment but couldn't resist. "You gainin'?"

"I'm fine," Jubal drawled. "Though Arthur here ... I had goats growing up and he's dumber than any goat I ever seen, yes m'am."

"How come you're so polite?"

"Taught that way, I guess." Their conversation felt like the milk, warm with a little slippery texture to it. In the lulls, the shed was silent save for Betty's milk whizzing into the pail. Arthur had figured out how to drink and emptied the pan in seconds. Jubal pulled away before the calf butted again. "He wants more," Jubal said, coming round Betty's rump.

Sally snorted. "He'd drink till he shit straighter 'n a pencil." She twisted her head on Betty's flank to look at Jubal. "Guess that ain't polite?" Suddenly, Sally felt embarrassed and wished she could think before speaking. "Southern girls swear?" she asked, hopefully.

Jubal grinned. "Never."

"Don't start in, Jubal Calhoun." Sally loved the name when he first introduced himself the day before, on their way into the house from the shed. "You been 'round my brother too long. Besides, I'm hoping a little of your politeness rubs off, but you keep up like that I won't have a chance."

"Ain't a fault to say what's on your mind."

"At the time, you mean?" Sally shot Jubal a look but didn't wait for a response. "Yeah, I do, but don't know if it's the best thing. Ma's always snapping at me 'cause of it. Says when I get older …" she finished milking and stood up. The pail was nearly full and Sally leaned back a little to balance its weight. "Your mother nice to you?"

Jubal's grin faded. The talk had turned so fast. "I'll be haulin' that fer ya," he said, taking the pail. He turned and carefully carried the milk through the shed door. Sally watched him go and bit her lip, wondering. Then she let Arthur loose to attack his mother's udder before following Jubal to the house.

―

The Norton farm was on a rise above the river, ten acres clear and double that wooded, though the good lumber had been cut off. Fields provided room for a huge garden, most of which ended up in thick glass jars and the root cellar, and enough corn and hay to keep Betty in milk half the year.

Jane Nichols was the fifth of eight children, six of them girls, daughter of a sea captain who was gone for years at a stretch. She grew up headstrong and willful, a constant trial to her mother. When her father came home between voyages, the same temperament that dominated all manner of seamen ruled his children. The boys quailed while the girls stayed out of his way, except for Jane. She resented authority, her face was too strong to be pretty, and a stubborn streak grew with every stricture the family imposed.

Generally, she would rather muck about on the clamflats or explore the bay in a little peapod with one of her brothers than learn to sew or knit. When Jane was sixteen, Captain Nichols found her behavior so intolerable on one of his visits ashore that he burnt the peapod, an act that completely underestimated his daughter.

'I ain't your crew!' she screamed at him, and stomped out of the house.

Four miles away, John Norton lived in a shack on a small cove, eking a meager livelihood from fishing the bay in a dilapidated Friendship sloop. An only child, orphaned when both his parents died the same week from whooping cough, John Norton had a stoic, easygoing way that didn't argue when Jane stepped aboard, nor when she straddled him in the cutty of his sloop.

The Nichols lineage came direct from upright, virtuous Puritan stock, and Jane's pregnancy sealed the estrangement with Captain Nichols, who never spoke to her again. The shack was a far cry from the substantial federal house on Main Street in Searsport, and as her belly grew Jane faced the gnawing price of freedom. Though Lester was an easy baby, the choices, or lack of them, infuriated her.

Inshore fishing was an independent life and a poor one. John knew the old sloop was too chancy for open water but he figured a few years' wages at sea could stake him to a bigger, safer boat in Maine. Before Christmas, he shipped out on a square-rigger hauling lumber from Bangor to Liverpool.

Sally had just learned to walk when he returned. While Lester was a lovable, good-natured burbler, Sally had her mother's bones and they battled from the moment Sally began biting Jane's nipples wanting more milk. By the time John landed, Jane looked a decade older, nearly crazed from living alone in the shack with two infants. Jane swore if he ever left again she'd sit in the shack with the children and burn it to the ground.

A season later, an old and tired but still sound fishing schooner came available on a share return basis. John leased the boat, hired a man, and went to Georges Bank, three days out, ten fishing, and two back, six months a year. Jane hated his absences but finally there was enough money. Lester started at the little one-room schoolhouse in Orrington, Sally and her mother fought to a draw most days, and Johnny came into the world.

In between fishing trips and during the winter, John Norton cut the white oak, hackmatack, cedar, and pine that had made the land valuable. Over four years, a thirty-four-foot boat rose on the Penobscot riverbank and Lester's earliest memories were of the small schooner's frame rising, his father daubing knees of hackmatack and white oak frames. The razor-sharp adze took off wood flakes that were perfect for Lester to carry down to the river and launch, just like his father said would happen with the schooner.

The loneliness, three children, and tearing a hardscrabble saltwater farm from the lower Penobscot valley sapped the fight right out of Jane, though not the latent spirit. Gradually, she adjusted, though it was easier while John was out on the Banks. When he was home the frustrations and withered illusions somehow were harder to bear, or easier to share, Jane wasn't sure which. As much as she longed for him while he was at sea, on land his presence was a constant reminder that he could go and she had to stay. By Lester's seventh birthday, John had finished the schooner and spent seven and sometimes eight months at sea, a week or so between trips. The house got bigger, the fireplace drew, a small barn rose, several more acres were stumped, and a good cast-iron cook stove appeared in the kitchen. As the homestead became comfortable, the parents said less.

Lester saw none of it. His imagination lived mostly at sea, for despite the boy's pleading, John kept him ashore with the admonition to listen to his mother and attend school. That pattern lasted until the October when John Norton went out to fish and stayed on the Banks forever.

Jubal surprised the Nortons with his one-armed industriousness but within several days, Lester decided he would have to find work while his friend's arm healed. The two boys ate more in a lean week than the women could consume in a generous month. Though spring was pushing in, it was too late for prime maple sugaring and too early for planting.

Ten days after coming to Maine, Lester pushed back from the dinner table.

"Come end of this week, Ma, we'll have 'nough wood put aside," he announced. "Then I'm going upriver."

Already restless, the prospect of hanging around the farm another month was more than he liked to consider. Frequently, he found himself thinking of his father, with the dawning realization that John Norton went to sea as much to leave as to go. Recalling boyhood memories of his father, Lester could imagine the man he must have been.

"There be fifteen, twenty million feet comin' down the river," Lester added. "Men got to ride that drive or logs'll end up snarled bad as a mile-long beaver dam. Decent money if you can keep your feet."

"And you slip and fall, how you supposed to get out with a bunch of logs on your head?" Sally challenged. The mere idea of falling in the river made her shiver. "'Sides, you weren't but a cook's helper last time."

Lester gritted his teeth, feeling the familiar urge to tell his sister to keep her mouth shut. On *Flying Cloud* Lester had talked about his winter in the lumber camps when he was thirteen, but the tale grew a little in the telling, and he wasn't particularly interested now in being specific with Jubal, who watched closely.

"They need good men," Lester huffed. "Told me anytime I was welcome back."

"Peelin' spuds?"

Lester didn't appreciate Jubal's amusement. "Can you imagine growing up with such a damn sass?"

"Lester!" Jane Norton slammed a fork down but Sally had already hurled a half-eaten potato at her brother.

"She started it, Mom!" Lester worked into a good, reckless lather. "Man doesn't have to put up with that!"

"You act like you're some capt'n or something!" Sally cried, realizing she'd crossed a line but having no idea how to gracefully back down. "You *were* peeling ..."

"That's enough," Mrs. Norton hissed, in a voice so hard both children went silent. "Go upriver, Lester," she ordered. "Jubal, you'll stay here until your arm is healed, then you either join Lester or do as you wish. You're welcome as long as we live here. And you," she pointed at Sally, "put your barbs away. Sometimes you seem to cut just for the fun of it."

Sally's lip quivered and she wanted to shout at her mother but was too ashamed. The conversation had taken an abrupt turn and dropped into the rancor that occasionally soured their family for days. Sally knew she was caustic and thin-skinned but couldn't help it—the nastiness sometimes just spewed up before she could stop herself.

Jubal watched with unabashed fascination, which provided Jane a lever. "Were children this harsh in your family?" she demanded. Mrs. Norton still looked ready to slap Lester or Sally, whoever spoke first.

"Didn't have none, really," Jubal replied.

"Sally, clean the table and serve pie," her mother ordered. "Lester, I'd like some of that good coffee you make." The children rose without a word.

"Now, Jubal, explain what you meant by that," Mrs. Norton continued. As Lester gathered a coffee tin he'd bought in Orrington and filled the pot from a copper urn on the cookstove, he listened intently. Getting a family history from Jubal aboard ship had been like melting ice to make water.

Jubal's free hand went inside the sling and massaged his arm. In the last few days he had started moving it some, finally beginning to sense healing. The muscle atrophy frightened him and he had divergent impulses, wanting to protect his arm yet use it to quickly recover strength and movement. Whenever he took the sling off to dress or bathe, the arm felt as though a stiff wind would break it again. The thought of a useless appendage was unbearable.

"Not very interesting, m'am," Jubal replied, his face settling into a self-deprecating smile.

Jane Norton tingled with anticipation. Something flared in her; she had never tolerated taciturn retreats from her husband and was not about to accept them in a young man.

"I'll be the judge of that," she replied, a smile belying the tart edge to her voice. The kitchen had become quiet, Lester and Sally moving as though on tiptoes. The children kept their eyes averted but a simmering fire in the cookstove was enough sound to exaggerate silence.

Jubal fought the urge to flee that rose every time someone asked him about his childhood. Aboard *Flying Cloud* it was easy enough; he just left the forecastle, regardless of weather, though it happened rarely. A ship was an intimate refuge and each man determined his level and boundaries of intimacy, accepted by his shipmates lest someone violate their own. The Norton kitchen was the forecastle's antithesis and he suddenly realized where Sally's temperament had formed. For the Norton women, boundaries were to be breached.

"Tell me about your mother," Mrs. Norton said.

"Don't rightly know, m'am," Jubal replied. "She died bearing me."

"At childbirth?"

"So I'm told."

"You believe that?" Jane even surprised herself at the question, though Jubal's expression gave her deep satisfaction. The boy sat stunned, opening and closing his mouth several times, unable to speak.

Jubal's hand went to his sparse mustache. At length he spoke in a slow, measured drawl. "I don't rightly know."

"Why do you doubt it?" Jane asked, her voice lowering.

"It's not that, exactly," Jubal replied. "Jes' never really knew. My daddy said she'd died when I was born."

"Who told you different?"

"That's the point. Weren't nobody, 'cept maybe ..." Jubal nodded to himself, "Emma."

"Servant ...?" Mrs. Norton pressed. "Slave?"

"Oh, she's slave. Ain't seen her in years."

"You remember her, though?"

Jubal could remember Emma, more the scent and feel of her than an actual presence. Memories were vague and fleeting, like shadows in a dream, tucked away in the deepest parts of his sleep. Emma was soft and dark, a musky, tropical fen when he buried himself in her arms after hurting himself, he couldn't remember how, as a very young boy, his earliest memory. Though Jubal couldn't be sure, he suspected she had been his wet nurse, as often happened in the slave quarters when children were orphaned. He must have shared her lap with her own newborn but couldn't remember, mother and children fading into the mists of his early childhood, replaced by the dusty, white light of an Alabama afternoon, of humid nights and the swamp chorus. Amorphous, blurred images piled on top of each other, punctuated by the sound of a jug coming to rest on the floor, a soft, definitive thump of home.

Sally watched him like a hawk, loving every syllable that rolled off his tongue. Jane was about to ask another question, but Jubal leaned forward and slowly stood up. "Y'all excuse me, believe I'll smoke my pipe. Sunset's do have a fine, crisp quality in this northern light." He reached for a jacket and swept it around his shoulders. With a respectful nod to Mrs. Norton, he left her sitting at the table, regarding him.

Sally looked at her brother with liquid eyes and could feel her heart racing. She had never seen a man face down her mother, a man that couldn't be dominated or at least brought to heel by the power of a formidable woman. Lester caught the glow in his sister and understood. Years of knuckling to a strong-willed mother had left him proud of her strength but weary of the struggle. Lester had learned to bend and avoid engagement, while Sally woke each morning prepared for battle. Neither had anticipated Jubal, who could stand noble without fighting and simply disengage with dignity.

Chapter Fifteen

"You still got your wages, right?" Jubal asked, balancing on the wooden sled as it slid across the hoarfrosted field. The day had come on crystal-clear, rising sunlight glittering over the hayfield. Lester steered Jake, the huge palomino Percheron draft horse, through an opening in a stone wall leading to the woodlot where they'd spent the last several days thinning and bucking small trees into firewood for the following winter. Jubal worked the horse while Lester chopped. Teamstering with one arm was awkward but Jake remained patient and the trees weren't big. Though Lester could just as easily have done the work himself he knew Jubal was stir-crazy.

"I do," Lester replied. "Nothing but the trip here to spend 'em on."

"Best make what you can on the river," Jubal said, breath vapor spilling into the sparkling morning. "Leave it all to your ma. I'll give half what I got—and don't be arguin'."

Lester knew if the situation were reversed, he'd do the same.

"Fair enough. I'll pack up tomorrow, ride north Monday mornin'. Be back in four, five weeks; then we'll pick us up a coastie for Boston. With luck we'll be running down our easting by midsummer—might even be in time to catch a hurricane coming north."

"The trades I miss," Jubal admitted, "though I been doing just fine with no hurricane. You've never been in one, so you can josh. Hurricane ain't a joke, like to beat that squall busted my arm all day and night."

"Ever seen one down home?" Lester asked, stepping to a foot-thick maple.

Jubal nodded, "One blew the shit out of the cotton crop three years ago."

Lester wound up with the ax but paused. "That why you left?"

"Had sumin' to do with it." Jubal worked Jake around to pick up the first twitch. He said no more. Lester waited, and then shrugged. Moments later the *thwack* of axe hitting frozen hardwood echoed across the still valley.

"Gimme your knife, Lester," Jubal said, taking his dinner plate to the slate sink. Lester pulled his sailor knife from its sheath, grateful even though he felt naked without the blade. Jubal had an uncanny knack for putting an edge to a knife.

"How come you don't sharpen your own?" asked Sally, still picking at her dinner.

"How come you're feeding like a bird?" Lester replied, knowing his sister was trying to be ladylike. She hadn't spoken to him in two days.

Sally's glance was pure malevolence.

"Y'all mind sparing us the dog 'n cat routine?" Jubal said, taking Lester's knife. "Gets old."

All three Nortons stared at him. Since his arrival, Jubal had been so mild-mannered they were taken aback by the direct, quiet drawl. Even Jane had come to tolerate his taciturn demeanor, though it was a grudging acceptance. No amount of prying short of rudeness had brought forth much information from Jubal about his family or childhood.

Lester didn't think twice about Jubal's long stretches of silence. The sudden lance stung, however, especially since none of the conversation had been directed at his friend. Jubal could be touchy but Lester didn't recall him barking at the endless bicker of shipmates aboard *Flying Cloud*.

Jubal read his mind.

"We're not aboard ship, Lester. When you and Sal get peckin' it fills up the house so, 'n the rest of us got to live with it. Besides," Jubal glanced at Sally, "'tis disrespectful to your ma."

Jane Norton laughed a full-throated, one-syllable peal. For once Sally was speechless, bringing a wide grin to Lester, whose feeling of annoyance evaporated as his sister lit up like a crimson beacon.

"Go up that goddam river, Lester," Sally hissed, "and keep going!" She shot up from the table and stomped upstairs. There was a moment's pause before her door slammed so hard the house shook.

"Goodness, Jubal," Lester grinned, "I don't envy digging yourself outta that stall."

"She'll be fine," Jubal said, feeling the edge of Lester's knife. He took a sharpening stone off the fireplace mantle and sat near the fire with the stone between his knees, beginning the slow, methodical stropping to hone the blade.

Jane Norton watched the young men, amused that they would converse almost as though she were invisible. Sally's blasphemy warranted a reprimand but the girl's volatility would have to lower before she could hear anything. Since Jubal's arrival, Jane noticed her daughter's behavior had gone from temperamental to erratic. She recognized the symptoms. With a mixture of curiosity and dread Jane Norton accepted the young handsome sailor mending under the same roof as a daughter in the full throes of change. Sally needed new clothes that wouldn't stretch her front buttons.

Later that evening in the boys' bedroom, Lester laid out an assortment of woolen clothes he'd collected a year earlier. The pants and red shirt had been mended several times, victim of branches and underbrush snags. While he stuffed a haversack with an old pair of hobnailed boots given him by a lumberjack, his mother came in holding two pairs of newly knitted socks. Lester cooed, knowing the socks would keep him warm even when soaked with frigid Penobscot water. Jane Norton sat in a small rocking chair as Lester packed the remainder of his clothes plus the new socks. While he rummaged through his duffel bag, looking for anything he might want to take north, his hand closed on the small leather satchel. Withdrawing the letter, he read its address aloud: "Donald McKay, East Boston."

"Captain Creesy," Lester waved the envelope, "gave it to us in New York. This McKay fellow builds ships in East Boston."

"You're going to see him?" Jane Norton asked, trying to keep the grief from her face.

"I expect so." Lester sat on the bed and leaned forward, looking at her directly. "How did you find Eleanor Creesy?"

"You were bound to follow your father, and I couldn't bear to lose you, too," Jane Norton replied. "I wanted you to go with someone who would keep you alive." The ghost of Johnny hung in the evening. Silence filled the room as Lester came over to his mother and kneeled on the floor before her. "I've never met the woman, nor had heard of her, for that matter," Jane took her son's hands and continued. "But your Aunt Dorcus knows her. Dorcus had just come back with Uncle Jediah from New York; he's been running a Liverpool packet for several years and Dorcus often goes along. I wanted Jediah to take you, but they were going to be ashore for the summer. Dorcus had met the Creesys at the hotel in New York where all the captains stay. Jediah and Captain Creesy sailed together as mates twenty years ago. Dorcus said there was a new ship being built that Captain Creesy would command, and she has high respect for Eleanor Creesy. You may remember your aunt doesn't respect easily."

Both Jane and Lester smiled at the understatement. Dorcus Fullam was the eldest Nichols daughter, a frosty, severe matriarch of the family. She had not seen her youngest sister since John's funeral but with a glance understood Jane's rebellion years had faded into the oblivion of shattered dreams. Dorcus' heart softened at losses already suffered, and Jane's request revealed a new, imminent sadness.

"Captains are not made kind," Dorcus replied, when Jane made her pilgrimage to the substantial Eastport house. "So we won't ask them." To Jane's astonishment, Dorcus offered her tea and then sat down to compose a letter to Eleanor Creesy in New York, "an extraordinary woman." She cautioned, "Make sure Lester understands he's an example of the family!"

Jane stroked her son's head. "I didn't want you to grow up so fast, and now you're the only man I have left."

"You going to be all right, Momma?" Lester asked.

"No," Jane Norton replied, through a flash of bitterness. "You'll be gone in a month, Sally will leave in a few years, and my Johnnys are dead. I'll grow old, alone, but it won't be in this house!" The last came with such force that it dried Lester's tears. He didn't know what to do.

"I'm sorry, son," Jane said, trying to smile. "It's been a dreadful year. Now don't make it worse." The vehemence returned. "Don't you dare lose yourself to that ocean! I will never forgive you if you follow your father!" Lester nodded dutifully, though struck by a preposterous thought. Admonishing the ocean to be nice sounded like a job for a mother; no sailor went to sea intending to drown.

"I'll be careful. The captain and Mrs. Creesy taught me right."

"What's she like?"

"Oh, it'd be like shipping with you," Lester replied, though he realized his mother was several years younger than Mrs. Creesy and looked a decade older.

Jane Norton's face broke into a sudden, wide smile that lingered for a moment before dissolving. "Are you joining the ship again?"

"*Flying Cloud*? No, she'll be gone by the time we get back to New York. I expect Mr. McKay will have a ship soon to sail, or know of one. I've found a ship once; the next time'll be easy, especially with Jubal. Two good sailors are valuable."

"Even so young?" Jane asked, quickly adding, "though, I know you're capable."

"There aren't many old men on ships, Momma. Climbing aloft at night, in a snowstorm …" Lester had the sinking feeling he should keep his mouth shut. Jane Norton shuddered and fell silent. He laid his head in her lap and held her, watching the shadows of candle flame flicker on the walls of his boyhood room and thinking it was time to go.

―

Downstairs, Jubal rocked near the fire, his mind aloft on a moonlit, tropical sea. Near him, Sally sat in the straight-backed chair using firelight to mend a pocket in Jubal's sea trousers.

"What'ja thinkin'?" she whispered. Only the tiny creak of the wooden rockers and an occasional pop of burning wood marred the silent evening.

Jubal raised an eyebrow and smiled. "Oh, how about a night in the trades? Every sail flying, pulling perfect, so fine and full you couldn't feel any strain, just the gentle roll of a ship gliding 'cross a sparkling sea. Moon hanging up there like a fancy New York streetlamp, bright enough to read a book at midnight."

"Sounds lovely," Sally admitted, though the sea held little intrinsic wonder for her. Sally was far more interested in places the sea connected.

"Beyond words," Jubal breathed, closing his eyes again.

Sally grew tired of the quiet. "How did you meet Lester?"

Jubal didn't open his eyes but his answer told her he was willing to talk. "He stumbled onto the ship," Jubal chuckled, "like he was lost. Think he was, too."

Jubal thought back to when he met Lester, on a late afternoon before leaving New York. *Flying Cloud* was taking in the last of her cargo, passenger luggage cluttered the wharf, and sailors still appeared alongside, many looking dazed with their duffel bags and sea chests. Jubal had been aboard for a week and spent most of his days aloft, where he was when Lester appeared at the gangway, wide-eyed and nervous, asking for Mrs. Creesy.

"Comin' on dark," Jubal said. "So he were happy to find the ship."

Sally stopped her sewing. "Lester ain't afraid of the dark."

"In New York he'd be, any sense to him. No place for the faint of heart, nor the foolish. Neither is a ship."

"You had any hard times?" Sally asked hopefully. "At sea? In New York?"

"My share," Jubal drawled, not a hint of humor to his voice.

"How much is a share?"

Jubal opened his eyes and looked at her. Sally's auburn curls shone in the firelight and he could smell a faint whiff of lavender soap. He smiled, knowing she had taken another bath. In the woods, Lester had grumbled about cutting deadwood for hot water, complaining that Sally had taken more baths in the last week than she normally did in a year.

"A share?" Jubal repeated, bemused.

"You had your fair share, you said," Sally chirped. "So …? What the hell … What's that supposed to mean?"

"I don't believe there's a question in the world you and your brother ain't thought to ask."

"That's 'cause asking you questions is like milking Betty in November when she's about dry," Sally sniffed. "Besides, I been fixing your clothes."

"What's my pockets got to do with questions?"

"It's a fair trade," Sally replied, biting a thread before examining the trousers.

"Takes two to trade, and I don't know what-all we're trading."

"Oh, yes you do, Jubal Calhoun! I fix your pockets and you tell me about yourself. Which means I get to ask questions and you answer them. That's required, and a fair trade." Sally threw him a challenging look that left Jubal tongue-tied. "You musta been a trial for your teacher. Now, we'll start again, slow and easy like. *What's your fair share?*"

Jubal's gaze returned to the fire. For a moment he felt the flash of anger and then put it aside with a sense of resignation.

"Well, I was born in Gee's Bend, Alabama."

Sally leaned forward, the sea pants discarded in her lap.

"And …" Jubal mused, suddenly veering uncomfortable and cranky, feeling interrogated. "That's where I grew up." He said it with finality and went back to rocking.

Sally sat opened-mouth and tense, waiting expectantly. In an instant, realizing Jubal had gone silent again, she stood and threw his sea pants in his face, hard.

"Mend your own damn clothes!" Sally cried, dashing up the stairs.

Jubal continued rocking, his face smarting from catching a button. He nearly threw his pants into the fire, then just dropped them in disgust and looked at his folded arm. "Heal, goddamn you!" he muttered. Above him the floor creaked, followed by slow footfalls coming down the stairs.

Lester slumped in Sally's chair and stared at the fire. "What the hell happened with Sal?"

"Think they can use a one-armed man in the lumber camps?"

"Nope, you'll have to stay. Be better anyway, you can't stove that arm up or we'll never get out of here. Lord knows, I'd rather face the Horn again than these women in the morning."

Jubal scoffed. "You're headed to the woods, I got to navigate these shoals alone. Where's Eleanor when a man needs her?"

Lester chuckled, trying to keep it quiet. Jubal broke into a grin and joined Lester laughing, both of them muffled to occasional snorts. "I can understand a Whampoa coolie better than these women," Jubal shook his head. "They ain't *never* met a question they didn't want to bring home."

"Ayah," Lester sucked wind. "Never knew why my dad seemed so ready to be at sea. I love Ma and Sal, but I can't wait to fly the royals again."

"Well, get up to the woods, 'n back. Don't bust nothin' up. You leave in the morning? How 'bout I come to Bangor, buy some supplies and come back, you keep going?"

"Are you gonna be all right while I'm gone?"

Jubal shrugged. "Likely not, 'less I move in with Betty." He started laughing again. "Just get back all of a piece so I don't have to wait for you to mend. Then we'll head for China or some other place where they don't ask so many darn questions."

Carefully, the boys mounted the stairs and tiptoed through the hallway. The bedroom was small, and they moved around each other like dancers in a comforting memory of the clipper forecastle.

"See you in the morning, Lester," Jubal said, rolling on his side.

"'Night, Jubal," Lester lay still, staring out the small double-hung window at the Big Dipper. "Good luck," he whispered.

Jubal was already asleep.

Chapter Sixteen

By the middle of May, Jubal decided he would remove his sling for good when the month turned. He was already beginning to use his arm, carefully gripping the purse line and hauling it with Jane and Sally Norton to empty the seine net each afternoon.

Before he died, John Norton had constructed a small weir in the river for the spring salmon run. Though the catch declined as Bangor dumped more refuse and sawdust into the river, each annual run was a necessary supplement to the Nortons' food supply.

Jane Norton hated fishing and every year swore she'd never do it again. The resolve died when meat became scarce in winter and her boys wolfed their dried fish. Each spring they lugged an old dory into the river again and set the seine net. Salmon on the drying rack reminded Jane of codflakes along the shoreline. The fish harvest was bitter irony; she had demanded John limit himself to similar work that killed him, depriving her of their life together, even if she had grown furious at him for being so decently dull.

Sally liked everything about the fish but its taste. Though winter hunger was a great leveler of food preferences, Sally swore she'd never eat fish again when she grew up and left. That she was leaving was a given, a sentiment often made clear to Jubal.

"Where you going?" he would ask each time, wondering if the new answer would be in the same hemisphere as the last destination.

"Mobile," Sally replied, one Saturday afternoon in late May. "Anywhere these damn black flies ain't!" The swarming flies made any day without a breeze almost unendurable.

"Yes m'am, they're another reason nobody in their right mind would live here," Jubal replied, swatting at the cloud biting any patch of unprotected skin and helping him stall for a moment. Sally's reply had startled him. "Of course Mobile's got skeeters a'plenty. You wouldn't look good in malaria."

"You had it?" Sally called. She had moved knee-deep in the river while Jubal towed the purse line out to an oak piling that secured the net's far edge. The weir was tucked behind a promontory where the river current slowed and migrating salmon came to rest. Fewer fish left the mainstream but that made for a net more easily managed by one man. Jubal's arm had healed enough to row gently and he could feel it grow stronger with exercise. He took his time, for the frigid river cooled the air directly above, holding flies to the riverbank. They were as bad as any bug assault he'd ever experienced in Alabama.

"Comes with being raised in the South." Jubal snugged the dory's painter to the weir post. "Don't know, but Mobile wouldn't suit you just right," he added, avoiding Sally's gaze.

"Too much of a loudmouth?" Sally challenged, hands to her hips.

Jubal breathed deep, wondering why he bothered, but then laughed as he rowed back to her, the dory crabbing slightly from two arms pulling with uneven strength. "You said it, not me."

Sally stared at him, her face beginning to color as he tied off the net. "How many girlfriends you had in Alabama?"

Jubal looked at her blankly.

"No lyin', Jubal Calhoun! You got a sweetheart down home?"

"Whatever you talking about?"

Sally started to blush. "Why, I can't think to make it plainer!"

Jubal's eyes shone and his lips pursed, trying to contain a smile. "Oh, well ... there be a passel of 'em. Place were full of heartache when I shipped out."

Sally's freckles showed like spotlights. In a sudden movement she wound up and brought her hand flat across the river surface, sending a sheet of spring runoff at Jubal so quickly he could only wince and seize up at the drenching.

"Oh, you will regret that," he said with a sinister chuckle, but Sally already struggled to clear the river.

"Mom!" she squealed, "Jubal's on the loose!" She raced up the riverbank, holding her skirt knee high, toes squishing in the spring mud.

Jubal grounded the dory and with his good arm dragged it ten feet from the river, the effort flushing him. He walked up to the women, growling at Sally, who giggled from behind her mother's dress.

Jane Norton slowly wiped her bloody, reeking hands over an apron already smeared with salmon guts. As she tucked in a wisp of hair an angry speckle of black fly bites showed at the base of her scalp. "Whatever you are," she said, her voice hauling fatigue, "I hope you eat black flies. God, they're infernal!"

"Ain't the only things," Jubal replied, wiping his face.

Jane looked at him quizzically; Sally eyes widened. Facing them, Jubal could see both expressions and for a moment the bloodline between them was so clear they looked like the same person at different ages.

"Sally, stop tugging at me," Jane snapped. Jubal stood ramrod straight, a tattered, wet shirt clinging to his muscular chest. As he put his arm back in the sodden sling, she could sense the current between him and Sally but felt too tired to deal with it. "Jubal, is that dory tied off?"

"Yes, m'am," Jubal replied, hiding a flash of annoyance. "I seen rivers rise twenty feet overnight. She's hauled right up the bank there."

"Then c'mon, you kids," Jane said, turning toward the house. Sally tried to keep her mother between them but Jane brushed her off with a snort of exasperation. Jubal scowled and Sally jumped back. "Enough!" Jane Norton commanded. "Sally, get the cookstove going. Jubal, bring a couple of these salmon up to the house. At dinner you can tell us about your rivers, the Alabama and the Cat-something?"

"Cahaba."

"Good," Jane nodded. "We'll have us a travelogue tonight, courtesy of Jubal." Anything to get her off this river for a few moments, she thought.

Sally lit out for the house, casting an exaggerated glance over her shoulder. She raced along the newly plowed field that had just been planted to beans, potatoes, and corn and ducked around two apple trees, heavy with blossoms. Even with only one good arm, Jubal had made short work of the spring plowing.

Sally had showered him with questions the moment he hooked up Jake.

"Where'd you learn to plow, Jubal?" she demanded, on the sunny morning when they first began working the fields. Jubal led Jake to furrow rows that barely quivered.

"Fella name of Jordon Hatcher. Mule would turn this straight as a spar. Jake here, he's better at twitching logs. Sparse dirt you've got; ain't black bottom."

By the time Jubal came up past the field ten days later with a large gutted salmon, they had turned the earth a second time, then planted the field. He stopped and shifted the fish to his lame arm, still in the sling, and felt a slight twinge at the weight. Jubal could tolerate the discomfort, almost welcomed it, because the fear of being crippled had finally left him. He reached for a handful of soil and crumbled the dirt between his fingers. The afternoon had cooled, sending the black flies to wherever they spent the night.

A sudden, faint call sounded from far away, overhead, and Jubal closed his eyes, breathing deep. The honking grew louder and his gaze followed the geese headed north, as though a flock of birds were reminding him that life teemed beyond the horizon.

Jubal did a slow circle, taking in the Norton farmhouse. Smoke puffed into the crisp afternoon sky as Sally worked the bellows at the woodstove. Beyond the house, across the road that led north toward Bangor, wooded hillsides climbed to the skyline. Commanding the valley floor, giving it ultimate definition, the muscular Penobscot churned around a low knob and disappeared toward a far trace of mist in the distance that marked the river mouth. Jubal nodded, acknowledging the sanctity of his refuge, grateful to feel almost whole again at last. Then he took the fish in his good arm and headed for the house.

Jane Norton was reading a letter when Jubal came in. Another envelope lay on the dinner table, already opened. A smile had transformed her, taking years off her face.

"From Lester," Sally said excitedly, washing her hands at the sink. "He's up to Passadumkeag, below Katahdin, says he'll be home in a week. Aunt Dorcus wrote, too. Can't hardly believe *that*."

Jane read Lester's note a third time. "Well, I don't know how he managed it, but his writing surely improved on that ship."

"Eleanor Creesy, m'am." Jubal said. "As a teacher, I doubt there's equal."

"I must thank Aunt Dorcus when we see her," Jane Norton said, pointing to the second letter. "She's invited us to Bangor next week. There's a professor from Bowdoin going to speak at the Bangor Hotel. Aunt Dorcus reserved rooms for us! Sally, Jubal, we're going to the city!" The anticipation felt like a tonic after so much drudgery.

Sally squealed and ran over to hug Jubal, who immediately stiffened. On several occasions Jane had meant to sit Sally down and discuss life with her, especially as the girl became more excitable. The boy had been gracious and friendly while maintaining a distance that stymied Sally and relieved her mother. For though Sally might not know exactly what she wanted, Jane had little doubt that if Jubal led, Sally would be more than willing to follow. With a sigh of resignation, Jane realized it was better for the boys to go. Without warning, she walked over to Jubal, who had extricated himself from Sally's clasp, and hugged him, kissing his cheek.

"Jubal Calhoun," she said, feeling a sudden, intense gratitude, "you can call this home as long as there's a Norton alive."

Flustered, Jubal sought to deflect the attention. "Passa ... what? Katahdin?"

"Indian names, places upriver, the big mountain," Sally chimed in. The sudden shift in her mother's mood could bounce, she knew, but it was infectious and the kitchen seemed to glow. The woodstove threw off a cozy heat that escorted the fading light into evening. "Any Indian names down there, where you're from?"

"Oh lordy, yes," answered Jubal, relieved to be on safer ground. "Cahaba, that's Choctaw. Means canebrake, river cane grows thick along the bottomland. Alabama's named after the Alibamas Indians, part of the Creeks—weren't a tribe's much as a confederation. Plus Chickasaw, Marapossas, Chattahoochees. Thick, they were."

"Are they still around?" Sally asked.

"Some," replied Jubal, taking a seat of safety in the rocking chair. "Though not enough to bother 'bout. Andrew Jackson thumped them hard twenty some years ago, before he came president. They've been pretty well pushed out."

"The rivers are red?"

"No. They're muddy down low, near the gulf, though the Coosa and Tallapoosa, I heard they're fine and clear, coming from the mountains up Tennessee way."

"Do you have river drives?" Jane Norton asked.

"Nope, though there's fine loblolly pine."

The last traces of adolescence had vanished, his voice had settled into a melodious baritone, and cheekbones etched by pain and anxiety on arrival had filled with health and vitality.

"Rivers are mostly for moving crop to market and goods from Mobile. Cotton goes down, everything else comes up, depending."

"On what?" the Norton women asked in unison.

"Well ..." Jubal stared at the ceiling, unconsciously rubbing his arm. "Your station, guess you'd say. Whether y'all was farmin' or plantin'."

"That the fall line, down there?" Jane Norton asked, quietly.

Jubal regarded her for a long moment, unaware he'd stopped rubbing his arm. Then he looked away, the rocker stock still. Sally sat motionless; her eyes darted from Jubal to her mother and back.

"Never thought of it that particular way."

"The planters in Alabama are the ship captains in Maine?"

Jubal considered. "Close. But probably ship*owner* is more right. Overseers are the captains. A planter in Alabama ... man's top rail on the fence, then."

"How come you're a sailor?" Sally asked. "Why didn't you want to be a planter?"

"Right now, I want to eat," Jubal replied, standing. "Sal, get me flour 'n some that lard. This here salmon, well, I'll show you how we fry catfish. Bake us some biscuits, too."

Chapter Seventeen

On the first of June, much to Lester's surprise, a brief note from his mother arrived at the lumber camp asking him to meet them in Bangor. A few days later Lester rode a log raft downstream, mustered off the drive, and walked through the sawmills lining the riverbanks. Though the thought of his first hot bath and dry bed in nearly two months made him nearly skip into town, he wondered how his family had afforded a room in the best hotel north of Boston.

Surprise turned to astonishment when Lester ran into his Aunt Dorcus on the steps leading to the Bangor Hotel.

"They won't let you in wearing those, Lester," she said, nodding to his river driving boots that tore small splinters in the wooden sidewalks. River drivers routinely ignored Bangor shop owners' admonishments about damaging public property. No self-respecting driver would take off his studded boots for the sake of a sidewalk.

"Aunt Dorcus," Lester stammered. The seabag draped over a shoulder nearly fell off as he halted, open-mouthed. The Nichols family had never been huggers, so he quickly doffed his hat and stabbed out an arm. To Lester's surprise, Dorcus grasped his hand in a firm shake and regarded him openly. His aunt looked every bit the stern matron he remembered, but while her countenance had barely changed, Lester could feel keen interest.

Dorcus Fullam hadn't seen Lester in several years. On her way out of the hotel that morning she had caught the amble of a riverjack, instantly obvious by the pants tucked into his high boots, narrow hips flaring to wide shoulders in a red woolen shirt, topped by a battered hat. When the driver strode directly for the hotel as if he would walk through the entrance door rather than open it, Mrs. Fullam's regard became a stare, as she grew increasingly certain the young man was her nephew. She could see how he had filled out, now almost six feet tall, lean and hard but still with the unlined, silky skin of youth. Lester hadn't paid any attention to the woman on the hotel steps until she spoke.

"You must be, what?" Dorcus Fullam looked him over, "sixteen now, Lester?" Her gaze was so intense Lester somehow felt on display.

"I will be, m'am, come winter."

"December."

"That's right m'am," Lester replied, hiding his astonishment. As a child, he had learned early the clear, though unspoken, message that the Nortons were at the very fringe of an extended Nichols clan, as if they were of the family, but not in it. The sudden incongruity baffled him. The woman who had been a remote witch in his childhood was indeed a formidable presence—and an immediate reminder of someone else.

"Thank you, Aunt Dorcus," Lester said. The gratitude was so abrupt she raised her chin in question.

"For recommending me to Captain Creesy," Lester continued. "And particularly, Eleanor Creesy."

"A fair voyage?" Dorcus asked, her twinkling eyes and the shadow of a smile softening the dryness. Two weeks earlier a letter had arrived from New York, sent from *Flying Cloud* a day before the ship set sail on its second voyage to California. Eleanor had kept her end of the correspondence, recounting Lester's maiden voyage and informing Dorcus that he would likely be bringing an injured shipmate north. Neither Lester nor Jane Norton would know that Eleanor Creesy's letter prompted Dorcus' invitation to meet at the Bangor Hotel.

"Lester!" Sally ran out of the hotel door and tripped on the top step, flying into his arms with a crash that nearly sent them both toppling. Lester hoisted his sister high and she squealed, trying to recover the back of her dress. "Stop going away so much!" she cried, thumping his chest before desperately embracing him again. Lester felt her nipples against his shirt and the incongruity flashed again, as if all his childhood certainties were knocked askew.

Holding Sally, Lester noticed the hotel doorman prepare to open the double etched-glass doors with a flourish. Jane Norton emerged first, with Jubal right behind, taking her arm. Lester immediately saw that both Jubal's hands were free, and he wore a new suit.

"Hallelujah," he whispered.

"What?" Sally spun around. "Look Ma! He's back and not even soaking wet!" She wheeled again to Lester. "How many times you fall in?"

"Not a once!" Grinning, he vaulted up the stairs to his mother. "Safe and sound," Lester reported, reaching for her.

Jane Norton blinked back bittersweet tears, for the joy in her son's face was shared. In the moment she recognized Lester, his gaze went beyond her and the boys' eyes had locked. However much Jane Norton had come to love Jubal, she hated sharing affection. There had never been enough, and now she would be left again, this time by the last man in her life.

Lester saw the tears even as he felt her hint of a brittle smile.

"Never expected to have a family reunion in downtown Bangor," he chuckled, hugging his mother. She released him quickly and turned to Jubal.

"We put up with your friend," she said. Then Jane couldn't resist and took Jubal's arm and kissed him on the cheek.

Aunt Dorcus stood aside. Sally's smile hardened.

"How ya been?" Lester asked.

"I'm good," Jubal drawled. "How yew?" They stood nodding and shaking hands, Lester with one arm still around his mother.

Sally felt completely left out and the boys' silly grins annoyed her.

"Captain Fullam," she called to the gentleman coming out of the hotel, "Lester's home!"

Captain Jediah Fullam walked deliberately down the steps, settling his top hat as he approached. Barely taller than his wife, he had a closely cropped beard that matched the gray speckle of his fine woolen suit. Both boys straightened.

"Lester, you've grown," the captain remarked. He hadn't seen the boy since the small memorial service for his father.

"I suppose, sir," Lester replied. The women watched in fascination as the boys stood as if ready to salute. "My friend, and shipmate, Jubal Calhoun," Lester offered, releasing his mother.

"Calhoun," the captain nodded.

"Sir," Jubal replied, extending his hand.

"Mrs. Fullam tells me you're back from a voyage," the captain observed. "*Flying Cloud* and that fine passage to the Golden Gate. Perk's the man to do it. How'd you leave it with him?" Captain Fullam's nonchalance magnified the question.

"We'll join them again," replied Lester, "soon as we can."

"Creesy's already outbound." The Captain readied a cigar. "But if you're looking for a berth, Donald McKay's launching another ship in Boston this month. I don't doubt but this one will be as fine as *Flying Cloud*."

"Come dear, you men can talk ships later," Dorcus Fullam interrupted. "We'll have dinner tonight after the Masonic Lodge. I think the lecture will be extremely interesting."

"Beg your pardon, m'am?" Lester said, clueless.

"Aunt Dorcus has invited us to an event tonight," his mother explained, "a professor from Bowdoin College is speaking."

"How long does that professor have to talk?" Sally asked, without a trace of enthusiasm.

"Professor Stowe will simply make an introduction." Mrs. Fullam replied. "His wife is speaking, as well she should, I might add, having written an exceptional series for a New York newspaper, just recently published as a book." She raised an arm to the doorman, signaling for a cab. "Now come, Sally, we're going shopping."

Mrs. Fullam instructed Lester to room with Jubal upstairs before motioning for the women and taking her husband's arm to a waiting coach.

"Buy something nice," Jubal said to Sally as she turned to go.

"Oh, Lester! He's bad as you!" Sally hissed, and pulled her mother down the stairs.

The boys watched the coach clatter away. "You survive all right?" Lester asked. "Five minutes tuckered me out."

"It weren't the palmiest days," Jubal replied. "Sally's growin' and she ain't Southern shy."

"Anything I don't want to know about?" Lester asked, untying his boots.

"Not yet," Jubal replied, as he took the seabag and headed into the hotel. "But let's get the hell outta here, I ain't no priest. Time we head fer Boston, find us one Mr. Donald McKay."

On his way through the lobby, Lester glanced at a poster for the evening lecture in the Masonic Lodge, and reminded himself to tell Sally the name of the professor's wife. Harriett Beecher Stowe, the poster advertised, would read from *Uncle Tom's Cabin*.

Chapter Eighteen

A half-hour before the lecture, Lester studied the poster illustration while waiting for the women. A man on horseback held a leash attached to the drooping, sorrowful neck of another man on foot. Beside him, an anguished woman gathered a sobbing infant to her hip, her outstretched arm beseeching the mounted man. The rider was white, the torn family, black. Lester grew uneasy before he even left the hotel.

At the Masonic Lodge an overflowing crowd greeted Harriett Beecher Stowe with a loud and long ovation. She was a shy willow of a woman with a voice that couldn't carry, and a hush spread over the crowd as they strained to hear. The drone of mosquitoes and occasional slaps were the only sounds marring the audience's silence as Mrs. Stowe read a passage from her book that included the whipping of a black slave at the hands of his brutal master.

Lester could see Jubal shut down, sitting rigidly upright as though carved from marble.

Mrs. Stowe finished reading to a hall that quickly heated from lecture to revival. Lester felt the hostility escalate as the small woman answered questions from her audience. Suddenly someone stood, castigated the "peculiar institution," and began expounding on the moral righteousness of abolition. Another listener leapt up, red-faced with fury, to interrupt.

"Any white man south of Mason-Dixon is a disgrace to humanity!" he roared. "God damn them to hell!" Decorum vanished as the hall erupted in a babble of condemnation.

Abruptly, Jubal rose, and ignoring Dorcus Fullam's icy glance, walked out.

Lester found him at the hotel, smoking his pipe on the verandah overlooking the river. He made no comment, other than to say that dinner was ready. Jubal emptied the pipe and walked past Lester with his jaw set.

The chowder had barely been served when Dorcus Fullam laid down her gauntlet. "You left, Mr. Calhoun," she declared. Sally swallowed at the formality and stared straight ahead as the silence lengthened. She knew Jubal wouldn't break it.

Jubal sat motionless except for a pulsing vein at his temple.

"You've no response, Mr. Calhoun?" Dorcus Fullam demanded.

"I didn't hear a question, m'am."

Captain Fullam paused, his soup spoon in midair, and looked at his wife. The table had the feel of an arena, with two combatants circling.

"Indeed," Dorcus said crisply. "Then be so gracious as to explain why you left."

Jubal put down his spoon and for a moment Lester thought he would simply get up and leave again. Sally and Jane glanced at each other, bracing as if for the ripping thunderclap that follows lightning over the river.

"With all due respect, m'am," Jubal said, "the evening had nothing to do with slavery and everything to do with judgment. In my opinion."

"Slavery is not something to be judged? Do you countenance enslaving another man?"

"A black man?"

"Black, yellow, green—I don't care about color!" Dorcus cried. "Any man!"

"That's my point, m'am," Jubal drawled. He sat upright at the table, dapper in his suit, a young man entering his prime though the mustache was still a wisp. "Slavery is about color. Black man in the South, a yellow man in San Francisco, red man here."

"Surely you're not comparing the Chinese or Indians to Negros!" Jane Norton interrupted. "Chinese or Indians can come and go as they please. Can a black man in Alabama?"

"Can an Indian here?" Jubal retorted.

"They're hardly slaves," Dorcus Fullam snapped.

"Yes, they have freedom to starve, or beg, or live off the scraps left by lumber money," Jubal replied, looking her in the eye.

"They're not bought and sold like cattle!" Dorcus Fullam exclaimed. "They may be poor but they can move. A Negro in Alabama can't even do that!"

"A free man can," Jubal dodged. "Nigras can be free."

Dorcus pounced. "Who frees them?"

"Whoever owns them, m'am," Jubal replied, his voice tightening. He made a visible effort at restraint.

Sally couldn't sit still any longer. "I just don't understand it, Jubal, and you never'll explain," she said, trying to help him, though she didn't know how. Sally had tried without success to prod Jubal into talking about life on the plantations. "Slavery just seems so cruel."

"I seen that," Jubal admitted. "Down home, most folk think slaves do jes' fine, don't have no cares, get fed, have quarters. Mostly Sal, I don't try to explain because I seen it tried. Unless you're Southern raised, you can't know. Slavery just is. It's the way of the country, a way of living. Snows here, don't it? Just does. Don't like it, then leave."

"You own slaves, ever?" Sally asked.

"My father did for a time, and I been around them since I can remember." Jubal had calmed and his voice grew quiet. "But me? No, I never owned 'em."

Dorcus wouldn't let up. "Do you want to?"

Jubal considered that for a moment, and looked at her. "Not there, am I now? You want to be someone down home, you own slaves. Owning and holding land's not enough. It must be cultivated in order to yield its increase. Cultivation means cotton, and cotton means slaves."

"It's not right," Jane Norton declared.

"I'm not sixteen yet, m'am, but already I seen a fair bit, and one thing's clear to me," Jubal said, reaching for his knife, "most people think they're right. Don't matter what it is, they hold the truth. I just don't see there's that much truth to go 'round."

"When are you sixteen?" Sally jumped in.

Jubal paused. "July. Seventeenth." Deliberately, methodically, he sawed at a piece of meat and stared at his plate, ending the conversation as surely as if he'd been struck dumb.

Lester had been chewing beefsteak, wishing he could enjoy his food. After six weeks of beans and bread he had relished the prospect of a real meal, but the conversation made it impossible. Jubal's birthday stopped him for a split second; Lester knew full well Jubal didn't know the month of his birth, much less the day.

Dorcus Fullam reached down to her handbag. "Well, here's an early present to you, Mr. Calhoun," she said, evidently deciding not to press him further. She pushed a book across the table. Lester knew the title without looking: *Uncle Tom's Cabin*.

Chapter Nineteen

Dorcus Fullam didn't exactly apologize to Jubal the next morning after breakfast, though she did acknowledge him in a way Lester would never forget.

The boys rose by sunrise, intending to buy livestock across the river in Brewer and drive it to the farm while Jane and Sally Norton hired a boat to take supplies the half-day trip downstream. They didn't exchange a word at breakfast, Lester quite aware Jubal sat like a cocked pistol. The day promised to be fine and they bolted their food before nearly galloping out of the lobby.

"Lester, Jubal," a woman's voice called as they reached the double entrance doors. They turned to see Dorcus Fullam descending the stair dressed in a brocaded robe, her hair flowing to the middle of her back.

Both boys gaped as if at an apparition. Sunlight sparkled through the pewter halo of her hair, washing any severity from the old woman's plain, wrinkled face.

"Shut your mouths, boys. Here." From the folds of her robe Mrs. Fullam took two small purses and handed one to each of them. "The captain told me you spoke of trade after dinner last night. Someday you'll have families. Make it multiply."

Lester stammered something unintelligible, but Dorcus simply opened her arms and taking their shoulders gently turned them to the street. "Time to go," she said, giving them a tiny push to the door.

The boys took the hotel steps in two bounds, their strides lengthening as they made for the river. "She ain't so bad," Lester whispered. Jubal had nothing to say.

Above and behind them, Dorcus Fullam watched as they strode downhill into the morning sun.

"Fine-looking young men," the doorman commented. "Family? Your boys?"

"I had daughters," Dorcus Fullam replied.

"Looks like they know where they're going," the doorman grinned.

"They're sailors, heading back to their element. Look at them ... off to run down the wind."

Jubal stayed mute until mid-morning.

After they'd bought a cow and her calf, four piglets, and a covey of chickens in Brewer, Lester tried to lighten the mood. "She give us each ten dollars," he pointed out.

"Payment for the privilege of humiliation," Jubal snapped.

"Well give me that purse, 'fore you throw it in the river," Lester ordered. "We'll add it to our stake, just like she said."

A few hours later, he tried again, commenting that Aunt Dorcus would never offer something to a person she didn't admire.

Jubal wheeled so fast Lester was taken aback. "That's horseshit, and you know it!" Jubal stood in the road with his chin out, belligerent as a bull. "Tell you what that gold piece is all about. That's niggah money!"

Lester took another step back.

"Just how stupid you want to be, Lester?" Jubal cried, his fists balled white. "You don't think good Capt'n Fullam never made no money off slaves? Oh, he didn't have to haul them, no, just the rum and sugar cane from the islands! Who you think picks that? Never hauled cotton or corn or tobacco to Liverpool? Who totes them bales? How come just about every cargo is loaded onto ships owned out of Boston, New York?"

Lester was lost. "Whatever are you talking about, Jubal?"

"Goddam it man!" Jubal stood in the dusty road, yelling. "I was on them riverboats the time I was ten doing niggah work! I kept my mouth shut, but I heard, God knows what I heard. Tell you what," he pointed a finger at Lester, "your ass is coming to the rivers. We'll watch them cotton factors in Mobile, see 'em grow fat using *Northern* money for the seed and hemp and tools and all sorts of fancy goods that go up the Tombigbee and 'Bama, bringing down that cotton. I'm gonna take you up to Cahaba, pay in kind. Then you can talk to me about your Aunt Dorcus!"

Neither said another word until they got home.

Sally glanced at Jubal as he came in to dinner. "Looks like dinner's with a keg of gunpowder tonight," she griped. Lester ignored her, and Jubal walked out before the plates had even been set.

"Begging your pardon, Mrs. Norton," he said, grimly, "ain't hungry tonight."

Lester found him after dark, down by the river. He brought some chicken and a hunk of bread, said nothing, and left his friend alone.

Later, in the middle of the night, Lester woke from a restless sleep. Next to him, Jubal slept on Johnny's old cot in the corner of the tiny bedroom. Lester listened for his measured breathing.

"Jubal," Lester whispered, "you 'right?"

The silence was long enough to suggest Jubal either slept soundly or didn't hear, but Lester knew better and waited.

"My arm's right, now," Jubal murmured. "I'll thank your Ma the rest of my life, Sally too, if she'd ever shut up. But I'm leaving in the morning, Lester. Come along if you like, but I'm gone."

Lester sighed. Nothing he could say would mollify his friend—not that Lester wanted to stay. He was just saddened to leave with the sour taste of that evening in Bangor now turning bitter, a legacy of what he knew would be his last time home in years. Lester reached out in the darkness and found Jubal's shoulder. "Give it a couple more days, Jubal. I'll get word to Clyde—I saw him coming off the drive, he's nearly loaded and'll take us to Boston. Meanwhile, don't pay Sal no never mind, she's just all wrought."

Jubal didn't answer, but gripped Lester's forearm tight enough to tinge an ache in his own arm.

Lester turned over and within a few moments his breath slowed and became regular. Jubal listened to his friend drift off, aware that sleep would elude him as his rage festered through the night. Too much had been said, not so much by Sally, although she could never leave well enough alone. When it came to prying, the girl was as relentless as a spring river, even as Jubal ignored her pestering attempts at debating something he had never questioned.

For the next several days, none of the Nortons could pry more than a few syllables from him.

Chapter Twenty

Three days after they had returned to the farm, a barely legible note arrived from Clyde Pingree telling them to meet him midriver as the tide ebbed the next day. Lester and Jubal were ready, having expected the note. They had packed their seabags and already brought a dozen hogsheads of fresh maple syrup down to the riverside. The boys had purchased the syrup from local farmers, hoping to make a profit in Boston.

The dory was loaded when Sally suddenly clambered in and grabbed the oars. Despite Lester's protests she wouldn't relinquish them, refusing even to talk. Sally's emotions were so uncontrollable they made her feel crazy. Despite herself, she had picked at the scab of the Bangor lecture until Jubal spent most of his time in the woods or fields, which only infuriated her and hurt all the more. Now she felt alternately bereft, weepy, snappish, and envious, especially since Jubal was silent as wood.

Jane Norton had refused to even come down to the river, having given her hugs and gone upstairs, where Sally knew she'd spend the better part of a week.

Lester couldn't wait to leave, it all seemed so thick and complicated and irreconcilable. He gave up trying to reason with his sister and sat quietly as she pulled the dory off the riverbank and held it near the salmon weir, out of the current, from where they could see the *Mattie Mae* in time to row out.

Close on noon, the dirty mainsail of Pingree's schooner hove into view and Lester stood to wave, though it was still half a mile off. Sally nearly spat something nasty but bit her tongue, then suddenly wanted to cry. Instead, she wrenched the boat around, nearly toppling her brother overboard. Jubal, watching, snatched at Lester to steady him but said nothing.

"All 'board," Cub Pingree squeaked. The day had turned damp and cool. "Be thick a fog 'n the bay," Clyde pronounced.

Sally held the toerail as the boys off-loaded their bags and cargo onto the schooner, already piled so high with lumber it looked more like a barge with sails. In moments, the dory rode high again, and Sally knew she couldn't tarry in the current. Lester stepped to her and she stood, Jubal instinctively reaching to steady the dory against the schooner's hull.

"I love ya, Sal," Lester said, his eyes glistening. "You take care Ma best you can. I'll write, and try to send some extra money."

"When will you be back, Lester?" Sally asked, staring at the river. She'd given up all pretenses at courage and her voice came shallow and misty, already in mourning.

Lester shrugged.

"I'll miss you," she whispered. "Be careful. Don't leave me with Momma alone." She was crying now, holding Lester by his woolen shirt. Then Sally looked up. "Jubal Calhoun, you take care my brother. Anything happens to either of you I'll never speak to you again."

Lester kissed her hair, then turned to the schooner and vaulted aboard. He kneeled on the lumber to hold the dory's gunwale. Sally stood still, looking at the water, her face a mask of abandonment. Jubal moved to her then and reached into his shirt. He held out something. Sally looked at him and shivered, pulling herself together, then wiped her face and reached tentatively for the offering.

"A bird," Sally said, softly, taking it in her hands. "Is it a goose?"

The carved bird was in full flight, its wingspan about the length of Sally's hand. Lester smiled at the beautifully detailed carving, aware at once why Jubal had spent long hours alone by the river in the last few days.

"Naw," Jubal replied, "an albatross. Me and Lester see 'em in the Southern Ocean. Sailors think they watch over us." He took Sally in his arms as her face disintegrated again and kept hold while her shoulders rhythmically heaved.

Finally, Clyde Pingree coughed. With a nod, Jubal let Sally go.

"He'll watch over you," he whispered, "I tole 'im to." Gently, he leaned and kissed her on the cheek, then turned and clasped Lester's extended arm. With one foot aboard the schooner he gave the dory a slow, firm shove and the boats parted.

By the time Cub Pingree brought the boys coffee, the dory was but a speck against the wooded shoreline, its oars working like tiny sticks over the dull brown water.

"Good trip home, Lester?" Clyde called from the wheel.

Lester held the tin cup, soaking up its heat. "Yeah," he sighed, "I suppose you could say that."

Jubal handed him a cheroot, then finished making up a pipe. Lester reached for his matches and cupped Jubal's pipe until he saw the glowing bowl, then lit his own smoke.

The *Mattie Mae* picked up speed as the ebb tide and spring current sent her into the bay. Sitting cross-legged on a lumber pile, Lester and Jubal silently sipped coffee and savored their smokes as the first, faint stirrings of the Atlantic ground swell met river's end.

Chapter Twenty-One

Lester and Jubal stood open-mouthed at the spectacle.

The McKay shipyard in East Boston teemed with activity bordering on an organized riot. They could see that three hulls were under construction, one in preparation for launch, a second in frame, and a third begun with the laying of its long keel. A derrick lifted squared timbers the width of kegs and fifty feet long into place. On both ends, twelve-foot diagonal keyed scarf joints readied to mate corresponding timbers making up a ship's backbone. The steady *thwack, scrape,* and *growl* of crosscut saws, adzes, mallets, jackplanes, drill braces, and chisels sounded in the afternoon, as men worked the wood. From massive trunks and huge, squared bolts came ribs, futtocks, beams, knees, planks, posts, railings, and spars.

Men sang and others laughed, an industrious and disciplined team of three hundred shipwrights and laborers that seemed to churn as one body. Not a man stood idle.

Beyond, alongside a wharf near the slipways, a fourth ship—her hull long, sleek, and jet-black—floated quietly. High aloft amidst a rigging web of lines and shrouds, several men, tiny as children, hung the last of the canvas.

"E gods, Jubal!" Lester breathed. "I seen shipyards before, but never nothing ..."

"Yes sir," Jubal nodded, equally impressed, "these boys are serious, all right." He lowered the seabag and flexed his shoulders.

Lester turned to a man walking by, who carried a broadaxe over his shoulder.

"We've got a letter for Mr. McKay," Lester explained, "could you tell us where we might find him?"

"Which one?" the man asked in a thick brogue, barely slowing.

"I'm sorry?"

"Donald be there, on the stocks." The man motioned toward a huge hull with his axe, holding it outright like a yardstick in a hand missing two fingers. "Ask for Lauchlan aboard *Sovereign*," he pointed the axe toward the wharf. "Likely he be seeing to the rigging of his ship."

The boys exchanged glances.

The axeman continued on his way. "Donald builds; Lauchlan commands," he called over his shoulder. "Good day, laddies."

Lester's throat dried. "This here letter's addressed to Donald. How 'bout I do the talking?"

The finished hull stood in her stocks, enormous against the bright spring sky. From the ground, a man had to bend backward to see the top rail, nearly thirty feet above. Painters had finished and the scaffolding was down, save for towers at either end where carvers were fitting a figurehead and detailing the counter. Several wagons were drawn around the finished hull, and men unloaded upholstery, mirrors, and marble fixtures in a steady parade that marched up a ramp extending to the deck.

As the boys approached a voice called "Donald!" They turned to see the broadaxe man, who had begun to square off a timber, gesture toward a figure standing under the stern counter of the hull. Though formally dressed, the man stood making chalk marks where he wanted his shipwrights to plane and shape the stern planking.

"Them laddies," the axe man yelled, pointing at Lester and Jubal, "carrin' a letter for ye inna their kit." He went back to his work, magically making a round log square.

The suited man acknowledged the boys with a wave of chalk before resuming his comments to several men. "Take her smooth here," Lester and Jubal heard as they approached, "the line direct from our planksheer so she be curvilinear through the stern, do you get my meaning now?"

Donald McKay clapped a man lightly on the shoulder and turned to regard the two young strangers before him. He stood over six feet, clean-shaven and dressed well despite the heat, his ruffled shirt and vest incongruously flecked with sawdust. Several woodchips had lodged in curly dark brown hair turning to gray. A clear and intense expression ended in a narrow chin that could have been hewn from hardwood strewn about the yard.

"Mr. McKay?" Lester asked, removing his hat and withdrawing the letter from his pocket. Jubal did a double take and glanced away. The letter looked as if it had been crumpled into a ball several times. "Pardon the condition, sir, we've been traveling."

Donald McKay scanned the one-paragraph note.

"Take this aboard to my brother, Lauchlan," he said, motioning to the ship at dockside. "Ask, or look for the tallest man. Perhaps later we'll have opportunity to speak, lads. I'm curious how *Flying Cloud* performed. If you will excuse me now ..." McKay's nod thanked and dismissed them.

"You certainly made a good impression," Jubal remarked, approaching the gangway.

"You handle Lauchlan McKay then!"

"Without a doubt," Jubal drawled, striding toward the wharf.

Approaching the ship, they stopped to admire the bold script across the stern: *Sovereign of the Seas*. Wide-eyed, Lester and Jubal felt the immense latent power barely moving against the wharf. "She's a fair bit bigger'n *Flying Cloud*," Lester murmured. Jubal nodded agreement as a hail yanked their attention aloft. Several riggers hung from the high forward yard, roving the web of Manila hemp that stabilized a foremast the size of a giant tree.

"Whew!" Lester marveled, "bet it's close on two hundred feet, top the main truck."

Jubal led up the gangway. On deck, a dozen men knelt, the musical *ching-ching* of caulking hammers and chisels resounding as they embedded oakum between the planks bringing the ship watertight.

Amidships, a broad-shouldered man, a head taller than anyone near him, surveyed the scene before heading to a large open cargo hatch where a ladder led below into the hull. Under a rumpled sea cap, sandy mutton-chop whiskers bordered a lined, weather-beaten face. Moving with the rolling gait of a sailor, he mounted the ladder and turned to descend but paused as he saw the boys.

Lester and Jubal unconsciously straightened as they felt his eyes make a quick, practiced appraisal.

"A letter, sir," Jubal called.

Lester quickly held it up. "Captain?"

Lauchlan McKay stepped back onto the deck as the boys hurried to him. Taking the proffered letter, he made a quick scan and looked the boys over again.

"Norton ... Calhoun?" Captain McKay had the surprising gentleness of a man comfortable with his uncommon size.

The boys nodded one at a time. McKay extended a hand the size of a bear paw.

"How old are ye?"

"Fifteen," they answered in unison.

"Looking for a ship?" The captain's tone was blunt, though not rude.

Both boys nodded again.

"Throw your bags on top the forecastle and go up to the main royals," the captain gestured. "Tell Mr. Reynolds—there, at the crosstrees—I want him to put you to work."

"Yes sir. Thank you, sir," Jubal moved without hesitation. Lester followed, feeling the excitement build. They tossed their bags off and headed for the starboard ratlines together. Jubal turned and whispered, "Race you to the royal top," and trotted across the deck for the port shrouds, Lester waiting at the starboard rail. At Jubal's nod they were off.

An hour later, Lauchlan McKay mounted the ladder from deep in the hold, satisfied with his final inspection.

"Good bones," he muttered, with a last look at the base of *Sovereign of the Seas'* main mast. Four feet through, the mast rested on the massive backbone of the ship: two keels bolted together, one atop the other, frames attached on top, two keelsons stacked over the frames, the whole assembly over eleven feet thick, fastened with inch-and-a-half copper and iron rod. Five-inch planking on both inside and outside of the frames, and above, fifteen-inch knees supported twelve-inch deck timbers. A pungent scent of oak and pine permeated the dim light. Lauchlan had the sensation of being inside a thousand year-old timber grove, freshly sawn.

"She's built for the Southern Ocean," Donald McKay observed from twenty feet above. He stood on deck with one hand on the ladder, waiting.

"We've an excellent offer from New York," Donald continued as Lauchlan gained the deck. "Purchase, with a one-year lease-back option."

"Take it," Lauchlan glanced aloft.

"I did," his brother replied, following Lauchlan's glance. "She's ready?"

"Tomorrow, perhaps the day after."

"Those boys sailed with Perk?" Donald nodded at two small figures at the royal yard a hundred-eighty feet above. "He wouldn't send that note if they weren't good."

Lauchlan watched the boys move easily, each with a tar brush, touching up the rigging. "I sent 'em up straight off," he remarked. "A man climbs the rigging, in ten feet you know if he's born to it or not. They're young, but they've been there."

Near suppertime, as shipyard workers filed home into the long sunset light, the rigging master ordered Lester and Jubal below and aft to the captain's cabin.

At Lester's timid knock, Lauchlan McKay motioned them in. He sat at his desk below the glass skylight, immersed in a leather-bound notebook filled with lists of tasks essential to complete before his ship sailed. Two etched-glass doors rested on the floor beside him, waiting to be hinged onto the built-in cabinet above. Like much of the captain's cabin, the doors were framed in mahogany inlaid with rosewood.

Lester and Jubal stood, absorbing the understated elegance, and waited for the captain to finish his notes. Despite diligent efforts aloft to avoid it, spots of tar speckled their clothing. When a drop caught Lester high on the cheek he had tried to wipe it but succeeded only in smearing the tar under his eye.

"It's just tar, sir," Jubal explained, when Captain McKay stared at Lester. Lester glanced at him uneasily and then caught his meaning. The smear looked like the remnants of a shiner.

"That's right, Capt'n," Lester blurted, "I'm too fast on my feet to get hit."

Jubal nearly groaned, wondering whatever possessed Lester to be so presumptuous. Jubal waited for the cold stare he would expect from an Alabama riverboat captain, but Captain McKay merely nodded and reached for another leather-bound book that lay open on a shelf of the built-in cabinet.

"Sign the manifest, if you're aboard," he instructed, coming to this feet. "The second mate would be charged with your enlistment but he's in Marblehead at the moment, burying his son. T'will be his decision where ye berth, but I'll make ye able seaman, accounting for your experience with Captain Creesy, whom I know to be a capable man. The term's till we land back in New York, though inbound from where and for how long I kinna say now. Are ye aboard?"

"Yes sir!" the boys declared. Lester almost saluted, filled with an unusual mixture of awe and delight. The captain towered over them, a figure that could easily make most men quail by his physical presence. But though firm and direct he had none of the cold, brittle edge of a hard-bitten driver. Even Jubal was impressed.

"Where ye staying?" Captain McKay asked.

"We heard from another fella there were places in the North End," Lester replied.

Jubal closed his eyes for a moment, afraid to see the captain's reaction.

There were only two reasons a sailor would spend the night in the North End—liquor and women.

"We brought our seabags, sir," Jubal interjected. "Come down from Maine, had to trade our cargo right off, then here. Be much obliged, sir, if you could recommend a place to board. Don't need nothing 'sides a pallet, sir."

The captain nodded forward. "Sleep aboard, once ye sign on. She'll be your ship then. Gather a noon meal at the dining hall. Bedding won't be aboard for another week, but the weather's fair."

An hour later they gathered their seabags into the forecastle aboard *Sovereign of the Seas*.

"Feels strange, don't it?" Lester whispered, unnerved by the eerie silence. The boys were alone, the first occupants in new bunks stacked like library shelves, smelling of fresh-sawn pine. Jubal headed for a far corner and tossed his gear into the bottom bunk. Lester followed, curious what compelled Jubal to take the safety of a corner, but he didn't ask. Nor did it occur to him to take any other bunk but the one above.

When darkness swallowed the shipyard, the boys turned in for their first night aboard. A small oil lamp over the mess table cast flickering shadows. Though a crew would quickly turn the forecastle into a swarming, sweaty place, Lester viewed the empty bunks with a mixture of anticipation and uncertainty. Captain McKay's comment came back to him, and he realized that they would be outbound for California but could end up nearly anywhere on the planet. After unloading in San Francisco, the sole determinant of their future would be Lauchlan McKay's best judgment of where the most profitable cargo opportunity lay.

"Think we'll be going back to China?" Lester asked Jubal.

"Dunno," Jubal mumbled from the precipice of sleep.

"Think McKay's good as Creesy?" Lester asked a few minutes later. He stared at the bunk a foot above him. The question faded into the night.

"You got the imagination of a rock, Jubal," Lester muttered, giving up thought of any conversation. After the day's adrenaline, a sudden surge of loneliness overtook him. He felt aggrieved, listening to Jubal's even breathing.

"Asshole," he muttered to the planking, "don't even care what happens."

Chapter Twenty-Two

California, November 1852

As she approached the West Coast, *Sovereign of the Seas* looked from a distance like a gigantic orchid springing from the sea. Lester and Jubal separately took navigation sightings, then compared them, a practice they had begun aboard *Flying Cloud* and continued on this voyage with Captain McKay's permission.

After conferring, they predicted landfall—the first since Cape Horn—off the Farallon Islands at dawn. The ship raised the islands just after sunrise and sailed through the Golden Gate on a cool afternoon, sixteen weeks out of New York and a month ahead of any ship that had left the East Coast with her.

After days of seascape, the first glimpse of land was so intoxicating that passengers and crew nearly lapsed into collective hysteria, terrified that someone might beat them to the goldfields. Within forty-eight hours of tying up at the Pacific Street wharf, only a dozen seamen and the boys were left. California swallowed the rest.

Lester knew Jubal was sorely tempted to jump ship, but he didn't worry. On signing the ship's ledger in Boston both boys had given their word and hand to Lauchlan McKay. Their action had been separate but they felt it applied indivisibly, and neither could imagine shipping out without the other. Nor had they been aware that McKay immediately noticed their precise signatures, which suggested that Eleanor Creesy had probably tutored the boys, her reputation well-known and highly regarded among the fraternity of New England captains.

On the three-month voyage Jubal and Lester were nearly inseparable, trading books from the ship's library and taking their daily position fixes with an old but accurate sextant Lester had found in a pawnshop before *Sovereign of the Seas* departed New York. Captain McKay immediately noticed their practice and thereafter queried either Lester or Jubal of the ship's approximate position. Seldom did the captain disagree with their reckoning, and as the ship closed San Francisco he called them to the quarterdeck to inform them of their usefulness upon arrival.

The fast, out-of-season passage proved a bonanza, and the boys worked long hours with the captain and Mr. Reynolds, the second mate, one assigned to each as aide. Lester accompanied Captain McKay into the city, where they met a variety of merchants, agents, and wholesalers. Most wanted the captain to consign the cargo to their warehouses for sale and distribution, but McKay politely brushed aside these entreaties, knowing full well the timing of his arrival added significant value to everything in the hold.

Lester took notes as the captain's scribe, drafting contracts and completing bills of sale, enjoying what he would later describe to Jubal as the "underestimatin'" of the sharp, sophisticated businessmen dealing with Lauchlan McKay. In the captain's presence, as silent witness to the tides of negotiation, Lester's imagination took full flight.

Jubal spent his time aboard ship. Most of the crew disappeared within hours of docking, so Mr. Reynolds gave him primary responsibility for managing the stevedores and longshoremen. Jubal went to the ship's chandlery, found an adze and removed the hickory handle, then attached a handsomely braided and whipped hemp loop to the latter's end. A clear-eyed, strapping young man holding a billy club commanded attention, and within half a day after the first crates of mining tools were offloaded Mr. Reynolds knew Jubal would have no trouble.

Fifteen days later the ship lay empty. After months of activity with hundreds of passengers and crew aboard, the sudden silence gave *Sovereign's* empty bowels the ring of a crypt. Surveying the deep, open holds, Jubal wondered what would fill them.

"Don't know yet," Lester replied, "Capt'n hasn't said, though I heard China tea is off. London price is low—it may not support the freight here to Whampoa and 'round Good Hope."

With unloading finished and the financial and banking transactions completed, the captain had given them three days' leave.

"How'd we make out?" Jubal asked, as they stood on the wharf. In New York, they had asked the captain permission to ship a small amount of goods on their own account. The practice wasn't uncommon, and Lauchlan McKay gave approval, with the admonishment that they bore all risk.

After talking and arguing for days, making endless lists of possible trade articles and comparing profit potential, the boys decided to buy a ton of one-inch chain and several dozen sleeves, couplings, and hooks. Lester's reasoning was simple: when a man needed chain, nothing else would do. Anything going or coming from the interior, and most every operation at the gold mines, would require chain. Jubal had agreed that in the worst case they'd probably break even on the hundred dollars—a year's wages—they'd amassed from Dorcus Fullam, the maple syrup, and their pay at the McKay yard.

"Not bad," Lester answered. Jubal's eye narrowed; Lester was noncommittal, which gave it away.

"Made out, didn't we?" Jubal grinned, unconsciously licking his lips.

"Nine hundred and eighty beautiful gold dollars," Lester replied, his face splitting into a wide smile as Jubal let out a whoop. "One helluva profit! 'Course, if another ship had beat us by so much as a day we could have made nothing, but that's why we've been driving so hard! C'mon, let's go find us Carmelita and your Chileano darlin'. I got us a couple hundred in cash; the rest is banked alongside the capt'n's. Said he'll give us a draft when we want."

A few hours later, the boys stood outside the burnt-out shell of Carmelita's old saloon. The fire had left the entire interior a charred wreck and part of the roof had fallen in. On either side, scorch marks were still evident, but the fire had been checked before consuming the adjacent buildings.

"Must have been deliberate," Jubal observed.

"Well," Lester sighed, "we ain't sleeping here." The sight depressed them.

By late afternoon, they found another place in the center of town and took adjacent rooms, connected by a bath, for the night. While Jubal took a nap, Lester ordered a bath drawn and luxuriated in a steaming, soapy tub, kept full by a small, androgynous Chinese porter bearing copper hot water buckets. After nearly two hours, three cheroots, and half a hip flask of whiskey in the tub, Lester felt as though he had arrived on land. Standing made him reconsider. He wobbled out and collapsed into bed.

Lester woke long after dark to a hand shaking his leg. Sounds from the dining room drifted up in a low hubbub. "What time's it?" he croaked.

"Time for me to eat," Jubal replied. "I had a downright fine nap, though you look peaked. Dinner, or is it more beauty rest? Which you could surely use."

Lester contemplated the world from a sitting position. "I'm hungry," he managed.

Jubal went into the bathroom and returned bearing a bucket of cold water. "Stick your head in," he ordered, pulling up a chair and plunking the bucket down. Lester stared at the black water, then tentatively put his face in the bucket. Jubal grabbed him by the back of the neck and dunked him good.

"Bastard!" Lester sputtered, but the fresh water cleared his head and he dressed while Jubal puffed contentedly on his pipe.

To Lester's chagrin, the suit he'd bought in Bangor no longer fit. "How come your clothes fits and mine don't?" he complained, trying to button his shirt at the throat without choking.

"You ain't matured yet," Jubal replied through a cloud of smoke. "C'mon, you look good as you can."

The hotel restaurant was full, but the maître d', a small wiry Mexican sporting a waxed handlebar mustache, reconsidered after Lester casually pulled a gold piece from his vest pocket.

"Gonna grease it like him?" Lester asked as they waited for their table, knowing Jubal was sensitive about his thin mustache.

"Man looks like he got whacked with a slab of bacon," Jubal replied, self-consciously smoothing his upper lip.

"Yours is probably better for tickling the ladies."

The maître d' put them at a small table in the corner and they relaxed with a bottle of tequila. Despite himself, Sally came to Lester's mind, and he pictured a bleak November tableau along the Penobscot. Early winter was his mother's hardest time, when she might descend into one of her black glooms that could last for weeks. Sally would face that alone; the thought saddened him.

Midway through the meal Lester took the Mexican aside for a word. Jubal raised an eyebrow but Lester didn't volunteer anything. The boys finished dinner in silence and enjoyed cigars the Mexican brought on a fine silver plate.

Finally, Jubal made to pay, but Lester said he'd taken care of the bill and they ought to retire upstairs. Jubal was surprised when Lester simply bid him good night and headed for his room. He shrugged, and unlocking his own door, walked in.

She waited in a corner chair, wide-eyed and erect. Long, straight black hair hung past her shoulders, framing a smooth, cinnamon-colored face. Jubal stared intently until the girl could no longer take his gaze. Lowering her eyes seemed to crack a mask, and she sat still, hands tightly clasped, a quiver flashing across her chin. Jubal doubted the girl could be more than twelve.

Moments later, Lester knocked from the bathroom door and stepped in. "I told him young," he sighed, running his fingers through his hair, "but ..."

"They're that," Jubal agreed. Behind Lester, standing in his doorway, a second girl stood, not five feet tall. Lester motioned and she timidly entered the room. The girls glanced at each other.

"Shit, they're younger 'n Sally," Lester said. "Think they're sisters?"

Jubal shrugged.

"You two get going on home," Lester ordered, pointing at the door. The effect was opposite to what he intended. Their eyes widened and the one in the corner stood, urgently speaking Spanish. "You get that?" Lester asked.

"You can put my Spanish in a spoon," Jubal replied. "But likely they leave, it'll go bad for 'em. We kick these girls out, might be they get whipped or end up with someone way rougher. It's your trade, Lester. Can't turn 'em out now."

"I didn't ask for kittens!"

"No matter, they're here."

Lester looked miserable. "C'mon little one."

In his own room, Lester undressed without looking as the tiny girl stood in the corner, waiting. In his drawers, he pulled back the covers and motioned for her to turn out the light. The girl swallowed and blew out the lamp. In the sudden darkness her shift rustled to the floor. She slipped under the covers and lay still as a stone, naked.

Lester reached around her belly as it were a sapling. Despite the throbbing in his groin, he knew he would never forgive himself taking a child.

Neither moved for the longest time, but finally, carefully, she turned on her side, away from him. Lester stifled a groan, did the same and they settled, back-to-back.

When he awoke at sunrise, she was gone. Lester lay awhile and soon heard his friend pissing into the chamber pot. Jubal opened the door, looking tousle-haired and sleepy. "Stay here, or the ship?" he mumbled.

"Yours gone too?" Lester asked. Jubal nodded.

Lester stared at the ceiling. "Throw'd my bacon right in the dirt." He swung out of bed. "Let's get out of here."

Jubal regarded him a moment longer before shutting the door.

Chapter Twenty-Three

Three months later, *Sovereign of the Seas* churned southeast through the huge gray combers of the Southern Ocean, bearing down on Cape Horn with eight thousand barrels of whale oil in her holds. Lauchlan McKay had driven the ship relentlessly from Honolulu, refusing to take down the royal yards as they approached the high southern latitudes. Looking aloft nearly made the first mate sick, for the masts bent like reeds and lee shrouds flapped slack in the gales and rainsqualls.

Lester and Jubal kept constant watch on the rigging and reported to Mr. Reynolds when the foretopmast sprung. In the mast, made up of four spars held together with iron hoops, one spar had split from the racking, insistent strain. A day later, the foretopmast sprung in a second place, and when the ship heeled over in a gust, the mainmast itself would protest with a spine-chilling shriek. Still the captain pushed on.

Several days before the equinox, the boys came on deck at dawn with their watch. The ocean sounds assaulted them as waves washed the deck. All night long the ship had slashed southward, surrounded by seas that sometimes towered to the topsail yard nearly eighty feet above deck. *Sovereign* sailed as if borne along a knife-blade, balanced between heroic grandeur and sliding down a wall of doom.

"Norton, Calhoun!" Captain McKay bellowed, "to the wheel!"

The boys struggled aft along the lifelines, Lester leading. Jubal caught Lester's arm to tie the soul-and-body lashing, a small cord around his wrist that closed the slicker sleeve from rain and seawater. Lester pulled himself forward with one hand, feeling Jubal work. Over the weather rail, another black squall line filled the horizon.

"Gonna be a wild one," Lester muttered under his breath, wondering how much more the ship could take. For two weeks he had gone into the ship's hold several times a day to check the bilge. She wasn't making much water but the hull sounded like a herd of thirsty cattle, one long lowing after another.

Two exhausted men gratefully relinquished the helm and staggered forward for breakfast. Lester and Jubal took their places, hands crossing at the top of the wheel. The spokes hummed in their grips, telegraphing the forces at work on the hull.

"Hold her steady, boys," Captain McKay said, his voice a conversational anomaly against the natural bedlam. "South by southeast."

Below them in the ship's waist, Mr. Reynolds and two able seamen slid to the lee rail. The scuppers were awash, seawater sometimes rising to their knees. Lester watched for a moment, then felt Jubal's tug on the wheel as a towering graybeard lifted the stern like a feather. In moments, the enormous ship began surfing down the wave as it broke, covering the deck in foam. The boys struggled to hold the ship as it fought to slew sideways; every man aboard froze, feeling the tremendous momentum as they roared down the wave face into a trough. Jubal was sure the bow would bury, but she came up without even wetting her bowsprit.

"See boys," the captain said, as though reading their minds, "she be a beautiful ship. The faster ye drive, the dryer she is, on account of being flat and sharp. Look how she rides, nearly the same speed as the seas—this swell may bear us a half-mile. Stand and hold steady, for unless I miss my guess you boys will witness this morning what no man has ever seen."

"Nineteen knots, sir!" Mr. Reynolds called, recounting the number of knots passing through his fingers.

"Again!" the captain called.

A seaman reeled in the knot line and the first mate examined the chip log workings. Quarter-inch manila line connected through the middle of an oak wedge about the size of a healthy pie slice, weighted with lead along the top curve. Short strands of manila ran from either corner of the wedge to a wooden plug, which attached to a socket in the line a few feet above the wedge. The lead and wooden plug acted together, holding the wedge perpendicular to the line and sea.

Satisfied, the mate pulled some slack off the reel, called "Watch!" and tossed the line overboard. Beside him, an able seaman held a small hourglass containing the precise amount of sand that would fall in fourteen seconds. The wedge disappeared behind the ship, line humming from the reel. Moments later a small strip of white cloth flashed through the mate's fingers, far enough forward on the line to ensure the weighted wooden wedge astern floated upright and stationary beyond the wake's turbulence. "Turn!"

The seaman flipped the hourglass, staring intently as the mate felt one small leather knot after another flash through his hand. As the last sand grain dropped through, the seaman yelled "Mark!" and the mate clamped his fingers to the unspooling knot line. Far astern, the sudden, jerking stop yanked the small plug loose and the wedge flipped flat to skip along behind the ship for easy retrieval.

The mate examined the line again, keeping his thumb and forefinger where he'd snubbed it taut. He was midway between the ninth and tenth knot, each exactly forty-seven and one-half feet apart.

The normal hourglass aboard thousands of ships held twenty-eight seconds of sand, the same precise fraction of an hour as the space between knots equated to a nautical mile in distance, eight hundred feet longer than a statute mile, so as to make a sea mile equal to one minute of longitude at the equator. Six knots passing through a mate's fingers in an hourglass of time meant his vessel would travel six nautical miles in one hour—sailing at a speed of six knots. Lauchlan McKay had ordered a custom-made, fourteen-second hourglass, halving the normal time, because at speeds above sixteen knots the spooled chip-log line ran out before the sand did. With the new hourglass, the mate had simply to double the number of knots passing through his hand to calculate *Sovereign of the Seas'* speed.

Lester and Jubal glanced at each other. They were sailing faster than any ship had ever recorded. At sunset the previous day, *Sovereign* had been tearing along at seventeen knots and had kept up her speed through the night while Captain McKay stood the quarterdeck.

"Now you may take in the royals, mister!" Lauchlan McKay called to Mr. Reynolds, whose immediate relief was obvious. The squall had drawn nearly upon them as the high sails bellied out and were snuffed by men in the rigging. At the wheel, Jubal could feel no diminution of speed as rain pelted them, blowing horizontal out of the west.

As the ship approached Cape Horn, weather had grown colder each day, and constant movement and sound dulled the men's senses. Sailors rarely spoke in the forecastle, manning their watches in exhausted silence, all save the captain. Lauchlan McKay rarely left the quarterdeck, often sleeping strapped into a sea chair near the wheel. His image affected the boys in different ways.

"Man's like granite," Lester whispered one late afternoon, trying to get warm in his bunk before taking the long evening watch. The ship was only a few hundred miles from the Horn, plowing due south in a snowstorm.

"I'd follow him anywhere," Jubal agreed. "Gonna lead, got to be the example."

"You want to lead that bad?"

The question seemed to startle Jubal. "Well ... what's the choice? You want to follow, always do somebody's bidding?"

Lester leaned back into his bunk, feeling the scratchy straw mattress. "This donkey's bed 'bout ready to go overboard," he groused. "Think you can't lead without suffering? That man has got to be ... Hell, we were a couple hours at the wheel and damn near froze. Capt'n *lives* on the quarterdeck."

"Yeah," Jubal concurred, "and because he does, you'd do anything for him. Set the royals in this snowstorm, he tells you. I come to believe, Lester, it's just the trade. Right, wrong, don't matter, just is."

"Jezus, Jubal, how much of life *just is?*"

"I know what you're getting at." Lester could barely hear Jubal's soft drawl above the moaning wind that slipped into every crevice of the ship. "And you can read that Stowe lady's book another few times, you like."

Lester kept quiet, not feeling to argue.

"What's today?" Jubal asked.

"The date? March something, twenty-eighth I believe, give or take."

"All right. Eighty, ninety days, Honolulu to New York. That'll put us in about May, first part."

"So?" Lester rolled over and looked at his friend in the bunk below.

Jubal pointed a finger. "You're not gonna be cold then, Lester, this'll all be a bad dream. Alabama in May is lots of things, but cold ain't one of 'em."

Chapter Twenty-Four

New York, April 1853

Lester studied the newspaper as he waited for Lauchlan and Donald McKay to finish their conversation in the captain's cabin.

"You see this?" he asked Jubal, sitting next to him in the lee of the aft deckhouse. Though it was a pleasant spring day in New York, the boys were huddled together, unaccustomed to cool breezes after a month transiting the tropics. Lauchlan McKay had not paid them out yet, though most of the crew had already gone.

Jubal grunted, intent on the maritime journal.

"We're famous!" Lester laughed.

"We?"

"Well, the ship. That run we made 'bove the Horn? It's news all over the country!"

"So why do you think them McKays got long faces?"

Lester could feel the setup. "You always got to be the authority, Mr. Know-it-all. All right, why?"

"Says seventy ships left the East Coast for San Francisco in the last three months. That place just isn't big enough to gulp a ship every other day. Rates are in the shitter! Lauchlan ran to Honolulu 'cause them barrels of whale oil were the best chance. Doubt they made much coming home."

Lester was about to answer when Jubal grabbed his arm, turning to the creak of a skylight opening a few feet from where they sat.

"How did she sail in the Southern Ocean?" Donald McKay asked, his voice distant but distinguishable. The boys held their breath.

"*Sovereign* sails fair, dry, and fast," Lauchlan replied. "What is it you are building now? How much bigger?"

"She's in frame," Donald's tone was defensive. "Four thousand, five hundred tons. Four masts she'll stand, three square-rigged, the last fore and aft, carrying fifteen thousand yards of canvas."

"*Sovereign* and half again? Twice the size of *Flying Cloud*? Good God, man, we're building the biggest ship that has ever sailed!"

Jubal looked at Lester open-mouthed. "Imagine trying to steer her," he whispered, "'round the Horn, a gale at midnight!"

Lester was bug-eyed. Holding up two fingers, he mouthed, "two *Flying Clouds*?"

"I need a brandy," Lauchlan McKay declared. "How much will we have into her?" The clink of glasses sounded through the skylight.

"About three hundred thousand, loaded," Donald replied. "Two to build."

"You don't like dice, Donald, yet we'll put everything on one ship?"

"*Sovereign* has treated us handsomely!"

"Last voyage yes, but Liverpool is chancy. And I believe California freight will decline further."

"Precisely why we need the *Great Republic!*" Donald cried. "Eighty million in gold came out of Melbourne last year alone, and the British don't have the ships to meet the demand. Everything—grain, people, equipment, general cargo—must land in Melbourne by sail and we need size for those waters, a large ship, fast and dry. One good voyage is all we need. And Lauchlan, can you imagine the amount of tea we could bring back from China?"

"Who will command her?" Lauchlan asked.

"You will, of course!"

Jubal and Lester grabbed each other.

"I'm running *Sovereign!*" Lauchlan protested.

"We'll lease it in Liverpool," answered Donald.

"The name," Lauchlan said, after a lengthy pause. The boys held their breath. "Why the *Great Republic*?"

"Longfellow," Donald McKay replied. "Have you read his poem, 'The Building of the Ship'? When I read that I thought to name her after our country, the Great Republic."

"Aye man, you've an appetite for risk!" The tension in Lauchlan's voice tightened Lester's stomach. "How do you know we can peddle the lease?"

With a sly grin, Jubal craned to hear, and Lester suddenly realized why his friend had picked this precise spot to sit out of the wind.

"I already have," Donald replied. "Do you remember James Baines? He visited us last year, from London, the owner of the Black Ball Line?"

Chapter Twenty-Five

Lauchlan McKay paid them off with an invitation to sail with him again when *Sovereign of the Seas* left for Liverpool in late fall. Jubal and Lester promptly agreed, trying to hide their elation, then bounded down the gangway and into the city. Finding lodging at a tavern near South Street, they spent the next week, dawn to dusk, plying the wharves, constantly discussing and arguing about relative risks and profit of various items they could ship to Alabama. Lester was adamant about investing most of their savings.

"Greenbacks aren't earning us anything, Jubal," he insisted. "We've got to trade. There's no point working a ship if it doesn't got our stuff on it." Each morning they made their way to the shipping houses on South Street, searching for a coaster headed south.

Eventually someone directed them to a decrepit wharf where a small schooner sat low in the water, dwarfed by the surrounding full-rigged ships. The *Cerbin Flanigan,* seventy feet at the waterline, had loaded jute, rope, farm implements, and fertilizer but was already three days overdue to sail for Mobile. When they found her, floating like a small, ugly duckling amidst a far larger and nobler flock, Lester took one look at the unkempt deck and turned on his heel. Jubal, however, bade him pause as he hailed the vessel.

Moments later, a man bolted from below. He was short and dirty, with the wild-eyed face of a man haunted. Stammering, the captain asked their business in a drawl so thick Lester found it nearly incomprehensible. As Jubal introduced himself, the man shivered.

"God bless, yer a Southern boy! Come aboard, straight away!"

"Let me handle this," Jubal muttered.

Two hours later, attacking a steak at a waterfront tavern, Jubal described the deal he had cut.

"His name is Captain Leonard Godbold, but he don't own the boat. She's property of a cotton factor, one of them traders that keep planters in goods for the cotton crop and sell it at harvest." He chewed carefully, considering. "Something ain't right; the man lost his crew. Dunno 'bout that, but our wages and the freight will wash, an even trade for him, and a helluva good one for us, don't you think? He can't handle her alone."

"Damn good," Lester agreed, ripping a chicken apart, "if he keeps his part of the bargain. The man's right strange, you ask me! What's to prevent him from holding our goods hostage in Mobile, maybe trying ..."

Jubal cut him short. "Capt'n Godbold, he's a Tombigbee boy. That's a river, runs into the Alabama 'bove Mobile. Hardworking folk them are, tearing a living out the woods. He'll do what he says, so long's we do. Fellow we went north with to Maine—Clyde weren't it? He ain't no different. Now then, think those teamsters can get everything down and aboard this afternoon?"

Lester nodded, uneasy, but aware the tables had turned. If they were shipping out to China, he would feel nothing unusual, but for some reason going to Alabama left him dry-mouthed and edgy. For the first time he appreciated Jubal's wariness a year earlier when Lester brought him home to South Orrington.

When Jubal and Lester returned they directed a teamster to pull his wagon beside the *Cerbin Flanigan* and then offloaded eight crates. The boys handled the cargo carefully and Jubal spent a half-hour at the deck lashings while Lester disappeared back in the city to return with a cartload of food. At sunset, with as much ceremony as if they were crossing the East River to Brooklyn, the boys cast off and Godbold steered the schooner into the ebb tide.

By midnight they were offshore and Lester, in his first words to the man, suggested the captain go below and sleep. In the dim light of the wheelhouse lantern, Godbold, who had said almost nothing since leaving New York harbor, looked to Jubal, who nodded.

Through the night, the *Cerbin Flanigan* bore off the New Jersey coast and made for the Gulf Stream under a clear, moonless sky. The boys alternated watches and decided to let the captain sleep.

"Man's completely shot," Lester said. Jubal grunted agreement, puffing on his pipe.

As dawn broke, they shared some cold coffee and watched the morning fill in. Far ahead, a line of weather hugged the horizon.

"Looks like it's going to get wet in a few hours," Lester remarked. He felt like talking.

"Why did you leave home, the first time?" he continued, bracing for the next drop into a trough. A building breeze blew out of the north, directly against the Gulf Stream flowing up the coast. Wind against current jammed the water into short, lumpy seas.

As the boat plowed into an oncoming wave Lester stepped forward of Jubal, intercepting the sheet of water flung across the deck, and winced as the seawater found a way down his collar.

Jubal grinned, standing easily at the wheel. "It ain't Cape Stiff cold." The Gulf Stream water was noticeably warmer than the air that blew over the Grand Banks.

"I left scared," he said, surprising Lester, who hadn't really expected his friend to reveal much. Jubal kept the schooner off the wind, concentrating on taking the seas as best he could so their cargo didn't get battered. "Was April, 1850," he continued, "when I stowed away on a bark outbound Mobile for New York—mostly in ballast, cause the cotton don't come in 'till fall. So 'course I was found out. Didn't have any money, much, but those bastards took it for passage. Ended up in New York, not a coin to my name … no clothes, family, nothing … One of the worse times of my life. 'Cept I'd just come from the worse time."

"How'd you survive?"

"Living in the alleys along South Street for days, I did all right. Leastways, I could eat. A kid can always scrounge. But nights got scary, just a matter a time before something bad found me. I saw a poster—couldn't read much then but enough to make 'er out—and asked around until I found the ship. A packet, the Liverpool run, out 'n back."

"Is Liverpool worse than New York?" Lester settled himself; the talk made him feel better.

"Dunno, never got off the ship. Too scared. But I did in New York, that's when I run into you. Eleanor Creesy—I like to tell you I'll remember that woman to my dying day."

"What was so bad down home—where we're going?" Lester tried to hide his fascination. "The 'worst time,' you called it?"

"Mind taking the wheel, Lester? Spell me while I make a pipe. Though we might want to jibe her, cut 'cross this current 'stead of fighting it."

Lester's nose twitched, he could smell rain. "There's a squall up there, sure as Neptune shits. This breeze is coming out of Canada and that ahead is Bermuda air. Going to be a tempest, yes sir."

Twenty minutes later Lester called out to jibe the boat and Jubal worked the sails while her stern went through the wind. When a wave came aboard and hit the foremast, washing several coiled lines off the belaying pins, Jubal struggled forward to clean up the mess.

As the *Cerbin Flanigan* steadied on her new course the captain appeared on deck, awakened by the commotion. In one glance Leonard Godbold took in Jubal recoiling lines on the foredeck, Lester at the helm, the weather horizon. Without a word, the captain returned below, and in moments the small coal stove smoked. Hot bowls of gumbo came on deck an hour later, and the boys nearly inhaled the delicious, spicy stew.

"Rain's about an hour to starboard," Lester warbled through a mouthful of rice. "How about you cook, Capt'n, and us boys'll steer?"

Jubal stopped in mid-chew, mortified, but Captain Godbold took no offense. A moment later, Lester stood open-mouthed, his spoonful of gumbo hanging in the evening air. He glanced at Jubal, and looked again at the captain.

Tears streamed down Leonard Godbold's face and his shoulders began to shake. "I jes' don't know how I'm gonna face Mother," the man sobbed.

Alternately keeping eyes on the approaching weather, Lester and Jubal listened in rapt silence.

Three days earlier, several hours before *Cerbin Flanigan* was to sail on the ebb tide at sunset, Leonard Godbold's two sons had begged to go into the city to buy something for their mother. Born a year apart, the boys—the oldest thirteen—were the captain's only crew. Their father told them to be careful, stay within two blocks of the wharf, and be back within an hour.

The boys didn't return. After a fruitless, then frantic, search through sunset, Godbold notified the police and spent the night along the wharves, knife in hand, calling for his sons. In the first streaks of dawn, he'd found a bruised drunk who mumbled about his escape from a gang of crimpers the previous evening, not a block from where the *Cerbin Flanigan* lay. Godbold raced to check the maritime registers. Two ships had cast off at sunset the night before, one bound for Helsinki, the other to Calcutta.

The municipal police shrugged. There was nothing to be done until the ships returned, if in fact the boys had been taken aboard, though the practice was common enough. Crimpers were human hyenas that pounced on unsuspecting, weakened, or young men, delivering them to departing ships, unconscious, drugged, bound and gagged, or in any other condition necessary to get them aboard. Captains of slow barks and brigs that plied world sea lanes needed bodies and often had few scruples. Once at sea, they were a law unto themselves.

Godbold searched until he could no longer stand but finally had to face the wrenching truth. His wife and seven more children waited on a rough inland farm in the Choctaw country of the Tombigbee valley in western Alabama, near the Mississippi border. Regardless of his tragedy, the schooner had to get off the wharf or would be seized for demurrage, provided someone didn't murder him first and steal the boat and its cargo.

Though almost out of his mind with anguish, Leonard Godbold feared his family would starve if he didn't get under way soon. Praying that someday he would see his sons alive again, he considered how to set sail. When Jubal approached and Godbold heard the boy's drawl, he knew it must be divine intervention.

The voyage down settled after they cleared the Gulf Stream, though neither Lester nor Jubal could forget the captain's tale. The plight of Godbold's sons struck deep. Both remembered the dark, dank bunks of their first voyages where they retreated to a fetal curl in loneliness so deep it almost crushed them. Memories made for a quiet trip.

Ten days out of New York, *Cerbin Flanigan* raised the Alabama coastline.

Chapter Twenty-Six

The light impressed him most. Sailing south from the New England spring, Lester had expected warmer weather, but he didn't know what landfall would bring. The low, flat coastline looked like an impenetrable green tangle, at once mysterious and exotic, almost malevolent.

Mobile Bay shimmered, the heat enveloping everything, filling the sails with a moist, salty breeze that cracked a man's lips. Herons and pelicans covered sand-spit islands seeping from the Gulf, and the pale blue water was ochre-streaked from inland clay. Neither sky nor clouds were discernible, just an endless chalky haze that hung overhead like a celestial bowl, smudging the sun and swallowing any line of horizon to seaward.

In the distance, Lester could make out a stick-like collection of masts marking the harbor roads. Squinting, he tried to discern where the ships stopped and the city began, but the water glinted and hurt his eyes. Instead, he looked again at Jubal, who wore an expression most anyone else would think opaque, though Lester recognized the longing.

"So, just what are we going to do down here?" Lester asked an hour later, as the outlines of Mobile materialized from the haze. "Sell that crystal first off?"

In New York, Jubal had decided to buy crystal, fine silver flatware, and porcelain china. "It's heavy for the amount of space," Jubal had explained, "and there ain't much room on deck. Besides, people like nice things and nobody makes this stuff anywhere nearby. We can sell it in Mobile, along the river, on the steamboats—lot's places. Think she'll be a fair trade."

"How do you know the worth of this stuff?" asked Lester.

"Don't," Jubal allowed, "but it's got to be relative. Couple hours in Mobile, we'll know. Sell her there or head upriver."

Lester remembered the exchange as he watched the water change color in the shallows. "You never got to the where we're headed part, beyond 'upriver,' that is. Mind telling me our course?"

"What's the difference?" Jubal replied. "You never been there."

Lester watched closely since Jubal avoided his gaze.

"I reckon you don't know where 'tis we're heading," Lester said, affecting an exaggerated drawl. "Guess we're jes' gonna go ramblin' 'round Al'bamer."

"Don't be fractious, Lester. You knew what were gonna happen in Maine? Hold on to yer boots. Look at her like's another adventure; we ain't had enough."

Lester let out a bemused, self-satisfied snort. "Never a dull moment with you, Jubal," he shook his head. "'Course, ain't many sharp ones, neither …"

As the schooner dropped anchor the Captain Godbold called the boys aft, and to their complete astonishment, asked them to take over the cargo. Though the captain dreaded breaking the news of their sons to his wife, he was anxious to leave upriver. Impulsively, he implored Jubal to deal with the cotton factor and return the schooner in good order, for which he would split the voyage earnings. They could either deposit or mail a draft for the captain's share.

Lester wondered if Godbold had gone mad, but Jubal took the request calmly. "Absolutely not, Capt'n. Deal's a deal. We'll take care of her and send you the full, proper amount. Go on to your family."

While Godbold fetched the manifest, Lester looked at Jubal with an open, unspoken question.

"Man knows we're good for it," Jubal said, quietly. "Now we got to figure what Lauchlan McKay would do, he was here."

The boys whispered between themselves, and when Godbold reappeared Jubal wrote out two copies of an authorization to the cotton factor on which Godbold left his mark, a sort of crabbed simile of his initials, the only thing he could write. The captain gathered his meager belongings while Lester got the small dory out of its chocks and overboard. Within an hour of dropping anchor, Jubal stood in the dory taking the captain's gear off, preparing to row for the town docks. Godbold lowered himself in, and Jubal had readied to his oars when Lester called from the schooner's deck.

"Captain, how much cash you got?"

Leonard Godbold sat upright in the stern, suddenly looking small and vulnerable. Despite the heat, he wore a topcoat and floppy, broad-brimmed hat. He patted his coat in several places and looked blankly about him.

Lester tossed a small pouch that Jubal caught and calmly put in Godbold's lap, ignoring the man's incredulity. Aboard, Lester went below to organize the unloading. Jubal pulled deep, enjoying the sun on his shoulders and the whistling of his friend fading into the dory's wake.

After sunset, a soft thump against the schooner's hull woke Lester. He had been lying on deck, mentally calculating the capital necessary to purchase the schooner cargo. He played with various scenarios, changing the interest rate, voyage time, or the potential effect of selling all or part of the cargo to one buyer. The numbers began as a ledger in his mind but soon became muddled. When Jubal returned at twilight, Lester sat up suddenly, realizing he'd fallen asleep.

"Fetch." Jubal tossed a package of stained newspaper. Mounds of breaded, deep-fried fish, crab legs, and cornbread greased the wrappings. Without a word, Lester began stuffing his mouth, pausing to catch a line from Jubal and tie the dory off.

From his hip pocket, Jubal pulled a small bottle. "Mr. Lester Norton," he announced, taking a swig, "may I introduce Miss Southern Whiskey?"

Chapter Twenty-Seven

Daylight greeted Lester with a pounding headache and a tongue that felt as if a pelican had nested in his mouth for the night. "You alive?" he croaked at the stirring nearby.

"No," Jubal managed in a strangled whisper.

A half-hour later, Jubal tried to rise, but his head spun. He lay in his bunk for several more minutes before forcing an elbow upright. "Lester, git up," he said, gritting his teeth. "We got a berth; man's expecting us wharfside middle of the morning."

Lester moaned, "What the Christ was that stuff?"

"Alabama likker. C'mon, bit of a breeze's up and the tide's flooding! Got to rid ourselves of this cargo."

When he heard the small capstan clanking, Lester forced himself on deck. Jubal back-winded the working jib and the bow swung around while Lester tied the wheel off amidships and went forward to help. When the anchor cleared, he wobbled aft as the schooner got under way. Jubal followed, lowered a bucket overboard and dumped the seawater over his head. He shook like a hound, then swung another bucketful aboard and looked at his friend. Lester just leaned over the rail, shuddering as warm saltwater doused him awake. Minutes later the small chimney vent began to smoke, and as the *Cerbin Flanigan* approached its Water Street berth, the boys sipped mugs of hot coffee, carefully taking in the port.

The night before, between swigs of whiskey, Jubal had spread a nautical chart of Mobile Bay in the schooner cabin and traced out the town and river channels for Lester. A maze of islands marked the mouth of the Mobile River, which Jubal explained ran only about forty miles inland to the confluence of the Alabama and Tombigbee rivers. As their conversation grew lubricated, Jubal rummaged around and found a pencil and paper, then drew a map of the state illustrating the river systems that drained into Mobile Bay. Jubal's map looked like an uprooted tree, and Lester could immediately see that the city was a funnel of economic vitality for everyone living in those watersheds. Suddenly, the cargo made visceral sense to him, and he excitedly went through the manifests, asking Jubal to identify the likely destinations for everything on board.

When Jubal described the riverboat traffic and mentioned that on the two-day trip to Montgomery, midway up the state, riverboats would stop almost a hundred times, Lester started pacing the cabin floor, three steps in either direction before running into cargo, and peppered Jubal with questions about the local economy.

"My land, Lester," Jubal smiled, enjoying the parade, "you're going to wear a track right through the sole."

Lester stopped abruptly, snatched the whiskey bottle and took another pull. "Jubal, we're traders! We been doing it already, only a little for sure, but we've started. Look where we been, last two years! We seen Perk Creesy, the McKay brothers do it! Those are the questions they ask. Sure they got lots of money now—*or can get it*—but they were young, too. I admit, this Southern licker helps a little, but we've just got to think bigger! I ask you sir, look at your map!"

Jubal laughed, his face aglow. "So ..."

"So we're getting a ship!"

Jubal went speechless, the light draining from his face like a spent whale lamp. "Oh, Lester ..."

Lester continued, unperturbed. "You mean to tell me that Leo Godbold's got bigger balls then you? Well sir, not me!"

"Godbold come on hard times and you know it! But fact is he might's well be a teamster. He don't *own* nothin'!"

"You're being thick, Jubal!" Lester pressed on. "That's the whole point, same as Lauchlan McKay just did. Didn't you learn anything following him 'round? They sold *Sovereign,* and then leased her back! Didn't pay for her, just to use her!"

"Yeah ...?" Jubal looked skeptical but the disdain had disappeared.

"Two, three years my friend," Lester leaned forward, tapping Jubal's chest. "We work the clippers, we never go *nowhere* without trading cargo, we ask questions—don't give a hard time—and we always keep our eyes open. Then we find us a small boat, something like this first. You don't always want be someone's boy? You want to lead? Well, it's going take some planning and now's the time to start, yes sir!"

⁓

Jubal stood at the bow, pointing his cup to direct Lester down the line of wharves toward the berth he'd been assigned the day before at the Cotton

Exchange. He had accompanied Leonard Godbold to the cotton factor's office in a nondescript building on Claiborne Street, but the man had left for the afternoon. Godbold took Jubal to the Exchange and left him in the hands of a clerk he knew from previous trips before hustling off for the riverboat landing to catch the afternoon steamboat heading upriver.

The berth was empty as the *Cerbin Flanigan* approached at midtide. Lester carefully eased the bowsprit alongside the tall black cypress logs that supported the wharf, several feet above. Jubal dropped the jib and lassoed a pier, and in a minute of unspoken communication, the boys tied off the bow and stern, then paid out four spring lines, snubbing the schooner secure. Lester stood near the stern, eyeballing the web of dock lines when he noticed Jubal looking upward.

A formally dressed man stood above them, his hands clasped like a parson watching his flock enter church. Of medium height, he was portly, clean-shaven, and wore a dark, well-tailored suit with a high-buttoned collar and bow tie. Beneath his wide-brimmed hat, Lester saw an open face, unemotional except for the man's eyes.

The boys returned his gaze for several moments. Jubal expected Lester to say something but his friend remained silent. The raucous cry of a gull overhead and shouts of longshoremen down the wharf seemed unnaturally loud. Finally, the man reached into his coat and withdrew a paper.

"Mr. Jubal Calhoun? Mr. Lester Norton?" he read in a low drawl, polite, genteel, and direct. He looked from Captain Godbold's authorization back to the boys.

"I'm Jubal Calhoun, sir, and this be Lester Norton," Jubal replied, his drawl more pronounced than Lester could remember.

The man seemed to consider that thoroughly. "Begging y'all's pardon," he said finally, "do you have a copy of this authorization that Mr. Doucet was so kind to give me? Said y'all be having a duplicate."

Jubal looked at Lester. He'd given him the copy upon returning aboard the night before, when they'd gone over the manifest together.

Lester stood rock-still, dressed only in cotton trousers rolled to mid-calf. His hair was mussed and salt-dried from the bucket shower. "Begging your pardon, sir, who might you be?"

The man turned slightly to regard Lester, until the barest hint of a smile played at his lips. "I'm Truette Stubbs. I own this vessel."

"Begging your pardon, sir," Lester repeated, "do you have identification?

Proof of ownership?"

Jubal watched the conversation carefully, realizing he and Lester were legally responsible for the ship and its entire cargo. Jubal felt a swell of pride for his friend.

"No disrespect intended, sir," Jubal said, bringing the man's gaze back to him, "but you can understand we're obliged to Captain Godbold, who's entrusted us with this here vessel. I'm sure you appreciate our duty."

The man paused again, as though he never reacted to anything without thinking first. To the boy's amazement, he nodded in almost a bow and his smiled widened slightly.

"Why, of course I understand," Stubbs replied. "And I do respect y'all's ... dedication 'a purpose. Unfortunately, I neglected to bring title with me—having known Mr. Godbold for several years. However, I do believe ... Just a moment, please."

Truette Stubbs turned, blew a piercing whistle that momentarily silenced the hubbub of the waterfront, and made a beckoning motion. The boys craned to see, but the schooner deck was head height below the wharf and they could only hear running steps echo under the wharf planking. Suddenly, two policemen appeared above them and eyed the boat.

"These boys been rascally, Mr. Stubbs?" the older one wheezed, catching his breath. "What y'all doin' aboard there, boys? Where's Godbold?"

Stubbs held up a hand. "No trouble, Ben, no trouble t'all. These boys doing right, oh yes. But we've never met, and ... well, you see, they're just being cautious, as appropriate to the circumstance."

Lester didn't know why he had asked for the man's identification; it just came out that way. He'd thought of Lauchlan McKay and how he might handle these sudden responsibilities.

"Godbold's gone upriver," Jubal said.

"And left y'all here?" the policeman demanded. He had caught his breath and was getting hot at the preposterous explanation. "What for? What happened?"

"He went direct to his missus," Jubal explained. "Lost his boys in New York."

"Lost them!"

Jubal nodded. "Could be headed anywhere now."

"A crimp, most likely," Lester added. "South Street's no place for young'uns."

No one said anything for a time. Then Truette Stubbs unfolded his hands.

"How old y'all?"

"Sixteen," Lester replied. "Coming on. Both us," he nodded to Jubal.

The three men on the wharf looked them over. Stubbs turned to the older policeman.

"Ben, could you watch the vessel while I accompany these boys to my office? I'll send a niggah here shortly, most likely Scott or 'Zekiel. Be much obliged."

―

The boys went below briefly to pull on shirts and boots. While Jubal dug out the hat he'd bought in San Francisco, which had become battered over time, Lester pocketed the rest of their money.

After taking the boys to his office, where he produced a title abstract for the *Cerbin Flanigan*, Stubbs inquired about the cargo manifest. Lester had brought a leather satchel with the ship's papers and handed it over, explaining they had not examined or loaded any of the goods so could not vouchsafe for them. Stubbs simply nodded and pulled a small cord behind his chair. The boys heard a faint bell chime; several minutes later, light knocks announced a slight, middle-aged black man. Stubbs addressed him as Scott and introduced the boys. Scott nodded, but averted his eyes and was so quiet as to be mute, barely moving his lips to acknowledge Stubbs' instructions for the cargo.

Jubal suddenly remembered the crates they had purchased in New York. Stubbs listened with that impassive, absorbing gaze until a trace of his mincing smile returned and he inquired how they intended to sell the goods and what their plans were while they were in Mobile. When Jubal explained that they were headed upriver to Cahaba, the man nodded and said he expected they would be his guests until they left. Before the boys could protest Stubbs held up a hand, and in that quiet, genteel drawl told them he would hear nothing to the contrary.

Turning to Scott, he directed him to prepare a "Havana turn'round," and then scribbled a note for the black man. As Truette Stubbs pocketed the manifest, he suggested the boys return to the schooner for their gear and also decide what they wanted to do with their cargo. The boys cast uneasy glances at each other. In New York, the exciting and romantic self-image of traders had turned cash into what now looked like a bunch of heavy, awkward crates with no known destination or buyer. When Stubbs casually added that perhaps he might be of some assistance in the cargo disposal, Lester almost offered to sell it outright for whatever the man would pay.

As they left Stubbs' small office building, Lester noticed a wide boulevard at the end of the street. From the nautical chart he'd seen the night before, he remembered that Mobile was laid out on a grid fronting the harbor.

"Are we looking toward the city center?" he inquired of Stubbs.

"Yes indeed," the man nodded, "and since I need to attend some matters at the Cotton Exchange, why don't you boys look around downtown and then we can all return to the *Cerbin Flanigan* and prepare a port manifest so you can legally release the cargo."

Within a block of the wharf, Government Street was paved with crushed seashells that seemed to absorb and reflect the heat. When Jubal bought two glasses of lemonade from a street vendor, Lester remarked how much better it would be with ice.

"You have any ice?" Jubal asked the vendor, an old woman who looked Cuban. When she shook her head no, Jubal turned to Lester. "What do you think? Two weeks down here, from Maine? How much would we lose on a load of ice?"

"Money or weight?" Lester asked, already doing the math.

"Same difference, ain't it?"

Lester laughed in the middle of a swallow and started to choke.

"Is, right?" Jubal grinned, whacking him on the back. "Remind me to ask Stubbs about ice."

They boys spent an hour meandering away from the waterfront, finding neighborhoods of handsome homes set back from the streets amid manicured, flowered yards. The houses were built with large columned porches and shaded by enormous oak trees garlanded in moss. In the older part of the city, where wrought iron balconies graced the front of narrow two- and three-story buildings, Lester remarked that it looked like the Spanish parts of San Francisco. Jubal gave him a brief history of the city and its serial occupants. French, British, Spanish, and finally Americans had coveted Mobile for its strategic location.

"Ain't this place been called 'Paris of the South'?" Lester sniffed. "Don't look all that much to me."

"When's the last time you been to Paris?"

Lester ignored the comment. "What do you think's down there?" he wondered, as they crossed Royal Street. A few blocks away, dozens of men milled about as more streamed in from side streets. Several empty wagons passed, headed in the crowd's direction. When Jubal didn't answer, Lester glanced at him.

Something in the way Jubal avoided his gaze struck Lester, and without a word he set off along Royal Street. Coming into a square, he noticed the street sign: St. Louis. As the sun climbed to high noon, Lester stopped on the eastern side of the street and stared beyond the gathering crowd to a small cluster of black women surrounded by children, some on the women's hips, others holding their hands or trying to hide in the women's long skirts. Behind them a line of black men waited, expressionless. The men stood in chains.

The color drained from Lester's face as he took in a small stage along the western side of Royal Street. Two men on horseback stood at either end, each holding a rifle casually across his lap. The air was redolent of heat and humidity, with the faint whiff of tension and spectacle. A tall, angular man in high boots and thigh-length coat, wearing a wide white hat, mounted the stage.

The auction began.

Lester could feel Jubal beside him but neither said a word for the next searing hour.

"Ladies 'n gentlemen!" The auctioneer opened his arms to welcome the crowd, as though he was about to begin an oration. "Good day to y'all, and I'm right pleased to see you! Today we have a fine passel of niggahs, several splendid bucks, some with good skills, carpenterin', blacksmithin', 'n the like. Got fine breeding women, good field hands all, and healthy young 'uns. Let's git started, now! Charlie, bring 'em on up here!"

One by one, the men were unshackled and brought on stage. The women followed, individually or with their small children, all dressed as if for church. Any child over the age of twelve was auctioned alone. The auctioneer pointed out the musculature of the men, the good hips and teeth of the women—pulling their lips apart as if displaying a horse's mouth—and the skills of both. The bidding was spirited, though decorous, and as each sale was made, the winner would move up to the front, sign a promissory note and receive a receipt, then motion the newly purchased slaves to wagons parked at the side of the square. The black women walked single file, some still suckling infants, but the men were either bound or shackled again in small groups. Not one of them made a sound, save for the brief, frightened squalling of small children, quickly hushed by the women.

Lester noticed many of the buyers stopping at a table several yards beside the stage. On a pole behind the table a sign read Southern Mutual Insurance Company. While the slaves waited, the new owner and an insurance underwriter considered the slave's value. When the auction was almost over, one buyer's conversation with the underwriter went to a haggle and became a dispute, audible across the square.

Lester turned to Jubal. "What's that about?"

Jubal said nothing for a time, considering the scene. "Can't say for sure," he answered, still watching. "Probably that fellow bought the woman and wants to insure her for more than he paid. Likely she's with child. Planter'll want to up the value for the unborn; insurer doesn't want to cover." Jubal stroked his mustache. "Just guessing, though."

Lester spun on his heel. He strode toward the docks, but halted midway and wheeled in the middle of a small side street. Jubal followed half a block behind, walking at a normal pace, his face expressionless. Even at a distance he could see Lester seething. Jubal stopped a few feet before his friend.

"Jubal, you gotta tell me plain," Lester said, straining to talk. "If we're going to do business with anybody owning slaves, then we're done! You see the way that woman looked back there, one you said were with child? That tall Negro, long arms? I bet was her husband and somebody else bought him! Seen that look between 'em! Jezus, breaking up families, you seed how scairt shitless those youngsters been? Couple of 'em on their own, weren't twelve!" Lester was enraged almost to tears.

"I was on my own, twelve," Jubal replied.

"Not as no goddam slave! And they ain't *on* their own, they're owned!" Lester flapped his arms like a wounded bird. "Tell me, Jubal! I swear you're the best man I ever known, but you want to do business with these kind of people, I'm outbound right here 'n now! Goddam it, you said that Stowe woman overdone it! Well sir, you ask me, *Uncle Tom's* ain't the half of it!"

"You want to throw that silver and china in the harbor, go ahead."

"We're not selling that stuff to planters!" Lester yelled. "You said lots people want that stuff!"

"Anybody with money is a planter," Jubal replied. "Maybe they don't have slaves, maybe they live in town, but slaves are money here. You think you could sell ice not to slaveholders? Just where's it stopping, Lester? Can't sell nothing to England because they're starving the Irish, or throwing Scots off their land so they can put sheep there instead? When we go to Liverpool, are you going to scream at Capt'n McKay like you're doing now, throw a tantrum on the dock?"

Lester's face changed from anger to bafflement, but Jubal would have none of it. "You believe Lauchlan McKay speaks the truth?" he demanded. Lester dumbly nodded.

"You talk to him about the world like I did," Jubal said, not budging an inch. "Well, you can *talk*, but I listened because I know I ain't really seen all that much. Them mills in Manchester live off cotton! Remember Eleanor Creesy talking about 'mud'! English going to war—going to *war*—Lester, on account of selling opium?"

Lester stood in the street, working his jaw and glaring at Jubal. Two men walking by stopped and looked at them. A horseman sauntered past, twisting in his saddle to stare at Lester before turning away and spurring his horse into a trot.

Jubal reached for Lester's arm and gently pulled him forward.

"Lester," said Jubal, his voice low. "I brought you down to see my country, not get you killed. We're not in Bangor, Lester. You holler like this back at that auction, someone's going take a whip to you. Think about where we been, what we seen. Remember them women's tiny feet in China, been bound up Eleanor Creesy said, when they was little girls? That wasn't pretty, but I didn't see you hauling them fellows' pigtails none. So just come about, take in your sails 'n heave to, Lester!"

Chapter Twenty-Eight

Truette Stubbs lived in a spacious, beautifully built house on Canal Street three blocks off the waterfront. The boys accompanied him in the late afternoon, after the schooner had been unloaded and their crates were stored in a warehouse near the riverboat landing. Jubal and Lester each had an upstairs bedroom that fairly crackled with cleanliness. Ezekiel, an old stooped Negro whose short, curly hair and wispy beard were snow white, drew them separate baths. They didn't see each other again until dinner was served at dusk.

The meal was splendid, though mournfully quiet, except for the jarring moments when Louisa came in from her kitchen. Truette Stubbs' cook and housekeeper had a voice that matched her frame, voluble, huge, and bursting with vitality. Otherwise, Lester's morose, monosyllabic mood cast a pall.

Lester knew he was being rude but didn't care. He had never been in the presence of slaves, much less been served by them, and he barely spoke through dinner.

From a kitchen she commanded as if it were her quarterdeck, Louisa served the men sumptuous pork roast, spring vegetables, and fresh-baked breads, each course accompanied by her booming laughter. As they finished dinner, Ezekiel cleared the plates and Louisa strode in with a platter bearing bowls of steaming peach cobbler.

"These here last 'a dem stewed peaches, Mista Stubbs, jes' a little sugar like you like 'em!" Her laughter bounced around the dining room as she passed out the bowls with hands the size of small hams. Louisa glistened with sweat and her musky odor lingered as she turned away. Ezekiel held the door as she strode back to the kitchen.

For the first time in hours, Lester smiled. "Wouldn't want to cross that woman," he finally managed, regarding the dessert. Then he looked up, his face drawn. "How long have you owned them?" Lester's question was studiously polite. Jubal stared, expressionless.

Truette Stubbs carefully took a spoonful of cobbler and savored it. "My, she makes a fine peach cobbla," he said, dabbing his lips with a napkin tucked at his chin. "What makes you think I own 'em?"

The question hung in the air. Stubbs held Lester in an impenetrable gaze for a few moments and then went on eating his cobbler. Jubal waited while Lester opened his mouth, but no reply came forth. Three times Lester almost spoke but stopped before he started. In the silence, Truette Stubbs methodically worked his way around the cobbler, from the outside to the center.

"Well, don't you?" Lester finally managed.

"No," Stubbs replied, taking his last bite of dessert. He reached for a silver teapot, gesturing to Lester, who shoved his cup across the table.

"Well ..." Lester concentrated on sugaring his tea. "Thought you owned them. Like Scott."

"I don't own Scott, either," Stubbs replied, pouring Jubal's tea before his own.

Lester took that in, and for a moment Jubal felt sorry for him. His friend sat with the blank look of someone whose certainty had vanished.

Truette Stubbs folded his hands and regarded Lester. Jubal was fascinated by the display of patience; the man had an uncanny ability to keep quiet.

Finally, Lester lifted his hands in a helpless, supplicating gesture. "I apologize, Mr. Stubbs. I never been here before, never seen slaves, never seen an auction of people sold—no offense intended—like cattle, or logs. This afternoon, after you left the dock, before we got our bags, a man come by demanding to see Scott's authority, had to show a note of some kind."

Stubbs nodded. "That's right, I wrote it this morning, y'all were there, at the office."

Lester looked at him quizzically.

"I don't own, Scott," Truette Stubbs explained. "I lease him. Another fellow in town owns him, but he's gone after the crop's planted." Stubbs dabbed his face with the napkin again. "You see, Mobile bustles like a beehive about half the year. Spring, when planting starts and everything required goes up river, then again come fall when the crop's in. Why then Mobile is jes' thicker than bugs, cotton shipping out to dozens of ports. New York, Baltimore, Liverpool, Glasgow, Bordeaux, Antwerp, London, Hamburg, Genoa, just all over. Then there's lots of fellows here, cotton factors like me, shippers, commission merchants, traders, all manner of folk. But between times, like summer when it gets hot, you could nap right in the middle of Government Street. So the niggahs don't have nearlys much to do and their owners can lease them out—or let them work on their own account—but they need to carry a permission note to the effect. Otherwise, the owner can be fined, or with Scott, I'd be fined, as the note's my responsibility. Now Scott, he can read and write, so I pay his man enough for his rent and pay Scott direct to work whenever a ship comes in. I own three schooners and keep them going. *Cerbin Flanigan* heads for Cuba, picks up cane, rum, and brings me back some of these fine cigars we're going to have us right now." He pushed his chair back. "Ezekiel'll bring tea. You boys drink brandy?"

Jubal and Lester settled into their chairs on the porch as Ezekiel lit a smoking candle to keep the mosquitoes down. Soon the cigar smoke added a wreath. The men were quietly sipping their brandy when there was a commotion from the house and Louisa bustled out the door, holding another tray. Proudly, she put down small dishes of ice cream, each with a sprig of mint on the top. Louisa stepped back and looked at the boys severely.

"Yew boys ain't drinkin' brandy? What y'all doin'? Mr. Stubbs, de's boys jes' barely growed! Servin' 'em brandy, they ain't hardly been weaned!" Louisa picked up their teacups, clucking like an aggrieved hen. "Drink's de devil, you boys be joreerin' and 'mount to nuthin'! Mr. Truette, it's a devilin' shame. Yew drinkin' brandy when yew's them age?"

"I was," Truette Stubbs smiled.

Louisa wheeled back into the house, still clucking.

"What were you doing, sir, your younger years?" Jubal asked.

"Your age?" Stubbs mused. "Well, I was born in 1800, so let's see ... 1816, thereabouts, I was soldiering with General Zack Taylor, in the Creek War."

"Who did you enlist with?" Lester asked.

"Myself—weren't no one to go with." Stubbs took a sip of brandy. "Seeing y'all aboard this morning, why, I was looking back thirty some years ago. Man grows right up when he don't have but one choice."

Jubal cleared his throat. "You've been alone ever since?"

"No," Stubbs replied. "That's why I like 'Zekiel and Louisa around. I've known 'em a long time. They're not married, to the best I know, but," he turned to Lester, "they're free niggahs."

"They're free, but Scott is owned?" Lester asked, confused, "and leased out?"

"There's what you'd call ..." Stubbs smiled, "permutations. Ezekiel and Louisa belonged to my wife's family. She swore that if anything ever happened to her, they was free. Her daddy was dead and he'd owned them since forever. In their young days, they must have been valuable, because he insured them high, sixteen hundred dollars for the two. Tessa—she was my wife, bless her—cashed the remainder of the policy and paid the bond not long before she died."

Lester stirred in his chair. "Bond?"

"If you going to free your niggahs, they got to post a bond, case they become a ward of the public."

"You don't own any slaves now, sir?"

"Never owned them." Stubbs twirled his cigar. "Slaves are good money and bad business. My opinion."

Lester nodded as if he understood, though he was baffled. "What happened to your wife, sir? If you don't mind me asking."

The night sounds suddenly crescendoed, as though the cicadas had come to full chorus in their nocturnal symphony.

"What happened to my wife?" Truette Stubbs repeated. He swirled the brandy in his glass, then downed it and sucked his lip. "The *Orline St. John*."

The night symphony shattered as Jubal choked on his brandy.

Chapter Twenty-Nine

As the steamer huffed and wheezed against the Alabama River current two days upriver from Mobile, Jubal pointed to charred trees and a few piles of rubble, the only remnants of the *Orline St. John*.

"It was three years ago, March '50," recalled Jubal, "I was a fireboy 'board her. Capt'n had seen me often enough at Gee's Bend 'n gave me a job. The last one I had 'fore I left these parts and went to sea."

The young men were standing on the top deck in the cool evening on their way to Selma, where Truette Stubbs said they could readily sell their silverware and china at one of several stores. The cotton trader had provided a letter of introduction to a Selma merchant and taken them around Mobile shops to compare prices, advising that each day up river, their goods' value would increase several percent.

"So that makes you about eleven, twelve?" Lester calculated. He had spent his day watching the riverbank roll by, fascinated with the fecund jungle that reached to the water's edge. Tall live oaks leaned over the riverbank, dripping hundred-foot strands of moss like scarves of greenery that splayed onto the chocolate river. Occasionally, a low, dense growth of river cane crowded the bank, especially in the lowland delta where the river broke into a labyrinth. Further upriver, higher hills covered in soaring stands of loblolly pine had Lester musing on lumbering possibilities. The only logs he had seen were deadwood and snags that the riverboat dodged with surprising agility.

"Yeah," Jubal laughed without humor. "On my own, just like Stubbs. Anyway, the *Orline* set out from Mobile in March, right into the spring flood. River's high then and rolling. Capt'n was pushing, trying for Montgomery—that was the railhead—before the train left northbound." He reached in his pocket and drew out pipe fixings. Lester bit off the end of a cigar Truette Stubbs had given him and scratched a match, lighting Jubal's pipe and then his own smoke. They both leaned on the rail of the promenade near the bow.

"Had to push hard against the river," Jubal continued, his voice lowering to a monotone. "You can imagine the way we went through that pine, burns so hot, 'n we had to load couple times a day. Any of the landings where we could lie to, well, we just loaded that jesse up, right to the furnace. Look back there now, that stack?"

The old riverboat's high-pressure steam boilers gorged on fat pine to turn the sidewinder paddle wheels, sending a steady cascade of embers sparkling from the boiler smokestack, whisked away downstream in glowing points that twinkled and disappeared amidst the gathering darkness.

"Coming on sundown and *Orline*'s pushing everything she's worth. I'm feeding the furnace, nearly passed out from heat," Jubal took a long drag from his pipe and blew the smoke out his nostrils. " I looked up and top the pile is afire. Wood's just slick with resin, summer cut, and within a minute we're a goddamn torch going upriver. Men in front, playing cards or watching, women back aft with the kids, fifty, sixty people aboard. The pilot heads for the bank so everyone kin get off the bow, but the river's up, see along that tree line, all them hanging out over? We just burn them trees but can't get in. Now the boat's afire, going right cross amidships, staircase in flames." Jubal took a deep breath, and pointed to the charred trees on the riverbank.

"Pilot can't steer, wheel ropes turned to ash, the boat's burning in half, fire's got hold of the boats. So I start putting the women and children over, on doors, mattresses, whatever I can get my hands on. Those women in big skirts, ones with the hoops in 'em? It would have been simpler if they grabbed hold of an anchor, went down like stones."

"How'd you make it off?" Lester shivered, looking aft as the riverboat rounded a bend.

"Finally jumped, got hold of a barrel. Tried to hold a girl, about my age, her dress tore, she's screaming and I lunged. Missed her and lost the barrel, that were the last I seen her, blonde hair disappearing in the bubbles." Jubal rubbed his eyes and let out a long sigh. "So I swum, or stayed afloat, 'till a deadwood nearly tangled me drowned, but I got a hold and rode her downstream. She run into Gee's Bend. River nearly makes a circle there. Niggahs on Gee's place found me next morning, walking circles in the fields, least they said. I don't remember. Thirty-nine dead. The women, children, every single one." Jubal voice had dropped to a murmur. "Never told a soul 'bout it, 'cept now."

Lester dropped his cigar into the river.

"Don't know if I was kid then," Jubal sighed, "but I surely weren't after that night." He tapped the remains of his pipe on the rail and watched the ashes disappear. It was almost dark. "Didn't want to tell the man, but I saw Truette's wife. Way he described her, I 'member the one. She was kindly and brave, the last off when she jumped. Dress caught on something and she just hung there, went up like a candle—clothes, hair, until she burned enough, something let go and she fell, never come up."

"Then you left?" asked Lester, laying a hand on his friend's arm. "What for?"

"Couldn't stay," Jubal replied. "My Uncle Whitmill and I fought, was the reason I was on the *Orline* to begin with. So I headed for Mobile and stowed away to get anywhere but near the river." Jubal grimaced. "I didn't have nothing, but if I'd been paid for nightmares ... woulda been right rich."

―

Arriving into Selma the next morning, they unloaded their crates and Lester stood watch while Jubal went into the city carrying a letter from Truette Stubbs to a local merchant. Jubal returned within an hour, riding in a wagon driven by a black man.

"The niggah told me he's one of two dozen this merchant owns," Jubal said, "Rodgers is the merchant man's name. Now if you don't like it, Lester, tell this niggah to move on; you can sell this stuff any way you want. I'll help, but won't be sayin' another damn thing."

Lester looked directly at the black man but the slave averted his eyes. Their crates lay on the landing wharf amidst piles of lumber, sacks of grain, and other assorted cargo that a team of slaves was moving into brick warehouses. The morning was humid and already hot. Overhead, huge clouds appeared to be boiling, promising a deluge by afternoon.

Lester sighed and pushed his hat back. "Trouble with being righteous is you got to eat." Between them, they had about twenty dollars in coins left. "Let's just see what we can do before this stuff gets soaked. Next time, we do our trading from aboard ship. Once we start moving cargo, it becomes a chore."

"You yourself said we make more," Jubal pointed out, not wanting to show his relief.

"More's fine if we can do the same or less. Hell, now we're just glorified teamsters. Might as well stay on the coast, be less trouble."

An hour later, in the back of a large emporium on Water Street, Absalom Rodgers carefully held one of the crystal glasses to the light. While he examined the cargo, Lester and Jubal craned their necks to catch glimpses of women window-shopping. Selma was obviously prosperous, with a half-mile commercial district that ran parallel to the river. Perpendicular to Water Street, several blocks of large, stately homes led inland. Women dressed in bell-shaped skirts and holding parasols strolled along the boardwalks, and the street bustled with wagons and men on horseback. In the distance a train chugged and tooted into town.

Rodgers thoroughly examined the china and tapped the silverware together, listening for tone, while the boys watched impassively. Finally, he took a calculated look at all the crates. "Seventeen hundred dollars," he announced in a reserved drawl. Rodgers was a tall man, white-haired with spectacles, who walked with a decided limp.

The boys looked at each other. In Mobile, they had spent a day examining products from Europe and New England. On the way upriver, whenever the steamer stopped at a town landing long enough, one of them ran ashore to price comparable merchandise. After much discussion, they decided that $1800 was the lowest price they would accept in Selma. Truette Stubbs had offered $1500, but urged them to ship the goods upriver, where he was confident they'd do better.

"Seventeen hundred," Lester blurted, as though he suddenly awoke from a stupor. "Done!"

Jubal ground his teeth, certain they could have raised their price, but he held out his hand to shake, surprising Rodgers. "One hand's good as the other," Jubal remarked.

Rodgers smiled for the first time since they'd met, a thin move in a hard face. "How long y'all staying in Selma?"

"Once we conclude this matter," replied Jubal, "we'll be returning south. A day perhaps."

"May I suggest a rest at the St. James Hotel? Y'all may have seen it above the landing."

"Thank you for your recommendation, sir," Lester replied, trying to think of a polite way to decline. The hotel looked expensive.

"My suggestion 'n recommendation. Indeed," Absalom Rodgers nodded, "my invitation …" The boys looked at him blankly.

"I own the hotel," Rodgers explained. "Truette Stubbs and I go a long way back. Fought under me with General Taylor when we were young men, not much older than y'all now. His letter," Rodgers held up the note, "is clear 'nough. By what cause did you purchase this particular crystal and china?"

"A woman," Jubal explained. "I accompanied a Mrs. Eleanor Creesy once, our captain's wife, in New York. Was a few years ago and she ... how'd you call it, Lester? She was a teacher, gave us much more than we realized at the time, I guess. Mighty good to us, they were."

Rodgers nodded. "Don't cost to be good to people, 'specially when they earn it. I suppose you think Truette Stubbs has been good to you?"

"Without a doubt, sir," agreed Lester.

"Yes, he's a good man to be with—especially in a fight—and a fine judge of character," Rodgers said. "Y'all might not thought—I don't know—but once aboard that schooner y'all could have gone anywhere, and whatever would Truette Stubbs've done?"

—

Enclosing a square central courtyard, the St. James Hotel in Selma stood three stories above the bluff that looked south over the Alabama River and boasted the finest rooms between Montgomery and Mobile. After several days sleeping on a cargo deck, the boys could not believe their good fortune. They had breakfast on the middle balcony adjacent to a spacious room where they'd spent the night, relishing fine, fresh-squeezed orange juice and rich black coffee while wolfing down flapjacks, pork chops, and grits.

"That fits right," Jubal belched, reaching for a cigar.

"It pains me, but I got to commend your New York good sense," Lester said, lighting up and tossing the matches at Jubal. They leaned back and smoked, content to savor the bright, warm morning, washed clean from a torrential rain the evening before.

Lester rose and walked to the balcony, surveying the river. "You know," he observed, "this place is a pile of contradictions. Polite and friendly folks ride around with whips, pleasant unless they get pissed off. Then they're ready to hang you. The whole economy—a man's station, opportunity, wealth, everything—why, it turns on something so chancy as the color of his skin."

Jubal stubbed out his cigar. "Let's get us some horses."

"Where we going?"

"Cahaba, and Gee's Bend."

"We just passed them," protested Lester. "River goes right by, why don't we float back?"

"'Cause we're riding," Jubal declared. "I want to be on horseback."

Chapter Thirty

The road paralleled the river, following its wide valley swings above the high water mark. Although normally placid, the Alabama River might rise sixty feet in a spring surge or hurricane rain, so the road sometimes ran miles from the river in the bottomlands before coming back along high, clay bluffs.

As their horses plodded along, Lester surveyed immense cotton fields that spread through rich red soil. Often, hundreds of slaves could be seen in the distance, laboring in the open under a blazing sun, little dark dots slowly hoeing a green quilt that rolled across the land. Overseers sat on horseback, sometimes tipping their hats to Lester and Jubal if they were close enough, other times just watching as the boys rode by. Occasionally, far off on a hill or wooded knoll, a large, imposing white house crowned the surrounding domain.

The boys didn't say much, nor did they hurry. In Selma they had bought smoked jerky, hardtack, and coffee. Watching the weather, they judged it safe enough to spend the nights beside a fire, camping along a creek, or on a knoll they could easily reach from the road. Both wore light cotton coats over the shoulder holsters that Jubal had purchased. Lester didn't question the need to be armed; between them they carried four hundred dollars and a bank draft for the remaining cargo profit.

Several posses had ridden by, on the lookout for runaway slaves. Each time, the armed men stopped, perfunctorily tipped their hats and regarded Jubal and Lester with open suspicion. Lester never said a word, allowing Jubal to explain their presence and intentions. The encounters always ended amicably, though with a faint, distinct flavor of menace.

"Y'all see a niggah, you ask for his paper," one leader directed. "Niggah more 'n eight miles away from who owns 'im, 'er been gone more 'n two days, y'all rope him, hear? That's law, and be doin' a good turn."

Lester stayed quiet. Especially after a posse had ridden away, he concentrated on mulling the costs of a slave economy. At the Mobile exchange he had seen cotton prices, and the slave auction had indelibly branded his memory with the dollar value of slaves. Land advertisements in the Selma newspaper gave him an idea of plantation costs. The numbers offered a refuge, providing safety from the sullen anger churning his belly. If a slave did run, where would he go? Negros breaking for freedom had almost no chance of surviving against mounted man hunters.

Two days south of Selma, they forded a small stream late in the afternoon and followed the road as it paralleled the watercourse. Just before dark, Jubal turned off on a narrow, well-trodden trail leading into the woods and came to a small clearing that looked as if it been a campsite for centuries of travelers. The stream was wider, flowing slow but clear to the southeast.

"This here's the Cahaba," Jubal announced.

Lester glanced at the river as he tossed his saddlebags down. "Pretty small to handle a barge."

"They don't quite come this far," Jubal replied, "couple miles further down's the first landing, and she gets wider 'till the town, at the confluence with the Alabama. We'll be there mid-morning."

"And do what?"

Jubal gathered some sticks, concentrating on making a small fire.

Lester was too tired to stir it further. His mental exercises had worn him out, but eventually the itch had to be scratched.

"Jubal, this here's how I figure it," he began, after his cigar was lit and drawing well. "Cotton on the river landing's about eight cents a pound, right, maybe nine? A bale's nearly five hundred pounds. You get fifteen hundred bales off a thousand acres, that makes sixty thousand dollars gross from the crop. Costs fifty to fifty-five thousand, what with all the growing, storage, shipping, weighing, drayage, the like, so you come to about a ten percent return. That's if you're not paying on the land."

Jubal stared at the fire.

"So the way I see it," Lester continued, puffing away, "it's good business—*if.* One big *if* after another. *If* you own the land ... *If* the weather holds ... the price stays firm ... the slaves you bought work hard enough to repay their purchase ... the harvest comes in on time. If you can get two crops a year, you make right out." Lester glanced then nodded, satisfied Jubal was listening.

"What I don't get is the slaves. Now, 'course if you own them, that don't take much thinking. But, here's another of those big *if*s. You buy them at what—average a thousand apiece? Ain't that what the auction price was in Mobile—seven hundred dollars a kid, twelve to thirteen hundred per man, right? A hundred slaves, a hundred thousand dollars. Take you ten years, two good crops a year, to pay 'em off. Might's well pay them wages, wouldn't cost anywhere near ten thousand a year and no bearing their freight over the winter."

Lester suddenly stopped, as if he'd had a revelation. "Ahh …" he gestured with his cigar like a pointer. "Just the initial investment, ain't it? You keep them in the fields and they multiply. The interest on your investment comes in newborns." He looked at Jubal. "So what's the crop here, really? These places grow cotton, or do they grow slaves?"

Jubal tossed his cigar into the fire and lay back. "You decide, Lester," he said, rolling over and pulling his hat down.

The boys mounted up in the vermilion light of dawn, a morning sky that at sea portended heavy weather. Before they'd gone a mile, Lester could feel Jubal's tension and he realized that during the ride from Selma his friend had barely said a word, and then only in response to either the posse riders or a direct question. They entered a long, dim stretch of wood where gnarly branches of live oak almost smothered in vine covered the road like a verdant prehistoric roof. Finally, as though emerging from a tunnel, they left the forest and rode into a young, succulent cotton field glistening with dew. As the first streaks of sunlight slanting across the road warmed his face, Lester decided he wanted to know what they were riding into.

"Don't rightly know," Jubal replied. "I spent a couple years here, living with a family that took me in, the Cocherans. Where I got my schoolin'." He sighed suddenly, and stopped his horse in the middle of the road.

"What?" Lester reined in, half a horse ahead, and quickly looked around, wondering if he'd missed a threat.

"I don't know … maybe we shouldn't go in."

Lester stared at his friend. Jubal had never been tentative about anything.

"Well, Jubal, we're going! You might never come back, but by God you'll know why, because you surely don't now. Whatever's got you like a fever ought be lanced. Eleanor Creesy were here right now, she'd take you by the ear and kick you through it!" Lester turned and spurred his horse into a trot. "C'mon Jubal," he called. "Let's go do our visiting and head downriver so we can get back to New York. Capt'n McKay's not going to wait outbound for Liverpool!" He rode on, afraid to look back.

Lester's horse tossed its head, wanting to run with the morning. Lester gave the gelding rein and they took off in an exhilarating gallop, both horse and rider reveling in the cool, delicious surge of wind past their faces. A mile later, when he glanced back, Jubal was far behind, having put his mount into a steady lope. Lester's horse had broken a hard sweat so he took it down to a trot. At the end of a long curve the boys were just about even when Lester pulled up short. Ahead of them, the road ran true as an arrow for another half-mile, ending in a bluff above the Alabama River. From the river's edge and leading several hundred yards back from the water, buildings rose on either side of the road.

Jubal stopped beside Lester. "Capitol Avenue," he said, quietly. "Cahaba, Alabama."

A noble brick house commanded the rivers' confluence. Four large columns supported a roofed porch that spanned the house's entire width facing the broad, placid Alabama. To the left, the Cahaba River, a tenth the size, came in like an errant thread trailing the fabric of a scarf. The boys pulled their horses to a halt in the dooryard and dismounted before Jubal took a deep breath and approached the house. A young woman came onto the porch, her coal black skin in sharp contrast to a bleached white apron and bonnet.

"Whut y'all want?" she demanded, hands going to her hips.

"Watch your tone!" Jubal bristled. "Go tell Mr. Cocheran that Jubal Calhoun is here!"

"He done gone," the black woman waved up river. "Missus die 'o fever and he took dem chillen wid 'im up north. Whut else you wanna know, ain't here?"

Without a word, Jubal vaulted into the saddle and spurred his horse.

Lester and the black woman exchanged looks, equally blank. He followed his friend; a few moments later the screen door slammed.

"Mind tellin' me ...?" Lester asked, as he caught up and the horses slowed to a walk through town.

"Goddam uppity ..." Jubal breathed. He shook his head clear. "I spent two years there. Mr. Cocheran, he'd take in kids sometimes, they needed it. We thought he talked funny; he'd come down from Syracuse or someplace like that. Good man, he was, me being too young to appreciate. And he paid for a teacher, there was about ten of us kids went to a little schoolhouse out back. I was there 'cause I kept running away from Gee's Bend. But I hated being in school, couldn't abide listening to everything going on outside. Birds, wagons, riverboats, horses—Lord, it was torture. I liked reading and stuff, but hated sitting still, kept ruckusin'. Finally, I just went back, figured I could handle Gee's Bend again." Jubal shook his head. "Wuz wrong about that. Near dead wrong."

Lester played a hunch. "Is that where we're headed?"

"Since when do you get to knowing what I think before I do?"

"Ain't celestial navigation," Lester laughed, "to see we're going out a different road than we came in on. Anything you want to get while we're here?"

Jubal stopped. "Like what?"

"I dunno. Somethin' for your friends, or family, or whoever else t'hell we're going to?"

Jubal's face wrinkled. "Yeah, thanks, I do. Down near the slide, there's a store there, we'll stop."

Lester spent a half-hour waiting for Jubal outside a shop that could have been a small twin of Absalom Rodgers' emporium in Selma. The wait exasperated him. When Jubal came out empty handed, Lester nearly said something sarcastic, but the forlorn look on his friend's face stopped him.

Jubal gave a shrug of resignation. "I don't know what to get." At Lester's bafflement, Jubal elaborated. "I ain't never bought nobody a gift before."

"Well," Lester said, all the starch suddenly washed out. "Well. Who's it for? Man, woman, or child?"

"Woman."

"Go back in there," Lester pointed, "and buy some of the shiniest, most eye-blinding fabric they got. Not a woman alive who don't like bright colors. Momma told me that—probably 'cause she never had none."

Jubal spun on his heel and disappeared into the store.

Lester waited, subdued. The mention of his mother reminded him he was remiss in writing, and he counted the months since sending a letter to Maine. He didn't know what to write and didn't want to tell his mother the truth—that he had no intention of returning for several years.

Jubal strode out, holding a small bolt of scarlet silk under his arm, in time to see Lester's downcast expression. "You swallow a lemon?" Jubal asked.

Lester waved him off, his gaze suddenly drawn to something else. Jubal turned to see a man approaching. Dressed in overalls and a floppy straw hat, tall and bare-footed, he was the blackest man Lester had ever seen.

"If it don't be Jubal Calhoun!" the man exclaimed. "I thought yew'd flopped your wings and flied!"

Jubal stood dumbstruck, mouth agape. He tipped his hat back and stepped forward. "By Gawd, Jordon! I'm good, how you?"

The black man laughed with the deep music of a born singer. "Why, Lord gimme 'nother day, well's to say! Who you brought, Masta Jubal?"

"This here's Lester Norton." Jubal's drawl had deepened to molasses and he grinned like a schoolboy. "Me 'n Lesta seen the world together! From Maine he is, way north. Lester, this here's Jordon Hatcher!"

The black man nodded politely. Half a head taller than Lester and broader in the chest and shoulders than Jubal, Hatcher was strong-featured, with high cheekbones, a large, flat nose, and full lips. The man had long, muscular arms and splayed toes on feet that never saw shoes.

Lester, flabbergasted that Jubal spoke as if the man had no color, immediately liked Jordon Hatcher. "A pleasure, sir," he replied, dismounting. "Jubal's told me absolutely nothing about you." He reached to shake hands.

Jordon Hatcher stared for a moment before his eyes darted to Jubal and back. He stiffened and briefly grasped Lester's hand. "The boy ain't given to talk," Hatcher agreed, stepping back and regarding Jubal. He seemed to relax. "But Lord, he kep' us in meat! Deer, turkey, possum, they's uncommon now. Beulah be expectin' yew to provide, first thing. Y'all comin'?" It was both question and command.

"'Spect so," Jubal nodded. "The boys in the fields?" He turned to Lester. "There's two Hatcher boys."

"No, sir," Jordon Hatcher replied, "got 'em workin'." The smile left his face and he regarded Jubal impassively. The sudden shift resembled a cloud shuttling under the sun and Lester realized this was the first time since his arrival in Mobile that he'd seen a black man make direct eye contact. "Uncle done sold us."

The air suddenly went taut. A songbird tittered once, sounding unnaturally loud. Jubal took a deep breath.

"Had to?" he asked, carefully.

Jordon Hatcher nodded yes.

"Who ...?" Jubal leaned forward.

Hatcher shrugged. "The judge bought me, but masta rides circuit, sumpin' 'bout a bank ruptin' when a man's business go bad. So I kin hire me 'n the boys from him some, working on time. I about done fixin' a house, edge of town. Daniel, Isaiah, be carpentering on the slide, o' there. " He nodded his head downriver where a shallow roof covered an open wooden platform at the embankment's edge. Both the platform and its roof extended into a narrow chute that slanted downward and disappeared out of sight.

On the trip upriver Jubal had pointed the chutes out, explaining they were used to load cotton. Lester wondered how far this one dropped, remembering a chute further downriver that had a 325-step staircase alongside. "You mean the bales slide down them?" Lester had asked incredulously. "A bale, five hundred pounds? I wouldn't want to be on the receiving end!"

"Bales are about four hundred eighty pounds," Jubal had corrected. "Slaves'll work up top but Irishmen do the loading on the boats. They don't cost nothing." Lester had just stared, realizing his friend was dead serious.

The faint rap of hammers rang from somewhere far over the embankment. Jubal shifted his feet, uncertain what to say. Jordon Hatcher saw the boy's confusion and his face softened. "Wha'ju got?" he growled softly, motioning to the bolt of fabric.

Jubal's lower lip quivered. "For Beulah," he whispered. Lester watched, touched by his friend's embarrassment.

Jordon Hatcher threw his head back with a booming laugh. Jubal turned red, shy but delighted.

"Oh my!" Hatcher clapped his big hands. "Yew better go shootin'! Beulah be wantin' to feed you right!"

"My rifle?" Jubal asked.

Hatcher's delight vanished in an eyeblink. "Yes suh," he murmured, "it sho do, sho do."

Chapter Thirty-One

Jubal remained silent as they rode single-file out of Cahaba. Lester, mulling the encounter, glanced back for a glimpse of Jordon Hatcher, but the man had disappeared over the embankment onto the slide.

Jubal reined suddenly and turned in his saddle. "Lester!" He reached for his friend's arm. "Jes' take this 'n not be pestering me, 'cause there's no explaining I can do that'll satisfy. Don't be shaking a nigra's hand. It just's not done, ever. White man sees you, knows straight away you ain't of a kind. Worse, that niggah'd be 'impudent,' could get him whipped bad, or worse. Jes' don't."

Lester thought of Jordon Hatcher's awkward, soft handshake, and didn't reply.

The track gradually widened to a wagon's width as it skirted long, flowing cotton fields that shimmered in the afternoon heat. Beside them, the woods rose in a jungle wall that could swallow a man on horseback as certain as if he rode behind a curtain. As the horses trooped into the afternoon, their heads drooping, Jubal described the history, as he knew it, of Gee's Bend.

Forty years earlier, Joseph Gee came into the Alabama territory, young and ambitious. The Chickasaw tribe was a shadow of its prime and Joseph Gee's marriage to an Indian princess may have been romance or calculation, but the result was new life in the bulb-shaped bend midway along the Alabama River.

"Gee died sometime in the twenties," Jubal related, "and passed it on to a nephew, I think: George. By then he had forty, fifty slaves. My daddy was overseer for George Gee, though I barely remember the man. He sold to a fellow named Mark Pettaway, seven, eight years ago. Pettaway came from Carolina, brought out another hundred slaves."

Lester snapped awake. "We gonna see your dad?" Jubal had never spoken of his father.

Jubal shook his head. "Died not long after Pettaway came."

"What happened?"

"Liquor," Jubal replied, "drunk to death. People told me different, said it was fever or something bad in his gut, but I knew otherwise. Didn't drink much, but when he made whiskey he drank 'till it was done."

The boys rode along in silence. "Well, I'm sorry to hear that," Lester said, finally. "You got no family?"

"Whitmill Rivens, he calls hisself 'uncle'," Jubal spit with sudden vehemence, "'count of marrying Pa's sister, Aunt Amelia. Last I saw him, he took a shot at me."

Lester nearly dropped his reins. "Your uncle?"

"That's his callin', not mine!" Bitterness etched Jubal's face.

On the midday ride across the bend, Jubal described the scene of his last visit, of coming home from the *Orline St. John* horror to a violent, screaming argument between his aunt and uncle, of hurtling pans and the feminine screech to be gone and 'take yer black cunties with yew!'"

Jubal had stood in the dooryard, barely thirteen, and seen his aunt come flying through the door, nearly ripping it off the leather hinges, and sprawl in the yard. His uncle came striding out, enraged, and got hit smack in the face by Jubal's rock, thrown reflexively to protect the bloodied woman. Rivens had howled, then wheeled back into the house. Jubal didn't need more warning and took off at a dead run.

He was a hundred yards away when the shotgun blast sounded, too far away to do any damage. Jubal kept running until he found the Liverpool packet.

"C'mon, rain'll come 'fore dark." He spurred his horse so hard the startled animal neighed and broke straight into a gallop. Lester hurried behind but it was too hot for the horses to last long at that speed, and they settled into a lope that ate up the miles.

The sun had disappeared behind the cloud line when Jubal slowed his horse to a walk. Lester studied the sullen-looking sky, heavy with rain, and knew they were in for a wet night. Suddenly, without warning, Jubal turned off the road and guided his horse directly into the impenetrable gloom. In seconds he was out of sight and Lester quickly spurred to follow, afraid of being left behind. He stayed close, soon realizing they followed a faint game trail through the forest. Watching his friend, Lester's fear subsided; Jubal was as relaxed and confident in the hushed, spooky woods as if he'd been reefing the main topsail in a blustery squall.

The boys followed the trail that seemed to track in a mostly straight line. Once accustomed to the light Lester saw that the undergrowth wasn't as thick as he'd thought. He was looking at the thick mantle overhead when his horse stopped abruptly and nearly pitched him forward directly onto Jubal's mount. In the sudden silence, a faint burble of running water rose from the forest floor. Jubal dismounted and led his horse through the undergrowth. Lester followed and scanned the surroundings before he saw it, close upon a natural spring bubbling from a rock basin.

Almost indistinguishable from the forest, a lean-to of lashed logs hung suspended between four huge trees. A mixture of bark, grass, woven branches, and decayed leaves, fallen in spots but mostly whole, created a roof high enough to shelter a standing man. Jubal handed Lester the reins to his horse, dismounted and walked to a large old gum tree nearby. At its base, a cleft had formed as the tree slowly died and rotted from within. Jubal picked up a stick, banged it around inside, and paused for a few moments to see if any snakes appeared before reaching in to withdraw a long leather casing tightly secured with rawhide. As he returned to the horses, Jubal untied the bindings and reverently opened first the leather, then a cotton sheath underneath, to reveal a single-shot, long-barreled percussion rifle. A faint sheen still showed from the residue of oil that coated the weapon.

"First time I shot this, was about eight," Jubal said. "Knocked me flat. Belonged to my daddy. He taught me to shoot with a smaller bird gun—this was hard to handle; I was too little. When he died I hid it, otherwise Whitmill would have stole it. Jordon Hatcher told me what to do, bringing it here, but a niggah caught with a rifle be hung, no question." He looked at Lester with a flash of insight. "Didn't appreciate it then, but he risked his life. Many times. For a boy." Jubal thought about that. "Mr. Hatcher couldn't shoot good because he'd never learned. Niggah better not, hereabouts. But Jordon Hatcher can *do* anything under the sun. Taught me how to use it and take a little powder out of each round so the discharge didn't flatten me."

"How'd you get the fixings?" Lester asked.

Jubal's grim smile took him back to the awful days after his father's death. "Daddy had some, and I stole the rest from uncle when he was drunk."

"He didn't know you had it?"

"I weren't 'round more than necessary. Stayed here lots, and with Hatchers, though I knew that was dangerous. Still, I could hunt, and I'd bring Beulah the game and she'd cook it, take care me, 'specially after Emma left."

Lester shook his head, trying to keep it all clear. "Who's Emma?"

Jubal looked into the treetops. There was little left of the day, and overhead the first patters of rain sprinkled the canopy.

"I'll get us some meat," he said. "Unsaddle them horses, will you, start us a fire? Best get a stick and make some noise, kick the deadwood 'fore you pick it up. Snakebite here ain't a good thing."

Chapter Thirty-Two

Beulah Hatcher stood in the dooryard of her low pine-planked shack, watching the boys approach. Her eyes twinkled as Jubal dismounted and walked into her open arms. She hugged him long and hard, then pushed him arm's length away and looked him over.

"Boy's gone," she murmured. "You sho 'nough a man now."

Jubal untied the fabric bolt, handing it to Beulah as if making an offering. Her eyes widened and she smiled. An abrupt, dark gap split her face; Beulah was missing four front teeth. She took the fabric and stroked it, unconsciously closing her lips.

"Oh, my lan'! This soon be my Sunday best," she said, reaching up to hug Jubal again. "Now where's yo' huntin'? Jordon tellin' me to expect y'all."

Lester pulled a leg over and slid down, untying a gunnysack that held the two pheasants, a fat possum, and a wild turkey. He hefted it over his shoulder as Jubal returned to his horse and pulled off the carcass of a mule deer, not much bigger than a large dog.

"Oh Mista Jubal!" Beulah crowed. "I'd knowed, yes I did! Who yo' friend?" She jutted her chin at Lester and grinned again, a vivid, pink tongue flashing against the gap in her teeth.

"Lester Norton, m'am," Lester replied, doffing his hat.

Beulah stared at him, stunned. "You got a fine mother," she recovered, before motioning them to follow.

Lester noticed a gaggle of kids who had been peeking from behind the corner of a shack. Seeing his glance they nearly stampeded trying to run away. He had noticed them furtively dart out from other dilapidated hovels that made up a tiny, ramshackle village carved out of the wood's edge, built in no discernible pattern.

"You chillin' come here!" Beulah ordered. The children skidded to a halt as if roped.

At dusk, Jordon Hatcher and his sons were greeted by the smell of roasting turkey as their wagon pulled up. Lester watched them arrive but his attention was drawn to another group of people, perhaps twenty in all, who approached from the opposite direction on foot. Instinctively, he knew they were slaves coming home from a day in the cotton fields. That afternoon, covered in blood and scratchy feathers from skinning and plucking game, Lester had felt entitled to ask more questions, and Jubal obliged, explaining that the village belonged to the Pettaway plantation, though some slaves might be working for Whitmill Rivens.

"Aunt Amelia," Jubal recalled, gutting the deer, "she was nice I guess, but don't remember her much. They lived on the other side the plantation, south shore of the bend."

While they talked, the children helped pluck the turkey and scrape the skins, then gathered vegetables and ground corn flour as Beulah prepared the bird and started a large kettle of stew in the outside kitchen. Jubal constructed a spit and skewered the deer to roast.

As dusk turned to darkness, people gathered round the firelight in small clumps and the sound of low conversations and soft laughter muted a growing night racket. Cornbread, dried peaches, and nuts appeared. Stewed jellies in old, thick clay jars, breads, and tubs of rice came from other homes. Anyone could take a wooden bowl and ladle the stew or slice a slab of roasted venison.

Lester sat with Jubal and Jordon Hatcher's boys, Daniel and Isaiah. Both were in their early twenties, they thought, and had been taught trade skills by their father. Legally the property of Ptolemy Harris, Wilcox County's bankruptcy judge, the boys were beneficiaries of the deal their father negotiated with Harris to hire out his own time and that of his sons. They all worked in the community, providing carpentry, blacksmithing, and wheelwright services. The family lived on the difference between wages they earned and the rent owed to Judge Harris for allowing them their own time.

Though initially cautious with Lester, the boys peppered Jubal with questions. Many of the younger children gathered around, drawing their elders with them, until Jubal found himself at the center of a crowd listening to his tales. A few times he asked Lester to join in but Lester demurred.

Jubal was in the midst of describing how they had re-rigged *Sovereign of the Seas* after a Pacific squall dismasted the ship when several men came running into the campfire light and grabbed Jordon Hatcher, bodily picking him up and hustling off into the darkness. The crowd hushed, magnifying the slow, clip-clop of an approaching horse. Like magic, the slaves and their children melted into the darkness. In less than a minute, only Beulah and her two sons remained with Lester and Jubal.

Lester's head whipped about, as if trying to fathom a trick. The warm hum of laughter and conversation had vanished. He looked at Jubal but his friend stared into the darkness, tense as a windward shroud.

The hoofbeats stopped. In the sudden silence, night sounds rose until they seemed to howl.

"Well," a voice drawled, slashing the racket. "If it ain't the prodigal, returned."

Silence stretched so taut Lester held his breath. He could see the faint glow of a cigar bloom and recede. Hoofbeats resumed and moments later a handsome roan horse stepped into the light carrying the dark silhouette of a tall, slouching man wearing a broad hat that shadowed his face but for an aquiline nose. A long coat and high boots gave his rangy frame the lean tension of a nightrider.

"Ain't changed much, have you, boy?" the rider said to Jubal. "Nary the courtesy to come by 'fore you eat with niggahs." He spit into the dust.

"Git out ma dooryard!" Beulah Hatcher hissed.

The man reached to his side and came up with a whip. "Listen yew nigga bitch, I don't own y'all no longer," he said quietly, pointing at the Hatcher boys, who had stepped in front of their mother. "But open your mouth agin, be the rest them teeth!" He looked around. "Where's that black buck niggah?"

Jubal stood. " What do you want, Whitmill?"

The man looked down at the Hatchers with undisguised contempt, then deliberately opened his coat and tucked it around the big revolver strapped to his hip. He turned his attention back to Jubal.

"Well, we growed some," Whitmill observed. "Manners don't come with size?"

"I was comin' by, tomorrow," Jubal replied.

Whitmill Rivens chewed the stub of his cigar. "Yeah. You do that, boy," he said, turning his horse. "Best do that." Rivens flipped the spent cigar at the Hatcher's hut as darkness swallowed him.

No one moved a muscle as the clopping horse hooves broke into a trot that soon faded amidst the night sounds. Finally, one of the Hatcher boys turned and let out a low whistle. Momentarily, the crackle of twigs and dry leaves announced the return of Jordon Hatcher and his neighbors. The man's face looked chiseled.

Jordon Hatcher turned to Jubal. "Best not stay long," he said, in a voice that matched his expression.

"Yes, sir," Jubal nodded, "first light." He hesitated. "I was hoping to give my regards to Emma. She still up to the big house?"

In the deepening silence, insect sounds grew almost deafening. Beulah looked at Jubal for a long moment.

"Emma gone to the Lord," she whispered, closing her eyes. Beulah slowly turned and walked into the cabin, followed by her men.

Jubal and Lester remained alone in the waning firelight. Without a word, Jubal slowly sank down, staring at the fire. Lester kneeled and touched his friend's shoulder.

"Tell me about Emma."

Several minutes passed before Jubal could talk. "She were an octoroon," he finally answered. His voice was flat, and his eyes didn't leave the fire. "She 'an Beulah, they were good to me, early on, before Emma went to the big house."

George Gee needed an overseer and Richard Calhoun needed a job. A few years before Jubal was born, Richard's sister, Amelia, had come to live with her brother briefly, before finding work in Camden, a small farming community on the other side of the Alabama River from Gee's Bend. Within a year, Amelia married Whitmill Rivens, and several months later bore a stillborn child. Meanwhile, Richard Calhoun had begun to realize his ambitions. In addition to overseeing the Gee plantation, he had leased cotton land and slaves from George Gee, with an option to purchase.

"I don't know all the details," Jubal explained, as Lester fed the fire, "I was so young. Guessing now, but I think maybe Pa couldn't manage everything, so he gets Whitmill—who don't amount to a pitcher of warm piss—to come over and help. Pa might have owned something by the time he died, but it went to Aunt Amelia, same as going to Whitmill. I doubt Whitmill could do much better managing the debt payments, especially after a hurricane wrecked the crop. Probably wrecked Gee too, and he had to sell to Pettaway, 'count of debt. So Whitmill probably owes Pettaway—the lease would have gone with the Gee place—and can't meet it, otherwise he'd never 'a sold the Hatchers. That clear? I know sounds complicated. Guess it is." Jubal gave a short mirthless laugh of sudden understanding. "Of course Pettaway, who come with slaves, would rather work land than lease it, so he calls the note on Whitmill, squeezes him, and gets both land

and slaves to settle. No wonder ..."

"Your father owned Hatchers?" Lester asked, trying to get it straight.

"Think so. Either that or leased 'em, and Gee sold the lease to Whitmill. Somehow they 'came Whitmill's property. So was Emma, but she were called to the big house, a year later, thereabouts, after that storm."

"You called her what, a octoroon?"

"Yeah, one-eighth niggah."

"You divide 'em up?" Lester scoffed. "Who knows who's been riding who? Or got records that far back?"

"The law gets almighty thick," Jubal admitted, shrugging. "Just the way it is around here. You seen enough already to know it ain't the North."

"You lived with your dad?" Lester felt as though he were putting together a puzzle that Jubal had never assembled, though he had all the pieces.

"'Till I was about eight, when he died."

"What was your ma like? He must of talked about her."

Jubal shrugged. "Pa never said word one about her."

"Are we going to your home tomorrow?"

Jubal shook his head. "Burnt a few days 'fore Pa died. Watched it, too," he sighed. "Then I had to live with Whitmill and Aunt Amelia, but I run away. My Aunt, I didn't see her much, they never had no kids after the first dead one. She seemed different, sort of sad, generally speakin'. Pa about lived in the fields, but Emma was around 'till I was maybe six, seven. Cora, too."

"Cora!" Lester sucked his breath, regretting the interruption.

Jubal didn't seem to mind. "She's Emma's daughter, I think by a slave named Curtis. He's least half Cherokee and Cora sure looked to have some that to her, straightest black hair you could imagine. They lived near here—one them places we passed comin' in—though Emma spent a fair while about our cabin most days. Cora often be with her. We played all the time as kids 'till Cora had to be in the fields. Then Emma moved to the big house—Sandy Hill—the plantation itself." Jubal paused for a moment, his stomach twisting at the memories—a knot of slaves staring at the smoldering ashes of his house, Emma and Cora standing apart in the white afternoon light, holding hands, tears streaming down their faces as Whitmill Rivens spurred his horse, taking the distraught boy away.

"Weren't there but a week or two," Jubal continued, "most miserable time you can imagine. I just walked home, 'cept there weren't nothing here. Jordon Hatcher built me that little hut because I couldn't live here with niggahs, sheriff would'a come, anyone hear that." Jubal snorted. "Whitmill didn't care and Aunt Amelia was a little crazy. Better part of a year or two I lived in the woods." He smiled, looking almost proud. "Was a good time—I liked it. Hunting 'n stuff, comin' here seeing Beulah 'n the boys, Emma when she'd be visitin' from Sandy Hill. Emma usually'd come with Cora, and sometimes that Curtis," Jubal continued, dully. "Now there's a niggah never said not word one to me. He weren't 'round tonight. Then Jordon Hatcher come and takes me to Cahaba, Mr. Cocheran's, place where I got a little schooling."

"Your uncle—Whitmill? What's he want?" Lester felt his stomach turn. He'd seen rough men in the northwood lumber camps and remembered Wainwright from *Flying Cloud*. "Hard man, you ask me."

"You think? Maybe ... though I'm surprised Jordon Hatcher didn't kill him, hitting Beulah." Jubal spit into the fire. "Best them fellas takin' him out, teeth 'er no teeth. He'd be hung straight away, if a niggah did something to Whitmill Rivens ..."

The boys spent that night and the next day under a hay shed as driving rain swept through the bottomlands. They debated whether Whitmill Rivens warranted five hours riding in a downpour, but Jordon Hatcher decided the issue. Jordon came to the hay shed an hour after the gray, soaking dawn with a pot of chicory coffee, cornbread, boiled eggs, and grilled venison that Beulah had prepared. As Lester and Jubal devoured breakfast, the black man sat answering mumbled questions. Hatcher said Amelia had died two years earlier of fever and Emma died unexpectedly a year later; it appeared a mule had kicked her. Then Curtis had made a break, stabbing Whitmill Rivens before heading south along the river. Hearing that, both Lester and Jubal stopped eating and waited.

"Curtis, that man could run!" Jordon Hatcher sighed as rain pounded off the planked shed roof. "So he tried foolin' 'n went cross-country, instead the river. Dogs knowed better, treed Curtis in a couple days. Men talked him down, then let them dogs loose. Tear'd Curtis apart right in the swamp. Drowned like a coon."

Jubal stared at Jordon Hatcher. "Did Whitmill do something to Emma?" he spit the question and answered it, throwing his food into the rain. He stood, fists balled tight. Lester gaped at this friend.

Jordon Hatcher held his chin. "Ought talk wit 'im."

"Ain't a mule alive'd kick Emma," Jubal snapped. "She'd soothe the orneriest ..."

The black man stared. "No diffunce, not now. You done good, goin' to sea. Best git back awhile." He glanced over to his shack. "Boys 'n me gonna build near town, leave 'way from here before one 'a us gits hung. Mista Jubal, you growed now, I kin't help you again." Jordon Hatcher's voice sank to a bare rasp. "Uncle 'n I ... we don't git 'long. Hear?"

—⁓—

Wild flowers and small saplings grew up through cracks in the rotting puncheon floor. Scattered pieces of charred lumber lay strewn about, and several broken bricks marked an old fireplace. Anything salvageable had long since been carted away.

Lester stayed mounted, looking over the sorry remains of Jubal's home. They had left the Hatcher village at dawn and ridden through the morning into the depths of Gee's Bend. Periodically, the brown slick of the Alabama River could be seen through breaks in the forest.

Jubal's old home lay at a fork in the wagon path, one track continuing to skirt the river and the other cutting off obliquely to split a huge cotton field in two. The land was uniformly green, lush, and empty of people.

"Slept over that corner," Jubal motioned, coming back to the decaying footprint. "Cornshuck mattress and an 'ol rag niggah doll, called him Boy." He smiled. "My daddy wanted to be a planter, so's that's what I wanted. Got to have niggahs to be a planter." He looked out over the cotton fields. "And land."

"Your pa lease this?" asked Lester.

"The house? No, came with the job overseeing. He leased land, though don't know if this here were it. We're about the middle of Gee's holdings—Pettaway's now. Take this track in front of us about fifteen miles right through the heart of it, and that's where Whitmill lives, the other side. About half way, another trail bears left, goes to Sandy Hill, the big house. Beyond is the river landing, top of the bend. Going to oversee the holdings, you want to be close on center."

The ride across the bend was hot, humid, and melancholy. Twice they passed small slave villages, each a squalid collection of huts that looked as if a stiff wind could flatten them. Most were shut tight. "Must be a boiler in there!" Lester exclaimed, taking a swig from his canteen. He couldn't seem to drink enough water.

"They don't like air," Jubal replied, "especially at dark. Something about vapors or spirits. Be buttoned up tight on an August night."

"Think it's like that in Africa?"

"Most of 'em are a hundred years or more from Africa. Probably been in this country longer than your people."

Late in the afternoon the boys rode up a shallow incline that crested like a hip before descending in a mile-long swale ending at the riverbank. Set back from the road along the crest, another pine-planked hut stood with a horse shed out back. Smoke drifted from a squat brick chimney, and the door and two windows were open, but no one appeared as Jubal hollered. The boys pulled to a halt several yards from the hut and sat for a moment, weary from the day's ride.

"Whitmill must have been tired," Lester remarked, reaching for his empty canteen, "riding through the rain." He watched his friend closely. This was the third mention he'd made of Rivens, and though a cord in Jubal's face wrenched each time, nothing more had been said.

Jubal looked at him as if he were a dolt. "You people don't know nothing anyhow. Every one them quarters he could take some young'un to warm his bed. How often you think the man sleeps alone?" He shook his head at the naiveté and threw a leg over to dismount.

The cloying heat had already made Lester cranky. Thoughts of Whitmill Rivens riding up in the middle of the night and claiming a young slave infuriated him, but his caustic reply choked off as Jubal froze in mid-dismount, one foot still stuck in the stirrup. Lester followed Jubal's gaze and his own jaw dropped.

A tall, barefoot girl stood in the doorway. The faded ribbon of a calico apron gathered her simple, sleeveless, knee-length shift, accentuating a slender, erect carriage and striking face. High cheekbones, a doe-eyed gaze, and straight, jet-black hair tied in a ponytail gave hints of Indian blood, but her nose had a slight, though distinct African flare above a wide mouth and lips dark as nutmeg. Watching the boys without expression, she slowly folded her arms and stood stock still, waiting.

Lester sat mesmerized, his breath stolen by the image. He could have looked at the girl until dark had not his head snapped back at the sound of Jubal's whisper.

"Cora."

Chapter Thirty-Three

The boys sat on a top rail of the corral, watching the sun disappear over the far bank of the river. Sometimes they'd glance down the road, looking for a glimpse of Whitmill Rivens who, Cora said, usually returned about dark. The girl was inside, cooking supper. Initially, she had greeted them coolly, but within an hour the boys were lugging water, chopping firewood, heating grease, and grinding potash to make soap. As the sun lowered she went in to prepare dinner, telling them in a quiet, direct manner to stay out of the kitchen.

"Can't say the woman's all that talkative," Lester complained, "though she ain't afraid of putting us to work."

"Oh, she can be," Jubal disagreed. "Used to chirp like a songbird when we was young."

"You grew up together?"

"Spent fair bit of time playing," Jubal recalled, making a pipe. "Wherever Emma was you'd find Cora. I don't know but that Emma was my wet-nurse. Must have been her, I think of it now."

"What was your ma's name?"

"Virginia, 'guess." Jubal noticed Lester's puzzlement. "Aunt Amelia said once that was her ma's name, my grandmother. Only name I ever heard tell of."

"Where's she buried?"

"Dunno. Someplace by the old cabin, I think … stands to reason. I went looking this morning. Pa once said there was a rock over her, but I never knew which one." Jubal lit his pipe and puffed heavily until his head was wreathed in smoke. He inhaled deeply and blew out in a long swoosh that brought his head low. "Appreciate you coming here with me, Lester. Sorry it's not so friendly as your place …"

"Get what you come for?"

"Dunno," Jubal shrugged. "I ain't got family. Just the way it is. Don't believe I may ever come back here. Nothing to come back to, though I do feel the country in my bones. Like an old pair of boots, just fits your feet even when they're about falling off."

Lester stared at the setting sun. "She was your first," he asked quietly, nodding toward the house, "when you couldn't …?"

Jubal closed his eyes. "Uncle tried to fetch me back; said he'd give her to me."

"You knew she'd be here, now?"

Jubal chewed the pipe stem. "I don't know that I knowed, but I ain't surprised." Slanting sunlight etched his jaw as he abruptly rapped the pipe on a boot heel. "He liked 'em young."

Whitmill Rivens returned at sunset and nodded them inside the two-room cabin, where Cora had set three place settings in the main room by the fireplace. She served the meal and returned to the kitchen out back. Whitmill ignored her except to bark once for a new jug. Cora briefly reappeared with the whiskey, pulled from a cold box buried behind the house, set the jug on the table without a word, and left.

Rivens looked exhausted but he was patient and methodical. Other than giving the briefest description of Maine, Lester stayed silent. Jubal wasn't much more talkative, but over the course of dinner Rivens extracted enough information to learn the boys weren't destitute and intended to become involved in the shipping business.

"Could be right useful," Rivens remarked, as he pushed away his plate and poured another whiskey. Lester felt light-headed and the room seemed stifling hot, though Jubal appeared unaffected by the liquor. Evidently the heat didn't bother him, for he wore his coat and usually sat back, holding his glass in his lap.

"Now then," continued the man, "I know we had a triflin' disagreement few years back and you left on bad terms. Your pa's sister were sickly, not doin' her best."

Jubal took a sip of whiskey. "Only one reason I come back for. I just want to know where my ma's buried."

Rivens looked him over. "Well, I was hopin' you were ready to do your share, bein' next in line. If this family's ever to be planters, take a station 'cording to how we should, I need help."

"You need money."

A flash of anger rippled through Rivens but he nodded agreement.

"True. See, I work my bones! Pushin' them niggahs for Pettaway and tryin' to make progress for us. But we suffer from a lack of capital. Why, your friend here," he gestured at Lester, "comes from the land of capital to the land of real work. You know that every dollar of cotton landed in Liverpool, 'bout half goes to Yankee shippers while I git eight cents? Them cotton factors, Mobile 'n New Orleans, they jes' agents providin' expensive credit from them shippers, but only if I agree on a futures price. Squeezin' both ends 'gainst the middle. I'm workin' for them!"

Rivens swallowed his whiskey and poured another. In the flickering candlelight, his lean, raw-boned face looked like creased, sweated leather. He leaned back in his chair.

"You left Jubal, 'n I got no one to share the load. Why, I'm workin' for them factors, 'n them Yankees behind 'em! I'm their niggah! But mine got no cares, fed, dry roof, no worries t'all, 'cause I do the worrin'! Not a care." He downed the whiskey and poured himself another, then filled the boys' glasses. Lester sipped only enough to appear polite; he didn't feel like drinking. The scene struck him as both pathetic and ominous; Whitmill Rivens aspired to the gentility of Truette Stubbs without a prayer of attainment, having neither the acumen nor style.

"You behind?" Jubal asked, his voice even.

Rivens' nostrils flared and he stared at the boy. "How can a planter git 'head when them factor bastards got hold his throat?" Bitterness spilled from the man. "Where the fuck you been? When you gonna do somethin' worth your daddy 'memberin'? Never done lick a real work, have you, Jubal? Couldn't stand the gait. When comes time fer a man to stand tall, you go crawlin' north! You think I work myself dead so's you can pick up my rights for nothing?"

Spittle glistened on his lips and he turned on Lester. "Yer a quiet sumbitch, 'n tha's goud! Come down here tell us how to run our niggahs, you'd best ride on. Politicians think they can tell us how to live, them sorry bastards! When you go back north, tell them fuckin' Yankee shippers we don't need 'em much longer!" He downed his whiskey, filled Jubal's glass, and topped off Lester's. "I ain't being rude, boy," Rivens said, "jes' tellin' you the Gawd Almighty truth!" His face worked furiously. "Goddam it, boy, you ought be here!"

"Where's my ma's buried?" Jubal asked.

Rivens snorted.

"What'ju got for capital, boy?" his palm slapped the table. "Growin' cotton requires hard work 'n capital! Look at me, sweated out and filthy! You seen them fields, dead green to my dooryard! Good harvest and I'll guaran' goddam-tee a fav'rable return."

"I know a bit about trading," Jubal said, his voice almost a monotone. "I don't know cotton. My mother ..."

Whitmill Rivens took a long slow sip of his whiskey, regarding Jubal over his glass, and then set it down with a deliberate thump.

"Cora!" Rivens' primal scream made Lester flinch. The kitchen went deathly quiet before the door opened and she stood there, her face inscrutable. "Tell 'im where his maw's buried."

Suddenly, Whitmill Rivens collapsed in guffaws. Lester's face went ashen, and his body felt like the inside of a reverberating gong. In the ghostly light, Cora's face came clear, the set of her forehead, the plane of chin, both a mirror of Jubal's. Only their coloring differed, and her nose was broader.

"Yew ain't smart 'nough, Jubal, ever amount ta a pile of horseshit!" Rivens slurred. "I told Amelia you were shiftless—better at bein' 'nother animal 'n the woods then doin' yore share!" He belched and poured whiskey. "Jes' look at 'er, boy! Yew took 'er early, broke 'er in good! Her maw come sassed me, that Beulah bitch with her. Coupla teeth weren't 'nough for one, 'n the mother thinking she gonna tell me what I can do with the daughter. Got right hot that niggah woman did, she don't know Whitmill Rivens 's no man to cross! Got what she deserved, denyin' me, yes suh! Then that big niggah took a knife, thought to cut my belly! Dogged that buck right to ground, did. See what you been missin', boy?"

Jubal's gaze hardened into pure loathing.

Whitmill Rivens sniggered. "You look hot, boy. I'm jes' keepin' it in the extended family, the one you're already in. Can't prove nothin', no sir, and these niggers ain't talkin', but don't think I don't know!"

The planter looked at Cora, then back at Jubal before taking another swallow of whiskey.

"Ask her where the grave is!" Rivens gaze turned to a sneer. "Your father spread the mother for years," he hissed, "'n I'm spreading the daughter." A lethal smile split his fury and he shrugged. "'Less you wanna come back, cross-breed her, take after yer old man."

Lester blanched and his stomach heaved. Without warning, Jubal leaped to his feet. Whipping his coat back, he pulled his pistol, aimed it downward across the table at Rivens' groin, and pulled the trigger. The shot crashed with an explosion that shocked Lester backward out of his chair.

Whitmill Rivens gave a blood-curdling scream as he crashed to the floor, writhing and twisting, hands clutching his crotch. Cora hadn't moved. Jubal took aim again, a maniacal glaze to his face.

Lester lurched for the barrel. "Jubal!" he screamed. A round blasted through the tabletop, splintering the puncheon floor.

Jubal Calhoun shook his head and took several deep breaths. He stared at Whitmill Rivens and his bloodstained crotch. The man had passed out.

"Doubt he'll be spreading anything again." Jubal holstered the pistol and looked at the young woman, who had neither moved nor changed expression. "Do the best you can here." He pulled the coin pouch from his jacket and set it on the table.

"Lester, we is outbound."

Chapter Thirty-Four

After a hard ride through the night, they reached the landing at Bridgeport by dawn. Leaving their mounts at a livery stable with payment for the horses' return to Selma, the boys boarded a downriver steamer to Mobile just as the sun cleared the high eastern treeline.

Late that evening, Ezekiel opened the door to see two travel-stained young men whose saturnine expressions prompted him to quickly fetch Truette Stubbs. The man had not yet retired and came down to the foyer in his evening robe. At a glance, he bade them into his library and rang the bell for Louisa. Within ten minutes the exhausted boys had cornbread, cold ham, and tea.

Truette Stubbs simply asked what had happened. Lester let Jubal do the talking, only interjecting to thank the older man for his recommendation to Absalom Rodgers. Stubbs waved that away, concentrating on Jubal, his eyes sparkling like obsidian pools. Occasionally, Jubal would pause, but neither Lester nor Truette Stubbs filled the silence, and eventually Jubal picked up the thread and more of the story emerged. Finally, when Jubal opened his hands and looked down at the floor, Stubbs asked only one question.

"Is Whitmill Rivens dead?"

"I don't think so," Jubal said. "I can't be sure the man didn't bleed to death, but he wasn't gut shot."

Lester shook his head; he didn't know.

"This appears to me a family matter," Stubbs said, staring at Jubal as he poured himself a small tumbler of brandy. "However reprehensible you might regard Mr. Rivens' conduct, nothing I heard is against the law. Contrarily, you have assaulted him because of some alleged offense. You'd be well advised to mitigate such anger. A successful man understands self-control. That kind of behavior can cost you dearly."

Stubbs tossed back his brandy and set the tumbler down with a sharp snap. "Y'all leave in the morning," he announced. "I've a schooner going to Havana. From there, get back to New York and stay gone for a time. For y'all sakes, I hope the man lives."

"We have a draft from Mr. Rodgers," Lester mentioned, a little uneasy. Jubal looked up from the floor. "And I believe we're carrying another four, five hundred, plenty for us." He turned to his friend. "We ain't talked 'bout this, Jubal, but ..." Lester swallowed and took a deep breath. "Mr. Stubbs, I'd like to cash that draft first thing in the morning, give you the funds."

Truette Stubbs sat still as one of the Buddha statues the boys had seen in China, his presence commanding Lester to continue.

"If'n it's all right with you, Jubal," Lester glanced at his friend, then took another breath and plunged. "Well sir, this is what we want you to do. Please take them funds—I think the draft's for twelve hundred dollars—and buy Cora. And release her, like your wife did Louisa and Ezekiel. Pay the bond. If there's a balance, we're good for it, God's word, as long as one of us is alive."

Neither Lester nor Jubal would ever forget Truette Stubbs' response. He had sat impassively through the entire conversation, but at this he visibly relaxed, though his folded hands didn't move from his belly.

"Here's a lesson I want y'all never to forget," he said. "Don't speculate on *events*. You can speculate on people and goods, but don't be predicting what might happen, not without security. Like land. I'll do my best with this young niggah woman, but surely I cannot make the man sell her. I know of Mr. Pettaway but not this Rivens fellow. Accordingly, I will not take the funds. If successful, I will expect to be reimbursed with reasonable interest, a business transaction. Absalom Rodgers' draft is as good for me as yours, so sign it over, and I'll give you a draft on my New York bank for the identical amount. Also, considering circumstances, y'all ought to leave little notice of your activities in Mobile. Come dawn, I strongly advise you to be aboard for Havana. Write me from the North. I doubt we've seen the last each other, but best y'all give this a few years."

Chapter Thirty-Five

Boston, October 1853

Against the flush, rich colors of a gorgeous Indian summer morning, the largest wooden ship ever built—a city block long and wide as a street—stood in imperious silence on the ways, her black hull a regal counterpoint to the eye-dazzling copper sheathing and white deckhouses. From the eagle figurehead at her bow to the semi-elliptical stern, graced by another eagle clutching an American shield in its talons, the *Great Republic* waited the day before launching, as if disdainful of the tiny men swarming over and around her.

Lester worked along the keel, slathering the ways with tallow as other workers carefully withdrew scaffolding that had supported the ship through her construction. Jubal stayed far overhead, helping secure the last in a web of lines and chains supporting the bowsprit that angled upward from the ship's prow like an enormous sixty-foot lance.

At six o'clock, a clanging bell sounded day's end and a stream of men trundled by the office building, many of them glancing to the window where they could see the master shipbuilder bent to his drawings.

As the shipyard emptied, Lester stood shirtless at a wash trough near the dressing shed. "You're supposed to lather the skids, Lester," Jubal remarked as he came from the deck. "Looks like they lathered you."

"Messy business," Lester groused. "I need a proper bath, cold water don't cut this grease."

Jubal laughed, a sound that might have annoyed his friend but for its rarity. Lester had grown accustomed to his friend's moods; sudden silence could descend on Jubal and last days. Lester usually let it be. Memories of Alabama could make him toss in his sleep. He could only imagine Jubal's dreams.

"Buy you dinner at Molly's," Lester said, as he toweled himself. "Welcome home present, couple weeks late."

"I'm the one got's our money," Jubal grinned, handing Lester his shirt. One or the other usually carried their cash.

"Your new status don't do much for me," Lester snorted, though he welcomed the banter. Jubal was finally coming out of the deep melancholy that had draped him like a mantle for months, from the predawn boarding of Truette Stubbs' Havana-bound schooner to the record-setting Liverpool passage after they had reached New York and rejoined *Sovereign of the Seas*. When the big ship landed in Liverpool, the McKay brothers—Donald had come to explore opportunities in England—each took one of the boys to act as scribe and aide de camp. Like sentinels, the boys witnessed strategy sessions, contract negotiations, financial transactions, and *Sovereign*'s sale to English owners before accompanying the brothers back to America on an westbound packet.

After disembarking in late July, Donald and Lester returned directly to Boston. Lauchlan and Jubal remained in New York to purchase and arrange transport of gear and materials necessary to rig the *Great Republic* before the gigantic ship was towed to New York for her final outfitting and loading.

"Come a long way, we have," said Lester, toasting Jubal an hour later at a rear table of Molly's Tavern. "Right hands to the most respected shipping men in the world."

"That's putting a hard shine to it, Lester," Jubal smiled, reaching for his pipe and settling into the corner. "Though, got us good teachers for sure. You keep learnin' how they're put together, I'll learn to run 'em." As he lit his pipe and leaned back, Jubal's coat opened, revealing the butt of a pistol.

Several hours later, Lester turned over and blinked wide-awake in the darkness. They bunked in the forecastle of the great ship and a flicker of fire had ripped him into consciousness on the edge of panic. Within moments he realized it was a lantern. No hint of dawn showed through the skylight and a sigh of relief almost toppled him back into sleep, but the flicker interrupted his reverie like an annoying moth and he wondered why Jubal would be reading in the middle of the night.

"What are you doing'?" Lester asked softly. Several other men were sleeping, sailors Lauchlan McKay wanted aboard on the maiden voyage.

"Reading," Jubal muttered, rustling a page. "Letter's from Truette Stubbs."

Lester rolled over so violently he nearly fell out of his bunk. "About Cora?" he hissed. "What's it say? Gimme it!" Lester leaned over, reaching for the letter.

Jubal moved it out of range. "Ain't addressed to you."

"Oh," Lester replied, almost as if struck. He swallowed hard to check a sudden, roiling stomach.

"Sorry, Lester," Jubal whispered, "I'm just being contrary." Lester didn't reply, but the light flickered and a moment later Jubal stood, holding the lantern and letter.

Lester reared to his elbows and avidly scanned a page filled with neat, flowery cursive.

September 6, 1853
Mobile, Alabama

Dear Mr. Calhoun,

This is to inform you of business developments discussed, in May, last. Due to recent inclement weather, this year's crop is uncertain. Duties here preclude a journey, however brief, into the country. I may not ascertain with due conviction that to which we are engaged.

However, I have notice that the worst case has not transpired, nor is likely, and inquiries indicate financial pressures exist sufficient to entertain purchase of assets that may be forthcoming. Such sale may well be distressed, but in any event will not occur before this year's turn.

A transaction here may precipitate actions beyond my ability to forestall; therefore, I advise you to pursue global opportunities forthwith. As events warrant, I shall correspond accordingly.

Yours sincerely,
Truette Stubbs

Lester forehead wrinkled as he looked at Jubal.

"Cotton's late—probably been raining heavy," Jubal explained. "Factors are busy right now. With the season, Mobile's at a hard gallop, so Stubbs can't leave and go up country before the crop comes down, gets graded, and warehoused. But he heard that Whitmill Rivens isn't dead. Pity, that."

"What's the rest?" Lester whispered.

"Pettaway is probably about to call the lease," Jubal said, "especially should the crop go against Whitmill. If he can't pay the debt he'll be forced to sell slaves again, like he did the Hatchers. Then Rivens could come north looking for the fellow who shot him and nothing Stubbs could do about it. So we might as well see the world. Guess I should write, tell him our plans."

A week later the boys were aboard *Great Republic*, dressed in their Sunday best, enjoying the panorama and excitement. Under a cloudless sky, fifty thousand people gathered from every direction, arriving on foot and horseback, in stagecoaches, wagons, buggies, and carts, and aboard ships of every size from square-riggers to sloops and dories.

At the stroke of noon, Donald McKay smashed a bottle to her stem, men slammed the chocks loose, and moments later the *Great Republic* began to move. At the stern, Jubal could feel a slight tremor, then her colossal bulk slid with surprising speed. He glanced aft and did a double take, incredulous at the sight of a small paddle wheel steamer leisurely crossing the ship's path.

Lester was oblivious to the steamer, fascinated by the ship's surge. To his astonishment, the friction against her cradle sparked and smoked with such heat that the oil-soaked ways burst in flame. Shipyard men raced to douse the fire as Jubal started yelling.

The *Great Republic* muscled into the harbor, sending up gouts of seawater that surged like a breaking waves, rocking dozens of boats and swamping several small craft. She barreled backward, four thousand tons of momentum bearing down on the little steamer. Jubal screamed while Lester let loose a piercing whistle. The steamer captain suddenly realized his peril and in a scene that would have been comical if not disastrous, the paddle wheel began thrashing frantically, as if it were a duckling desperate to avoid a whale. The boat made it out of the way, barely, though not without losing her stern flagstaff to the huge ship as it plowed past.

Two harbor tugs came alongside and rafted to the *Great Republic*, belching black smoke into the crystalline skies, trying to slow her down. Aboard, Lauchlan McKay swiveled his head from the tugs to the aft skyline, where the Chelsea Bridge loomed larger. The captain's face tightened, his fingers clenching like claws.

"Let loose the anchors!" he suddenly bellowed. The boys raced forward and joined a dozen other sailors to release the anchors on either side of the bow. Lester tripped on a block and caught his foot in the anchor chain but Jubal yanked him away, ripping Lester's coat mere seconds before the six-inch chain links sang out like fishing line. Captain McKay ordered the chain belayed and as his ship pulled the catenaries of both anchor cables rigid, every man could feel the enormous strain. The *Great Republic* finally came to a halt fifty feet from the Chelsea Bridge.

"Would've smoked right through," Jubal remarked, breathing easier. Lester could only shake his head, sobered by how quickly the gay spectacle had turned.

Chapter Thirty-Six

New York, December 1853

A dusting of snow graced The *Great Republic* as she lay at her South Street berth the day before Christmas. Overhead, the ship's rigging looked like an angel hair wreath. From a few blocks away the scene was beyond beautiful, as if a meticulous, celestial elf had delicately frosted every line.

"You actually go to the top of that?" Sally Norton asked, gazing upward. Jane Norton didn't bother to look and huddled in her woolen shawl against the cold East River wind. A horse shuffled and snorted nearby as the coachman patiently waited for his party to clamber aboard.

Lester nodded proudly. "Hull down from the Narrows, we'll have everything flying. She's near full now: wheat for Liverpool, then emigrants to Melbourne. Captain wants us aboard the day after Christmas, and we're outbound the next."

"Look all you want," Jane Norton said, raising her skirts to step into the carriage and its relative warmth, "I'll wait inside." Jubal offered an arm to support her. A moment later, Sally followed and took Jubal's arm but her grip was markedly different. The mother accepted assistance; the daughter reached to hold. Jubal smiled politely, feeling the distinct pressure that lingered longer than necessary.

Lester knew his mother hated the big ships. Though delighted as a schoolgirl on her first trip to New York, Jane Norton's excitement vanished along South Street. The woman so thoroughly detested the ocean that she thought of returning to Bangor by land, a notion that struck Lester as ludicrous. "See Mom, if you go back overland," Lester said, lurching with the coach, "why, you and Sal would be a mass of bruises, even if you don't freeze in a nor'easter." The four had packed into the carriage, knees almost touching.

"We're not going overland; Mom just hates the ocean," Sally retorted, glancing at Lester. "Don't worry Momma, Aunt Dorcus always travels in style."

The siblings' look was the silent message of co-conspirators, part of the plot to get Jane Norton from the confines of a saltwater farm in December, one of the meanest months in her year. Sally also looked at Lester to keep his eye off her knees, especially the one pressed against Jubal's leg.

Sally's letter to Lester in Boston a month earlier had been a plea. Each autumn, as sunlight dwindled and the north wind grew raw, Jane Norton descended into a gloom that might last weeks. This year looked bad. By mid-November, their mother had become almost incapacitated, sometimes spending several days in bed and barely uttering a word. Sally still walked or rode Jake the six miles to school and back, but when her mother withdrew she was forced to do all the chores and maintain house alone.

An auger of guilt chewed Lester as he read Sally's letter at the McKay shipyard, but he wasn't about to come home, regardless of his mother's condition. The mere thought of returning to a settled life in Maine felt stifling. Later, he talked it over, and to his surprise Jubal came up with an intriguing idea.

"Write Dorcus Fullam," Jubal had suggested. "She's family. Maybe she'd want some company next trip to Boston or New York. Don't blame your ma, I'd go crazed up there, too."

"No colder than Cape Horn," Lester pointed out.

"I don't live on the Horn," Jubal scoffed. "Bring her here, or to New York after we get there."

The machinations took some doing and more money than Lester had hoped, but Aunt Dorcus did help, arranging transportation on a coastal steamer to New York and reserving hotel rooms for her sister and niece with a plan to join them Christmas Eve. The Fullam family matriarch knew that Jane Norton wasn't the only woman who bent under the weight of caring for a family alone in the endless northern winter. Dorcus' own husband had taken command of a new ship and was somewhere off the Cape of Good Hope on his way home from China.

Jane Norton felt as if an enormous burden had been lifted. Though the three-day steamer trip down had been a ghastly, heaving ride in the backside of a gale, the Manhattan holiday throngs and downtown vibrancy were a merciful tonic to the bleakness of saltwater Maine. She emerged from her emotional cocoon to flourish with an almost manic enthusiasm before falling into bed each evening.

Although Sally relished her mother's vivacity, she knew it was brittle and there would be a harrowing price when they returned home. New Year's Day would barely be the beginning of winter along the Penobscot. While Lester swelled with vitality as he showed them the city and ship, Sally's emotions swung from pride in her brother to resentment and fury at the injustice of their respective lots. Two days before Christmas, after a day of shopping on Broadway, Jane Norton retired to their room after dinner while her children and Jubal gathered for hot cider near a fireplace in the small hotel's lounge.

Sally hands cradled the steaming cup. "You're a selfish bastard, Lester," she declared, without preamble.

"Beg your pardon?" Lester blinked. He looked at Jubal, but his friend was no help. Jubal had taken his customary seat in the corner, back against the wall.

"You got to beg for more than that," Sally replied. The frosty day had reddened her cheeks, accentuating a freckled nose. Auburn hair cascaded to her shoulders in natural, tight ringlets that looked like twirled Christmas ribbons. Lester had decided his sister was striking, though her features were too strong to be beautiful. She had turned fifteen and carried herself as a young woman, with a flawless complexion and youthful, unlined skin, save for rough, raw hands and cracked fingernails.

"The last couple years haven't been easy," she continued. "While you been off to all parts of the world, I'm home watching Momma, keeping her from just going mad."

Lester sat back, defensive and ready to dismiss the exaggeration.

"You think I'm exaggerating?" Sally challenged.

"Now Sal," Lester began.

"Now Lester! When are you coming home? She's our mother means she's *your* mother, too!"

"Sal, what can I do?" Lester cried. "You want me home so we can all be miserable? Go lobstering on the bay, work in a quarry just so you and Mom have company? Sally, there's a *world* out there and I seen it! I'm a man, dammit!"

"Oh?" Sally's face began to glow. "Does that mean I'm supposed to sit around the farm, wait till some moon-faced boy shows up, then be like Betty, calve a new baby every year until one day I got time to join the church choir? All because I'm a woman?"

"You don't have to get crank with me, Sally!" Lester snapped.

Sally spun at Jubal. "Are you this stupid, too?" She glared at him, and then slowly leaned back in her chair. "Appears so." Jubal looked like it would take a metal bar to pry anything from him. Lester was about to reply but stopped, seeing his sister's face quiver.

"Lester, don't you think I'd like to see the world?" Sally whispered. Her voice gathered strength. "Don't you think I want see San Francisco, or China, or anywhere? This three, four days have been the best of my life. But I can't, 'cause I'm all Momma's got. You just go. Live. Explore, have adventures, get big-headed. Well, I'd like the chance to get big-headed! Lester, you can decide if you want to come home. I can't even decide to leave."

Lester stared at the table for several moments, then at his sister. "Somehow I'll try to do right by you, someday." His palms opened, beseeching her. "But I'm not coming back to Maine. I just can't."

Sally turned away. "I know," she said, the resignation plain but bitter. "You'd be a pain if you did come home, and Momma's enough. But don't think your freedom's free, Lester."

Lester could feel tears at the edge of his eyes. "I love you, Sal." He didn't know what else to say.

Sally rubbed her eyes. "I love you, too, Lester." She sighed and looked around the lounge. "I'm going to live in this city one day," she declared, before standing and turning to Jubal. "Let's go. Gimme yer arm."

Dorcus Fullam arrived at the hotel the next afternoon. Her steamer landed at South Street two hours earlier than scheduled, courtesy of a blustery northwest wind that had been building all day. Aunt Dorcus directed a courier to the *Great Republic* wharf with an invitation for the boys to dine at the Astor House Hotel, a prospect that Jubal regarded with all the enthusiasm of a tooth extraction. Lester teased him some, hoping to deflate any argument.

Dinner passed pleasantly. The two sisters, though almost fifteen years apart, seemed to have grown closer. Dorcus Fullam made only one oblique reference to slavery, in an off-handed question that took both Lester and Jubal by surprise.

"What do you think of Dred Scott?" she had asked Jubal as dessert was being served.

"Huh?" Jubal blurted. He didn't know what she was talking about. Neither did Lester.

"You might want to read about him," Dorcus Fullam said and left it at that. A half-hour later, begging fatigue from her steamer trip, the older woman rose from the table. Dinner ended as though the curtain had dropped on an act in a play.

Outside the Astor Hotel, Lester hailed a carriage and had just instructed the driver to drop the women off first when a small fire wagon went clanging by, immediately followed by another, large tanker wagon, its driver whipping his six-horse team. Moments later, a shouting phalanx of men surged from the Astor Bar.

"*Fire!!* To the ships!" someone cried. Lester and Jubal nearly threw the women aboard and dove in after them as several other men clambered up, cramming into the carriage and hanging to its side rails. Sally scooted onto Jubal's lap as the livery driver cracked his whip and sent the carriage swaying around a corner. From the window, Lester could see men running along the streets and other wagons and cabs wheeling toward the East River. Two blocks from South Street the carriage halted in a snarl of traffic. The men bolted and Jubal tossed Sally aside, following Lester into the bedlam.

Several blocks in from the river and north of the *Great Republic*, a roaring fire etched the night sky as it consumed a four-story building. The northwest wind howled, fanning flames like a giant bellows. Lester watched in horror as the building collapsed, sending fiery embers skyward where the gale hurtled them downwind, directly into the tops of the huge ship. Glistening with tar, her tall rigging suddenly seemed to stand as an enormous wick, beckoning the flames.

Firemen fought through the melee as the high rigging sputtered, caught, and then fanned into tongues of flame that leapfrogged along the spars. Though the firemen managed to connect pump wagons, their hoses sent water only to the topsail yards. Within minutes the upper rigging began to let go and burning debris showered the men. As large pieces of tackle, shrouds, and spars rained down, the fire captain ordered his men to safety on the wharf.

Lauchlan McKay seized an axe from a fireman and leapt aboard his ship, roaring, "cut her down!"

The captain attacked a shroud as crewmen emptied the ship's chandlery of mauls, saws, adzes, and axes and began hacking away at the enormous masts, oblivious to the horror above.

The deck became a field of combat. As a man went down, struck by falling debris, sailors dragged their wounded shipmate to safety and another man took his place. Lester chopped at the mainmast with all the precision he had learned felling trees in the north woods while Jubal stood at the upwind rail sawing through dozens of shrouds he had carefully reeved to support the high masts. Once he glanced up but the scene was so horrible he forced himself not to look again. The sky seemed to be an open furnace.

Jubal could see firemen frantically hooking up more pump trucks but the overall effect was pathetic, like trying to extinguish a bonfire with squirts of water. Someone screamed, and above the tumult Lauchlan McKay's voice roared a warning. Moments later, the main mast toppled overboard, taking most of the mizzenmast. Forward, the seventy-foot topsail yard sagged, then crashed to the deck like a spear and shattered. Beside the *Great Republic*, another clipper had burned to the waterline, a total loss. In the middle of the river, tugs held a ship in the current as flames engulfed it like a floating torch.

By dawn, the proud ship was a smoking hulk. The *Great Republic* had been shorn, with every mast, yard, and sail gone by the board. As firemen poured water over the decks, Captain McKay surveyed his ship with the bleak look of a commander who had met the enemy and lost.

That afternoon Donald McKay stood bareheaded on South Street, staring at the ruin of his masterpiece, clutching the telegram that had been delivered in Boston at midnight. Beside him, Lauchlan described the horror in a monotone. A small bakery had caught fire on Front Street, its flames igniting an adjacent warehouse packed with flour. The conflagration swept downwind to the docks; by daybreak, four clippers had been completely destroyed and a dozen other ships damaged. The *Great Republic's* coach houses were littered with debris, but the deck fires had been put out. At sunrise, a hundred firemen gathered hoses and equipment before returning to firehouses all over lower Manhattan.

As Captain McKay and his bedraggled crew surveyed the carnage suddenly the forward hatch exploded and a sheet of flame shot into the morning sky. The captain, already numb from despair and exhaustion, summoned up his quarterdeck voice once again and ordered men onto the river in whatever launches or small boats they could find. Hours earlier, at the inferno's height, the foresail spar had speared through the deck. The fire below had smoldered all night until finally igniting just after the firemen left. With no other alternative, Captain McKay directed his men to chop holes through the hull to scuttle his ship.

The five-inch Georgia pine planking, hard and waterlogged, yielded to the exhausted men slowly. In a small skiff, Lester and Jubal took turns with an axe, sickened with the feeling of butchering priceless artwork. Finally, the boys came ashore and slowly trudged to the McKay brothers. Dozens of men stood solemnly, but no one said a word. Donald and Lauchlan murmured occasionally but after a time everyone just watched the ship slowly sink, sputtering and hissing, until she settled onto the East River mud.

Chapter Thirty-Seven

Within a week of the great fire, salvage contractors began building a cofferdam around the scuttled ship, estimating that it would take a year to lift and repair the *Great Republic*. Lauchlan McKay dismissed his entire crew and the boys returned to Boston with the brothers, accepting Donald McKay's offer of employment. The boys were so numb that when McKay made his terse offer, loss and loyalty combined with no better alternative to carry the boys north to the East Boston yard. Donald McKay threw himself into work, and by January the boys bunked in the forecastle of *Lightning*, a new clipper scheduled to launch in six weeks.

Jubal hated the Boston winter. The high rigging was unforgiving at the best of times, but roving shrouds in February, when his fingers stuck to the frozen manila hemp, put him in a mood so black he would barely speak to Lester at night, particularly since his friend didn't mind the weather.

Lester thrived in the bowels of a newly rising ship, carefully calculating the dead rise, crawling around the orlop deck with calipers, taking precise scantlings for the butts and knees. In the East Boston yard he felt an almost sensual thrill bearding a plank to the cutwater or stem. The creation of a ship filled him with wonder and pride. Though Lester knew his friend was miserable, several times he reminded Jubal that they'd be outbound when Lauchlan McKay was ready.

On a bitter winter evening in early February, Jubal returned to the forecastle and nearly wrapped himself around the woodstove. Lester was in his long-underwear, reading by a lantern. He didn't look up as Jubal stamped the snow off his boots.

"Heard?" Jubal asked, feeling utterly frozen. He put his hands over the stove as if he were about to fry them. "Insurance payment came through—fifty thousand less than she cost. Lauchlan's done, not taking another ship."

Lester put his book down and stared. "Good Christ! They have a falling out?"

"Ask 'em. No matter, we're beached."

Lester considered for a moment, and then shook his head. "Nope, we're not," he said. "Let's go."

Jubal's eyes narrowed. "Where?"

"Liverpool! McKays don't own us. Lauchlan's one of the best captains on earth, but he don't have to be our last. You can't stand the North, this ship'll be outbound in a few weeks, and neither of us have ever been to Australia."

"Thought you liked it here."

"I do," Lester grinned, "but you look like a bird that migrated the wrong way. Go talk to Lauchlan, ask him to get us aboard *Lightning*—he must know the captain."

The next evening Jubal brought two letters into the whale oil lamplight beside the woodstove. The first was anticipated; Lauchlan McKay had provided a recommendation. The second was totally unexpected. Truette Stubbs had written from Mobile.

January 28, 1854

Mobile, Alabama

Dear Mr. Calhoun;

Pursuant to our understanding, I have recently executed a contractual agreement with Mr. Mark Pettaway in regards to an asset recently acquired. As this transaction reflects financial duress of the seller and holder, requiring a change in their holdings, a prudent regard for continuity compelled Mr. Pettaway to protract asset liquidation. Therefore, I negotiated and concluded an irrevocable option to purchase said asset three years from the 1st of this month, past.

The above developments may affect your affairs. I urge you to insure appropriate measures, as the volatility in our markets is apparent. Further, I advise you to pursue global opportunities at your very earliest convenience unless you are prepared to respond aggressively as events may warrant.

The option price is $500.

Yours sincerely,

Truette Stubbs

Lester read it through twice. "This mean what I think it does?"

"Depends what you think," Jubal replied.

"You're feeling spunky," Lester observed. "Reckon this says Whitmill Rivens got jammed on his interest, had to sell stuff, including Cora. Pettaway isn't in great shape either, but wants to keep her around because he fired or got rid of Whitmill and she probably knows enough to be useful. How am I doing?"

"There's hope yet. Keep going."

"Truette did some sort of three-year deal for five hundred, we owe him now. Cora's free in three years, but this says 'option,' so I guess the balance comes due then, whatever it is, if Truette still wants her, his choice. I wonder what she fetched? Bastards. Meanwhile, Whitmill's going to be paying a visit north, probably because he's unhappy you shot his balls off, and Truette thinks it'd be a good idea if you disappeared, unless of course, you developed a death wish and want to greet him, talk things over."

"I ain't afraid of Whitmill Rivens."

"Spare me the courage," replied Lester. "I am. Man with no pecker's got nothing to lose." Lester pulled a cheroot from his pocket, bit off the end, and struck a match to it, then pointed the glowing end at his friend. "Here's what we do. Tomorrow send Truette a bank draft. Then use Lauchlan's recommendation. We'll be outbound Liverpool when *Lightning* goes. Stay on her if we can, and head for Australia."

Lester waved the cigar smoke from his face. "Jubal, give a thought to what we should ship on our account and ask around about Australia. See what we can learn about that trade. And before we leave, remind me to send a note to Mom 'n Sal. Australia's a poke from here—this is gonna take us awhile." Lester regarded his friend. "Which ain't a bad thing. That option doesn't mature for three years. I doubt Whitmill Rivens will wait that long."

Chapter Thirty-Eight

Liverpool, December 1855

A ship's boy ran up the stairs and skidded to a stop before the third mate. "All secure forward, Mr. Calhoun, sir!"

Jubal nodded, concentrating on the aft lines being made fast to the bollards on Albert Dock. Ten minutes later, satisfied that the *Donald McKay* was safely secured in its berth along the Mersey River, Jubal went below to make a last log entry, before reporting to the captain.

Lester was in Captain Warner's cabin when Jubal arrived, detailing a list of dockyard repairs that would be necessary before the ship left again for Melbourne. The captain carefully examined Lester's list, for the nineteen-year-old was the youngest bosun ever to serve under him, a position occasioned by the loss overboard of two senior men in a cyclone off New Zealand. The bosun—or "boatswain" of ninth century Norse and English splice—did not stand regular watches, and might combine, as Lester did, all mechanical, carpentering, and sailmaking maintenance duties for working a wooden ship.

Finally, he nodded, and looked to Jubal. "See to these, Calhoun," he said. "Norton, I expect also to see your report to Mr. McKay. Send it to the Connaught." Warner donned a Shetland wool overcoat, clapped a beaver hat atop his balding head, and bid his young officers a happy new year before leaving for the city.

Lester looked at Jubal, his irritation plain. Private correspondence with the McKay shipyard was none of Warner's business, but antagonizing a captain made no sense.

Jubal shrugged, and picked up a copy of the *Liverpool Maritime Gazette* lying on the captain's desk. "Looking at this, we're lucky to have a ship," he said. "New York is hardly building, jobs tough to find, the whole California trade's in the head." He tossed the paper onto the console, but picked it again, noticing something. "You see this? *Charles Mallory* and *Staffordshire*, both lost, one off Brazil, the other run aground, Cape Sable. *Sea Witch* went down off Cuba, and *Oriental* burned in the Min River. *Dauntless* left Rio for the Horn and's not been heard from again. We haven't done bad, considering."

Lester didn't answer. He was tired from the voyage, eighty-six days from Melbourne, the third round trip in two years, each on a different McKay ship. They had left the McKay yard and gone out to Australia and back in *Lightning*, then made a run on the *James Baines* before the most recent passage aboard the *Donald McKay*. When they had first arrived in Liverpool on *Lightning*, Lester and Jubal had jointly written a letter to Donald McKay, describing the sailing characteristics of the ship. On their return to Liverpool from Melbourne seven months later, McKay—carrying on without Lauchlan, who had returned ashore to their boyhood home in Nova Scotia—answered the letter with a request, also made of James Baines, one of England's richest shipping magnates. McKay wanted "his associates" transferred to the successive new ships the East Boston yard had contracted to deliver for Baines' Australia service, the Black Ball Line.

Jubal glanced at Lester, feeling the fatigue himself. "Think we ought to hang around?" *Champion of the Seas*, McKay's fourth ship, was sailing inbound from Melbourne, and due to dock in three weeks before immediately returning to Australia.

"Let's see if Truette Stubbs or Eleanor Creesy got anything to say," Lester replied, anticipating the mail awaiting them at James Baines' office. Eleanor Creesy's letters were chatty and always carried an admonition to read more, including titles that she thought appropriate, while Truette Stubbs' communication was quite formal, though invariably packed with news and suggestions for commercial opportunities. Stubbs had asked the boys to arrange shipments of agricultural implements from England to Mobile and trade whatever they could from Australia. Most recently, before sailing from Melbourne, the boys had brokered several tons of wool for delivery to England. On each trade, they received a five percent commission, and within two years, Lester and Jubal had made almost five thousand dollars.

James Baines rose from his desk as Jubal and Lester were shown into his office. A high-back chair upholstered in rich wine-color brocade sat behind the desk, a century-old remnant of Javan teak pulled from the opulent captain's cabin of a Dutch East Indiaman. Resplendent furniture glowed in the afternoon light streaming through silk-curtained windows twice Lester's height. The founder of the Black Ball Line had taken a shine to the raw-boned American boys, who looked all sinew and corded muscle, yet were unfailingly polite, instinctively avoiding the Persian carpet dominating Baines' office. Though he wouldn't say as much to anyone, the boys reflected his own memories. An impoverished childhood in the Glasgow slums had marked James Baines for life.

"She's a good ship, sir," Lester reported, uncertain why the shipowner didn't speak directly with his captain. In fact, Baines liked the uncensored reports on his ships. Captains were more circumspect, especially as the worldwide economic slowdown kept clipper ships idle for months in some ports. The boom days of California were over, and word from his New York agents indicated that East River departures had dropped dramatically. "Made for the forties," Lester continued, "she handles those latitudes wonderfully, though your passengers don't fare so well, not being seamen."

Baines waved that off. "People only emigrate once. Now tell me about her in all weathers!"

For an hour the boys talked as the Scotsman questioned them intently, alternately describing the mechanics of her rigging, how the *Donald McKay* performed in light winds and heavy, from all points of sail, and the record speeds she made surfing down the huge combers of the high latitudes. After what seemed an interminable discussion, the shipowner thanked them and bade them good afternoon.

Tall, Palladian windows filtered a waning winter sun that suffused the anteroom with pale light but little warmth. The boys sat on a hard bench under the windows reading their mail. By unspoken agreement, the journals, newspapers, and letters went on the bench, available for either to read as he chose, excepting Sally's letters. She had written each of them separately. Lester read his sister's letters three times, his heart sinking with each turn, holding the most recent in his lap while re-reading other letters.

Eleanor Creesy and her husband had made two circumnavigations via California and China, and Donald McKay wrote tersely about the shipbuilding slowdown chronicled in the maritime journals. Truette Stubbs described a thriving cotton industry despite talk of an impending depression. Boston, New York, and Mobile newspapers reports were largely sensationalist; the Mason-Dixon Line had become a political canyon, growing inexorably as attitudes toward slavery hardened in the North and South.

The news accounts were depressing. Spending most of their time in different hemispheres at sea allowed Lester and Jubal a merciful ignorance of politics at home. Truette Stubbs alluded to the North-South sectarian tension by means of his increasing emphasis on sheltering income through European transactions and English banks. The boys had been direct beneficiaries of Stubbs' hedging, and their Bank of England account swelled through trades on his behalf. Though gratifying, to Lester their profits had a scent of hypocrisy, like the whiff of druxy.

As the light faded in the anteroom, the world news felt increasingly remote and unimportant. A letter in Lester's lap grew heavy as stone, and at length he just stared at his oblique, lengthening shadow on the shiny parquet floor.

"Better head home, Lester," Jubal said.

The sad sympathy in his friend's voice cut through Lester's stoic façade. A tear welled and he nodded.

"Don't sound good, does it?"

Sally's letter, postmarked the previous March, conveyed weariness and resignation. Their mother was failing, shrinking before her daughter's eyes as the winter deepened; Sally did not know if Jane Norton would live to see spring. "Whenever you get this," the letter said, "please come home."

Lester felt a hand squeeze his shoulder. Jubal walked to the door of James Baines' office, knocked twice, and entered unannounced, closing the door behind him. After a few minutes he returned and gathered the mail.

"C'mon, Lester," he said, taking his friend's elbow. Lester rose to his feet, feeling like an old man. The boys were standing in the failing sunlight, Jubal holding Lester's arm, when James Baines opened the door from his office.

"Your friend," the English shipowner's rich Scottish brogue addressed Lester, "has confided that family calls ye to hearth. Take this," he extended a letter, "it's me authorization for passage to Boston. You've a berth aboard my ships on your return. Godspeed to you."

Outside, the Mersey was streaked with a rippling, mauve sunset. Lester shivered against the chill, still accustomed to southern summer. Even Cape Horn had been comparatively mild, and the long run up the Atlantic had seen such idyllic weather that their return to northern winter felt downright rude.

"Day or two don't make much difference," Lester said, his voice feeling disembodied. "Truette wants us to expedite that shipment of cloth, ought to do it first before we head out. Though I don't understand why he's importing fabric."

"He's not," Jubal replied. "It's his cotton, shipped here on speculation. If the market is off when it lands here, he'll pay a tolling contract for the milling and ship the cloth back home. The Brits either pay him decent for the crop or they do the weaving, he keeps ownership, and sells it back home. He's just taking what the market gives."

"Why not send it to Massachusetts?" Lester countered. "I heard there are more spindles in Lowell than in all eleven Southern states combined. Hell, if he was thinking future, Truette would finance a weaving operation in Alabama."

"Don't fit," Jubal explained, "not aristocratic enough. Planters are the top of the heap. Trade is for them that don't have the family, money, or blood for growing cotton. It ain't called 'King' for nothing."

"What did Sal have to say?" Lester asked.

Jubal was taken aback. Lester never pried into his letters from Sally. "She said your ma come on sickly," he replied, after a moment. "Talks about visiting Philadelphia sometime."

Lester stopped in the street, baffled. "That's the first I heard. What's in Philadelphia?"

"Somebody she heard talk in Bangor, same place we heard that Stowe lady. Sally said the woman's name is Lucretia Mott."

Chapter Thirty-Nine

Maine, February 1856

Jubal marveled at the virginal Maine landscape of midwinter. Swathed in pristine white, the hillsides seemed to undulate like a fluffed cotton blanket toward the sea. He'd thought they would land at the riverside near the salmon weir, but Lester explained that without snowshoes, tromping up through waist-deep snow would leave them wet, frozen, and exhausted. Instead, they walked from Winterport, the head of winter navigation, ten miles upstream, where the river began to freeze. The road was smooth as a table, packed hard, and glazed by horse teams that rolled the roads after each snowstorm. Approaching the farmhouse, Jubal noticed the path to the barn was a corridor cut through snowdrifts higher than his head.

Sally stood gaunt and hollow-eyed at the stove when the boys came tramping up the frozen steps. She heard them first, for nothing but blurred shadows were visible through the thick hoarfrost coating the windows. Sally had stopped going to school at Thanksgiving, afraid that she would come home to find her mother dead. The house already felt like a tomb. When the sudden clomping sounded on the porch, Sally had the crazy thought that Jake had kicked his stall down and wanted to come in the house. Then Lester was in the doorway, seeming to fill it, and she just stood there and nearly sagged, too spent for tears.

Jubal hugged her tentatively, shocked at the narrow face and drawn cheeks. Below his Scottish sheepskin coat—Lester had told him it would be cold and even the warmest coat he could find in London was only adequate—Jubal could feel Sally's ribs against him. The gesture seemed to give her a small measure of relief.

"Lester, you brought home a sheep," Sally said, her shallow, tired laughter mixed with sniffles.

Lester knew what to expect but still wasn't prepared when he pulled off his boots and quietly entered the corner room where Sally had moved their mother. Though Sal had kept a basin filled with balsam shoots and rosehips, the room smelled of sickness. Beneath a pile of quilts, Jane lay like a delicate bird, her body wasting away.

Sally had written that the doctor called their mother's malady "consumption," though that could mean anything with a cough attached. Mostly, Sally wrote, in a statement that struck Lester with the force of a blow, "Momma just seems like a woman who decided her time had passed and she'd rather die than be trapped, barren, and old."

Jane Norton slept peacefully, her face toward the frosted window. Lester stared, unable to move. Sally came in and linked arms, then stood on tiptoes—Lester was now a head taller—and kissed him lightly on the cheek, before leaving him be. He could hear Jubal and Sally talking softly in the kitchen. After awhile the front door closed and a moment later, Jubal's wide shoulders passed by the window. Soon the rhythmic thud of an axe splitting wood sounded near the barn.

Perhaps something about the powerful swings vibrated their way through Jane Norton's unconsciousness, for her eyes fluttered and opened briefly. Too weak to turn her head, she lay there as though getting her bearings. Lester knelt, bringing his face close to hers.

"It's me, Lester," he said, starting to cry. "I'm home, Momma,"

Jane's eyelids moved and her lips quivered. She barely stirred, and Lester reached under the covers for her hand, feeling as if he was taking hold of a wren. Jane closed her eyes but he could feel the slight, deliberate pressure of a grip that had once held him with the ferocity of a mother, that memory now a mere shadow as she gave a last grasp to her son. He knew that she could feel his presence and it made him weep with sorrow and shame, the loss washing over him like a deluge of guilt for being away so long. He buried his face in the quilts, sobbing. Sally came and stood beside him, stroking his hair, murmuring that everything would be all right.

Their mother never fully regained consciousness, though she sometimes seemed to acknowledge Lester's presence when he fed her broth each day. Mostly, she departed life with more patience and grace than she ever lived it, taking her leave in a long, slow glide that saw the winter out, as though with her last act she intended to join her youngest son directly.

Sally woke one morning in late April to find her mother had gone in the night. Lester was out in the barn and knew immediately by the look on his sister's face when she came to him. He had risen before dawn with Jubal, intending to twitch a last load of hardwood from the woodlot. As the ground thawed, they worked earlier and shorter hours, quitting by mid-morning when the overnight frost melted on the twitching trail.

Jane Norton had waited to pass until the frost was out of the ground. She had seen people die in winter and pickled in brine or just left in the sheds to freeze hard as oak, then covered with sawdust, preserved until the ground was soft enough for digging. The children remembered how she hated those who didn't have the dignity to die in warm weather. Jubal dug her grave on the hillside above the farm, at the foot of a huge umbrella-shaped maple tree just budding to spring. A few feet away, two granite markers rested upright, one canted slightly from a frost heave. Jane had been specific: she wanted to be buried next to her son. The tombstone slab of her husband held little emotion for her. After news of his loss, she'd had the headstone carved and then carelessly slammed it in the ground, damning John Norton's bones to the ocean floor. Even as she lay dying, Jane wouldn't forgive John for leaving her so early, to face rearing the children alone.

Lester hitched Jake to the wagon so his sister could drive into South Orrington, stopping at neighboring farms along the way, and then telegraph Dorcus Fullam when she reached the town post office. They had decided to wait a few days for the burial, until a Sunday, when people who wished could come. From the dooryard, Lester stood for a moment, watching what remained of his family. Sally turned and waved from the wagon, and he could see Jubal working under the apple tree. The sadness gripped him again but he swallowed it and headed for the barn to build his mother's coffin.

Nearly forty people came to wish Jane Norton onward. To Lester's astonishment, a schooner had made it up the river and anchored off the fishing weir. Captain Fullam was between voyages and he brought five of Jane's sisters along with their husbands and children, sailing up from Eastport rather than risk getting bogged on the muddy roads. Lester and Sally had seen some of the women only a few times and had the awkward sensation of welcoming close family members whom they barely knew. Neighbors and family gathered under the maple tree.

As the local pastor recited a parting psalm, Jubal looked into the afternoon sky and shuddered. Overcast had settled in from the south, an advancing harbinger of spring rain. Between the leaden sky and coarse, unforgiving soil, Jubal realized he had his own choice; to let the last flicker of his family's flame expire with his own death, whether at sea, in a tropical port, or along the ochre river of his youth, or to create a lineage and legacy worthy enough to call such people as this to his grave.

Jane Norton was put to rest and buried by the men, while the women returned to the farmhouse and set out supper, where Dorcas took over with the undisputed authority of a Nichols matriarch. The older woman had known what would be necessary, and each boy came up from the river bearing a basket of food. Sally watched with amazement, appreciating the lifelong ambivalence her mother felt in the presence of such a powerful sister. The dynamic between aunt and niece was utterly different, however: within an hour Dorcas and Sally recognized themselves kindred souls. As people surrounded the table and filled every nook and cranny of the house, balancing plates on their knees, Dorcas asked Sally what she intended to do next.

"I'm to spend the summer in Philadelphia," Sally replied, attempting to hide her uneasiness, "in the employ of a prominent family."

"Oh?" Dorcas Fullam frowned, as though a chambermaid's job was beneath her people. "Might I know of them? And how did you secure such ... employment?"

"I wrote and requested the position," Sally said, her face beginning to shine. "Last fall I was inspired by a speech in Bangor and decided that if Momma should pass, I would seek my fortune."

"Your fortune!" Captain Fullam exclaimed. "Whatever are you talking about?"

"I'm to work in the home of Mrs. Lucretia Mott," Sally declared, with a hint of defiance straight from her mother.

"Bravo!" Dorcas Fullam exclaimed, leaping to her feet. "What inspiring news! Oh, splendid, I am so proud of you, Sally!" The sight of a sixty-year-old woman suffused with schoolgirl animation stupefied everyone, save Captain Fullam. Dorcas Fullam looked at her husband, delighted at his consternation. "Lucretia Mott will be one of the most important women in American history," she declared, as though it was the equivalent of spring following winter. "How many of you have heard of the Declaration of Sentiments?"

Silence.

"Ignoramuses, all of you!" she scolded. "Seneca Falls, New York, 1848, the Declaration of Independence for American Women, and about time it is!"

"Drivel," growled her husband. "A group of ..." he bit the pejorative off but it was too late.

"Of what?" Dorcas and Sally cried in unison.

"Of blustery ladies who think the responsibilities a man shoulders ought by rights also be the provinces of women!" Captain Fullam retorted, getting to his feet. Lester had the distinct sense this wasn't the first time a storm had gathered over the topic. "If you ask me, my dear girl, you'd do very well to find a good husband! Lester will give a share of this farm, no doubt. I'm sure you'll attract suitors."

Dorcus Fullam swatted the remark aside as if it were a mosquito. "She didn't ask you, John. Besides, that sentiment is rubbish."

Jubal's jaw dropped and he watched the captain's face color. "The sun is setting, my dear," he barked, "and the tide turns. We shall weigh anchor in one-half hour exactly," Captain Fullam looked at his watch. "At 4:45. Lester, see to the ladies' wraps." The captain slammed on his hat and offered a rigid arm to his wife.

Dorcus Fullam looked bemused. "Time for you to go to sea, dear," she said. Turning to Sally, she took a step and embraced her quickly. "How I wish I were your age again!" she whispered. "Write to me."

Using both the schooner's peapod and the farm's dory, Lester and Jubal shuttled the families to the schooner. After the last trip, as the peapod was hauled aboard, Captain Fullam leaned over the rail and spoke quietly to Lester, who steadied the dory against the current. "If you're on this coast in August you've a berth with me. Sooner, then I'd advise you to head to New York. *Flying Cloud* is outbound California, first of June."

"Does Captain Creesy still command?" Lester asked.

"And how does she fare?" Jubal added. Circling the globe five times in as many years would test any vessel.

"He does indeed. She will need refastening soon enough, though I have not seen her and cannot say." Captain Fullam tipped his hat. "Fair winds, men!"

Lester stood off as the captain bawled orders and the men aboard raised sail. "Perk won't take her if she's tired," he murmured.

Jubal nodded. "You can bet Eleanor will have something to say about it."

Within an hour, the schooner disappeared around the bend, running for the bay in the full grip of river current and ebb tide. Lester, Jubal, and Sally walked back up to the house without a word, trying with little success to avoid the sucking April mud, churned to a mess by the departing family. The day seemed to have abruptly closed, leaving a lingering sadness. They were back at the house when Sally broke the silence.

"How can the captain and Aunt Dorcus love each other and still have such different opinions?" she wondered, drawing her shoe across the boot knife embedded in a granite slab by the porch. Sally carefully peeled the mud off in clumps, standing on one foot to examine the other after each pass. Neither boy offered a comment.

"How'd you learn of this woman, Lucretia Mott?" Lester asked later, still adjusting to his sister's maturity. He remembered a headstrong girl but now regarded a formidable young woman. Lester felt on uncertain, uncomfortable ground.

"You're surprised at me, aren't you, Lester?" Sally smiled, feeding the cook stove. She had gained weight since their return, and looked less haggard. Firelight glowed off her face as she stirred soup for dinner. "Betty can hide a thought better than you."

Jubal sat near the fireplace under an oil lamp, enjoying the heat and light, thinking that Jane Norton's death was like the crossing swell that signaled a sea change and fresh weather. He buried his nose deeper in a book.

Lester gave an exaggerated sigh and accepting the inevitable, folded his hands, waiting.

"I'm free, Lester," Sally said, with the quiet force of a judge gaveling her verdict. "We're selling the farmhouse. You want something here, take it."

"What are you talking about, Sal?" Lester's voice rose. "You got no right to negotiate a sale!"

"Who does? You? It's mine, much as yours. You said yourself you're not coming back, and I sure as hell won't be the hen here, keeping it warm 'till you decide to show up again."

"But ..." Lester sputtered, "it just isn't right!"

"Oh, that's downright lame," Sally scoffed. "Lester, you got money, I can see your clothes are good enough. Jubal too, that post of a friend over there. You want the place, you're welcome, just pay me my share. Half."

"Well, I dunno Sal ..." Lester temporized, feeling like he was trying to get traction on a frozen pond.

"You don't have to know," Sally replied, her voice hard and even. "I'm not mother, Lester. I admire you, mad as it sometimes made me, and I'm going do just what you've done. I'm reaching for the world. Philadelphia's my first stop."

Chapter Forty

New York, June 1856

Sally slammed the newspaper shut and threw it at Jubal. She stomped to the wharf's edge and kicked a piece of wood into the East River, then stood there fuming, oblivious to the sparkling sunlight or South Street's usual, clattering commotion.

Jubal's lower lip worked, and for a moment he felt like walking up to the young woman and kicking her square in the rump, except he'd have to haul her out of the filthy river. He glanced at the newspaper, knowing by her reaction what he would find. Beside him, Lester grimly surveyed the ships clogging the wharves.

The *New York Tribune* headline screamed Sacrilege in Kansas!! A half continent away the national slavery drama approached climactic proportions, a tenor of violence known as "Bloody Kansas." The territorial border with Missouri was a fault line, separating slave state from free.

Sally, who had read every newspaper she could find on their trip south, was incensed. Her outrage had grown with every mile from Maine, exacerbated by Lester's ambivalence and Jubal's downright refusal to discuss politics or abolition. Clyde Pingree's coastal sloop, now commanded by his son Cub, had taken them to Boston, where they stayed a few days before boarding the train to New York.

En route, the boys had called on Donald McKay at the East Boston yard. The shipbuilder was gracious but distracted, and Lester and Jubal could immediately see why. Energy and activity at the shipyard was a shadow of the halcyon days, with fewer men and smaller ships on the ways. McKay's face showed the pressure, and though flashes of passion still remained, the responsibilities of competing in a shrinking market had taken their toll. Holding onto his men even as business slowed, he was finally forced to let many go. Donald McKay had waited too long, however. Loyalty had drained him financially and the yard struggled. As they left, Jubal remarked that the man reminded him of a captain weathering the front side of a hurricane, knowing the backside could be worse.

The ride to New York was silent until Sally found another newspaper, which stoked her emotions. Blaring stories detailed secessionist depravity and spoke of runaway slaves stabbing their children to prevent them from being hauled south. On the South Street wharf, Sally wheeled and marched back to them.

"You men can gallivant around the planet," she ranted, "but your country is coming apart! Don't you see? Don't you care? You're going to come back around the Horn"—she spat it with an artificial swagger—"and find this place in flames." Sally waved a finger in Jubal's face, oblivious to the grins of stevedores and longshoremen who had stopped work to watch. "I know you Jubal Calhoun, you're not mean. I *know* you don't countenance owning the sweat of another man, tearing families apart for sale, or claiming the abominable right to sexual congress with slaves!"

Lester gasped despite himself. He had not said a word to her about Cora and couldn't imagine Jubal confiding anything. Jubal stared at the river.

Sally looked bitterly from one to the other. "All you two care about is trade! Shame on you!" She grabbed the paper, inadvertently ripping it. "This madness is spreading and all you can think about is your next ship! Go ahead, sail away and fight the weather. I'm going to Philadelphia and fight for something worth the effort! Abolition, emancipation, the rights of woman!" Sally was flushed and breathing in snorts. "Oh, goddam you both!" She wheeled in place and Lester had the urge to try and calm her but was afraid he'd get slugged.

To his complete astonishment, she did slug him, a short, hard jab to the chest. Sally turned and delivered one to Jubal as well, leaving both boys too stunned to move.

"Oh, just take me to the train station," Sally said, suddenly looking exhausted. With a start, Lester realized his sister's emotions. A sad truth etched Sally's face; neither knew when, or if, they would see each other again. In two hours, his sister would board the Philadelphia afternoon express while he prepared to sail the far oceans of the globe.

"Hello!" A cheery voice interrupted the pall settling over them. Everyone turned to see Eleanor Creesy waving from a carriage that had just pulled to a stop along South Street. Lester and Jubal whipped their hats off as Captain Creesy came around the back of the carriage and helped his wife down. Jubal glanced at Lester, who looked equally puzzled. Several travel chests lay securely strapped to the carriage roof.

Upon arriving in New York the day before, they had headed directly for

South Street to find *Flying Cloud,* but neither the captain nor his wife had been aboard. They found them at the Astor Hotel, where the boys learned that after five circumnavigations, Captain Creesy had recommended to the owners that the ship be refastened. As the captain described *Flying Cloud's* condition to Lester and Jubal, Sally and Eleanor Creesy chatted pleasantly until Sal mentioned her job in Philadelphia.

Eleanor Creesy's response was quieter but no less demonstrative than Dorcus Fullam's. She immediately extended an insistent invitation for all of them to dine that evening, an elegant affair that had lasted until ten. The attention left Sally flushed and radiant.

Now, dismounting from the coach, Josiah and Eleanor Creesy's countenances showed opposing expressions. The captain looked dour and moody while his wife was ebullient. She waved at the boys and embraced Sally like a long-lost sister.

"When is your train, dear? Isn't it the afternoon express?" Mrs. Creesy asked. Sally tried her best to look cheerful.

Captain Creesy noted the boys' confused expressions and tersely explained. "Nat Griswold refused. He thinks the ship is good for another voyage." The captain reached into his coat for cigars, passing one to each of the boys.

"So ... ah," Lester stumbled, not sure how to proceed. "What's your plan, sir?" Jubal waited, sudden anxiety gripping him.

"Nat Griswold be damned!" Eleanor Creesy declared. Captain Creesy hadn't even removed his cigar to speak. "He doesn't think the ship needs refastening, but Perk does! So we're not going, not to California, anyway. We're leaving for Boston right now." She turned to Sally, "I'd be happy if you'd join us to the station, dear. You'll be traveling one way while we go the other, and then we'll just have to write. Oh, I'd love to go with you!"

Captain Creesy looked like that might not be a bad idea. Lester and Jubal stood still, shocked that their plan had blown away like cigar smoke. The captain grunted, then motioned down the wharf. "Do you know Joshua Patten, a young fellow out of Rockland?"

Lester had never heard of him, but the town of Rockland was at the entrance to Penobscot Bay, no more than thirty miles from the Norton farmhouse.

"I spoke with him not an hour ago at the Astor," Captain Creesy said, "while the missus was packing. If you see him right off, I believe he'll treat you fair. Tell him I sent you. But be quick—there's plenty men on the waterfront needing a ship."

"Where away?" Jubal asked, turning to look along the forest of masts.

"Four, five ships down," the captain nodded. "An extreme clipper, sixteen-seventeen hundred tons, heavily sparred. *Neptune's Car.*"

Chapter Forty-One

New York, February 1857

Under cover of a leeward awning that protected them from freezing rain, Lester and Jubal watched the steamship make her way against the ebb tide streaming through the Verrazano Narrows. Jubal was morose, buried in his bulky sheepskin coat and shifting his feet trying to keep warm, though careful not to slip on the treacherous, icy deck. Lester grinned, lit a cigar, and passed it to his friend. Jubal grunted, champing on the cigar without moving his arms.

"Balmy welcome," Lester remarked. He lit a cigar for himself. "We won't be here long, Jubal. Besides, think of that fellow waiting to die. Could be lot worse than cold."

"I'm going to die warm," Jubal declared, though he pitied Captain Patten, who at twenty-eight, had an attack of brain fever two weeks after *Neptune's Car* left New York. Incredibly, the captain's eighteen-year-old wife had taken over the ship and commanded it to San Francisco. Mary Patten was eighteen and only realized she was pregnant as they approached Cape Horn.

"Couple of weeks," Lester assured him, "month at most, we'll be sweating in the Gulf. Man can go to extremes in no time running the longitude." Two weeks earlier, they had left the port of Manzanillo in Panama. "What do you think? Steam, or find us a coastie going back south?"

"We're sailors," Jubal replied. "Steamers are faster but this ship ain't worth a shit in weather. Rivers are one thing—the sea's altogether another."

The return trip north from Panama reflected their entire voyage, equal parts challenge, opportunity, and nightmare. After Mary Patten had taken over for her husband west of the Cape Verde Islands—an event that neither Jubal nor Lester could have thought possible if they hadn't been aboard—the ship's first mate objected with such vehemence that the diminutive woman ordered him confined to the ship's brig and advanced Jubal to take his place on the quarterdeck, where he nearly lived during the seven hellacious weeks it took to drive *Neptune's Car* around Cape Horn. One howling gale after another pummeled the ship, at times driving her within a day's sail of Antarctica. Mary Patten didn't change her clothes for fifty-two days.

Lester and Jubal marveled that a young woman their own age could command forty hardened sailors in the harshest seas on the planet at the worst time of year. Yet her courage was contagious, and despite the extraordinary hardship of ice, snow, mountainous seas, and incessant headwinds, not one sailor was lost nor badly hurt. Four months after leaving New York, *Neptune's Car* anchored in San Francisco Bay where Lester and Jubal promptly carried a prostrate Captain Patten to the steamship wharf. The clipper was left in the hands of the ship's agent, and accompanying Mary—now six months pregnant—they departed six hours after arriving in San Francisco, steamed south to Panama, crossed the malaria-infested isthmus by train, and immediately boarded an Atlantic steamship packet, racing to get Captain Patten back to a New York hospital before fever killed him.

On the passages to and from Panama, Lester and Jubal learned the utility and danger of steam. There was little of the placid beauty of a clipper, flexing its wings to a tropical breeze. A steamship was constant racket and incessant vibration from a gasping engine; its cavernous boiler sounded like a prehistoric mastodon stomping through an aquamarine garden.

The experience still haunted Jubal. Despite continual, loathsome noise and the inadequate power in heavy weather, he could see steam spelled the eventual death of sail. When Lester insisted on making a financial plan to purchase and operate a ship, Jubal questioned whether they should wait several more years, then buy a steamship.

"This progress isn't going backward, Lester," he argued. "Imagine going around the Horn, regardless of the wind! It's jest a matter of time."

"You want to wait?" Lester countered. "Meanwhile, keep shipping out, maybe on these deathtraps?"

"The point is," Jubal replied, "I don't want to be a Donald McKay, bless the man. Work half your life, then it falls apart because the world moved on without you."

"I agree! But we climbed aboard *Neptune's Car* because we didn't have anything better to do. Just taking another trip, making somebody else rich, like all the jack tars we've know over the years. Mary Patten is uncommon strong, but you ran that ship, Jubal. 'Tis high time we do it ourselves."

Neither would forget the pathos of debarkation in New York. The boys brought Captain Patten off the steamship first, literally half the man he had been six months before. Mary followed, gingerly descending the gangway. A black cloak and white scarf lent her the semblance of a waddling penguin teetering to a stop in the open arms of her brother, who had come from Boston to meet them at the wharf.

"She's just our age," Jubal marveled, waving goodbye as Mary took her husband to the hospital.

"Yes sir," said Lester, "her course is laid right out, a rail really. Doubt she can get off. Ours now, well, we got the blessing and curse of freedom."

"What's cursed about it?"

"It can get taken away. Josh Patten, he's done having the choice. Neither does Cora. You don't suffer freedom if you don't have it."

"Philosophy's hardly your calling, Lester," Jubal snapped. He hollered for a livery cab. "Let's head for the Astor, get the hell out of this weather."

As they settled into the cab opposite each other, Lester fingers drummed his knee. "Expect we'll have any word from Truette?"

Jubal snorted. "How the hell should I know?" But a moment later, he leaned forward. "First things first. Either we stay north—don't matter to me whether's New York, Boston, or Philadelphia, and wait to hear from Truette after we send him a telegram this afternoon—or we go direct to Mobile. Either way, we can't commit to anything until we know our obligation. It's been better than three years. We gave the man our word."

"You're right as rain," Lester sighed, with a sinking feeling. "What do you want to do?"

"I want a hot bath. We'll telegraph Truette, ask him to reply to Philadelphia. Tomorrow we'll take the train 'n go see Sally."

Chapter Forty-Two

Lucretia Mott sat with her hands folded, reminding Jubal of a female Truette Stubbs. Phlegmatic and courteous, Mrs. Mott seemed bemused at Sally's obvious discomfort. Lester wished his sister would relax but knew she desperately wanted them to make a good impression.

The boys had arrived unannounced, shortly after midday. Sally nearly fainted when she answered the door, and her squeal brought John and Lucretia Mott to opposite ends of the entry hall, more out of curiosity then alarm. In their thirty-year marriage, the couple had raised five children.

From her gray eyebrows and lined features, Lester judged the woman to be about sixty. A close-fitting white bonnet framed her face in an oval, accentuating clear green eyes that reminded him of the winter sea off Maine. She shook his hand in a firm, bony grip.

"Pleasure m'am," Jubal bowed slightly. Lucretia Mott's eyes sparkled, hearing the drawl. The boys shook hands with John Mott, a portly mutton-chopped man neatly dressed in a suit tailored earlier than his present girth.

"Sally," Mrs. Mott said, "could you offer some tea to our guests please, and join us in the library?"

Within minutes, Lester and Jubal felt as if they were on display before a pair of sagacious owls. Jubal was instantly on guard, feeling a sudden wish to be aloft. He noticed tiny indentations on his palm and recognized marks from Sally's fingernails.

"Please excuse the intrusion," Lester began, fiddling with his hat, "we left New York rather suddenly and I don't doubt we beat the telegram. It might be with the post here." Jubal proffered several letters, which he had taken from the postman as they passed through the picket gate into the front yard. The Motts lived in a fine two-story brick home on a wooded residential street in North Philadelphia.

"Sally has spoken of you often," Mr. Mott said as his wife accepted the mail. Sally came in with the tea, trying not to rattle the crockery as she poured and served.

"Thank you both," Lester said, nodding in turn to the Motts. He grinned at his sister. "You look wonderful, Sal."

Jubal smiled, still wary, though it was a struggle to keep from staring at Sally. The year had vaulted her into womanhood, with cheeks glowing beneath a crisp white bonnet and curly hair that shone in the rectangular shafts of winter sunlight streaming through double-hung windows. Sally wore an ankle-length dress and white apron, but though it was a domestic's uniform, she showed little of an employee's deference.

"You are sailors?" Mrs. Mott asked. "From where have you come?"

"Start at the beginning Lester," Sally said nervously. "I keep talking about you, but ... Well you've been everywhere!"

Lester began their story again, finishing with their leaving Mary Patten in New York. Jubal kept quiet, with the growing knowledge that his time was but delayed. He had noticed the mail, letters from Frederick Douglass and Elizabeth Stanton, copies of the *North Star* and William Lloyd Garrison's newsletter. This was an abolitionist house. Despite the courtesy, he had the sense of swimming in deep water where razor teeth lurked below.

"Where are you from?" Lucretia Mott asked Jubal, when Lester ran out of words.

"Cahaba, Alabama, m'am." Jubal's drawl was more pronounced than Lester had heard in years.

"Nobody's going to bite you, Jubal," Sally said. Lester saw the gleam in his sister's eye and realized Sally was thrilled. Jubal also felt the emotion, becoming even more uncomfortable. He didn't mean to be rude, but it made him testy that everyone would look at him like he was some kind of oddity just because of his birthplace or speech. Being in the North always felt like walking through a hostile jungle, a sensation that never arose in Britain or Australia or, for that matter, on the West Coast. Anywhere above the Chesapeake, however, Jubal knew it was only a matter of time.

"What will you do if the Republic splits?" John Mott asked.

The question was so direct that Jubal drew back. He searched the man's face but saw no judgment.

"I haven't but given it a thought, sir."

"I can see that," John Mott said, "and commend thee. It's uncommon of late."

Sally settled back, her nervousness settling. She had written of Lucretia Mott with undisguised adoration, extolling the woman's humility, wisdom, and devout spirituality. Suffrage and abolition were the temporal expressions of a profound Quaker faith, causes to which she applied an acute political mind.

While Jubal's reaction was guarded, Sally gazed at him with shining, liquid eyes, willing him to stand and proudly reveal himself.

"How do you mean, sir?" he asked John Mott.

"You sit before us," Mr. Mott explained, "seemingly oblivious to your different heritages." He glanced at his wife, who nodded, though she didn't take her eyes off Jubal. "Quite refreshing, I should say."

The young men stared at him.

"The national discourse has deteriorated," Mr. Mott continued, "with basest calumny replacing common norms of dialogue and debate. It is gratifying to witness young men between whom the issue of North and South, slave or free, has had no derogatory effect."

Lucretia Mott sipped her tea. "How do you do it?" she asked.

"Do what?" Jubal asked, perplexed. "Get along?" He looked at Lester who opened his hands, also mystified.

"Well," Jubal's face split in a wry smile that quivered Sally's loins, "we don't, much."

"Lester's always been a trial!" Sally laughed.

"Thing is," Jubal continued, "guess we grew up together. I suppose also, we've mostly been away. Right and wrong depend a good deal on the port you're in. Then there's right and wrong on the water, and the ocean's always right."

"Do you intend a life on the seas?" Lucretia Mott asked.

"Not really sure, m'am. It's what we know."

"So what are you doing next?" Sally chimed in, radiant as a spring rose. "You boys getting married?"

"Sally," Lester almost groaned, "I haven't see you in months. Can't we catch up a bit?"

"You're avoiding me, Lester. I know you both well enough; you'll be gone in a couple days or hours for God knows where—beg pardon, Mrs. Mott—and you'll tell me all about it when you show up again. I'm your sister. I can ask."

"We're likely going south," Lester said, trying to contain his exasperation. "Mobile."

"What's there?"

"Trade."

"Trading what?"

Unconsciously, Lester drummed his fingers on the chair. Jubal took a sip of tea, though the cup was empty.

"Would you wish to stay with us?" Lucretia Mott asked suddenly, readying to stand. "The children are grown, we have room and you are welcome."

Sally prepared a roast with vegetables and fresh-baked bread, and after Lucretia Mott said grace in a long, eloquent soliloquy, Mr. Mott served the food: three modest proportions and small mountains for the boys. The table was quiet, a silence that later felt like the prelude.

"How long may we expect thee?" Lucretia Mott began, innocently enough.

"Be going back to New York tomorrow," Lester replied, salivating at a slab of roast.

"Then?"

"Mobile," Lester mumbled, wishing he could pay attention to eating.

"What's there?" Sally probed. "You said trading? What?"

Neither Lester nor Jubal answered immediately, hoping the other would say something.

"Cargo," Lester said, his face almost in the plate.

"Human cargo?" Lucretia Mott asked.

Jubal dropped a blob of mashed potato in his lap. Lester choked. An ant walking across the dining room floor would have been noisy.

At length, Jubal replied. "I don't rightly know." He was losing his appetite.

Lester put down his napkin. Might as well be now, he thought, looking at his friend. "What *are* we gonna do?"

"Dunno, Lester," Jubal drawled. He looked at Lucretia Mott. "There's a young woman Lester and I are buying." Sally's eyes widened, but Mrs. Mott had no reaction other than to watch intently.

"You wouldn't own someone, would you?" Sally cried.

The silence grew so deep Lester could hear the ticking of a grandfather clock somewhere in the house.

"Don't think so, no …" Jubal answered. "Unless I was growing cotton in Alabama. If my birth had been different—if I'd come into this world in the big house and not the fields … Why, yes Sally, I would be owning people. If I were born in the far north or along the African coast I'd probably have me more than a few wives. And if I were a nobleman in Russia or Persia, I'd likely have serfs or concubines. And consider it normal. Say what you will, but in the South, well … slaves are part of the landscape, much as red dirt and the canebrake."

"What is significant about this woman?" Lucretia Mott asked.

"She's a slave now; our purchase will free her," Jubal drawled, longing for his pipe and a tumbler of brandy. "I've known her since I can't remember. She's ... was ... It's unclear her ownership at the present time ... But she's been the property of a bad man, fellow I know well and with whom have had strained relations."

Lester rubbed his jaw, marveling the understatement.

Jubal ignored him. "We engaged on our behalf, on Cora's—that the women's name—a cotton factor out of Mobile, fine man. Mr. Truette Stubbs has secured an agreement which is due to be exercised early this year, perhaps already been done. Don't know—we're waiting for word. We'll be going there, in any case."

Mr. Mott cleared his throat. "To claim property, which you will then release?"

The boys nodded.

"What do you plan for her?" John Mott folded his hands at their silence. "Regardless of circumstances, the Lord praises your action. However, manumission without preparation may simply allow this young woman a direct road to perdition."

Lester's mouth hung slack.

"Is she educated?" Mott asked, and got no answer. "I thought not. Without succor, funds, prospects, assistance ... she has scant hopes to expunge her history. The times are excessive. I can think of numerous avenues to penury, but not one, save providence, to her salvation in this life. Have you not thought you are freeing her from one bondage to another, yet unknown, quite possibly as, or more, odious?"

Obviously, they had not. Lester regarded Cora's freedom as a vague, though potent, talisman. He often dreamt of her, shaken with the allure of memory yet safe by distance.

Jubal had occasionally wondered what would become of Cora once she settled in Mobile. He had taken Truette Stubbs' maidservant, Louisa, as his example, assuming that Cora would find work at the home of someone whose innate decency mirrored Stubbs. In the unforgiving honesty of Lucretia Mott's dining room however, he recognized this fantasy as hopelessly naïve.

Jubal looked at Lester.

"They be right," he sighed, resigned to a more complicated situation than he had ever foreseen.

"William Still!" Sally exclaimed with a clap that startled everyone.

"Who?" Lester demanded. The conversation had depressed him and he felt a fool.

"I will ask him," John Mott agreed.

"If need be, I will gladly surrender a portion of my wages to support her!" Sally pronounced, flushed with excitement.

"William Still is a freedman," Lucretia Mott interjected in her steady voice. "A Negro, modestly successful in business, a devoted family man and respected member of our community. If you bring this woman here, rest assured, she will find refuge."

"And tell Cora she will read," Sally declared. "I will teach her."

Chapter Forty-Three

Philadelphia left a long silence on the New York–bound train, but the effect vanished on South Street that evening when Lester let out a whoop and pointed to the low-slung schooner rafted near the aft end of an unloading barkentine. The *Cerbin Flanigan* waited patiently, like an old friend.

Leonard Godbold pumped their hands repeatedly, clenching his remaining teeth and nodding.

"Mr. Stubbs telegraphed the shipping house here, told me to find you boys," Godbold said when he could talk, "and Lord sakes, y'all saved me the trouble, no doubt 'memberin' how I hate this city! Come 'board now, we got some gruel that ain't good but it's hot. Tommy! Abel!"

Jubal jumped lightly onto the *Cerbin Flanigan*'s deck as Lester followed. Overhead, a streak of lavender signaled the last rays of sunset and Venus hung beyond the harbor narrows like a diamond stud above the horizon, promising a cold night. He hoped the schooner would be leaving soon and Godbold had berths available.

"Boys, this here's Mr. Calhoun and Mr. Norton," Leonard told his sons, "and they'll be our shipmates homeward bound, I hope to say!"

Two boys appeared out of the companionway, one about seventeen, the other younger.

Jubal stepped forward to take an extended hand. "I'm Tommy," said the older one. The sheath and hath of a huge bowie knife hung from his belt. By his side, the younger lad opened his mouth and stood awkwardly, trying to make a sound, until he stuttered out his name, "Aaaabbel." It came out in two syllables, one tortuously long, the other a truncated chop, sudden as the snap of fingers.

"Gratified y'all have us 'long," Jubal said. "My mate, Lester."

As the five of them crammed together in the small forecastle, Lester looked around, trying to imagine owning or leasing a ship this size. Immediately, he could see she was too small for the transoceanic trade. They needed a ship half again as big and twice the capacity.

Leonard Godbold noticed Lester's appraisal.

"This be her last trip, leastways under us. Truette's gonna sell. Made mention of another ship, a topsail brig he got in trade, some sugar factor outta Havana got 'overextended,' Truette called it. This here does pretty well runnin' the coast to Hispaniola 'er down Mona Passage to the Windwards, but she ain't really a bluewater boat."

"How big?" Lester asked.

"The brig? Three hunnert ton, there'bouts."

Jubal had made the same quick study. "Are you going to command her?"

Godbold shook his head. "No, I'm a small-boat man. 'Sides, I'm gittin' old fer this, 'n the farm provides. Boys'r comin' on, not so many mouths to feed. 'N I miss Mother."

"What do you figure Lester, a dozen men?" Jubal mused, seeing his friend's mind race with the math of cargo, tonnage, and distance.

Lester nodded. "We'll have to talk with Mr. Stubbs. A brig…" He thought of a small, two-masted ship, foremast carrying square sails, the amidships mainmast flying a large triangular sail. Probably not fast, but mobile and seaworthy. "How old's she; what's her cut?"

"Twelve, fifteen years," Godbold replied, reaching for a cigar. He offered one to Lester and another to Jubal. "Ain't seen her, but Truette thought she were fair sharp, though don't know that he's good judge 'a them things. Built North, he said."

"When are we outbound?" Jubal asked. He glanced at Lester and nodded at his friend's direct gaze.

—

Two weeks later, the *Cerbin Flanigan* passed between Sand Island and Mobile Point into Pelican Bay at high noon, ghosting along in a light breeze over water that was painful to the eye, almost like staring at a mirror reflecting sunlight. Lester stood forward, already parched from the unaccustomed heat. He tried to watch for shoals, doubtful he could see anything in time, thankful that Leonard Godbold knew these waters like he knew his hand.

Jubal joined him forward, shirtless and tanned the color of burnished chestnut, reveling in the subtropical warmth of early March. He hadn't worn his shirt since they turned the Florida corner. Jubal's face had a look of possession, the marrow-deep pride of coming home. Neither said anything for the next hour, until they had left Fort Gaines astern and passed into Mobile Bay. Godbold intended to sail through the afternoon and anchor by twilight before moving into the harbor roads after daybreak.

"Hope Sal was right," Lester said, finally able to look ahead without squinting as the lengthening angle softened the sun's reflection.

"Women buy stuff," Jubal replied, "and they'll be here now, cotton coming on. Besides, we hedged a bit."

Before leaving New York, the boys had visited the financial district and secured cash with a letter of credit they had thought to bring from their Liverpool bank. *Cerbin Flanigan* was fully loaded with fertilizer and farm implements for the new cotton crop. The only other space left to add a little general cargo was in their bunks, so Lester and Jubal resolved to fill one berth with their own cargo, and then hot-bunk, alternating watches with one sleeping while the other was on deck.

In Philadelphia, Jubal had off-handedly asked Sally if she had any clever ideas for cargo. She thought for a moment, then replied with a wicked smile, "Taffeta and crinolines." Jubal must have blinked, for she stood back, hands on her hips.

"Just because I'm living with Quakers doesn't mean I intend to dress like one forever!" she told him. They were standing in the train station, waiting for the express back to New York. Lester was aboard already, having grabbed their seabags to stow them beneath the seats. Sally waited for a response, but Jubal didn't know what to say. The blast of a steam whistle came as a relief and he reached to hug her. Sally took the hug, then threw her head back and blazed a look before kissing him on the lips, brief and hard. She broke just as suddenly and stared at him before leaning forward again. Jubal anticipated a nice, longer kiss but had to stifle a sharp cry. Startled, he realized Sally had bit him.

"Every time the salt spray stings," she whispered, "you'll think of me. Jubal Calhoun, you get back here!"

As the afternoon sun set over the Gulf of Mexico, Jubal rubbed the tear in his lip, now almost healed. The salt spray had its intended effect. He could still feel Sally's strong back and the grip of her fingers in his hair. Later, in New York, he had looked at each roll of silk thinking how it would dress Sally. The crinolines were a different matter. Neither he nor Lester had the faintest idea what size to buy, but a matronly saleswoman had helped. When the *Cerbin Flanigan* cleared Sandy Hook, one bunk held two crates of crinolines telescoped atop one another, with bolts of fine taffeta silk wedged inside the centers, a nearly $2000 investment in total.

Lester wasn't worried about their cargo, but he couldn't stop wondering what had become of Cora. The whole experience in Gee's Bend had faded into a mist of memory, her image softening until she had retreated into a fog of blurred features, the shadows in that cabin flickering and dimming until he didn't know exactly what he remembered. Of Whitmill Rivens they had heard nothing, save Truette Stubbs' oblique comments that the man had survived and was intent on vengeance. Otherwise, Rivens had vanished.

Truette Stubbs greeted them at the dock with a wide, unrestrained smile.

"Y'all left your youth at sea," he marveled, looking them up and down. "I can hardly address you as 'boys' anymore, though forgive me if I think of y'all as such."

Earlier, after word of the *Cerbin Flanigan*'s arrival had reached his office, he had hurried down to meet the schooner. The wharves were crammed with equipment and supplies for plantations upriver, and within minutes a half-dozen slaves were offloading the schooner's cargo onto wagons for transshipment to the riverboats.

Lester and Jubal greeted Truette Stubbs with restrained emotion, though both were so deeply moved they blinked back tears. The trust this man had placed in them, gratifying at the time, now seemed utterly munificent. Through letters and long-distance financial instruments, the three had conducted commercial transactions totaling thousands of dollars. Lester had a journal of their activities on five ships and ten passages, balanced to the penny, accompanied by sealed letters from the Liverpool bank detailing their formal records, all of which Truette Stubbs accepted almost as an afterthought. Unbeknownst to Lester or Jubal, copious correspondence with his English bankers had long confirmed his instincts.

"Come to the office," Stubbs urged, "and we'll discuss matters of business before dining. Of course, y'all be stayin' at Royal Street; I've alerted Louisa. Y'all may remember Louisa—she is not one to disappoint."

Before they left the schooner, Lester directed the Godbold boys to offload their crates. When Stubbs learned of the contents he chuckled. "I know just the party'd be interested in that merchandise," he said as if savoring a private joke. "We'll make a call later today, and I advise you boys be sharp. And hold your price whatever the inducement."

At noon, they walked to an inn downtown where the clientele looked to be urban aristocracy. Lester and Jubal felt uncomfortable amongst the businessmen and ladies, all dressed in fine suits and full dresses. Among this gentry, the boys looked particularly rough-cut, wearing cotton blouses open at the throat and duck trousers stuffed into their seaboots. Some of the men looked at them askance and might have objected to their presence had Truette Stubbs not escorted them with aplomb, quietly enjoying the guarded, searching glances of several women. He led them to his table in the courtyard, apart from the crowd and pleasantly situated in the midday sun.

"Welcome to Mobile, gentlemen," Truette Stubbs toasted them with a glass of rum punch. "Fine to see that you boys have done so well. We've much to discuss, but first may I recommend the crawfish or snapper here? They do a marvelous job with snapper, lightly poached."

Halfway through the meal Stubbs finally raised the option. "Do y'all intend to proceed?" he asked, in the dead silence.

The boys exchanged glances. "Yes sir," Lester replied, squirming, "though I don't reckon we know exactly how. We're hoping, maybe … if you could advise us. First time I've ever encountered the situation. You, Jubal?"

The idiotic comment distracted Jubal for a moment but forced him to think. "What do we do, sir?"

"Though the option became current January last," Stubbs replied, assuming his Buddha pose, "the woman remains in Gee's Bend. As y'all may recall, the option price is to be deducted from the total sale, plus interest 'course, seven percent. The sale terms were nine hundred principal, less the option fee. With interest, balance is approximately four hundred ninety dollars."

"Four ninety," Lester repeated.

"That's correct," Truette Stubbs said. "For her."

Something about the way he said it singed the air.

Lester and Jubal stared at the older man, ignoring a fly that buzzed between them.

"The option," Stubbs folded his hands, "did not include the child."

The insect landed on Lester's forehead. At length, Truette Stubbs reached across and gently shooed the fly on its way. Jubal sat as if he'd had a stroke.

"Wha … When …?" Lester stuttered. "Hmmm … well, sir." He shook his head to clear the cobwebs; his breath let go in a whoosh. "How old's the child? What's … she … like?"

"Two," replied Truette Stubbs, regarding him with an unblinking stare. "The boy's … mostly white."

Chapter Forty-Four

Lester and Jubal spent the early afternoon in shock. After lunch they recovered their seabags and, at Truette Stubbs' instruction, extracted a small sampling of merchandise from the shipping crates. Ezekiel pulled separate baths, which suited them just fine. Lester had little interest in conversation and Jubal none.

Truette Stubbs returned late from the cotton exchange in high spirits, explaining that after remanding much of the cargo to wholesalers and shipping agents he had gone to his lawyer's office and finalized documents to exchange the schooner for the brig, which was expected from Havana any day. "Tonight," he said, donning a freshly laundered shirt, "we've considerable to discuss. I intend to take full possession of the brig soon as she offloads. Don Miguel signed the sale last week while I was in Havana."

"He's trading the schooner for the brig?" Lester asked. The sale made no sense, the bigger vessel likely twice the value of the *Cerbin Flanigan*.

"I'm the one trading," Stubbs explained. "Sugar and cotton share the same necessities of factoring, both being capital- and labor-intensive, with the return depending on harvest. Lots can happen between growing and selling—therein lays the risk. I shorted his sugar."

The young men looked at him blankly. They were in Stubbs' dressing chambers as he shed his business attire for a finely tailored caramel-colored suit. Earlier, following his suggestion, Lester and Jubal had laid out their own suits, which Ezekiel pressed into reasonable shape. Unlike Stubbs' lightweight cotton, the fabric was heavy for Mobile's climate. Already, both boys were sweating, and to their dismay, they had grown. Neither suit fit well; compared to their elegant mentor, they felt like bumpkins.

"Sugar's done nicely," Truette Stubbs continued, carefully tying a saffron velvet tie, "after a storm nearly wiped out British plantations in Tortola and Antigua a few years back. He leveraged on a futures price per ton but I figured those crops would come back fast enough this year to swing the market. Price is off eleven percent. He's obligated to fulfill the contract or buy it back."

"What's the difference?" Jubal asked.

"Price per ton is now less than when he borrowed," Stubbs replied, regarding himself in a full-length mirror. "I'm making that spread. The man is cash short—it's not the only bet he's lost this season—and the brig's worth the *Cerbin Flanigan* plus the spread. I offered a trade. He's not out of pocket, no cash transaction to tax, and he gets a schooner that'll run the Cuban coast better than that brig. I get a ship that can go direct to Liverpool with Mobile cotton."

"He still loses several thousand!" Lester objected.

Truette Stubbs nodded. "He'd lost that already, and it's another lesson for y'all. *Your first loss is your smallest loss*. You take a hit, take it. Holding for better days prolongs the pain, makes it worse. You might not like losing an arm, but if it's torn up you got a choice: your arm or you."

The young men looked a little sheepish, like they'd stumbled in something a bit too big for them. Truette Stubbs pointed in the mirror. "Just watch yourselves," he smiled. "Best keep that in mind, shortly."

They walked through a semitropical portrait of spring, startling in its contrast to New York and Philadelphia. Slanting sunlight caressed pastel-colored buildings and refracted off fragrant city streets abloom with dogwood and magnolia. A faint, warm breeze rustled off the Gulf. Lester carried several fine silk bolts, and Jubal some crinolines without obvious embarrassment, both gratefully enchanted with the gorgeous Southern weather. Any shadows of a mulatto woman and her child lay far upriver, beyond the realm of concern.

Truette Stubbs stopped before a storefront, tossed his cigar into the street, and discreetly struck the knocker. Jubal craned his neck to the read the sign above the door, whispering to Lester. "*Tout le Monde* ... Fine tailoring for the woman of distinction." Almost immediately, a peephole snapped sharply.

"*Oh, mon dieu*, Monsieur Tru-ehhta!" The door flew open to reveal a middle-aged woman who looked like her head carried a wasp's nest. "*Chèri! Viens m'embrasser!*" She barely hugged him while kissing both cheeks with a flourish. Lester noticed that despite the loud display, her glossy lips never touched the man's skin.

"Gentlemen, may I present Madame Françine Giroude," Stubbs bowed, "proprietress of this fine establishment, seamstress par excellence. My associates, Mr. Jubal Calhoun, Mr. Lester Norton, most recently arrived in Mobile with merchandise that may be of interest."

"Ah *chèri*, such bew'tiful young men," Madame Giroude gushed. Jubal nodded but Lester bowed and kissed her hand, adding a barely audible click of his heels.

"Such marvelous hands!" the woman purred. "Do you play ze harpsichord?"

Lester gulped. "Nope ... ah ... No m'am, I don't. Sorry to say." Madame Giroude looked at him with her head slightly cocked, as though inspecting a horse. Her face was powdered, with rouged cheeks and lips. A beauty mark dotted her lower jaw and another lay on her shoulder, exposed by the dress that ended just above an ample bosom.

"Ohhh, *donnez-moi, s'il vous plaît,*" she cooed, keeping hold of Lester's hand. "*Les* taffeta silk, ah ... *très bien*, is *Chine?*"

"The finest in Canton, m'am," Jubal offered, remembering their first trip to the Pearl River on *Flying Cloud* and thanking Eleanor Creesy yet again for all the lessons she had given them. In New York he had followed Sally's suggestion and gone shopping in Chinatown.

Madame Giroude fingered the material, clearly knowing fabric and her business. "I think maybe Zhauzan, *non?*" she replied. "No ze best, but ... *très bien.*" She held the silk high to the window light, but not satisfied, then bent low to examine it, offering a voluptuous chasm that nearly made Lester swoon.

"What is ze price ...?" inquired Madame Giroude as she straightened. The blood had pooled in her throat and chest like a morning rose.

"Well ... ah," Lester's tongue knotted. "Whatever you ..."

"Forty dollars a bolt," Jubal replied, crisply.

Madame Giroude looked from one to the other. "Which is ze man?" she asked, pursing her lips.

"We're partners m'am," Jubal replied. "But I'm the authority on fabric, so ..."

Lester looked to him as if he were a lunatic.

"Two crates, thirty bolts and fifteen crinolines per crate, m'am," Jubal continued. "Twenty dollars for the whalebone, apiece. Three thousand will do it, m'am."

The woman gave him the demure smile of a panther, turned with a flourish and walked several steps to a tall cabinet. Her dress was cut to the middle of her back.

Madame Giroude beckoned the men as she poured liqueur. After toasting, she sipped while turning her full attention to Jubal. The smile was still radiant but by her eyes he knew she had marked him as an adversary. Lester quaffed the liqueur.

"I will conzider ..." The woman turned to Lester. "Ze colours ... how many like zis?" She motioned to the bolts he carried; Jubal had picked ones Lester wouldn't have chosen but he liked them now. Lemon yellow, peach, a gauzy purple, and emerald—each was vivid and rich.

"Oh, 'bout dozen in all, wouldn't you say, Jubal?" Lester didn't have a clue.

"Fourteen," Jubal replied.

"I needs to zee all colours, and ze price ees *très grande, mais possible*," Madame Giroude decided, in a manner that spoke finality. "*S'il vous plaît, demain*, at ten hours, you will bring all ze silk, no? *Oui, très bien! Moment, excusez-moi*." She walked like a graceful pendulum into her office.

Moments later Madame Giroude returned, offering Truette Stubbs her hand. He graciously bowed, as did Jubal. Lester bent low, kissing her hand, and she laughed lightly, pressing her other hand to his before seeing her guests from the shop.

~

The men walked in silence for several blocks before Truette Stubbs suggested they stop at a tavern for rum and Cuban cigars. They had barely seated themselves before Jubal turned to his friend.

"That note she slipped you is probably a nice little invitation to get your eyes screwed backside your head. Wouldn't you think, Truette?"

"I'd have to read to been sure," Stubbs replied, his belly shaking.

"Bastards, both you," Lester said, thrusting a hand into his pocket. He had walked as though his arm was wooden, trying to conceal its contents.

"Just make it plain you ain't negotiating with your dick," Jubal said, with a touch of envy. "Perhaps be best if you tell the lady afterwards, or you might not get no forwards. Don't know why she took such a shine to your slobber, though I'd wager you're in for a ride."

"Truette?" Lester had had enough of the ribbing. "What's the deal with this brig?"

"Deal?" Stubbs replied, all merriment vanishing.

Lester drummed his fingers on the table and took a slug of rum, clicking the glass down. "Jubal and I—you can ram in here anytime, Jubal—we're thinking of starting a company, selling shares in it. Doubt we could get a bank to finance us, but we've got a plan, maybe approach several men, investors. We're hoping you'd be one."

"Y'all want to buy the brig, I'll carry your paper, is that it?" Stubbs asked.

"We're thinking, yes," Lester replied.

"Where's the principal coming from?"

"Our own funds, plus what we could raise in New York, Boston, and Liverpool, hopefully. It would take us a bit of time, and firstly we needed to discuss with you. But she's your ship, what do you intend?"

"Makes no sense selling the brig against paper," Stubbs replied, tightly, "to young fellows who've never commanded before. Now over the years, I have developed a fair bit of trust in y'all's ability to conduct yourselves appropriate, keep your word, make good business decisions, and get things done as necessary. But y'all are crawling now, about to walk. And thinking you can run." He stared at Jubal and Lester in turn.

The young men flushed, feeling like they'd been spanked. The business scheme that Lester had spent so much time refining suddenly seemed presumptuous and riddled with assumptions. Stubbs' brutal honesty was a bitter pill, but not unfair; Lester and Jubal knew they had overreached.

Truette Stubbs could read them like a newspaper. "It is fine to be ambitious, you fellows. Just be clear of your capabilities—therein lies your credibility." He leaned forward. "Now here's a deal. Value of the brig is about twenty thousand. I'll offer you each ten percent interest for two thousand, individually or jointly, as y'all choose. Additionally, you put in another two thousand dollars operating capital, man the ship under *my* captain, for which you get ten percent per man direct interest in the cargo—profit *and* loss—apart from the five percent brokering of other material, as the case or opportunity arises."

"Your captain?" Jubal asked.

Stubbs replied. "Y'all got good heads, but you're green, and don't forget it. Pride's an essential thing in a man, long's he knows its limitations."

⌒

Lester stared at the ceiling as Françine snored softly into his shoulder. A delicious waft of perfume and sweat brought a languorous smile, and he decided that forever after, the smell of fish would remind him of waking after sex the night before. Alternately tender, adroit, acrobatic, and frenzied, the woman had raked Lester's back, locked him in the vise of her legs while he held the wrought iron bed to stay mounted, and buried her nipples in his face as she urged him to gallop. He lay exhausted, emptied four times, stunned at the wanton power of a carnal woman. As he drifted off to sleep, Lester's only regret—if he could call it that—was the fear that forever after no woman would hold a candle to Madame Giroude.

Late the next morning, the contents of three crates were strewn about the shop. Jubal and Madame Giroude haggled, the young man stubborn as a mule, the woman demonstrative, loud, and by turns coy and viperish. Occasionally, she would smile sweetly at Lester, but for the most part, she ignored him.

At midday the boys walked into the Bank of Alabama with Madame Giroude's draft. The Frenchwoman had completely emptied their crates, fingered the goods until every single item was strewn throughout the shop, and finally, after several tantrums, told Jubal to take her price or collect all the material and get out.

"She better be good for this twenty-four hundred," Jubal snarled, "or I'm going to pay her another visit and burn that goddam shop to the ground. Shit, barely made ten percent for all that messing round."

Lester thought it prudent to keep silent.

"Good thing we're going upriver. Give me time get my bearings," Jubal ranted. "Some dumb bastard tries to drive a hard deal now I'll liable shoot him in the knees. Gawddam it. What time we leaving?"

"Two," Lester replied. Truette Stubbs had instructed them to meet at the riverboat wharf for the overnight trip upriver to Gee's Bend. The final transaction for Cora would take place at the Pettaway plantation.

The bank draft did clear, mollifying Jubal slightly, though he took two shots of whiskey and smoked a cigar before and after lunch. He had stopped talking, and Lester kept quiet.

Jubal didn't loosen until Mobile lay astern, simmering in the wake of the riverboat as it chuffed upriver. Truette Stubbs stood beside them at the taffrail watching the green jungle close in on either bank.

"So Lester," Jubal turned, his voice a syrupy drawl. "Do you play ze harpsichord?"

Lester reached in his pocket and pulled out three Cuban cigars, lighting his companions' before getting his own going well and regarding it lovingly. "No, can't say that I do." He smiled and blew a smoke ring. "Though I did have one hell of a lesson."

Chapter Forty-Five

An overhead fan did little to lift the oppressive, late-afternoon humidity on the verandah of Mark Pettaway's stately plantation, Sandy Hill. Lester sat at the edge of the circle, his wet shirt clinging as if half-laundered. Rivulets of sweat burned his eyes and he fought the urge to scratch an itchy crotch.

Jubal and Truette Stubbs seemed unmindful of the heat. Across a low, tulipwood table, neither Mark Pettaway nor his lawyer, William Oates, took any notice either. Lester forced himself to stay awake and alert, though he most wanted to take a nap. Erotic dreams and the riverboat engine's huffing had deprived him of two nights' sleep so the torpid, inland heat made him drowsy and boring conversation didn't help. The men casually meandered around the perimeter of politics and local news.

Trying to stay awake, Lester concentrated on Pettaway and Oates, as different as two men could be. The plantation owner was a quintessential Southern gentleman, silver-haired, gracious, and courtly, attentive to the comfort of his guests. Mint juleps and pastries littered the table.

Oates was the complex opposite. A newly admitted member of the Alabama bar, the young man looked only a few years older than Lester or Jubal. While he projected a professional reserve in the presence of his client, Lester suspected this was affected. Occasional, reptilian eye movements and a pulse at his temple insinuated deeper traits. The older men dominated conversation. Pettaway and Truette Stubbs discussed the sugar business, trading gossip, and impressions of the commercial climate.

"You find it an acceptable level of risk?" Pettaway asked, with polite skepticism. "My experience with Spaniards has not been positive. Words get slippery, and a contract may evolve contrary to the understanding—nothing's quite clear or for sure. Damned unfortunate when a man's hand cannot reflect his word."

"Havana's often a jumble of promises and intent," Stubbs agreed. "Of course, it doesn't help when Louisiana Cajuns like Pierre Soulé run off to Ostend, Belgium, and come up with a damn fool manifesto saying Cuba's part of America's 'inevitable destiny.' Spain doesn't take kindly to our ambition when it conflicts with hers. Can't say I blame 'em."

"You don't think Cuba ought be brought in as a slave territory?" Pettaway asked, an edge to his voice. "By God, if those Kansas John Browns have their rein ... Sir, I say it's damn difficult to protect our way of life when the federal government is in the hands of politicians dedicated to our oblivion! An elected representative of the U.S. Congress sentences to hell the hardworking men who produce upwards of fifty million dollars of cotton each year, the taxes on which support those same rapacious sons-a-bitches in Congress. The time is coming when it's either stand for the rights of free men or succumb to a tyranny of the bare majority. Why, we fought for that cause eighty years ago!"

"And we'll do again, sir," William Oates interjected.

Lester's drowsiness vanished. He glanced over to the far corner of the porch. Sitting with his back to the table, a small coal-black, silver-haired man worked a cord that ran to the fan above them. The slave tugged at the cord with numbing regularity, wafting the muggy air as if in time to some perfect, internal rhythm, apparently unmindful of the white men's discussion.

"Let us hope it does not come to that impasse, gentlemen," said Stubbs, locking fingers across his belly. "The chief justice recently ordained that Dred Scott be remanded and the fugitive slave laws have been widely observed in the North. There's cause to believe reason will prevail."

"Do you, sir," Pettaway raised his eyebrows, "believe slave and free states are not ultimately, inevitably impermeable—that the juxtaposition of such diametrical viewpoints is not irreconcilable?"

"Disputes are part of life," Stubbs shrugged. "But threatened suicide is hardly an effective negotiating posture."

"I beg your pardon, sir!" blurted Oates. He backed off just as suddenly. Lester watched him, now convinced his intuitive sense was accurate.

"An agrarian society, which is what slavery has induced, is no match for an industrialized competitor," Stubbs maintained, his own voice hardening. "I am as passionate as any man regarding a way of life, the freely expressed and realized conduct of society, and especially for the freedom of trade, which is under such constant threat, be it in Havana, Madrid, or Washington. However and notwithstanding, virtually *every* material thing that enables Mr. Pettaway to plant and harvest a cotton crop comes from the North or abroad. I defy y'all to go into a store in Mobile and outfit yourself for *any* manner of undertaking with goods manufactured south of

Mason-Dixon. Fact is, our rhetoric flourishes theatrical, while our conduct remains obtuse."

"Perhaps ..." Mark Pettaway said. "Dred Scott may, in fact, portend a rational appreciation for property. Perhaps it will make Whitmill Rivens' work more effective."

The overhead fan stuttered. Every eye went to Mark Pettaway, but the planter's face was a mask.

"I see ..." Truette Stubbs pondered the remark. "May I ask if this pertains in any way to the business at hand?"

"As a matter of fact, yes," Pettaway countered. "Which is why I've invited Mr. Oates here today. Given the condition of my acquisition of the niggah woman in question, I thought it only fair to allow Mr. Rivens the repurchase of his former property should he wish to do so. Such has been the case, as conveyed by mail to Mr. Oates. Mr. Rivens is often North, engaged in the recovery of property unlawfully absent its rightful owner."

Lester and Jubal glanced at each other. The news that Rivens had become a slave bounty hunter was noxious, but fit.

"And who, sir, are you representing?" Stubbs asked Oates, his voice so even Lester knew he was furious.

"Nominally, Mr. Rivens," Oates replied, "though at the suggestion of Mr. Pettaway, I'm here as an observer."

"To observe the execution of our agreement?" Stubbs asked.

"Mr. Pettaway has informed you of Mr. Rivens' intent, sir," Oates answered stiffly.

"I need not remind you, sir, the parameters of contract law?" Stubbs replied. "We are not in Cuba, sir. Three years ago I accepted an *irrevocable* option to purchase—my option—for which I paid as per the letter of the contract. Is there anything about the word 'irrevocable' that is unclear? Sir?"

Oates flushed and gritted his teeth, but didn't answer. Stubbs turned from him with the iron face of dismissal.

"Mr. Pettaway, according to my calculations—I have them here for your perusal—the balance due for the niggah woman Cora and her child is four hundred and ninety-seven dollars." Truette Stubbs passed over a sheet that listed the financial data in his careful, flowing script. "Here is my draft for that amount. I beg to conclude this matter on terms agreed and my associates will accept possession of my property forthwith. And thanking you in advance for your hospitality, we shall take our leave."

"Mr. Stubbs," Pettaway replied, all pretense of gentility cast aside, "I have given my word to Mr. Rivens—and I intend to keep it!"

"Just how many words do you have, sir?" Stubbs snapped. "I, too, have your word, and your hand, and your signature!" He leaned forward and raised a finger slightly. "Mr. Pettaway, sir, I intend to enforce this contract. I will not resort to untoward persuasion, but should I be forced to leave due to the rupture of your solemn commitment, I make one of my own, sir. As the Lord is witness, I will return with the sheriff to claim what is rightfully mine. Thereupon, I shall commence to subject you to every available stricture the laws of the state of Alabama afford me. I declare before these present, sir, that I shall not rest before justice is addressed. *And served.*"

Truette Stubbs stood. Jubal and Lester abruptly rose with him. Mark Pettaway remained seated, his face impassive.

"Mr. Rivens knows where to find me," Truette Stubbs lowered his voice. "I've no doubt your agreement with him was made in good faith, and he may negotiate with me in similar fashion or address whatever grievances he endures through the courts. Perhaps Mr. Oates can advise him in this regard, having been 'observer' to this transaction. If you would be so kind, I do believe prompt action will allow us to board the evening boat downriver, directly."

Mark Pettaway took a deep breath. Though galled at Stubbs' adroit suggestion, the planter was no fool. Standing, he bowed slightly. "Very well," he said, accepting the plausible retreat from his untenable position. "I shall refer Mr. Rivens to your office."

Calling to the old manservant, he curtly ordered him to bring the "niggah woman, Cora."

The old Negro shuffled off the verandah and across the yard to some outbuildings a hundred yards away. Several minutes of silence ensued, broken only when Truette Stubbs brought some cigars out of his pocket and passed them around. Another servant appeared with glasses and brandy. Without a word, Pettaway poured. Stubbs pulled out a document and handed it to Pettaway. The planter looked it over, then went into the house and returned a minute later, handing the document back. Stubbs checked the signature and, satisfied, returned it to his coat.

Jubal and Lester saw her at the same time. She was barefoot, taller than they remembered, with her hair tied in a bandanna. One hand carried a satchel; in the other arm Cora held a small tan boy who hid his face in her neck, sucking his thumb.

Truette Stubbs offered his hand to Pettaway and then to Oates, who hesitated before taking the handshake. Jubal and Lester followed Stubbs' lead. Truette Stubbs raised his brandy glass and all followed suit.

"Gentlemen," he proposed, "may we live long and prosperous." Downing the brandy in one gulp, he pulled on his hat and tipped it to Mark Pettaway before descending to the front yard. Jubal and Lester followed and met Cora as she came directly to the wagon they had rented at the river landing. She gave no sign of recognition. Jubal reached for the child, who squirmed, but Cora whispered something in his ear and he relented. After Lester helped her into the wagon bed, Jubal made to pass the child.

"The boy stays!" William Oates folded his arms.

There was a moment of complete stillness marred only by buzzing flies. Then Cora snatched her child from Jubal, hugging the little boy tight.

Truette Stubbs vaulted off the wagon seat and strode directly at Oates. The young lawyer's eyes widened and he readied himself. Jubal's hand crept inside his coat. Mark Pettaway looked mortified.

"Is the boy your property?" Truette Stubbs seethed, his face six inches from Oates.

"No sir," the younger man didn't flinch. "However ..."

Stubbs turned away contemptuously and addressed the planter. "Mr. Pettaway, a word with you, sir. In private, if you will." Without waiting, Stubbs walked to the end of the verandah and stood gazing over the fields.

Pettaway couldn't ignore a gentleman's request. He walked over and waited, frowning until Stubbs turned to him. Only the low, unintelligible whisper of a conversation reached the boys, and since the planter obscured Stubbs, neither Lester nor Jubal could tell who was talking. Suddenly, Truette Stubbs extended his hand. It hung suspended for a moment before Pettaway's own hand rose, palsied with tension, and the two man shook. Stubbs immediately walked back to the boys.

"Let's go!" he said, ignoring Oates and briskly striding to the wagon. The boys trotted after him and jumped in, Lester grabbing the reins. Cora sat behind in the bed with the little one in her lap. The wagon wheeled out of the yard and onto the road that led down to the river landing. No one looked back.

They were silent for perhaps a mile before Lester cleared his throat. "Just what did you say, sir?" he asked. "If you don't mind me asking?" Jubal listened intently, glad for once that his friend could never keep quiet long.

"Offered him six hundred for the boy," Truette Stubbs replied. "That's the high side of fair for a niggah child, though he's close on being an octaroon if the man Rivens is his father. Don't doubt but we ain't heard the last of this."

"How will you pay Pettaway?" Lester asked.

"Told him I'd settle when the crop's in," Stubbs replied mildly. "Deduct as necessary."

A smile came over Lester's face and he glanced at his friend.

Jubal didn't quite get it. "You gonna trade, or something?"

"No," Stubbs said, "just credit his account. Y'all weren't 'round at planting, but there was a fair bit of rain—fact is, a little too much. So the crop's going to be off some, even with these fine conditions rest of the summer. Like a lot of men, Pettaway sells futures against his crop so he'll have cash to operate. I bought a fair few; they're commercial paper and get traded. I told him we'd settle when his crop—my crop—lands in Mobile."

Lester could only shake his head in admiration.

Chapter Forty-Six

By the stars it was an hour before dawn, but Jubal couldn't sleep, restlessness bringing him on deck.

Just as unsettled, Lester joined him at the taffrail high above the riverboat's prow, after checking that Cora and her child slept safely among cotton bales two decks below. "What are you looking at?"

The half-moon had already set and only a lighter shadow of darkness revealed the serpentine back of the river against black riverbanks. In the deepest part of the night, aside from its pilot and a few deckhands, the boat slept.

"Libra," Jubal replied. "Can't quite tell if I'm seeing Zuben Elgenubi or Eschamali, one the two."

"You plotting a course?" Lester asked, amused, knowing Jubal could find any of the fifty-six navigational stars.

"No. But we ought to," Jubal murmured, the darkness hushing all sound save the rhythmic strokes of the paddle wheel astern.

Lester sighed, having no idea what to do. "Well, we're in for another six hundred, but I guess that's just the way of it. Sal said she'd help."

"Sally didn't know nothing about a child," Jubal pointed out. "We going to just send her up to Philadelphia, let her fend for herself? Lester, that woman probably's never been more than ten, fifteen miles from Gee's Bend. I doubt she knows how to read or figure. Not even sure she knows much about money. Truette Stubbs hasn't said anything, but I can tell what he's thinking. He done his part, kept his word, and now it's up to us. We started this—how we going to finish it?"

Lester threw up his hands. "I'll telegraph Sal. We've got a ship with cargo and ought to be feeling lucky. They're calling this the panic of '57, depression that'll affect the whole country, maybe Europe too."

The boys fell silent for several minutes.

"I hope Truette's captain ain't a imbecile," Jubal said, disappointment evident in his voice. Though young, his confidence had embroidered potential ownership of the brig into his first command.

"We got a little ahead of ourselves," Lester replied, knowing his friend. "Lauchlan McKay or Josiah Creesy would have laughed at us pitching them shares. We need a few more years under our belts, then buy the brig from Truette and start a shipping company. That's what we know—leastways, what we're learning."

Jubal reached for his pipe. "I'm more concerned about the here and now. We gonna free a niggah woman carryin' an infant? To what? Just put her on a steamer to New York, call it good, wish 'em the best? Land sakes, Lester, you remember your first time in New York? She'll barely make it a block from South Street before the pimps close in!"

"If we go north with Cora, we'll miss the ship," Lester objected. "Truette intends the brig's going direct to Liverpool soon as she's loaded."

"I was present," Jubal growled, "so there t'is. Take care of ourselves or take care of her and that kid. I don't see one doing the other."

"That was your choice, too," Lester said.

"I know, dammit!" Jubal lit his pipe but it didn't settle him. "Was three years ago, 'n best of intentions. Now it's a long row to hoe."

"What do you want to do," Lester huffed, "send her back so she can be some other white man's pallet?"

Jubal's voice lowered in warning. "Don't wave that savior shit at me, Lester Norton. We give our word to Truette and we'll keep it. That doesn't mean it ain't messy."

Lester studied the embers flickering from the riverboat stack and disappearing into the inky night. Cora's manumission gave them stark options: either shepherd her north or continue their own course and hope she survived without them. Lester knew that his friend's anger stemmed from absence of choice.

"We'll sort it out," he said, though the pledge sounded hollow.

Jubal grunted and smoked his pipe, waiting for the first sign of dawn.

The riverboat docked at Mobile's quay in early afternoon. Truette Stubbs directed Lester to see Cora home while Jubal accompanied him down to the waterfront. Stubbs had seen the silhouette of the brig in the inner roads and wanted to get aboard immediately to inform the captain that at his direction Jubal would ship out as first mate with Lester as carpenter's mate.

Lester hired a livery cab and stopped at the post office to telegraph his sister. Cora hadn't said more than half a dozen words since they'd left Gee's Bend and the boy would not let go of her for a moment. Lester found their presence disconcerting, as if he suddenly had new appendages that he could no more leave behind than his elbows. He had tried making small talk but Cora stayed nearly mum, though she never stopped examining her surroundings. Lester couldn't tell if she was fascinated or overwhelmed.

Only when they reached Stubbs' house and Cora met Ezekiel and Louisa did she relax, as though the black couple extended an instantaneous, unspoken bond the moment mother and child appeared. Louisa reached for the boy and he opened his arms to her without a sound.

"Wha's yo' name, boy?" Ezekiel asked.

"S'all right," Cora said to her son, "go 'head ..."

"Curtis," the tiny voice whispered. The boy turned away and gnawed on a hand.

"Curtis," Ezekiel repeated with a wide grin, "dat be a fine name. Bet you're a fine boy, too. C'mon, Curtis, I'll show you a nice bed to rest. Must be tired." The boy's face trembled but his mother pointed to the old man and nodded. Louisa set the boy down and Curtis reached for the man's extended hand, then, with a backward glance at his mother, padded away behind Ezekiel.

Lester went on the porch to smoke a cigar. He watched the afternoon sun settle, waiting for Jubal, but before long his restlessness pushed him into Truette's library, where he borrowed some paper before returning to the porch. Ezekiel appeared later, bearing a pitcher of lemonade and a flask of rum. By the time Truette and Jubal returned, Lester had filled his sheet with calculations and settled back to enjoy the gaining twilight.

"What'd you roll in?" Lester asked.

"The ship's hold," Jubal replied. "The brig's called the *Regina Menegario*, and I guess she'll stay that way 'cause Truette wants to keep her on the Havana registry. Thought he'd do Mobile or New York, but he said he liked it offshore. Peculiar, you ask me. She's going to run back to Havana tomorrow noon, I'll deliver the ownership papers to the registry, provision there—it'll be cheaper in Havana—then head for Liverpool. Our friend James Baines is doing the landing there. Damn small world."

Lester nodded, taking a swallow of rum.

Truette Stubbs came onto the porch and placed several documents on the table. In his other hand, he carried a decanter made from thick, ornamented glass.

"Option release, bill of sale, manumission papers, bond," the older man said, "that should be it." He gestured to the decanter. "Some celebratory brandy, a present from my father-in-law, which I've been sipping over thirty years."

Stubbs carefully poured three rounds and then replaced the stopper with almost religious concentration. "You must properly seat this, right off," he explained. "Wine wants to breathe some but this brandy don't like the air. Never, ever leave her open, no sir. That's why she's been so fine all these years." He smiled at the decanter, as if it held a treasure trove of memories.

"There's a fellow coming by for dinner tonight," Stubbs continued, "who might be able to assist. Gustavas Horton, been in Mobile near on twenty years, though I think originally he's from Syracuse, or up that way. Raised his family here, couple of fine boys and a girl, around the same age as you. Horton's a merchant and a lawyer, goes to New York several times a year. I believe he is heading there later this week."

"You think he'd accompany Cora?" Jubal asked.

"You don't ask, you don't get," Truette replied. "He's a good man, headed that direction, his wife likely going also. Got someone who'll meet the niggah woman?"

"Sally will take her in, one way or another," Lester replied. "No doubt there, unless her situation's changed."

"Ain't that doubt?" Jubal queried.

Lester looked at Truette, feeling a little mellow from the rum.

"Jubal's got a case of buyer's remorse."

"Go to hell, Lester," Jubal groaned. "Now then, admit a distance between plans and results. Same as expecting a fair season sail to Liverpool and getting the snot kicked out of you in mid-ocean, storm blows up hard. That's all I mean. Regardless, I'll feel better when that woman leaves Mobile astern."

Both Truette and Lester stared at him.

"Rivens," Jubal answered quietly. "Believe you're right, Truette. Ain't seen the last of this."

They were mulling his comment when Gustavas Horton and his wife came through the fence gate.

By the time the Hortons left close to nine o'clock, Lester was almost asleep on his feet. Jubal excused himself as they departed, saying he needed to check on the final disposition of cargo at the wharf and didn't expect to return for a few hours.

Twenty minutes later, he was at the waterfront. The night was still and the cooling land sent a soft, warm breeze seaward. Looking across the inner roads from the city wharf, Jubal made out the brig's masthead lantern before he hailed the night watchman, flipping him a coin before setting off in a harbor punt.

Vessels cluttered the inner roads, swinging to the wind and outgoing tide like a brood of gigantic ducks. Jubal looked them over briefly, mentally matching rigs to the maritime listings at the cotton exchange. Most were shuttling the Atlantic from American ports on the eastern seaboard or northern Europe, though a few had come in from China or India. Mobile was a hinge on which the entire Alabama economy swung, from the plantations outward to the world coming in.

The moon had set when Jubal finished roaming the ship, crawling along the hold to inspect stacks of cotton bales for any sign they might shift in a seaway and checking every lashing on the deck hatches. Rowing back to the wharf by starlight, he slowed several hundred feet from the *Regina Menegario*, to regard her dark shadow. The brig was diminutive compared to a clipper ship, but he had no doubt she would teach him.

Shortly after eleven he returned, coming in through the alley and side yard of the house. To his surprise, the back door at the kitchen pantry was locked. He was about to knock but thought better of it, not wanting to make a disturbance. Suddenly feeling very tired, he trudged around the block and came up to the front gate, hoping Lester would be waiting on the porch with some brandy and a cigar.

The porch was empty and dark, though a light showed in the curtained parlor window. Jubal opened the front door slowly and stood in the entry hall listening. The house was still, utterly silent.

Jubal glanced back to the porch. One of the chairs was a bit askew; he noticed a half-smoked cigar lying on the porch beside it. Shutting the door quietly, he walked across to the parlor, muting his boot heels on the marble tile. The parlor door was ajar; he knocked lightly.

"Y'all may enter," Truette Stubbs' voice called. Jubal stood for a moment, weighing the plural y'all'. Now taut as a leopard, Jubal gently pushed the door open halfway.

Stubbs sat in an easy chair, still dressed for dinner, his face in shadow from the lamplight at his shoulder. As the door opened he reached for the elegant brandy decanter on a side table next to him. Withdrawing the stopper, he poured a small amount in a goblet and set the decanter back down. Stubbs carefully raised and passed the stopper to his other hand, twisting it slightly so the cut glass sparkled against the light, before he set the tapered bulb on the table with a soft, deliberate *click,* the tapered end askew, pointing behind the open door. With his free hand, he slowly raised the goblet and sipped his brandy, eyes unblinking as he stared at Jubal.

Never, ever leave her open, no sir.

Jubal took a step forward and violently kicked the door. A split-second later an abrupt crash, and then thud, rattled the room. Ducking into a crouch, Jubal charged in, wheeling to catch sight of Cora standing wide-eyed in front of the fireplace, Lester splayed prone and motionless at her feet. Wheeling past the door, Jubal rushed fast and low at Whitmill Rivens, going for the short double-barreled shotgun the man held in one hand. He grasped Cora's boy Curtis by the neck with the other hand.

Rivens had tried to twist away as the door smashed open but it had caught his shoulder and he staggered, groping to regain his balance. The boy was frozen with fear, stumbling as Rivens moved backward. Cora leaped for a porcelain vase on the fireplace mantle.

Jubal went at Rivens and knew instantly the shotgun would level faster than he could reach it. With a snarl, the taller man kicked at the child and got the gun loose just as Cora hurled the vase. Rivens ducked but the vase clipped the top of his head, knocking his hat off and giving Jubal the extra fraction of a second to dive at the barrel and push it aside as Rivens pulled a trigger.

The deafening blast shattered the door panel and spun Rivens from the recoil. Jubal slammed him in the gut with a shoulder and kept moving, oblivious to Rivens' free hand chopping at his neck. Bulling the man backward, Jubal sunk his teeth into Rivens' wrist with such ferocity that he could feel bones break in his bite. With a howl of pain, Rivens dropped the shotgun and clawed at Jubal's face as both men toppled over a chair and into the doorway that led to Truette Stubbs' library.

Cora snatched up her boy and fled toward the entryway, throwing Curtis at Ezekiel as the old man appeared behind the splintered door. She turned frantically to see Jubal and Rivens roll out of the parlor and into the library. The library door slammed, kicked shut by one of the men as they thrashed into the room. Cora looked to Truette Stubbs, who opened a small drawer in the side table and pulled out a pistol. He stared at the library door, his jaw clenching with the sounds of breaking furniture.

A sudden crash wheeled Cora's attention back toward the library. She spotted the shotgun and lunged for it, cocking both hammers, and then leveled it at the library door as silence again claimed the house. Holding her breath, she stared at the door handle, waiting.

Time seemed to stand still. Truette Stubbs pointed his pistol at the library door while he took another sip of brandy. On the floor by the fireplace, Lester moaned and stirred. Cora glanced at him but whipped back to the doorway as the handle moved.

The knob turned slowly, tentatively, until the library door swung open. Jubal stood wavering, bleeding from gouges on his face and chest. His shirt hung in shreds. A scarlet bubble popped at one nostril and he spit out a tooth.

Cora looked beyond him to the man lying on his back. In two long strides she reached Jubal and yanked him past her. He nearly pitched forward but managed to stay upright, dazed and staring at the floor as Cora stepped into the library.

Whitmill Rivens groaned, and tried to raise himself on an elbow. His nose was smashed and one eye had already swollen shut. He stopped as his other eye focused on the two black holes staring at him. Cora kicked the door shut behind her.

A hammer snapping on an empty chamber rang from the library. Moments later, the shotgun blast shook pictures and rattled china.

Nothing moved until the library door opened again. Cora strode out, thrust the gun at Jubal, and went to find her son.

As Lester stirred, Truette Stubbs moved quickly to the doorway, ready to fire his pistol. He stood momentarily and then lowered the gun. Jubal leaned the shotgun against the shattered door and staggered to Lester, hauling him to his feet. They looked at each other numbly, until a scratching sound registered. Truette Stubbs, back in his chair, scribbled furiously. Stubbs finished the note, reread it, nodded, tossed down the last of the brandy and called to Ezekiel as he stood. The old man appeared almost instantly.

"Get Louisa in here," Stubbs ordered. "Then fetch the boys' things."

Ezekiel darted out and Stubbs moved to Lester, taking him by the cheek and checking the bloody scalp where Rivens had clubbed him with the gun butt.

"Hard-headed one, ain't you?" Stubbs muttered. He looked Jubal over, gave him his handkerchief, and then went back into the library. Jubal sponged his bloody nose, trying to jam the tooth back into his jaw though he looked as if two fingers could topple him. Several drawers clattered onto the library floor before Truette Stubbs reappeared with a leather folio. Louisa came into the parlor.

"Lester, listen to me!" Stubbs looked closely to make sure he was lucid. "Here! Ship's papers, manifest, some cash. Ezekiel'll get you to the wharf. I've ordered the captain to leave immediately. Twelve hours early, tide ought to be close. The law's going to be coming shortly to investigate this here attempted robbery, and you two are complicating factors I don't need. Send word from Havana."

"Rivens?" Lester whispered.

"There ought be enough to recognize."

Jubal staggered over to the desk and taking the tapered crystal, carefully stoppered the brandy.

Truette Stubbs nodded grimly, then pointed to the door as Louisa took Lester and Jubal by the arms. "Y'all go. Now!"

Chapter Forty-Seven

Philadelphia, July 1857

Sally Norton fanned herself against the afternoon humidity while waiting for a break in the wagon traffic that jammed the street. She darted across and into a small store to buy a bag of hard candy for Curtis. The shy boy couldn't resist the sweets Sally used to tempt an opening into his confidence.

She had never known a child so careful with adults, and despite seeing him every week, Curtis still treated her warily. Sally's heart went out to the boy. She could only imagine how stunning the change must be from life on a plantation to a large, bustling city. At least the heat must be familiar, she thought, wiping her brow.

She made her way into a neighborhood of good homes where the tree-lined streets were narrow and free of horse manure. The city bustle quieted and birds darted overhead, disappearing into the foliage. Sally turned up a short cul-de-sac that looked like a tunnel carved from the canopy of elm trees and came through the gate at William Still's house.

Cora answered the door wearing a simple cotton dress that nearly touched the floor, half covered by a white apron. As usual, her hair was pulled back in a bun, and she still walked around the house barefoot, although Sally figured a northern winter would change that habit. Tucking a wisp of hair behind her ear, Cora ushered Sally in without a word.

Cora looked remarkably settled, considering all that she had been through. Lester's letters had described the unexpected situation, but Sally was not prepared for Gustavas Horton's telegram announcing Cora's imminent arrival. In a panic, Sally had gone to Lucretia Mott, who read the telegram and immediately penned a note, directing Sally to William Still's home forthwith.

"Mrs. Still's pregnancy is advancing," Mrs. Mott explained. "I think this is her fourth, and she will need help. The Stills are no strangers to sudden company." Sally wondered at the enigmatic comment, but said nothing.

William Still had graciously invited Sally in as he scanned Mrs. Mott's note. Of medium height and solidly built beneath a modest suit, Still had a striking face marked by a wide mouth and eyes aligned with the outer edges of a broad, flat nose, giving him the look of a scout or hunter, savvy without being threatening. While he read, Sally noticed the crisp, careful part of his hair and a brilliant white shirt that set off skin the color of cocoa.

"Is she alone?" William Still asked.

"I presume so," Sally stammered. The thought had never occurred to her.

"No matter." Still pocketed the letter. "Would you be so kind as to bring her directly here? I can send a man if you wish."

"Oh no, please don't bother!" Sally blurted. "I'm so grateful you can help! Lester," she went on in a rush, "that's my brother—said she hadn't much schooling and I thought ... well, I could tutor her."

"I doubt she's had any education," William Still replied. "Whatever assistance you could offer would indeed be helpful. Now, if you'll excuse me, m'am, I have guests ... But remember, come directly."

A week later, Gustavas Horton had brought Cora and her son Curtis from Mobile, with a note and one hundred dollars from Lester.

When Sally first saw Curtis at the train station she had to stifle her shock and bewilderment. Mother and son were equally terrified, the boy nearly burrowing under Cora's dress to hide from the crowds. Sally gave an inward snarl at her brother for this surprise, but took Cora's arm and headed into the clamor outside Union Station. In the livery cab, Sally recalled William Still's remark doubting Cora's education so she asked for the manumission paper. Cora handed her an entire packet of documents.

To Sally's great relief, the Still household needed a maid. In brief conversations with Letitia Still, Sally learned that both she and her husband had been born to free families, though some of his brothers were still slaves living in the South.

"His daddy bought freedom," Letitia explained once, "but William's mother escaped and changed her name. She had four children at the time but could only take two. Bore eighteen in all; William's the youngest."

Initially, Cora's silence seemed almost congenital, muteness that only relented when absolutely necessary. Gradually, Sally realized what could be mistaken for shyness was actually Cora's innate character, flavored with a dose of self-consciousness that eased as Sally tutored her twice a week. These lessons included Curtis, though the combination of a wide-eyed child and intent adult woman made for an unusual class. When it came to reading, one had no more experience than the other. To the delight of both women, Curtis loved listening to Sally help Cora read, though his concentration span blew the lesson apart in a half-hour. The boy played freely with the three Still children, all under ten, and with their banter, his speech soon discarded the cadence of Southern slave shacks. Cora's self-consciousness at her plantation speech also diminished as the lessons went into summer.

"I'm not giving any demerits for dem, dis, 'n dees'," Sally had scoffed, "so stop this reticence! The Motts aren't exactly gossipers, and I need someone to carry on a conversation."

The literacy lessons took place in late afternoon while the Still children had their naps and before Cora began cooking the family dinner. Lessons often provided time for the two young women to talk quietly while Cora laboriously traced the alphabet and sounded out words in elementary school books that Sally borrowed from the Motts. Although Sally enjoyed the tutoring, it was also a means to explore Cora's life, and through her, Jubal. Every lesson included several questions about Alabama, especially concerning Cora's family and Curtis's father.

To Sally's consternation, however, Cora was adept at minimalist answers, deftly parrying the questions with an absence of guile that suggested a keen mind. The speed with which Cora learned to read and write—learning in a month the equivalent of a school year—helped her dodge Sally's inquiries by always supplying a new literate question.

"Are you a ..." Cora paused to look at the pamphlet again, "one de Hicksite Quakers? Or orthodox?" Both words required Cora to concentrate. Sally remained quiet until Cora succeeded sounding out the syllables of both Quaker sects.

"I'm not either one," Sally laughed. "Austerity doesn't hold much appeal. Going around with a bonnet is about as dumb as those stovepipe hats men wear, though they court fashion, while women are supposed to express virtue and chastity."

"What's dat—*that*—mean?" Cora asked.

"Polite," Sally sighed. "Not aggressive. Certainly not enticing." She looked sideways at Cora. "Not obviously wanting a man." Sally paused and seemed to be waiting.

Cora held her gaze without blinking.

"Damnation," Sally exclaimed, "you're as bad as Jubal." Her voice dropped to a whisper. "What's it like, really? Is it ...?"

Cora remained silent.

"… Wonderful? No? Bad? Difficult? What?" Sally blushed and let her breath out. "By Jesus, Curtis didn't just drop out! What did you feel? What was his father like?"

Cora's wide nostrils flared. "Dat boy even thinks bein' his daddy, I strike 'im down!"

Sally recoiled.

"Oh, I love him, Curtis, best I can," Cora said, her back straight as a knife blade snapped open, "but you want be took, mounted like a damn mule? Man come at you hard, like to being kicked! Pawin', yankin' my hair whenever he take a fancy, makes no diffunce you be bleeding. The real trade, you want to know? His seed for my blood! Jes' a man's meat, all we is!"

Cora's eyes closed and Sally could see she fought to restrain herself. In the sudden, harsh silence, Cora's jaw started to tremble. Finally, she regarded Sally with glittering eyes.

"Why you want a man?"

Sally licked her lips and swallowed. "I want to be held," she replied. "Lock my legs around a man I believe in, trust. Lucretia Mott might wear a bonnet all day, Letitia Still's got kids pulling her every which way, but look at them! They're strong and resourceful, 'cause they not alone! I watched my momma live alone and wither! Whatever that man did, he gave you a beautiful boy!"

"Give?" Cora flared again, standing. "He *took* every day, taking all he ever knew! 'N take some more!" She nearly shook with rage. "That man killed my mumma!"

Sally held out the pamphlet. "Cora, anger will never bring her back."

"Anger kept me alive!" Cora spat, snatching the paper, "'till I kin …" Her face shuddered.

"Until it kills you!" Sally shot back. "Worse, it'll kill everybody round you, especially that boy! You want him like his daddy, then stay angry! He'll be gone in ten years, just like my brother. Why shouldn't he, living round a nasty, mean-spirited woman picking at her wound because it's more comfortable than healing? Safe, it is. Just keep saying they're all takers, and you won't ever have to give!"

The two women had come toe-to-toe, but suddenly, as if by mutual consent, stepped back. Sally felt lightheaded, almost reeling.

Cora regarded her critically, as if inspecting every inch of her face. "You the first white folk ever treat me human," she said finally, touching Sally's cheek.

The touch brought a tear. "Lester did," Sally whispered.

"Yeah," Cora said, softening. "You right 'bout that. He did. Guess that makes you three—'cause Jubie he always did, too, 'cept nearly once." An image of Gee's Bend whispered by her face on a cloud of memory. "Them boys …" Tears welled and trickled down her cheek. Cora gently touched her face and regarded the moist finger. "First time since Mumma went … 'n I swore never to cry no mo'."

"Then you're started to come back," Sally said.

"A piece, maybe," Cora murmured, "findin' pieces." She took a deep breath. "Let's us read, Sally."

Chapter Forty-Eight

Liverpool, August 1857

Lester sat at the desk in the captain's quarters looking over a copy of the *Regina Menegario*'s bill of sale, dated for the next day, August 4, 1857. Above him, the open skylight caught a zephyr of afternoon sea breeze and he could hear Jubal hollering at the longshoremen on Wapping Dock stacking the last cotton bales coming off the ship.

Truette Stubbs' message awaited them in Liverpool, sent by telegram from Mobile to New York and then carried on the fast packet that arrived three weeks before *Regina*, addressed to them through James Baines' office.

Stubbs' directions were clear and concise: sell the ship.

"He just bought it," fumed Jubal, waving the telegram that James Baines had sent by messenger to the docks.

"They're moving troops out of Crimea," Lester replied, having scanned the newspapers. "Sending 'em to another shitteroo in India, a mutiny of some kind."

Lester knew his friend's indignation was founded in enormous disappointment. For the first time in his life, Jubal had taken command after they left the brig's captain in the Azores at a hospital to recover from malaria, a remnant of their provisioning in Cuba. On the run from Ponta Delgado to Liverpool, Captain Calhoun was never off the quarterdeck for more than a few hours.

James Baines could also read the young man. "That brig is too small for the trade," he said the next day, over lunch in his private dining room. "A fine sentiment to be captain of a small brig rather than mate on the big ships, but there's no romance to trade. Capacity and speed—the money is in how much you carry and how fast."

The Scotsman could see Jubal listening to what he did not want to hear. "You lads are twenty, now?" he asked. "How long to sea?"

"Six years," answered Lester.

"Seven," Jubal said, leaning back. He had little interest in food.

"A few more," Baines observed, "you'll be ready. Stay with the big ships ... with mine, to be exact. Most particularly, McKay's beauties, for you know them intimately. Whitehall has chartered three of my ships to transport British soldiers to Calcutta," Baines continued, finishing his mashers with gusto. "*Champion of the Seas* and the *James Baines* are in Portsmouth, outbound in a week. I'm going there day after tomorrow." Baines pushed his plate away and poured a shot of brandy. "Pity I don't have more McKay clippers. More's the pity that Donald probably be done."

Baines regarded the astonished young men.

"McKay closed his yard. That panic in America devastated the shipping business. No doubt he'll build again in some capacity, but you'll never see the likes of his greatest ships again."

Jubal completely lost his appetite. With a twinge of shame, the dispiriting loss of his command went hollow compared to the unfathomable bitterness Donald McKay must have endured, as everything he ever worked for became irrelevant.

Lester set a full forkful down and his shoulders sagged. The memory of Donald McKay dressed in a fine, sawdust-flexed suit, instructing him how to loft a frame or square the stem, would stay with him forever.

"One man's failure is another's opportunity, gentlemen," James Baines said quietly. "You know McKay's ships and I need you now. The *James Baines* leaves for Calcutta a week yesterday. I want you to serve her: Calhoun as first mate; you, Norton, as carpenter's mate. We'll take care of the closing tomorrow and have the cargo settled in a few days. Then I'll expect you to join me in Portsmouth. Will you, now?"

"Of course, sir," Jubal nodded, still numb.

"There's two boys who've shipped with us, Mr. Baines," Lester said. Tommy and Abel Godbold had come from Mobile. "May we roster them? Good boys, they'll be fine, rugged seamen. Our word on them."

"Of course," Baines said, reaching for the port. "Each ship will have a thousand soldiers—plenty to do."

Five days later, they stood in the *James Baines'* waist gazing northwest. The sun was low in the sky, a velum sphere of iridescent purple clothed by the coal haze above Portsmouth harbor.

"Allllll's weeeell, Mista Caaalllhoun," interrupted Abel Godbold. The young boy had appeared soundlessly from the foredeck, where he'd last been ordered by Jubal to coil the lines properly.

"Very good, Godbold," Jubal said, his voice brusque and distant. "You're dismissed, though you'd be advised to take the time with your manuals.

Before we weigh anchor, I'll want rhumb lines past Spithead or down the Solent, depending on wind; then a mark fifty miles off the Lizard, where we turn to run down the southing, with a heading for Finisterre. By morning watch, do you hear?'

The boy saluted and trotted forward to the forecastle. Jubal watched for a moment, remembering Eleanor Creesy, with whom he still corresponded. Their first voyage aboard *Flying Cloud* seemed a lifetime ago.

As he watched the sun balance atop a low hill, Lester bounded up the stairs to the quarterdeck. With Jubal's increasing responsibilities, Lester assumed most of the letter writing required to manage their financial affairs. He'd spent the afternoon finishing correspondence to London, Philadelphia, and Mobile.

"Wrote them all," Lester reported. "Gave Truette the deal terms and shipped a hundred tons of cloth back, like he asked. Told Sally we'd probably be a year," he went on. "I promised we'd be back before '58's out and sent her a draft for five hundred dollars. Figured ... Well, just seemed right."

Jubal nodded, watching the last arc of sun disappear behind the seaport.

"As for Cora ... Hard knowing quite what to say," Lester finished. "I don't know how much she can read, though no doubt Sal's been hard at her." He fell silent, feeling the pit in his stomach that usually accompanied such thoughts.

Beside him, Jubal took a deep drag of his cigar and blew a long stream of smoke into the lengthening dusk. "Coupla years ..." he muttered.

The India turnaround took eight months, capped by the unforgettable December afternoon when the *James Baines* and *Champion of the Seas* charged together up the Hooghly River toward Calcutta on a skysail breeze. Regimental bands played on deck, and thousands of soldiers cheered wildly as the ships spun to weather and dropped anchor off Sand Head. Later that evening, Lester penned a note to Donald McKay in Boston, describing as best he could the emotion of being aloft on the finest ships in the world. Jubal added a postscript, but the letter felt bittersweet, like a plaintive coda to a melody that was fading into silence.

The *James Baines* returned to Liverpool in April 1858 and tied up at Hutchinson Dock, scheduled to board another troop of soldiers embarking for India. Because of the crammed port facilities, it was two days before longshoremen and stevedores could offload the ship. Jubal and Lester used the time at the shipping offices of James Baines, consigning their small portion of cargo to agents and picking up mail. Lester also helped Tommy Godbold find a ship home. The boy carried a polished box for his mother holding the ashes of Abel Godbold. The youngster had died of dengue fever in Calcutta and been cremated along the banks of the Hooghly.

"Leastways, she'll have something to bury," Tommy had choked, when Jubal handed him the cotton bag of ashes, still warm from the pyre. Several days later, Lester gave him the dovetailed box, made from sandalwood he'd bought in the market.

Among their mail was a letter from Philadelphia. Sally had written a short, curt note that simply said she'd bring them up to date *when* they got home. The men looked sheepish, passing Sally's letter back and forth. Truette Stubbs also wrote, inquiring when they might return to Mobile to discuss business opportunities to the south. "Must mean Havana," Jubal opined.

To their surprise, another large package of books had come from Eleanor Creesy. Lester tore open the package and scanned the note inside. "Eleanor says this Whitman book—*Leaves of Grass*—is for the both us, though might be more to your taste. Grass don't have leaves, last I checked."

"Poetry'd be difficult for you," Jubal replied, distractedly. The note from Sally hurt. "One more round to India, then I guess we'd better haul west."

Lester nodded agreement, though an hour later those plans turned to ashes. Returning toward Hutchinson Dock, they saw a familiar, grim sight that made them both groan. A half-mile away, billowing smoke from a massive fire wrinkled the sky. Sprinting to the docks, they found an army of firefighters battling the inferno enveloping *James Baines*.

"Least it ain't freezin'," Lester threw up his hands.

"We insured?" Jubal asked, sickened at the sight.

Lester nodded. "Though payout'll be another story." Firemen tried to contain the blaze, but vivid memories of the *Great Republic* kept the young men spectators, knowing the fight was futile.

Jubal looked at the maroon satchel Lester carried. "That all you've got?"

"Our papers and what I'm wearing," Lester nodded. "A few books at Baines." He spit, shaking his head and gnawing a lip. "By God, that's a horrible sight!"

"Lordy, how many more we gonna lose?" Jubal turned, unwilling to watch another proud ship burn to the waterline.

Lester fought back tears. "She were a fine ship."

"Not no longer. And we're beached; no hold on us here now. So let's find us a packet tomorrow, get back before that sister 'a yorn disowns us." He pushed his battered derby back as they walked into the city.

At a busy intersection they stopped for traffic. "Lester," Jubal muttered, "I don't want ever to see another ship burn in my life. Never again."

Chapter Forty-Nine

New York, July 1858

The Liverpool packet sailed into New York harbor and eased to her South Street berth in mid-afternoon, early enough for Lester and Jubal to head directly for a Broadway haberdashery. The men bought new suits before discarding the clothes they had worn to rags since losing their entire wardrobes in the *James Baines* fire. Shortly after dawn the next morning, Lester telegraphed Sally while Jubal bought tickets on the southbound express. Before boarding, they visited a newsstand and accumulated a dozen newspapers and periodicals from major cities in the United States.

Neither said much on the ten-hour train ride, but read with the voracious intensity of men who had been at sea for a year. Nationwide, rhetoric had reached incendiary levels. The country seemed wracked by geography. Depending on the writer's politics, columnists in Boston, Charleston, Pittsburgh, and Savannah poured scorn and vitriol on partisans of abolition or slavery.

At midday, when the train conductor announced that the dining car was open for lunch, Lester tossed a copy of the *Southern Literary Messenger* on top of the *New York Tribune*.

"You'd think Hammond and Seward were from different countries," he said, finishing the text of speeches by senators from South Carolina and New York, a barbed counterpoint of moral superiority and vilification, the former extolling King Cotton as the latter derided agrarian aristocracy.

"Different planets," Jubal muttered, having already devoured the same news. "Vile stew ..."

Several hours later, Lester awoke with a start and elbowed Jubal as the train clacked through the switching yards bordering Philadelphia. A brief thundershower had passed through, leaving puddles and a pleasant crispness to the afternoon light. As the express disgorged its passengers onto a platform already thronged with people, Lester took the satchel while Jubal shouldered a small seabag that held their books and new clothes. Easy gaits, deep tans, and watchful confidence marked them as seamen, but otherwise they caused no notice nor expected any. Approaching the terminal, Lester glanced at Jubal to say something when his friend's eyes widened and he coasted to a stop. Lester turned and halted dead in his tracks. Twenty feet away, partially hidden by a column at the platform entrance, Sally and Cora waited.

Both women wore full ankle-length, long-sleeved dresses that drew tight at their waists. Sally's auburn hair fell from beneath a bonnet in ringlets to her shoulders. Cora, the taller by several inches, wore a small, flat hat over hair pulled back in a twist. Her hands gripped an umbrella tightly and she stared at the young men.

Sally's smile made her face luminescent. As she took a step forward, Lester did the same. They broke for each other simultaneously and crashed together in a wonderful, resounding clump that filled Jubal with a burst of starlight. Sally whimpered and laughed as Lester buried his face in her shoulder. Cora had not moved, though she managed a small smile at Jubal's glance.

"I missed you so much … It's been so long," Sally breathed, looking at her brother with a mixture of adoration and admonition before hugging him again, relishing the feel of his hard chest and shoulder muscles.

Jubal shifted his feet, waiting. Suddenly, he swiped his hat off as if it were smoldering. He realized Sally had been watching while holding Lester and her gaze unnerved him. A moment later Sally's gay laugh turned her brother, and he too grinned. Even Cora smiled. A blush worthy of poetry lighted Jubal's face and his embarrassment grew measurably when Sally released Lester to take Jubal by the arms. Standing on her tiptoes, she kissed him square on the lips. "Took yer time, didn'ja?" she scolded.

Jubal swallowed, and looked to his friend for help.

Lester shrugged. "Couldn't keep him away from the ladies."

Sally pointed a finger at her brother. "You ain't changed a mite, Lester!" She turned back to Jubal. "He's been bad, hasn't he?"

Jubal nodded. "Wicked terrible," he replied, mimicking Lester's downeast accent.

"Figured," Sally sniffed, so happy she wanted to dance. "Think you fellows can dig in that sea kit and find some manners, say hello to Cora?"

Both men nodded self-consciously, and Lester stepped forward, extending his hand, trying to be gallant but nonchalant. He found her so striking it was difficult not to stare. Cora's smile froze and suddenly she handed him her umbrella. Not knowing what else to do, Lester took it and stood there feeling foolish as Sally started to laugh.

"You try," she said to Jubal.

Jubal bent and extended his hand, looking for a moment like he'd fall over. To Sally's astonishment, Cora meekly shook Jubal's hand, as a line of color rose in her face like a vase filling, until the two of them averted their eyes, one blush fueling the other.

"Priceless!" Sally clapped.

The awkwardness softened and in a moment of connection, they locked eyes. A rigid cord seemed to bind and separate them until Cora moved. Slowly but firmly, she pulled Jubal's hand until he took a small step. Cora's arm came around his back and carefully brought him close in an embrace both intimate and reserved. Then she stepped back and gently touched a forefinger to his nose.

A knowing smile came to her face and Jubal lowered his eyes, the shadow of a sheepish grin touching his lips.

"Like when we wuz little," she murmured. Cora turned back to Sally and Lester, who were standing as though the world had stopped.

"Let's get going," Jubal ordered.

Sally reached for Jubal and grabbed hold, turning him toward the passenger terminal. Lester offered his arm to Cora who took it with a moment's hesitation. The couples silently made their way through streaks of pale afternoon light slanting across the crowded terminal and walked onto the street outside.

—

Within a week, the men were restless. From long habit, they both arose at dawn and idled each day before calling on Cora and Sally for an evening walk. Though both women were thrilled to get out, by the time Cora was finished with her supper duties, Curtis had exhausted himself. Lester rented a buggy so the boy could fall asleep in his mother's arms, though that cramped Lester's efforts to keep close to Cora.

Jubal didn't have that problem. He and Sally sat together as if glued, though Sally did most of the whispering between them. The street lamps had been lit by the time the women were dropped off at their respective homes. Every evening, Jubal and Sally moved into a shadow on the porch, while Lester waited, jealous that he couldn't do the same with Cora because he held a sleeping boy in his arms. Besides, he still wasn't sure how'd she respond.

The men stayed at a small hotel near the port and spent much of the glorious summer weather along the docks, watching the bustle of a major seaport. Often the clap of filling canvas sounded across the water and both men stopped and watched. When a clipper slipped her moorings and rode an outgoing tide, steadily raising sail, Jubal nodded approval.

"Pretty good," he muttered, knowing his commands would be in much the same order and he'd expect them to be carried out with as much dispatch. "Funny, ain't it, Lester? At sea, we always can't wait to get into port—don't matter what part of the world—and then we get there, can't wait to get going again."

"How come it's hard to stay still?" Lester asked.

Jubal paused, taken aback. "Dunno," he finally replied. "Standing 'round doesn't produce anything, I suppose. You know how it is in the doldrums, nearly going mad as the canvas slats about, drivin' us nowhere."

"I can't explain it to Sal," mused Lester. "We aren't going to be around long and she'll just get mad again."

"You want to stay?"

"And do what?"

"Damned if I know. Figure out how Truette does it? Become some sort of trader—find a business that needs doin'."

"Neither one of us would last a week being a merchant. Imagine showing up to the same place every day, selling stuff. Though I bet Sally's been pestering you." Lester reached for a cigar, so Jubal knew his friend was agitated.

"You're right, she'll likely be angry," Jubal agreed. "But I don't know what to do about it. Ships I can understand but I doubt I'll ever say the same about Sally. Would you want to spend all day worrying about making a woman angry?"

"Are going to spend your life roaming?" Lester retorted.

"Didn't answer my question."

Lester pondered, eyeing the diminishing clipper. "Mom weren't exactly the mild type," he said at last. "Used to call it 'white heat,' when she'd clam up for a few days, throw food on the table, and just as well say to hell with you little bastards. We knew she didn't mean it but I'd rather face a she-bear in springtime. Sometimes the worst was I didn't even know what I'd done."

"Is Sally going silent, like your Ma?" Jubal wondered. She hadn't been silent or submissive with him, quite the reverse. Sally Norton had a habit of looking Jubal right in the eye.

"Lord no! But I feel like there's weather, the other side the horizon. Just my bones, but if it were me I'd double the watch."

Two days later Sally proposed a Sunday afternoon picnic after the church service. Lester dragged Jubal along to morning worship at United Presbyterian, where a well-known local preacher, Henry Highland Garnet, was scheduled to sermonize. Lester had never heard of him, save for Sally's casual remark that the man was a stem-winding orator.

Neither Lester nor Jubal expected anything but a pleasant and uneventful day when they arrived from the livery Sunday morning at the Still residence in North Philadelphia. That nonchalance disappeared when a half dozen black people came from the house with Sally and Cora, filling the carriage Lester had rented. Sally had made an offhanded request for a carriage, "not a buggy," and Lester had indulged his sister even if it was twice the expense and more aggravation. Breezily explaining that the guests were visitors she had invited along to church, Sally was certain that Lester and Jubal wouldn't mind.

Neither man knew the specifics of William Still's activities but it didn't take much imagination—Philadelphia was a known way station on the Underground Railroad, as it was now called—to suspect that the four Negro men and two women, with rough hands and ill-fitting clothes, all refusing eye contact, were not native to the city.

When the party arrived at church, Jubal took the reins and said he'd watch the team. Cora marched the visitors directly to the front pews where they were seated near the outside aisle in close proximity, Lester noticed, to the corridor that led into the back of the church. Sally left briefly and returned a few minutes later with a proprietary hold on Jubal's arm. The men glanced at each other as Jubal dutifully sat down next to Cora.

The congregation was almost equally mixed between races, though Lester noticed almost all the buggies and carriages outside had carried whites. Black members walked to church.

In a pamphlet provided in the pews, Lester read that Henry Highland Garnet had been born a slave in Maryland about 1815 and then fled north with his father thirty years later. Garnet's missions had taken him throughout the North and to Europe several times; recently he had been elected president of the African Civilization Society. Lester wondered if that thread would be woven into the sermon.

"Fifteen years ago," Garnet began, in a deep, carrying voice, "I was disowned by the Anti-Slavery Society for my declaration that slaves had the right to murder their masters."

Anyone who hadn't been listening sat up.

"Gratefully, God gives man humility with age, and sometimes wisdom. I do believe, however much you and all of us may desire it, there is scant hope of redemption without the shedding of blood. But answering murder with murder has lost its righteousness, for which I thank people before me today." Garnet extended a hand. "Many who abhorred my vehemence then did not forsake me, as they have not forsaken you." He looked directly at the small group Sally had brought, and then leaned forward, pointing at the congregation.

"Over two centuries ago the first of our injured race were brought to the shores of America. They came not with their own consent; neither did they come flying upon the wings of liberty to a land of freedom. But, they came with broken hearts, from their beloved native land, and were doomed to unrequited toil and deep degradation. Nor did the evil of the bondage end at their emancipation by death. Succeeding generations inherited their chains, and millions have come from eternity into time, and have returned again to the world of spirits, *cursed and ruined by American slavery*."

Sally reached for Jubal's hand, but he pulled away, crossing his arms.

"To my white brethren here today," Garnet opened an extended hand to Jubal and Lester, "a word, for my message has long been to the black community. However much we appreciate white allegiance, *ultimately this a black struggle*. It is our skin that enslaves us, that, and our tolerance of bondage ..."

Jubal stared straight ahead, into the past, to the ivory heat of home, smoke lazily wafting away from the cabin chimney as he walked barefoot along the dusty track beside the cotton fields. In the distance he could see his father astride a horse, surrounded by bent backs weeding the crop and the soft moan of singing. The drone of Garnet's sermon became the incessant hum of dayflies and he felt the sleepiness that often took him under the shade of a live oak, a boy curled for a nap in the heat of midafternoon. Jubal closed his eyes and could see that boy, sleeping alone. He wanted to reach for him, stroke his head, when a shadow appeared and slid over the boy's face. Jubal opened his eyes.

Cora's hand rested in his lap, fingers open, the creamy pink of her palm a stark, beckoning command. Jubal lifted his gaze to the pastor.

"... Could this congregation remove to reconvene a scant two hundred miles away? For the black people among us today the result would be chains, a lynching tree or the brothels. Color determines this choice: *liberty or death*—or—*slavery or death* ..."

Slowly, as if a chain pulled inexorably at his arm, Jubal's right hand settled into Cora's. Her fingers curled into his like sinewy roots around a rock. Jubal closed his eyes.

"... To confront the white Baptist minister who, in the name of God, terrifies his flock that abolition will force amalgamation between Negroes and children of the poor white men of the South ..."

His father rode to him out of the setting sun, the boy on the step waiting, hearing sounds of Emma setting the table for supper.

"... To mock the calumnious politician who rails that poor white men will be the slaves of Negroes ..."

The father swaying on his feet, in the fields since dawn, tousling the boy's hair ...

"To that sweeping, abysmal belief throughout the South that slavery is of God, his natural and intended condition for the black race ..."

... the thump of a jug on the puncheon floor, the little boy crawling into Emma's lap next to a sleeping Cora, nuzzling as the slave woman stroked his face with a callused, gentle hand, softly humming a spiritual that carried him away ...

Henry Highland Garnet raised his hands high. "Jesus!" he roared, "has told us a house divided cannot stand! And will not! For I tell you, *it shall be torn asunder!*" Garnet slammed the pulpit, scanning the congregation.

Beside him, Lester could feel Cora stiffen, and he stole a glance in her direction. She looked rigid as a statue, her hand gripping Jubal's as if for life.

"My call to rebellion—as fervent today as fifteen years ago—is born in the bosom of liberty. Forget not that you are native-born American citizens, and as such, you are justly entitled to all the rights that are granted to the freest! In the name of the merciful God, and by all that life is worth, let it no longer be a debatable question whether it is better to choose liberty or death. I say again: *Let your motto be resistance! Resistance! No oppressed people have ever secured their liberty without resistance!*"

Garnet paused and took a long drink of water, holding his audience spellbound.

"Do as you will," Garnet intoned, "and your courage shall not be in vain.

But to my black brethren, *the time is now!* Remember the stripes your fathers bore! Think of the torture and disgrace of your noble mothers! Think of your wretched sisters, loving virtue and purity, as they are driven into concubinage and are exposed to the unbridled lusts of incarnate devils!"

Sally gripped Jubal's bicep with both hands, burying her fingernails.

Henry Garnet took a deep breath. "The decoction of our lives," he began, his voice low but audible throughout the sanctuary. Then, opening his arms and throwing his head back, the cry trumpeted to the rafters.

"*Slavery must die!* A house divided cannot stand! The South is but the foundation! The house is this nation! *It shall be torn asunder!*"

Lester heard little else. The sermon had been like water torture, slowly becoming so intolerable he felt he would scream. His head ached and he bent forward, feigning listening but willing himself away from the vehemence until he could see the horizon in all its grandeur and indifference.

Gradually, as Garnet closed his sermon, Lester returned to the sanctuary. Blinking, feeling dazed, he realized something was odd, unusual. It took him several moments trying to piece together the sensation that made him swallow. Cora had cupped her hand around his arm and barely, but perceptibly, leaned into him. He glanced across at his friend, astonished to see Jubal's head bowed, as if in prayer, though he knew Jubal was not communing with God but had gone to their place of safety, high in the royals, on a trade wind run across the blue back of an immensity that was law unto itself.

Cora released both men to stand for the closing hymn. After the benediction, when they turned in the pew for the aisle, Lester gently put his hand on the small of her back and felt her lean into him again. He took hold of her elbow until reaching the front vestibule, where a clutch of people had stacked against the church entrance. Cora pulled her arm in, sandwiching Lester's hand to her waist. His heart was pounding but he wasn't afraid.

"Where's the little one?" asked Lester, guiding her into the sunny morning and down the front steps of the church.

"I gave him to one of the woman come yest'day," Cora answered quietly. "She sucklin' her own 'n not wantin' to be out." Lester could hear but leaned close, savoring Cora's smell.

"Is he coming on our picnic?" Lester asked, assuming they were headed back to the house.

"No, he ain't."

Thankful for the crowd that kept their intimacy secret, Lester and Cora slowly made their way through the throngs toward the carriage standing in the shade of a massive chestnut tree. Inside, Lester nonchalantly crossed his leg, resting it against Cora's thigh and he stretched an arm on the seatback behind where she pinned it firmly with her shoulder blade. They waited twenty minutes for Jubal and Sally, Lester willing them to be lost.

"What about ... your visitors?" he asked, suddenly. He had seen the four men and two women, shepherded by a bonneted woman and austere-looking elderly white man, slipping out the back corridor.

"They's leaving," Cora replied.

So much the better, Lester thought, his curiosity piqued at her finality.

Finally, Sally and Jubal came out of the sanctuary following William and Letitia Still. Lester raised an arm but Sally pulled Jubal over to greet Lucretia Mott and her husband. Lester watched as Sally once more tugged at Jubal, but this time he ignored her, setting out for the carriage with such determination she nearly lurched keeping up with him.

Any prospect of a pleasant and uneventful day melted in the morning sun.

Jubal took the carriage reins and drove silently, with a coldness bordering on rude. Sally grew increasingly agitated as her chatter elicited clipped, cursory responses. She tried to make conversation with Lester and Cora but Jubal kept the horses at a trot, the steady clop of hooves on cobblestones eclipsing any conversation. Sally finally gave up but held firm to Jubal's arm.

Jubal steered the carriage northeast on the Benjamin Franklin parkway until reaching Fairmount Park at the city's outskirts. In full summer bloom, the park was an extravagant, aromatic landscape of flowers and majestic trees. Jubal slowed the team until finding a spot that offered plenty of shade and the flutter of a small brook, where he hauled the horses to a stop. In the sudden quiet, a butterfly meandered, its flight so whimsical that all four sets of human eyes followed it to a flowering rosebush. As if on cue, songbirds exploded and the wood resumed its summer buzz.

Sally contained herself barely long enough to spread the quilt across a grassy patch above the creek. "Jubal, you can say something!" she exclaimed. He was standing a bit apart, his pipe smoking like a chimney. Cora watched, but Lester just sighed and reached for a cigar.

"Goddam it, Jubal, look at me!" Sally sat up, tossing the plates she held onto the quilt. "Why do you have to take things so personal?"

Jubal turned to her. "You telling me it weren't?" Lester had never seen his friend so angry.

"It was just as much about her as you!" Sally said, throwing an arm Cora's way. "But she isn't standing there, snorting like a bull just got nipped!"

Jubal contained himself, though it clearly took a major effort. With an inward groan, Lester realized Sally had been holding back far too long—when she let go the surge would be no more controllable then a dynamited log jam.

"When are you going to face it, Jubal?" She cried. "The only people that love you are right here! Look at Lester, as close to a brother as you'll ever have! Look at Cora! *Look at your sister!*" Sally was on her feet, eyes blazing. "Don't tell me you don't know! Christ, look at you two, a moron could put that together, different color is all! Stop running, for Godsakes!"

Just as suddenly, Sally crumbled. "Because I can't catch up ..." she implored. "You just don't ever put that guard down ..."

The songbirds had stopped. Only the soft babbling brook interrupted a breathless silence.

Sally stood, watching Jubal, tears beginning to stain her cheeks. She approached tentatively, hoping for something, but he was immovable. Sally slowly reached out and touched his nose with a forefinger.

Jubal recoiled, as if she had trespassed on something inviolate, then spun on his heel and strode away. Sally looked in terror at her brother.

"Better go after him, sis," Lester murmured, chomping his cigar.

Sally ran but Jubal had a good start and his long, furious stride ate up the park grounds.

Lester leaped to his feet. "Jubal!" he roared in a quarterdeck voice that made Cora brace. His friend stopped in midstride but didn't turn around. Sally didn't care; she went at Jubal and tackled his back at a full run. The two figures staggered to stop nearly a hundred yards away.

"Well, either they will, or won't," Lester remarked, plopping square-legged on the quilt. Cora came beside him and folded like a deer, looking at him with a smile. Lester tossed his hat aside and gave her a quick kiss on the lips. "He *is* your brother, isn't he? How long have you known?"

"Long's I remember," Cora shrugged. "I don't recall the man much, but Mr. Jordon 'n Beulah say Jubie's daddy been kind to Mumma." She licked her lips.

"Who's who down there?" Lester wondered. "Must be pretty complex."

"Thick as the swamp," Cora agreed, sitting upright. Lester noticed she always did that when concentrating on her speech. "Mumma 'n Beulah, they sisters of the same woman. Grandma, she was tree parts white. Beulah's father were black, but Mumma's wuz white, made her 'roon. She nearly all white, except one-eight, so she be a slave."

"Who told you all this?" Lester marveled.

Cora relaxed, looking at him as if he were odd. "Family. Ain't white folks talk?"

"So what happened?"

"Jubie's daddy, he's layin' with two woman, both with child. You seen how it is. He was in Mobile, getting ready for plantin'. His white woman—wife—gets the death of fever, 'n a baby can't live inside if its mother dies. Mumma had Jubie. Not 'xactly the same time, but near enough, so his daddy don't know, or care enough. He can't tell Jubie ain't been white forever, when he come back. Mumma knows her choice. 'N a few years later, Mumma has me. I don't 'member Curtis much, but Daddy must have been done with Mumma."

"It's all fractions," Lester mused.

"What's 'fraction'?"

"Pieces of the whole. Your momma was an eighth, so Jubal is one-sixteenth, though he looks straight from Scotland."

Lester marveled for few moments and then glanced over his shoulder. Sally had managed to get Jubal turned around and was talking earnestly, holding him securely by the waist.

"Please Jubal, listen to me ..." Sally whispered. "I've never begged in my life, and I swear this is the only time's ever going to happen, so listen good. I loved you the moment you come through the barn door—Betty nearly stomped my milk pail. But you're so damn hard to love, cause you're never around and then you keep hiding. Just stop running! Please! Whatever happened was just what happened. You were a child. You and Cora ... she forgives, if that's the right word. Rarely says anything about you, but it's always *Jubie,* in that soft drawl of hers. What are you so afraid of?"

"I ain't a niggah!" Jubal exclaimed, through clenched teeth. "Maybe Ma was Cora's ma ... I don't know; I couldn't face it. But I ain't a niggah! Don't know how they feel, and I don't feel it! I never been one!"

"It doesn't make you anything more or less than what you are!" Sally pleaded.

"I been on the edge all my life," Jubal countered. "The edge the canebrake, edge of town, of family, hunger ... on the edge of respectable folk, *all my life*. You know how that feels?"

"No," Sally whispered, "and I don't care. For me, Jubal Calhoun, you're not at the edge. Jubal, you're my center. You go anyplace, doesn't matter where, I'm right there." She pressed her finger to his heart. "And you're staying here," she breathed, taking his hand to her breast.

Chapter Fifty

Three weeks later, Lester and Jubal sat in a waterfront tavern waiting out an afternoon rainstorm. With nothing to do, they poked around on the docks where the smell of cordage, Stockholm tar, and harbor mud brought some comfort. The strolls had become a daily ritual.

Lester pulled out the letter he'd picked up at the post office a few hours earlier and reread it for the third time, glancing at his friend. Jubal fooled with his pipe before he spoke, nearly driving Lester to distraction, finally muttering, "Truette says he'd like to see us, we ought to go. Man's never fouled our lines."

Lester waved the wreath of smoke away and squinted out a dirty window. "Then let's check the trains. Rain's slacking some. I don't know what Stubbs is thinking, but something's up."

The rain left steaming humidity and they were soon sweat-soaked, but walking felt good and Jubal stretched his shoulders, thinking this was the longest period of inactivity he could remember. Although the picnics with Cora and Sally were usually enjoyable, Lester and Jubal spent their time hanging around, waiting several days for a few hours when the women weren't consumed with domestic duties. Waiting had become as oppressive as the July heat.

"I'm hungry," Lester announced, scanning a train schedule. "Tired, too."

"From a sliver of a walk?" Jubal retorted. Lester turned on his heel and walked off. Jubal followed, both bemused and annoyed. "What are you so crank about?" he asked as Lester flung a door open to a small steakhouse two blocks from the train station.

"From just doing nothing!" Lester railed as they took a table. "If we can't work nothing out of Mobile, eight or ten ships a month are leaving South Street for 'Frisco again; won't take us long to find a berth."

"When you gonna tell 'em?"

"You're a cowardly one," Lester snorted. "You tell them."

"She's your sister."

"And she's yours!"

"Cora won't blink," Jubal said. "Sally's the one that'll get hot."

"Well, I been dealing with her all my life," Lester complained. "You're her bull now. Chrissakes act like it!"

"I am," Jubal grinned. "I'm running. Bull goes sniffing an ornery heifer, gets a hoof in the teeth. No thank you."

A barmaid brought whiskey and Lester drank half of it in one swallow, relishing the rasp in his throat. "You'd think Still were her old man," he grumbled.

The situation galled him. Neither woman had much time, Cora particularly, and even when she could free a few hours, Cora's boy didn't like to be separated. Curtis tolerated Lester to a point, which always seemed to coincide with being left behind. Then he'd wail frightfully and spoil Cora's mood for a walk or buggy ride. The times when he could see her alone felt chaperoned because Lester's desire to be with Cora ran smack into William Still, who insisted on knowing when they would return from any outing. The man had sternly told Cora, in words plainly meant for Lester, that he would not countenance an improper relationship.

Jubal grinned as the barmaid brought sizzling steaks and a steaming bowl of mashed potatoes. "Well, right now I guess Still is," he remarked, dumping a mound of potatoes on his plate. "The man is no fool. You want Cora, *he's* going to make damn sure *you* make an honest woman of her."

"Snub tight, Jubal," Lester protested. "No one's saying anything about marrying!"

Jubal raised an eyebrow before stabbing at his steak. "You're the one that's got to ask."

"I ain't asking nothing until I know I can support a family! And how we gonna do that, sailing the seven seas? Ever think that's why the Creesys didn't have any kids? Ought to have asked her."

Jubal scoffed. "You wouldn't have asked her even if your back been whipped to ribbons."

"Sally drapes you like a cloak, but I don't see you going on your knees!"

"Those women are in collusion," Jubal opined. "Must be."

Lester grunted in agreement and ripped into his dinner as though it were the enemy. The train schedule, he realized, had goaded him; nothing was going to change until they changed it. "So tomorrow?" he mumbled through a mouthful of meat.

Jubal shook his head. "Only if you tell your sister. Me, I'd wait for Sunday. Best have a picnic before the storm."

Four days later, after another sermon excoriating slavery, the four of them enjoyed a buggy ride on a beautiful summer's day. Cora left Curtis to play with the Stills' children. When they arrived at the park, Sally made no pretense at a common gathering and simply grabbed a picnic basket with one hand and Jubal with the other, lugging them both off to a private spot a hundred yards away. Lester stood open-mouthed, before realizing that Cora headed in the opposite direction to a cluster of beech trees on a small knoll. The day was blazing hot.

Cora spread a quilt on the ground and rummaged in their picnic basket as Lester doffed his suit coat.

"A scorcher," he said, undoing his tie and stretching out to lean on an elbow.

Cora passed him a glass of lemonade, still cool from the sawdust-packed cooler. The sweet, tangy drink felt like cold nectar and Lester drank the entire glass, smacking his lips to smile at Cora. She leaned over and kissed him.

"That's all you git, Lesta Norton," Cora said gently, as she broke away.

"Wha' ... you talkin' about?" he mumbled through his astonishment, unconsciously mimicking her speech.

"I'm talkin' you ain't gonna lay with me 'less done by the grace of the Lord."

Lester's shock was too childlike to be contrived. Cora laughed and stroked his face, her hand feeling like a rough pine board. She turned and lay at right angles to him, putting her head in his lap.

"I know you want me, Lester," she began, looking at him. "And I want you, if that be the feelin'. Ain't one I ever knowed ... on account of only one man forced me." Cora stared, daring him to look away.

Lester held her gaze. "That man is dead. The past is past ... It won't come with us unless we bring it, and I'm not going to."

"But Curtis come wid me."

Lester gently touched his forefinger to Cora's nose.

"You're bad as your sister," she said, turning away as if annoyed. Lester reached for her again and Cora knocked his hand aside, laughing. He kissed the top of her hair; she smelled of honeysuckle.

"None 'a my business," Lester said, "but what's that about?"

"That's right, none your business!" Cora agreed. She laughed again, an infectious sound. "Back we was little, Jubie and me sat in the fields, playing our nose tag game. One touched the other the most soft—but we had to feel the finger, weren't no cheating allowed—they won. Mumma was still alive then."

"Did he know?" Lester asked.

"Jubie?" Cora shrugged. "Probably ... though 'spect he *felt* more than *knowed*. I think that's why he couldn't take me when Uncle said go 'head. Mounting me would been the same as stabbing Mumma, hardly no diffunce. Whatever he knew ..." Cora sighed and a mist came to her eyes. "Jubie loved Mumma."

Lester lay back and stared at the sky, idly running his fingers through Cora's hair. A high thin haze held the heat in and he thought of floating under a similar sky in mid-ocean. He softly whistled up a breeze.

Cora rolled onto her stomach and looked at him. "When you goin'?" she asked, softly.

Lester's whistling chopped silent. He shook his head, marveling. "In the morning," he replied, still staring at the haze.

"Where?"

"Mobile, to see Truette Stubbs. Then dunno ... we'll see."

"When you coming back for me? For us?"

"How long do I got?"

They stared at each other.

"How long you need?" she wiggled closer.

Lester sighed, and looked up again. "'Till ... I can put us in a good home and have a future I can see. Jubal and me, well, we been together so long, kind of think alike ..."

"You gonna wed me or Jubal?"

"You're as bad as my sister."

Cora grinned suddenly, flashing pearly teeth. "Sally will take care of that!" she chuckled. "Jubie's never been no match for a woman. I give him another year, two, before she have her way with him."

"She'll do that whenever she wants," Lester replied, bemused at the shifting cadence of speech, as if Cora slipped in and out of her past life. "Though, if those two get to playing a game of stubborn, it could go on forever. Granite against marble." He glanced at Cora and saw she was staring into the distance. Lester twisted, spotting the speck of quilt that spilled across the park lawn like a discarded napkin. A tiny basket could be seen, and nearby one of the horses swished its tail; otherwise, the park was still and empty.

Sally gasped and shuddered, her body twitching atop Jubal's arching back. His hands clutched the back of her thighs, pulling their bodies so tight the slippery lotion of her oozed against his fingers. Slowly, Sally's rhythmic panting subsided until she pulled her head from his shoulder, looked at him or a brief moment, and licked his lips before burying her tongue in his mouth.

Sally broke free, giggled, kissed him, and quickly wiping herself with her slip, scurried up to the top of the rise, peering out like a scout. "C'mon, Jubie, get up here, make like you know me," she hissed. She reached under her dress, hitching her bloomers up snug, then brushed the leaves and twigs off her backside.

Jubal came up besides her, buttoning his pants. He suddenly felt quiet and unaccountably shy. Sally noticed immediately and looked at him hard.

"What am I gonna do with yew?" he drawled.

"You'll leave," Sally replied, satisfied. "Like you always do. But you'll be back or I'll come after you. You know that, don't you?" She stared at him and Jubal nodded, opening his arms.

"No matter what," she added, coming to him again.

Chapter Fifty-One

Truette Stubbs looked older and more portly. Sitting on the veranda as they came through the gate, he rose with a look that radiated joy and shook their hands interminably.

"Y'all look mighty good!"

Both Lester and Jubal found themselves tongue-tied.

"Come out back, let's sit for a spell," Truette motioned as Ezekiel appeared like a genie to take their bags, "where it's cool as it's going to get. Private, too."

Lester and Jubal followed him through the house, both examining the repaired door to his study. Truette led through a beautiful, subtropical garden to a cypress gazebo separated from the alley by a tall hedge. He reached into his coat and passed out long stogies.

"Cuba's finest," he grinned, as Louisa backed through the house door, nearly taking it from its hinges, and strode across the yard like an African queen. She thumped a decanter of Kentucky whiskey and a tub of ice on a nearby table before smothering the young men in either arm.

"Woo-ee,' dem ladies be standin' in line!" she cried, whacking their chests as they stood awkwardly, embarrassed by the attention. Cackling, Louisa waddled back to the kitchen.

"Firstly," Truette began, clinking ice cubes into three glasses, "recapitulate your travels since y'all were here last. Then we've some financial matters to discuss before looking forward ... to the horizon, as Lester might say." He chuckled, making himself comfortable and nodding them to start.

By turns they talked for an hour, describing the Australian runs, various trade deals, and making such brief mention of Philadelphia that Stubbs' eyes narrowed. Jubal ended their tale with an oblique question about any aftereffects from Cora's brief visit to Mobile.

"A few of my neighbors congratulated me on killing a thief," Truette Stubbs replied, evenly. "Bounty hunters don't carry seraphic reputations ..." He nodded the matter closed. "Now then, let me elucidate my recent journey to Cuba. I've 'come rather fond of Havana, the Spaniards notwithstanding. Also, I've brought property in St. George Harbor, Bermuda. Call it a strategic choice, if you will."

Stubbs leaned forward.

"Conflict is coming, gentlemen," he declared. "How you will face it is up to y'all, and I shall not ask where your allegiance lies except to require it first with me." Settling back and swirling his whiskey, Stubbs stared into the glass as if it were a crystal ball. "The future of this country, gentlemen ... will be settled in blood. I foresee incalculable suffering."

"What are your plans, sir?" Jubal asked, working to get the words out.

"I've a contract on my holdings here, excepting this house," Stubbs answered, "and shall transfer my operations to Havana, with a small ancillary effort in St. George. In the event of hostilities, there are trade advantages to both ports. As for you, I propose the following."

He added ice to the men's glasses carefully and poured more bourbon.

"I have structured a transaction with James Baines," Stubbs began, "a product of your experience in the wool trade from Australia. As you are no doubt aware, California has strengthened considerably. At this moment, under a demise charter, a ship is loading in Liverpool with cotton and wool goods bound for San Francisco via the East Coast. Perhaps she has left already, but in any case I expect her in New York by early September."

Lester and Jubal leaned forward.

"I propose you ship aboard our charter," Stubbs continued. "A one-year, global contract. Act as my representatives and employees, first mate and carpenter's mate, respectively, from New York, under the command of Captain Asa Caldwell, a man of impeccable reputation. In San Francisco, use your best judgment regarding cargo opportunity, although we are committed to loading spring tea at Foochow for either London or New York. Again, I shall rely on your judgment at that time. In addition to your wages, as determined by Captain Caldwell, and a three percent fee on any trade from New York through the course of the charter, I offer shares in the voyage at par."

"What's the ship," Lester asked, "outbound New York?"

Stubbs' smile savored the irony. "*Romance of the Seas,* McKay-built, a breed with which I recall you have great familiarity. Baines thinks that man is the best shipbuilder in history."

Chapter Fifty-Two

New York, October 1858

Cub Pingree brought every stick of white pine the *Mattie Mae* could carry down from Bangor and rafted alongside *Romance of the Seas,* just in from Liverpool. Lester had telegraphed Clyde Pingree from Mobile and arranged the trade, and then bought cargo for Pingree's return trip to Maine. Six frenetic days later, *Romance of the Seas,* so deeply loaded she had barely ten feet of freeboard, passed the ochre-colored woodlands of Staten Island on a brilliant, blustery day.

Regardless of weather, Lester knew it was bound to be a wet ride. Reeving a block at the *Romance's* maintop, he could hear Jubal far below in the ship's waist, ruling the starboard watch. At the windward quarterdeck rail, Captain Caldwell's tall, spare silhouette stood motionless, taking the measure of his new first mate. As the clipper's sails were set in disciplined, professional order, Lester felt a flash of pride for his friend, before it faded again against the unsettling memory of their brief, daylight visit to Philadelphia. They had not talked yet but would, Lester knew, sometime before the Horn.

Philadelphia had been a wound. Lester tried to lance it the day they left New York, while they still could send a telegram, but Jubal perfunctorily turned away from the offhanded query about Sally.

A few days earlier, after the South Street loading had been completed by midday and with *Romance* ready to cast off the next morning, the boys gained permission from Captain Caldwell to leave the ship for eighteen hours. Jubal and Lester raced to the train station and just caught the Philadelphia express, leaving no time to send a telegram. Consequently, they arrived unannounced at the Mott's home near sunset.

The men had not been in Lucretia Mott's parlor more than a few minutes before Sally thrust two books at Jubal. "Oh Jubal, you must read this!" she had exclaimed breathlessly, thrilled to see them. "*The Impending Crisis,* by Hinton Helper—he's from North Carolina!" Sally seemed to think Hinton's birthplace confirmed the book's veracity. Her sparkling excitement changed to consternation as Jubal's face hardened, and he curtly nodded.

"Sally," Lester complained, "Jubal and I have worked all night, been eight hours getting here, and we're outbound tomorrow supper, high tide. Can we just ..." he flapped his hands, suddenly feeling the exhaustion of preparing a ship for sea. It vexed him that his sister just could not seem to appreciate that first and last, Jubal was Southern.

Lucretia Mott appeared and graciously invited them for dinner, momentarily postponing what later felt like a slow roasting. A woman named Mary Brown was present, plus two black men, Robert Purvis Jr. and James Pennington. Just the sound of Jubal's drawl was enough to set the table on edge. Sally asked Purvis how he had been so successful in business as to force a nearby township to reverse its policy of excluding Negro children from public schools by withholding his substantial tax responsibilities. Then she sweetly requested that "Reverend Pennington" describe the marriage ceremony he had performed for Frederick Douglass and his wife nearly twenty years earlier.

Mrs. Brown, a pinched-looking woman in a severe brown dress and tightly drawn bonnet, said little, explaining she was in Philadelphia to meet her husband, John, now away on business. Jubal only made one comment, after Purvis inquired if Lester and Jubal's experience in England had given them any insight that could help explain the British tax policies for Scotland, which seemed to be driving people off their land.

"Value's relative, according to who's taxin' or gittin' taxed," he replied, in his thickest bottomland drawl. "Earl 'a Sunderland, he's jes' burnin' them Scots out, care 'a the Highland Edicts, 'cause they're squatters. Sheep pay better. Guess he's a good host though ... that Mrs. Harriet Stowe, she were his guest of honor on her trip to England. The *Gazette* said she had a fine time." He pushed his chair back, politely nodding to the Motts. "Apologies m'am, sir. Gotta get the night train, catch our ship."

Lester winced and rose with him. After good wishes and handshakes, Sally showed them to the door, her face ashen. "You don't have to leave," she had said anxiously, as they gathered coats in the parlor. "I'll see you in the morning?"

Jubal turned on her. "I'm getting good and goddamned tired of your righteous education, Miss Sally Norton. Take a fine look at me. If you're so desperate to change a man, go find yourself another one."

Sally tried to stop him, but Jubal pushed past her and walked out. She wheeled to her brother with a pleading look. "I need to talk with him!"

"When it comes to thick," Lester remarked, "sister, you met your match. I suggest you learn something about listening first." He hugged her as Sally started to cry.

"Lester, I *must* talk with him."

"Best let him cool down. And he will, but not right off. We'll be gone a year, give or take. You can write to us at Houqua Wharf, Shanghai. We might get it in six months. Right now I'm going to call on Cora, before it gets too late."

"Don't bother," Sally had sniffed. "She's not at the Stills."

Lester stepped back, his face quizzical.

"Cora's gone for a time," Sally replied, staring at him. "Lately, she sometimes has to leave suddenly."

"What for?" Lester rasped, alarmed.

"You two are always leaving," Sally replied. "Don't think we're just knitting until you get home." She regarded her brother, than looked at Jubal, standing in the street, waiting. "Cora hasn't forgotten where she came from. Ask her yourself what's she's been doing ... whenever you get back."

Chapter Fifty-Three

For two weeks, Captain Caldwell ran down the easting, leaving the Cape Verde Islands astern before the trades began to die away. On a blistering afternoon in late October, *Romance* ghosted over a greasy sea, the breeze light as a sigh. The starboard watch was on deck, unfurling and going over every inch of the heavy Cape Horn canvas they would carry in southern waters, when the masthead lookout sang out. Jubal went aloft and squinted his eyes into the white haze before spotting the smudge of canvas far ahead on a converging course.

Two hours later they were still a half-mile away when the vessel's signal flags asked permission to come aboard. Jubal ordered a boy to fetch the captain as he studied the ship through his telescope. She was a topsail schooner, about one hundred fifty feet in length.

"Mr. Calhoun?" Asa Campbell took the proffered telescope.

"*Wanderer*, sir," Jubal replied, watching a small launch being lowered from her side.

Captain Campbell suddenly slapped the telescope shut, startling Jubal.

"Smell her?" the captain asked, in a flinty New England accent. "Abolished better than fifty years ago, but those bastards are still at it. Heave to, Mr. Calhoun. Fetch Mr. Norton. They'll want water." Asa Campbell walked to the rail and spit, looking like a man that wished he had a cannon.

The whiff of sewage suddenly wrinkled Jubal's nose as he ordered the helmsman to head up into the breeze. Men peeled off the windward rail and raced for their stations, some scrambling aloft while others manned the braces. Jubal took the steps three at a time into the ship's waist.

"Off tacks 'n sheets!" he roared. "Lower skysails! Lower royals! Mainsail haul!"

The big clipper gracefully horseshoed, shedding canvas as if she were molting. *Romance* coasted to a stop and lay in the swell, her few remaining sails trimmed so the bow pushed one way and stern worked opposite, leaving her idle in mid-ocean. As they drifted to leeward, the heat settled on them and men stayed clear of the iron fittings, almost hot enough to cook eggs.

The longboat approached and from its bow a man rose, dressed formally despite the heat. "Ahoy there, what ship?" a Southern accent drawled across the water.

"*Romance of the Seas!*" Jubal roared in a hail that carried across to the schooner itself. "Sixteen days outbound New York for San Francisco! Y'all?"

"*Wanderer!*" the man replied, smiling at the accent. "Three weeks from Cape Town, bound for Savannah."

"Bullshit!" Lester snapped. He had joined Jubal at the rail. The stench now was almost overpowering, as if the top had been torn off a huge privy that carried an entire village's night soil. "No way that schooner made it up the African coast in three weeks."

"What do you require?" Captain Caldwell demanded from the quarterdeck, his manner cold as the day was hot.

"Begging your pardon, sir," the man said, turning to the tall, gray-haired Captain. "Gazaway Alexander, at your service." He tipped his hat.

"No begging necessary," Asa Caldwell spit back. "*What do you want?*"

Every sailor aboard *Romance* was on deck or aloft. Several glanced at Asa Caldwell, stunned that their captain's aloofness had turned to such plain animus.

Gazaway Alexander stiffened at the tone. "Water! Sir! If I may be so bold as to request your consideration!"

"Calhoun! Norton!" the captain ordered, "a dozen casks to the slaver. Move lively now!" He turned back to the launch. "You'll have water, goddamn you to hell! Now stand off!"

Alexander recoiled as if he had been hit. His hand went to his coat but stopped as a pistol magically appeared in Asa Caldwell's hand. "Stand off!" the captain snarled. Alexander promptly turned and sat down. A moment later, the launch crew backwatered fifty yards to drift in the swell.

Jubal heard the curse but was already ordering men to lower a longboat while Lester headed below with several crewmen. Empty barrels were brought on deck and filled at the pump abaft the mainmast, with enough air left in each so the barrels could float awash. *Romance's* launch towed them across the silent ocean, momentarily marking a dotted line connecting the only two tiny specks in an immense void.

Lester and Jubal pulled at the oars with four other men. As they approached *Wanderer,* the lowing sound of humanity packed like livestock seeped through the hull. An oily sheen of sweat, piss, shit, vomit, and blood surrounded the ship. Lester gagged at the water's halo of revulsion, nearly puking from the stench.

The *Wanderer*'s longboat had been pulled aboard, and Gazaway Alexander stood at the rail, directing his crew. Jubal remained silent except to answer Alexander's question, 'Where is home, sir?"

Lester's tensed in anticipation.

"Alabama," Jubal replied, in a remote voice that closed further conversation. Alexander's teeth clenched and he spun on his heel. Moments later another man came over the side into the longboat to help with the transfer. The schooner crew hoisted barrels on the lifeboat davits and emptied them into a catch basin on deck. Occasionally, a moan or cry emitted from deep in the hold, but otherwise the work proceeded in peculiar silence. As the last barrel came dripping out of the ocean, Lester glanced at the seaman returning to *Wanderer*. "How many souls aboard?" he whispered.

"Five hunnert," the man replied in a laconic drawl, "when we left the Guinea Coast. Down 'bout thirty right off. 'Spect we'll land four hunnert 'er better, Savannah. This here water'll help. Obliged y'all." He nodded and trotted up the sea ladder, hauling it up behind him as the longboat pulled back to *Romance of the Seas*.

Later, as dusk settled on the ship, Lester stood at the quarterdeck rail, staring at the white smidgen on the horizon until all signs of *Wanderer* disappeared. As he turned to go forward, a chunk of water-blackened mahogany came from under the ship's counter and slipped astern. Lester idly wondered what currents it had ridden from the African coast when suddenly he turned back again. He had noticed Jubal on the other side of the quarterdeck, staring aft. The mahogany rode up the ship's wake like a small log before the wash flipped it back over.

Suddenly, Lester realized he wasn't looking at wood. The chunk was a small pair of bloated legs, torn at the waist. Of the child's torso, nothing remained.

Chapter Fifty-Four

Spring 1859

Out of curiosity, Lester did a sun sight at noon on the March equinox, shortly after *Romance of the Seas* weighed anchor at Shanghai and cleared the Yangtze River with nineteen thousand chests of tea bound for New York. Lester still practiced celestial navigation but his skill couldn't compare with Jubal's. Through the years, Jubal had gained the ability to take one look at the starlit heavens and figure their position within a few hundred miles anywhere on earth.

Three months later, *Romance of the Seas* tied up to the South Street wharf, a splendid run against the monsoon. Captain Caldwell acknowledged as much, informing Jubal he was ready for command and offering to write a personal letter of recommendation to the Maritime Board if Jubal wanted to take the master's examination. After remanding the cargo, Lester had settled accounts and gone ashore to deposit $15,000 in the Bank of New York.

"Did you wire Truette?" Jubal asked, after they'd gathered their seabags and descended to the quay. "We get any mail?"

"Sent a telegram to Mobile," nodded Lester. "I also mailed him in Havana and Bermuda, there's no telling where he is. Sally and Cora, too, though none have answered yet. A letter's here from Eleanor Creesy. She and the captain have gone ashore. That's it." Lester didn't hide his disappointment and he knew his friend shared the sentiment.

The year had leavened Jubal's anger—even he couldn't carry a grudge around the world. A dozen letters addressed in Sally's clear, flowing script had awaited him in San Francisco. Every week she had written, bereft that he had left angry, and pleading with him to understand that she did not judge him. Though she could not countenance slavery, particularly as runaway slaves passed through William Still's home—a revelation confirming Jubal's suspicion that the house was on the Underground Railroad—she treasured Jubal's memory, every night caressing the carved wooden albatross he had given her years earlier in Maine.

The last message was less a letter than cryptic note: "Darling, I love you forever. You must come home to us."

The overland mail took less than a month, and Lester received two letters from Cora, spaced six weeks apart. The second was longer and more expressive, handwritten evidence of her growing literacy. Proudly describing Curtis's blossoming development, Cora also displayed the keen observations of a newcomer to Northern life, noting that Negroes were free, but hardly equal, and in many parts of Philadelphia, barely tolerated. The overt racial violence of the South was illegal above the Mason-Dixon line, but no less prevalent. A stridency had crept into her letters, with veiled references to a "mission" that commanded her attention, if even the price was to "leave my Curtis with Sally." The letter that reached San Francisco had been postmarked in November. Cora's last written words braced Lester: "Come home. Bring Jubie."

There had been no word in Shanghai, and now nothing in New York.

Lester fingered Cora's letter. "I think there's some sort of sea change in Philadelphia."

Jubal nodded, carefully putting Sally's letters in his kit. "Can't hardly say, though ..." he shrugged. "Well, we got here, that's better than some others. Dock news is we missed the worst winter off the Horn since the '40s. The ice crushed *Fleetwood;* her mate and a few seamen were picked up, but the captain's boat, with his wife and son, were never found. The *John Gilpin* hit a 'berg and went down, and the *John Milton* smashed into Montauk at night, in February. Inbound from the tropics they hit a howlin' snowstorm, every man jack aboard washed ashore frozen, still sunburnt from the doldrums."

"As a reward for surviving," Lester exhaled in long sigh, "I want to eat breakfast in a hot bath." The morning was cloudless, and a warm summer sun had brought the city into the streets. Hailing a cab for the Astor Hotel, they paused for a newsboy, but a quick glance at the morning paper was enough for both Lester and Jubal to fold it up. The front page fulminated with a nation's anger, every story illustrating the schism between North and South.

"Every time we get back here," Lester observed, "everybody's madder. Shit, the Chinese are packed in like pogies and they get along. What the hell's the matter with Americans?"

"It shorly don't look good," Jubal agreed.

At the Astor Hotel's reception desk, the clerk handed them a letter with their room keys. Jubal tore open the envelope and quickly scanned the page. "You're not getting much of a bath," he announced. "We're going to St. George."

Lester read the letter and then stared at his friend. Stubbs had written one sentence ten weeks earlier from Bermuda, after receiving letters Lester sent when *Romance of the Seas* first reached Shanghai. The handwriting looked shaky, but the message was clear: "Come when you receive this."

Lester and Jubal found Truette Stubbs in his new home in St. George, Bermuda, built on a hill overlooking the harbor. The building was slung low, with a surrounding verandah planted to hibiscus and frangipani that Stubbs had imported from Tahiti. Truette Stubbs' home looked like serenity on earth.

Ezekiel met them at the front door and immediately they knew something was wrong. The black man's sadness showed as he bade them through a spacious living room and onto a small patio set back from the house. Truette sat under a palm-frond awning taking spoonfuls of soup from Louisa's hand. The man's appearance shocked them like a fist to the stomach.

Remembering a demeanor ranging from Buddha-like to cherubic, Jubal and Lester found a shadow of that man. Truette had lost his glow and vitality. Despite living in a semitropical Eden, he had shrunk, as if he were wasting away.

"My land, you men are fine sights!" he rasped.

Lester tried to keep the dismay from his face and couldn't talk. Jubal was stricken, but he managed a soft-spoken "What?"

"Bright's Disease," Stubbs explained. "My kidneys'r giving out."

"Can we do anything, sir?" Jubal asked, in a tone of reverence that made Lester turn his head away.

"Y'all did right by comin'," Stubbs answered. He winced from some internal spasm, and then ordered Ezekiel to bring his brandy. "The last of it," he smiled.

Stubbs waved his hand to Louisa, signaling no more soup, and she left. He waited until Ezekiel brought the brandy and poured three glasses, handing one to Truette, who smiled, cupping the glass with both hands.

"To my brandy," he said, his eyes moist, "and good boys, become fine men."

Truette wetted his lips with Ezekiel's help and then closed his eyes as another wave of pain coursed his face. The old black man watched as Truette breathed. Without looking at either Lester or Jubal, Ezekiel gently took the brandy glass and set it down. He forced a mournful smile and left.

"Y'all got here in time, I'm grateful," said Truette. "Don't have much left, I'll make it plain. I'm askin' y'all to handle affairs on my death, which can't be long off, truth to tell. Been a good trade, yes it has." He looked at Jubal and Lester, and motioned a finger for them to drink their brandy. Both obeyed, hardly tasting the smooth liquid.

"I knew y'all would be back for me," Stubbs continued. "So I had the necessary documentation prepared; jes' have to sign. If you're agreed, of course. There are accounts in Mobile and Havana, but the bulk is in London. I established a new company, you each own a third, my estate owns the rest—everything I have is in it. Invest as you think wise. Y'all have that talent now. However, if you ever disagree, Lester you vote my share. Jubal, you're a tougher captain, but Lester's smart and shrewd. I look at y'all like the sons I never had, but this is business."

The talk exhausted him and he fell silent. For several minutes, intermittent calls of songbirds and a rustling, tropical breeze were the only sounds beside Stubbs' labored breathing. Finally, Truette gained enough strength to speak again.

"Get to Mobile," Stubbs wheezed, "execute my last cotton contract and deliver it to James Baines in Liverpool—he's expecting you. Then buy a ship, medium clipper. Sharp but capacious beam; capacity's important. Railroad's to Missouri already, be to the West Coast in five, eight years. Panama railroad's going to gut the Horn traffic. So, find an American ship in England. Buy it right. They're discounted severe, presently. Own it with James Baines on a five-year call, he's majority shareholder by two percent. That's important. Got that deal in hand, but y'all pick the ship. Hear?"

Lester and Jubal nodded in unison.

Truette Stubbs closed his eyes, gathering one last effort. "The company dissolves in ten years; y'all have to figure your buyout then. Take care of Louisa 'n Ezekiel, long's either one is alive. Last thing. War is comin'. *Stay out of it!*" Spittle gathered on his lips, and he forced himself to continue. "That's why Baines's got to own more than half. I want her English registry, case of what might happen. Now give your hands and your words. Take care them nigras, and each other. Hold to that wonder you had as boys. Don't let the madness yonder destroy it. Hear? Good. Gimme yore word."

    Lester and Jubal extended their hands and clasped Truette's little bird claw of a grip.

    "We'll take care of 'em, Truette, long as one of us breathes," Jubal said, nearly choking.

    "Promise," Lester whispered, tears streaming down his face.

    "You're good boys," Truette Stubbs said. "Now go on, back to sea. Yes, suh—go live your lives."

    The man panted lightly, and his eyes sparkled.

Chapter Fifty-Five

Mobile, July 1859

Truette Stubbs' Mobile house was surprisingly cool, though it retained a pale whiff of sickness. Standing in the study, Lester regarded the parlor door and nodded approvingly at the joiner who had repaired its shattered remnants after the shotgun blast. Footfalls sounded on the stairway as Jubal came down, having gone to his room to change a shirt completely sweated out from the suffocating humidity of the Mobile waterfront.

"Any word?" Jubal asked, coming into the study.

"No," Lester replied. "After sending three telegrams in as many days I'm stumped. Do you think they've moved someplace?"

"I got as much idea as you do."

"Well, I don't know what to make of it."

Jubal went around the desk. "Think Truette would mind if I sit in his chair?"

"Think you'll pick up some of his smarts?"

Jubal shook his head, his eyes glinting. "By God, we owe that man." Slowly, as if reverent, he sat in the chair. "Cotton's loaded, she's outbound on the evening tide." A two-masted barkentine running the Liverpool trade lay anchored in the harbor roads. "We can book passage right up to sailing."

Lester leaned against the wall. "Last we heard from the women, they seemed to be telling us to get our ass to Philadelphia. Maybe we could beat that barkie to Liverpool, if the weather cooperates. But it don't feel right, not doing what Truette asked of us."

"Seemed more like an order, to me," Jubal agreed. "Leastways, that's how I feel about it. Like we're obliged, everything he done for us. 'Sides, how often you remember the weather cooperating?"

"How long you think we'd be tangled in Philly?"

Jubal snorted. "A day, a month, a year?"

Lester ran his hand through his hair. "We'd have to take them with us. That'd be a hard chance."

"I think we ought lock this place tight," Jubal decided, "'n get the hell out of here. Take passage with the cotton, do our business with Baines, find us a ship and bring a load back. Them women would be hard-pressed to keep us beached if we had our own ship."

"Three weeks out," Lester agreed, "three more to scour the docks in Liverpool, four back. Three months, shouldn't be more than four. Sally won't like it, but the world isn't going to fall apart before the end of October."

Jubal rose and looked around the study. "I do believe I'll remember this room clear as the day, rest of my life." He sighed, uneasy, but seeing no better alternative. "Let's get her done, Lester. Grab our seabags and go."

Chapter Fifty-Six

Liverpool, October 1859

A cold, sullen rain soaked two figures standing on Wapping Dock in Liverpool. Looming above them, the medium clipper *Mastiff* floated quiet and still, deeply loaded with manufactured goods from the mills of Manchester.

"What do you think, Captain?" Lester asked. "Home by Thanksgiving?"

Jubal shrugged. "You know the western ocean in November well as I do," he replied. "Four weeks ought to do it, unless we stop in Bermuda first. Though I thought we'd be unloading at South Street by now."

"We've done the best we could," Lester said. "I wrote the women we'd have turkey and ham aboard *Mastiff*. So, it'd be best if we cast off in good shape."

"Ebb tide tomorrow," Jubal agreed, "if you're ready. Banks, contracts, bills of lading, insurance—all set?"

The voyage from Mobile had taken twice as long as anticipated, courtesy of weathering a hurricane that dismasted the trader. Since landing James Baines' cotton in England at the end of August, Jubal and Lester had traveled between Liverpool, London, and Portsmouth examining ships. They had even crossed the English Channel to Cherbourg, France, comparing construction caliber and prices for various rigs and tonnages.

During one of their trips to London, Jubal applied for a seat at the British Master's examination. Over the years, he had kept a log of his experience detailing the requisite sea time and mate responsibilities and he also came armed with letters of recommendation from Lauchlan McKay and Asa Caldwell. Jubal's credentials, his service on British-registered ships, plus James Baines' influence at the Admiralty, helped gain him entrance to the exam. On examination day, Lester waited several hours outside the hall and then took a triumphant new captain out for the finest meal in Liverpool.

In their ship search, Lester had tried hard to be impartial and judge every vessel on the merits of its condition and original construction. However, once he learned that a Donald McKay ship was for sale in Liverpool there was no further debate.

Mastiff lay in ballast, a victim of her owners' overextended leverage against the North Atlantic and European markets, where shipping rates had fallen. The ship had spent much of her time shuttling between London and the Mediterranean, occasionally crossing to America.

"She's had her share of weather, but nothing real bad I'd think," Lester relayed to Jubal. "By her logs she's been in the Southern Ocean only twice, out to India and back. Tight, not a sign of hogging yet. Caribbean pine on oak, spruce spars, iron-strapped. McKay-built, right through, I can almost see where Red Jackie daubed out the scarfs. Must have been one of their last ones—remember them days?"

A thousand-ton medium clipper had the same sharp ends as her extreme sisters but more beam, a flatter floor, with smaller spars carrying less canvas. Though she lost time to those sisters in light air, *Mastiff* could sail almost as fast in heavy winds, and her greater cargo capacity would more than compensate in profitability.

Lester negotiated and closed the transaction with Baines—forming a separate corporation—Truette Stubbs & Company—to own the ship and finance a maiden cargo, while Jubal scoured Liverpool's docks and assembled a crew. The first mate was a Finn; the second mate, German; and the rest were from Norway, Newfoundland, Spain, Italy, and Australia. Excepting the cook, Baptiste, a Creole from Hispaniola, no one aboard was older than thirty, and the youngest was a ship's boy from Bath, Maine. Lester had found him wandering the docks, looking for a ship after stowing away in Portland on a brig. The boy reminded him of a brave fawn. Within a minute of their meeting, Lester just ordered him aboard ship. Barely thirteen, Peter gave a shudder of salvation before scampering up the gangway and reporting to Jubal.

At sunset two days before departure, Lester and Jubal stood at the quarterdeck rail discussing the last provisioning details when a courier made his way through the wharve scrum to the gangway asking permission to come board with a letter for the captain. Lester thought nothing of it as Jubal signed for the letter, but a glance moment's later stopped him cold.

From the slump of his partner's shoulders and bowed head Lester knew something was amiss. As Jubal passed him the note Lester recognized James Baines' handwriting. A welling dread went bone deep.

October 25, 1859
London

Gentlemen:

I regret to inform you of word from my Bermuda agent just received: Mr. Truette Stubbs of Mobile, Alabama, and, most recently, St. George, Bermuda, passed from this life September 21, 1859.

A more honourable man I never encountered.

Yr most obedient and humble servant,
James Baines

———

At dawn two days later, *Mastiff* dropped her tug at the mouth of the Mersey River and headed northwest. Jubal stayed on deck for the next thirty-six hours until they cleared the North Channel and left Rathlin Island and the Firth of Clyde astern. Lester kept an eye on Urho Kekkonen, the big Finn, though it became apparent Jubal had chosen his mates well. When the second mate took over the watch, Lester let Jubal sleep through two watches, though he knew it would annoy him. The crew was still mulling the unusual relationship between captain and carpenter's mate, for Lester seemed more of a factotum than a member of the ship's company. Lester didn't care what they thought. He was an owner.

Mastiff rounded the north coast of Ireland and was plowing through the long rollers of the Atlantic on a slicing, cold, southwesterly breeze when Jubal awoke. Baptiste came into the captain's cabin dressed like a black Eskimo, already complaining.

"When we gittin' close to Cooba?" the man chattered, his shivering rattling the breakfast tray. Jubal, listening to the sounds of his ship, didn't even bother to answer. When he'd finished half a cup of coffee, Lester finally pitched him the latest newspapers from the Atlantic packets that gathered just before leaving Liverpool. The *New York Tribune* headlines of October 20, 1859, thundered of events three days earlier, when John Brown had attacked Harpers Ferry, Virginia.

Thanksgiving found *Mastiff* south of Newfoundland with a foot of snow on her decks. Jubal's maiden voyage as captain had been savage. One frigid gale after another slammed them in the eastern Atlantic, often almost stopping the ship in its wake. Iced rigging became so dangerously top heavy in towering seas that Jubal was forced to dip far south into warmer waters, where the ship languished two weeks before fluky western winds. Finally, nearly seething with frustration, he sailed north again only to catch the full blast of an Arctic snowstorm barreling out of the Gulf of St. Lawrence. The month had turned before *Mastiff* came into New York harbor and picked up her tug off Governor's Island.

"You were right," Lester said, leafing through newspapers tossed aboard from the tug. "They hung Brown yesterday. In Virginia."

Jubal nodded, paying more attention to the East River current. "Serve's 'im," he muttered.

"Think that'll be the end of it?"

Jubal spun to his first mate. "Mr. Kekkonen, make ready jib and foretopsail!"

Urho's instant roar sent men scrambling into the rigging. Jubal gestured to his second mate, "Mr. Fischer, that tug smokes again, cast off! I won't have us tethered to a lame duck if her steam dies." He took a deep breath. "Get the snot kicked out of us and can't wait to get in, except it's a damn sight more dangerous in this current with nothing up."

Lester looked around briefly and then resumed reading, thankful again he didn't carry the unremitting duty of a captain. "Brown was passionate crazy," he remarked. "Eloquent too, though bloodthirsty beyond doubt. Like he wanted to hang."

"What's California freight doing?" Jubal asked.

"Frisco's holding up. Looks good enough to make a run."

Despite the brutal passage, Jubal and Lester had made time on the voyage for several long quarterdeck discussions to plan their next year. Deciding that the trade patterns they'd learned from a decade at sea would be their best course, they had tentatively scheduled *Mastiff* to load in New York for San Francisco, rounding South America late in the southern summer to avoid Cape Horn's worst weather. From California, they would make for China and load tea for Melbourne or London, whichever market looked more attractive at the time. Lester hoped to bring Australian wheat or gold back to England, but so many variables of weather and trade could intervene that he had only promised James Baines they would be back within a year.

A week after *Mastiff* arrived in New York, she again lay low in the water, her orlop ballasted with tons of iron train rails and the next two decks stuffed with fabric, sofas, clothes, agricultural implements, plus twenty upright and three grand pianos.

Jubal was meticulous with the loading. Meanwhile, Lester went all over Manhattan, securing the contracts, insurance, and banking arrangements in the name of Truette Stubbs and Company. Waiting impatiently as beetle-eyed copy boys laboriously compiled the multiple drafts of paperwork, he then tore into the shopping district and up to the stockyards with Peter in tow, provisioning the ship for a four-month voyage to California. By mid-morning Tuesday, the ship was nearly ready.

"Let's go," Lester said, when he returned.

"Our demurrage runs through tomorrow," Jubal replied, "and this rain ought to blow through. What's your hurry?"

"Philadelphia," Lester said. "Ship's loaded, provisioned, watered."

"Think the mates can keep the crew?"

"They're your mates. If they can't, we've got bigger problems," Lester shrugged. "They'll mind her."

As the two o'clock Washington Express huffed out of Pennsylvania Station, Lester and Jubal leaped aboard with only the clothes they were wearing and a sheaf of newspapers grabbed at a kiosk by the station entrance. Though both men glanced at headlines, the shrill clamor around John Brown's raid and subsequent execution made for depressing reading. Within a half-hour, Lester had fallen asleep and Jubal nodded off not long after. Neither moved until well after dark, when the train clattered over a bridge.

"Delaware River," Lester yawned, rubbing his eyes. "Couple more hours and we'll be in Philadelphia, maybe less. This express is faster every year."

Jubal stretched the stiffness and glanced at his pocket watch. "In around ten, thereabouts. Pretty late to be showing up at the Motts' place."

Lester didn't relish the situation. "Sal won't mind and those Quakers will just have to get over it. Otherwise, we could wait till morning, but that won't leave time to call on Cora."

"You captain this one," Jubal said, pulling his hat down.

Lester tried to follow Jubal's example, but he was too uneasy to sleep. After a week of feverish activity, the sudden delay felt like skidding to a stop in the middle of a footrace. He picked up the papers again.

John Brown had thrown a rapier at America's heart. One newspaper after another screamed of the North-South divide, as if they were polar opposites ripping apart. *Disunion,* a word that chilled Lester, cropped up repeatedly. The coming political conventions to nominate candidates for the 1860 presidential election seemed poised for fratricide. "A rugged year coming," he murmured, turning down the gaslight overhead. Beside him, Jubal slept lightly.

Two hours later, they asked the driver to wait under a streetlamp, dismounted from a livery cab, and stood in the quiet street before Lucretia Mott's home. Aside from a light in the library, the house was dark.

Lester took a breath. "This is right stupid. But we're here ..." He squared his shoulders, marched up and stuck the knocker lightly, trying not to make much noise.

Jubal winced as the brass clapped like a cannon shot.

A figure stirred in the library and Jubal came up behind Lester to wait. Moments later, John Mott opened the door, dressed in a robe and obviously wary. Then he recognized the men.

"Mr. Norton, Mr. Calhoun ... Well," he said formally, "good of you gentlemen to return home."

"Thank you, sir," Lester said, removing his hat. Mott's stiff reserve unnerved him. "Beg your pardon for this late intrusion," he stammered. "Truth is sir, our ship's loaded. Commercial contracts, responsibilities, deadlines ... I'm sure you understand, sir. But I'd be dearly remiss if I couldn't give my regards to Sally. Could you be so good as to call her, sir?"

"Remiss? Yes, indeed." Mott stared at Jubal for a long moment and shifted his gaze back to Lester. "Your sister no longer lives here. You'll find her at E Street, number fourteen, top floor. I trust she'll see you. It's about time, gentlemen. Good night." He looked them both over once more before closing the door with a metallic click that felt like a slap.

Lester exhaled slowly as the cab driver flicked his pony into stride. "Cold as the Labrador current, that man."

"Wore out our welcome," Jubal nodded. "Why do you suppose she moved?"

"Can't hardly say," Lester shrugged. "Maybe she got mad." The pit growing in his stomach deepened as the cabbie left the tree-lined neighborhoods and entered an older, dingy part of town where narrow row houses had been neglected for years.

At 14 E Street they looked up to the dark window in a small, narrow dormer. Jubal dug a candle stub from his pocket and climbed three flights, the flickering candlelight illuminating flaking wall paint and a few missing balusters on the stairway. The top was vacant, save for one door. Lester glanced at Jubal, took a deep breath, and knocked twice.

Nothing. He knocked twice more, but still there was no sound. Finally, just as he turned away, they heard soft footfalls and a faint rustle.

"Who's that?" a voice demanded. Lester's face lit up, he recognized Cora.

"It's me! Lester! Jubal, too!"

A chain jingled and the door opened a crack. "My lan'!" gasped Cora, as she flung the door wide. "Where in the Lord's name y'all been?" She reached across the threshold for a handful of Lester's coat and hauled him in. He swept Cora into his arms before she had a chance to say another word, lifting her until she grunted.

"Let me down, Lester!" Cora scolded. "Can't breathe, hardly!"

Lester let go and stared, his eyes shining at the sight of Cora's black hair falling past her shoulders. She looked thinner, but the full lips and high cheekbones still made his knees weak.

Cora looked him over with a restrained smile. A flash of fear jolted him as he realized a year might have changed her feelings. He wanted to ask her right then, but the creak of a hinge stopped him. Lester turned to see his sister standing in a doorway, curly hair partially obscuring her face.

Sally's toes showed under a loose, floor-length shift as she pulled a robe over her shoulders. She came in, pushing her hair back and blinking off sleep before the jolt of recognition stopped her. Lester threw his arms open and covered the space between them in three strides. Sally accepted the huge hug, but gently pushed back with a throaty chuckle.

"Hope we didn't rush you," she said smiling with big, wide eyes that held him for a moment and then shifted beyond.

Lester stepped back as Jubal and Sally stared at each other. Neither moved and the tension built until it became almost unbearable, Lester was certain that his sister would stand rock-still. Jubal finally unfroze and handed the candle to his friend without looking, then took slow, tentative steps forward. He reached for her hands and brought them to his throat.

"Sally," he whispered, and opened his mouth to say more.

The sound of a tiny cough stopped him.

It came from the next room. A moment later, another little cough sputtered, followed by the first, whimpering cries of a baby. Sally stared at Jubal a moment longer before turning into the bedroom. The cry quieted and Lester could hear his sister cooing.

Sally slowly came out of the bedroom rocking a small bundle at her chest, humming softly. She stopped a few feet from Jubal. The room hushed except for a faint, slurping burble, as the baby nuzzled into its mother.

"Meet Emma," Sally said.

Chapter Fifty-Seven

Jubal stood transfixed, his mouth hanging open.
    The baby nuzzled and slurped, then went silent. Somewhere in the room a clock faintly ticked. Lester wanted to say something but couldn't make his voice work. Both women stared at Jubal. Finally, Cora pushed.

"Jubie, go take your daughter."

Jubal's Adam's apple moved as if he were swallowing an egg, whole. He took two or three breaths and teetered, alarming Lester, who tensed to catch him. Jubal stepped forwards, shaking his head as though to dispel a dream, paused, then took another step. Sally didn't move.

"About time you came," she said, her eyes glistening.

A low moan escaped Jubal as he reached for his child. Sally carefully handed their baby to him, touched by the sight of his large, gnarled hands nearly enclosing the infant. Jubal held Emma close and stared with the intensity of a man counting each eyelash. The baby stirred, and Jubal's nostrils quivered as he inhaled for the first time in his life the ecstasy of a baby's sweet-sour smell. He bent forward and brushed her little face with his nose. Lester exhaled like the last gasp of a steam engine.

"Can I sit down?"

"No," Cora replied. "Go fire the stove, the corner over there. Coal's in the bin behind." She turned to a set of cupboards and in short order lit two lamps and ladled water from a pail into a cast-iron kettle. "Heat this, Lester. Doubt we be sleepin' soon."

Emma slept in Jubal's arms while the adults sat near a coal stove sipping tea until dawn lightened the dormer window. Their chairs came tight, interrupted only when Lester had to slowly pace off the heart-clutching sight of Jubal rocking his daughter. The women spoke of their year, slowly at first, but with less caution as the men listened in rapt attention. Occasionally, either Cora or Sally would ask about the ocean, but Lester didn't say more than a word or two before asking another question. The surrounding furnishings were sparse, and both women carried the drawn look of mothers living through insufficient sleep and unending effort. While neither complained, the struggle was plain.

Cora continued to work at William Still's house and had two other part-time jobs while also taking a reading class organized by Lucretia Mott. When Sally's pregnancy began to show, the Motts were offended, but they would not have turned her out. Sally's pride did that.

"I just didn't want to live with their judgment," she said, sitting with her feet tucked under her. Lester had taken his coat off and wrapped it around his sister, alarmed at her pallor. "Cora came, too," Sally sighed.

The men continually looked from one woman to the other, marveling at the quiet fortitude and bone-deep strength. Every trace of young girls was gone. In the dead of night Lester flinched when his sister made some flippant, edgy comment that was an uncanny echo of their mother.

"You're wondering why I didn't say nothing, I know," Sally said sometime before dawn. "We never knew where you were, or if anything written got to you. Besides," she continued, testiness creeping in, " it wouldn't have made any difference."

It was the only time Jubal spoke before dawn.

"I wish you had," he murmured, smelling his daughter.

After leaving the Mott's home, Sally got a job as a seamstress—"They let me bring Emma"—and came home to spend the evening with her daughter and Curtis before going to another job at a bakery from three to seven in the morning.

"Whoever's home watches the chillin'," Cora shrugged. "There's a couple other girls here ... We take a care of each other."

Lester noticed her language and speech had become an amalgam of plantation and classroom. When relaxed, Cora sounded of red clay soil, but often she made a visible effort to enunciate and drop the bottomland cadence. Lester was touched, wanting to tell Cora he didn't care how she talked.

"Why didn't you spend the house money, make it easier?" Lester said, turning to his sister.

"I used some already," Sally replied. "People coming north with nothing—I tried to help, best I could. There's still some left, but I didn't know what I might need." The comment was reproach simply by its fact.

Jubal kept rocking Emma.

The first rays of sunrise dimpled the dirty window when the women ran out of energy. Sally sighed, looking completely spent. "Norma at the bakery's going to be mad," she said with a shrug. "I've got to sleep before going to the dress shop."

"You're not goin'," Jubal said.

Sally looked up at him. Then she glanced at Lester.

"Where the hell have you men been?" she said, her anger surfacing in a rush.

"Bought us a ship, sis," Lester replied. "Jubal's captain."

"How nice!"

"I keep it floating and handle the tariff," Lester continued. "Jubal's captain at sea, I'm captain on land. Muscle 'n brains."

Sally looked at Jubal and snorted. "When are you leaving again? Today?"

Jubal nodded. "Tide turns just before midnight."

"Oh, goddam you both!" Sally cried, slapping the arms of her chair as she vaulted up. "Give her to me 'n get the hell out!"

"Emma's comfortable," Jubal replied, unperturbed. "You go pack. Give her a hand, will you, Lester?"

Lester stood. "C'mon sis, you heard the captain. You too, Cora."

Cora looked at Lester, Jubal, and Sally in turn. "Y'all gone crazy?"

"No," Lester replied. "We've got a ship full-loaded for California ready to cast off the moment we're aboard. Got to be moving, let's go."

"What do you think you're doing, Lester?" Sally challenged, working to a fury. "Just walk in here and rescue us? Did you buy arrogance with that ship?"

"Rescue?" Lester looked at his sister, then to Cora. "Be a cold day in hell before you two need any rescuing. We just didn't know how it was with you. Now we do. Besides, it's time. Jubal and I've known that since we was last here. We just had things to do."

Cora rose tall, her face flushing in the pale light. "You jes' walk in here after a year and start tellin' me wha' I's gonna do? Who you think you are, mister? I gonna take my Curtis and come on dat ship jes' 'cause you says?" She was hot and Lester's smile made her even madder. "Pay heed to your sister! Git outta here!" She stamped her foot and pointed to the door.

"Shush," Lester replied. "You'll wake the neighbors. I'll help get our things; you get Curtis ready."

"So's I can be yo' pallet on that ocean?" Cora snarled. "Been done that, Lester Norton! Find yourself 'nother tramp out on the street!"

"For just once in your lives," Jubal said, rocking placidly, "would y'all do what you're told?" Emma started to stir. "This caterwaulin's waking the child. C'mon, light's rising."

The women looked at each other as if they were dealing with madmen.

"That William Still's a minister, right?" Lester asked, reaching for his coat. "Or he must know one."

Cora's anger went out like a popped bubble. Sally stood open-mouthed, a mirror of Jubal a few hours earlier.

"Jubal'll give you away," Lester nodded to Cora. "I'll give Sal."

"That'll work," Jubal agreed, nuzzling his daughter.

Chapter Fifty-Eight

The Reverend Henry Highland Garnet was in the midst of breakfast when William Stills called. An hour later the pastor stood in his office at the United Presbyterian Church, holding his grandmother's old, battered Bible, a book the woman was never able to read but held nonetheless each Sunday on a South Carolina plantation until her death. Garnet had learned to read with that Bible.

Witnessed by William and Letitia Still, their two eldest children, Curtis, and, after a fashion, Emma—the infant slept through the proceedings after Sally nursed her in the carriage taking them to church—the Reverend Garnet began to conduct a dual wedding. In lieu of wedding rings, Lester had braided manila loops for the women from a spare sail thread he always carried in his satchel.

"We know a fellow in Canton," Jubal murmured. "He'll make us proper rings like nowhere else on this earth." The Reverend Garnet smiled at the ingenious knotting, done with the precision of a skilled sailmaker.

"When does your ship sail?" he asked, as he gestured for the couples to stand before him.

"At Jubal's command," Lester smiled. "He's captain."

"The ebb tide at dusk," Jubal explained. "So, begging your pardon, sir, could we proceed smartly?"

"Very well." The Reverend's deep, melodious voice was as commanding as a ringing gong. "In absence of your specific request, I present the vows as brought to us in St. Paul's Epistle to the Ephesians."

Reverend Garnet pulled a white cashmere stole over shoulders and opened his Bible.

"Will you, Lester Norton, have this woman, Cora, and you, Jubal Calhoun, have this woman, Sally, to be your wedded wives, to live together in the holy estate of matrimony as God ordained it? Will you nourish and cherish her, as Christ loved His body the Church, giving Himself up for her? Will you love, honor, and keep her in sickness and in health, and forsaking all others remain united to her alone, as long as you both shall live? Then say: I will."

The men's voices rang in unison.

Reverend Garnet addressed Cora. "Will you, Miss Cora, have this man

Lester Norton, and will you, Miss Sally, have this man, Jubal Calhoun, to be your wedded husbands, to live together in the holy estate of matrimony as God ordained it? Will you submit to him as the Church submits to Christ? Will you love, honor, and keep him in sickness and in health, and forsaking all others remain united to him alone, as long as you both shall live? Then say: I will."

"I will." The women stood straight, both in floor-length, full-sleeved, simple white cotton dresses Sally had made months before.

Reverend Garnet bowed slightly. "I pronounce you, Lester and Cora Norton, man and wife." Turning, he waited for a moment as Emma burped in her sleep, dribbling milky spittle on Sally's sleeve. With a smile, he continued, as Sally took Jubal's proffered handkerchief and cleaned their daughter's face. "I pronounce you, Jubal and Sally Calhoun, man and wife."

Each couple kissed, Lester and Cora gently, shyly, Sally and Jubal brief and strong.

William Still glanced at his pocket watch and cleared his throat. "The train …"

"Thank you, sir." Jubal, all captain now, nodded to the reverend. "Begging y'all's pardon," he looked about the small assembly, "we must step lively now."

"Not just yet," Cora said. "Reverend, do you have broom?"

The Reverend Garnet laughed, the wonderful cascade of a rock fall, joined by William and Letitia Still. Lester and Sally were flummoxed, but Jubal smiled.

"Indeed, I do," the Reverend replied, making for a corner cabinet. In a moment he handed Cora a straw broom.

Cora took Lester's hand. "This custom has been in our people longer than any of us known. The straw is all separate but the handle is one, just the way we were before 'n the way we are now. We're goin' to jump the broom, sweep the past behind." Cora lay the broom on the floor and took Lester's hand. "Ready? Now jump!"

As one, Lester and Cora hopped over the broom.

"Sally, Jubie," Cora ordered, "jump the broom!" They did, to robust applause.

Lester thrust his hand out to Reverend Garnet. "We'll never forget you, sir. Thank you! Now, we've got to go. I know my captain; Lord help us if we miss that tide."

Chapter Fifty-Nine

Mid-Atlantic, December 1859

As *Mastiff* approached the equator on New Year's Eve, Curtis fell asleep under a coruscating night sky. The boy loved to lie in Jubal's arms on the quarterdeck as the captain used his small index finger to trace constellations and describe the zodiac. Though only four, the boy had adapted to the ship faster than his mother or aunt, who were both only beginning to get their sea legs.

For the first two weeks aboard, Cora and Sally spent much of their time vomiting. As the days went by and *Mastiff* sailed away from the northern winter, Lester had stopped his grumbling—"helluva honeymoon" he complained to Jubal several times a day—and worried as the women weakened. Emma kept squalling because she didn't get much milk so Lester found himself primarily occupied as a nurse, once he'd repaired several spars and sails damaged in a nor'easter that had blasted them two days out of New York.

Jubal had nearly lived on deck since their departure. At dawn the first day he knew they were sailing into weather and he had driven the ship under all sail to clear the Gulf Stream and make as much easting as he could before the gale caught them. The storm came up the coast—deep, intense, and fast—and when Jubal decided he had enough sea room he turned to beat southwestward rather than running before the winds taking them north.

"You going deeper into it?" Lester had screamed above the rising winds. Jubal nodded, preferring the risk of weathering the gale's center in deep water to riding onto the Grand Banks, where the shallows would turn the sea into a maelstrom.

The excitement of their last whirlwind day on land quickly vanished for Cora and Sally. They had been unable to sleep much of the night after clearing the Verrazano Narrows at dusk. A sea was already building and Jubal didn't want to anchor off Sandy Hook, so the women were queasy before midnight. Curtis and Emma slept soundlessly but their mothers crawled by morning. The wonderful Astor Hotel dinner that had been their farewell to New York went spewing into chamber pots in the captain's cabin. Cora didn't appear on deck for eight days and Sally ten, though their first acts on seeing the horizon were to lurch with the ship's roll and puke over the rail. Word quickly passed that if a woman came on deck, any seaman nearby was responsible to keep her from falling overboard.

Gradually, through Lester's ministrations and Baptiste's preparation of broth, soup, and then slurries of solid food, the women began to keep down more than they threw up. Since Emma was being forcibly weaned, the cook also mashed bland imitations of the women's food and Lester began to feed the little girl each day, first with his finger and then a small spoon.

Under other circumstances Jubal would have been furious at the delays in getting sails and spars repaired, but he took it with reasonable equanimity now, mostly because he didn't have any choice. Nothing had ever rattled him like Emma's crying. When unhappy, the baby could frazzle the entire ship, so her father accepted a lesson in patience.

Lester required the same, getting so testy they didn't speak for a few days.

"I can't be in every damn place at once," he hissed at Jubal one night in the sail locker, out of earshot from any crewman. "The crossjack and mizzen royal be fixed in another day or two, but the fore topsail is blown to smithereens, and will have to wait. What with them women nearly turned inside out and that lil girl got's her father's lungs ... Well sir, you stay topside!"

Lester's outburst amused Jubal. They would only lose a day or two on the voyage, which he knew could easily come from a score of other factors. Plus the crew had adapted well to the presence of the families, though he'd never forget the dumbfounded amazement of every man aboard as they watched their captain and bosun, who had left as a pair, appear a day later, matter-of-factly bringing wives and children aboard.

As *Mastiff* picked up the northeast trades and turned south, the women began to appear more frequently, usually in the afternoon to watch the sunset from the safety of the quarterdeck. Curtis learned to scamper along with the sailors, most whom spoke to him in their own language. The boy routinely terrified his mother because he seldom wanted to hold her hand, but gradually Cora grew to trust that the crew always kept eyes on the boy.

Finally, as the ship entered the doldrums and sailed placidly under light winds, Sally and Cora became accustomed to the motion and pace of life at sea. The relentless rollers in the trades subsided to a long, gentle swell, and *Mastiff* flew every sail for days on end, rarely altering course.

Lester set up hammocks as the weather grew hot, and the women often slept under the stars with their children. Along with routine tasks required to keep the ship and sails in order, Lester had also remodeled two of the guest staterooms, creating a large cabin for his family. As they approached St. Paul Island, a few degrees above the equator, he decided to celebrate the arrival of normal life aboard a ship that had only begun its circumnavigation. Knowing the placid latitudes would allow Jubal to relax as much as he ever could at sea, Lester enlisted the cook and hosted an intimate dinner in the captain's cabin. Trolling off the quarterdeck at dawn, Baptiste caught a large tuna that became the splendid dinner centerpiece.

Emma sat propped in a clothes' basket at Sally's elbow and Curtis squirmed on a stool next to Cora, dressed like the adults in his Sunday best.

Jubal raised a glass of wine. "To beautiful women and fine children."

Sally felt herself again, enjoying the spicy food with her foot curled inside her husband's under the table. She regarded him with undisguised pleasure.

"Never thought I'd see a woman adore you, Jubal," Lester grinned. "Best not get used to it." He had never seen his sister so happy.

Sally made a face. "He's already used to it. Not many women lucky enough to have a handsome captain on their arm."

"You adore me, too, Emma?" Jubal asked. She chewed on a slobbery hand and burbled. "I thought so."

Cora stayed quiet. Lester had grown accustomed to her reticence, realizing he had only begun to know the woman. By temperament she was an introvert who seldom said something without having thought it through first. Later, at sunset, Lester pointed out the faint rub of St. Paul's Island on the eastern horizon. They were standing at the taffrail where Cora could keep her eye on Curtis, who was in the ship's waist with Cub Pingree. Four weeks earlier, when a coastal sloop had arrived in Bangor with news that *Mastiff* was loading for San Francisco, Cub had gone to his father asking for a year to see the world and experience life as a clipper man. The young Mainer waited on the quay when Lester and Jubal returned with their new brides from Philadelphia, nervous that the men might not consider his request to ship aboard. Jubal hired him on the spot.

"How's my darling?" Lester asked, refraining from putting his arm around her. He knew Cora didn't like public displays, and it would do morale no good to give the sailors any more imagination than the forecastle already provided. Lester could predict the envy and comments circulating with every glimpse of Cora's full figure. Also, Cora was definitely not white, a topic of some curiosity, though the crew came in a variety of colors.

"I'm alive, again," Cora smiled. "Spent nigh on two weeks thinking Gee's Bend was better."

"That bad?" asked Lester, shocked.

"Oh sweet Lord, I'd like to died! A woman can only retch so much. No joy in staring down a chamber pot."

Lester grinned like a kid. "I swear you're the most beautiful woman in the world."

Cora glanced sideways at him. "What you got in mind?"

"I've been waiting three weeks and better."

Cora looked away, embarrassed. "Ought be patient."

"I have," Lester declared. "And now I'm about ready to haul you into that longboat, throw the tarp over atop us."

Behind them, Jubal stepped from the companionway. He looked every inch the commander until he spotted Curtis standing with his little arms astride his hips. In all but the worst weather, the boy could melt the captain with his high, musical *Uncle Jubie?* Lester knew the sailors had picked the name up, but none would dare to use it outside the forecastle.

"C'mon darlin'," Lester said, "captain's on deck. Curtis will be fine." With a glance to her son, Cora turned and went below. A few seconds later, Lester followed.

He didn't come back on deck until the middle of the night, after the quarter moon rose. Cora lay sleeping, and he covered her with a silk sheet before leaving, gently wiping the last perspiration from her hairline. Earlier, in the fading light, she had been tense and stiff for the longest time as he stroked her body under the sheets, until at last he lay still, uncertain what to do. Cora had turned to him then.

"I'm scairt," she whispered.

"No one's ever going to hurt you again," Lester breathed. "Cora darlin', you've come home."

She came to him then and Lester let her unfold at her own pace, feeling her breath and pulsing heartbeat quicken in fits and starts. He stroked her smooth back as she pressed her face into his neck. Cora's nails raked him, as if she was stripping away demons to unveil her own wellspring. Lester bit his lip until it nearly bled before finally throwing the sheet aside and pulling her on top of him. Cora rose and took all of him, sitting upright with a low, guttural grunt that threw her hands to the deck beams above.

—

Sally began to read again as *Mastiff* cleared Cape St. Roque. Perhaps it was the shadow of the Brazilian mainland as they passed, or Lester's recalling their first voyage with Eleanor Creesy. In any case, Sally decided to learn navigation, and Jubal directed her to the maritime volumes. As she practiced with the sextant, Sally asked about Mary Patten's skill, for her brother had also told that story around the dinner table in the captain's cabin.

The women tried to make dinner a time for the families together, which was fine with Jubal as long as weather permitted. Sally became accustomed to her husband leaving the table abruptly, without explanation. When it first happened she was offended, until about three minutes later when the wind suddenly increased and the pitter-patter on deck quickly changed to the snare drum sound of driving rain.

"How'd he know?" she asked Lester, as the squall overtook them. Her brother sat with his ears cocked.

"Because he's captain," Lester said, although the ship telegraphed just as clearly to him. "The only difference between the keel and Jubal is he occasionally uses his voice. A captain doesn't just command—he *is* the ship. This crew under a different man would be an entirely different ship, one you'd hardly recognize."

Cora also read voraciously and demanded that Curtis continue to learn.

The boy tried, but his attention span was short, particularly since *Mastiff*'s crew cosseted him, showing the boy knots, splices, scrimshawing, and all manner of seamen's tricks.

As the ship sailed deeper into the Southern Hemisphere, dinner conversations often revolved around the two dozen newspapers that Lester had gathered on South Street an hour before sailing. The news had lain unopened until *Mastiff* cleared the equator. Two small pieces of news from these brought Lester and Jubal up short. Buried in the back pages of one of the maritime journals was a report that *Sovereign of the Seas* had run aground and broken up on the Malacca reefs coming home from China. The men took the news stoically, though they could barely hold a conversation the rest of the evening. A few days later, Sally opened dinner with grace and a prayer for Mary Patten. When both the men stared in astonishment, she gently told them of reading the young woman's obituary in the *Boston Herald*.

"Died of consumption at twenty-three," Sally said. "Left a young son—Joshua."

The sudden pall cast around the table alarmed Curtis. Lester saw the boy's distress.

"It's all right, son," he said, though the news saddened him deeply. "Another boy, just about your age, as good a lad as you, no doubt. A most courageous mother, yes sir."

Jubal excused himself from the table shortly thereafter, and Lester picked at his food a bit longer, before saying he had a spar that needed varnishing before nightfall.

Mastiff sailed through the Golden Gate in April after a passage of 115 days. The women stood at the taffrail talking excitedly, while Curtis sobbed into his mother's dress, nearly beside himself with frustration. He wanted to be on the quarterdeck near his uncle, but Cora held the boy's hand like a vise, ignoring his cries. At one point Curtis yanked her arm so hard she cuffed him on the rump, but even a sniveling tantrum on the deck didn't move his mother. She could see Jubal commanding the quarterdeck with eyes that missed nothing. When his ship neared land, the captain tensed like a big jungle cat, ready for anything.

Cora had quickly understood the invisible gulf separating Jubal from everyone aboard ship, even Lester. For Sally however, it had taken a major, begrudging adjustment to accept that the cabin threshold was also a border between her husband's intimacy and the merciless demands on deck. She savored the power of her captain but hated taking second place to anything, living or floating.

As Jubal ordered the anchor let go, an agent's longboat came alongside for the ship's papers and delivered a bundle of newspapers and mail.

"Baines' letter got here faster from Liverpool than we did from New York," Lester remarked. "He wants us to bring wool from Melbourne and cotton fabric out of Bombay if we've got room."

"In ballast to Australia?" Jubal asked. He noted Lester's unease and felt it, too. The speed of communication and just a glance at the newspaper headlines confirmed that change had become less evolution than a hurtling, headlong rush.

Lester shook his head, fluttering a document. "Contract for tea out of

Whampoa to Port Jackson," he said. "We're full most the way. If these margins hold we'll make a good run."

The next day Jubal left the mate in charge of unloading and the families moved ashore to sumptuous rooms at the Oriental Hotel. Lester ordered the staff to find a nanny so Cora and Sally could luxuriate in hot baths before going out to shop. The women indulged themselves like divas and then went off giggling to window-gawk at fashions from the East Coast and Europe. Despite their husbands' encouragement, they did much more looking than buying. Neither could shed the abiding fear of poverty that had loomed a season ago. San Francisco prices were also exorbitant for most items, an exception being used books, which came off ships in crates. Sally could justify books much more than dresses, so within a week, *Mastiff's* library had quadrupled.

Late dinner reservations allowed the adults a crystal-and-silver repast without the interruptions of fretting children. That freedom, plus a little wine, loosened up Sally to the daily news.

"Jubal, I never understand this Southern attachment." Her manner was earnest but careful. "I know they think it's hypocrisy, calling Irish and Scot immigrants free when they're paid a pittance, but at least they're not owned! How can people think their slave property is so content and better off, while fearing that those same slaves are primed for insurrection? Can someone be happy and want to kill you at the same time?"

"Sally," Jubal sighed, "get it through your pretty head that it isn't about slaves. True enough, it goes right to the heart 'n soul of Southern life, but Jefferson had slaves, Washington too, for a time. It's about submission, not secession. That's a distinction might be lost on you, but people live and breathe it in Alabama. Federal authority'll never replace states' rights. You can dissect the Constitution all you like and not get clear. Jefferson and Marshall argued about it for thirty years!"

"Jubal, just read that *De Bow's Review!*" Sally's face had flushed and her curls flounced on her shoulders. "They think Stephen Douglas is some sort of heathen beast! But it's the Democratic Party that's frothing at the mouth!"

"It'll be hot at that convention in Charleston," Jubal agreed. "Southern and Northern Democrats have only got the party name in common. I don't doubt it may split over who gets nominated. Point is ... well, that's it. A point. Someone sticks a sword at your throat, says do this or that, there's few men won't fight if they've got the means. Especially those with independence running through five, six generations of folk."

"Jubie," Sally said, reaching for his arm, "just look at your sister. This is about a million Coras."

Jubal looked at Cora, then back to his wife. "Is 'n it isn't, Sal; depends on the ground you first walked. Comes to it, who's to say what happens on that ground? Man who walks it, works, lives, breathes and dies for it, or somebody in a government building hundreds or thousands of miles away? Popular sovereignty is like giving authority to a herd. Men who refused to be herded settled this country. Your brother and I spent the last ten years becoming our own men—and if we weren't, *y'all wouldn't be wanting us.*" He stared at his wife, and then at Cora before sitting back. Jubal might as well have struck a gavel to the conversation.

"Jubal, you're just doing it again," Sally whimpered. "Ignoring politics, just like your family, a mule happy in his blinders!" She suddenly got up from the table and fled, causing an immediate lull throughout the dining room.

Lester studied his plate, saddened by how quickly the dinner had been ruined. He glanced at Cora and was surprised to see her staring at Jubal. Lester's eyes flitted back and forth between them, wondering who would dominate, but it was no contest. Jubal tossed his napkin to the table and went after his wife.

"Mom always said Sally's very first syllable was *no*," Lester observed. "Can't get enough attention, always the last word."

"She's scared," said Cora. "Just started a life together and those politicians fixin' to wreck it. Sally just sees lil' Emma, her man, and herself against the world."

Lester scratched his head and gave up trying to make sense of it. "Still want dinner?"

"Sho' do," Cora replied. "One of 'em will find the other."

Chapter Sixty

Mastiff crossed the Pacific in ballast, anchoring at Whampoa in late June. The crossing was idyllic, with day upon day of brilliant trade wind sailing. The ship rode high and easy, giving the crew time to sand, finish, and polish every surface from waterline to mastheads. There was no reason to drive the men hard and Jubal didn't try. Spirits were high and he welcomed a happy ship. The second mate had been a lone sour note but he'd been stupid enough to get drunk in San Francisco and disparage captains who brought women aboard. Jubal threw him off his ship.

To the surprise of everyone except Lester, Jubal advanced Cub Pingree to third mate and left the second mate position unfilled. The young man had only been a coastal sailor, but Jubal recognized a born seaman. Before the ship reached China, *Mastiff* had another credible navigator.

Curtis was upset that Cub didn't have as much time to spend with him, so Jubal ordered Peter, the ship's boy, to watch the child, especially as Curtis now terrified his mother by climbing into the rigging. Cora started a journal when Lester suggested she draft a family genealogy, and the extended passage gave Sally time to resume painting, a hobby she had developed while working at the Motts' home in Philadelphia. She spent a few hours every fine day at her easel, often with some of the off-watch crewmen silently observing, after they had somehow determined the captain wouldn't mind.

Sally rather liked the audience. She also continued her navigation study, and learned sailmaking from her brother, picking up the stitching skills quickly, though she had to learn layouts and cutting. The ocean also seemed to have given her another fledgling, for Peter bounded around with the energy of a puppy, helpful and enthusiastic in a clumsy, besotted way.

From the quarterdeck, Jubal felt the master of his world, sometimes glancing to the heavens with thanks for the benediction of seven magnificent weeks.

Off Canton, they stayed long enough to fill the holds with tea. By the time Jubal weighed anchor, the Chinese jeweler had done his work, producing rings for Lester and Cora that mimicked in gold the woven sail thread of their original rings. Jubal and Sally each had rings in the shape of a parting sea, with a diamond set off by a ruby on the right and an emerald on the left, colors of the brilliant nighttime lanterns on the masthead and port and starboard sides.

The run down to Australia was not nearly so pleasant. Though the weather was fine, *Mastiff* sailed against the southwest monsoon, what was left of it. The ship often beat against light, baffling winds, looping east of the Philippines and south through the Molucca Passage. Jubal picked his way amidst the islands sprinkled east of Sulawesi, making for the Arafura Sea. After nearly a month of constant tension in shallow, reef-studded tropical waters they cleared the Torres Strait into the Coral Sea and beat down the eastern coast of Australia.

Any romance of the sea had worn off for Sally. In Whampoa, Chinese restrictions on foreigners outraged her, an attitude Lester compared to ranting at the moon. She wanted to explore and suggested they go to Shanghai, but Jubal curtly reminded her that *Mastiff* was not a yacht. Sally's mood might have gotten worse but she made the mistake of addressing her husband sarcastically on the quarterdeck in front of his men. She quailed at his reaction, never again wanting to witness such cold fury. Jubal took Sally's arm in a grip that left bruises and escorted her to their cabin where, in syllables like bullets, he informed her that if such conduct was ever repeated on his quarterdeck she would be confined to their cabin until they reached port—whereupon he would book passage and send her directly to New York.

Sally pouted for a few days and though Cora was of some solace, Lester wouldn't even speak to her about the incident, other than a tart comment that "The captain means what he says." Only in coming through the Spice Islands did Sally come to fully appreciate her husband's responsibilities, for he ordered men into the rigging to watch for breaking reefs and sandbars while he paced the deck, armed with pistols in case of pirate attack.

Emma also diverted Sally's attention. The infant contracted a high fever out of Whampoa that lasted a week, giving Sally an awful fright. After it broke, Emma recovered quickly and started to crawl.

When *Mastiff* finally rode the big Pacific breakers past Sydney Heads and anchored in the finest natural harbor Jubal had ever seen, he began to relax. The entire crew was ready for shore leave and couldn't wait to hit the taverns and whorehouses of Port Jackson. The port teemed with the energy and mayhem of early San Francisco, so they decided to sail for Melbourne immediately, before their crew dissolved along the waterfront. Jubal sent Urho and Cub Pingree ashore, but the young Mainer was back within six hours, needing help because the mate had stopped for just one dram and that was the end of him. Lester and Jubal spent the next twelve hours lugging one drunken sailor after another back and finally weighed anchor with four men missing. Jubal left word at the wharf that their ship would be in Melbourne if the men wanted a ride home.

Sally was furious at the truncated layover but her anger evaporated when she saw *Mastiff*'s sailors stumble aboard with black eyes and missing teeth. Even Urho, a master knife fighter among Finns, came back with a crescent gouge to his cheek that took a dozen of Sally's careful stitches to close.

With the cargo holds temporarily empty, Lester relaxed enough to read several issues of the *Sydney Morning Herald*, an enterprising daily. Though news from American and Europe was generally two months old, the deteriorating situation in the United States dominated world headlines.

"Election's going to be between four men," Lester reported at dinner. "Douglas and Breckenridge for the Democrats—you called it Jubal, the party did split North 'n South—then there's Lincoln for the Republicans, and Bell for a new one, something called the Constitution-Union Party."

"Fellow from Indiana, is he?" Jubal asked. "Lincoln?"

"Illinois," Sally corrected. "Read those debates he had with Douglas, I've got them somewhere here in the books. That man comes from the same stock as us."

"Meaning?" Jubal asked.

"From next to nothing," Sally replied. "No money in that family. He worked for what he got. And he says what he means."

"Doesn't matter," Jubal observed. "A Republican president is a Northern president."

Lester nodded. "Southerners are calling him a 'mobocrat'." He motioned to the newspapers on the chart table. "It's rabid enough, and you can bet the *Herald*'s just picking up a sliver. Apparently, black men are about to marry every white woman below the Potomac."

"A president is a president," Sally insisted.

"He gets elected," Jubal said, setting down his napkin, "the country will crack like a nut." He gestured to the women. "Best eat well," he said, his voice going gentle. "When we turn the corner, it'll get rough bucking the Bass Strait. The Southern Ocean funnels through and can get colorful."

That was one way to describe a wild twenty-four hours. Riding empty, *Mastiff* cleared the eastern coast and bounced like a cork into the head winds and high, stiff seas of Bass Strait. The children were tied into their bunks while the ship labored around the southeast tip of the continent. Jubal pounded into the prevailing westerlies rather than be caught on a lee shore. Finally, after a harrowing night, they passed into the safety of Port Phillip Bay and anchored off Melbourne.

Sally and Cora came on deck in mid-morning with the children as Cub Pingree readied the longboat alongside. Jubal and Lester came to help their families disembark, and Sally extracted a promise that they would all spend several days together in Melbourne. Cora wanted another picnic, for they reminded her of home. The men were dutifully nodding when Lester stopped and stared through a dozen ships anchored in the roads.

"By God, Jubal, am I seeing right?" he exclaimed, pointing into the distance.

Jubal snapped his telescope open and stared for a moment before a slow smile raised his mustache. "I'll be damned," he marveled. "Yes sir, Lester, that there's the *Great Republic*."

Chapter Sixty-One

Melbourne, September 1860

Captain Joseph Limeburner escorted Sally and Cora through his massive ship while describing her reconstruction after the great fire. A few hours earlier, Jubal had sent a note over, briefly recounting his and Lester's experience, to which Captain Limeburner replied immediately, inviting them for dinner aboard.

The *Great Republic* looked markedly different from the masterpiece Donald McKay had built. Her mighty spars had been cut by almost a third, a mast had been removed, she was shorn of deck housings, and much of the beautiful interior detailing was gone. Lester and Jubal felt sadness at the once-magnificent creature's dowdiness. Still, she was one of the largest ships afloat.

"Even with a smaller rig, she holds the record from New York to the equator and the Horn," Limeburner declared. "Once did nineteen knots—that's average, mind you—for nineteen out of twenty-four hours on a run in the Southern Ocean. Her size is telling."

After the tour, Captain Limeburner spread a sumptuous dinner in the *Great Republic*'s stateroom. Having arrived into Melbourne from San Francisco only a day earlier than *Mastiff*, he was full of the latest news, none of it good.

"The election campaign has made a frenzy," he reported. "I don't know your politics, sir," the captain looked at Jubal, "but Abe Lincoln doesn't believe Jefferson Davis and his bunch will attempt to ruin the government, though I'm not so sure. What do you think, captain? Is this not more bullying tactics, the likes of which we've seen for years?"

"Who is the bull, sir?" drawled Jubal. "Sounds to me like two of them slobbering, each daring a charge."

"Indeed," Captain Limeburner replied, unhappy with Jubal's response. "The election will tell the tale, I believe, one way or another. You're bound to India, then England? Yes, you'll know by Liverpool I expect."

Joseph Limeburner's comment returned to *Mastiff* with the diners and remained a constant, unspoken presence on the slow passage to Bombay.

Despite the rhythms of life at sea, anxiety and uncertainty could not be whisked away on the monsoon winds. As their ship retraced its track north around the top of Australia and sailed westward to follow the coastlines of Java and Sumatra into the Indian Ocean, the men and women grew pensive, each contemplating the unknown journeys that lay ahead.

Sally and Jubal, by mutual, silent consent, relished the brilliant tropical air, luscious breezes, and sublime sunsets, avoiding all talk of America. The delights of family were too precious. Jubal was confident of his ship and crew, the weather held, and Emma started to walk.

Occasionally, the men would speak of business on the taffrail, where they had a running discussion as to why James Baines wanted them loading cotton in Bombay. *Mastiff* was nearly full, and if they sailed directly for Liverpool, the world voyage would show a handsome profit.

"So why the hell take us nearly two months out of the way?" Jubal wondered as they approached the distant outline of Ceylon.

"I've been wondering the same," Lester said. "Best I can figure, Baines is hedging."

"Hedging what?"

"England's economy would buckle without cotton," Lester replied. "Five, six ports below the Chesapeake ship a million tons every year; that was our bread and butter, too. But if Lincoln gets elected and the snarling starts, who knows? Virtually *any* spat's going to send cotton up. Two fellows start shooting, and the price'll go through the roof. So if you're a shipper ... He's doing the same as you, checking the horizon. India, Egypt—hell, James Baines don't care. He wants another source, and India's not far out of our way. Maybe he sees weather we don't."

Jubal looked out at the clear horizon. "Could be."

⁓

The cyclone hit them on Thanksgiving, a hundred miles southeast of Mauritius. From Bombay, where they loaded two hundred tons of raw Indian cotton, *Mastiff* enjoyed three weeks of good weather before a high, thin wisp of cloud cover muddied the sunset. When Urho woke Jubal at dawn to report the barometer falling like a stone, the captain took one look east and had the entire ship on deck within five minutes. Turning crimson, the first rays of sunlight came overhead in blood-colored streaks that splayed the underside of the cloud cover. Shafts of lurid, fire-burst orange lit the sun's path until the horizon almost quivered in anticipation. Charcoal clouds boiled out of the ocean and a sticky, fluky wind skittered across the sea. Even the waves seemed nervous. Sally had followed her husband on deck, but one look at the sky made her nauseous. She had never seen Jubal frightened but he was staring at the coming weather like a man in the shadow of an erupting volcano.

"Sally dear," he said, in a hushed, urgent tone. "Fill the water jars, get some bread, whatever food Baptiste's got handy. Tie Cora and the children in their bunks, then yourself. Go on, do's I say." He kissed her cheek. "We'll be alright," he whispered, before turning away. "Rico!" he roared to a dark Spanish seaman. "Tell Mr. Norton I'll have Cape Horn duck on the jib and mizzen staysail! Mr. Kekkonen, strip everything else! Now lads, *now!*"

Sally gulped at the hideous horizon and raced for the galley.

Several minutes later, Lester burst into the captain's cabin, took one look at the fastenings and tore the flimsy knots apart. He grabbed stout line, ordered the boy to curl next to Cora, and tied his family as if lashing them to a stretcher.

"Lester," Cora objected, "I can't get to the chamber pot!" Curtis huddled to his mother, trembling like a leaf.

"Yank this bitter end to free yourself if you must," Lester said, his hands flying, "but you'll toss 'round like a ball. Sal, get in that bunk with Emma. Hear it, she's coming!" The wind came upon them, heralded by the siren of a distant whistle bearing down on the ship. As the sound went from moan to a keening wail the sensation was physical, making Cora's skin tingle. Lester lashed Sally and her little girl before dashing out. The *Mastiff* heeled suddenly, swinging the cabin door shut with a crash that vibrated into their backbones. The women looked at each other, white-eyed, as torrential rain came like the drumming hoofbeats of a wild horse herd. There was a final pause before the deafening stampede shook them almost senseless. Cora felt but could not hear her son's scream.

On deck, the deluge continued until Lester had no idea where the ocean stopped and the sky began. Within an hour the sea had been whipped into frothing dementia and the ship careened like an acorn in a spring waterfall. *Mastiff*'s jibboom, rising fifty feet above the deck, frequently buried itself completely. In a sudden wind shift, the entire ship whipped sideways and fell off a wave, crashing into the trough with the impact of being dropped from a building.

Like a punch-drunk fighter, the ship kept staggering upright, only to get battered down again. The longboat tore loose and was reduced to kindling in seconds. A comber blasted over the bow and smashed the forecastle. Men lashed themselves to the pumps, struggling to keep their footing, neck deep in water. Lester was completely submerged at the mizzenmast while trying to raise a staysail to hold her bow into the wind. Halfway up, it exploded in shreds. For hour after hour, the surrounding, engulfing, harrowing scream of wind pressed them almost prostrate, until all thought and hearing and sight became indistinguishable.

During the darkest night, blinding lightning streaks sizzled and popped in the driving rain. A bolt hit the foremast, splitting it from royal yard to the topgallant doublings. Cub Pingree struggled onto the shrouds, but before Jubal could yell, *Mastiff* rolled on her beam, wrenching the splintered mast and yards out of the crosstrees and into the sea. As the ship came up again, the mass of wood and rigging surged back aboard and caught Lester like a gnat in a spider web. He would have drowned on the next roll but Jubal grabbed an ax and with a banshee scream chopped his way through to his friend as another green sea swept the deck, miraculously dumping Cub back aboard.

A moment later they all were washed into the taffrail so hard Lester felt his ribs crack. Jubal had kept hold of his ax and crawled back to the confused tangle, desperately hacking away before the mess holed the ship or dragged astern and tore off the rudder. Lester could barely move, but Cub held him fast until Urho saw them in a lightning flash. Dragging Cub and Lester aft through waist-deep water, the big mate tied them at the mast before staggering forward to help the captain.

Finally, often unsure if they were on the ship or in the ocean, Jubal and Urho cut the wreckage clear. Most of the crew managed to tie themselves to something or struggle to the quarterdeck, where dawn found them huddled and beaten. Jubal had lashed the wheel, leaving the ship to fend for itself, praying for divine grace. He had no idea where they were in relation to Mauritius or its reefs.

Throughout that day and into the night, the ship endured intense squalls that brought such unbelievable quantities of rain men had to hold their noses and breathe through pursed lips to avoid choking. Baptiste had never seen such a wild ocean in thirty years at sea. As the second night swallowed them Jubal despaired, fearing his ship could not stand another sustained battle before something let go and they foundered.

By daylight, the storm was gone almost as suddenly as it came. The morning grew stifling hot and breathless above a crazed sea. As the swells slowly subsided, Jubal went below to check on the women and children. The captain's cabin was in shambles, looking as if it had been in a salt shaker, which Jubal realized, was not too far from the truth. Sally slept, spooning Emma in her embrace. In Lester's cabin, Cora was up, kicking aside the jumbled mesh of clothes, broken drawers, and books that emptied from every shelf. Curtis sat in a corner, staring at the cabin sole, chewing a blanket.

Seeing Jubal, Cora froze. "Lester?"

"He got banged up but'll be all right. When this sea calms down, give the cook a hand, will you? Nobody has eaten in two days."

Back on deck, Jubal traversed the ship, amazed she still floated, and thanking the men in Donald McKay's shipyard for building a vessel that could withstand such a beating. Around him, men appeared like zombies, moving with the daze of warriors who had somehow survived a slaughter.

All except Rico. Sometime in the night, the sea had claimed him.

Chapter Sixty-Two

Truette Norton was born on January 11, 1861, and his birthplace entered into the log as *N46°W14°*. Jubal had driven *Mastiff* as hard as he dared to reach Liverpool before Cora's term, but by the Azores he warned his wife to be ready for childbirth at sea.

Bad luck dogged them. Jubal had spent a week looking for Rico but finally turned west again to round the Cape of Good Hope. In the Atlantic, just above the equator, *Mastiff* lay becalmed nearly a week, only to sail two thousand miles north into a snowstorm three days before Cora went into labor. Sally prepared the captain's cabin and then ordered Baptiste to keep water hot on the stove while reading a treatise on midwifery she had thought to buy in San Francisco.

Ten hours after Cora's water broke, Sally called Lester in to see his son for the first time. The wrinkled, almond-colored face was fast asleep on his mother's breast, a picture that seized Lester's chest with such force he struggled to breathe. Cora looked at him with glassy-eyed serenity and the faintest hint of a smile.

"Fine job," Lester finally managed, barely, and his wife rolled her eyes and laughed softly. Curtis wanted to hold his brother but was content to give a puckered kiss and pet the tiny, damp head.

Later, Jubal visited. Smelling of cold and stinking wet wool, he shook the sleet from his sleeve and barely touched the newborn with a reddish, raw hand larger than the baby's head.

"How's True?" he asked, glancing at Lester with respect and appreciation. The name had come as a deeply gratifying surprise when Sally told him an hour after the birth.

"Believe he will be a captain," Cora replied, nuzzling her son. "I kin feel it to 'im."

For the next week, Lester fussed and fretted over his wife as the ship plowed homeward through the building winter. Cora quickly tired of his worry and shooed him on deck when the south coast of Ireland hove into view. They ran the Irish Sea in two days before a howling southwesterly gale, finally turning into the lee off Birkenhead and picking up the Mersey pilot ten days after Truette was born.

"One year, two months, make it twenty-six days," Jubal said, as he and Lester watched the dockworkers snub *Mastiff*'s hawsers. They shook hands with a brief nod to each other. "How'd we do?" Jubal asked.

"Market's moved a fair bit in our favor," Lester replied. He'd been studying newspapers brought aboard by the pilot. "A fellow could get rich watching his country rip apart."

"How bad?" Jubal queried, leaning over the railing. "You sir!" he roared to a longshoreman, "another fender amidships!" He looked back to Lester, who hadn't answered.

"The nut's cracked right around," Lester said, "though the halves aren't split yet. Lincoln is president and South Carolina's passed an 'ordinance'—whatever that is—dissolving their union with the other states. Apparently, they're just the first."

After a lengthy pause Jubal asked, "Alabama?"

"Doesn't say," Lester shrugged. "Half-dozen legislatures have been meeting. Regardless, cotton, wool, wheat, and lumber are up five percent."

"Futures?"

Lester rifled through several pages. "Up fifteen ... climbing nearly a point a day this last week."

They both looked up as a four-horse coach clattered to a stop. A derby-hatted gentleman stepped down and straightened out his greatcoat before spotting them at the ship's rail.

"Captain Calhoun, Mr. Norton!" The men recognized James Baines' secretary, McTavish. "Splendid to see you!" McTavish strode to the pier's edge. "Exquisite timing, gentlemen, a handsome return per ton, indeed. Positively tidy! Our esteemed desires and expects you to dine forthwith at Baines House. Your coach, sirs!"

"I'm not yet bathed," Sally wailed, when her husband delivered the invitation. "And I don't have my land legs! I'll weave into his salon as if I'm drunk!"

Jubal smiled. "I'll catch you, darling. You'll like Baines. He's a little dandy, spit 'n fire jes' like you. There must be some Scot in those fair curls of yours, far enough back. Tartan, I'd bet."

"Tart yourself, Jubal Calhoun!" Sally waved a finger at him. "Emma's got to come. Peter can watch her and Curtis while we're there; I'm not leaving them aboard!"

"Fine," Jubal agreed. "I expect Cora will bring Truette."

Sally sighed as if her husband were a moron and pushed him from the cabin before she stripped to her bloomers, humming with the sponge bath.

―

An hour later, James Baines strode into his parlor and stopped in shock. Expecting two young partners, he found an extended family, four pairs in all, men, women, boys, and infants.

"The Lord said 'go forth and multiply'," Jubal explained.

"By God Captain, ye takin' the Almighty seriously!" Baines exclaimed. "Welcome ladies, welcome!" He turned back to Jubal with an incredulous smile. "Begging your pardon, man, but what have ye done?"

Jubal made the introductions as the women curtsied and the boys bowed. Lester's grin told Baines that a little rehearsal had occurred, certainly of Peter and Curtis.

"Well," Baines clapped his hands, turning to the butler. "Charles, a larger table! Can the children eat in the breakfast parlor? I expect the talk will be beyond their ken." As he spoke, the door chime rang again. "That will be our other guest, no doubt," he said to Jubal. "A countryman of yours, Mr. Charles Piroleau, of Savannah, Georgia, I believe."

Lester knew immediately Cora didn't like Charles Piroleau. As the evening progressed, he wondered if she would reveal whatever was behind the molten eyes and careful rocking of her son. Piroleau's obvious regard for the boy's namesake—he had heard of Truette Stubbs by reputation—didn't move Cora an iota. Nor did the news Piroleau brought.

"Yes m'am, I do believe it will," he replied to Sally's query about the possibility of the United States splitting apart. "Momentum is such that no existing body of Congress could produce plenary concurrence to an alternative plan. Indeed, there are constant prognostications of demarche, but I consider them dubious at best."

"You're speaking of revolution," Lester observed.

"Call it what you will," Piroleau replied. "Passions unleashed are not easily stemmed."

Lester nodded. "Reminds me of the *Great Republic* launching, years back. Remember Jubal? Such fanfare, and set in motion with a few strikes of a sledge. Stopping her was another thing altogether."

"Could you excuse me, please?" Cora asked, though the main course had just been served. The baby had started to snuffle. The men stood and James

Baines escorted her to another room.

"Why are you here?" Sally asked Charles Piroleau, after Cora left. "In Liverpool?"

"I am agent of a local import firm, Fraser and Trenholm," Piroleau replied. "And what are your plans?"

Sally smiled at the deflection and let it pass. She had no wish for a political argument on their first night ashore after months at sea. Deciding to steer clear of controversy, she kept Piroleau talking about world trade until she could gracefully join Cora and let the men retire to a sitting room for scotch whiskey and cigars.

Charles Piroleau passed up the cigar, though not the whiskey, pleading other "pressing" engagements, and soon bid the gentlemen good evening. As he left, Piroleau added an offhand comment to Jubal that perhaps they would meet again.

"What'd we interrupt?" Lester asked, after the Georgian had left.

Baines shrugged. "Trade, of course. Fraser and Trenholm, in Savannah, is one of the biggest exporters of cotton to England. If this 'Confederacy,' as Piroleau calls it, actually be formed, another sovereign country comes into existence. Treaties, tariffs, protocols, all the workings of state need be created. Cotton is the American South's air; ships are its blood supply. They must have commercial contracts in Britain to protect their most vital resource." James Baines poured himself another whiskey. "Piroleau's pressing engagements tonight no doubt include the most influential parliamentarians and lords in Liverpool, to ensure a continued supply of raw material, come what may."

The men absorbed the information silently. Jubal stared off to a spot on the ceiling.

Baines looked from one to the other. "The Chinese have a curse," he mused. "May you live in interesting times ..." The Scot leaned forward, his eyes shining. "Cotton futures are rising. What do you propose we do about that, gentlemen?"

Jubal looked at Lester, who opened their satchel and passed over the Bombay cotton contract. Baines adjusted his reading spectacles and skimmed it quickly.

"Prescience and sagacity, gentlemen, are rare and wonderful qualities at any age," he nodded. "Now then, your voyage, the whole of it."

For the next two hours, Jubal and Lester recalled their circumnavigation, detailing the cargoes, amounts, and margins of transactions during the previous fifteen months. Finally, in round numbers, they calculated the voyage had produced a gross profit of nearly $80,000. After paying off *Mastiff* entirely, the partners would split nearly $50,000, with half of the Americans' share going to Truette Stubbs' estate.

"The ship needs careening and other yard work, I expect," Baines said, when Lester finished his tally. "A month perhaps, maybe more depending on those plonkers in the shipyard. Why don't you take a bit of time—for the families, of course? My country estate is at your disposal, though the weather's likely to be abominable this time o' year. Or a trip to Paris should bring your wives delight."

"There seems to be no hurry, sir," Jubal drawled, with the look of a tomcat twitching his whiskers. Lester watched, also wondering why Baines would extend the turnaround.

"*Mastiff* is due outbound March first, gentlemen," James Baines said, refilling their glasses. "Machine tools, Sheffield-made—the finest in the world—fifteen hundred tons, a very profitable cargo. John Griswold expects them in New York by late spring."

James Baines lit another cigar. He looked at the match before carefully, almost ceremoniously, extinguishing it with a long, slow breath. "One other thing, gentlemen, a piece of advice, if you will. Of course, profits are yours to do with as ye wish." The Scotsman leaned back, tapping the ash from his cigar. "But I suggest you keep a sizable portion in England."

Chapter Sixty-Three

Liverpool, February 1861

If Jubal thought he would stay in Liverpool to supervise the overhaul, his wife had other ideas. On the coach ride to the hotel from Baines House, Sally announced the "tribe," as she called the families plus Peter, was going to London and France. They had seen enough water, Sally informed her husband, and she intended to see the world by land. Jubal relented, having traded a promise that they wouldn't leave before he had negotiated the overhaul contract and his ship was in drydock. Though it nearly snapped Sally's patience, Jubal held out for the two weeks necessary to make agreements for ship repair and replacing the longboat.

Lester and Cora were delighted to stay or travel. Their hotel suite had a small coal stove that became the center of their young family's quiet nesting. For the first time in memory, Lester felt no need to accomplish anything while having the financial means to do nothing but rock his son and play with Curtis. Cora read, wrote letters to the Stills and every member of the Hatcher family in Gee's Bend, regardless of whether or not they could read, and rested. By the time Sally booked their train to London, Cora felt whole and fully recovered from her pregnancy.

From London, the party took a train to Portsmouth and boarded a coastal schooner for Cherbourg. Expecting the long, rolling swells of mid-ocean in a muscular clipper ship, Sally found the small vessel intolerably uncomfortable as it bucked and bounced in the nasty chop of the English Channel. To her chagrin and embarrassment, they weren't even halfway across before she threw up. Curtis laughed at his aunt and got whacked for impertinence.

France enchanted them. Paris was their hub and they spent days walking through the city. Cora decided to follow Sally's example and indulge for the first time in her life with the luxury of mornings in bed. Periodically, they took the train in every direction except north, visiting the Alps and finding inns in Provence and the Loire Valley. Even Sally didn't mind the cool weather, warning Jubal that they would someday come back to France for a long stay in late spring, when the charcoal drawings she made most days would become paintings. Time ebbed like a slow, languorous nap until, by late February, no one looked forward to Liverpool. Even Jubal struggled to recapture the drive and initiative of command, finally preferring to simply wait until he stepped aboard *Mastiff* again.

Crossing the English Channel on an unusually mild and sunny day, the adults each had the same silent thought: their tribe was coming back to reality. For nearly a month they had heard only snippets of news and been spared blaring headlines of the catastrophe brewing at home. The women watched their husbands' faces harden with each mile closing the dock after the schooner raised Portsmouth Harbor. On the train back to London, Lester and Jubal immersed themselves in the daily newspapers while Cora and Sally sat holding their children, staring out at the English landscape as if it were the passing of a dream.

Seven American states had seceded from the union and sent delegates to Montgomery, Alabama. Days later, the Confederate States of America had been born. Proclamation, organization, and election of its founding president had been accomplished in short order; a convention was gathering to draft and ratify the Confederate constitution. Lester shook his head reading an article on the back page. A South Carolinian senator had assured his constituency that little hardship or violence would result from events. "The man says," Lester muttered, "won't cost 'no more than a thimble full of blood'."

A week later March turned, and *Mastiff* was only half-loaded. Jubal spent much of the day barely speaking, and then only to admonish Urho about the positioning of the huge crates as they were lowered into the hold. The cargo set his jaw on edge. The presses, lathes, and industrial castings, some the size of a rail coach, seemed almost a personal affront. Hundreds of cases filled with sparkling Enfield rifles, deadly at a thousand paces, jammed the hold to capacity.

Lester had anticipated Jubal's reaction when he saw the bill of lading before passing it along. The ship was being warped from the drydock to the railway pier. As she tied up, lying high and empty, a chuffing steam jockey had pushed the first flatcar alongside, and Urho readied liftlines off the loading derrick. McTavish came aboard with assorted cargo documents, handed them to Lester, and turned to watch the loading. Jubal glanced at the documents and frowned.

"McTavish," he said. "Are these what I think?"

The agent turned and raised a chin, the black beaverskin derby tugged taut to his hairline. "Beg pardon, Captain?"

"These machine tools," Jubal said, slapping the documents. "They're cannon castings, rifling lathes, barrel molds, is that not correct? Five hundred cases of rifles?"

"Why yes, Captain, I believe they are," McTavish sniffed. "Master Baines has secured quite the coup, don't you think? Handsomely profitable, I should say."

"Excuse us," Jubal said through clenched teeth. "A word with you, Lester!"

They walked to the quarterdeck and stood at the taffrail, staring away from the loading and down river. Jubal breathed deep several times.

"Did you know 'bout this?" he drawled.

Lester folded his arms. "We ain't been apart but a half-day since Bombay."

Jubal held his forehead and groaned. "Are we going to run arms?"

Lester stared at him. "This is a British ship, Jubal. Baines is a majority owner and we owe the man mighty. You recall what Truette Stubbs said about not getting involved? Well, this is the best we can do." He took a deep breath and his voice went flat. "Remember how indignant I was about trading cotton until we went to Alabama? There's no righteousness about this machinery, neither. That fellow Piroleau would send us to Charlestown if he could. Why, I bet he's tried with Jimmy Scot already, probably offered more money, but Baines isn't greedy enough to cross John Griswold. Jubal, this isn't about honor. It's about trade. Put plain, this is about money." He looked up as a carriage clattered onto the wharf. "Speak of the goddam devil."

Charles Piroleau stepped out of the carriage.

Lester turned to Jubal. "You deal with him," he said, grimly. "I'll be in the hold, to make sure this stuff stays put."

Twenty minutes later, Jubal found Lester inspecting straps and chains securing the massive crates. To the unspoken question, Jubal shook his head, as if trying to dispel a nightmare. "Piroleau's here for the same reason John Griswold wants this cargo. Offered to buy her outright, offloaded Charleston. Dunno, Lester ..." his voice trailed off and he rubbed at his eyes. "I can't believe but there's got to be a great mess of people who just did not believe it would come to this. Lincoln's inaugural might be the last chance, but I think you're right—this vessel's being launched by men who can swing a sledge but don't have a God's prayer of stopping her once she gets going.

They couldn't handle a pond, let alone this hurricane." Jubal ran a hand through his hair. "Christ, what are we going to do when we land? Head for 'Frisco again?"

"What's the weather going to be on the day we raise Sandy Hook?" Lester retorted. "God knows, but I don't—and neither do you. Nobody does. Maybe Sally's right and the man is 'Honest Abe.' Only thing I do know is I'm takin' five thousand dollars along with me for the family. In gold. So don't get us sunk."

Jubal winced. "When did you decide that?"

"I didn't," Lester replied. "Cora said." He felt a twinge of guilt, betraying a confidence of his wife, but he didn't want his partner to see the bank withdrawal without knowing why.

"Jesus …" Jubal took out a cigar and viciously spit the end off. "Gimme a match, will you? Sally'll want the same, probably already talked, them two. The world 'goin upside down, women thinking to manage our funds. Shit, Lester, what happened to the days with Lauchlan McKay?"

"They're gone, good as that East Boston yard," Lester said, taking the cigar Jubal proffered and striking a match. "Let's load and get out of here. May as well run home while there's something left of it."

Lester regarded his lit cigar, and then his gaze shifted to Jubal. "If I ask you at sea," he said, his voice tightening, "I'll be obliged to do whatever you order. So we ought to lay the course now. Is it New York, or Charleston?"

Jubal shrugged. "Don't matter what the world does, a contract is our word." His shoulders slumped as if he had taken up a load. "New York. We made that deal."

~

Mastiff cleared the Mersey in mid-March and Jubal sailed south, trading a fast passage for a smoother one. Urho had strapped the machine cases in every direction, but Jubal knew if a ten-ton die broke loose in a storm and got moving, it would slice the ship's four-inch planking like a hot knife through butter. *Mastiff* sailed southwest for two weeks before curving westward in the mid-Atlantic, where the weather was balmy, with warm days and cool, clear evenings. The sea was a vivid, deep blue, and dolphins frequently followed, cavorting in the bow wave with such grace and speed that Curtis wanted to join them when he grew up. Cora often lay with him in the bow netting, marveling at the sleek, silver rhapsody and wondering where they all went when suddenly, as if on signal, twenty dolphins would be gone in a blink.

Lester joined her one night when the dolphins made phosphorescent trails that looked like instant, momentary streaks of the northern lights. Above them, the dome of heaven offered ten thousand stars, and *Mastiff* flew every sail in a perfect pyramid of brilliant white canvas, each sail bellied perfectly to the northeasterly wind.

"What we goin' home to?" Cora asked, as she suckled Truette.

Lester shook his head in the darkness. "I'm afraid to learn."

"Freedom ain't for the faint-hearted," Cora breathed. "Them runaways, in Philadelphia? Every one of 'em wantin' to find a new day and scared nearly to death of it."

"William Still's place was a stop on the Underground Railroad?" Lester asked. He had suspected as much, but they had never talked about the changing cast of strange, silent Negroes that Lester had noticed in Philadelphia.

"One of 'em," Cora replied. "Quite a few other places in that city, though those slaves had to be real careful. White folks in Philadelphia don't like niggahs any more than in Gee's Bend."

Three weeks later, Lester was in the rigging at high noon, preparing to reeve a new halyard through the skysail lift block, when he saw a sail to windward. He hailed the deck and took another glance before resuming his work. Periodically, he looked up and made out the lines of a topsail schooner converging on *Mastiff*'s course. Flags fluttered on her afterstay and he read the signal: Request heave to'. Lester knotted the line, then descended and headed aft to the quarterdeck where Jubal studied the schooner.

"She's got cannon." Jubal didn't take his eye from the telescope.

"How far are we from Bermuda?" Lester asked. Jubal had sailed a parabolic course, and *Mastiff* was now headed northwest, less than a week out of New York.

"Hundred fifty miles southeast," Jubal replied, "Hatteras is near due west, five hundred. Ought to be in the Stream soon."

"What does he want?" Lester asked.

"Seen a telegram?" Jubal replied, sounding more worried than sarcastic. He turned to the first mate. "Mr. Kekkonen, strike the royals 'n topgallants, bring her 'round and heave to!" The schooner was still a half-mile off, but Lester could see her crew preparing to lower a boat. Thirty minutes later she lay fifty yards off the clipper, each ship slowly riding six-foot swells. The schooner's longboat came alongside and soon the Finn greeted two men on deck, one middle-aged, the other no more than twenty, both bearded and armed with pistols. Kekkonen brought the visitors aft to the quarterdeck.

"Captain Calhoun, sir," drawled a thick Southern accent. Jubal knew in five syllables the man was Georgian. "Howard Tilly, CSS *Charles Lamar*, at your service, sir. My second-in-command, Lieutenant Caleb Croft."

Jubal introduced Lester, who shook hands as his mind raced through possibilities of how these men could know *Mastiff*'s position, much less the name of its captain. Piroleau, he realized, must have sent word by a fast packet sailing two weeks earlier for any one of several Southern ports.

Tilly tipped his cap to the women, who stood in the companionway watching, and then turned abruptly to Jubal.

"A word with you in private, Captain?"

Jubal stiffened. Although Captain Tilly was calm, his subordinate had sweated through his shirt, a smell of fear.

"This way," Jubal said, heading for the companionway. The women stepped aside, expressionless.

As Jubal closed the cabin door below Tilly removed his hat and gestured to Lester. "Beggin' your pardon, mister, I'd be obliged ... duty requires I speak with Captain Calhoun privately."

"This is as private as it gets," Jubal replied. "Mr. Norton is my partner. His word is mine, sir."

Tilly looked from one to the other. "I am authorized, by the elected representatives of the newly adjoined Confederate States of America to buy your cargo sir, for fifty thousand dollars in gold, upon presentation to any port south of Chesapeake Bay. I shall avail my ship of whatever services you may require, sir, to convey, escort, and protect as necessary." He produced a document and passed it to Jubal, who glanced at it briefly before handing it to Lester. Tilly's offer accurately reflected the short, concise letter that had been signed and sealed by George Trenholm.

"Of Fraser and Trenholm?" Lester asked, a cold edge to his voice. He returned the letter to Tilly. "We carry contracts with a New York house, enforceable under the laws of Great Britain and the United States."

"Sir, I must inform you," the Georgian replied, "that a state of war exists between the Confederate and United States. Fort Sumter surrendered to General Beauregard three days ago, sir. I beg you reconsider."

"War?" Jubal intoned.

"*This is a British flagged vessel,*" Lester spit. "Do you understand, sir?" His voice rose in fury. "Be so good as to take your pistols and your traitorous odors off this ship!"

Tilly went pale and Lieutenant Croft's hand strayed to his sidearm.

"Gentlemen, go to the quarterdeck, please," Jubal gestured. "Wait there."

"Captain Calhoun," Tilly said, containing himself. "I am authorized by Mr. Trenholm to inform you that, should your ship land in New York, there are no assurances of your freedom. If you command this ship into a Southern port every person who so desires will be transported to a neutral country. Can your associate offer the same guarantee? I think not. I entreat you, sir; now is the time to choose. Now is the time to act as Thomas Jefferson and Patrick Henry did! Sir!"

Jubal bristled. "Who would detain me, and for what?"

A knock on the door split the crackling tension. "Sail ho, Captain," squeaked Peter. "On the port quarter."

Captain Tilly pulled on his hat. "I don't doubt that is the *Stephen Douglas*." He glanced at Lester, gritting his teeth. "A ship of our enemies, the Union Navy."

Tilly pulled a document from his coat and wheeled back to Jubal. "I am also to deliver your commission as a naval officer of the Confederate States of America." He thrust the document in Jubal's hand. "Captain, we are at war! You have two minutes. Honor and country call, sir!" Tilly brushed by them and vaulted up the stairs to the deck, followed by Lieutenant Croft.

Sally burst in as the visitors ascended the companionway stairs. "What is happening?" Rankness lingered in the cabin.

Jubal stood motionless, staring at the commission letter, his face a wooden mask. Cora waited in the doorway. No one said a thing.

"My God, what is happening?" Sally screamed, running at Jubal and grabbing him by the shirt. "Say something! What is this?"

"It's started," Jubal replied, staring at his wife with a look that went right through her. He turned to Lester. "I cannot deliver this cargo to New York."

Lester didn't blink. "Tilly knew your name. Do you really think you could be arrested in New York if Piroleau, and this Trenholm character, hadn't set you up? They're playing both ends against the middle."

"It's a fight to the death, Lester." A deep breath of infinite weariness coursed through Jubal. "But it ain't that ... I can't ..."

Lester stared at his friend. "You can't *what*, Jubal? We've both seen this coming. Honor is the first casualty."

Jubal stared at Lester silently, struggling for words. "Can't ... fight against my state. If I land this cargo, I'm killing my people."

"That's the deal," Lester whispered. He closed his eyes for a brief moment, took a deep breath and then clenched his teeth. "Choose."

"My God, Lester!" Sally cried. Her brother's face looked hewn of unpolished oak.

She wheeled back to Jubal. "Are you going to fight for two thousand landowners so they can own six million slaves?" she cried. "What will you tell your children?"

Jubal went ashen. "I have to go."

Sally could see Jubal drawing inward and she gripped his shirt fiercely.

"Jubal! We're your people. We're your family ... *your family* ... My God! *We're your family*! You gave your troth," she cried. *"As long as we both shall live!"*

"We all face the Lord, Jubie," Cora murmured, "come Judgment Day."

"It's my home, Sally," Jubal said, his lip trembling. "I don't rightly know why, after all these years, but ... it's ... Alabama. She's my bones." His breath came out in a straggled gasp. He took Sally's wrists and pulled away, before turning to Lester. "You keep our word 'n take the ship. But I can't."

"I will not leave you!" Sally cried.

Jubal kissed Sally's hands. "Go to New York, darling. You and Emma will be safe there. I'll get word to you soon as I can ... when this madness is past—it can't run long. I'll come for y'all. I do swear."

Sally stared at her husband, wide-eyed. Suddenly, she broke free and grabbing Cora by the arm, bolted into the corridor.

Jubal watched his wife leave, tears welling in his eyes.

Lester felt a sudden chord ring through him like a pealing bell, leaving an immense sadness as it faded away. "You always was self-possessed ... a hard one." He stared at the deck for a moment and then looked up, the tears streaming now. "You know Jubal? We never fought. Not one time, not really."

Jubal closed his eyes and looked upward as though praying, then stepped forward as Lester did the same. They embraced and held each other as if forged, until a shiver passed through them and they drew back. Lester slowly bunched his fist and thumped Jubal's chest.

Jubal buried his fingers in Lester's shoulder. "I need you to watch my family."

Lester could only nod.

Jubal mounted the companion steps with the trudge of a man climbing the gallows. Lester came on deck as Jubal swung over the rail. From twenty feet, they nodded to each other a last time. Then Jubal dropped over the side.

Urho coiled the longboat's painter and made ready to throw as Captain Tilly spoke urgently to his rowers. Lester glanced to port and saw the topsails of a brig bearing the unmistakable flash of the Stars and Stripes and knew immediately that James Baines, always the prudent Scot, had sent word to New York by fast packet. The ocean was vast but by simply crisscrossing the shipping lanes directly above Bermuda a ship could be intercepted.

"Jubal!" Sally screamed, running from the companionway, Emma swaddled in her arms. Cora came behind, carrying a buckled suitcase. Sally stumbled on her skirts and almost fell, but kept going. She ran to the railing and started to climb over, but Cora stopped her.

"Give me Emma! Go, I'll hand her down!"

Sally wheeled and looked at her brother, a flash of love and terror and resignation. She clutched her breast for a brief moment before jumping into Jubal's outstretched arms. Cora carefully lowered Emma to Sally in the longboat, leaning so far over she would have fallen but for Urho holding her by the waist.

Meanwhile, Lester had darted below. In the captain's cabin, he reached for the key under the bunk and unlocked their strongbox. Withdrawing three flat bars of gold, he yanked open a small drawer, grabbed the pistol and stuffed the gun and bars in Jubal's seabag. Abruptly, he unstrapped his own knife and sheath, adding it to the bag before whipping the straps shut. Taking the companionway three steps at a time he raced to the rail. The longboat was pulling away as Lester leaped atop the rail and hurled the seabag, which hit Captain Tilly in the chest, nearly knocking him out of the longboat.

Jubal knew instantly what it was from the heft. Holding the bag tight, his other arm went around Sally, who hugged Emma close and leaned into her husband, clutching the last thing she had taken from *Mastiff*. Tight in her hand, Sally felt the soft edges of a small, carved wooden albatross. Neither moved as they watched *Mastiff* recede with every urgent stroke of the longboat's rowers.

Lester and Cora stood at the railing until the longboat came alongside the schooner as her crew raised sail. To leeward, Lester could see the *Stephen Douglas*, an armed brig, charging across the open sea, her gunports open.

"Mr. Kekkonen," Lester's voice boomed, as he moved from his wife. "Haul 'round the forecourse, ease the spanker, steer north by northwest!" Lester's concentration went to *Mastiff*'s masthead pennant and then to the two ships, one bearing down as the other fled. "Fall off a bit," Lester muttered, knowing a schooner could sail twenty degrees tighter to the wind than any brig. "Give her some time … she's got at least a half-mile and the weather gage."

Mastiff began to move as the sails filled, slowly making way, as if drifting across the brig's deadeye course toward the schooner.

Cora had disappeared but came up beside her husband a few minutes later, holding Truette. The boy was growing rapidly and looked at his father with big brown eyes.

"You're lucky, boy," Lester smiled, "your mother's such a handsome woman." He looked at the brig bearing down, now looming large and throwing a gushing bow wave, before glancing back at the schooner.

Cora glanced over the sea from one ship to another. The schooner sailed tight to the wind, her longboat bouncing along as if it were a stray child struggling to catch up, while behind them the brig had been forced to detour around *Mastiff* and now sailed even further off the wind, passing a hundred yards astern. Even from a distance Lester could see her officers staring, clearly furious at his sloppy seamanship.

Satisfied, he saluted them before turning to his wife.

"Sally be with child again," Cora said simply.

Lester smiled for the first time.

"That's wonderful. Another reason she had to go with him."

Lester stared at the schooner, now almost hull down in the swells. She looked like a young bird that had flown its nest. The brig flew every sail she carried but couldn't sail nearly as close to the wind. Already their courses yawned open.

"I imagine this must be happening everywhere," Lester reflected. "Families going the way of the country."

Cora said nothing, gazing southward. Truette started fidgeting and she shushed him.

"Kapitan Norton?" Urho approached Lester. He paused and took off his hat, stunned but obedient. "I take da vatch, Kapitan? You go aloft?"

Lester smiled and nodded to the big Finn. "Thank you, Mr. Kekkonen," he replied. "But I'll stay. Set all sail, if you will, sir. North by nor'west. " Urho saluted and bounded into the ship's waist, roaring at the crew.

"You like it aloft." Cora stepped close to her husband.

"I do," he agreed. "But a captain's place is on the quarterdeck."

Lester put his arm around Cora, guiding her to the aft railing. Below them, *Mastiff*'s wake boiled up and bubbled astern, leaving a long, straight seam that the sea gradually reclaimed. At that very point where ocean swells dissolved the last remnants of their passing, the *Charles Lamar* showed as a small, shining patch against the horizon.

They stood watching, breathless. A moment later, the white thread fluttered, became faint, and was gone.

Chapter Sixty-Four

New York, May 1861

*M*astiff's lines were made fast, and within an hour Lester drummed his fingers on the polished taffrail, resisting an urge to vault over and bring order to the mayhem below. A wagon loaded with freight from the ship across the wharf had left dockside when an incoming teamster cut his team too hard and the wagon's rear wheels caught. An axle snapped with a splintering crash that dropped the loaded wagon bed onto the wharf. Three crates shifted as one, snapping their hemp ties. Men scattered as the crates toppled and shattered, spilling eight-inch cannon balls that careened toward the cobblestones of South Street. A dozen horses dodged; now thoroughly spooked, they tangled in their traces, iron-shod hooves sparking on granite. Howling with fury, the teamsters whipped their horses and then went at each other.

South Street and its wharves were a clogged, churning mass, looking from the *Mastiff* masthead as if the top had been ripped off an anthill. A sea of top hats, derbies, flat-brimmed Stetsons, checkered bandanas, blue sea caps, and an occasional, lacy parasol bobbed like flotsam on a human tide. Black laborers hauled fully laden carts; sailors made their way to ships; men on horseback and in carriages rode along the East River edge. Stevedores and longshoremen manning rope hoists grunted, swore, yelled, and laughed in the midday humidity while hawkers and peddlers sold food, clothing, newspapers, cheap medicines, and trinkets from every corner of the planet.

Cora stood beside her husband, amazed at the spectacle. She glanced skyward, hoping the thunderheads would wait a bit longer before turning the landing into a complete muck of mud and manure. Truette hung from a sling off her chest, oblivious to the commotion, sound asleep.

"Ahoy *Mastiff!*" A voice boomed like a thunderclap.

A silver-haired man stood at the far edge of South Street pointing at Lester, then began to make his way up through the crowd. Tall, lean, and elegantly dressed, he moved with dignity and authority. Teamsters tipped their caps as coolies nodded with averted eyes. John Alsop Griswold was a sixth generation merchant whose family had shipped and imported goods from all over the world for two centuries. Since shortly after the American Revolution eighty years earlier, their offices had been located along South Street where Griswold's father had followed his great-uncle Nathaniel in building one of the oldest, most venerable trading houses in New York City.

Lester met Griswold at the top of the gangplank and introduced Cora. Griswold doffed his top hat and regarded the woman openly; he had seen Negro women in the company of white men, though in his five-plus decades, this was the first introduced as wife.

"A pleasure, suh," Cora curtsied slightly. Lester held his smile at the accentuated drawl. Usually, Cora worked at educated diction, but if riled or challenged the plantation cadence instantly reappeared, an impulse she shared with Jubal. The drawl was often Lester's first clue that his even-keeled wife had reached a limit of some sort. Griswold's regard must have qualified.

"A fair voyage?" the tall merchant inquired.

"No," Lester replied. He gestured to the companionway. "Will you join us below? Lunch is set in our cabin, where you may also review the manifest."

"Indeed, I ..."

"Griswold!" A second voice, higher pitched but just as commanding, sounded from the wharf.

"That will be General Meigs," Griswold explained. "We dined this morning at the Union Club. He asked to meet us aboard. May I?" The merchant beckoned to the weathered face of a bearded, barrel-shaped figure, who despite his girth, darted through the throng and scurried up the gangplank.

"Mr., ah ... Mrs. Norton," Griswold began as the man bounded on deck, "may I present General Montgomery Meigs?"

"Sir," Meigs extended a handshake, taking polite but brief notice of Cora. Lester immediately heard the trace of a Southern accent but couldn't place it. He glanced at John Griswold.

"General Meigs was recently appointed quartermaster general," Griswold explained.

Meigs yanked a handkerchief from inside his coat and wiped his sweaty, balding brow and graying nest of beard.

"With the authority and means," Griswold continued, "to purchase this cargo in its entirety, forthwith."

Lester glanced at the New York shipper. An idea ignited: until Griswold signed the bill of lading, *Mastiff*'s cargo was legal property of Truette Stubbs and Company.

Montgomery Meigs replaced his handkerchief but didn't move. "Where's Calhoun?"

Lester stared at the General.

"We had information this cargo would be hijacked to Charleston," Meigs continued.

"I am co-owner and captain our ship," Lester replied, his suspicion confirmed now as to why the USS *Stephen Douglas* had reappeared north of Bermuda but stayed several miles to windward, shadowing *Mastiff* to New York. His voice tightened. "This way, gentlemen."

General Meigs examined the manifest and nodded. "Yes, John, this material is vital. We can use these as templates, particularly the rifling lathes. Do you know their capacity?"

"Begging your pardon, sir," Lester interrupted, "how do you know Mr. Griswold?"

"I am frequently in New York, young man." Lester could feel the man's prickliness but felt some of his own.

John Griswold had no intention of allowing a clash. "General Meigs expressed interest in the cargo. I invited him to examine these materials; the English machine tooling is of unparalleled quality."

"Normally," General Meigs gaze bored into Lester, "this would be a matter for my subordinates but I have urgent business in the city. Your cargo has no comparative in this country at a time of particular severity."

"The times have lost all regard for normalcy." Lester agreed, his idea percolating. "What can I do for you, sir?"

The two men regarded Lester as Cora poured tea—Meigs requested coffee—and offered the fresh fruit and bread she had ordered Cub Pingree to fetch the moment *Mastiff*'s dock lines were made fast, as Sally had in many ports.

Cora glanced at her husband and swelled with pride. Over the last week, as they closed the approaches to New York harbor, Lester had hardened before her eyes. Now, dressed in an open shirt and sailor's dungarees, he faced formally attired, mature businessmen without a trace of intimidation.

"What has become of Captain Calhoun?" Meigs asked.

"My partner took leave, likely for his home in Alabama."

"To serve their rebellion?"

"You would have to ask him of his purpose."

Montgomery Meigs continued to stare at Lester, as if squaring this young, unlined face with the direct confidence of a perhaps-shrewd businessman. At length, Meigs declared, "I propose to purchase the entire cargo at a fifteen percent premium to FOB Liverpool."

To Meig's astonishment, Lester refused. Even Griswold, a man who had negotiated all his life, could not contain his surprise, particularly since he had commissioned the cargo. At breakfast, Griswold had described the contents to Meigs, who immediately declared he would inspect the ship that afternoon before returning to Washington. Now, newly aware that the Meigs must have known of the cargo all along—it might even be the reason he was in New York—Griswold thought to let this play out and see what the young man could do.

"I intend to make inquiries and may sail for Boston or Philadelphia," Lester explained. Cora nearly spilled the tea.

"Mr. Norton!" Meigs bristled. "Excuse me, *Captain* Norton. I know full well the English price of this cargo and shipping costs. I have no intention of paying an exorbitant tariff!"

"One doesn't simply add to the other," Lester replied. "A cargo's value depends on market conditions upon arrival ... as I have experienced in San Francisco, Liverpool, indeed at every port I have made in the world. I would not expect you to pay anything you considered exorbitant, nor should you expect me to accept any amount I believe insufficient to the moment."

"We are at war, Mr. Norton." Meigs spoke rapidly, his bearing having all the subtlety of a bull's. "If necessary, I may expropriate the cargo in the name of the United States government. Exigencies require alacrity; a rebel force is being raised in Virginia as we speak! Personally, I have a great deal to do. Only the intelligence of your cargo and John's description bade me personally take interest."

Lester extended a plate of fruit to General Meigs. "I doubt expropriation is a precedent lightly invoked; the consequences can hardly be predicted. A situation not unlike the present state of the country."

Griswold watched closely.

"With all due respect, sir," Lester continued, "the Union Army requires this cargo, and the Navy will need ships. I will accept twenty-five percent, Liverpool, plus sixty thousand dollars for this vessel, or an equivalent five-year lease. *Mastiff* is well-founded I assure you. One contingent upon the other."

Montgomery Meigs glared with such ferocity Lester thought the man could as easily explode as sip his coffee. "Young man, I have no time to haggle!"

Lester stared at him, unblinking.

Finally, with a flare of nostrils, the bearded man slapped his lap.

"Done. I'll lease her." Meigs leaned extended his hand.

Without hesitation, Lester took it, a beefy slab with the grip of oak.

General Meigs stood. The man's affect softened; he regarded Lester with frank appraisal.

"Now then, *Mister* Norton. Witnessing your skill in trade, with consideration for Mr. Griswold's opinion of character—he tells me you have associated with men of the highest integrity for years, an uncommon claim given your youth—and since you no longer have a ship ... I—that is, the *country*—have immediate and critical need of men who understand trade, transport, finance, and logistics, men of intelligence, mobility, perspicacity, integrity ..."

General Meigs paused for what Lester could imagine was only dramatic effect.

"I offer employment working with me for President Lincoln."

Chapter Sixty-Five

Bermuda, May 1861

Emma stirred and made a half-hearted cry, but still full from nursing she drifted back to sleep as the hammock resumed its lullaby. Sally sat beside her beneath the ship's skylight, opened to the speckled night sky. Moonrise wouldn't be for another hour and the sea air was so crystal clear she could see brief meteors streak across the heavens.

Sally had dozed despite the turmoil in her belly. The little one—Sally thought any baby this rambunctious must be a boy—seemed to be having a snit, kicking and punching with the force of hiccups. Sally often rubbed her belly with a hot cloth, which sometimes quieted the unborn, though not tonight. Then Emma had complained.

Footfalls sounded abruptly on the companionway; by the vibrations Sally recognized Jubal, who seldom descended steps less than three at a time. Moments later a light knock sounded at the cabin door and then his broad shadow filled the doorway against the corridor lantern glow.

"You've got to sleep, Sal," Jubal murmured.

"How?"

"I'll rock Emma. Sweetheart, we're safe here. There's nothing in St. George that will harm us."

"We're going to Mobile," she replied, her voice flat.

Jubal didn't reply.

"Just because you haven't told me about the blockade doesn't mean I'm stupid." Sally looked at her husband, then blinked as the unborn child let loose a foot hard enough for Jubal to notice the skin bubble on Sally's belly. She buttoned her blouse and rose, turning toward the bunk. "When do we leave?"

Jubal came in and gave the hammock a shove to resume Emma's rocking before helping Sally turn down the bed in the narrow bunk. As she settled he pulled the light cotton coverlet over his wife's rounded belly.

"Do you want tea? The galley stove is still warm."

"Yes." Sally closed her eyes. "When do we leave?"

Jubal paused, then kissed her forehead with love and resignation.

"Tomorrow," he murmured. "Sunset. In Charleston, we'll take the train to Mobile."

The door closed softly, light footfalls fading as Sally rolled toward the hull and buried her wet face in a pillow.

Chapter Sixty-Six

Five days after landing in New York, Lester stared into the shadowy night, swaying with the clacking rail coach as it rolled through the New Jersey pinewoods toward Philadelphia. Truette slept nestled in his arms; Curtis had spooned into his mother on the coach bunk opposite, neither moving but for their deep, regular breathing.

Lester was still too stunned to sleep. After a decade sailing the world, he wondered if he would ever set foot on a ship again. Settling the cargo and ship lease, less monies sent to James Baines, had netted $37,000, now deposited in the Bank of New York along with the gold bullion Cora brought from England. Other than the four trunks carrying their possessions, it was all they had. But not five in a hundred men would ever accumulate such wealth.

As the train clattered through the first switchyards north of the city, a vivid, red horizon rose from the mist of early light foretelling a storm offshore that would likely soak the coming day in Philadelphia. Surveying the horizon and then glancing about him, Lester's mind moved with the train's cadence, flitting amongst the tasks that would descend within a few hours.

First and foremost, the family needed a home, and Lester knew nothing about Philadelphia real estate. City banking relationships had to be established linking the New York, Liverpool, and London accounts. Cora and the children must be left safe. He would need to see John Mott and William Still.

General Meigs expected him in Washington by week's end.

Two weeks earlier, as *Mastiff* bore down on Sandy Hook, President Lincoln had appointed then Colonel Meigs to be quartermaster general of the United States with orders to organize the effort necessary to equip, provision, and resupply a field army that had increased tenfold in less than six months. Uniforms, weapons, ammunition, food, horses, fodder, wagons, boats, ships, warehouses, armories ... the list of goods and materials necessary to fight a war were staggering.

Lester closed his eyes at the memory of General Meigs' offer, and his own acceptance. He looked at his sleeping family and nearly wept, imagining the visages of all their losses, of his closest friend, his sister, their children—each family built together, now torn asunder. Meigs' voice echoed.

"... I expect you in Washington; there is much to do. Brevet Captain Norton, United States Army, Quartermaster Corps? Your commission to be forthcoming."

General Meigs glanced at Cora, then back to Lester. He gathered his things, a man in a hurry.

"Your country calls."

Chapter Sixty-Seven

Charleston, June 1861

Running the blockade proved easy. The Union Navy had neither the ships nor officers to choke the port effectively, though Jubal thought that only a matter of time, for the entrance to Charleston harbor was narrow. A few Union ships patrolling beyond the range of Fort Sumter's cannon would dissuade any merchantmen, and blockade runners were too shallow-drafted to bring in much cargo.

The *Charles Lamar* ghosted in on a moonless, midnight tide hard upon the shattered ramparts of the captured fort after approaching from the south along the coast. Jubal had stayed on deck, impressed with the quiet competence of Captain Tilly, whose exceptional local knowledge of the shifting seabed brought them so close to land that despite thick darkness they could see breaking waves flash and feel the backwash from shore.

As a humid dawn broke and the port came into view, Sally joined her husband on deck, Emma still asleep in a wicker basket. Jubal glanced at the child and realized she would soon be too big to fit the basket and too heavy for Sally to lift. A pang of sadness coursed through him. He had bought the basket from a street peddler returning from Truette Stubbs' grave on a bluff looking eastward from St. George into the ocean.

In that picket-fenced graveyard, adjacent to the modest coral monument over Stubbs, another Christian cross rose where Ezekiel had earlier buried Louisa.

The faithful black man was not the least surprised to greet Jubal at the island house, at once giving him a leather case left by Stubbs containing the deed, instructions to sell the manor, and trustee authority to do so. Also inside were copies of Ezekiel's manumission papers and the Mobile bonds that allowed him freeman status in the South. Between the documents and Ezekiel's meager travel bag, already packed, Jubal understood that Truette Stubbs had anticipated and prepared for events. When he and Ezekiel returned to the *Charles Lamar* together, Sally's surprise immediately gave way to immense relief and she hugged the little old man, knowing and gladly accepting he would be with them the rest of his life.

Sally looked about the harbor, noticing a small harbor sloop tacking in their direction from the distant wharves. "So this is it?"

Jubal didn't acknowledge the edge to her voice.

Sally turned to Ezekiel, who had followed on deck, lugging a travel bag in each hand. "Did your people come through here?"

"Don't rightly know, Missus," Ezekiel murmured.

Sally surveyed the city as they approached. Already a hum of activity built and she could hear distant bugles and church bells.

"All these slaves you're fighting to keep," she looked at Jubal, "isn't this where most of them were dropped first? How many people, free in Africa, set foot right there"—Sally pointed to the wharf—"never to be free again? Because of their skin."

Jubal's jaw tightened. "I didn't expect you to come." He eyed the harbor sloop closing on the *Charles Lamar*.

Sally let it pass. She just wanted to stop, sleep for several days, and awake to find this nightmare gone.

"Except it's daybreak," she muttered.

"Beg your pardon?"

"Don't ever beg, dear. But don't you go forgetting." Sally grunted as the unborn booted her in the ribs. "Now what will you have us do?"

"A few days here to rest," Jubal replied. "Then the train to Mobile."

"Rest?"

The sloop had come about into the morning breeze and hove to as the schooner approached. A distinguished-looking silver-haired man moved on the sloop's deck as Captain Tilly left his quarterdeck for amidships. Crewmen lowered a Jacob's ladder.

"Who is he?"

"Never seen him before," Jubal replied.

Sally's voice hardened, her teeth tight. "Who is he?"

Jubal sighed. "George Trenholm, likely, a cotton broker."

"Fraser and Trenholm?" Sally spit into the harbor. "You knew this would happen."

Jubal stared at the sloop.

Chapter Sixty-Eight

Philadelphia, September 1861

The filthy hand swept in from behind, covering her mouth and yanking Cora into the narrow, weed-choked passage between two brick houses. Curtis, who had been clutching his mother's dress as instructed, lurched with her, dropping the cinnamon donut he had been savoring. Neither had noticed the thief as they returned from the butcher, though later Cora would realize she had been an obvious target, her arms filled with baby, groceries, and a purse. As the late afternoon streets came alive from the heat and humidity of midday, the man had sauntered inconspicuously behind but sprung quickly after they turned the corner onto Dauphine Street.

"Just be quiet, so's I don't have to hurt the boy!"

Cora suppressed the urge to twist and fight the attacker, fearful for her children. The weight of her purse vanished as the strap was sliced free.

"Oh, you're a right plump niggah bitch," the voice hissed. Cora's face twisted to the man as he turned her around. An unshaven scowl stared from six inches, rotten teeth spewing spittle fouler than dead low tide. The man's knife hand pawed at Cora's breast as he tried to fondle her privates with the other, though the purse made him clumsy.

"Please masta, don't do nuthin' to my chillen!" Cora's voice cracked as she stifled sobs.

The thief snickered, groping beneath her skirts. Fumbling for better advantage, he lost the purse but snatched to retrieve it.

Cora drove her knee so hard into the thief's crotch his eyes bulged and he gasped, beginning to double up. A vicious kick to the ankle from the hard street shoes—she couldn't tolerate wearing them at home—sent him to his hands and knees. She aimed her other foot. Several blackened teeth disappeared into the weeds as his head crashed against the brick wall.

Cora looked around. "Curtis, take this!" She thrust the bag of groceries at her son, rifled the unconscious thief's pockets of several small purses, a bag of coins, and a wad of bills, which she quickly stashed in her purse, then grabbed the groceries.

"Git movin,' boy, step yore gait!" Cora strode back onto the main street, glanced in either direction, urged Curtis for half a block and stepped into the street to hail an approaching cab.

The cabbie slowed and called out as Cora fished in her purse. "I don't drive niggahs!"

Cora tossed him a gold coin and held up a second.

Though only three blocks from the small stone two-story house Lester had purchased for cash, Cora directed the cabbie on a circuitous route away from the neighborhood. Returning from the opposite direction, the cab traversed a busy intersection where Cora noticed two policemen patrolling on foot. The thought of reporting what had happened never crossed her mind. An appraising look one of the policemen gave her as the cab passed recalled the counsel of William Still, who had repeatedly emphasized that few people were as disdainful of, or more brutal with Negroes, than the Philadelphia police.

Directing the cabbie to drop them at an alley entrance, Cora waited as the teamster turned the corner out of sight before she took Curtis along the alley and entered the one-carriage, ramshackle stable in back of their house. Finally, in the tiny backyard she had already begun to turn into a vegetable garden, Cora felt safe again. Inside the modest but comfortable house, still with so little furniture she could only sit in the kitchen, Cora barred the door before settling the children for brief naps and turning again to a dictionary lying atop the open letter filled with Lester's handwriting that had appeared in the postbox a day earlier.

Riverboat Ohio Queen

September 26, 1861

My Darling Cora,

Darkness has swallowed the shore land, a foliage riot showing many varieties of green, now fallen asleep. I face the hollows of Kentucky; behind me rise the steeper hills of Ohio. This placid river is a boundary, though I cannot imagine how a people could be slave on one side and free on the other. In Maine, a decade past, I remember an evening of lecture, after I had first sailed with Jubal and he was home with us, his arm mending from a break when a squall at sea had gone badly. An author reading her book Uncle Tom's Cabin—I urge you to find a copy at the Library Company on Fifth Street—founded by Benjamin Franklin, no less—which described the flight of a Negro slave woman across ice floes upon this very river I now travel.

I think and yearn of you and our children. I mourn for Jubal and cannot fathom how his childhood should guide his actions against the judgment won from so many perils at sea between distant ports. Though I do not rightly worry of Sally—she has the strength and durability of my native state's granite—I can only imagine her anguish.

How will this catastrophe end? General Meigs opines that it has barely begun, and I have formed a high regard for the man. Of his prognostications, I will discuss when home. I do not doubt but I will return within a fortnight and hopefully sooner. I miss you beyond words.

Your devoted and loving husband,
Lester

Chapter Sixty-Nine

Mobile, October 1861

Ezekiel opened the bedroom curtains to the afternoon sea breeze, which kept the house cool despite the broiling afternoon sun. Sally wiped her brow and considered the cluttered bed. In Charleston, she had bought clothes for herself and Emma to replace those left aboard *Mastiff* in the Atlantic, and now she considered how to store them in the upstairs rooms of Truette Stubbs' mansion in Mobile.

Ezekiel glided past her, his head down.

"Ezekiel, are you all right?"

The gnarled old black man turned, and to Sally's astonishment she could see he was crying. "Oh, my dear man, what has happened?"

"Beggin' forgiveness, m'am," Ezekiel replied in his ghost of a voice. "Just ..."

Sally went to him and took his hands. "What?"

"We's back here, agin. Mr. Stubbs, he such a fine man, a good man. Lord dun takin' care him now." His voice trailed off to a strangled whisper. "Lotta years in this house, Louisa and me."

Ezekiel sagged and Sally brought him into her arms. "I miss her so, Miss Sally. Ever' live-long day, I miss my Louisa."

Sally blinked back her own tears. "The Lord's taking care of Louisa, too."

"Oh, 'spect so, I sorely do." Ezekiel gently freed and collected himself. "I goin' down to docks, Missus. Boats coming in from the day, get us a good fish for dinner. Mr. Jubal, he suppin' tonight?"

"I don't know, but cook enough for him," Sally replied. "He's downtown, tending to his business."

Alone again, Sally surveyed the room. Already uneasy at sleeping in Truette Stubbs' old bed—it seemed somehow a sacrilege, using the same bed he had shared with Mrs. Stubbs until her death—Sally resolved to make use of a smaller guest bedroom. Emma was napping down the hall; by the time the new baby came Sally thought perhaps she might think differently about this room. But for now, the sea breeze would blow through and take the mustiness with it, as the house became a home once again.

For this she would be eternally grateful to Stubbs. If the family had to be in Mobile, there was no better place. After two months living in a Charleston hotel, Sally longed for a home to call their own, a particular need after the interminable train trip through the South, over three different lines, each with a different gauge of track. Jubal said they were among the best lines in the South. Compared with the railroads of the Northeast, the Southern lines were a pathetic afterthought. Though she knew nothing of military matters, Sally thought if the Charleston-to-Mobile experience were representative of the Southern transportation system, winning independence through war would be no easy matter. Even Southern newspapers alluded to the challenges ahead; the euphoria and pugnacity of spring had vanished into editorial exhortations for vigilance and noble sacrifice on behalf of the new Confederacy.

In Charleston, Jubal had spent most days at the offices of Fraser and Trenholm. Before the war, the company had been one of the largest cotton traders to the English market and now had leveraged trade relationships in Liverpool and London to become the Confederate states' main international banker.

Sally had only spoken of Jubal's "work" once. Deliberate ignorance allowed a semblance of family comity, though Sally knew it was temporary.

"James Baines said cotton was the South's lifeblood," Sally observed one night, while she watched Jubal finish a late supper in their hotel suite. Again that day, he had left at sunrise and returned after sunset.

Jubal, instantly wary, didn't respond. "So how," Sally continued, "are you going to finance this 'war of Northern aggression,' as people around here are calling it?"

"We'll manage," was all Jubal would say, though quietly impressed with his wife. In fact, George Trenholm had enlisted him to run the Union blockade with a load of cotton to exchange for hard currency in England, and thereupon to commence purchases of armaments and ships for the Confederacy through Charles Piroleau, and a new man, James Bulloch, now en route to Liverpool. A fifteen-year veteran of the U.S. Navy, Bulloch intended to build a Confederate navy in Liverpool shipyards. Fraser and Trenholm's British office would become a front for Confederate war purchases and ship contracts with hard currency converted from cotton sales.

"You know ships, cotton, and finance," George Trenholm had explained, urging Jubal to return to Liverpool. Tall, patrician, charming, and cunning,

Trenholm's shrewd instincts in the cotton business had made him one of the richest men in America.

"To win independence," he continued, "we must infuriate the maritime industry that supports Lincoln. Raiders will carry the war to the North, terrorize the coastal population, and threaten Northern ports to divert their blockade. Our objective is to destroy Union merchant vessels, disrupt their commerce in the Atlantic, the Caribbean, and the China trade routes, and influence British interest in our success. Your work in England with James Bulloch—he's already there, and an exceptional man—is absolutely vital. You must go! Our Confederacy will depend on men like you!"

Jubal regarded his wife, his stomach wrenching with the knowledge he could share none of his feelings without prompting outright domestic warfare.

"Not one sliver of our gold will you contribute to this government," Sally said, staring as Jubal pushed aside his plate, appetite gone again. "And if you leave before I bear our child you will never share my bed again."

"Sally," Jubal retorted, "I've had enough …"

"Don't you 'Sally' me," she flashed. "I vowed 'for better or worse'—the latter of which your slave-holding brethren are doing their lethal best to provide!"

Sally stood and turned sideways, pulling up her dress. "Do you see this belly, Jubal? I carry *your* child! Have the good decency to at least lay eyes on it before you sail off to defend slavery!"

Jubal stared at his wife's back as Sally walked from the room. Standing slowly, he went to a cabinet and pulled a decanter of brandy and poured half a glass. He stared at the decanter top.

"*Never, ever leave it open to the air*. Ain't that what you said Truette?" Jubal stoppered the brandy. "I can do that. But 'stay out of it'? Said that, too."

Jubal sighed and took a swallow of brandy. "Wish I could."

Chapter Seventy

Philadelphia, November 1861

Cora shifted in her sleep, keeping a leg entwined with Lester's. In the deepest night, Philadelphia cooled with a northern weather front, and Lester reached for the wool blanket to pull back over their shoulders. Moonlight softly etched Cora's skin and he stirred at the swell of her breasts, idly trying to imagine the miracle of milk slowly filling for Truette, who had begun to crawl into his mother's lap en route to anything within reach.

The family had furniture now, nothing fancy, but better than Lester ever remembered from the South Orrington farm. Cora slept on the most comfortable mattress she'd ever known in her life.

Lester scratched his loins, now drying but still sticky. When he was home, after the children were in bed, they could not keep their hands off each other. In the privacy of night Cora would fling off the sheets and envelop him, as he would her, alternately a carnal and tender tangle, loving, gentle, and using every muscle in their bodies to shake the bed. Lester stared at the ceiling, feeling this moment was as close as he would get to heaven on earth, a wonderful slide to sleep.

At sunrise he awoke, reached for his wife and felt only bed. A shuffle and soft crackle of firewood came from the kitchen and then the delicious smell of brewing coffee cleared his head. Moments later, a sharp sizzle of bacon pulled him upright.

"You awake?" Cora smiled from the doorway.

Lester scrunched his eyes. "I'm going to call you Luscious."

"Call me anything you want if you mean it." She came to him and he nuzzled her belly. "You want 'nother one?"

Lester looked up beyond the mound of her robe, awake now. "Luscious?"

"I can feel me," Cora said, serious, "ready again. But I dunno ... two young un' be a handful. How often you gonna be gone?" Suddenly she turned away. "That bacon'll burn if I don't get to it!"

Lester pulled on a nightshirt and moccasins and walked outside to empty the chamber pot. The morning was crisp; frost would come soon—maybe even tomorrow, he thought.

Cora pulled the skillet off the cookstove and laid three fried eggs on a thick slab of pumpernickel bread. She'd never tasted German bread before Philadelphia but loved chewing the crusts. Lester sipped his coffee.

"Just about the full moon, isn't it?" he said, though he knew exactly the phase of the moon, a sea habit that would be instinctive however long he lived. Lester smiled at his wife. "A good time to travel—otherwise our family is growing."

"Where you goin'? When?"

"Washington. This morning, but I should be back late with my orders. I don't know what the general will want next, but I heard him say that the Union forces approach six hundred fifty thousand men. A year ago there were less than twenty thousand."

"How long you be gone when he tells you?"

"At least until after the full moon," Lester grinned, but his face grew pensive, a vision of the coming day. "It depends where he wants me to go. But this is building, on a scale I never thought possible. By spring we will see war everywhere."

"Lester," Cora wiped her apron, "I ..."

Never, since he had first laid eyes on her coming onto the porch at Whitmill Rivens' cabin, had Lester seen her nervous. He watched, fascinated, as she twisted her apron.

"I want to go to school," she said in a rush.

"For what?" Lester replied, dumbfounded. "Where?"

"I wuz with Letitia Still few days back, and we seen Lucretia Mott, 'member her?"

"Oh, by Jesus, yes." Lester's Maine accent rang.

"I heard her say another Quaker woman goin' to start a school. For women. A medical school."

"Here?" Lester was incredulous. "In Philadelphia?"

Cora nodded. "Mrs. Mott says she would help me find a tutor. Come next September, I could start."

"What about the children?"

"They'll be fine, I see to that. Or you ken stay to home!"

Lester grinned wide. "You've still got snap. When did you get this idea?"

"I been thinking 'bout Sally. And Beulah Hatcher."

Mention of his sister struck Lester like a blow, though he thought of her often, and of Jubal. Some mail still managed to travel between North and

South via private carriers, but no word from either had arrived.

Cora removed her apron, poured coffee, and sat across from her husband.

"Why Beulah?" Lester asked.

"She's knows everything about a child coming out, don't know that she's ever lost a one. Women come from miles around, sometimes travel a few days so's Beulah will bring 'em home safe, momma and baby. I tole Sally to find Beulah when her time comes."

Cora blew on the steaming cup and took a sip. "I do love coffee," she mused. "That child's coming soon, maybe's already here. Where do you think they is?"

"*Are*. I've got no idea," Lester replied. "Nary a one."

Chapter Seventy-One

Alabama River, December 1861

Coosa's paddlewheels held the steamboat alongside the wharf at Camden, a small town on the opposite bank of the Alabama River from Gee's Bend, long enough for Jubal to help Sally waddle down the gangplank. Ezekiel followed, holding a bag and Emma's hand. The wharf was largely empty—two other riverboats had stopped earlier in the day—save for a single man, a prosperous planter, by his dress.

"Ezekiel, mind that bag," Sally called, her New England accent as heavy as Jubal could remember since leaving Maine years before. She's ready for battle, he thought. Heavily pregnant, Sally leaned on him so as not to lose her footing.

"Mrs. Calhoun," Mark Pettaway tipped his hat. "Welcome to our locale." He extended his hand to Jubal. "Mr. Calhoun, sir. Fine to have you here. I have a skiff at the end of the wharf, if you'll follow me. And who might this lovely young lady be?"

"This is our daughter, Emma." The little girl hid behind Ezekiel, unwilling to look at Pettaway. Jubal smiled at her, bemused by Pettaway's casual demeanor, which he knew to be forced since the planter teetered at the edge of bankruptcy. So much cotton crowded the Mobile wharves, its export stopped by the Union blockade, that riverboats no longer would haul the crop south, much less stop at plantation wharves. The planter was being strangled in cotton; otherwise, he would never sell a slave so cheaply.

Four black men manned the skiff. Wordless but with rhythmic efficiency, they rowed across the river to the empty landing at Gee's Bend where a coach stood waiting. Within an hour of disembarking from the riverboat, Jubal looked again at Sandy Hill, the plantation manor he had never thought to see again.

"Is this where you bought Cora?" Sally's disgust was obvious.

Jubal nodded. Mark Pettaway sat stiffly opposite them, rising immediately as the coach circled to a stop before the front porch. A Negro footman hurried to open the coach door.

Pettaway helped Sally down and she looked around imperiously, pulling a shawl tightly around her shoulders to ward off the chill seeping in with dusk. She marched toward the front steps.

"Show Mrs. Calhoun her room," Pettaway ordered an aproned black woman waiting on the porch. "M'am, Mr. Calhoun and I shall await you in the library. Come at your leisure and we shall dine. Mr. Calhoun, a brandy and cigar before dinner?"

"Jubal, bring Emma up before you join our host." Sally called back, knowing she should remember her manners, but courtesy was too much effort. Everything about the plantation offended her, from the subservience of the ten slaves she had encountered already to cabins she could see in the distance, where the house servants must sleep. "Ezekiel, bring the bag."

An hour later, Sally walked into the library unannounced, interrupting Jubal's and Pettaway's discussion on the importance of securing British and French diplomatic recognition for the Confederacy. Sally carried the bag she had entrusted to Ezekiel.

Startled, both men scrambled to their feet. "You look refreshed, Mrs. Calhoun," Mark Pettaway purred, though she appeared drawn and haggard. He offered his arm. "Shall we dine?"

"I'm not hungry," Sally replied. "May I sit down? I wish to conclude our business and retire for the evening."

Jubal gritted his teeth. Although his wife looked so rounded and heavy she might topple, he was ashamed of her severity.

"Oh, I am sorry, m'am," Pettaway replied, without a trace of sympathy. "I assure you our slaves have prepared a splendid repast. On my honor Sandy Hill's table is second to none in Alabama!"

"No doubt." Sally settled herself as comfortably as she could, feeling big as a cow. "They ought to eat it. Now then, as Jubal has expressed to you, we wish to buy the Hatcher family. Beulah—isn't that her name, Jubal? Her husband, Jordon, I believe, and their two sons. Or, Jubal, is it three?"

Pettaway glanced at Jubal, his gaze plainly wondering how any man could tolerate such a wife.

"Mr. Calhoun said nothing about the family, only the woman. She is my property; Judge Harris owns the man and his sons. Two. The boys are married."

"Does the judge own them, the wives, too?" Sally grimaced. "Such a humane tradition." She folded her hands over the purse in her lap. "It doesn't matter. Buy them if necessary."

"Excuse me, Mrs. Calhoun?"

"Go to Mr. Harris and tell him you him you want to reunite the family." Sally snorted at Pettaway's blank look. "The judge wouldn't understand such a sentiment? Hardly surprising. I don't care how you do it, just buy them."

"I beg your pardon, Mrs. Calhoun," the planter worked to keep his composure. "I do not expect my guests to insult me in my own library!" Jubal shifted his feet, ready to go for the small, double-shot derringer in his boot if Pettaway erupted. Had Sally been a man, Jubal thought the planter angry enough to demand a duel right then and there.

Sally pulled a document from her bag and handed it to Jubal. "You are aware that last week we procured your outstanding note from the Bank of Mobile?" A week earlier, Jubal had, at Sally's direction, bought Pettaway's loan. The bank, which held dozens of similar unpaid obligations from other planters, none with hope of early settlement given the blockade's chokehold on cotton exports, had readily discounted and assigned Pettaway's note against Jubal's Liverpool accounts.

"I give my word as a gentleman that you shall be repaid at my earliest opportunity," Pettaway replied, sitting stiffly. The Mobile banker's notice to him had arrived on a mail boat three days before, along with Jubal's letter saying they would be visiting to discuss the planter's obligation and his wife's intent to buy Beulah Hatcher.

"I propose 'early' be *now*," Sally declared.

"Mr. Calhoun," Mark Pettaway spit, "may I speak with you in private?"

"You may not," Sally interjected, the disgust in her face plain.

"I beg your pardon, m'am! No man, nor woman, shall address me such! Anywhere, at any time, much less in my own home!"

"I propose to buy this plantation."

Mark Pettaway's jaw dropped. Jubal stared at his wife.

"The land, buildings, every slave, equipment, food, furniture, everything. You may take your personal effects."

Sally reached into the bag and withdrew a bundle wrapped in cloth. Jubal relaxed, suddenly understanding, as his wife peeled away the cotton layers. On her lap, a gold bar fairly shimmered in the soft lamplight.

Jubal adjusted the window in the Sandy Hill guest bedroom to let in a night breeze, knowing Sally slept better cool, as he would also, since lying next to her was like sleeping with a woodstove. She had turned away, trying to get comfortable on her side.

"Sally," he whispered, his mind racing.

"Would you tell this child to get born?" Sally growled. "I can't eat, can't sleep, my feet feel like bricks, I've got to piss every twenty minutes, and I need holsters for my chest. You get pregnant next time!"

Despite himself, Jubal chuckled. "Can I do anything?"

"Stay."

Silence lengthened; then far off, an animal screamed in the night. Finally, Sally began rocking from side to side. "Roll me over."

Jubal helped her as she grunted with the weight of the unborn.

"Find Beulah," Sally whispered, holding his face. "The baby is dropping. He's coming soon—I know he's big and I'm scared. How I'm ever going to push him out without tearing in two …"

"I'll be with you," Jubal swallowed, holding her close. He could feel the child kick. "You certain it's a boy?"

"Got to be. He's ornery as you."

"There's the pot calling the kettle black!"

"I know—I was rude to Pettaway. I can't abide the man."

"Whatever were you thinking?" In retrospect, Jubal couldn't believe he hadn't connected Sally's constant admonishments to Ezekiel about the bag with its contents.

"If I asked," Sally replied, "you'd had a hundred good reasons not to buy this place."

"I still have them. You don't know a thing 'bout planting cotton …"

"We'll plant something else," Sally interrupted. "Cora told me Beulah Hatcher was the best midwife she ever knew, has seen to dozens, maybe hundreds of births. You yourself said planters brought their slaves from fifty miles around to her."

"Buying her is one thing, but the whole damn plantation?"

"I'd rather be here than in Mobile, especially after you go."

Jubal paused, and the silence lengthened. "We haven't spoken a word …"

"Don't insult my intelligence Jubal, just because I did the same to Pettaway. You're going to Liverpool sure as I'm having this baby."

Silence again filled the bedroom. In the darkness, Jubal gazed at the shadow of his wife's shoulders, marveling again at Sally's instincts, thinking that she often knew what he was going to do before he did.

"I don't want to know what you're going to do there," Sally continued. "Especially since you'll regret it the rest of your life. But while you're gone, I've got the children. You saw Pettaway look at the gold bar? Watch, he'll be gone tomorrow before I change my mind; he knows things could get much worse. Hell, they will—those goddamn bankers were tripping over themselves, you said, to sell that note, at what, a forty percent discount? We've got land now and people—slaves, but they won't be for long; I'm gonna free every last one of them—to help us. We'll have plenty of food, and we're near the river so we can move fast, either direction, if the war comes here."

"I can't imagine the war could come here, since it won't last that long," Jubal whispered, the thought putting a pit in his stomach. "Pettaway might not be able to buy the Hatchers," he added, though he knew better.

"That planter's got the spine of a noodle," Sally scoffed, "but he's not stupid. Wanna bet?"

"No." Jubal knew Pettaway was hopelessly buried in debt, but the gold bar—gaining in value every day as the Confederate paper dollar inflated—offered immediate salvation from bankruptcy. By making the plantation purchase contingent upon first buying the Hatcher men, Sally had ensured that Pettaway would reunite the Hatcher family to save his own financial freedom. The irony was not lost on Jubal, and again, already more times than he could count, he wondered what compelled him to serve his state and turn away from everything he had ever loved. A profound sadness came over him, deepening as Sally's breathing slowed and she and their unborn child drifted off to sleep. He knew it wouldn't be long now.

Sally stirred. "Jubal," she murmured. "Get those other bars melted into coins. 'Case I need 'em, little bit at a time."

Chapter Seventy-Two

Nashville, February 1862

The gangplank had scarcely banged onto the Cumberland River wharf when Lester descended in long strides from the gunboat USS *Conestoga* and headed up Broad Street.

"Norton, wait for me!" yelled the *New York Times* reporter who had peppered Lester with questions after noticing several of the gunboat's officers addressing him as "Sir." Lester had been evasive, unwilling to say much about his mission, certainly to someone waiting to write down every word.

"Nice to meet you," Lester called back before loping up the street. The warm spring afternoon soon brought a sweat beneath his deep blue greatcoat, but he carried on, looking in vain for a cabbie. The city had the feel of a place suddenly abandoned, as indeed thousands of Nashville residents had done after news of Fort Donelson's fall a week earlier. The remaining residents stared sullenly, stunned that the state capital, full of martial bombast, a Confederate army, ten thousand tons of stores—flour, ammunition, feed, meat, enough provisions to outlast a yearlong siege—had been surrendered without a shot. Two days earlier, the Confederate Army simply melted away, though not before looting half the stores.

Several blocks inland, Lester stopped for a troop of horsemen, perhaps twenty in all, trotting toward the capital building. From the quality of their mounts and their mud-splattered legs, he could see they were mobile cavalry, recently in the field. At their center, a small bearded man rode easily, chomping a cigar. U.S.—for "Unconditional Surrender"—Grant, the *Times* reporter had called him. Though Lester recognized the general, he had never spoken with the man, having no need. Grant's quartermasters would know what the troops required.

General Meigs had already determined Nashville would be the major U.S. Army supply depot in the west. Five railroads intersected in the city, and from the river, gunboats and barges could supply several armies and navy flotillas as the Union pushed south on the Mississippi, Tennessee, and Cumberland Rivers into the Southern heartland. One look at the map was all Lester needed to understand Meigs' intent: the quartermaster general had sent him to Nashville to find the best army officer available to build the depot.

As the cavalry troop trotted by, Lester turned to follow. From across the intersection, a wagon started forward, driven by a middle-aged woman. Beside her, a young girl sat silently with a boy about ten. Despite the unseasonably mild day, all three wore coats. Two large luggage lockers were strapped down in the wagon bed.

On impulse, Lester hailed the woman. Surprised and wary, she held the two-horse team as he approached.

"Begging your pardon, m'am," Lester said. "Are you by chance leaving the city?"

At his accent, the woman's eyes flashed. "What business," she retorted, her Tennessee cadence unmistakable, "is it of yours?"

Half of Nashville had fled and this woman and her children were dressed for the road. "Should you travel south, m'am, may I ask that you take a letter? To my sister in Mobile?" On the gunboat, Lester had written a brief note to Sally, addressing it to Truette Stubbs' home in Mobile, the only place she might plausibly be, though he considered the odds long that the note would find her even if he could find someone heading south.

"We are going to Corinth," the woman replied.

"I do not know the place, m'am."

"In northern Mississippi."

"By yourselves? I trust you will be careful."

"My husband rides with Forrest," she sat straight as a rod. Lester had no idea who she was talking about but her sentiments were clear. "May they drive this rabble from our home! You have no right to be here!" Her son stared with the hatred of a boy whose father had gone to war.

Lester said nothing for a moment. "If you will do your best to post this, as if it were your own family, I'd be much obliged." From his pocket, he thrust a gold coin and the letter into the startled boy's hand.

The woman took the letter from her son. Glancing at the address, she softened, barely. "The Mobile and Ohio railroad passes through Corinth. I will post your letter," she said, "but only because of your sister. Far as we're concerned, God can damn you Northern bastards to hell!"

Chapter Seventy-Three

Mobile, March 1862

The gale rolled in from Mobile Bay as the ship made ready to cast off with the tide. Jubal had waited nearly a week for a moonless night and an offshore breeze, but the gale was a huge added gift. Though it would be a wet ride, the *Celeste* would be cloaked by rain as it ran at hull speed through the Union blockade. Jubal knew this bay and he had brought along an old oysterman who in fifty years had fished nearly every foot of the bottom.

Seven hundred cotton bales jammed the coastal schooner's hold; fourteen men waited on deck for his orders. He had financed the ship from his Liverpool accounts, a risk he would not thought of taking but for Sally's suggestion, and her demand that he include the Pettaway cotton at their personal discount.

"All ready, sir!" the first mate declared above the wind, rising out of the north. "Tide be turning."

"Stand by," Jubal nodded, watching the water barely begin to move seaward along a wharf post.

Wondering if this was his last look ever at the Mobile waterfront, he waited another minute, then signaled forward and aloft. Slipping her lines, *Celeste*'s jib and mizzen sail filled, and a half-mile out, Jubal raised everything she could carry. With eyes to the compass and the oysterman casting a lead line at the amidship rail, Jubal flung his ship into the storm's leading edge.

As the wind moaned and night deepened, Jubal tethered himself to a lifeline and strode back and forth between helm and the oysterman. A cautious plan to hug the mainland and move through the shoals under Dauphin Island blew away in the night. Steering opposite the storm's path, Jubal knew the wind would clock and spit him through the narrows of Pelican Bay passage into the Gulf of Mexico. Though Yankee gunboats patrolled the narrows, they would nearly have to run *Celeste* down to see her. In any other time or place this would be madness, Jubal knew, but these were his home waters and this was war.

Throughout the night, the schooner charged into pitch darkness. If the old oysterman misjudged and they grounded on a sand bank, Jubal knew the schooner's hull would plow to a stop in ten feet and everything above deck—rig and men—would hurl forward, catapulted over the bow.

The old oysterman never got the slightest bit nervous.

At dawn, the sky was leaden but the wind had warmth in it, and by the sea color Jubal knew they were well into the Gulf, alone.

"Steady as she goes," Jubal ordered the helmsman. "Make due south." Rather than sneak through the Florida Straits where Union ships would likely patrol, Jubal made for open water, intending to sail a long loop underneath Cuba and back up through the Mona Passage into the Atlantic making for Bermuda. There, he'd sell the boat and transship with the cotton to Liverpool. All of it, save the actual sailing route, Sally's idea.

"If you've got to do this homeland stupidity," she declared, a day before bearing their son, "use what you learned since you left me in Maine." Jubal had shaken his head; she just couldn't resist. "Trade something," Sally directed. "This family is going to live a long time."

Going below decks, he turned sideways along the narrow corridor between cotton bales to his cabin, made smaller by the two large bales stowed there. Bone-tired and laying fully clothed on his bunk, he looked at the carte-de-visite tacked on the bulkhead above. In Mobile, Jubal had learned of a French photographer, recently arrived from Paris, selling a newly discovered photographic process. Hauling the Frenchman up to Gee's Bend, he had set Sally and the newborn in a rocker on the Sandy Hill porch, Emma standing beside them. Jubal paid a hundred dollars in gold—a month's fine lodging in Mobile for the Frenchman—for four cards.

By the flickering whale oil lamp, Jubal stared at the photograph. Sally was smiling. Though the photographer insisted his subjects always chose to look serious, she ignored him.

Somewhere between memory and dream, Sally's voice came to him again. She whispered, utterly exhausted from fifteen hours of fierce labor. Beulah sat in a chair beside the bed, watching, though she too was completely spent. The baby had tried to come out shoulder first, as if already muscling into life, but Beulah had slowly twisted him right, though it took the night and well into a bright morning.

Jubal had rocked hours in the hallway outside the bedroom puffing on his pipe, fetching hot water off the woodstove as Beulah instructed. At noon he was dozing when he heard the women growing louder, Beulah exhorting

"*C'mon, Miss Sally!*" Then came a short lull, broken by a baby's cry.

Ten minutes later, Beulah opened the door. "Boy's fine. Mamma's tired," the black woman looked on the edge of old and she turned to slump in the chair. "She be comin' long all right."

Sally lay with the boy wrapped snugly, sleeping on her chest. Jubal reached into a bucket of lukewarm water and wrung out a cloth, gently wiping Sally's splotchy face and stringy, damp hair.

"Turn him over," Sally whispered.

Jubal could barely talk. "He's all tuckered out."

"Go 'head, he'll be all right." Sally gave a weak grin. "You oughta satisfy yourself."

Jubal started crying as he rewrapped the infant.

After a time, Sally sighed. "What do you want to name him?"

"Lester."

"That's nice." She stroked the baby's head. "Though some day they'll get mixed up."

"I'm going to call him Buck."

"Buck? Why?"

"My daddy called me that. One of the only things I remember."

Chapter Seventy-Four

Philadelphia, May 1862

The recoil nearly spun Cora around, but Lester caught and steadied his wife. He pulled a wad of cotton from her ear.

"Now reload—push the lever down and away from you, that brings another cartridge into the chamber and cocks the hammer ... That's it, but keep your finger away from the trigger—now aim. Put the center of the target right in the crotch of the sight." Lester stuck the cotton back but Cora swatted his hand and adjusted the wad to her ear.

A hundred feet away, against the gravel pit banking, Lester had mounted a target. He turned to the wagon that had brought them six miles outside the city to the abandoned pit, a place where he could show Cora how to handle the weapons he had brought from factories in Connecticut. Curtis stared from the wagon seat, his foot rocking a cradle holding little Truette.

Initially, Cora had recoiled at the lethal-looking Henry repeating rifle and a short-barreled .44 Colt pocket pistol.

"Learn the rifle first," Lester had explained, "then the pistol will seem easy."

"I don't want to shoot nobody."

"You have before. And the next time some thug aims to rob you, don't even pull that pistol out of your bag. Shoot 'em right through it!"

Bam! The recoil belted her but she was ready. A black hole showed in the target. She looked at Lester.

"Nice shot, now try again a little lower and to the left," he said. "Let's back up another ten yards. Curtis, you right?" Lester looked to the wagon as Truette started squalling. Curtis rocked the cradle so fast Lester knew the boy was furious.

"Let me try!" Curtis yelled.

"When you're eight!"

"What happens when he's eight?" Cora asked.

"Nothing. I'm just trying to shut him up now. Go on, shoot the magazine, four or five more, then try the pistol, but we'll have to get closer. From here you'd have a hard time hitting the wagon. The pistol is for close work, as the cavalrymen say."

"I don't want you to go fighting," Cora said.

"I already am," Lester replied. "Best way I know. Sooner this slaughter ends ..."

He glanced away, the memory still fresh, more horrific each time he dreamed.

"What?" Cora lowered the rifle, looking closely at her husband.

"Nothing. Try a few more."

"Don't you 'nuthin' me, Lester Norton."

Lester blinked several times before drawing a breath. "Twenty thousand men."

"What?" she whispered. "What did you see, honey? Where?"

"Last month. General Meigs ordered me to Nashville, we're building a fort to protect the supply depots. A courier came suddenly ... a big battle on the Tennessee River; they needed medical supplies. I went on a gunboat, a place called Pittsburg Landing. Never seen ... imagined even ..."

"Seen what?"

"Men. Dead, wounded. Horses ... trees blown to shreds ..."

Lester shook his head as if trying to dispel the dream. "Don't worry, it was over the day before. No danger for me."

"By that little church? Shy-something?"

"Shiloh. How'd you know?"

"You tole me to read the papers." Cora took his hand.

"Yeah ... I did." Lester swallowed. "I got to this place, they called it the Hornet's Nest, looked like some crazed giant had taken a scythe to an oak grove. There wasn't a sound. Every bird had flown."

"Let me try!" Curtis howled.

"No!" Lester wheeled. "You mind yourself! Mother and I will be right along!"

"He's just a boy," Cora breathed.

"I know. Let's go now, shall we?"

"It was bad, wasn't it?"

The memory returned. Lester approached a Union officer at the edge of the wood, bordering a field carpeted by bloating bodies swarming with flies. Black men dumped corpses, many missing pieces of limbs, in long trenches. The stench made him cover his mouth with a kerchief but he still gagged. He stopped in his tracks, staring at the face of a young man, barely older than a boy. Still with his blue cap at a jaunty angle, the soldier looked puzzled, as if wondering how his head—just his head—had ended up in a tree fork ten feet off the ground.

"Lester ..." Cora shook his arm.

"There was an officer there, tallying the dead and wounded. Ten thousand a side, give or take." Lester took Cora's rifle and put an arm around his wife. "In two days."

Cora's eyes closed as she laid her head into Lester's shoulder.

"He said they'd met the elephant."

Chapter Seventy-Five

Liverpool, June 1862

Jubal sat alone, his back to the corner of the Liverpool Hotel dining room. Patrons had begun to leave in the late evening, sunset at this latitude as the summer solstice approached, and he could see both James Bulloch conversing with a dining companion and the Union agents that constantly shadowed Bulloch, three tables apart.

When Bulloch and his companion rose, Jubal recognized Charles Piroleau, the Fraser and Trenholm agent that had bought his load of cotton smuggled out of Mobile a month earlier. Piroleau was simply Bulloch's front, selling the cargo to British mills at double the price he had paid Jubal. Bulloch was grateful and impressed that Jubal had allowed a margin to help finance the Confederate war effort, not knowing, nor did Jubal tell him, that the cargo was entirely the product of Pettaway's plantation at Gee's Bend. Piroleau had used Fraser and Trenholm funds to pay for the cotton Sally had thought to buy at a bankruptcy discount. At a five hundred percent profit, Jubal could afford to be patriotic, though he knew the moral disingenuousness was a clumsy amend for leaving Sally and the children.

Jubal waited for Bulloch to signal where they would meet at midnight. If the South Carolinian put his hat on before leaving it would be Albert Dock; if not, then across the Mersey at the Laird and Sons shipyard in Birkenhead, where the future Confederate raider CSS *Alabama* stood in drydock, three weeks before sea trials.

James Bulloch showed Piroleau out the door, donning his hat as he left. Almost immediately, two men rose from their table and followed. Both were short and squat but moved quickly, not even bothering to tip their bowlers to the barmaid who brought another tankard each of ale.

"Bloody hell, were ye thinkin' 'a not payin' fer ye pints?" she cried, as the men yanked open the door. One turned and tossed a couple of coins before they disappeared. "Buggerin' bastards!" the barmaid spat, then shook her head and turned back to the bar. She stopped, noticing Jubal's raised arm. He beckoned her over.

"I'll take 'em both," he said, "if you'd also bring a portion of shepherd's pie."

The barmaid, ample and middle-aged, suddenly smiled. "Where ye from, laddie?" Neither rotten teeth nor age would dissuade her from flirting.

"Memphis, m'am," Jubal replied, thinking she needed a bath, "in America."

"Now just where might that be?"

"In the middle."

"In the middle of the fight, are ye? Well, you've a mother who raised a proper gentl'man, she did! But I won't have ye pay for another man's pint! And them blokes, I be seein' 'em agin. Shall give a piece 'a me mind! Bloody hell!"

"Who are they?"

"Dodgy wankers pryin' inta others business, that's who!" She looked around, and lowered her voice. "But they be brass bastards, if ye get me meanin'! Don't be triflin' with 'em. No good will come ta ya!"

Jubal nodded.

"Now ducks," the barmaid beamed again, placing the tankards down. "Be back straight away with yer pie. Don't ye fret a mite!"

―

A half-hour before midnight, fog had settled into the dockyards, turning each streetlamp into a ghostly flicker that Jubal avoided as he kept in the shadows of the massive brick warehouses around Albert Dock. In a corner alcove off a narrow back alley leading to the quay, he drew moccasins from a small canvas rucksack beneath his cloak, exchanging them for the boots he wore. Gathering the cloak about him against the chill, he pulled the hood low until he was indistinguishable in the dark.

The moccasins, made of moose leather, suddenly brought Lester to mind, and their nights ten years earlier at the Norton farm in Maine. Lester had sewn the moccasins then for Jubal to wear around the house, and the moose hide had been around the world several times since.

Memories seized him, a sudden wracking anguish at the absence of everyone who had ever loved him, now thousands of miles from this dank, dark doorway where he waited for the mastermind builder of the infant Confederate Navy. Doubt bloomed, and he wondered what compelled him to leave Emma and Sally and their newborn son to support a rebellion that depended on foreign recognition by powers whose interests would be best served by an America dismantled.

The tower clock's bell boomed midnight and he listened for steady footfalls on cobblestone, knowing Bulloch would be punctual. On the twelfth ring, he heard steps, and moments later Bulloch walked past. Jubal tapped the brick with a foot-long piece of lead pipe the thickness of his thumb.

"Sixteen," Bulloch whispered, never breaking step. He disappeared around the corner.

The sounds of his boots receded until snuffed by the night. Jubal waited, listening intently. Hearing nothing more, he shifted his weight, about to follow when the slightest shuffle made him freeze. A furtive, confused patter approached, paused, and resumed. Shadows passed, topped by the silhouettes of two bowler hats. They stopped to peek around the corner and dropped in their tracks as Jubal whipped his pipe fore and backhand between their heads. Soundlessly he stepped over the unconscious men, deliberately crushing a bowler, and scurried down the stone quay past a row of varied working boats to the old, flat-bottomed coal sloop moored at wharf sixteen.

James Bulloch waited inside the tiny wheelhouse staring out the one small, dirty window that looked back at the quay.

"Followed?"

Jubal grunted softly. "Not now."

"Well?"

"A bark, *Agrippina,* 350 tons. Found her in Cardiff. I had her captain—a Scotsman, McQueen—sail for London. She's British-owned and -flagged and can carry anything she wishes."

"I will leave a packet at the Adelphi Hotel, they will hold it for you. What name will you use?"

Jubal thought for a moment. "John Norton."

"We should get you a British passport. I have a man in the ministry." Bulloch listened for a moment, then continued. "Load the bark within a month; we must be under way by mid-July, earlier if we can, but no later. Run everything through Piroleau."

"July?" Jubal asked, smiling to himself. Bulloch's understated brilliance sparked memories of Truette Stubbs. Though a modest man, Bulloch combined a financer's acumen and a trader's instincts with the cunning of an intelligence agent, layered beneath a diplomat's polish. Employing an uncanny sense of timing and manipulation, he maneuvered to build Confederate raiders in British shipyards even as the U.S. Consulate, suspicious of everything

Bulloch touched, tried to sabotage his every move.

"The Foreign Office may yet decide to seize the ship," Bulloch spoke softly, his fatigue evident. "The double game—tacitly supporting our cause while hiding behind their Neutrality Act. We pay the English to build our ships, but if Whitehall decides it is in their best interest they will declare them articles of war, subject to confiscation. England has allegiance to no one but itself."

Does anyone? Jubal thought, but kept quiet. In the darkness, he could feel Bulloch regard him. The silence lengthened.

"Where will we meet *Alabama* to arm her?" Jubal whispered. Bulloch maintained the fiction that Fraser and Trenholm were building a merchant ship launched in Liverpool to be sold in Spain to Spanish investors, so it would have no armament of any kind. The cannon, gunpowder, shot, and ammunition stores would be shipped from London. Bulloch had assigned Jubal the task of finding a suitable vessel somewhere in the British Isles, loading the armaments aboard her, and making the rendezvous.

"The Azores. Stay in touch from London and be ready to leave at a moment's notice."

Chapter Seventy-Six

> July 4, 1862
> Sandy Hill
> Gee's Bend, Alabama

My dearest Cora,
A letter arrived by way of Mobile today, from Lester, and I was so elated I shrieked with joy. Within moments Ezekiel, Jordon Hatcher, and his sons—I can never remember their names nor tell them apart—ran up the stairs to my rescue, Jordon ready with an axe! Beulah said I must set a better example since I am the new master here.

How could this have ever happened, that I, so contemptuous of slavery, now own 123 men, women, and children? By law no less!

Jubal and I have bought Sandy Hill. My beloved husband has abandoned his family for England to build a Confederate Navy, he says, so that we might continue to own human beings. His conviction nearly drives me mad, but I cannot debate this with him any more than I can argue with the magnificent live oak in our front yard. Indeed, the tree might be more talkative, witness to a century of this perfidy. (I like that word, having learned it from my reading, which I try to do every day when the children—Lester Jordon Norton, two months old—take their afternoon nap). I usually fall asleep reading for it is infernally hot. How anyone can work in the sun in these summer afternoons is utterly beyond me; I would die in the fields.

But isn't that where it all started—in the heat, in the fields?

The library here, a very good one, is the only thing that pathetic wretch Pettaway left of consequence. I heard he fled to France, which sounds in character; the almighty plantation owner would cower before anyone who would fight him back.

I do not know what we will do. I am a foreigner in what was once my country. In Mobile, after Jubal left, people were so uncivil, rude, and arrogant, as if my accent made me an enemy, that I gathered the children and Ezekiel and returned here. Perhaps I judge those pretty, vapid (I love that word) ladies harshly, for in truth, I am their enemy. Proudly, I am their eternal enemy.

I do not know how I will ever hold Jubal in my arms, or lie with him, again. How could he leave us? My heart is broken beyond bearing, but our children must not know. If their father lives he will face them one day, and then let him explain to them, as he can never do with me.

So, for now, we will stay and live, and wait for Jubal to return. Here, pious, righteous hypocrisy rules. The North oppresses a free Southern people who will fight to the death for the right to oppress and enslave another people. The contradiction leaves me speechless. Do you know how many times I have been told "You just don't understand?"

I will have Ezekiel send this by a Cuban man who may travel, he says, freely between the lines. He called on us in Mobile, intending to visit Truette Stubbs, and was much saddened by news of his passing.

You must write, I beg of you. Though surrounded by people—my slaves!—who would die for me, I am lonely beyond measure. Nights are the worst, utterly empty. Without my children I would feel hopeless, but for them I will never give up hope, though I no longer know of what. Peace, I suppose, and family. Is that asking too much?

I ordered the cotton crop to be burned in the fields and replanted to potatoes, corn, peas, and okra, though I can't stand the taste of that vegetable. Whatever happens, we will eat.

I would not thought to have burned the fields but for Jubal. Before leaving he rode to the cabin where you had been prisoner, he said, where Lester had met you.

Jubal burned it to the ground.

I do not know what we will do, but I love you and will bring my children into your home someday. My arms surround you and my brother; please give this to Lester, who is the finest man in this world, and I miss him so much—even if he brought me an impossible husband I cannot help but love despite himself.

> Forever,
> Sally

Chapter Seventy-Seven

Azores, August 1862

From high in the rigging, Jubal sighted his telescope along the coastline of Terceira Island, though the heavy swell gave him only a few seconds at the top of each swing to focus. Eleven days out of London, the *Agrippina* plowed slowly along, deep in the water from the weight of iron and steel below decks. Seven naval guns were lashed in the hold, from cannons firing a thirty-two-pound ball to a rifled behemoth, ten feet long and thick as a mature tree that could sink a ship at fifteen hundred yards with hundred-pound shells.

Aft, below decks, a hundred barrels of gunpowder, shells—solid and grapeshot—fuses, primer, and twenty boxes of new Enfield rifles lay atop 350 tons of coal. Also in the invoices Jubal had picked up at the Adelphi Hotel, were orders for uniforms and materials to clothe crew and officers, plus staples of flour, salt pork, corn, cases of rum, and the myriad small stores necessary to sustain the CSS *Alabama* for several months.

Jubal had seen to *Agrippina*'s loading in London before returning to Liverpool for further orders and had just arrived at Fraser and Trenholm's offices when Bulloch rushed in, ordering him to race over to the raider lying at dockside across the Mersey River with instructions for the master to set sail straight away. Bulloch had received word from a covert Foreign Office source that British Custom House officials would seize the ship the following day. Bulloch had christened the raider *Enrica* in Liverpool to promote the subterfuge that she was simply a steam-powered trader destined for Spanish owners. Once she made international waters he intended to rename her *Alabama*. The U.S. mission knew as much—their spies were just as diligent as Bulloch's aides—and had finally convinced Lord Russell, Britain's foreign minister, that the Lincoln administration would consider British provisioning of warships to the South an act of war.

That afternoon *Enrica* slipped its berth with a skeleton crew as Jubal took the train directly to London to ship aboard *Agrippina*. By nightfall the raider made the Irish coast and turned north to sail above the island and into the open Atlantic, intending to avoid any Union ships, before backtracking south, bound for her Azores rendezvous.

Agrippina had a slow, stormy, wet passage, but Jubal didn't mind—he was at sea again, with his memories and the constant question, Why am I doing this? He asked himself, repeatedly. Though James Bulloch could eloquently express his conviction that the Confederacy was but the latest historical example of a people rebelling against the bonds of oppression, Jubal could not forget Sally's anguished pleas nor the face of Beulah Hatcher, handing him tiny Lester a few hours after his birth. For several nights, alone at the rail as *Agrippina* rolled and plunged through squalls, he could not be sure if his face was wet from rain and sea spray or the wrenching toil from his heart. For the first time since he could remember, Jubal was grateful not to be in command.

At the masthead approaching land, he trained his telescope as the ship rolled upright.

"A point to port!" he bellowed below. The master waved aloft and the helmsman swung her until *Agrippina* pointed at the dark dot of the raider at anchor five miles dead ahead.

~

A week later, Jubal stood at the back rail aboard CSS *Alabama* as it lay in international waters fifteen miles off the Azores. A band aboard made a racket of "Dixie," and then crewmen raised the flag of the Confederate States of America, christening the ship.

In five days of unrelenting effort, Jubal had supervised the transfer of all the armaments, ammunition, stores, and most of the coal from the *Agrippina* to the CSS *Alabama*, a steam-sloop that was now one of the swiftest, most lethal warships in the world.

"You should be proud, sir," Jubal turned to James Bulloch, who had arrived several days earlier on a third ship, the *Bahama,* out of Liverpool, accompanied by the captain and officers of *Alabama*. This completed the complex minuet of building, arming, and manning a Southern warship with British connivance despite the vehement protests and machinations of Union officials. In fact, Bulloch had pulled off a logistical, political, financial, and intelligence masterpiece.

"We have reliable people and our cause is just," Bulloch replied. "Do you know of Raphael Semmes?" Bulloch nodded to the new captain, about to address the assembled crews of the *Alabama, Bahama,* and *Agrippina*, a motley collection of English, Irish, Dutch, and Spanish sailors, with a few semiliterate American wayfarers mixed in.

"No. I've heard the name, a naval captain of some experience, isn't he?" Jubal pondered the situation. "What inducements will be given to join? He needs at least sixty men." Bulloch had brought Semmes and a dozen American officers, but the crew would be selected from the sailors now listening.

"He wants a hundred," Bulloch replied, as Semmes mounted the quarterdeck and prepared to speak. Already, the new captain had acquired the nickname Ol' Beeswax, given by irreverent English sailors amused at Semmes' habit of repeatedly twirling his handlebar mustache, which indeed glistened in the morning sunlight. Backed by his uniformed officers, Captain Semmes looked every inch the taciturn naval commander, braids and epaulets complementing the fine, pewter gray uniform tailored to his trim, compact frame.

"Gentlemen," Semmes began, "permit me to read my commission from the honorable Jefferson Davis, president of the Confederate States of America, and orders for the CSS *Alabama*, as directed by the secretary of war, the honorable Stephen Mallory."

Jubal listened, enjoying the subtropical breeze yet feeling detached from ceremony. Captain Semmes finished his proclamations, handed the documents to one of his officers, and placing his hands behind him, appealed to his audience.

"It is well known that the United States, being a manufacturing and commercial people, while the Confederate States have been thus far almost wholly an agricultural and planting people, had within their limits and control at the commencement of the war almost the whole naval force of the old government. They have seized and appropriated this force to themselves regardless of the just claims of the Confederate States to a portion of it— and a large portion, as taxpayers out of whose contributions it was created. The United States are thus enabled to blockade all the important ports of the Confederate States."

Semmes' voice hardened. Jubal could feel the man's outrage.

"It must be admitted that we have equal belligerent rights with the enemy. One of the most important of these rights in a war against a commercial people is that of capturing his property upon the high seas. The citizens of the United States are waging an unjust and aggressive war on the Confederate States, which I have, with this ship under my command, the honor to represent. Who among you will join us to reject such tyranny?"

Captain Semmes looked over the assembled expectantly, but though a few sailors shuffled their feet uncomfortably, no one said a word.

That dog won't hunt, Jubal thought.

"As a people," the captain continued, "maintaining a government de facto, and not only holding the enemy in check but gaining advantages over him, we are entitled to all rights of the belligerents." Semmes paused, "including prizes, contraband cargoes, and ships of the enemy. I can and do promise you men signing bounty, double wages—both paid in gold—and prize money for all destroyed Union ships, paid by the Confederate Congress, should you serve for the length of our voyage!"

The sailors exploded in cheers. "Hear! Hear!"

Captain Semmes turned to his officers. "Mr. Kell, Mr. Sinclair, sign these men, if you will!"

A scrum ensued amidships, as the two officers descended and sailors clamored to sign on.

Jubal turned to James Bulloch. "These men won't be easy." Whatever the noble, patriotic sentiments that drove Bulloch, Jubal knew the *Alabama* would be a pirate ship with political legitimacy, manned by a crew interested only in prize money.

"Semmes is an uncommon man," Bulloch replied. "I don't doubt we will hear of his work soon."

Jubal said nothing as the captain approached.

"An exceptional ship, Mr. Bulloch." Semmes extended his hand. "I think I can make her answer to the purpose."

"Much depends on you, sir," Bulloch replied. Jubal noticed the wistfulness in the man's voice, as if Bulloch himself had hoped to command the ship he had built. "I will be most curious to learn how she performs."

The captain tipped his cap. "I shall entrust my communications to you by Captain McQueen, when we are resupplied by *Agrippina*."

Bulloch glanced at Jubal, who remained studiously noncommittal. Having dealt with McQueen for the better part of two months, Jubal considered the man a competent mariner, when he wasn't drunk.

Semmes' eyes narrowed. "I have not had the pleasure of your introduction, sir," he said to Jubal.

"Ah, of course," Bulloch interjected, "my associate, Jubal Calhoun, of Mobile."

The captain started. "Mobile? It is my home; I practiced law there for several years. Calhoun, you say? I know Calhouns, but they are in South Carolina. Are your people there?"

"My wife and family are in Mobile but I have been there infrequently in the last ten years. As for family elsewhere ... no, not that I know of."

"Your occupation, if I may ask?"

Jubal thought for a moment; no one had ever asked him the question.

"Trading, shipping. With my partners," Jubal's stomach suddenly tensed and he felt the unexpected flush of emotion, "we owned and operated a ship." With these men he could not go silent as he had with Sally, but he'd had enough of the conversation. "Did you know a Mr. Truette Stubbs?"

"Truette Stubbs! Of course I knew the man! He was one of Mobile's most respected citizens, a man of impeccable reputation, splendid character indeed. How did you know him?"

"He was my partner."

To both Jubal and James Bulloch's astonishment, the captain smiled for the first time since coming aboard.

"Are you one of the boys ...? Pardon me, sir, no insult intended, but at the Metropolitan Club where we dined on occasion, he spoke of his 'boys'."

Jubal straightened and blinked, clenching his teeth. He nodded.

Captain Semmes looked closely before turning to James Bulloch.

"Sir, I propose the following: may I enlist your associate in our initial voyage, if Mr. Calhoun is willing? When we are resupplied by *Agrippina* in three months' time—I shall sail to the Northern coast and then work south into the Caribbean where we shall rendezvous—Mr. Calhoun may return to Liverpool with Captain McQueen. I should be honored to have him serve aboard my ship—you may not know of Truette Stubbs but I vouchsafe that he was as shrewd a judge of character as any man I have ever known. No doubt Mr. Calhoun's opinions of our conduct and capacity shall prove of utmost, illuminative value."

James Bulloch looked at Jubal, who returned the glance, then regarded the captain.

"You would deprive me of a valued and capable man, sir, but ..."

"My seabag is aboard *Agrippina*," Jubal said at length, feeling caught in a vise between patriotism and doubt. "Allow me some minutes to pen a letter for Mr. Bulloch to convey."

Chapter Seventy-Eight

Philadelphia, September 1862

On a fine, Indian summer afternoon, Lester burst through the front door on Dauphine Street so unexpectedly Curtis nearly fell off his chair, sending his drawing sheet fluttering off the dining table. Beside him, Truette stared wide-eyed from a bushel basket, bib and face covered in fresh blueberry jam he had licked off a biscuit crumbling in his little fist.

"Cora!" Lester strode to Curtis, picking up his drawing. "It's all right, True," Lester grinned, for the boy's face worked, about to start bawling. "Where's your mother?" He raised his voice to a yell. "Cora!"

The rear door slammed and Cora ran in, still in her school uniform, an apron bulging with ripened tomatoes.

"Wha's da matta? The boys …?" She looked frantically from one son to the other.

Lester grinned again, amused that Cora's plantation cadence flashed back in an instant whenever she was stressed.

Cora didn't think it funny.

"Darling," Lester hugged her and she pushed him away.

"What come over you? 'Nough now, I'm droppin' tomatoes! Don't step on 'em! By the Lord!" She looked at him suspiciously. "What you been doin'?"

"Sit down. Right there, next to Curtis. Listen, all of you—you too, Truette."

The children and mother exchanged glances as Lester snapped open a newspaper. Cora sat, pushed aside her dictionary and schoolbooks, and began to unload tomatoes from her apron onto the table, looking wary.

"The *National Republican*," Lester announced. "Front page."

"A Proclamation," he began. "I, Abraham Lincoln, President of the United States of America, and Commander-in-Chief of the Army and Navy thereof, do hereby proclaim and declare …" he scanned the column to find the portion that had fired his excitement, "That on the first day of January in the year of our Lord, one thousand eight hundred and sixty-three, all persons held as slaves within any State or designated part of a State, the people whereof shall then be in rebellion against the United States," Lester raised his voice, "*shall be then, thenceforward, and forever free!*"

Lester glanced at his wife; Cora sat rigid, holding Curtis' arm with one hand and a tomato in the other, clenching it so hard a tickle of juice seeped through her fingers.

"And the executive government of the United States, including the military and naval authority thereof, will recognize and maintain the freedom of such persons, and will do no act or acts to repress such persons, or any of them, in any efforts they may make for their actual freedom."

Lester's eyes flitted down the column. "And I do hereby enjoin upon and order all persons engaged in the military and naval service of the United States to observe, obey, and enforce, within their respective spheres of service, the act, and sections above recited. Done at the City of Washington this twenty-second day of September, in the year of our Lord, one thousand, eight hundred and sixty-two, and of the Independence of the United States the eighty-seventh."

Lester lowered the newspaper and came to attention.

The house went dead quiet. A bird cawed outside. Suddenly, Cora leaped to her feet, the remaining tomatoes flying from her lap. Snatching the newspaper she sped past her astonished husband and out through the open front door into the late afternoon light.

Lester stood open-mouthed, looked to his sons, both just as startled, and took three strides to the doorway in time to see Cora throw up her arms. With back arched and head lifted to the sky, she let loose a cry that could be heard through the neighborhood. "*Glory, Glory, Glory Hallelujah!!!*"

Starting to sob, Cora sank to her knees.

Lester turned. "Curtis, bring Truette."

He came to stand by his wife, watching her shoulders heave as she kissed the ground. She turned to him, tears streaming, soil glistening on her lips, and reached upward. Lester lifted and enveloped his wife, filling with the smell of her hair.

From far away, he heard a church bell ring, then another, and a third. Finally, Cora released him, and still sobbing quietly, gathered the apron to wipe her tear-streaked cheeks. Ever so gently, she took the damp cloth to Truette's wide-eyed, blueberry-stained face.

Bells rang into the night.

Chapter Seventy-Nine

Mobile, Thanksgiving 1862

Ezekiel answered the knock at the front door, expecting to find the carriage driver he had secured for their short ride to the riverboat landing. Instead, a boy of about twelve or thirteen stood solemnly on the porch.

"May I help you, young masta?" Ezekiel whispered.

"I am Oliver Semmes," the boy replied, quite poised for his age. "I bear a letter from my father to Mrs. ..." he looked at the envelope, "Mrs. Calhoun. Do you know where I might find her?"

"And who might your father be?" Sally asked, bustling to the doorway. "Ezekiel, can you fetch my bag upstairs, I'm ready."

"Captain Raphael Semmes, m'am, captain of the warship *Alabama*."

Sally drew a breath and her hands shook as she reached for the letter. "How did you come upon this, young man?"

"A blockade runner came through from Bermuda." The boy looked her over and relaxed, no longer cautious. "Is it true what they say about you, Mrs. Calhoun?"

"Probably," Sally replied, bemused and annoyed. "It is a small place."

"Mobile is a great city!" the boy exclaimed. "Isn't it?"

"New York is a great city. Paris is a great city. Mobile? Well, I urge you to see the world, young man, as soon as you are able."

"As soon as we win the war I will," Oliver answered in a swaggering drawl. "Though I hope it doesn't end too soon. My momma won't let me enlist for five years."

"God help us," Sally snorted, "if this war lasts one more year!" She turned, anxious to read the letter. "Thank you for ..."

"Why did you invade us? We didn't do anything to you."

Sally bit off a retort. He was just a boy after all, but the question still smarted. "Let me ask you something, may I?"

Oliver nodded, as alert and intelligent a child as she had ever met. Sally shuddered with the sudden premonition he would be dead, that this war would consume him.

"Do you think yourself better than Ezekiel?"

The boy gaped. "He's an old nigger!"

Sally reacted as if slapped. "Thank you for the letter. Good day. You may get your wish after all!" She turned and slammed the door.

Oliver stared after her, perplexed. People had said she was ornery. Maybe she was also, as rumored, a little crazy.

In the hallway, Sally yelled upstairs. "Ezekiel, where the hell is that coach? I want to get out of here now! These bigoted pigs!" Sally muttered, stomping into the kitchen to stuff another bag with foodstuffs she had brought from Gee's Bend a few days back. She had left intending to stay in Mobile for a week, but after three days—of clipped conversations, turned backs, everyone in the city treating her as if she were a leper—Sally was so mad she thought it best to return upriver before she did something stupid.

"Like spit at the next bastard who rails at me about oppression!" She pointed a finger at Ezekiel who now stood in the doorway with their carpet travel bags. "And I'm gonna!" With a start, she remembered the letter and tore it open.

"You all right, Missus?" Ezekiel whispered. Sally held her mouth; he could see the note was short.

"Jubal will be home as soon as he can," Sally said, her voice flat. "Says he misses us terrible." She folded the note and tucked it in a dress pocket. "Let's get out of here."

The next morning they disembarked at Gee's Bend—Sally had given the riverboat captain an extra fifty Confederate dollars to stop at the dilapidated wharf, which pleased her because he could not reasonably refuse extra payment, even if inflation had eaten half its value. She had no intention of paying him from the gold coins Jubal had stashed in a safe hidden amongst the root cellar stores before leaving Mobile. Sally kept a limited number of coins at Gee's Bend, always fearful that a jealous, resentful local would connive some way for the authorities to confiscate Sandy Hill. By now, she figured, everyone in the county knew she was Unionist.

Coming by buggy from the river landing, she wondered suddenly if the seizure might happen now. Four horses were tied to a hitching post beneath the enormous old live oak.

A man stepped from the house as Jordon Hatcher coaxed the mules to a stop.

"Your name Calhoun, m'am?" The man didn't remove his hat.

Sally snatched the buggy whip from Jordon Hatcher, gathered her skirts and jumped down. She took the front steps in just short of a run and strode right by the man, ignoring him, going directly into the large vestibule. Beulah Hatcher had opened the screen door without a word, her face frozen.

Three men, two old and graying, one not yet in his twenties, with a face scarred from smallpox, stopped in mid-conversation. The two older men stood; the younger lounged in a chair.

"Emma, Lester?" Sally demanded of Beulah. The black woman nodded, her eyes lifting to the second floor. "Mae's got 'em," she said, referring to her daughter-in-law.

Sally glanced about. None of the men had removed their boots; mud from the previous night's shower streaked the floor.

"Were you born in a barn?" Sally yelled. "Get out!"

The men were taken aback but the young one recovered and chuckled, pulling a cigar from his pocket and snapping a match along his pant leg. "Well, ain't you a ..."

The whip cracked in his face, sending the cigar flying.

Astounded, the young man leaped to his feet. "You Yankee bitch! I'll ..." He stopped as if his speech had been slashed in half. Sally had lifted her skirts; staring at him was a Lefaucheux six-shot pocket pistol, as cold and lethal-looking a weapon as he had ever seen. Jubal had bought the pistol and a garter holster in England. His last instructions to Sally before running the Union blockade were to carry it, concealed, always.

At a shadow on the floor, Sally wheeled and cocked the hammer, stopping the man she had passed on the porch in his tracks, straddling the doorway. She took two steps backward to easily cover all four.

"Who are you?" Sally hissed at the young man. Despite his youth, this one was downright sinister.

Slowly, his hand went to the welt rising on his pockmarked face. Lean, with a sallow complexion and greasy hair, he stood with a permanent stoop. Sally noticed one arm hung limp and she had the sudden thought he must have been a breach birth.

"Rivens," the young man answered through clenched teeth, and she nearly shot him. "Sam Rivens."

Sally swallowed, willing her trigger finger to ease. The memory was crisp as the fall morning; Jubal had told her the story of Whitmill Rivens in their sea cabin on that first passage to China from San Francisco. She could hear his voice now, ending the tale: "Don't know that he had family. Heard of a few brothers in Georgia, but if a Rivens ever threatens you, kill 'im, no questions. Ain't just one rotten apple to a barrel."

Sally took a breath and looked at the oldest man. "I've six shots in this pistol and no one will contradict a single woman defending her home from four thieves. Now get into the dooryard and state your business."

Covering them as they filed out the door and down the steps, she took three quick, soft steps sideways and shot the gun out of Sam Rivens' hand as he wheeled, startled that she wasn't behind him as he'd thought. "My husband taught me to hit a coin at fifty paces," Sally said, staring at Rivens. "Your eye is about ten."

The oldest man glanced at the ruined pistol lying in the wet dirt, then back at Sally. "We come for the niggers. Him," he gestured to Jordon Hatcher, "and his boys. Need 'em up to Selma, gotta build a foundry."

"I need them here," Sally replied. Her lips peeled in a cold smile. "And I own them. Isn't that what your fellows are fighting about, except you're too old and junior here is crippled." Rivens winced and Sally knew she'd regret her meanness but for the moment didn't care; her blood was up.

"The Conscription Act passed by the Confederate Congress, this past April ..."

"Didn't apply to slaves," Sally snapped. "You can't have 'em. Now get goin', right now ... or you're thieves."

They stared for a few moments, uncertain, but then without a word the three older men turned and mounted their horses. Sam Rivens stared at Sally before bending for his shattered gun. Sally cocked her pistol.

"Touch it, you're dead. Go."

Beulah Hatcher came onto the porch as the men cantered away, Rivens taking one long look back. Jordon joined the women, silently watching until the horsemen became specks against the tree line.

"Woo-eee, Miss Sally," he exclaimed. "Jubie taught you, yes suh, done did I declare."

"A coin from fifty paces?" Beulah couldn't believe it.

"Well, actually it was a melon," Sally smiled, satisfied. "And the paces were mine, not his. But they were fifty. I counted."

Chapter Eighty

At sea, January 1863

Jubal gathered his seabag and made his way along the deck to the amidships gangway, careful not to touch any metal. At midday, the tropical sun was blinding against the water. Several hundred yards away, the low scrubby outline of the Aracas Keys rose a few feet high, too meager and isolated to be inhabited, precisely why Captain Semmes had chosen the site for his rendezvous.

Agrippina and *Alabama* lay rafted together under the lee of the sandspit keys, anchored in eight fathoms of the clearest water Jubal had ever seen, eighty miles from the Yucatan Peninsula and far from the shipping lanes where Union warships now patrolled. From confiscated Northern newspapers, it seemed the damage *Alabama* had done in four months went far beyond the collective cost of the twenty-five ships she had captured. Semmes had burned twenty-two, whalers and merchantmen, and bonded the other three to take crews off of the destroyed ships. The marine insurance costs of Union shippers had risen sharply.

"You're leaving," Lieutenant Sinclair joined Jubal at the rail, "despite the Captain's entreaties?" He stood hatless in an open shirt, a few inches shorter than Jubal though just as stocky, watching crewmen transfer the last of *Agrippina*'s bunkered coal. Early in the voyage, Jubal had taken an immediate liking to the Virginian. Both were the about the same age, though Jubal still hid ignorance of his exact birth date.

"I am expected in Liverpool," Jubal replied. "Captain does not need me."

"Yes," Sinclair agreed, "Captain Semmes knows how to keep himself near to the hearts and confidence of his men without descending from his dignity in the slightest degree, or permitting direct approach. They're proud of him, in their way, and he returns the sentiments in his." Sinclair's eyes shifted and Jubal followed.

Captain Semmes, dressed as always in full uniform despite the heat, descended the quarterdeck stairs and approached. "Mr. Sinclair," the Captain ordered, "you will see to it that the coaling is completed satisfactorily. I do not wish to linger. You stand ready, Mr. Calhoun?"

"Yes sir."

"Will you not reconsider? I sail for Galveston to engage the Yankee blockade squadron. Your presence would be most useful."

"I extend my gratitude, Captain, but gave my word to James Bulloch."

"The exigencies of war, Mr. Calhoun, often require reconsideration."

Jubal regarded Captain Semmes, seeing again the brittle righteousness he had come to recognize in a man who hunted and burned ships so efficiently the Union had placed a $50,000 bounty on his head.

"I gave my word."

"Hardly, Mr. Calhoun. I was there."

Jubal said nothing. Finally, Captain Semmes clenched his jaw and extended his hand. "I expect you shall give a full and fair report to Mr. Bulloch. Extend to him my best, and to Mrs. Bulloch the same."

"I will, sir."

"Very good." Semmes wheeled and strode up the quarterdeck steps.

Jubal looked after the captain, wondering if he had made an enemy.

"Not many men refuse the captain," Sinclair remarked, returning from his inspection. "All ready, sir!" he called aft.

"Take care, Arthur," Jubal said. "Godspeed."

"We will soon fight the Yanks, Jubal."

"I would sooner build ships than burn them."

"You will build warships to burn ships. I don't understand the distinction."

Jubal nodded. "Neither do I, quite. But I don't have the necessary appetite for destruction." In truth, watching the first ship they had set alight, a whaler five days west of the Azores that flamed like a torch, had made him sick. "When I was sixteen, I watched a ship I had helped build burn to the waterline. Do you remember the *Great Republic*? A terrible memory I never wanted to repeat."

"This is war, Jubal."

"I understand, Arthur. I'm as much of my country as you. But now, a burning ship at sea is no longer a plea asking aid. Indeed, it is warning for others to flee."

Captain Semmes had perfected the maritime ambush, setting fire to ships and then standing off with sails down to wait for a rescuing ship to arrive, before capturing and burning that ship also. Jubal appreciated the tactic but regarded it equally dishonorable to Semmes' practice of firing on unarmed ships to intimidate them into heaving to. The captain ordered the ships boarded and burned, if he saw fit.

"I don't fear a fight with any man but piracy I cannot abide."

Lieutenant Sinclair stiffened.

"This is a commissioned warship of a sovereign nation. Besides, the Union did not sign the Declaration of Paris five years ago outlawing privateering. The captain is a maritime lawyer! Certainly he, more than most any man, understands international law at sea!"

Jubal gripped Arthur Sinclair's shoulder. "No doubt you are right. I regret if I've offended you. Captain McQueen will not wait for me any more than Captain Semmes would."

"The captain will take your leave personally."

"I am as loyal as the next man, Arthur," Jubal replied, his voice hardening. "I will do my duty in Liverpool." He extended his hand and Sinclair took it firmly. Stepping back, they saluted each other.

Jubal swung the seabag to his shoulder and climbed the short steps to the gangway. "Godspeed, Arthur," he called, as cries coursed forward and aft to release the spring lines rafting the ships.

An hour later, *Agrippina* weighed anchor. *Alabama* was already hull down on the northern horizon.

"Calhoun! Welcome aboard!" Captain McQueen stomped up, his eyes alight and breath smelling of Scotch whiskey. "James Bulloch has ordered us directly home. We'll have a fine week or two before the weather turns, as surely she will, and then another turn of winter in the North Atlantic." The captain spun to the helmsman. "Make north by nor'west! All sail! Step lively, ye bloody tars!"

Captain McQueen wheeled back to him with a wicked grin. "Did you make a fine pirate?" Jubal knew the bottle must be half gone.

"Hardly."

The captain clapped him on the shoulder, roaring with delight.

Chapter Eighty-One

Philadelphia, February 1863

"Wake Daddy up, Truette, tell him time for dinner." Cora watched her son nod and pad purposefully into the living room where Lester had fallen asleep in a chair, the newspaper still in his lap. She smiled, cherishing the child's good nature. Truette rarely fussed, and though not yet speaking much, the boy understood most everything.

"Curtis set the table, then serve them potatoes. We got ham and peas goin' with 'em." She worked the cookstove, also tired from a string of eighteen-hour days.

The medical college courses were harder than anything she had even imagined. Each day she left the boys at Letitia Still's, walked four miles north to the college, and went to six hours of classes before walking to Lucretia Mott's where Mrs. Mott tutored her for two more hours. Then collect the boys, return to Dauphin Street, feed and put them to bed, clean the kitchen, and study an hour before collapsing into bed herself. Six hours later, if she was lucky, it was up again and back at the cookstove. Saturday she took her children to the markets, Sunday to church.

Lester came into the kitchen, still groggy from his nap. Little Truette held his father's hand, pulling him along.

"Anything I can do?" Lester mumbled.

"Right now you look hardly able to eat," Cora replied. "Sit down."

"I tell you what, wife, I am sick of traveling. Sick of trains, steamboats, horses, buggies, anything that moves. Sick of hotels and fleabeds, lousy food and drunkards and hustlers. I believe I've been to every state, every depot in the North, heard every scheme a shyster can dream up to fleece the government. Think I'll sit here for a year or two."

"And sleep in the chair?" Curtis asked. "How you gonna pee?"

"Curtis!" Cora scolded.

"Truette pees his pants," Lester looked at the seven-year-old, "so why can't I?"

"Tha's 'nough, both y'all!"

Lester and Curtis grinned at each other. "Momma's got the same bones as ol' Louisa," Lester said. "You remember her?" Curtis shook his head no.

Lester had made the comment without thinking; now he regretted it. The lightness went out of him like an extinguished lamp ... too many memories.

Cora helped Truette into his basket. "Curtis, say us some grace to the Lord."

Curtis made a face; he hated saying grace. "Thank you God," he murmured, head bowed, "for Mommy and Daddy and my brudder, and can I please get a puppy? Amen."

Lester tried hard not to laugh, but Cora couldn't help herself. "Whoever heard of asking for a dog sayin' grace!"

"Curtis just did!" Lester said, enjoying the boy's pluck. "Pass the ham, son, please. If I find a good puppy, I'll bring 'em home."

"What are you talkin' 'bout?" Cora straightened. "I got my hands full, what with taking the boys to Letitia Still's 'fore I walk to school, all day there 'till no more room in my head, then walking back to Motts and here, you mostly not to home. Never had to work this hard in my life!"

Lester stared at her, the humor gone again.

"Well, I'm sorry," Cora amended, "that ain't at all right. You hear me, Curtis? I'm sorry Lester, that were a bad thing to say. I been so ever blessed, hardly can imagine. I jes' get tired, too."

Lester chewed his ham. "Why don't we get someone here to look after the boys? We can afford it. Besides, I just got an advancement."

"When was you gonna tell me that?"

"I just did. General Meigs told me today. I've been promoted to major."

"What's that mean?"

"Nothing different for the moment, but ten percent more pay. So why don't we find someone to watch the kids, there's lots of ..." Lester grew careful, "new people who've come into the city." Thousands of former slaves had fled north and settled in camp slums on the outskirts of the Philadelphia. As black men looked for any work, white laborers resented the competition and racial tensions had soared.

Cora watched him closely. Lester could have no idea of the daily indignities she endured. Catcalls, obscenities, cheating at the markets, assumptions by teachers at school that she had less native intelligence even though she knew full well some of her classmates took hours to understand what she could grasp immediately.

"Negroes don't stand much different here than at Gee's Bend," she replied, "free or no."

"Why don't you take the trolley to school?"

"You not listening to me? Negros can't take no trolley, count of ..."

"Have you tried?"

Cora slammed her fork down. "Stick your head in the stove ash 'till you're good and dark, like me! Then you try!"

"Calm down, darling." Lester headed for safer ground. "We should get you some help."

Cora regarded her husband with a mixture of love and resignation. He could never know. "There's a woman jes' come," she said, taking a deep breath. "William Still tole me about her."

"Come from where?"

"Kentucky. Ran away from a farm, s'got nuthin'. But she knows children, real good with 'em, Mr. Still says." Cora stopped, as if screwing up her courage. "Maybe she could live here, help us."

"Where would she sleep?"

"Get us some carpenters, build a little room out back."

"It would be pretty small."

"I lived smaller."

"Is she alone?"

Cora nodded. "Her name's Edmonia. She's got two children, maybe three, I ain't sure. They wuz sold, count of their father being hung." Cora reached to help Truette with a potato he'd dropped. "She had to leave 'em in Kentucky."

Lester had his traveling rucksack packed by daylight and fired up the kitchen stove before Cora finished dressing. She came into the kitchen, buttoning her school uniform, surprised to see Lester cracking eggs into a skillet.

"How come you cookin'? I thought you were leaving this morning. Where you goin' this time?"

"Boston. I'll take the second express."

"Leave that blanket you're carrying. It ought be washed."

"No, don't mind that blanket, "Lester replied, turning his attention to the skillet. "I've got time."

Cora looked skeptical but after a moment she shrugged. "I'll roust the boys. But I ought'n to wash that blanket."

"Leave it be!"

She paused and looked to her husband, baffled.

Lester tugged Cora's skirt, pulling her close. His nose nuzzled her ear. "It smells like you," he whispered.

Purring, she went to wake the boys.

Two hours later they approached William and Letitia Still's home, Lester finally admonishing Curtis to hurry up after holding his exasperation in check for at least an hour. Between the two boys, there was always an interesting earthworm, bug, or piece of trash that merited investigation.

"How do you ever get to school on time?" Lester asked.

"Forget when you was a boy?" Cora laughed. She didn't know why Lester had chosen to walk with them this morning and decided not to ask. Besides, the morning was lovely, and for the first time in months, she didn't have to shepherd the boys alone.

At the Stills' house a middle-aged Negro woman dressed in plain calico cotton answered the door. Short, with the lined face and rough hands of someone who had worked outside most of her life, she reached for Truette. Lester immediately saw the boy was comfortable enough to go right to her. Curtis sped into the house, yelling for the Still children. The Quaker schoolhouse they all attended was a short walk away.

"Curtis, git back here!" Cora ordered. "Say good-bye to yore daddy!"

"When you comin' home, Daddy?" Curtis ran back, throwing his arms around Lester's legs.

"End of the week, son. I'll bring you something. Now be sure to mind your mother while I'm gone." Curtis peeled back into the house, shouting for his schoolmates.

"Lester, meet Edmonia." He thought Cora would say something else, but that was all.

Edmonia dropped her eyes and slightly bowed her head, then waited.

"I'm sorry you had to leave your children," Lester said, surprising all of them.

Edmonia glanced to Cora, but she had recovered and stood expressionless. Finally, Edmonia nodded, her face working as she struggled not to cry.

"We'll make room with the boys," Lester continued, "until we can build a suitable space for you. If you'd like to come, that is." He settled; this felt right. "We would welcome you into our home."

"Thank you, masta," Edmonia averted her eyes.

"Oh, no ..." Lester began.

"No mastas here," Cora declared. "Did you ask Mr. William, like I told you to?" Edmonia nodded.

"Lester," Cora continued, "he'll be home the end of this week. Then you come, hear?"

Edmonia nodded again.

As they walked away from the Stills' place, Lester turned to Cora.

"Didn't take you long to start giving orders," he teased. "Does she talk?"

"You likely wouldn't understand her," Cora replied. "She been sold three, four times, growed up way down Georgia, almost near Florida. *I* have a hard time understanding her someways."

They had reached Federal Avenue, where a horse-drawn, northbound trolley rumbled toward them. "C'mon," Lester exclaimed, pulling her forward. "There's the trolley."

"Lester!" Cora objected, but he was already flagging the conductor, who pulled on his reins and stopped the car. Lester helped Cora aboard, scoffing at her reluctance. He held her arm, steering her to a seat.

The trolley didn't move.

Cora sat motionless, her face rigid. Lester looked around; a dozen people, men and women, all white, stared back. The conductor tied his reins off and came to stand in front of them. "Niggers ain't allowed."

"I am a major in the Union Army; this is my wife. Proceed."

"Sorry, Major, against the law. No niggers 'llowed on public cars."

Lester controlled himself. "Did you not read the President's Emancipation Proclamation?"

"That weren't about streetcars."

Lester gritted his teeth, about to reply, when a two men boarded. Cora immediately knew they were drunk. Her hand went inside her bag.

"I will in me arse!" one man slobbered to the other in an Irish brogue. The second man, short, and broad-shouldered with a boxer's nose, stepped forward and cast a wet-eyed stare at Cora, then to Lester.

"What you waitin' on, eegit?" he growled at the conductor.

"No niggers. Ain't supposed to ride."

"Hear it, doxie? Pull yer socks up."

Cora didn't move.

"Mister," Lester held up his hand.

"Shut yer gob! Now, horrie," the man wavered and hooked his thumb, "piss off!"

The words were barely out of his mouth before Lester's fist was in it, driving the man back into his mate, who stumbled on the steps.

The Irishman had been hit before. He came roaring back, throwing a haymaker, but Lester had halved the distance and cocked his head as the punch clipped his ear and sailed past. In close, he drove a fist into the man's midsection so hard the Irishman retched up his last three ales. Lester stepped forward and drove his foot into the other man's knee, folding it backward with the sound of ripping canvas. Shrieking, he fell into the street as Lester grabbed the puking fighter by the hair and slammed his forehead into a rising knee, then chucked him onto the gasping drunk sprawled in the gutter.

Lester turned to the driver. "Now!"

The driver backed away, farting. "Don't hurt me Major! Please! I got six kids and me missus to feed!" He stared at Cora. "Beggin' yer pardon, lass—I mean, lady!—but I'll lose my job!" Wringing his hands, his eyes widened. "It ain't my fault!"

Lester turned from him, disgusted. "This way, dear." He stepped down and held Cora's hands as she came off the trolley.

"Ye broke me bloody leg!" the drunk howled, vainly trying to push his partner off.

Lester ignored them. "Taxi!" he bellowed. A hackney pulled over from the curb, where the driver had watched the entire incident.

"Where it will be, sir?"

"North College Avenue," Cora replied. "The Female Medical College."

Chapter Eighty-Two

Gee's Bend, March 1863

Twilight lingered above the ground fog forming over their freshly plowed fields, just greening with the first shoots of vegetables, corn, barley, alfalfa, and tobacco. Two hundred acres had gone in, the labor of one hundred people and a dozen mules.

Jordon Hatcher sat on the front steps of Sandy Hill smoking a corncob pipe, knowing he would never get comfortable enough to sit in the rocking chairs with Sally. Beulah had no such reservations; she rocked away, also smoking a pipe.

"We shore do 'ppreciate the thought, Miss Sally," Beulah blew a cloud of smoke, "taking us north. But the boys, wives, the chile'—Charity don't have but another two months most—how you ever going to keep us together for weeks, us never been away from here?"

"The Home Guard will be back," she replied. "It's just a matter of time." The idea to take them all North was half-baked, Sally knew, and maybe crazy, but worry knawed at her.

"Still," Beulah persisted, "how you gonna do it? Where we going? Boys, they'd get caught up in a minute, one army or t'other, what's the diffunce? Then what you think'll happen to them women and chillen?"

"You said the crop should go in first. It's in." Sally shifted Lester from nursing one breast to the other. "You don't look like a Buck to me," she said to the infant blissfully pulling at his mother's milk. The mere mention made her think of Jubal again, as she did about twenty times a day. "I miss that man terrible," she said aloud. "Bastard."

"Ezekiel says he give your letter to someone in Mobile," Jordon Hatcher's baritone voice rumbled, "will git it outbound."

"Did he pick a good ship?"

"'Spect so." Jordon's answered in a voice mild enough that Sally knew she shouldn't question Ezekiel's judgment. But between a new baby, running the plantation, and an absent husband working to ensure independence for a new country she detested, Sally was depressed and knew it. "We were so happy, that first voyage …" She looked up, recognizing half a dozen navigational stars. "Jubal taught me the night sky."

"He be coming home, Miss Sally," Jordon said. "I shore of it, Lord knows."

"If he lives," Sally replied, her voice almost breaking. She shook herself, trying to fling off the gloom on such a lovely evening. "We've got to get you out of here."

"Don't see how, Miss Sally," Beulah repeated. "Me and Jordon, we stayin', leastways."

"You are?" Sally sat up, interrupting Lester, who promptly burped on her dress. "Oh, Buck," she wiped herself and his face, and held him to pat out another burp. "What will you do here?"

"Same as we do now," Beulah shrugged. "Live."

"Boys'll be safe again this year," Jordon knocked his pipe on a step and refilled it from an old pouch. "Judge Harris—you 'member him, Miss Sally? Said we's needed in Cahaba, me and the boys. Ain't far, you know. We'll get paid."

"'Course I know the Judge," Sally replied, miffed. "I bought you from him. The man didn't say anything to me."

Neither Jordon nor Beulah said a word. Lester burped again. "Lester, for Chrissakes, you chucked half of it! I'm not milking you much longer!" Sally caught herself, wondering why she was so crabby. Though she'd bought the Hatchers, she didn't *own* them. But the idea that they would do something without consulting her was unsettling. Sally suddenly winced, aware she had come uncomfortably close to understanding how Southerners thought of their slaves. Doubly uncomfortable was her intuition that both Jordon and Beulah knew exactly what she was thinking.

"What does the Judge want you to build?" Sally recovered. "He is paying you, right?"

"Said so," Jordon replied, lighting his pipe again, his carbon black face glowing against the dark. Sally looked up; twilight was gone and the night had come in. Thousands of stars speckled the clear, moonless sky.

"What does he want you to build?"

Jordon puffed, his pipe glowing. At length he replied. "A prison."

"A *what?*"

No answer.

"What for? Where?"

"Cahaba, like I said." Jordon Hatcher rose to his feet and approached Sally.

She watched his shadow come to her, her eyes wide with alarm. "Whatever for, Jordon?"

Jordon Hatcher knelt before her.

"I's sorry Miss Sally. But's the best thing. Boys'll be safe from them fellas for a time 'cause judge says they got to have this prison."

Sally waited, feeling sick. Lester fussed. "Shush!" she snapped.

"There's a war, Miss Sally. Lots of prisoners, I hear. Some of them gonna come this way."

Chapter Eighty-Three

Liverpool, April 1863

Deep in the guarded Laird shipyards, Jubal examined the scantlings—thickness, width, and length of every bone in the ship's skeleton frame—against the specified dimensions James Bulloch had provided when he contracted with Laird Brothers.

"Do ye think we dinnae know how to read?" Laird's yard foreman huffed, insulted at Jubal's careful inspection.

"Would you spend a hundred thousand pounds without knowing what you bought?" Jubal replied.

The foreman scoffed. "This be number two ninety-four and her sister two ninety-five! Now, why, lad, would we number 'em so? 'Cause there be near on three hunnert ships built in this very yard, long before ye ever locked onto yer mother's tit!"

Jubal ignored him, though satisfied the yard hadn't shortchanged the drawings. Handing a lantern back to the foreman, he climbed the ladder and emerged from the hold into a misty, gray morning. Charles Piroleau waited on deck, huddled below an umbrella.

"Sure isn't a Charleston spring," he grumbled as Jubal joined him.

"Go home."

Piroleau looked morose despite his elegant suit and bowler. "We better win or none of us will ever go home."

"They're ugly," Jubal replied, "and I would hate to weather a blow in them, but these rams surely are made for trouble."

"If we can get them out of here." Charles Piroleau shifted on his feet, clearly nervous.

"What's happened?"

"Nothing. Everything. We're borrowing money we don't have, selling bonds that may be worthless. The Foreign Office is besieged by them damn Yankees—and they're smart and ruthless. The *Alabama* isn't helping." Piroleau lowered his voice. "Even Bulloch is nervous. He thinks the English are going to wait until they're launched, then impound them."

Jubal raised an eyebrow. "Watch us use our money to build their ships?"

Piroleau snorted. "The French would do the same. They're playing both ends against the middle."

Jubal flinched. Word for word he remembered the phrase, one of the last things Lester had said two years earlier, almost to the day.

"What's the matter?" Piroleau asked.

"I used to think the ocean was hard, unforgiving," Jubal replied. "But at least it's honest. Men and countries at war ..."

"I've got to see the Laird brothers, they're demanding a payment."

"They've met the contract. I'll check the other hull and meet you tonight."

As Piroleau left for the Laird offices, Jubal pulled his oilskin tight and went to the ship's rail, regarding hull 295 rising in the parallel stocks fifty yards away.

The sister ships were squat and ungainly compared to McKay's elegant clippers, mules against thoroughbreds. Donald McKay built for speed; these ironclad "rams," named for the seven-foot, solid-iron prow that stuck forward from the bow like a pugnacious chin, were built to kill. Iron layered upon teak, they would be the most lethal warships ever launched, though heaven help them, Jubal thought, in a hurricane. Cannonballs and shot would bounce off the hulls, making them impervious to Union ships. Two ships scouring the East Coast, blasting away with turreted deck guns, ramming wood-hulled Union vessels at will, they could "bring Yankee commerce to its knees," just as James Bulloch intended.

Jubal had returned to Liverpool aboard *Agrippina*, planning to supervise the building of shallow-drafted wooden blockade-runners, quietly anticipating he would command one of them. James Bulloch had other ideas.

"When the *Monitor* and *Merrimack* fought to a draw last year," Bulloch said, over a fine dinner his wife had prepared the day after Jubal arrived, "naval warfare changed forever. Great Britain has the greatest fleet in the world—made of wood. Half a dozen oceangoing ironclads would swipe them from the sea like so many bugs, and the English know it. As do the French and the Russians. Strangle a country's commerce, you strangle them."

Jubal had not responded, the irony obvious. When Bulloch pulled the new ironclad drawings from his private safe, Jubal's first reaction was curiosity layered with disdain. Remembering his first glimpse of *Flying Cloud* a dozen years earlier, Jubal regarded the smokestack, jutting prow, and muscular iron armament, musing that everything he had ever learned at sea was in the service of staying afloat, while the sole purpose of these warships was to execute the opposite.

"Do you feel it so strongly, Mr. Bulloch," Jubal asked. "That we must resort to this for independence?"

"I do. To become a nation, we must be prepared to be a nation. Without a modern Navy, we have no hope. Do you think this will be our last fight? Just look at European history. The British Empire exists because the British Navy destroyed the French and Spanish navies. Go further back ... Dutch, Portuguese, Venetians, Genoese, Greeks, Phoenicians ... maritime power is national power."

"We should be building these in Mobile, Charleston, or Savannah," Jubal replied.

"We will, if we win. To win, we must first build them here."

Now, in mist blowing through the Laird shipyard, Jubal studied 295's ugly silhouette and thought of every machination Bulloch had masterminded to get the two rams out of Liverpool. Charles Piroleau, on behalf of Fraser and Trenholm, had ordered the warships—fictitiously labeled "merchantmen"—for an obscure French company representing the Egyptian government. Everyone—the Laird brothers, Bulloch and Piroleau, the American consulate, the British Foreign Office, French and Russian spies—knew this was preposterous, but technically it wasn't illegal, yet.

Jubal knew Bulloch was absolutely right, that the subterfuge was clumsy and unsustainable. Skullduggery and maneuver had already become wearing. Jubal found himself dealing with false invoices, fake shipments, double billing, constant surveillance, sleeping with a pistol under his pillow—and always looking over his shoulder, wearing a money belt in case he needed to flee at a moment's notice. In the gray, bleak light, Jubal felt the weight of doubt, compounded by a chill of fear echoing in the words of Charles Piroleau: *or none of us will ever go home."*

Jubal's shoulders slumped. He felt empty, except for the small core of heat that seemed to smolder in his breast pocket, where Sally's note and the family photograph lived.

Arriving on a Dutch trader coming through Cuba a week earlier, the note was unsigned, though not unmarked.

The note was simplicity itself: *Come home to your family,* and nothing else, save for a memento from France, where his wife had deliciously ignored every church teaching about cosmetics.

In rich, carmine red, Sally's lips kissed him. Beneath, two thumb prints, one small, the other tiny, dotted the lavender scented paper.

At the Laird shipyard, mist turned to rain.

Chapter Eighty-Four

Boston, May 1863

The shipyard had seen its halcyon days. Where three massive clippers once stood in the stocks surrounded by swarms of men there was nothing now standing, only piles of salvage scraps. A dozen men worked careening a tug laid over on her side so they could clean the copper bottom.

A dozen years ago, almost to the day, Lester had shipped out from this place aboard *Flying Cloud* and his life had changed forever. Now, he surveyed the scene and was about to turn away, his disappointment almost unbearable, as if a wonderful childhood dream had reappeared with none of its magic, only the cold, hard reality of a mirage. Lester stopped, recognizing the figure, now white-haired, of the first man he had ever worshipped. Donald McKay still had the stride of a man in motion.

Lester shook his head clear, reminding himself that McKay probably wouldn't even recognize him.

In Washington, General Meigs had mentioned that one of the new monitor-class ships would be built at an East Boston yard, piquing Lester's curiosity. On impulse, Lester had continued on to Boston after visiting Connecticut armament factories to negotiate terms for another forty thousand rifles, and taken a ferry across the harbor. There was only one major yard in East Boston, but while Donald McKay was a magician with wood, Lester couldn't imagine him building an ironclad. The shallow-drafted coastal patrol vessel was basically a floating, cigar-shaped gunboat without masts or adornment of any kind.

One look at the shipyard, however, was enough for Lester to realize McKay likely had no choice. The clipper era was dead, sad as it was certain.

Lester saw McKay pause, noticing the lone figure near the yard entrance. They stared at each other before Lester approached. McKay waited, curious. Lester knew for certain then that the yard was idle. A decade earlier Donald McKay never would have paused.

The shipbuilder had aged considerably but was still splendidly dressed, though his clothes were a bit threadbare. He cocked his head, uncertain exactly who the young man could be.

"Lester Norton, sir, I ..."

Donald McKay's face broke into a wide smile and he looked Lester over nodding.

"The boy came home a man. Did you take a lesson from Josiah Creesy?" McKay chuckled. Lester blushed beneath his beard, recently grown, which he kept as neatly trimmed as he remembered the captain's.

"Your ships, sir, indeed made me a man. I cannot describe my gratitude."

McKay enjoyed the sentiment. "Weren't you partners with another young fellow? I can't remember his name."

"Calhoun. Jubal Calhoun."

"Yes, right, I remember him. The quieter of you two. What has become of Mr. Calhoun?" The expression on Lester's face wiped the smile off McKay's.

"Jubal fights for the Confederacy."

"I see." Donald McKay shook his head. "Not quite brother against brother, but ... close. I'm sorry. You know that Mrs. Lincoln's brothers fight for the South?"

"I'd heard. Is your brother at sea?"

"No, Lauchlan has retired to Quebec. He's building ships, but no longer commanding. I believe my brother is done for the quarterdeck." Donald McKay crossed his arms and he smiled half-heartedly. "What brings you to East Boston?"

"You will build a monitor-class now? I learned of this in Washington—I serve with General Meigs' Quartermaster Corps."

"Really? Why don't you come to the house, Mr. Norton, and dine with us? I'm sure Mary will be delighted."

At lunch, Lester recounted the many voyages with Jubal and described their respective families, though without the detail of Cora's slavery. Mary McKay was clearly curious, but Lester continually steered the conversation back to ships. Though he was proud of his wife, Lester had tired of the searching looks and abrupt cool reception their story could produce, as if an interracial marriage was too uncomfortable to acknowledge.

"Jubal and I did well in the shipping business," Lester remarked, "but I don't know that I will ever return to it."

"This phase with iron will pass," Donald McKay insisted. "The bottoms foul within months, cutting two or more knots from their speed. Trade calls for speed, and iron will never be faster than wood. Look how much success the *Alabama* has had, outrunning any ironclad. She is the greatest warship in history and she's wood. Every Union ship in the fleet searches for her, including," McKay remembered, "Josiah Creesy."

"Captain Creesy is a Union naval officer?"

"Indeed. The USS *Ino,* a medium clipper, and fast. Creesy took her from here to Cadiz in thirteen days. He's been hunting the *Alabama* from South Africa to Newfoundland. No luck, yet."

"Is Mrs. Creesy still navigating?" Lester asked. "We corresponded for years, but I haven't heard from her since the war began." Nor had he written, Lester realized, with a pang of guilt.

"No, she is in Salem, not twenty miles from here. The *Ino* was built a clipper but is a Union warship now. You should call on Mrs. Creesy. I'm sure she would be delighted. I remember her fondness for you and Mr. Calhoun. Eleanor was quite proud of you." Donald McKay regarded Lester with undisguised respect. "With good reason."

Lester hired a coach for the fifteen-mile drive north along the Post Road to Salem. The town no longer was the vibrant port of the early 1800s when it had been one of the most populous in the country and a center of the China trade. A silting harbor couldn't accommodate the larger cargo ships now using Boston and New York. Orders in shoe factories and tanneries and the local cotton mill had softened with the shipping decline, leaving merchants hard-pressed to afford the fine houses that had made the city a showcase of Federal architecture.

As the coach drove through city streets, Lester hailed the driver to a brief halt and bought a newspaper, intent on perusing the real estate advertisements. House prices were less expensive, relative to Philadelphia. An idea percolated. If they needed to build an addition to the house for Edmonia, why not sell the house and buy something bigger in Salem after Cora finished school? As he considered various financial ramifications, the coach pulled up to a splendid Federal-style house on Chestnut Street. Lester smiled, knowing that if Eleanor Creesy was home, she was just the person to ask for an opinion.

Knocking on the front door, he suddenly felt foolish. Arriving completely unannounced could hardly be described as courteous, and for a moment he hoped she was at sea with her husband or out visiting someone. But Eleanor Creesy herself opened the door. Gray-haired now, her face not so tanned but deeply lined from years in the sun, dressed in a beautiful blue, full-skirted dress, she recognized him immediately.

"Lester!" She threw her arms around him, giving him the sudden thrill of his sister, who would do the same thing. Eleanor Creesy abruptly pushed him to arm's length.

"Lester Norton, you have not written in three years! And no word from Jubal, who is worse! Though he was never much of a writer."

Lester swallowed. "Well ..." He shifted feet, twisting his hat. "I thought of you. Often. Truth is ..." Suddenly, he couldn't talk.

Eleanor looked closely. "Where is Sally? And Jubal?"

"They married," Lester managed.

Eleanor Creesy clapped her hands. "How splendid! And where are they now?"

To Lester's deep embarrassment and frustration, he choked up. "I don't know."

"Oh, Lester ..." Mrs. Creesy nodded with sudden understanding. "This cursed war ..." She pulled him into the vestibule, a beautiful room highlighted by the most magnificent spiral staircase he had ever seen.

"Come in here, now. I'll make tea, and then we'll sit in the garden and you will tell me everything."

As the afternoon lengthened into evening, Lester slowly related the events of seven years, since he and Jubal had last seen the captain and his wife before shipping out on *Neptune's Car*.

"Seems a lifetime ago," Lester said.

"It was. Now go on. Cora ... she had a son already? How did that happen?"

With the patience of a detective, Mrs. Creesy pried into every nook and cranny of Lester's life. Though initially uncomfortable, he eventually felt relief flood over him, as if he could unburden himself in the safe embrace of a sage.

"I believe Jubal may be in Liverpool," Lester mused, "that would fit. But he could be anywhere. He's an exceptional horseman, did you know? Jubal could handle most any living thing ... but from the way we parted ... I doubt he's fighting here."

"And Sally, do you think she's in Mobile?"

Lester shrugged.

"I am going to make some inquiries," Mrs. Creesy decided. "The consul in London is a good friend. Charles Adams—same family as both

Presidents—has a home on Beacon Hill; Josiah and I have known him for years. I wonder if I could get a letter to Mobile, though I'm not sure if... Now then, Cora and your two boys are in Philadelphia while you," Mrs. Creesy ruefully laughed, "you're still trading and shipping, but now on land, and for the government? Well, it must be done. Cora is in medical college, you said? Lord, I want to meet that woman."

Eleanor Creesy drummed her fingers briefly and then gave Lester a look that nearly made him laugh, a picture-perfect image of the no-nonsense schoolmistress he remembered from the quarterdeck of *Flying Cloud*. Her words did make him chuckle, for she continued to order him as if that education were yesterday.

"Here is what you will do. This summer bring her here—and the boys. I still have my father's house in Marblehead and there is no better place in the world to spend July and August. Especially since summer in Philadelphia will be infernal. I don't think Josiah will be home, and I get lonely. Bring them here, or send them if you can't stay. Do you hear me?"

"Yes m'am," Lester sighed, feeling a burden lift, one he had not known he carried. "I will.

Chapter Eighty-Five

Philadelphia, June 1863

The widow showed Lester and Cora through the eighty-year-old wood-framed farmhouse on Rabbit Lane, a narrow dirt track off Market Street on the outskirts of West Philadelphia.

"I know it's rough," Lester whispered to Cora, before they climbed the narrow, steep stairs to the second floor. "But there's three acres come with the house, we can get a buggy and keep it in the barn—it'll need some shoring, I'll do that …"

"When?" Cora interrupted.

Lester brushed that off. "Edmonia can stay above the stable, we'll fix that, too. Why, we'll fence the back, too, so you can have a garden and keep a few goats if you want."

"I ain't ever having another goat in my life."

Lester grinned. "Gettin' uppity."

Cora wagged a finger in his face. "Not gettin'. I am."

The widow showed them unfinished rooms in what had been an attic, the ceiling so low Lester could only stand upright in the center. "It'll be fine for the boys." He turned to the widow.

"I'm sorry about your husband. He fell at Fredericksburg?"

"Yes, the charge at Mary's Heights." She was a small, pinched woman and spoke with a slight Southern accent. "Five months … They took his leg at the knee, but the infection … Then again below his hip. I don't know how he survived that … and pneumonia … He just couldn't. Finally he gave up and went to the Lord." The lines in her face showed fatigue and bitterness.

Lester remembered his mother, the lingering smell of sickness in the back bedroom downstairs reminding him of his last spring in Maine.

"That is a terrible blow. What will you do?"

"I'm going home."

"To …?"

"Virginia," the widow replied, an edge to her voice.

"Alone?"

"I'm sure I can pass through the lines. Now, do you need to see anything else?"

"No m'am. Your price, do I understand correctly, is six thousand dollars for the house and land?"

"Yes, to the back tree line. I am selling the one-acre woods separately."

"How much for that?" Lester asked.

"Fifteen hundred."

"We'll give seven thousand for both," Cora said, as Lester was about to reply. He looked at her, startled.

The widow acted as if Cora wasn't there, and Lester suddenly realized she had never addressed Cora, nor even looked at her.

The widow regarded Lester. "Seventy-four hundred for the both."

"Seventy-one hundred," Cora snapped.

"Seventy-three fifty," the widow said to Lester.

Cora abruptly turned to the stairs. "I don't want it." She stomped down the stairs and through the front door.

Lester found her in the yard, fuming.

"Are you ...?" he waited.

"Wrong person went to the Lord!" Cora hissed through gritted teeth.

"Well, I bought it."

"How much?"

"Seven thousand, one hundred and fifty."

"When is she goin'?"

"Thirty days."

"She here at thirty-one days I'm gonna throw her out myself! You know why's she's going south alone, don't you?"

Lester shook his head, no.

"'Cause that Rufus—her niggah!—he knowed what she was going to do. No way he's going to Virginia, no sir. That good soldier died for him, and so Rufus buried the good man and just went up and gone! Good fer him!"

Keeping quiet, Lester helped his wife into the hackney that waited to return them across the Schuylkill River to Philadelphia. Cora had heard about the widow from Rufus, a black servant who came into the city frequently. Unknown to the widow, Rufus was also a confidant of William Still and used the widow's closed coach to transfer runaway slaves to trains headed north. Other Quakers along the way would house and protect them on their journey to safety and freedom in Canada.

Lester waited until Cora breathed normally again. "Forget about her, my love. She's just ..."

"What is wrong with white people?" Cora interrupted. "Some of them are like a well got dug with such deep hate I jes' don't ever understand. You don't know—you can't. See the way people look at Curtis, at little Truette? Me, I just get mad. But they *hurt*."

"Cora, this will make it easier. You're closer to the Medical College, and Satterlee Hospital isn't more than a mile. Chestnut Street Bridge will be done in a few years; there will be more people. We can divide the property. If Sally ever comes we can make room for her."

Cora looked at him sharply. "She'll never come without Jubal, no matter what happens. Not Sally."

Chapter Eighty-Six

Washington, D.C., June 1863

As Cora gathered the children and prepared to board the morning express for New York, Lester passed a news kiosk and stopped in his tracks.

"To Arms! Citizens of Pennsylvania! The Rebels Are Upon Us!" The June 28, 1863 *Philadelphia Inquirer* was hysterical he thought, but it made him pause. For three weeks, Pennsylvania citizens had anxiously followed reports from the west, where the Army of Northern Virginia marched northward toward Harrisburg. The Union Army of the Potomac shadowed General Lee parallel to his line of march. Lester knew Philadelphia was buffered; the Rebels would have to fight through a hundred thousand Union troops before they could threaten the city.

"Come now, Lester," Cora called, as the train whistle tooted a warning blast. "Let's get our seats."

Settling into a comfortable berth, Cora held Truette to the window alongside Curtis, who stared wide-eyed, so excited he couldn't keep still. Lester quickly scanned the news article, dismissing it as another wild, totally inaccurate, and probably profitable attempt at alarming people into buying the newspaper.

Looking up, he suddenly was not so sure. A Western Union clerk had leaped into the train compartment just as the conductor called *All aboard!*

"Major Norton? Urgent telegram for you, sir!" The clerk thrust it into Lester's hand. The train lurched.

Threat to Harrisburg.
Ensure safety of depots.
Leave immediately.
Meigs

Cora looked at him as he rose. "Where you going, Lester? The train is moving!"

Lester grabbed his bag and kissed her, dropping the telegram in her lap. "Got to go, I'll join you in a few days."

"Then we're coming!" Cora made to get up.

"No, take the boys!"

"I've never met Mrs. Creesy!" Cora was alarmed now.

"I'll wire her, ask her to meet you in Boston. Change trains in New York!" Lester was already moving along the aisle as the train began to move. The Western Union clerk had made the door and leapt onto the platform. "Same station in New York. Just ask, you'll be fine! Love you, I'll send a telegram!"

Lester came off the train and started running back to the window where Cora, Curtis, and Truette all stared at him, wide-eyed and distressed. He waved as the train gathered speed and they pulled away. Wheeling, he sprinted for the stairway leading for the bridge spanning the platforms, where the western express was already making steam.

—

By sunset, Lester rode into Camp Curtin on the northern outskirts of Harrisburg, one of the largest Union camps in the country. The state capital was a major manufacturing center, and trains going in every direction on railway bridges spanning the wide Susquehanna River made the city a vital link between the Atlantic seaboard and the Midwest. When Camp Curtin became mustering point for soldiers from Maryland, Michigan, Minnesota, New Jersey, New York, Ohio, and Wisconsin, General Meigs located a major supply depot in the city. A prisoner-of-war camp had also been built, both making Harrisburg an irresistible target for General Lee.

Lester rented a roan mare from stables near the train station and galloped to the camp, intending to meet the commanding officer. Instead, he found bedlam. Troops mustered to march, caissons clattered by and officers shouted, trying to bring order out of chaos. Only a captain remained at headquarters, muttering as he pawed through a mound of telegrams.

"You want to know, too?" the captain replied, slapping the pile of telegrams. Lester had asked for a status report, and since he wore a uniform coat with his major's stripes the man had to pay attention. "Meade, Stanton, Hooker, everybody wants to know what's happening. I don't know! Reports are fragmentary and unreliable. But the Rebs come through Mechanicsville today, not five miles west. We're putting up fortifications on Camp Hill now."

"Where's Camp Hill?" Lester snapped, uneasy at the captain's nervousness. In the distance he could hear sporadic cannon fire.

"Two miles west, along the Carlisle Pike. In the morning ..." The captain stopped. Lester had already bolted out.

The roan was spirited but skittish, so Lester spurred her hard, galloping across the Susquehanna as night fell. He wanted to inspect the fortifications before it got too dark and then find an officer who could apprise him accurately of the Rebel concentration. With thousands of available troops from Camp Curtin, they ought to be able to hold off an attack until the Army of the Potomac arrived, though Lester was uncertain where the bulk of Meade's army was at the moment.

A sliver of moon provided enough light to see a lane cut through the trees, and Lester dropped the roan to a canter, eating the distance. He passed a troop of soldiers and paused to ask for directions, but the lieutenant in command said he was only told to go left at the fork another half mile down the road.

"Which direction?" Lester asked.

"Left, I was told," the lieutenant repeated.

Lester tried to curb his exasperation. "Camp Hill—is it straight on, or bear west?"

"Sir, the colonel said to go left."

Lester gave up and spurred his horse another half mile until he made out the fork. A smaller road cut off to his right, heading northwest, and he tried to make sense of the dark, squinting at treetops to determine if the land rose toward a hill. Finally, he urged the roan forward on the pike, bringing her to a trot for a few hundred yards before slowing to a walk.

The night grew quiet and Lester listened carefully. Shouts came from far to his right but he couldn't distinguish the source. A distant rifle shot echoed from the same direction, and in the sudden stillness afterward he heard the gurgle of a stream. The moon had lowered and he could just make out the pike lane against treetop silhouettes.

"Barely see a thing," he said to his mount. "Guess it be best we turn back." He pulled the reins.

A twig snapped. The horse froze.

"Halt!"

There was no mistaking the drawl.

Lester jammed his spurs and came nearly unseated as the roan leapt straight in the air, lunging into a gallop. A hornet flew by, the rifle blast almost simultaneous. A fusillade rang. His hat flew off, another bullet nicked his forefinger and cut through the reins, a round tore the middle ribbon from his arm sleeve and his boot heel was lost to the marble-sized ball that plowed into the mare's heart. Three more full strides and she folded, dead before her nose hit the turnpike. Lester pitched straight forward, slammed into ground he couldn't see, somersaulted and went into an uncontrolled cartwheel before crashing head first into a hickory post.

The only road marker within a mile read Camp Hill. Below the lettering an arrow pointed left.

Chapter Eighty-Seven

The sun was low in the sky when Jordon Hatcher and his sons gathered their tools along the prison wall and trudged to the waiting wagon. Sally held the mules still as the men piled the mauls, pickaxes, and shovels into the bed. As the brothers climbed aboard, she handed Jordon a burlap sack bulging with cornbread, cooked bacon, and jugs of cold spring water.

"They giving you fellas tomorrow off?" Sally asked, as the men tore into their food. "It's Independence Day."

The men looked at her blankly, too tired and busy to respond.

"Don't suppose so," she snorted. "That'd require being independent."

Sally slapped the reins and the mules started forward, settling into a rhythm that would bring them back to Sandy Hill by dark. Ordinarily, Beulah drove the team, but she was busy tending to a young, frightened woman enduring her first childbirth. Sally continued along for a few miles and then turned to Jordon Hatcher.

"Had enough? Come up here," she slapped the seat beside her, "and keep me company. Fill me a pipe, too."

Jordon did as he was told, bemused that Sally had taken to smoking a corncob pipe when there weren't any white people around. He pulled out the fixings from his pouch and passed her the unlit pipe, readying a match.

"Oh, just light the damn thing up!" Sally said. "Your spit wouldn't hurt me any more than if I kissed you."

Jordon was so startled Sally burst out laughing. "Go 'head, light it!" She traded him the reins for the smoking pipe and took a puff, enjoying the sensation of blowing smoke through her nose. "I know, not too ladylike, but then, Jordon, you're a tolerant sort. Now, how many men are in that stockade back there?"

"Heard 'bout six hunnert, gonna be, maybe half that now."

"You're almost finished?"

"A little more to do on the guard catwalk. But we ain't doing the roof."

Cahaba Prison consisted of a requisitioned, unfinished brick cotton warehouse, half-roofed, adjacent to a flat, open yard, all surrounded by a twelve-foot wooden stockade wall enclosing an area of about fifteen thousand square feet. Guards constantly manned the catwalk and had stationed two cannons, one at either end that could rake the open courtyard between the warehouse and stockade walls. Newly captured Union prisoners arrived almost daily, a sight that so horrified Sally the first time she witnessed their arrival she swore she'd never visit the town again.

However, a doctor lived in Cahaba, and when Emma suddenly developed fever from a beesting, Sally forgot any oaths and galloped back to town. Though the doctor thought Emma would recover fine, he kept her under observation overnight in his small clinic. Since Beulah Hatcher remained with Curtis at Sandy Hill, Sally stayed with Emma in Cahaba.

A young prisoner was also at the clinic, an Ohio soldier so gravely ill from an infected wound he died during the night. The doctor was not surprised, observing that prisoners existed on such meager rations—"We can hardly feed *our* boys on the field"—they had hardly any capacity for healing.

Returning with Emma to Sandy Hill, Sally made a simple announcement to Jordon Hatcher. "We'll have to figure out how to feed those prisoners," she said.

"Ain't possible," Jordon replied, pulling Sally up short. She had never before heard him disagree with anything she wanted.

"Like to be five-six hunnert prisoners by winter. No m'am, we's got to eat, 'n these fields can't hardly feed a thousand folk." Sally pondered that for a few weeks.

Now, as the twilight crept in, lulled by the swaying seat and relaxing tobacco, she fought the urge to nap. "We're growing more than we need, aren't we, Jordon?"

"Growin's one thing, harvestin's another," the black man replied. "When we put away what we need, give 'em the rest. 'Cept, Miss Sally," Jordon glanced her way, "best think how people bound to git riled, you being a Yankee and wanting to feed Yank prisoners."

"I'd thought of that. Bastards. But the doctor said a new 'commandant'—I never heard that word before—was coming, and he's a Methodist minister. He can't be all bad."

"Tell 'im to fix the water for them men," Jordon said. "'Jes an open trench now, comin' out the town and flow through the prison, out the other side. Folks do their washin', dogs leavin' their business, hogs rootin' in the mud ... Why, that water ain't fit for a privy before it even git to Castle Morgan. Drink that water, bound to get the death 'o sick."

"Castle Morgan?"

"Tha's what folks come to call it. After some Reb general."

"Is that supposed to be funny?" Sally could feel herself getting hot again. She was sick of being mad, But how can I help it? she asked herself. "This country has gone mad."

"Somethin' else ain't funny. A new guard showed up today."

Sally waited, noticing the candlelit windows of Sandy Hill in the distance.

"'Member that young fella, bad face, arm all stove up?"

"Sam Rivens?" Sally puffed her pipe but it had gone out. "How much more work have you got on the catwalk?"

"Few mo' days. Couple'll do it."

Chapter Eighty-Eight

Marblehead, July 1863

A warm breeze rippled the harbor surface as Eleanor Creesy spun the little sloop into the setting sun and let the back-winded jib nestle them against the float.

"Quick, Curtis," Eleanor commanded, "step ashore, tie the bow off—I'll toss you the stern line. Then hop back aboard and we'll lower the sails."

Cora sat with Truette in her lap, watching Curtis and Mrs. Creesy put the boat to bed. Truette cooed, a sound Cora thought seemed to capture the entire spirit of day and place, and this huge-hearted woman. At midday, they had sailed into Massachusetts Bay and made for a small, uninhabited island where Mrs. Creesy beached the boat and spread out a picnic lunch. Later, while exploring, Curtis had seen a lobster buoy bobbing offshore and implored his mother to let him wade to it. Cora adamantly refused but the fear in her voice brought an immediate reaction from Mrs. Creesy.

"Does the boy know how to swim?"

When Cora paused, then shook her head, no, Mrs. Creesy harrumphed. "Well, we must remedy that!"

Cora avoided her glance, a mistake.

"Do you?" Mrs. Creesy demanded.

Within minutes, all four of them were down to their knickers and in the water. Curtis, initially terrified, soon realized he wouldn't die in Mrs. Creesy's arms and within an hour took to the water like a duck, shrieking with excitement. Truette splashed in the shallows, fell over once while Cora was learning to float, and coughed up a mouth full of seawater. The little boy didn't even have time to cry. Mrs. Creesy hauled him to up, gave him a whack on the back and then back in the water.

"You're fine, just hold your breath like this, see?" The matronly woman demonstrated and wagged a finger at Curtis. "Watch your brother while I show your mother how to swim."

All of them were exhausted by sunset. As they climbed the steps leading to the old captain's house that sat overlooking the harbor in one direction and the open Atlantic in another, Cora thought she had never had a more magical time in her life.

Mrs. Creesy treated her with the interest and courtesy of Lucretia Mott without the righteousness. Meeting them at North Station, Eleanor had hugged her as naturally as a long-lost sister, hoisting Truette into her arms, ordering porters to take the bags, hailing a cab as if she were captain on a quarterdeck. Within minutes, Cora instinctively knew Eleanor Creesy was an example of everything a woman could be.

She was fearless.

"We're having lobster, clams, mussels, new corn, and blueberry cobbler," Eleanor announced. "And some lovely Madeira Josiah brought back from Spain. Curtis, you and your brother need to go to bed early because tomorrow there's the Fourth of July parade!"

"Is Daddy coming?" Curtis asked. He had jumped back in the water from the harbor float and was now shivering, wrapped in a long towel.

"No," Cora replied. "He had to go somewhere important. We'll hear from him in a few days." She tried to speak distinctly, wanting to make her best impression.

"Don't you worry," Mrs. Creesy said to Curtis. "He'll be here just as soon as he can. I've known Lester for a long time—met him when he wasn't too much older than you—and he's a very capable fellow. Now come sit down and have your supper, then off to bed so your mommy and I can have a nice long talk."

Eleanor handed the Madeira to Cora. "Open that."

Chapter Eighty-Nine

Awakening at dawn with a throbbing head and his shoulder feeling as if it might be broken, Lester blinked into a cold, hard face that looked vaguely familiar but he couldn't recollect from where.

"I know you," the face said. "Five, six years ago, you killed my client."

"What?" Lester tried to get his bearings.

"Alabama. The Pettaway place, you were on the porch with that fucker Stubbs, and your buddy, what's his name?"

"Who are you?" Lester lay in a wagon bed, the man standing beside him staring over its short sides. "Where am I?"

"Colonel William Oates, 15th Alabama. You're in Chambersburg, prisoner of the Confederate States of America. My prisoner. You were spying."

Though his head pounded, Lester pulled himself up and looked around. He was in a large encampment, bustling with men breaking down tents, readying draft horses, hitching wagons and caissons, and mustering into marching formation.

"I'm a major, United States Army." Lester had come fully awake, knowing full well the distinction: a captured soldier was a prisoner, subject to the rules of war; a spy could be summarily shot.

"You ain't in uniform," Oates sneered. Lester had no idea what became of his coat and insignias. "I say you're a spy. Git up!" Oates grabbed his collar and threw him the length of the wagon. Lester caught himself from falling, his shoulder aflame.

Oates turned to his men, ordering them to hobble Lester as they would a horse. "He touches them ropes, shoot him dead."

For three days, the hobbles stayed on. Lester walked south with the 15th Alabama from Chambersburg, arriving on the outskirts of a small town where twelve roads intersected: Gettysburg.

Each successive day, above the constant din of cannon fire, endless rifle volleys, charging, screaming, wailing men, and galloping horses, Lester and several other prisoners and slaves hauled Confederate wounded from fields left abandoned as the battle surged to another part of the line. Constantly within range of a Rebel guard's shotgun or a spent Union bullet, they struggled with the carnage from places they'd never heard of before, indeed were only descriptions blurted by survivors: the Peach Orchard, the Wheatfield, Devil's Den.

The bearers carried and dragged men with graying beards, men barely old enough to shave, men from Mississippi farms and the north Georgia woods, North Carolinian shopkeepers, Virginia blacksmiths and Alabama traders, fishermen from the Outer Banks, Florida trappers and Texas cattle drovers, men dazed and moaning, crying for their wives and mothers, crawling, staggering, or simply staring in disbelief at bullet holes and shredded limbs. Lean men, tall, thin, short, squat, muscular men, educated and illiterate, intelligent and slow-witted, some so excited or terrified their rifles held half a dozen charges on top of each other, none fired. Covered in dirt and dust, chaff and immature grain, pouring sweat, reeking of effort and fear, stunned by their own blood, blood everywhere in splotches and pools, intestines and brains on peach blossoms and summer wheat and green corn.

At night, covered—indeed drenched—in the blood of these fine, brave men, his shoulder nearly paralyzed, Lester tried to sleep, arms tied behind his back to a tree.

In three days, he ate once. Two miles to the east, across a ridge that rose south of the town, a low line of smoke lay like a fog bank through the scorching daylight. Each dawn, Confederate troops hurled themselves at that ridge, falling back at nightfall, readying to repeat their effort at the coming daybreak.

The second day, near sunset, Oates returned, disheveled and soot-streaked, exhausted on his feet as he approached the wagon where Lester had been shackled.

"One more regiment, I'd a taken that hill, turned his flank." Oates moaned, punching the wagon in frustration. "Woulda smashed you fucking Yanks, drove you from the field, inside two days been burning Lincoln's bedroom!" Oates wavered and stared at Lester, then suddenly snapped and pulled his pistol, pressing it to Lester's forehead. "I left my brother on the field! You fuckin' Yankees!" Fighting to restrain himself, he snarled like a wounded lion and pulled the trigger.

Click.

"Colonel," one of his men touched Oates' shoulder. Oates spun away from his man and hurled the empty pistol, catching Lester square in the face. Lester went down.

On the third afternoon, a cloudless, throat-parching furnace of a midsummer's day, a two-mile front of Confederate cannon unleashed an hourlong thunderstorm of fire. In the sudden silence that followed, Lester watched through a swollen black eye as twelve thousand men tramped across what a few days earlier had been a non-descript farm field in an unknown town. For twenty minutes, excepting the wave of men moving forward, the world seemed to stand still. Then the far ridgeline erupted in a flash of flame and smoke until the screams of hell were visited upon the earth.

An hour later, half the men returned.

By nightfall, Lester couldn't move, no longer caring if Oates or anyone else beat him to death. Everywhere he turned there was death. He spent the night chained to a wagon full of men he had hauled from the field, all drunk with the stupor of violence and injury, of men cursing and spitting at his aid because he wouldn't take their pistols and put them out of the agony of being gut shot, teenagers staring at severed arms or listening to burbles of bloody air coming from holes in their lungs, stoic men trying to hold torn intestines from spilling into the trampled grass.

All night long Lester lay still, hearing the hideous screams from men still left fallen on the field, howls that carved like sharpened fingernails into his psyche.

"O God, why can't I die!"

"My God, will no one have mercy and kill me!"

"I am dying! I am dying! My poor wife, my dear children, what will become of you?"

In the morning, as the Confederates waited for a Union counterattack, Lester hauled men to the surgeon's tent, then carried them back to wagons without hands or arms or feet, or added discarded legs to piles already five feet high.

By late afternoon, the wagon train readied. General Lee would retire his army from the field.

Oates rode up to Lester and ordered his hobbles cut loose once they had chained him again to a wagon.

"We're headed south, Yankee." He spit at Lester. "You're walkin'!"

Chapter Ninety

Jubal tried to ignore the Limeys at the bar. He thought they were probably off the British packets that regularly made the transatlantic run to New York and had heard him order his ale, recognizing the Southern accent, a slip that annoyed him.

"Happy Fourth, mate!" one man chortled, thumping Jubal on the back. "Independent Day for you Rebs, too?" Four of them roared. "Blimey, let's drink to you bastards, fighting like us!"

Jubal took a swallow of ale and tossed a gold coin on the bar top. "A round for the plonkers," he said to the bartender, turning to leave. Generally, he spoke as little as possible, doing his best to stay in the shadows, away from the constant, furtive eyes of surveillance detectives paid by the U.S. Consul.

The Limey grabbed Jubal by the coat, ripping it as he spun him around. "You be a cheeky bugger!" he thrust his chin. "Too good to drink with the likes of us?"

"Hardly," Jubal replied, picking up his tankard and chucking the remaining ale in the man's face.

Sputtering, the man pawed his face but suddenly stopped as the guffaws in the bar died. Jubal pressed the short double-barreled derringer into the Limey's eye.

"Enjoy your mates and leave me alone."

Knowing that whatever came after the silence wouldn't help him, Jubal made quickly for the door and ducked into the crowded street, moving fast. Admonishing himself for losing patience and drawing attention he made for the labyrinth of dockyard flophouses along the Mersey, an area he often used to lose a tailing detective. No one followed and he breathed easier, though the episode cautioned him. The stress of constant tension had begun to show; Jubal knew if any of the other Limeys had made a move he would have pulled the trigger and turned his derringer on the threat, but two bullets wouldn't have been enough to get out of that tavern alive.

Taking a ferry across the river to Birkenhead, Jubal walked a circular route to his lodgings in the house of an elderly, almost deaf British woman, the widow of a sea captain who rented rooms in the large brick mansion left by her husband. Jubal had rented the room as John Norton, a trader from

Wales, whose occupation required frequent visits to other cities in England, with occasional forays to northern Europe.

Jubal lit the lamp in his room and decanted a brandy, noticing that every single time he pulled the stopper Truette Stubbs' memory came to mind. The room was pleasantly furnished, certainly comfortable, yet Jubal had never felt so lonely in his life. Lighting a cigar, he sat in silence, sipping the brandy. Faintly, he heard the ticking of a grandfather clock in the hallway outside his room. Chimes began, the top of the hour. Jubal counted to ten.

As the echo receded and ticking resumed, Jubal stubbed his cigar out. Taking paper from his traveling case, he filled a pen from the desk inkpot and stared at the blank, white linen.

July 4, 1863

Liverpool

My beloved Sally,

Yesterday I returned from France, staying at the Cœur de la Cité Hôtel Bordeaux Clemenceau—do you remember it from our visit with Lester and Cora while our ship Mastiff was careened in Liverpool? Mr. Bulloch and I made arrangements to sell our merchandise to a French company.

Jubal pondered; best to be circumspect, he thought. Though the letter might languish for months before he would entrust it to someone heading for Mobile, if indeed, Sally and children were there—or anywhere in Alabama, for that matter—he considered it prudent to gloss over the details. Besides, he wondered, how could he explain or describe the latest twist of James Bulloch's endless game of outwitting Union agents so that the Laird rams would ultimately scour the Southern coast of blockading Northern ships?

The U.S. Consul berated the British Foreign Office for violating the Neutrality Acts, complaints that had become so increasingly shrill that Bulloch had cooked a plan to sell 294 and 295 to French bankers representing the Khedive of Egypt. Bulloch planned to rename the ships *El Toussan* and *El Monassir* and repeat the *Alabama* escapade, sailing the unarmed ironclads toward Bordeaux, where they would be outfitted and armed offshore before heading for the American coast. Jubal couldn't see how it would work. Exploits of the *Alabama* were front-page news in Britain, an uncomfortable embarrassment that had English newspapers predicting impending war with the United States.

Jubal set the pen down in despair. He relit the cigar, doused the match, and promptly stubbed his smoke out again.

I miss you and our children beyond measure. Buck must be walking—is he talking yet? And darling Emma, you must teach her to read. If not for Eleanor Creesy, I would have been forever clumsy with words, and I want so much that our children become educated. England has given me only one thing that I do not regret: books. Late into the night I read, my only solace, for without books I would be incapable of living without you.

Every day I must write: contracts, instructions, and specifications to the suppliers of our material. The evenings come—I dread them—alone, quiet, the sound of time passing by, of moments I will never recapture with you and our children. The clock marks life passing by.

While the British calculate the latest news—Lincoln's Proclamation has turned the English public against us; Lee's brilliance at Chancellorsville gives renewed hope—Britain conspires to destroy American shipping by supplying the means of our destruction so that she may sail, literally, into the breach and reclaim her maritime commerce supremacy that we worked and sailed the world to earn. I think of the McKay brothers, Truette Stubbs, poor Captain Patten of Neptune's Car, his dear, courageous wife Mary dying so young, of Lester and I! Now Britain will take the fruits of our destruction that she sows and we reap!

It is too painful to contemplate.

I am sorry, my dearest Sally, that I cannot write of more pleasant things, of remembering the sunlight in your hair, the beautiful laughter that made my heart soar, the strength you give to our children. And yes, though I never thought I could, how I do miss your endless questions and sentences that brook no doubt.

And the smell and taste of you in the darkness ... and your skin in the morning.

Wait for me, dearest love. Protect our children. Remember all that we endured. I am coming, though cannot now say when.

I love you forever,

Your obedient, humble husband,

Jubal

Jubal folded the paper, then opened and reread the letter. For a moment he considered editing—*obedient* and *humble* hardly sounded right—but the effort had drained him and he decided to walk off the nagging depression in hopes he could soon sleep. Stashing the letter in one of his books, he relit his cigar and turned down the lamp. Quietly locking his room, he plucked a single hair, wetted it with spittle, and pasted it across the door near the bottom. Bulloch had advised him that English informants at the Foreign Office spoke of pervasive activities by Union agents desperate for any information that would sabotage Confederate efforts to launch the Laird rams. Nothing the Union Navy had could withstand these ships; on them, Bulloch insisted, could hinge the entire war.

Checking the street, Jubal set out in cool twilight, walking fast. Overhead, the first green flickers of the aurora borealis pulsated against a stunning sunset as he headed for Birkenhead Park, an oasis of greenery where he could walk alone. The bucolic woods and open paths reminded him of Alabama, and he could find a bench and sit and listen to the wind, away from the stench and bustle of the shipyards and counting rooms that consumed his days. Birkenhead Park was the only place in England where the turmoil of conflict between heart and head quieted, and he tried to spend a few hours there each week, restoring himself for unrelenting clandestine warfare.

At his favorite bench, he leaned back and watched the aurora borealis build, now splashing reds and purples across the heavens as the evening lengthened. Settling, he became aware of a burr on the bench. Extending his hand, he pushed off and shifted a few inches.

Thunk!

Jubal started. A short, feathered stick protruded from the bench back in the narrow space between his arm and chest. Momentarily flummoxed, he realized it was a thin arrow. Looking up, he saw the Limey sailor calmly aim the crossbow again.

Diving beneath the second shot, Jubal somersaulted and was on his feet at a dead run. A bullet whistled by, kicking up the sod beyond him and he ducked low as a second round sailed over his head. Instinct led him downhill, toward a stream that ran through the park. Too wide to leap, the watercourse forced him laterally, deeper into the park, and he headed for the Swiss bridge, a small covered bridge the park designer had added based on similar bridges in Switzerland. Too late, Jubal realized the gunman might cut him off. He slowed, pulling the derringer from his coat, and failed to see the third man waiting amidst the shadows inside the bridge.

The man stepped out and put a shoulder into Jubal, sending him sprawling into the dim light of the covered bridge. He rolled, raising the derringer but the third man's boot slammed his arm, pinning it just as the gunman ran up. Seconds later the Limey skidded to a stop, his crossbow loaded and aimed at Jubal's chest.

"It's us plonkers, Yankee boy," the Limey chuckled. "They be tellin' us to stop ye, but nobody was sayin' how! But firstly we'll be showing ye what comes from a pistol in the eye. Are ye listening now? Cut his nuts off!"

Jubal could see the Limey cover him while the gunman passed his pistol to the third man and snapped a switchblade open from his pocket. He leaned down and sliced open Jubal's pants, grabbing his genitals. With a backward swing, he came down to cut as Jubal reared and stiff-armed his forked fingers straight in the man's eyes.

Jubal felt the slice in his shoulder but clutched the knife hand and stabbed sideways into the leg jammed on his arm while yanking the blinded assailant across him. A cry sounded and the pressure came off enough for Jubal to wrench his pinned arm free and fire upward. The knifeman's blinded agony cut to a guttural grunt as the crossbow arrow meant for Jubal drilled his spine.

The Limey looked in amazement at his crossbow, then at the feathers sticking from the knifeman's back. Next to him, the man staggered, dropped his gun, and collapsed, clutching at his shirt.

"I'm shot!"

The Limey ignored both his fallen mates and stared into the derringer pointing directly at his eye.

This time, Jubal pulled the trigger.

⁓

James Baines answered his back door well after midnight. Seeing Jubal, he lowered his own pistol. They had not seen each other in almost a year.

"Good God, man, what's become of you!" the Scotsman exclaimed. He looked older, and lined. Jubal wondered if indeed the rumors of Baines' difficulties—overly extended in steamships, an aging, waterlogged wooden clipper fleet, investments in a bank that had collapsed—were true. "I'd given ye up for lost!"

"I'll explain," Jubal gasped, "but sir, I need your help."

"Once a partner, always," Baines replied. The Scot had known of, understood, and accepted Jubal's mission for the Confederacy. "Man, you're bleeding!"

"A knife wound. Can you look? It's a slash. Messy but not deep I think."

Baines yanked the coat off and wiped the wound with the sleeve of his nightshirt. "No, shallow enough, though it ought be mended."

Jubal smiled tightly. "No doctors—stitch it as you would a sail."

"Yer on the run, lad," Baines declared, matter-of-fact.

Jubal nodded. "Do you have a ship, outbound?"

"Aye. Tomorrow, from London."

"I must be on it."

"Ye shall. McTavish will put ye on the first morning express at sunrise. Now come, we must clean and splice this, and ye will tell me all what has happened, though I kin guess. Forgive me fer sayin', but I told ye to stay out of it."

"You did indeed, sir. Where does she sail?"

"Melbourne, on the noon tide. Come now."

Chapter Ninety-One

Marblehead, July 1863

A week after the battle of Gettysburg, Cora still had heard nothing from Lester. Each day, she had walked the children to the telegraph office and come back empty-handed.

"That's not like Lester," Cora worried to Eleanor Creesy, her concern affecting the otherwise idyllic vacation. Both boys had become so enchanted with the water Eleanor laughed that Curtis "spends more time in the ocean than out of it."

Every Northern newspaper was full of news from the battlefield but the panic of Lee's invasion had abated as the Army of Northern Virginia marched south.

"Why don't you telegraph the Quartermaster General's office?" Mrs. Creesy asked. "They should know where he is."

"Can I?" Cora recoiled. "I'd never think I could do such a thing."

"Land yes!" Eleanor scoffed. "You're his wife! Let's go right now, I'll do it."

Cora was astonished by Mrs. Creesy's boldness and even more deeply impressed by the woman's nonchalance. Authority or ceremony meant little; if Mrs. Creesy wanted something, she said so or did something about it.

"Now forgive me for saying this, Cora," Eleanor said as they walked back from the telegraph office, "but take a lesson from Curtis." The boy was chasing a butterfly. "Nobody can tell you what to do. Just because your skin is darker than mine—why among the Masai tribes in Africa, I'd be ugly—doesn't mean you're less capable. How many white American women are studying to become a doctor? Mind you, men aren't going to like it any more than they like the idea of us voting, but believe me, this will happen. Do you know why?"

Cora shook her head, no.

"We will make it so. It starts with each of us, every single woman. It starts with you."

"Yes, m'am."

"Good," Eleanor smiled. They approached the captain's house. "Have you ever had sangria? No? Well, they know how to live in Spain. Let's make some."

The afternoon drifted by as the women sat on the porch, keeping an eye on the boys playing in a tidal pool below the house. The sangria gave Cora a mellow glow, and she put her anxiety about Lester aside to enjoy the afternoon. Later, when Curtis had come up from the water to show them a small, flattened stone shaped like a fish, smooth as silk from centuries of surf, Mrs. Creesy found a short length of thread and made him a necklace, which made him very proud. Cora put the boys down to nap in a hammock under the huge oak trees out front and was dozing herself in a lawn chair when the telegraph courier galloped up.

"Telegram for Mrs. Creesy!"

Eleanor came from the house and ripped it open. She sucked a breath and clutched her mouth.

"What?" Cora demanded. Without a word, Mrs. Creesy handed her the telegram.

Regret to inform Major Lester Norton missing in action near Harrisburg, July 1.

Pls convey to wife.

All efforts to determine status.

Meigs

Cora made directly for the house, calling behind her. "Curtis, wake up! Get dressed! We're going home! Right now!"

"I'll come with you to Boston!" Mrs. Creesy was right behind. "Go pack." She turned and called to the courier, a young man she had known since he was a boy. "Louie, go back to the post office and telegraph the Shore Line Railroad, I want a sleeping berth to New York City tonight!"

The courier tipped his cap and vaulted into the saddle. "Yes m'am, right this minute!"

An hour later, Eleanor Creesy helped them settle into a sleeper cabin, ignoring the looks of white passengers in the same car. She had thrown together some leftovers and joined them in the dash to South Station where they arrived ten minutes before departure.

"Now, Cora," Eleanor said, "go right through New York. Don't stop, just transfer to the Hudson ferry. You know the way? From Tenth Avenue, uptown to the terminal, it's around ten blocks?"

"I know," Cora nodded. "We come that way."

"Don't stop. I saw yesterday's papers—the president ordered conscription a few weeks ago and there were protests this weekend in New York."

"What's 'conscription'?" Curtis asked, stumbling on the pronunciation. Cora was grateful to the boy; she didn't know the word either.

"Calling men up to fight the war. Making them go, unless," Eleanor shook her head, "they can afford to buy an exemption. The poorer people don't have the money. That's what they're upset about, mostly new people from Ireland and Germany. That's in Europe, across the ocean. Didn't you go there?"

Curtis shrugged and looked at his mother. "Did we?"

The train whistle cut a reply and Eleanor Creesy gave quick hugs and bustled from the car, coming back along the platform as Cora lowered their window.

"You must come again, it's been wonderful to have you!" Mrs. Creesy exclaimed. "Have a good trip, boys! Cora, wire me when you get home!" She stood on the platform waving as the train lurched and began to move.

"Thank you so much, Mrs. Creesy," Cora leaned out the window, reaching to touch her. "You've been so good to us, such a …"

"*Extra! Extra! Read all about it!*" A newsboy came trotting in from the terminal, roaring at the top of his lungs. "*Fresh off the press! Draft riots in New York! People gettin' killed!*"

Mrs. Creesy scurried to the newsboy and ripped a paper from his hands. He protested and demanded payment but she ignored him, scanning the paper. Suddenly she gathered her skirts and ran after the train as it gathered speed.

"Cora, you can't go! Get off!! There are race riots in New York!! Get off!"

The train had picked up speed and her voice already faded, but even from a distance Eleanor Creesy could see Cora's look of iron determination. Mrs. Creesy cupped her hands.

"*Don't stop!*"

Cora waved and then sat back, stunned. Curtis looked at her.

"What's a 'race riot'?"

"I don't rightly know. But we be fine, don't go worryin'."

Curtis looked at his mother too intently and she shifted in her seat, fiddling with Truette.

"What's 'race'?"

"Don't you go worryin', hear me?"

"Mommy ..."

"It's the color of your skin. White people, black people, red people, yellow. All kinds of people. Negroes, Chinese, Choctaws, Ireland. Now lie down, time for you to sleep."

"No it's not, sun's still up. What am I?"

"What are you what?"

"What race am I? Me and True?"

Cora exhaled and was quiet for a time but Curtis outwaited her. "You Negro."

"What makes a Negro? Are you one?"

"Skin color. Yes."

"Is Daddy?"

"Lester? No. He's white. Now stop askin' questions and do what I tell you."

"Is Lester my daddy?"

Cora stifled a grunt, feeling like she'd been kicked in the belly. "Lester loves you. Curtis, you being the luckiest boy in the world."

"Is he my daddy?"

Cora gathered herself, willing not to cry in front of a child she loved with every fiber of her body, as much as she loathed every fiber of the man who had given her this boy.

"No. Your daddy is gone, dead, and now Lester's your daddy. Someday when you're older, I'll tell you about ... everything. But not now. You just gotta trust me, Curtis."

"You promise?"

Cora blinked rapidly, willing the tears not to fall.

"Yes, child. I promise."

The train chugged through rainstorms overnight but the day dawned clear. Cora woke the children as the express glided to a stop at the Tenth Avenue station. Truette was still sleepy and became grumpy, uninterested in the few biscuits and apples that his mother offered, the end of the provisions that Eleanor Creesy had thrown together. There was nothing left to feed the boys.

"Truette, stop your fussin!" Cora scolded, looking around for a porter. "We'll get some breakfast 'fore we go home, but we've got to get the ferry.

Curtis, mind your brother."

The station was strangely quiet, with none of the porters she had seen passing through on the trip north. Cora looked about, uncomfortable, wondering if the porters didn't come to work until later in the morning, but she was anxious to continue and hoisted their canvas bag and her purse and set out along the platform for the 30th Street exit.

Behind her, Truette still squabbled and Curtis half-walked, half-dragged him until Cora grew exasperated and grabbed the younger boy, hoisting him on her hip.

"Curtis, take my purse," she directed. The canvas travel bag would be too heavy for him. "But hold it close, don't let go of it for nothin'!"

On her trip north, the train station had bustled and surrounding streets were crowded with pedestrians, cabs, and freight wagons. Walking into the street from the Boston overnight express, she was surprised to see it empty, except for two single-horse cabs. The drivers looked around furtively, one standing on his wagon seat and looking down the street. An older black woman ran by.

"Get goin'! Get off the street!"

Cora stared in shock. The woman was a man! A commotion sounded from a few blocks away; both cabbies abruptly snapped their whips and their horses trotted away. From a block down on the avenue a shopkeeper bolted out of his store, still in an apron. A Negro, he waved at Cora, yelling, "Run for your life!" before dodging back into his store, slamming the door.

The commotion grew louder until she could make out the sounds of ragged chanting. Suddenly a crowd came out of 32nd Street and spied the disguised man.

"Hallo! Blackie!" Jeers turned to taunts; then a teenager screamed. "That ain't no woman!"

A dozen men set upon the fleeing man like a wolf pack, ripping off the dress and clubbing him to the ground. The flash of brass knuckles winked in the morning sun as others closed in, laughing, kicking and stomping the prostrate man.

From the opposite direction another mob poured onto the avenue, making for the store. Two men tried to kick the door in—"Open 'er you bloody nigger!"—but drew back as several other men kicked in the storefront window. As it shattered, a flaring bottle sailed through the opening and exploded in gouts of flame. The crowd cheered, though a kid who had gotten too close howled, his hair aflame. Two men tackled the boy.

"Curtis, run with me," Cora hissed. "Run!" They dashed across the street, Truette starting to cry.

"Mommy!" Curtis looked terrified. "What's happening?"

"Come on, no time. I don't know. We gotta go. Go! Go!"

A voice hailed, "Hallo!" They'd been seen.

Cora ran as fast as she could but holding both Truette and the travel bag made for an awkward waddle. Looking back, her heart went into her throat. The crowd had surged around the corner, giving chase. Suddenly the leading edge pulled up short, yelling and pointing. In front of Cora, a double-horse team had barreled around the corner off Eighth Avenue, charging directly at her and the boys. A policeman whipped the team while another rode beside him, his shotgun etched against the rising sun.

Snatching Curtis, Cora darted into a doorway as the wagon clattered past, packed with policemen carrying billy clubs. As the wagon pulled to a stop, the police poured out and with clubs flailing, waded into the crowd of men now howling and throwing paving stones they'd ripped from the street. The shotgun roared and pistol shots rang, the melee turning into a battle. Cora grabbed Curtis and fled deeper into the city.

An explosion rippled off to her left, uptown, and a building burst into flame. She heard the chant of a crowd another a few streets over and suddenly could make it out: *No draft! No draft!* From the opposite direction a voice shrieked "Kill the niggers!"

Cora peered around the corner and stifled a scream. Before a laughing, chanting mob, a boy, no more than fifteen, pulled the half-burned body of a Negro man through the street, tugging on a line tied around the dead man's testicles.

Doubling back, Cora pulled Curtis along and turned into a side alley, trying to find some place to hide from the madness she could hear building. The alley reeked of refuse and she tried every door; all were locked.

"Hallo!" The cry sounded behind her. Four men surged down the alleyway howling with laughter. "Let's get us some black pussy!"

Cora dropped the canvas bag and grabbed Curtis by the collar, running into the next street. A shop owner saw her from the doorway, frantically motioning. The family hurried across the cobblestones as fast as Cora could go.

Curtis tripped.

The child went sprawling as Cora turned, still holding a piece of collar. Hoisting him to his feet, she looked up to see the men charge around the corner. They pounced like rabid dogs.

One man tossed Curtis aside while two others swarmed Cora, trying to pull Truette from her. She fought like a banshee, clawing, kicking, and biting with such ferocity the men backed off slightly. The ringleader stepped forward and swung a club but Cora ducked, catching the blow on her shoulder.

The man reared to swing again but stopped short and screamed. Curtis had attacked from the rear, burying his teeth in the man's thigh. He kicked out and Curtis fell away, spitting fabric and flesh. Two men tackled Cora, and she went down, trying to shield little Truette. She kicked upward, catching an attacker in the crouch, and he folded like a jackknife, moaning in the street. The other man punched her in the mouth but she hurled herself at him, biting his face, feeling the crush and splinter of his nose. The last man tried to kick her but she was rolling away. He picked up Truette instead and chucked the crying toddler aside.

Curtis was on his knees, clutching his mother's purse, trying like a snapping turtle to bite the ringleader clubbing him and tugging at the purse. Enraged, the men picked up Curtis by the hair and grabbing his jacket, took three long strides and threw the boy and purse right through the storefront window. From her knees, Cora screamed and came at the ringleader like a tigress but he sidestepped with the skill of a soldier and used her momentum to throw her through the part of the window Curtis hadn't already shattered. Cora landed hard on her son and rolled into a stocked shelf, sending it crashing into its neighbor. Bottles broke, barrels overturned, the floor became wet and greasy. She lay for a moment, stunned.

With a crash, the shop door flew open, kicked off its hinges.

"I'm gonna fuckin' strangle her!" The man Cora had bit came on, blood pouring from his face, but the ringleader slapped a fearsome paw on his shoulder.

"Not so fast, cluchy," he said, working at his belt. "Not 'till we've had a go!"

The ringleader booted her legs apart but Cora kicked him in the shins.

"Fuckin' doxie! Hold 'er legs!" The man limped, but dropped his pants; he was stiff and rising, his face sweating with anticipation. Cora spotted her purse and rolled, snatching it to her chest. Panting, she looked at the three men standing above her, the ringleader's erection quivering.

"Don't hurt my boys," she begged, swallowing.

The ringleader laughed, a sinister chuckle, and motioned to his mates. "Her legs! Hold 'em wide! Kick me again, cuntie, 'n I'll beat yer brains to cobbler!"

The men spread Cora and ripped off her drawers as she fussed in her purse. "Ohhh, lookee that growler," the ringleader salivated, settling on his knees. He stared at Cora's nakedness, then leered at her, grinning, as she shot him in the face.

The ringleader flopped backward as the two men stared in astonishment at the small, smoking hole in Cora's purse. Another hole appeared in the purse, then a third. One man went down with a bullet in his throat, the other with a severed aorta.

"Mommy," Truette cried. He stood in the doorway crying, and bleeding from his forehead. Cora crawled to him, sweeping the boy in her arms.

"Mommy," another voice gasped. Cora wheeled to Curtis, who lay prone where he'd landed, coughing. "Mommy," he whimpered.

Keening, Cora scurried across the floor on hands and knees, ignoring the cutting glass shards.

"Curtis, Curtis, you a'right? Tell Mommy you're a'right!"

Curtis struggled to talk, his little chest heaving. "It hurts, Momma."

"I'll git help!" Cora took his shoulders. "Can you move?"

Curtis let out a soft cry that twisted her heart. "Ohhh, Mommy, it hurts!" His voice was feeble, his eyes glassy. She pulled her hand away and it caught something, making her gasp. A tickle of blood showed from a fresh cut on her hand. Then she nearly fell completely apart.

The jagged edge of a glass shard protruded from Curtis' chest.

Holding her breath, she touched it; the shard was rigid. She pinched the end, pulling gently. Curtis gasped.

"Is Daddy ..." His voice faded as he took a small breath, then another, smaller, and his breath became faint "... coming home?"

Curtis went still as the light left his eyes. In a moment, he was gone.

Cora knelt, willing the small chest to move again.

"Curtis," she whispered, repeating his name, pleading, and then begging. Finally, choking and laying her head on the small, still chest, she collapsed into wracking sobs that seemed might break her apart.

Suddenly, a bottle crashed ten feet away and burst into flame next to an overturned urn of whale oil. In moments the urn exploded upward into a smashed case of olive oil. Instinctively, she threw an arm up to protect her face as fire leapt to the ceiling.

"*Mommy!*" Truette screamed. The olive oil sizzled; cries sounded from upstairs.

Cora scrambled back to the boy as the olive oil ignited, then wheeled and dove for her purse before crawling and rolling again for the door, trying to extinguish the flames on her dress and sleeves. She staggered into the street dragging Truette and saw the last man, who had recovered from her kick and fired the store. He sneered at her but his eyes widened as she pulled the pistol. Bolting for the alley, he nearly made the corner when two bullets between his shoulder blades sent him crashing into the far wall at a full run.

Cora turned back to the store, now engulfed in flames. She covered her head and gritting her teeth against the intense heat, took two steps to the doorway but another explosion knocked her back.

"*Mommy!*" Truette wailed.

An hour later, a police patrol stopped as a black woman wandered up Tenth Avenue, bloodied and bruised, her hair singed, burnt clothes hanging in tatters. A mute baby boy sat on her hip clutching a purse. In the woman's other hand a pistol pointed at any man that so much as looked at her.

The police captain approached, talking softly, advancing cautiously, until she lowered the pistol. His men gathered around and offered to help but finally gave up and put the mother and her child in a paddy wagon.

No matter what the policemen said, the woman wouldn't talk. Neither would she relinquish either her silent son or the gun, and the boy wouldn't let go of the purse.

Chapter Ninety-Two

Gee's Bend, August 1863

Sally fanned herself against the humidity, squinting into the white afternoon haze as she came onto the porch at Sandy Hill. One of the housekeepers had run in with a report from a field hand: four riders were approaching from Cahaba.

Sam Rivens pulled his horse to a halt at the front porch stairs. He carried a double-barreled shotgun across his lap, casually pointed past his horse's neck. Sally could see one of the hammers already cocked.

"Looking to make some mischief?" Sally smiled without a trace of humor. "Come strolling into my dooryard with a ready shotgun?" She looked the men over—they were all armed—and regarded Rivens. "Sure it's not too big for you to handle?"

"Yankee bitch, you got a big mouth!" Rivens spit a stream of tobacco juice.

"It's my house." Sally drawled, giving a ladylike swing to her dress.

"We come for the niggahs," one of the older man said, hoping to settle things before they spun out of hand. He had warned Rivens not to get riled, but the northern woman had a way of putting any man on edge.

"Why don't you *leave* for the Negroes?" Sally replied.

"We got to build that foundry in Selma, 'nother one in Montgomery," the older man declared. "This here order is from the governor, State of Alabama. We can requisition niggahs as," he slapped the pages of a document open, found his place and read, "necessary for protection and preservation of all material essential to the Confederate States of America." He folded the document and stuffed it in his shirt. "Says so here, we got the legal right."

"Let me see it."

"No need m'am. I read it right."

"Doesn't look like any one of you can read," Sally retorted. "Do you two mutes," she nodded at the other men, both strangers, "know your letters?" The men looked at each other, then back to Sally. "Nope, didn't think so," she said.

The older man lost his temper. "Gawdammit, where are they?"

"Where is who?"

"Them Hatcher boys, been working on the stockade. They're blacksmiths 'n we needs every smithy we kin find! Cannon, rifles, we got to make us iron! Now dammit, we come to git 'em!"

"Find them," Sally replied, knowing Ezekiel was already taking a circuitous route around the fields to warn Jordon and his sons. Sally had ordered them to pack for hard travel. Both Daniel and Isaiah Hatcher were married, the older with a baby girl. Jordon Hatcher had said they would slow them, but Sally wouldn't even think of leaving any of the family behind.

"This is the last time I'm tellin' yew," the old man declared. "We'll pay when the time comes."

"When what time comes? With worthless Confederate paper, not fit for my privy?" Sally knew she was pushing their limits but didn't care. In disgust, she turned away. "Get out of my yard."

"They don't come," Sam Rivens straightened in the saddle, "we'll hang them fuckers."

Beulah Hatcher flew out from behind the front door where'd she been listening and hurled a frying pan at Rivens. Beulah's aim was true; the cast-iron spun through the air like a saucer and caught him full in the face, busting his nose and nearly knocking him from the saddle.

"You heard the Missus!" Beulah screamed. "Git your sorry asses out our dooryard!"

The shotgun blast nearly cut Beulah Hatcher in two.

Rivens spit several teeth and cocked the second barrel, raising it toward Sally. "I'll kill you, too!" he sputtered through blood turning his scraggly beard scarlet.

The older man lunged at the shotgun as it fired, shattering the window beside the door. Sally shuddered; the charge had whistled by, a few pellets tearing at her sleeve.

A body dropped inside the house and someone screamed. "Mae Belle!" Sally bolted inside, nearly vomiting at the sight of Beulah's intestines. Jordon and Beulah Hatcher's daughter-in-law lay crying on the floor, blood soaking the right side of her dress. Another house servant screamed as bloody bubbles covered Mae Belle's lips.

"Water and towels!" Sally yelled. Horses hooves galloped away and she raced for the gun closet, pulled out one of Jubal's rifles and rushed back to the front porch, checking the chamber. It was empty. The horsemen were already hidden in clouds of dust.

Sally turned back to Mae Belle. The young woman lay motionless, staring at the ceiling, her blood pooling onto the floor.

"It's all my fault, Jordon," Sally wailed, when the black man and his sons rushed onto the porch and skidded to a stop, taking in the carnage. They had heard the shots and waited until the horsemen rode past, whipping their mounts hard, before running a mile back to Sandy Hill.

"I baited them, couldn't keep my mouth shut! Beulah and Mae Belle would have been alive if I'd just kept my mouth shut!" Sally started sobbing uncontrollably.

Jordon Hatcher had seen much death in his life and knew its face; he took several deep breaths. His son Isaiah pushed by and ran into the house. A moment later, the young man cried out in agony.

"Daniel," Jordon kneeled next to Beulah, wiped his perspiring forehead, and reverently kissed his wife's eyes closed. "Prepare your mother."

After nightfall, fifty slaves gathered around pine coffins that Daniel had quickly built, singing spirituals as Jordon and Isaiah washed the feet and faces of their wives by torchlight before gently placing them in the rough-cut coffins. Daniel nailed the tops shut and six men lowered the coffins side by side, in the red soil. Sally stood by the graveside as dirt thudded on the hard pine, holding herself and rocking as if in a trance.

When the earth was settled, Isaiah pounded two crosses into the fresh graves. Finally, Jordon put his arms around Sally, the first time he had ever held her. She whimpered into his chest.

"It's my fault!"

"You didn't do the shootin'," he said, his voice deep, quiet and stoic. "It's done, the Lord called."

"I made them mad!"

"Shush, now," Jordon Hatcher stroked Sally's hair. "Beulah thought you wuz the strongest woman she'd ever seen, the only good white woman she ever knowed. Said she never knowed white people could be good, 'cept for you and Jubie."

"Oh, Jordon, what will we do?"

"Got to go now. Not tomorrow, maybe not fer a few days. Me and the boys got work to do. Then, we shorly got to go."

Sally swallowed. Something in Jordon Hatcher's voice, the way he stiffened, told her she didn't want to know what "work" they had to do.

Two days later, Sally, carrying tiny Lester and holding Emma's hand, boarded a steamboat headed upriver. Five slaves came with her—three men, a woman, and her newborn baby. The men were loosely chained together, and Sally, affecting a drawl, ordered them about.

"Where y'all headed, m'am?" asked the purser, looking over the slaves. Jordon's sons hauled duffel bags while he toted a canvas rucksack. Charity, Daniel's wife, had their infant daughter on her back and carried a large bag.

"Far as there's 'nough river," Sally drawled.

"Been hell-fire hot, but wet this summer. River's high 'nough up to Wetumpka, foot of Devil's Staircase. No going beyond them rapids. Gonna sell these niggahs in Montgomery?"

"I don't ask people their business," Sally sniffed. "Show us to my cabin, if you will, please." She pulled a key from around her neck and unlocked Jordon from his sons. Her voice toughened. "Take that bag from Charity," she ordered, "and follow this man. You boys go below. Watch them bags, y'all hear? If you know what's good for ya!"

The purser's face set at the rudeness and he didn't say another word to her, as Sally intended. She didn't want prying eyes or questions, nor to give anyone reason to suspect the duffels contained boots and coats for overland travel, Jubal's three rifles and two pistols, plenty of ammunition, plus several days' provisions of rice, beans, and smoked bacon. Jordon's rucksack contained gold coins they had taken from the cellar safe.

Sally had hugged Ezekiel, leaving him with his notarized bond and a power of attorney to use Mobile bank funds for maintaining both the city mansion and Sandy Hill. "Wait for Jubal," Sally ordered, though she had no idea where her husband was or if he were still alive. She did know Ezekiel didn't want to go north and might be too frail for the arduous trip.

The old man simply nodded.

In her stateroom, Jordon opened the shutters and Sally looked out as the steamboat cast off from the Gee's Bend landing.

"Think we'll ever see Sandy Hill again, Jordon?"

"Can't say, Miss Sally."

"How'd you get so fatalistic?"

Jordon looked at her, perplexed.

"Accepting of the unknown," Sally explained. "We've got no idea what the future will bring and that doesn't seem to bother you a bit."

Jordon Hatcher shrugged. "I lived a good long life. My Beulah's gone; only thing left for me to do in this life is protect my boys—see to it, if'n I can, they don't have to take what I took."

"You think we can make it?"

"I know the country top 'o this river. Beulah and I wuz born up to the hills. Jubie's pa brought us down when we wuz young, Beulah not even a woman yet. But you," he lowered his voice, "gonna have to get us through. We jes' be quiet, ain't sayin' nuthin'."

Sally nodded. "I'm thinking how." They'd formed a plan, but she knew it would surely change.

Traveling upriver by steamboat as far north as the river level would allow, hopefully above Montgomery, the party would travel by wagon or horseback over the height of land and into the Tennessee River Valley, where Sally intended to buy a flatboat and float the length of the river to Paducah, Kentucky. Two thousand miles, a month or more, two armies to cross through, depending on where they were fighting, a hundred different ways of being stopped, raided, robbed, arrested, or just "disappeared."

Jordon had used just that word before dawn, when he and boys had come to the house, covered in mud and reeking of rotten eggs. Sally knew that smell, the stench of Ten-Mile Swamp, a thick, tangled low-lying area in the southern crook of Gee's Bend that flooded throughout the year when the river rose from hard rains and then sweltered as it slowly drained into the lowering river. Sulfur springs gave the swamp a noxious odor that people avoided; night vapors terrified the superstitious and very real ten-foot alligators could drag in a mule or deer that grazed too close to the swamp edge.

"You stink to high heaven," she had said to him then. None of the men would look at her. "What did you do to him?"

"Who dat?" Jordon asked.

"That murdering cripple."

"Sam Rivens? Heard he wuz 'disappeared'."

"Did you kill him?"

"Whatever make you think that, Miss Sally? Be a sin to kill a man. No, m'am, not us."

The men left her to wash and get dressed and fed, readying to leave Gee's Bend forever. Jordon saw no reason to tell her that they'd taken Sam Rivens at midnight—he'd come out to answer the knock at his door, both hammers cocked on his shotgun, which did him no good, for Isaiah could kill a rabbit at thirty paces with a rock from his slingshot so Rivens' forehead at ten provided an invitation. True to his word, Jordon hadn't killed him, simply made a small slice in the man's throat, enough to sever his voice. They left Sam Rivens bleeding and hogtied to a tree in Ten-Mile Swamp; the alligators would visit soon enough.

There being no reason to waste a good shotgun, Jordon packed it in one of the duffel bags, where it now lay as the steamboat chuffed upstream and Gee's Bend merged into the trees hanging over the riverbank astern.

"Are you fine now, Miss Sally?" Jordon asked. "Believe I'll go down to the cotton deck with the boys." The tall slave bowed and left Sally with her children to go below and join his, who he rightly suspected were already doing what he intended, taking a nap in the August morning sun.

Chapter Ninety-Three

East Tennessee, September 1863

Lester untied the rope holding up his pants and shambled into the woods again, the fifth time in as many hours. Two weeks of dysentery after trudging six hundred miles had left him staggering. He just managed to squat before a liquid stream gushed and splattered the forest floor, but he was relieved not to shit his freshly washed pants. An hour earlier he hadn't been so lucky, and had to stand in the cold, ankle-deep ripples of Chickamauga Creek rubbing his ragged trousers free of corn kernels that with a little rinse looked as if they had never passed through his stomach. The stream had cleared overnight, no longer copper-colored from the blood of a thousand wounded soldiers.

A young bluecoat watched him return.

"How long you been with 'em?" the trooper asked as Lester dropped to his haunches. Several dozen Union soldiers sat huddled together under guard at the rebel encampment, captured on the first day of the Battle of Chickamauga by General Nathan Bedford Forrest's cavalry.

"Gettysburg," Lester replied. "Where you from? How'd you get captured?"

"21st Ohio Infantry," the soldier replied. "We got cut off, can't see a thing in them woods. Least we're alive. Seen them lanterns last night?"

Lester nodded, depressed. Women had gone through the battlefield after dark, trying to identify loved ones, or simply helping the wounded. A ground fog had settled in the thick woods and the ghostly, moving flickers looked like a swarm of fireflies meandering through a moaning forest. Lester was too weak to join them and didn't see the point anyway. If a man hadn't made it off the battlefield yet, either through his own effort or carried by comrades, chances were slim he would ever rise.

"Whaddya think'll be the butcher's bill?" Ohio asked. He was a young man, in his early twenties, mustered in at Columbus three months earlier, which he'd explain to anyone who would listen.

"Likely one of the biggest towns in Maine," Lester replied, surprised at himself. He realized that lately he rarely thought of Maine—or much of anything else, for that matter. Mostly he tried to keep Cora and the boys to mind when he wasn't thinking about food.

"They were the only thing that kept me going the length of the Shenandoah Valley," he said aloud.

"Huh? What are you talkin' about?"

"Nothin', don't pay no heed."

"How'd you get here?" Ohio asked, looking at Lester's battered, calloused feet.

"Walked."

"You look it. Thin as a beanpole."

"Doesn't matter, we'll be busy soon, picking up the pieces, I reckon." Lester sighed; he just wanted to sleep.

"Doing what?"

"Burying a few thousand good men."

Horse hooves trotted close and stopped. Lester stared at the ground and paid no attention until a chunk of bread landed in his lap. Startled, he hesitated and then tore into it before looking up. William Oates tossed a piece of meat that Lester snatched.

"You've gotta tighten up, Yank."

Lester eyed him, stuffing the meat in his mouth.

"Careful," Oates said, throwing a leg over his saddle. "You're gonna chuck it. No more where that come from." Noticing the other Union soldiers eyeing the food, Oates drew his pistol. "I don't give a fuck about y'all. This man's my prisoner; I want him alive. So much as think about poaching that food, I'll shoot every last one of you."

Oates holstered his pistol. "Ten minutes, Norton, come down the line with me to that cabin yonder. Stay quiet. Make a run for it, I'll hang you *and* these prisoners."

Lester grunted. "I can't run any more than I can fly."

Oates grinned, despite himself. "You've got gumption, Norton, I'll say that much. Ten minutes." He spurred his horse.

"How come you're special?" Ohio demanded.

"Walk home and maybe someone will throw you piece of rotten beef," Lester groused. He hadn't talked to a northerner since Harrisburg, and after this one had no desire to talk with another. Inwardly groaning, he hauled himself upright and made for the cabin.

Rebel cavalry officers milled outside a squat, chink-log structure that looked at least fifty years old. Likely it had been built by one of the first pioneers pushing into land that for centuries had been Cherokee territory before the tribe was nearly exterminated, its remnants forced onto the Trail of Tears, a thousand-mile walk to the Oklahoma territory. Now the thickly wooded hills were being fought over yet again.

A magnificent gray horse stood before the cabin, its long head drooping, as a young trooper brushed the horse's sweaty flanks.

"That's Forrest's horse," Oates said, noticing Lester eye the stallion. The colonel stood beside his own mount, waiting for orders. "Splendid animal, isn't it? Though not likely for long. Forrest has had a dozen shot from under him; can't say that I give this one much prospect."

"Why do you want me?" Lester asked.

"You usin' yer finger agin?"

Lester looked at the stub of his index finger. The bullet wound at Harrisburg had become infected on the fields at Gettysburg and by the time General Lee's retreating wagon train had reached Williamsport ford on the Potomac River Lester's finger was swollen with infection. A rebel surgeon had examined the wound, promptly put Lester's hand on a wagon bed and in one swift, accurate chop, cleaved the finger at the middle knuckle. As red-hot iron cauterized the wound, Lester nearly passed out.

Ever since, the smell of roasting meat made him queasy.

"I liked that finger," Lester said.

"That ol' sawbones likely saved your hand, or your arm—maybe your life."

"What do you want?"

"You're staying with Forrest. Drive one of his wagon trains 'till they send you."

"Send me where?"

"We'll be stayin' with Longstreet, movin' east and north, likely. Forrest is going the other way, dependin' on what General Bragg says." Oates nodded to the cabin and lowered his voice. "Though he's about ready to shoot Bragg and I don't blame him. Never should have let the Yankees back to Chattanooga. We should have hit them when they were on the run!"

Union troops had fled the field after two ferocious days of fighting that took Lester right back to the memories of Gettysburg. The roar of battle rolled over and through hills and dense woods, one constant, sustained tumult of cannon fire, musket volleys, explosions, shrieks and cries of horses and men, the laughter and howl of victory, anguished moans, and the silence of the fallen. In the rear, Lester had taken men to the field hospital and moved them again after their amputations.

"They'll be back," Lester said.

"You damn Yankees are so fuckin' sure of yoreselves!"

Lester shrugged. "Most of your supplies come from what you capture. Who's making those weapons, provisions?"

"We've got the best generals," Oates insisted, but he couldn't sustain the conviction, shaking his head. "And the worst. We've got to outlast you."

"You started this."

Oates slapped his gloves on an open palm. "The Union was a voluntary one! That it was no longer a safeguard and protection, but a menace to our rights, we resolved to withdraw from it and form another union. One we believed where there would be peace, harmony, and security of rights resulting from homogeneity of interests!"

"You sound like a lawyer again." Lester replied, bemused that Oates' language could change from a red-dirt farmer to an educated attorney in one sentence.

"I ain't going to miss you, Norton."

Lester regarded Colonel Oates. Though he had detested the man, two months in his company, walking hundreds of miles with the Alabama infantry, even if as a prisoner, had tempered his opinion. Oates was headstrong and hot-tempered but courageous, steady in battle, and loved by his troops. A hard, tough man, he was neither mean nor cruel. A week after Gettysburg, Oates had actually apologized to Lester for almost executing him, admitting he had become unhinged from the loss of his brother in their desperate attempt to turn the Union flank at Little Round Top, and his despair at coming within a few minutes, a few feet of success—so tantalizingly close—but still falling short.

"What shall become of me?" Lester finally asked. The numbness of captivity had ebbed into resignation, and though initially considering escape, he had come to the conclusion that if he ever wanted to see Cora and the boys again his best chances lay in waiting for an opportunity to flee into the forest. At the Potomac crossing he'd given his word to Oates that he would wait for a prisoner exchange, and since then had mentally wrestled whether an oath given under duress must be honored. Within a month, however, it was a moot debate. He felt too weak to survive any flight. So he put one foot in front of another and tried to husband his strength, mostly successfully until the dysentery.

"You're going south, to a prison camp. From there, arrangements will be made for your exchange."

"Why are you doing this?"

"After that incident with Stubbs, I wasn't predisposed toward any affection to you. At Gettysburg I despised you. But since, my feelings have tempered. Indeed, I have watched you. Never a complaint, compassion and good cheer for the wounded, an honorable man of his word. To those of us born and bred in the South, honor is all." After crossing the Potomac, Oates had released Lester from his chains and hobbles in return for that oath. "Besides, truth be known, I couldn't stand Rivens. A whiner, no backbone t'all. You didn't kill him?"

Lester shook his head.

"I believe you," Oates said, handing the reins of his horse to Lester. An aide had waved from the cabin, summoning the colonel. "But your friend did?"

"Someday perhaps I will tell you the story," Lester replied, as Oates brushed his trousers, readying himself for his audience with General Forrest. "But I would have gladly killed Rivens if given the chance."

"I imagine you would," Oates replied, and then strode for the cabin. A few minutes later, he returned, hurrying.

"I go with Longstreet," Oates said, taking the reins and swinging into the saddle. He extended a gloved hand.

"If we both survive, perhaps our paths will cross again."

"You know your path. I don't know mine."

"Alabama. You are to be sent south, as I said, to a prisoner of war camp. The commandant is a decent man, to the best of my knowledge."

"Where?"

"Not far from our first meeting." Oates looked Lester straight in the eye. "Cahaba."

The colonel saluted, and galloped away.

Chapter Ninety-Four

Tennessee River, October 1863

Jordon Hatcher wrapped the boy carefully in the sling. "You ready, Buck?"

"His name is Lester," Sally admonished the tall black man. "You're as bad as Jubal." She adjusted her son's tiny mittens as he tried to touch her breath vapor in the crisp dawn.

Jordon laughed softly, the deep musical rumbling Sally had sought. She loved the sound, as if it were a reminder from eons past that whatever life's hardship, there would always be goodness. Sally was ready for some goodness.

"Tha's why I call him Buck, for his papa. I can see Jubie in him plain as day." Jordon caught Sally's look. "Jes' like I can see Emma in you."

"You mean me in Emma?"

Jordon's rumble made her smile. "Same diffunce, Miss Sally," he said, holding the amiable infant as Sally gathered the sling around her shoulders. "Now gimme your foot, we'll put you atop this old fella."

He hoisted her onto the graying mule, the most mild-mannered of the three she had bought at a livery stable outside Wetumpka. Jordon reached for the shotgun leaning against a tree and passed it up to Sally. Northern Alabama wasn't as rabidly racist as the southern plantation land but there was still no way he would be seen holding a rifle in any populated territory. Even around Sandy Hill, Jordon or his sons would only hunt if Sally were nearby, so she could claim the weapons. Though his hair had gone white since Beulah's death, Jordon's keen eyesight at distance had made him as capable a hunter as his sons.

From their vantage on a flat rock outcrop, they could see a thin ribbon of the Tennessee River several miles north and a thousand feet below. On the southern riverbank, smoke curled from a small town.

"That's got to be Guntersville from the looks of it." Sally consulted the last of her maps, bought from the surveyor's office in Wetumpka upriver from the confluence of the Tallapoosa and Coosa rivers, which formed the Alabama. Wetumpka, on the Coosa, was the last steamboat stop up the river system from Mobile before a series of falls, gorges, and rapids made the next hundred and fifty miles impassable.

"You trust them with Black Fox?" Sally looked back to the cave where the Hatcher boys waited with Charity and the children. A white-haired Cherokee sat on his haunches at the cave entrance, a place he told Jordon his family used to hide during the Indian wars three decades earlier.

"Can't say. We're here on 'count of him; ain't led us astray."

"He still won't talk to me!" Sally grumped.

"You're white."

"So is Emma; he'll talk with her!"

Regardless of her repeated attempts, the old Indian remained mute with Sally, though he answered in broken English any question Emma posed. Sally had to admit her daughter was full of questions.

Jordon had found the old Indian begging in Wetumpka while Sally went to buy tickets for the stagecoach that mostly paralleled the river north to Greensport. There, the upper Coosa became navigable again and they could board another steamboat for Gadsden, two hundred upriver miles further north, not far from Georgia at the foot of the Appalachian watershed. Sally planned to disembark there and make the fifty-mile trek northwest over the stagecoach road that traversed a series of Appalachian ridges into the valley of the Tennessee.

Sally had variations on her story, depending on the level of curiosity shown to a single woman traveling with several slaves. She was either widowed, necessitating selling her property at the most advantageous locale—always someplace further on—or her husband had been wounded in East Tennessee and they traveled northward to search for the hospital where he lay suffering. Naturally, her slave men would bring him home for the proper, loving care only she could provide.

Sally knew her story was all too plausible. After two years of war, a dozen horrific battles and countless skirmishes, there was no shortage of widows for a thousand miles in any direction.

That story didn't impress the stationmaster, who questioned her closely about her plans with "them niggahs" he had seen disembarking from the steamboat that morning.

"You got papers?" he had demanded.

"The man that questions me will answer to my husband," Sally responded, with a practiced mixture of aloof disdain and prickly southern pride.

The stationmaster backed off. "You ought go to Anniston," he pointed to a wall map. "That foundry there, and ammunition works, too, both needs 'em. Everyone got to sacrifice, all due respect to your husband."

"So kind of you. I'll consider that," Sally lied, noticing the town was generally in the right direction—north—though on the east side of the Coosa and she wanted to stay west. She left the station before the man could pry anything more from her and returned to the riverside where the others waited, uncertain what to do.

Sally had found Jordon talking quietly to the old Indian, who from his wizened bronze complexion, high cheekbones, and sharp nose looked to be full-blooded. For the sake of appearance she acted imperious, pulling Jordon aside to quietly express her uncertainty. Under no circumstances did she want to get close to Anniston. Questions would only get sharper.

To Sally's astonishment, Jordon said they needed three mules, one for Sally, another for their belongings, and one to spare. He'd explain later. Despite misgivings, she took Jordon to the livery stable, bought the three animals he picked out, and by late afternoon, announcing to the livery owner her party was bound for Anniston, they set out. Five miles outside of Wetumpka, Black Fox stepped from a clump of underbrush, led them to a ford back across the Coosa, and continued directly onto the forested hillside west of the river.

When safely out of town, Jordon had explained that the old Indian subsisted on handouts and living off the land. For a price, Black Fox offered to guide Jordon north along a safe route to the wide river. From the Tennessee, they would be on their own.

While they were taking a huge chance, Jordon's instincts never wavered. Over the next several days, Jordon learned that none of Black Fox's family had survived the Trail of Tears. When his last child died of smallpox on the banks of the Mississippi twenty years earlier, he had left the remnants of his tribe, disappeared along the river ice, and walked home to live amongst the mountains in the old ways, wandering occasionally into civilization to beg or steal, whatever the opportunity. When the white men again started war, this time against each other, slaves started fleeing north. Black Fox knew the look of a runaway slave. He had already made the trek several times, not just to help the slaves but to vex the white men who had destroyed his family.

Traveling through densely wooded valleys he had known since childhood,

Black Fox displayed all the craft of a woodland animal, smelling the air, watching flights of geese, eagles, and hawks, listening for bird calls or deer barks to avoid humans of any kind. Several times he had taken them deep into mountain glens to avoid a Rebel cavalry or Home Guard troop, camping in thickets and caves as long as he thought necessary, sometimes for several days after a rain so the ground dried, making tracking more difficult. The Hatcher boys hunted. All the supplies were gone and they had taken nearly six weeks to travel two hundred miles, but now the wide river flowed only a few miles distant.

On the rock outcropping atop the Tennessee River Valley, Sally looked back at Black Fox. Emma had joined him, sitting cross-legged, mimicking the Indian.

"I hate leaving her," Sally said, as Jordon took the mule's reins.

"Isaiah and Daniel will watch 'em. We ought be back tonight."

After considering the best possible lie, she had decided to enter Guntersville as if looking for her soldier husband, reported wounded around Nashville. A single woman traveling with an old family slave was understandable, certainly if she carried the anxiety of her husband's fate.

"I hope this is the last time we have to ride," Sally complained, "though that Indian was right about these critters." The mules were steady and sure-footed on the mountain tracks traversing the undulating ridges of the Appalachian Mountains.

By mid-morning, Jordon and Sally walked into the town, heading for the river landing. They didn't draw much attention, as the townspeople seemed intent on their own business. Half the buildings were in ruins, blown apart or burned with only the chimneys left standing.

Directly below the river landing, a long low shed resonated with the sounds of a steam sawmill. An old, peeling sign on the roof advertised Gunter's Landing. Next to it, from another shed, a chorus of hammers and the steady slam of a steam pile driver reverberated across the valley. Sally and Jordon glanced at each other and then headed that way.

"Excuse me, sir," Sally called to a blacksmith pounding iron at a forge to make some part for a small, narrow barge being built by laborers close to the river. The pile driver snorted and puffed, raising its pile to drive oak logs into the embankment. A wharf was under construction, beside the charred remains of a previous structure.

"Can you tell me when the next steamboat arrives going downriver?"

The blacksmith held his hammer with a forearm the thickness of a tree limb. He was short, stout, and bearded but copper-skinned and wore his silver hair tied in a ponytail.

"No steamboat going down, missus. Yankees would sink her if Forrest didn't stop her first. Only thing on this river is barges, but they got to be small this time o' year."

"The river looks plenty wide," Sally observed.

"Muscle Shoals is downriver two miles, then you've got eighty miles of wet rocks. Why you want to know?"

"My husband's a prisoner in Nashville. I'm trying to get there."

"Go overland, through the lines," the blacksmith said. "They'll let you pass, though doubt the nigger can. If the Home Guard don't confiscate him the Rebs will."

"Jordon's been with me all my life," Sally drawled, "I couldn't leave him."

"Ever ask him how he feels 'bout that?"

Sally stared, uncertain. "Beg your pardon?"

"Never mind," the man snorted.

"You don't believe in our cause, sir?" Sally asked, doing her best to mimic a southern belle.

"You ain't been here before, have ya? North Alabama's not so trigger happy as you folks down south. Sending boys to die so rich planters can rock on their porch?" The man spit tobacco juice. "Let them sons of bitches work! Like I do! Now if you don't mind, I got things to do." He turned away and pumped the forge bellows.

Sally and Jordon glanced at each other.

"You own these works?" Sally asked.

The blacksmith stopped and turned to her, exasperated. He pointed to the sign. "My father founded this town. M'am, I got things to do. So if you please."

"Gunter?"

"John Gunter. He married my mother, daughter to Chief Bushyhead, the Paint Clan. That's what whites called him."

"What happened here? Looks like a big fire."

"You mean a big fight? Unioners shelled the town from across the river. Start a fire, ain't so easy to stop. Tell your folks down Mobile way that."

"Oh."

"'Cause the Rebels were here. Started the war, they did. Then just rode off after they got the place all wrecked."

Sally leaped. "How much for that barge?"

Gunter looked at her as if he hadn't heard right.

"That barge there," she pointed, "will it make it over Muscle Shoals?"

"Depends how high the river is. Better know what you're doing."

"How much?"

"It ain't done." Gunter's hammer hung loose. He appraised her, and then looked at Jordon, his eyes narrowing. "Black Fox brought you?"

Sally blanched. Despite herself she gulped, and then nodded.

"Figured. He was Paint Clan. Nothing left of 'em."

"Will you take fifty dollars?"

"Fifty Reb dollars ain't worth wiping my arse, beggin' your pardon."

Sally dismounted and walked directly to the man. She took a breath. "Fifty dollars gold," she said, speaking soft but clear in her Maine voice. "And the mules, too. Load her with enough lumber to build a shelter, a bag of beans, one of rice, smoked bacon if you can."

The blacksmith's eyes narrowed. "Where you from?"

"We're from Mobile. I was born in Maine. I'm going home. And if you so much as whisper that to a soul, I swear to God I'll shoot you dead. Begging your pardon, mister."

The blacksmith looked over at his men. Curious, they had stopped building the barge, but seeing Gunter's scowl, they quickly resumed hammering.

"You'll never make it."

"I meant what I said."

The blacksmith drew himself straight. "I got—I had—two sons. One went blue, the older; the young one—he was hotheaded—gone gray. Both of 'em with my mother now, smallpox took her in the '40s. Klaus come home shot to hell at Vicksburg; he joined a troop from Huntsville went with Sherman. A month later, three weeks back, Henry fell upriver at Chickamauga; Polk got him killed." The blacksmith swallowed and talked through his teeth. "Goddamned if I didn't bury 'em all 'count of them planters!"

Sally sucked a breath. "I ..." she stammered.

"Don't say nothin'!" The blacksmith looked away, as if he just wanted to throw his heavy hammer into the river. "There ain't nothin' to say."

"Will you?" Sally whispered.

"Will I what?"

"Sell me the barge."

"What kind of hut you want on it?"

"We'll take care of that. It'll look better if I leave with a load."

"To trade, you mean?"

"It'll give me a story, when I need one. The widow ..."

"Is your husband gone?"

"I don't know where he is."

The blacksmith looked them over, and decided. "Two more days, at dusk. Wait 'till after the men go, but don't tarry. I'll break 'em in two if they call the Home Guard—can't stand them scum. But get gone."

—⁓—

Two days later, at dusk, Sally left the mules and five ten-dollar gold pieces with Gunter and they set off in the gathering darkness, making a mile downriver before Jordon spotted a small campfire on the southern shore. Black Fox waited with the others, smoking geese he'd downed with the shotgun Jordon had left him. At dawn the following day, the Indian took the sweep and led them into the top of Muscle Shoals, water his people had run for thirty generations.

Though Black Fox knew the river, the barge wasn't nearly as nimble as a dugout canoe and they frequently grounded or bounced off the sharp rock sides of narrow chutes. Each night the Hatcher boys repaired the boat with a few hand tools Gunter had packed aboard. Deep into the series of rapids, they pulled into a secluded stream and camped for two days while the Hatchers made more repairs and built a false floor under which they could hide. A small hut barely tall enough to sit in went overhead, providing concealment and protection from rain or an early snowstorm.

Though the river was cold and thin ice formed overnight, Black Fox forbade fires except in the early fog of morning and then only to cook and smoke fish they had netted the night before.

Resuming downriver, the Hatchers stayed inside the hut as they passed a Rebel encampment on the south side. When a sentry hailed and then sent a musket ball overhead, Sally, her silhouette obvious in full dress and bonnet, sent a shotgun blast back, to the faint laughter of troops on shore.

In late afternoon of their fourth day, Black Fox smelled camp smoke from the northern shore. Steering for the southern bank he told Sally—having finally decided to talk to her, though she didn't know what she'd done differently—they would wait overnight and pass the Union encampment just before dawn, when there was just enough light to pick a route through the rocky riverbed.

That night a thunderstorm rolled in from the west, jammed up against the mountains, and wrung itself out over twelve hours. By dawn, the river had risen two feet. No longer passing through bony ground, the river pulsed and buckled through the last ten miles of Muscle Shoals.

At the first hint of dawn, Black Fox looked the river over and directed Jordon and his sons to rig a front sweep. They didn't get under way until well after dawn. Within moments of casting off, Black Fox yelled for Jordon to man the forward sweep, and they fought to keep the barge from slewing sideways in the current. Riding Muscle Shoals resembled surfing onto an ocean beach, and the barge quickly began to fill. In the hut, Charity held the children as Sally and the Hatcher brothers bailed with anything that would hold water. Black Fox and Jordon struggled to hold the barge in midriver, barely glancing at the large Union camp two hundred yards through the mist on the Tennessee shore.

The first shot was a light cannon round from the southern shore arcing overhead to explode in the Union camp. Their range established, a quick Rebel volley followed before the Union cannon erupted, shells sizzling through the rain. The sharp crack of rifle fire came from both banks as sharpshooters peppered the opposite shore. Black Fox ducked low, bullets whistling above and behind him. One round, then another, hit the hut with loud smacks.

Enraged, Sally appeared with the shotgun and sent a blast toward the Union lines.

"Stop shooting!" she screamed, her cry lost in the din. "We've got children aboard!"

The next rifle report was altogether different, a low, brutal echo. A Henry buffalo gun fired .50 caliber bullets the size of a man's thumb that could drop a one-ton bull in its tracks at half a mile. The marksmen missed forward a yard but his next shot tore a huge splinter off the sweep, ripping it from Black Fox's hand. A third round plowed right through the hut planking.

On her knees in the hut entry, Sally heard Lester cry out. She wheeled and saw her son through the dim light of the hut ten feet forward, sitting in Emma's lap and bleeding from a splinter that stuck from his cheek like a needle. Another inch higher and the boy would have lost an eye. The bullet had ripped Daniel's pantleg as he lay across Charity, shielding his wife and the baby.

The skirmish receded upriver, ending as abruptly as it had begun. Muscle Shoals' rocky moraine petered out and the river settled and doubled in width as the barge floated broadside to the river in the morning rain. From shore, the little wooden craft looked abandoned as it passed steamboat ports on either side of the river below the shoals.

Further downstream in late afternoon, a small red man took hold of the splintered sweep and gradually steered to an old abandoned river landing. In the cold rain, he jumped into knee-deep water, shoving the barge back into the current before wading ashore, carrying a shotgun above his head.

A woman crawled from the barge's hut, her dress drenched and hanging limp. The old Indian watched from the shallows as she steered back into the river. As the main current took hold she turned and, ripping off her bonnet, fluttered it in a forlorn wave, which he returned. Then, as if on signal, the woman turned back to the river and he walked from it, onto the overgrown, forgotten trail of the Natchez Trace, disappearing into the forest.

Chapter Ninety-Five

Philadelphia, November 1863

Near the crackling fire, Lucretia Mott gently rocked Truette, who sat on her lap, paying rapt attention.

"Listen my child and you shall hear ..."

Cora stood in the doorway, watching her child hang on every word the wizened Quaker woman read. A snow-white bonnet tightly encased the woman's silver hair and lined face.

"... of the midnight ride of Paul Revere."

The new stone fireplace drew splendidly, throwing welcome heat into the old living room. Two stonemasons, runaway slaves escaping from a North Carolina plantation, had rebuilt the crumbling colonial fireplace, replacing it with Pennsylvania bluestone.

Cora glanced again at the urn atop the mantle, a private look; she had told no one the urn contained several handfuls of ash.

"Did you understand all that?" Mrs. Mott asked the boy.

Truette nodded, smiling.

"What did you understand?"

He let himself down and padded to his mother, burying himself in the folds of her dress.

"Don't you go hiding behind my skirt! Go out now, and help Rufus with the firewood."

Rufus had come through the door from the woodshed with an armload, dumping it in the box beside the big Atlantic cook stove. Rufus looked at Edmonia as she stood at the stove stirring a large iron stew pot and was rewarded by a gleam in her eye, as if telegraphing what might happen later that night now that they had married.

Rufus winked at Truette and held out his hand. "Let's get us some more stove wood. Man's got to work to eat, don't you know?" Rufus laughed as the boy skipped to him, reaching for the man's hand. "And you's got to eat, seeing as how you gonna be one big man!"

A rare smile creased Cora's lips and she looked at William Still, who had stopped his interview with the runaway slave to watch. The fugitive slave, just arrived the night before, didn't know what to make of the easy banter and relaxed surroundings, though he instinctively knew the taut, Indian-boned black woman who rarely spoke was no one to cross. She ruled the house with the authority of a queen, but behind that dignity was the clear ferocity of a warrior.

"He'll talk again," Lucretia Mott observed.

Cora shrugged. "Can't say."

"Give him time. He understands everything."

Cora nodded; she knew that. Truette had not said a syllable since New York; his last word had been *Mommy!* just before she grabbed him. Both had barely escaped as the store's second floor collapsed in a crashing shower of flames. Three days—spent in the police station—had passed before the Union Army restored control. The draft riots had claimed the lives of over two hundred people, and eleven black men were lynched, but none of those numbers registered with Cora, nor did the fifty stores that had been burnt to the ground—save one. She had returned there dragging her son, who shook with terror as his mother climbed through the charred tangle of beams, sifting through mounds of ash until she found what she had come for.

The blackened stone shaped like a fish hung from her neck now. After one of the escaped slaves had drilled the stone, Cora looped a gold chain through and not removed it since, even as she bathed. No one would see the stone either, unless her husband returned, though there had been no word from nor of, Lester.

Cora noticed the flicker of delight between Rufus and Edmonia, who had fallen in love as easily as toppling off a park bench. Rufus returned to the house shortly after she and Lester had bought it from the widow, asking if they needed a house servant. Lester had balked, claiming Edmonia was more than enough. New York changed all that.

Letitia Still had met Cora and Truette at Union Station when they returned to Philadelphia. Cora was still so numb and traumatized she could barely function, while Truette remained absolutely mum. William Still and Rufus showed up at the Rabbit Lane house several hours later, and Rufus never left.

"Tell me," Lucretia Mott had not taken her eyes from Cora, "how do your medical studies proceed? Come, sit here with me." The Quaker woman motioned to the other rocking chair, also a product of a runaway slave, one of perhaps a hundred that had already passed through the barn Rufus had supervised building out back. In fact, it was much more dormitory than barn, another way station on the Underground Railroad.

"Entertain an aging woman with some new knowledge," Mrs. Mott directed.

Cora could hear the resumed murmurings of William Still in the kitchen, intent on cataloguing the story of every slave who passed through Philadelphia before he arranged their passage north. Cora's barn had increased their capacity to house fugitive slaves, hundreds of whom used the chaos of war and absentee owners to flee every state in the Confederacy.

"What you want to know?" Cora asked.

"What *do* you want to know."

Cora sighed, annoyed at the correction. Lucretia Mott simply stared, and Cora suddenly chuckled, knowing the woman knew of her annoyance and didn't care. "Yes m'am. I get a little tired is all."

"Women can't afford to get tired."

The back door slammed and Truette came into the living room, climbing directly into his mother's lap. Sucking his thumb, he nestled and immediately closed his eyes.

"Don't go sucking your thumb, True," she said, pulling his thumb from the boy's mouth. He immediately put it back in.

"Daddy would be telling you the same thing."

Truette opened his eyes and stared at his mother. Slowly, he withdrew his thumb and snuggled closer to his mother's chest.

Chapter Ninety-Six

Jordon Hatcher steered the battered barge as best he could, knowing he had to stop soon for repairs or they would simply disappear into the river. The barge lay so low in the water it was more raft than boat. Isaiah and Daniel had given up bailing and sat huddled on deck in the lee of the hut while Sally lay curled in a ball at their feet where she had collapsed at sunset the day before. Emma and little Lester slept with Charity and her baby, covered by the last dry blanket. Below deck, two feet of sloshing water had ruined the food and soaked their gunpowder.

Overnight, they had left the barge to the river, too exhausted to do anything but let the current take them where it would. In pitch darkness the rough water sounded terrifying and the barge had banged against several rocks, but each time had spun off and continued downriver.

Before daybreak the sky cleared, with a cold wind out of the northwest, the direction in which the stars told Jordon the river had turned. He began to lean into the sweep, steering for shore. At sunrise, smoke rose ahead and he resolved to stop regardless of which army or what kind of people inhabited the landing. The only other choice was to drown.

"Miss Sally," he gently shook her awake. "We comin' to a town. Got to stop 'count we hardly 'float. C'mon, we need you now." Jordon's voice took on a different timbre. "Daniel, Isaiah, roust yoreselves! One of you take 'hold the sweep!"

Sally got to her knees and blinked, trying to orient herself. Shivering uncontrollably, she looked a mess, standing barefoot with matted hair, her dress filthy and ripped. As Isaiah stumbled back to steer, Jordon hoisted Sally and enveloped her in a bear hug for warmth.

"What's that say?" He pointed to a sign on a building that stood on high stilts above the river. Several boats lay tied to the bank, one flying the U.S. flag. As they floated closer, Jordon could see it was a gunboat, bristling with cannon.

"Pickwick Landing," Sally read as her vision cleared.

The barge grounded in the mud below the steamboat landing. Daniel jumped ashore and tied the barge to a tree and helped Sally off, carrying her to dry land.

"Someone ought stay," Jordon said. "Isaiah."

"No."

"Me neither," added Daniel.

Sally didn't know what to say. Jordon gaped, shocked at his sons. Emma stood on deck holding Lester's hand, watching.

"Jes' need t' feel the earth under my feet," Daniel breathed.

"Jordon, get my bag." Sally was too tired to argue but she had come fully awake at the sight of her children. "We've got to eat. I'll find out where we are. Isaiah, give me a rifle. Daniel, take Lester; Emma, stay with Jordon. You too, Charity."

Charity shook her head. "No m'am, we're going with Daniel."

"Oh, for God sakes!" Sally exclaimed. "Just stay here 'till we get back!"

"Stay with me, child," Jordon agreed. "Ammunition's no good, Miss Sally."

"Well, give me the rifle anyways. We'll go down swinging."

The Hatcher boys helped Sally up a flight of stairs onto the low bluff where half a dozen old buildings comprised a small village. As they ascended, a blue-clad Union office came out of the gunboat wheelhouse and stared but said nothing.

A single cross street intersected the muddy track that paralleled the river for a hundred yards before ending in a tangle of trees. A tavern and the steamboat station office occupied the riverbank, while a motley collection of sagging wooden buildings faced the river. At the intersection, a rough-planked general store sprawled around the corner, and they headed in that direction. A few townspeople stared as they walked abreast, but Sally ignored them, expressionless, as if in a dream. Lester let out a fuss, wanting Sally to carry him, but she shushed the boy so harshly he turned away, burying his face in Daniel's shoulder.

Three splendid horses bearing shiny military saddles twitched their tails in the morning sun, reins slack to a hitching post in front of the general store. As they approached short steps that led onto a wraparound porch, the front door swung open and a soldier stepped out, holding it for someone coming behind. A Union officer strode onto the porch but abruptly paused, as shocked at seeing Sally and the Hatchers as they were to see the black officer. In a handsome blue uniform with gold epaulets, his Colt pistol jutting from a gleaming black holster, the man stopped in the act of pulling on spotless calfskin riding gloves. Clean-shaven, he was every bit as black as any of the Hatcher men, as was the soldier holding the door and a third trooper emerging.

"Who are you?" Sally blurted.

"Beg your pardon, m'am?" The officer stiffened. The third soldier stepped beside him, slightly raising a short-barreled shotgun, while the trooper at the door already had one hand on his sidearm. Individually and together, they looked as tough as any men Sally had ever seen.

"Are you a Union soldier?"

"Sergeant Hiram Douglas, 6th U.S. Colored Heavy Artillery, m'am."

The Hatcher brothers gaped.

"Who are *you*, m'am?" The sergeant's expression was solemn, almost severe. "And these men?"

"Sally Calhoun. Of Mobile ... and Orrington, Maine. We've come from upriver. These are my ..." Sally stopped, looking at the Hatcher boys. Suddenly her eyes misted.

"Your slaves?" Sergeant Douglas demanded. "If so, I declare them contraband by orders of General U. S. Grant, United States Army." He looked at Isaiah and Daniel directly. "If you were not free men before, you are now!"

"They've been free since the moment I bought them," Sally snapped. She caught herself. "Is this northern territory?"

"Indeed. We died to make it so. Shiloh lies not ten miles north."

Sally could hardly believe it and looked closely at the officer. Slowly, absorbing the news, she turned to Daniel, extending the rifle. "You hold it from now on. Give me Lester."

"Where is your destination, m'am?" Sergeant Hiram relaxed. He eyed the Hatcher brothers as if calculating.

"North," Sally replied, still marveling at events. "Philadelphia, maybe Boston ... I'm not quite sure."

"And you men?"

Daniel and Isaiah looked at Sally.

"They're coming with me," she said.

The sergeant regarded the brothers. "Is that your choice?"

"Huh?"

"We are making the rounds of towns in West Tennessee, enlisting men in my unit, activated June 20, last, upon our occupation of Corinth. Would you consider serving?"

"Us?" Daniel blinked. "Soldiers? I'm married."

"So am I."

"Our pa is below, on the barge," Isaiah looked from one soldier to the next. "We wuz gonna take Miss Sally downriver."

"I suggest, m'am," the officer tugged his gloves tight, "you go direct to Corinth, a half day west by this road, and a good one it is. Board the Memphis-Charleston railroad. Steamboats leave daily upriver from Memphis. You would make Pittsburgh in less than a week."

Birds twittered in the silence; a line creaked from one of the moorings on the river below. Finally, Sally turned to Isaiah Hatcher.

"Get everybody and whatever is left worth bringing."

Chapter Ninety-Seven

Alabama, December 1863

"Stop! Oh. for God's sake, stop just for one minute. Take me out and leave me to die on the roadside!"

Lester sat bolt upright, the dream still so vivid he whirled, unsure what was reality. Someone moaned; a faint light showed through the boxcar, the train swayed, slowing. He realized where he was.

Closing his eyes and swallowing, willing the nightmare of that twenty-seven-hour walk south from Gettysburg to wherever it would lurk until next time, Lester concentrated on his belly. He imagined kidney pie in Liverpool, steak and buttered biscuits in San Francisco, apple pie his mother used to make, buckwheat cakes and maple syrup Sally prepared at the woodstove in Maine, the eggs, grits, and bacon Cora served the boys in Philadelphia.

The delicious meals, so real he could taste every morsel, vanished as a jolt snapped him fully awake. The train began to move but stopped after a few feet. He waited, but only heard the sound of wind. The ache returned to his belly.

Lester wanted to salivate but had no moisture left. The water in the boxcar was putrid before it had been poured in a tub four days ago; now he could barely stand the stench, much less drink it, though some men did. A few hours later, they would vomit onto the shoulders of the men in front and another fight would break out. Put three hundred men in a forty-foot boxcar and keep them totally confined four days, something was bound to happen. At least a dozen prisoners were dead and beginning to smell. Packed like apples in a barrel as they were, the crowding offered only one benefit: no one had yet frozen to death.

Another lurch woke him awhile later and he could see by the shafts of light coming through the boxcar's sides it was late morning. The train coasted to a halt and prisoners stirred, hearing the shouts and sounds of civilization. As the car clattered over several sidings, the clamor grew louder, a racket of steam whistles, cracking whips, and braying animals. The car banged to a stop.

Nothing happened for another hour, and the light grew bright enough that men tried to peer out through the cracks. A young soldier pressed the planking and called out. "We're in some town!"

Someone screamed and soon the entire car erupted in shouts.

"Let us out! Water, for God's sake! Mercy! *Let us out!*"

The prisoners would have torn the car apart but had no room, nor energy. Suddenly the doors creaked and slid open, the noon sunlight so blinding everyone shielded their eyes.

"Git down!! Everybody out! Make trouble, you'll be shot dead!!" The drawls were so pronounced Lester immediately knew they were in the deepest South.

Prisoners shoved and pushed and Lester gingerly jumped down, careful to land solid. He was weak and stiff, his clothes hung on him; a broken ankle was good as a death sentence. After six months among Rebel soldiers he knew half of them were malnourished, so there would be little left to feed several hundred prisoners. Lester was one of the few not in uniform and certainly among the thinnest.

Most of the Union troops had been captured in Tennessee battles, though some came from Virginia and North Carolina. To Lester's surprise, their spirits were strong—though captured, they weren't beaten. Nearly three years of war had tempered all the combatants he had met, North and South. Nobility had shattered. This was a fight to the death, and the North was simply stronger. Every prisoner thought it a matter of time before the Union prevailed. Lester agreed the Rebels were ferocious, fearless fighters, but Southern railroads, food supplies, clothing, weapons, and horses were all inferior.

"Form ranks!!"

The prisoners shuffled to obey, mustering in an open field on the outskirts of a town. Mounted guards surrounded the troops, mostly old men, all armed with shotguns they pointed at the prisoners.

"March!"

The prisoners walked on a dirt road that was vaguely familiar to him, and Lester kept turning to find landmarks he might recognize. A wide river came into view as they left the town behind, but at one point the river did a wide sweep and looking back Lester saw a building he was certain he'd seen before. Then it came to him: the St. James Hotel.

"We just left Selma," he whispered to the man next to him. "I been here before; this is the Alabama River."

The news passed up and down the lines. Now Lester could pick out the landmarks. He knew this part of his journey was almost over.

That night, six prisoners made a break, running into the forest. Within an hour, bloodhounds had caught the scent and their baying kept the entire troop awake all night. Very late, the darkness exploded in distant howls. A burst of distant rifle fire followed. By dawn, three prisoners returned, each carrying a body, herded by the mounted posse. Guards, prisoners, and dogs watched as the captured escapees were summarily hung from a huge, weeping live oak and left swinging in the rising sun. As the day wore on, six more men collapsed in the heat and were left to die along the roadside.

Two days after leaving Selma, 264 prisoners shuffled down Capital Avenue to the stares of Cahaba residents, gawking as if these men were strangers from the moon. They were marched past the emporium where Jubal had bought Beulah Hatcher's bright fabric, and the cotton chute leading to the river.

Just beyond rose a high stockade.

"Well, Jubal, you son of a bitch," Lester hocked and spit though there was little spittle to it, just brown, nasty bile. "I'm back."

Chapter Ninety-Eight

Rufus and William Still decorated the Christmas tree while Edmonia and Letitia Still supervised preparations for dinner. Several men attended a large pig roasting in the field out back, keeping watch on a dozen children laughing and playing kickball. Suddenly, Edmonia turned and hurried toward the barn, and the women chuckled, remembering sensitive stomachs in the first trimester of their pregnancies.

Cora accepted the bustle and cheer of the proceedings as she helped with the chores of table setting and making sure all was prepared for the Christmas dinner. But beneath her pleasant demeanor a dispassionate heart watched, as if she were a spectator. James Pennington and Henry Highland Garnet discussed politics and the coming election campaign, while Truette toddled around trying to pull things off tables, generally unable to keep his mind on anything for more than thirty seconds though he still would not utter a word. Cora had given up trying to corral the boy and had just directed everyone to "make sure he doesn't break nothin'."

The door chimes sounded and she answered the door to welcome Lucretia and John Mott. Soon the house was a babble of conversation and laughter, the antics of children and squabbles of adolescents, a vibrant mix of accents and colors, opinions and knowledge, a human celebration of living and the joy of Christmas.

Cora did her best to be part of it, though she felt little joy. Sometimes she wondered if the light had gone from her life. At night, alone in bed, she would stir and touch herself as Lester had, missing him with an ache that left her pillow drenched in tears. But during the day at school she remained stoic and cool, unflappable even amidst dying men or terrible surgeries gone awry. Both the teachers at the Medical College and physicians at Satterlee Hospital had come to recognize her intelligence and ability. Cora carried herself with regal dignity, but they all knew she could spring into action in an emergency, still calm as a summer dawn regardless of the crisis.

The house at Rabbit Lane had become a gathering place of sorts, always a temporary home to a dozen or more runaway slaves, while students from the college and nurses at Satterlee often showed up for readings or discussions on emancipation, medicine, suffrage, politics, women's rights, and religion. Cora had been frugal, mindful of Lester's admonition to be careful with money—she had learned enough numbers to budget a hundred dollars per month for the family, figuring that way she had enough to raise the children until they were on their own.

Nor was she too proud to accept contributions from William Still and others in the Philadelphia community who knew and admired her character and sacrifices. Cora used that money for the souls passing through.

William Still often visited, interviewing escaped slaves. Though he did not speak of Lester's loss, nor of the New York horror, word had filtered through. Cora's strength simply drew people; she provided everything she could and asked for nothing.

A commotion at the back door preceded the entry of men bearing steaming plates piled with roast pork. Children crowded inside, lining up at the slate sink to wash their hands as the women put out heaping bowls of yams, potatoes, peas, and tubs of gravy for each of the several tables, adults in the dining room and children in the kitchen, where Lucretia Mott gave the adolescents strict instructions to keep order. Letitia Still opened the oven door and smells of fresh biscuits filled the house.

Soon thirty people held hands, bowed their heads, and listened as Henry Highland Garnet gave thanks.

"Our Heavenly Father, we ask of you this day your blessing as we, the children of your creation, do solemnly gather to honor and praise this day of your son's birth, who gave his only earthly life so that we may live forever in your grace ...

"Bless the children here, and those who have fled oppression and subjugation that they might live as free men and women, as you intended all humanity to live ...

"Bless our beloved president, as he toils to vanquish the evils of slavery and the heinous acts of those who would enslave us ...

"Bless this bountiful repast, that it may nourish our bodies with its abundance and our souls with its evidence of your munificence ...

"Bless all those who may not partake of your glory, the loved ones missing, lost—those gone to live with you forever ...

"We pray you will protect those we know of not ...

"And we ask your blessings for this good woman whose home we share and who has welcomed those among us who for the first time may experience the joy of your son Jesus Christ in the full measure of freedom ...

"We give thanks in your name …"

As one, the entire assembly intoned, *"Amen."*

After several moments of silence, the hubbub of conversation resumed, children laughed, and cutlery clattered as serving bowls emptied and people dug into a truly bountiful Christmas feast.

From her place at the head of the table, Cora rose to fill a bowl of green beans as the door chimes sounded again. Rufus, closest to the living room, scuttled to answer. Puzzle expressions and shrugs were shared at the tables—no one else was expected. Cora had her back to the dining room door when the conversation suddenly stopped. Startled, she spun around.

Jordon Hatcher held his hat in one hand and cradled a small, wide-eyed boy in his other arm.

Cora dropped her serving bowl.

"Miss Cora," Jordon nodded, tears already staining his cheeks. He turned slightly, to a thin, pale, drawn woman who stepped into the dining room and the little girl peering out from behind her dress, both bundled against the December cold.

"Well," Sally sighed, pulling her shawl back and leaning against the doorjamb, "we made it."

Chapter Ninety-Nine

Havana, January 1864

"Señor Norton?" The Cuban customs official looked over Jubal's forged British passport, having no firm idea what a man from Wales should look like. "*Quál es su trabajo?*"

"*Azúcar,*" Jubal replied, knowing a sugar trader landing in Havana was hardly strange. With a flourish, the custom official scrawled his initials and waved Jubal on.

Finding an inexpensive room overlooking the harbor, Jubal emptied his single bag onto the flimsy cot and snapped open his German telescope to examine every ship at anchor. In Melbourne he had spent three weeks looking for the right vessel—owned by a neutral country with no interest in the American conflict that was bound for a port somewhere in the Caribbean. After walking the dockside taverns and questioning local stevedores, he had decided it safer simply to keep watch, so he bought the finest telescope in Melbourne. Finally, he had found a Dutch barkentine bound for Amsterdam via Rio de Janeiro and Havana. The trip would be long, nearly four months, almost twice the time it had taken the fast clipper out of London to reach Melbourne.

Jubal hadn't minded the voyages and kept to himself. Relieved to be simply a passenger, he felt no responsibility as first the clipper, then the bark, weathered the harsh Southern Ocean weather. To his unexpected pleasure, the clipper had an extensive library and he read voraciously, particularly American authors. Every volume aboard by Hawthorne, Dana, Thoreau, and Emerson, came into his cabin. A traveling Jesuit had given him a Bible, which he read and then reread twice more. Most intriguing was a recently published book by an Englishman, Charles Darwin. *On the Origin of Species* and the Bible were the only two books in his bag now, along with his drawing quarto, a change of clothes, and his pistol. A derringer always occupied his pocket, as did a stiletto his boot.

In Melbourne, he had bought a book locker and scoured the local bookshops, buying volumes by a Frenchman, Victor Hugo, Greek classics, and treatises on the Roman and Persian empires. Having the time, and no inclination to be social, he spent long hours in the new library delighting in the science texts of Copernicus, Kepler, and Tycho Brahe before embarking to South America.

Six months of science and literature, without one substantive human conversation beyond the weather, had stretched him far beyond the confines of Liverpool or the distant American war. When his eyes tired of reading he sketched anything that struck his fancy: seascapes, horizons, passing ships, birds, other passengers or sailors at work, all coming alive as the latent talent Eleanor Creesy had encouraged became a developed skill. As his hand stroked the cotton pages of his quarto, Jubal felt as if Sally watched, commenting on his interpretations, needling occasionally just so he didn't become too vain, 'like me!' He could hear her laughter.

The reading and drawing filled his days and evenings, a distraction and attempt to forestall the crushing loneliness he experienced thinking of his children. Though he did not regret his choices and accepted their consequence, the fervor and patriotic certainty that had driven him to Liverpool drifted from weariness toward ambivalence as the sea miles fell astern.

Six weeks outbound from England, the emotional drift came into stark relief when the clipper rounded Cape of Good Hope into the Indian Ocean. On deck for a break from what he had begun to think of as his studying, and pensive with the musing of *Civil Disobedience,* he spotted a distant sail briefly, far to leeward, closer to the unseen African shoreline. Weather had been foul with evening coming on and Jubal couldn't be certain, but he'd have bet a substantial portion of the English pounds in his cabin that the shadowy silhouette he strained to identify through the mate's telescope was the CSS *Alabama*.

She had vanished into the night, leaving him to wonder how much more of men's effort and livelihoods Captain Semmes had destroyed in the name of freedom, and of the vessels beyond the horizon on which the sea wolf would soon feed.

Three days after arriving in Havana, Jubal made a morning scan of the harbor and spotted a small, jerry-rigged longboat sailing into the bay, overloaded with sailors. Donning a newly purchased flat-brimmed hat and light coat, he set out for the quay, his dress and nut-brown tan making him indistinguishable from Spanish traders frequenting the wharves.

Standing at a discreet distance, he watched as the Cuban custom officials questioned the longboat helmsman as he came broadside to the wharf.

"We been sunk," the captain called. "Damned Yankees fired on us, we was fishing! Burned to the waterline, we were! Had three boats and this is all we's got left!"

The Cubans talked among themselves in Spanish but Jubal turned away. The accent was Cajun and these sailors were no more fishermen then he was. A blockade-runner, he thought, caught by a Union frigate, which would likely have forced a captured vessel into port and seized the cargo as contraband. The privateers had either fought and lost or tried to outrun the frigate and failed. The Union blockade had indeed tightened, confirming reports Jubal had read in Melbourne.

The captain's fairy tale gave him an idea, and he set out for the fishing village at the far end of the harbor. Rather than risk running the blockade into Mobile, Jubal went looking for a fisherman who could land him in Matamoros, at the mouth of the Rio Grande in Mexico. He patted his breast pocket, where he kept the folded note from Sally and the family photograph, both now almost in shreds: *"Come home."*

"I'm comin'," Jubal muttered to Havana harbor.

Chapter One Hundred

Philadelphia, March 1864

Sally stepped from the carriage she had taken from Union Station and swept little Lester into her arms. The little boy had seen her through the window at Rabbit Lane and come running, squealing as he skipped across the lawn. Emma had heard him and came flying down the stairs hard on the heels of her brother, their cousin Truette close behind.

"Have you behaved?" Sally demanded of her children, "and listened to Aunt Cora and Edmonia? You'd better have!" Her smile belied her tone, and the children pawed through her purse and luggage looking for the presents they knew their mother had brought.

Emma pulled out the hinged chess set and turned it in her hands, puzzled, but before she could ask her mother what it was for, Truette snatched the box and dumped its contents on the ground.

"Truette!" Sally admonished, but Emma yanked the set back and belted him in the head. In seconds, the two were wrestling on the ground, and Sally had to hand her son to Edmonia to pull off Emma, who was already rubbing Truette's face in the grass. Edmonia, obviously pregnant, parked young Lester on her belly; both marveled at the sudden mayhem.

Freed of his attacker, Truette bounced up and flung himself back at Emma just as Cora arrived, striding from the house. As unceremoniously as if she were picking up a sack of flour, she grabbed her son by the hair, hauled him a few feet away, and gave him a solid whack on the rump before ordering him to his room upstairs.

Truette stared at Emma, his fists balled tight, but then wheeled and ran into the house.

"It was his fault!" Emma declared.

"If you played with him," Sally replied, "he might be friendlier."

"I'm not playing with him until he talks! He can. I know he can!"

"How do you know?" Sally asked, bemused.

"'Cause! He talks in his sleep."

Cora nodded. "She's right, he does."

"Well, help me pick up these chess pieces," Sally directed. "Buck, you help, too." Though she had always resisted using her son's nickname, Sally changed her mind when Cora had immediately smiled, a delighted, full-faced blossom, the first time she heard Jordon Hatcher address the boy that way.

"Yes indeed," Cora chuckled, "Buck. Tha's what we called Jubie."

Somehow it made Jubal closer, though Sally still had no idea if her husband was even alive. One letter a year earlier from Mobile was all that she had heard. Increasingly, she fought between letting him go forever and holding onto his memory. The hoping had become too painful, and finally she had felt herself scarring, though each night she kissed the wooden albatross that lay on the nightstand beside her bed.

"Where's the kings?" Sally asked, after they'd picked up the pieces. William Still had taught her to play and she thought it would be good for the children to learn, though she admitted the complexity that made her head hurt would probably bore them in minutes.

Cora chuckled; Emma and Sally stared at her.

"Truette!" Emma wailed, and ran for the house.

"That little bastard," Sally laughed, balling her fists as the boy had.

"Welcome home," Cora handed Sally's bag to Rufus, who had come in from the back where'd he been supervising several runaways chopping and putting in the next winter's firewood. "Supper's ready. Come on in and tell me about Washington."

"I went to New York," Sally said, surprising Cora, who had put her on the Washington train five days earlier.

"You got some explaining to do."

"I made us some money," Sally said.

⁓

The children were asleep and the house quiet when the women finally sat in the rockers before the fireplace with their tea.

"You were right," Sally began, taking a long sip. "Ohh, isn't this delicious? Makes me think of our first trip. I got mad at Jubal in China … remember …?"

Cora waited.

"I miss Jordon," Sally sighed. Jordon Hatcher had stayed in Philadelphia only long enough to see Sally settled and then set out to rejoin his sons and Charity at the army camp in Tennessee. Daniel's wife had refused to leave her husband, immediately finding work with the washerwomen doing the troops' laundry.

"Those boys be doing what they should, enlisting," Cora replied. "Now what ain't you tellin' me about Washington?"

"General Meigs wasn't expecting me, and his staff said I'd have to make an appointment. So I just walked into his office."

"I bet you did."

"I stood in front of him—he was looking at some papers, it's not like I was interrupting anything—and said Lester Norton's my brother, that I hadn't come from Mobile to wait to see him, Mr. Meigs, that is, and we'd been partners, Lester and I. Now I had to support our children, his and yours and mine. So I told him about our resources in Liverpool—didn't mention Jubal, didn't think that a good idea—and said I would do just what you said Lester was doing, buying supplies for the army. But that I would buy them and resell, and he owed us that much."

"Did he look at you like you was crazy?"

"*Were* crazy. Yes. And I admit, maybe it was a bit bold."

"You don't say?"

Sally wagged a finger. "I know you's being sarcastic."

"*Are* being. What'd he say?"

"Well, he was pleasant enough. Said if I could purchase shoes, blankets, and cloth at a particular quality and price, for these quantities—he showed me all the specifications—he'd buy them. So off I went to Union Station, up to Lowell, Massachusetts, and Lewiston, Maine, stopped in New York first to see John Griswold and get introduced to the New York bankers again, went north and through around ten or eleven factories, and signed the contracts. I've got to make sure everybody delivers, but two percent on a hundred thousand dollars ..."

"We didn't have no hundred thousand dollars!"

"We've got fifty."

"Fifty ain't a hundred."

"*Isn't*. I borrowed fifty from John Griswold. So do the figuring."

Cora calculated. "Ummm ... two thousand?"

"Well, yes. But I split the commission with Griswold, fifty-fifty."

"One thousand, then?"

"Nope. On his fifty, he gets one percent: five hundred dollars. Fifteen hundred for us."

"Where'd you learn to do this stuff?"

Sally looked surprised. "Jubal and Lester—that's what they did." She sipped her tea. "Lord knows if they could, we can."

"That will hold us awhile."

"Nope. We're going to buy land."

"We are?"

"Weren't you paying attention last Sunday? Lucretia Mott said the Friends were going to start a college. A woman's college, Swarthmore, didn't she call it? What's that mean?"

"Mrs. Mott said it was someplace in England, where the Friends began. Weren't you paying attention?"

"Let's find out where they're going to put it and buy as much land around it as we can. A woman's college? That's going to grow."

"How do you know?"

"Because we're going, and half this country's women are like us."

―

Three weeks later, Sally came into the Rabbit Lane kitchen after dinner waving a document. "Here's the deed," she cried, and then stopped. Cora had just arrived a few minutes before, her dress streaked with blood. "What happened to you?"

Cora swiped her hair back, looking exhausted. "The hospital ..." She handed her coat to Rufus and slumped in a rocker, staring vacantly into the low fire. "I don't think he were eighteen. We took both legs, one arm. He woke from the ether, picked his head up, looked at hisself, put his head back down ... and died." She sighed. "Can't blame him a mite."

Sally took a deep breath, put the deed on a table and went into the kitchen cookstove and prepared tea. Joining Cora, she settled onto a rocker and stared at the fire. "When will this madness end?"

"We got land?" Cora asked.

Sally nodded. "Thirty acres, next to the Benjamin West house. That's going to be the first building."

"Well's to say ..." Cora mumbled, staring back at the fire. The front door chimes rang, repeatedly. She started, spilling her tea.

The door chimes rang again, urgently.

In moments Rufus strode past to the front vestibule and pulled back the peephole, examining the visitor. He opened the door and they heard a familiar breathless voice.

"Cora Norton, is she here?"

A moment later, Eleanor Creesy swept into the room.

Sally and Cora had both turned, mouths open, dumbfounded.

"Sally?" Mrs. Creesy exclaimed. "Isn't it? What are you doing here?"

"I'm ..." Sally stuttered.

"In a minute! Cora this came, first thing this morning!" Eleanor waved a telegram. "General Meigs wasn't in—I guess my address is the last one the war office had, the telegraph people. I had to come ... the express trains ..."

Cora stared, swallowing, her face ashen.

Eleanor Creesy's eyes teared.

"Lester's alive! They found him!"

Chapter One Hundred One

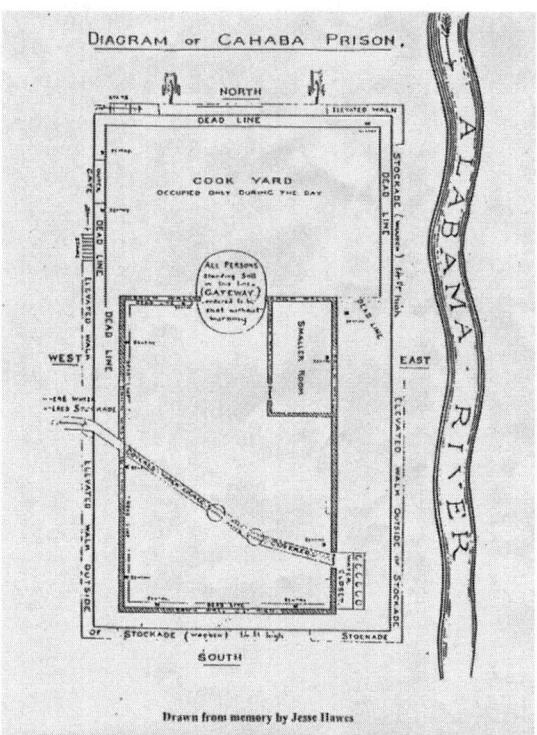

"Norton, what's the date?" someone asked in the dark. By the accent, Lester recognized one of the New York troopers who had never been out of the city before being drafted. Among the prisoners, it was general knowledge that Lester could determine the calendar within four or five days by the night sky.

"Around the end of March," Lester replied, annoyed that he'd lost precious time on the bunk to sleep. Orion was low in the southern sky after sundown; Lester knew it was close to April but didn't know the exact date, nor did it really matter, except the ground would be warmer as spring lengthened. On alternate nights he could sleep on a plank bunk, but there was only four hundred bunks for nearly seven hundred prisoners. The winter earth stayed so cold stronger men sometimes slept on sicker, weaker men too feeble to protest.

Breathing deep and regular, as a *sadhu* had demonstrated to him a lifetime ago in Calcutta when Abel Godbold had died, Lester tried to concentrate on nothing. With a start, he remembered the holy man sitting near a gutter, explaining that his English came from service in the British Raj until those troops mutinied and were slaughtered. Imprisoned, the man found solace in meditation and religion, later to adopt the holy life.

Shall I become a priest? Lester wondered, and then dismissed the notion, trying to will himself asleep.

Smiling suddenly, he stirred in the darkness. An image of Cora's nipple had come to mind and savoring the image, he exhaled long and low, tracing his finger gently around the dimpled silver dollar–sized chocolate as her nipple hardened, rising full and rich, pulsing in his mouth as he …

"Bastard!" Lester swiped at the rat nibbling a piece of corncob off his heel. He kicked out and caught two more before he brushed his feet clean so they'd bother someone else. One more night, he thought, gazing overhead at the dark roof. Make it through one more night, and then make it through one more day.

"Think Henderson'll keep his word?" the New Yorker whispered.

"Shut the fuck up!" another trooper snarled.

"Your mother can suck my cock, asshole!"

"Too bad your sister ain't here, she'd hump us all!"

"I think so," Lester muttered.

The troopers quieted. Even in the dark, prisoners within earshot strained to hear. Norton was a man you paid attention to. He'd organized the hunger strike to get the commandant's attention, demanding the water now bisecting the prisoner stockade in an open stream—freighted with garbage, dead rats, and pig, dog, cat, horse, and occasionally human shit, so fetid the prisoners relied on rainwater to drink—be piped in clean, or they would simply starve themselves.

Lester didn't know if the other men were strong enough should their bluff be called, but he was. Even if he could close his eyes and hold his nose long enough to swallow, there was little sense in drinking water that would be dysentery in the time it took to go from his mouth out his ass.

Commandant Henderson agreed and promised to do his best, though he had little control. A decent man, Henderson managed a prison camp that flooded in spring rains, had twice as many occupants as he had food to feed them—and that only rancid bacon or pork fat, bug-infested peas, and moldy cornmeal, more crushed cob than grain.

Lester had heard the commandant was a former minister, and he snorted at the irony, a man of God in charge of hell on earth. "He said he'd sent those telegrams for us to be exchanged. He probably wants to get rid of us before another trainload comes in."

"Think more's comin'?" New York asked.

"This war isn't done," Lester replied, rolling over.

Chapter One Hundred Two

Dropping to his haunches, Jubal sipped, looking upriver and down. The Mississippi was frigid from snowmelt, running fast and nearly a mile wide. Overhead, a star—it must be Rigel, he thought—flickered through, but the rest of Orion wasn't bright enough to break through the misty fog hanging over the river, nor could Jubal see the eastern shore. A light showed in midriver and he watched for ten minutes as the dark shadow of a gunboat steamed past and disappeared around a bend, spewing boiler cinders into the night that reminded him of phosphorescence at sea.

He looked around the landing where a small stream barely the width of a house entered the enormous river. Committing the site to memory, he rode south four miles and into Vidalia, heading for the inn.

Jubal had traveled nearly a thousand miles from the Matamoros ferry on the Rio Grande, first on the "cotton trail" from Brownsville to San Antonio by stagecoach, then over the old El Camino Real to Natchitoches in Louisiana and on to Vidalia, opposite Natchez on the Mississippi River. Employing a passable Welsh accent—as much as anyone in South Texas could recognize one—he had used his forged John Norton passport whenever necessary, kept to himself, and continued almost nonstop, never removing the leather vest he'd had made before leaving Havana.

Hidden under a tailored coat he had also designed to mimic the latest London fashions, the vest held an inner lining securing several dozen gold coins. Though the vest felt like carrying rock, Jubal had it made to serve as his personal bank and shield. Rumors of Union troop movements had been rampant, and bandits and deserters prowled the countryside. On many of the runs, the drivers asked Jubal to sit up top, cradling a shotgun with other armed passengers. The stagecoach became a galloping battlewagon.

After a night in Vidalia and the first bath he'd had in a month, Jubal bought the finest horse he could find and a Spencer repeating rifle to join the two new pistols he had purchased in San Antonio. Though no one had challenged his story—yet—he could feel the tension grow at every stage stop closer to the big river, which still shielded most of Texas from the Union Army.

The innkeeper had been blunt.

"You be foolish to travel yoreself t'other side the river. Natchez ain't been burnt but the delta is crawling with Yankees. Sherman burnt Meridian, Corinth's gone; never know what's gonna happen. Fellow git himself killed hardly askin'. How come you're set on it, Mr. Norton?"

"I dare say, it won't be a problem, what?" Jubal sniffed. "I'm hardly a combatant. I shall do some illustrations of the countryside, write articles for *The Sunday Times*—you've read it, of course, published since you had the bloody cheek to revolt—and generally have a go. I'm not about to have a few piddly horsemen put the willies up me!"

The innkeeper looked at him with such incomprehension that Jubal was hard-pressed to keep a straight face.

"Just put me ashore somewhere quiet, good man! Where shall that be? To whom shall you to direct me? A spot of gold coin to the good, isn't it?"

"Go straight 'cross to Natchez, then. Ask anyone in town—they'll tell you where to go. Where are you goin', anyway?"

"I'll just have to follow my nose, good fellow. Now be so kind as to find me a ferryman, first thing day after tomorrow, before sunrise. An extra guinea for the right man!"

Two days later Jubal sat astride his horse, a tall black mare the livery stable owner had called Henrietta, and waited at the landing. Healthy, with good feet and young enough to still be lively in the morning, Henrietta had quieted and enjoyed the oats he'd given her, sniffing and nuzzling him for more. He had ridden through the town as the first roosters crowed and made the landing before the boatman arrived. Dawn purpled the eastern sky and a low mist hung over the river, the best conditions to cross. Sound would be muffled, and the low barge, only big enough for a few men and horses, would stay hidden. Jubal planned to skirt Natchez if could and make directly overland through cropland for the piney woods. Though he didn't know the country, traveling by the sun and stars was second nature. If accosted, lies or his weapons would decide the issue, but he planned to stay as far from the main roads as possible.

The resolve to be home had hardened. In San Antonio, he had learned that four months earlier the British had indeed seized the ironclad rams he, James Bulloch, and Charles Piroleau had worked so hard to build: *El Toussan* and *El Monassir*. Jubal scoffed at the memory, the perfidy rankling. He could imagine the crushing disappointment that Bulloch must be feeling, though Jubal knew the man would consider it only a battle lost, not the war.

From the cool smell of spring dawn and raucous cries of birds by the thousands, a sense of home came stronger. Gee's Bend lay only 250 miles east as the crow flew—a week if he didn't push Henrietta hard, three days if he was willing to ruin her. Jubal knew of the country by story and tale—it was mostly old Choctaw territory, sparsely settled, and other than connecting roads and the Mobile and Ohio railroad line, it would be mostly woodlands except in the Pearl and Tombigbee bottomlands, the only two rivers of any size before he hit the Alabama.

The first ten or fifteen miles might be chancy. Getting out of Natchez without encountering a Union sentry was unlikely. He would just have to talk his way through. But he felt certain that if he tried to run the Union blockade and got caught, they'd eventually learn his identity. Then, without doubt, his association with the CSS *Alabama* meant the gallows.

Henrietta's ears perked forward and she looked up the small stream. From the overhanging trees, a small barge appeared with an old man at the sweep. Jubal knew instantly he'd have to work hard or they'd be far downriver before making the eastern bank.

"Are you alone?" Jubal affected his accent.

"I'm 'nough."

"Quite the powerful current, wouldn't you say?"

"Sweeps the bend and snaps up a'gin, midstream," the old-timer replied. "Bring that nag on—tie 'er gud."

Jubal dismounted and led Henrietta, despite her reluctance, onto the barge, enticing her with another handful of oats.

"Where you from?" the old man asked after a time. He handled the long sweep with skill, quartering the barge into the current. Jubal had lent a hand, watching the water ripple, swirl, and spin. Though the river was full, the broad bend snapped the current like a whip, becoming more pronounced in midriver, until the barge actually rode the current *upstream*.

"Jolly good!" Jubal exclaimed, impressed by the boatman and enjoying his own pantomime. "From Cardiff, in Wales."

"Thought them was a fish."

"Whales are very big fish, indeed! Wales—no *h*, mind you—is a country to the west of England. British Isles, don't you know? Now then, where shall we land?"

"Under the hill, if'n you want to meet Yankees, down below if'n you don't." The old man looked at Jubal, expressionless.

"No," Jubal replied, feeling a bit foolish. Perhaps the accent was transparent. He stared at the old man, then brought out his shortened shoulder pistol, checked that every cylinder had a cartridge and did the same with the Colt on his hip before drawing the repeating rifle from its scabbard and loading six shells from a box in his saddlebags.

"Got any baccy?" the old man asked.

Jubal reached back into his saddlebag and brought out tobacco and a magnificent briarwood bulldog pipe he had found on his only trip to Cardiff.

"Lemme see that," the boatman said, admiring the pipe. "A beauty—fellow made that knew his trade." He hitched an arm over the sweep, pulled a handmade corncob pipe from his ragged coat and expertly filled and lit his smoke.

"Like you know yours," Jubal remarked, preparing the bulldog.

"Were me," the boatman said, "I'd come off, make south 'long the river 'bout half mile 'till she starts gettin' wet. Not too far—that nag'll bog. Head directly into the sun, follow 'er just as she rises 'till above the treeline, and go directly north. Yo'll be beyond most o' them Yankee camps. Go past Forks of the Road, keep goin' onto the 'ol Trace, heads north 'n east. Me, I'd keep to 'er a day, maybe two—ain't no one uses that no more. In the day, I was young, went to Nashville more 'n once all the way. Natchez Trace ain't what it was then ..."

The boatman examined the river. "Goin' slack and then'll pick up quick."

Jubal could see vague outlines of steamboats, gunboats, barges, and assorted river craft as they slowly drifted past Natchez Under-the-Hill. Atop the bluff, he could just make out the roofs of majestic mansions that fronted the river.

A half-mile south of town the boatman steered into a mudflat at the base of the sloping bluff and tossed a hook into the trees to hold the barge fast. Jubal dropped the small gate and led Henrietta into the shallows and out, tying her while he fetched the hook.

"How might you be returning, my good fellow?" Jubal asked.

The old man regarded Jubal, his eyes twinkling.

"Land the other side, break 'er down, sell the wood 'n walk home." He held out his hand and watched, eyes widening, as Jubal dropped a gold coin into his crinkled, dirty palm. The old man mouthed the coin, his face splitting in a toothless grin.

"Keep 'em loaded, Whaleman."

Jubal tossed him the hook and shoved the barge back into the current. Reaching into his vest pocket, he flipped the old man a second coin.

A sentry did stop him outside town but it was a desultory order; the man was bored and sleepy. Union troops had taken Natchez a year earlier without a fight and there had been no conflict since. Jubal produced his British passport, explained he was lost, and asked directions to the commanding officer's quarters. He obediently turned north and let Henrietta walk slowly for Liberty Street, the main road into Natchez. They paused at Forks of the Road, an intersection known all over the south where slaves had been sold for nearly a century at one of the largest slave markets in America. A collection of rough wooden warehouses occupied the land where the road broke into a Y. Three stately mansions lay within a few hundred yards, easy hailing distance to the slave market. Jubal stopped Henrietta out of the Union sentry's sight.

Tens of thousands of humans had been sold on the very spot. Rights to own and market, buy, sell, and command these slaves—forever—had propelled half a million white men to fight to the death over two thousand miles of countryside and nearly every ocean on earth.

Jubal spurred Henrietta. Startled, she broke into a gallop. Quickly, he reined her back, not wanting to be conspicuous, and put the mare into a lope that ate the last half-mile to the woodland cut, now almost overgrown.

This lane had first been trampled by a few thousand years of buffalo herds migrating to grazing lands and salt licks four hundred miles north in Tennessee. Later, Indians had used the buffalo "trace" and stitched it into a trail that thousands of fur traders and settlers had also used. It had been the only road that linked the original American colonies with the Gulf of Mexico. Pioneers had walked back to Kentucky and Virginia after floating their keelboats down the Ohio and Mississippi Rivers. With the coming of steamboats and railroads, long stretches of the Natchez Trace had become irrelevant and were abandoned, but the land had not yet entirely reclaimed the deep rut left by millions of footsteps.

Without a look back, Jubal and Henrietta disappeared into the brush and onto the narrow but distinct trail, finally slowing to a walk, becoming just two more wary animals in the surrounding forest.

After four nights, Henrietta was hungry and exhausted. Jubal had held to the Trace for two days and then struck out overland, due east, crossing the Pearl River the evening before. The spring woodland had been greening but was open enough for Jubal to see a wolf pack stalking them until he pulled the repeating rifle and shot three, including the big male, in quick succession. At night the screams of panthers had kept him feeding the fire until daybreak, and the mare was too spooked to graze much. Then the bear attacked, almost costing Jubal his horse when Henrietta nearly tore her mouth apart trying to pull away from the bit.

Jubal had stopped at midday in a clearing to roast a haunch of the wolf he'd carried for two days, figuring the blood smell would deter others—and it might have, though it also probably attracted the bear. He had tied Henrietta off with a double length of stout leather to a large tree, leaving her plenty of slack to graze. If the tree had been smaller, the mare would probably have uprooted it when she smelled the bear, coming in fast from downwind. Henrietta screamed and bucked frantically, finally rearing to fight before Jubal managed to fire all six rounds from the Spencer's magazine, finally dropping the brown bear, still lean from hibernation but standing as tall as the mare's back, not five feet from where Henrietta had shit herself empty. She was so frazzled that Jubal doused the fire, carved a chunk of half-cooked wolf to carry, and set off again, reluctantly deciding he needed to find a stable for the night or his mount might collapse.

At sunset, he pulled up on a narrow, lightly traveled dirt track and surveyed the crossroads town a few hundred yards ahead of him. A sign on one of the six buildings read Butler, Alabama, County Seat. Jubal had heard of the town before and he knew the Tombigbee River was only about ten miles away. From there, he could either go by steamboat to Mobile or ferry the river and continue straight another fifty miles to Gee's Bend. He hadn't decided which yet.

One more day ... the thought suddenly clutched at his chest. Would Sally and the children be at either place? Two years had passed; Emma would be talking and Lester walking. The thought of his son suddenly made him smile.

"Can't wait to see you, Buck!" he said aloud.

"Who's Buck?" a voice asked.

Jubal wheeled, drawing his pistol.

"Whoa, hold that horse, mister," a lean woodman rose from where he had sat, motionless, above the road. Dressed in buckskin, he looked as if he'd been a trapper all his life. "Little jumpy on such a quiet day, ain't you?"

The Welsh accent was pointless.

"Who are you?" Jubal asked.

"Chalmers. You?"

"You live here?"

"On furlough," the hunter walked into the road. "Forrest's Cavalry. Miss Madison, she has rooms down there, for folks come in for business at the county seat. I do some huntin', venison and the like." Chalmers gestured back to the carcass of a mule deer, lying in the underbrush. He looked Jubal over. "You come a ways."

"Where's her place?"

Chalmers pointed. "Four corners, southeast one, with the long barn out back. You can stable yer mare."

"Obliged." Jubal tipped his hat and spurred Henrietta forward. He had talked enough.

"Stranger! You mind cartin' this meat down? I'll gut it, jus' git 'er there."

—

Miss Madison, a stout, graying woman, heard Henrietta clop into the yard and came onto the front porch, wiping her hands on a full apron. At a glance she relaxed, making a quick appraisal; the deer draped over the mare, the road-stained traveler on a wrung-out horse, Chalmers walking some way behind.

"You need a bed, mister?"

Jubal simply nodded.

"Stable your horse. There's oats and hay; ten dollars for the bale."

"Ten dollars?" Jubal started. "For a bale of hay?"

"Well, you want to work any, I'd rather have it," Miss Madison declared, hands going to her hips.

Jubal tipped his hat, calculating how to pay. Confederate currency was almost worthless, but for a man trying to be inconspicuous, payment in gold would be like screaming. He headed for the barn.

Dismounting, he led Henrietta through the big open door but stopped so abruptly the mare ran into him. Two horses, good, strong mounts, stood in the stalls, sweat drying on their flanks. On adjacent racks, cavalry saddles hung. Jubal looked closer. Each had a brand in the leather: CSA.

He stared at the saddles, feeling his teeth grind: *Confederate States of America.*

Footsteps approached and Jubal's hand went to his holster. Chalmers came into the barn.

"One of these yours?" Jubal drawled, deciding he would have to play the situation.

"Nope," Chalmers replied. "Mine's hobbled out back. She ain't tired." He untied the deer carcass, hauling it off Henrietta. "Oats in the bin over there. There's a niggah who'll brush down the mare, soon's he's back from the river. They been trying to blow the snags fouling the river 'tween here and Mobile—steamboats ain't run for a week. Major Horton," Chalmers nodded his head to one of the horses watching, "he didn't want to wait."

"For what?"

"Going north, Columbus. Forrest left two weeks ago; the major came to Mobile. They'd put his pa in jail. We got to rejoin the unit, but there won't be anything left of these nags. Just skin and bones if we ride there. Forrest, I tell you, sir, that man's hard on horses."

"Identify yourself!" The order, crisp and hostile, spun Jubal around. A short, compact Confederate officer with graying hair stared at him, his lanky orderly a step behind holding a short-barreled rifle as casually as if it were an extension of his arm. Both men had appeared soundlessly in the barn door.

Jubal looked the two men over and said nothing.

"Mister," the officer stiffened, "I don't know you, but you're of fighting age on a good horse far from the lines. We've had our fill of deserters!"

Jubal flushed. "I'm seeing three good horses and men of fighting age, far from the lines!"

The rifle rose and pointed at him.

"Shoot that, you'll both hang," Jubal snapped at the orderly.

The major, a man unused to feeling threatened, paused. Doubt flashed in his face. The orderly waited. Chalmers stepped back.

"Identify yourself," Jubal commanded.

"Major Franklin Horton, 1st Cavalry Division. Lieutenant Carter, my orderly, here, and you've met Corporal Chalmers?"

"Jubal Calhoun, special agent to Secretary of War Stephen Mallory."

The three soldiers stared, flabbergasted.

"What are you doing here," Horton recovered, "sir?"

"None of your business. Now if you'll excuse me, gentlemen, I intend to wash off the road." Jubal walked directly at the lanky Lieutenant, who instinctively stepped aside.

"Mr. Calhoun?"

Jubal paused, turning to the Major.

"Excuse me, sir," Major Horton continued, "did you know a cotton factor in Mobile, Mr. Truette Stubbs?"

Jubal's knees went weak.

"My parents, Gustavas and Eliza Horton. Do you recognize the name?"

Jubal shook his head, no.

"Six, seven years ago, I remember your name; my mother told me. You and a Yankee bought this nigger woman, sent her north. Right? My father took her to New York or Philadelphia, someplace. Stubbs asked him."

A feeling of dread came over Jubal. "Chalmers said your father was in jail?"

"He's Union," Horton replied, his voice tight and defensive. "Refused conscription."

"Born in Syracuse, wasn't he?" Jubal remembered. "Your mother and father on one side, you on other?"

"Yes, sir. Me, my brother, and sister, all born and bred here."

Jubal suddenly felt exhausted. "Let's pray it doesn't happen to us and our sons." He turned to the house but stopped as the major spoke.

"Where are you headed, sir?"

"I need to contact Richmond," Jubal lied. "I'll go to Mobile in the morning."

"Best come with us sir, telegraph will be better through the Army. Sherman's marauding in Georgia, the lines are cut that way."

"Regardless, I need to stop in Mobile first."

"Begging your pardon, Calhoun ..." Major Horton shifted his feet. "There's not many Yankees in Mobile. My parents know 'em all—at least them that are honest about it, like Mrs. Calhoun."

Jubal stared, his dread flaring. "You know of my wife?"

"Not direct, sir; we never met. But Mother speaks of her. They was friends, being Yankee and all."

"Was?"

"Oh, I don't know that anything bad has happened ..."

Jubal stared through the man.

"Well, Mother says she's gone, Mrs. Calhoun, and her children."

Jubal nearly threw up.

"Where?"

"North. Can't say where, I don't know. A time back, Mother said."

"How do you know?"

"Mrs. Calhoun, she didn't get along with folks much, except my parents. She made quite a hollerin' when my father was arrested. I finally had to come, straighten things out. But I admire her, standing up for my father. That wife of yours got a reputation, if you know what I mean."

Jubal nodded. "Thank you." He turned and walked to the house. His head ached and he wanted nothing more than to smoke his pipe in the tub and figure out what to do next.

But as he approached the back door, a small smile creased his travel-streaked face and Jubal muttered under his breath.

"I know what you mean."

Chapter One Hundred Three

Washington, April 1864

At mid-morning, General Meigs came out from his office into the anteroom, fingering several telegrams. Sally, Cora, and Eleanor Creesy rose as one.

"Mrs. Norton," he said, "your husband is at the Confederate prisoner-of-war camp in Cahaba, Alabama. It's in ..."

Both women gasped. The general eyed them.

"We know the place, General," Sally explained, "well."

"We don't, other than there are probably a thousand men there. I can't speak for their condition but as of a week ago, Mrs. Norton, your husband is alive. Knowing the man, I have the utmost confidence he will prevail."

"When will he be exchanged?" Cora asked.

"I believe within the next few weeks. Certainly by the end of the month."

"Should we not hear from your office," Sally declared, "we will visit again May first." Eleanor Creesy glanced at her; Sally took the hint. "Thank you for everything you've done."

"Indeed," General Meigs replied, amused at the forthrightness of the woman, who reminded him of his daughter. "Major Norton's situation is distressing; it would be for me, were he my son, and my men are not far removed in my feelings. Yet I have benefit of a soldier's expectations."

"Is your son serving?" Eleanor Creesy asked. She had heard of Meigs. Josiah held the quartermaster general in high regard and there were precious few men about whom she could say the same.

"John, my eldest, yes. In Sheridan's Corps, now in the Shenandoah Valley."

"God bless him," Cora said, "and you, sir. Thank you."

General Meigs bowed to the women.

Later that afternoon, the eastern express pulled into Philadelphia's Union Station, en route northeast. Cora and Sally gathered their purses.

"You must telegraph us the moment Lester is released," Eleanor instructed. She was continuing on to Boston. "Josiah will want to know."

"Is he home?" Cora asked.

"I expect him later this month. Then he's done and I doubt we shall leave Salem again. You must come visit."

"What will Mr. Creesy do?" Sally asked, the sharp pain of longing twisting her stomach. Mostly she had become inured to her loss, but at unexpected moments—Eleanor's invitation had stabbed like a needle—Sally felt utterly bereft.

"Oh, he'll figure something," Eleanor replied. She could sense the young woman's anguish. "You mustn't give up, Sally. It's not like Jubal to just …"

"Just what? He left!"

"He just did what he had to do," Cora said. "You did the very same. He'll be back."

"If he lives …"

"Lord'll decide that."

The women went silent. Finally, Eleanor gave them both hugs. "Off you go. Cora, send word immediately! I'll see you next week, Sally?"

"I'll wire you," Sally promised.

As they stood back on the platform, waiting for the train to leave, Cora turned to Sally. "You're going next week?"

"Five or six days," Sally replied. "Maine for shoes, New Hampshire blankets, knapsacks in Connecticut, and then back home."

Cora smiled, admiring Sally's skill at using Meigs' sympathy to win brokerage contracts for Union supplies, though Sally insisted the general was the most virtuous man she had ever met and showed no favoritism. "He'll spend fifty million dollars and account for it to the penny!"

The train lurched, gathered momentum, and pulled away. "That's as fine a woman as we'll meet in this life," Cora sighed, waving to Mrs. Creesy.

"They both said that," Sally mused. "Lester *and* Jubal."

"They'll be coming home."

"What if they don't?"

"Then we'll just go get 'em."

Chapter One Hundred Four

Mississippi, April 1864

Jubal rode north with Major Horton and his men from Columbus, Mississippi, the head of steamboat navigation on the Tombigbee River, arriving in Corinth a week after leaving Butler. Other than saying he intended to go by train to Richmond and report to the secretary of the Navy, Jubal had kept to himself, preferring the company of his horse to soldiers. Henrietta had rested and settled on the boat trip upriver, the good weather held, and with a dry road she made the two days' hard ride to Corinth in fine spirits.

The town itself was shattered. After Shiloh and a two-day battle that burned or leveled half the buildings, the Union Army had occupied Corinth for a year before pulling back to Memphis, a hundred miles west.

On the trip north, Jubal knew he was moving as flotsam would in a river, but he would soon have to choose. The British passport remained in his vest, unmentioned and unseen. He could remain a patriot and make his way to Richmond for orders or desert somewhere along the Tennessee or Mississippi river, use the passport and slip north to Pittsburgh, then head for Philadelphia. If Sally and the children weren't there, he'd travel on to New York or Boston or Maine—just keep going until he found them. Somehow he would find his family.

Unless he was caught. Deserter or spy, Jubal figured neither side would hesitate to hang him.

The Corinth stationmaster decided the issue.

"There's no service now. All trains move by government order, troops and munitions," he declared, when Jubal asked when the next express left headed east. "Besides, you'll never get to Richmond, not until Hood or Johnston takes care of Sherman. He's right astride the line in East Tennessee, cut us in two at the middle. That's why Forrest been through here, raiding north. Taking the pressure off, make them pay attention and fight here."

Major Horton said the same. Though he had not pressed Jubal on the journey north, his suspicions were aroused by the man's tight restraint.

"Carter, Chalmers, " he had ordered his subordinates as they disembarked the steamboat, "keep a watchful eye on Mr. Calhoun but don't be obvious. His story is a bunch of pieces that don't rightly fit."

"He don't speak much about his wife," Chalmers observed.

"The woman a man marries says a good deal about him," Horton replied. "I seen her once and wouldn't want to tangle with her."

At the Corinth station, Horton had followed Jubal onto the porch. "You've got a good horse. General Forrest isn't two days' ride north, and we need men. Calhoun, you ought come with us."

Standing in the sunlight with three wary Confederate cavalrymen, Jubal knew the time had come. Instinct developed by a decade at sea prevailed. Approaching an uncertain landfall with a storm bearing down, Jubal knew he wouldn't hesitate to shorten sail, look for sea room, and wait out the weather.

"Let's go, Major. Find us your General Forrest."

⁓

After two hundred miles in four days, Henrietta was about spent. They had continued north into Tennessee, following the road that Forrest and several thousand men had ridden nearly three weeks earlier. Nearing the Mississippi River, they heard distant cannon fire, and Horton ordered Carter and Chalmers ahead.

"Found 'em!" Carter reported on their return. "The general attacked Fort Pillow this morning. We're ordered left, Bell's brigade; couple of his officers been killed."

"What's the objective?" Jubal asked. He had watched Raphael Semmes stalk a ship, gauging the wind and adjusting tactics according to the sailing characteristics or fighting capacity of his enemy, but he had never seen a land battle.

"The general figures to destroy Fort Pillow, then move downriver to Memphis."

"Why doesn't he just go direct to Memphis?"

"Union horses," Carter replied, gesturing to Henrietta, whose head drooped, looking for something to graze, "and supplies."

"How many defenders?" Horton asked.

"Six or seven hundred. Half, maybe more of them, are niggers."

"Nigger soldiers?" Horton exclaimed. "In Yankee uniform?"

"Yes, sir. Nigger Yankee troops."

"They're dead!" Horton declared, spurring his horse.

Jubal followed, but Henrietta was winded and they soon fell behind. The cannon fire grew louder, and as he crested a hill and came to a stop, the panorama of a battle in progress laid out before him.

Fort Pillow had been built on a bluff overlooking a sharp bend of the Mississippi; cannon could easily choke traffic either upriver or down. In the bend opposite the fort, a Union gunboat steamed against the current, holding in place. Inland from the fort, concentric semicircular trenches had been dug behind an earthen parapet fronted by a ditch.

On first glance the location looked impregnable but the parapet was littered with bodies of Union troops. Puzzled for a moment, Jubal realized with a flash of understanding that it was a matter of time; General Forrest had used the fort's defenses to overwhelm it.

Union infantry in the trenches were protected by the earthen berm but they had no direct line of fire at Confederate troopers outside and below. General Forrest had stationed sharpshooters on the high ground Jubal now occupied and they picked off any Union soldier firing from atop the wall. Likewise, the Union gunboat shooting up from the river couldn't lower its guns enough to damage the Confederate infantry protected by the berm.

On the left, two barracks at the southern end of the fort were crawling with Rebel forces that had managed to storm the buildings. Jubal had read of the military term *enfilade* and now understood the devastating effect, for these troops had flanked the trenches, firing along their lines much as Raphael Semmes had avoided an enemy's broadside cannon and cut across their bow or stern, his cannon raking the length of the ship.

Horton urgently motioned them over to a conference of officers. "General's given them twenty minutes to surrender! They refused and he's bound to drive 'em into the river before they git reinforced! Already had three horses shot from under him!"

Jubal could see General Forrest on a hillock half a mile away surveying the battle through field glasses. The gunboat belched fire. Seconds later the ground exploded near General Forrest's party, scattering most, though Jubal could see two horses fall. One of the riders bounded to his feet; the other lay crumpled.

Suddenly, the piercing blast of a bugle carried across the field followed by the full-throated roar of five thousand men. Jubal's heart leaped as sharpshooters around him opened fire. Troopers in the buildings laid down a flanking fusillade as Horton and his men galloped forward and down the slope toward the embankment. As if swept forward in an avalanche, Henrietta surged after the other horses. Jubal heard himself screaming, pulling his Spencer from its scabbard.

A wave of butternut uniforms leapt into the ditch and pressed against the embankment. Hard on their heels, a second phalanx came over them, using the first wave's shoulders to climb atop the berm, then reaching back down to haul their comrades up. The gunboat opened fire, but a savage volley of rifle fire answered, peppering the iron sides with a sound like corn popping in a giant skillet. In quick succession, the gunboat's ports slammed shut. Like clockwork, Rebel sharpshooters held their fire as men atop the embankment surged forward, firing at the massed defenders in the trenches below.

Jubal yanked Henrietta to a halt before a third wave of troopers preparing to storm forward and leaped down just as a grapeshot canister exploded in their midst. Simultaneously, he felt blows to his face and chest before the concussion knocked the wind out of him as he went flying. He landed hard and stared into a clear sky, bewildered at the sudden silence and struggling to breathe. Sticky liquid dribbled into his eyes and he rolled to his elbows as battle sounds began to filter through the ringing in his ears. He sucked a breath at the stinging burn on his forehead and wiped a sleeve across it, pulling away something that plopped and rolled down his coat. Jubal fingered the dark brown lump and gasped at its heat. Slowly he realized it was a shard of metal trailing a bloody scrap of cloth.

Jubal winced and spit blood, tossing the shrapnel aside where it landed on the severed forearm that had punched him in the face. His stomach heaving, he rolled away and shrieked from a sudden, searing stab of pain so violent he flopped back, gasping for breath. Pain pulsed and radiated from his hip, as if a six-inch sewing needle probed at bone. He couldn't feel his legs.

Flailing in agony, his hand struck something sticking from his hip and he screamed again. Panting, spitting more blood, Jubal yanked at whatever had impaled him until something cracked like a twig. Staring, he gaped at the shredded piece of uniform clinging to a bloody white stick. With a cry of horror, he flung the bowed, jagged rib into the heap of shattered soldiers to his front. Gulping, whimpering, he felt his wound; dizzying shafts of white light radiated from a splinter still embedded.

The battle roar changed; no longer a full-throated cry of courage, it became a howl of rage. Shrieks, cries, bestial roars of triumph, agonized pleas cut short with gunshot, the bellowing of General Forrest and his officers urging troops onward or to cease firing, Jubal couldn't tell which—none of it mattered as he struggled to clear his mind and find the will to rise. With a heave, he sat up. Pain exploded before his eyes like rocket bursts.

The afternoon sky swooped and swirled into darkness.

―⁓―

"Jubie ... Jubie." The voice came to him in a dream and he wondered where he was, struggling to make sense of the vague light, a blurry shadow above him, the buzzing in his head. The shadow dissolved before he could focus; I'm dreaming, Jubal thought, still trying to get his bearings.

Stirring, a sudden, shooting pain in his hip brought him awake and memory of the battle slowly returned. Jubal wondered if he had lost his hearing—the low light was too quiet. Concentrating on one thing at a time, he tried to focus and gradually distinguished distant, muted sounds of men and wagons. The light was rising; he realized it must be morning.

Carefully, dreading what he might find, Jubal took inventory. One arm worked, then the other; one hand felt his throbbing forehead, the other gently explored a broken nose. Drawing one leg up, he tried the other but couldn't feel it. The attempt made him gasp and stars flooded his vision. He lay still, exhausted.

"Water," he croaked after a time, trying to stir awake. "Need water."

"Here," the dream voice returned. "None too fast, y'hear?" A face shadowed the cloudless sky overhead. "Pull on this. Need to wash yore face."

Delicious cold water trickled over his parched lips and a soaking wet cloth gently pressed against his teeth. Jubal sucked tentatively, then pulled hard, the liquid coming like nectar into his arid throat. Water washed over his face and he closed crusted eyelids, surrendering to the sublime, cool massage that cleaned his forehead.

Opening his eyes, he stared into the face above. Jubal closed them again, willing the dream away, then blinked several times to clear the hallucination.

"Jordon?"

"You cut up, Jubie." Jordon Hatcher looked down at him. "Messy 'cross the head, but ain't deep."

"Jordon, is that you?"

"Jubie, it's me. You ain't goin' be so handsome with a nose all busted. I ought set that straight."

"I can't get up. My hip."

Jordon Hatcher looked at the wound carefully. Gently, he probed; Jubal gasped.

"Still somethin' in there," Jordon said, the deep voice rumbling. "Doctors all be busy; they thought you was dead."

"How did you …?" Jubal stopped, utterly perplexed.

"My boys. Come here to be with 'em. Been working the fort, teamsterin' and they was soldierin'. Charity, she here, too, a washin' woman."

"Daniel, Isaiah? Where are they?"

The black man tried to speak but couldn't, and his face dissolved in anguish. Jordon Hatcher sobbed silently.

"Jordon …" Jubal reached for him.

"Daniel be right there," Jordon's rumble became half-strangled. He pointed toward the trench, sobs wracking his chest. "I just grateful his momma never'll see 'im." Jordon Hatcher wiped his eyes with the rag that he'd used to clean Jubal. "Isaiah, he layin' down to the river. How come they stab a soldierin' man, 'gan 'n agan … like he had no right to fight 'em?"

Jubal swallowed, remembering Major Horton's *"They're dead."*

"Here," Jordon swallowed, struggling to collect himself. "I'm gonna leave ya this canteen. Gotta get us a wagon and a mule, get you to a doctor."

"What … are you going to do?"

"Takin' my boys home, bury 'em with their mother. Beulah'd want that."

"Beulah's dead?" Jubal mind reeled. "Home?"

"Yes, suh, Masta Jubie. We's goin' to Gee's Bend. Goin' home. 'N you kin tell me how is it you being here."

"Jordon. My horse, we'll need my horse."

"Ain't nothin' left here alive, Jubie, 'cept you."

Chapter One Hundred Five

Washington, May 1864

An aide showed Cora and Sally into General Meigs' office. Behind the general, a huge map filled the wall, showing both Union and Confederate army movements and positions.

"Looks like the entire country is fighting," Sally remarked, studying the map.

"The spring campaign has commenced," General Meigs replied. "I take no pleasure in predicting that May will be an horrendous month. Though your husband, is imprisoned Mrs. Norton, he is perhaps safer than were he with either Grant or Sherman. Both those armies will soon see severe action."

Cora glanced at the map but wasn't interested. "When will Lester be exchanged?"

General Meigs cleared his throat, rose from his desk, and came around to face her.

"Do you know of the massacre at Fort Pillow, in Tennessee on the Mississippi River?"

"I heard the name," Cora replied, "but don't know the details. I've been in school and at the hospital."

General Meigs relaxed and leaned on his desk, nodding. "Medical school, isn't that correct? Mrs. Mott, or perhaps Mrs. Creesy, mentioned as much. I can't remember which. What are you studying now?"

"Anatomy."

"Do you ..." General Meigs paused, as if wondering how to ask the question. "Is it interesting?"

"Metal and lead do terrible things."

General Meigs folded his arms.

"We dissect a new soldier every day," Cora continued. "Every student has their own, every day."

"Death is teaching you life."

"I don't understand it," Cora agreed. "Do you know how amazing we are? I never believed in miracles—my people do, but I never took notice much of spirits—but when you see how the Lord built an arm, or a hand ... Do you know how many bones are in a hand?" She held out her own, the rich copper skin of the back contrasting with the brilliant pink palm, flexing, pinching, pointing. "Play piano, sew, pull, grasp, salute, poke ..." Cora looked at the general, dead serious, her voice a mix of plantation and education. "Ever think how many things you can do with a hand? And it's just one miracle. Eyes, ears, feet, digestion ... Can you tell me, General, why our minds make such a mess of these miracles? And a young, beautiful man, barely older 'n a boy, gets torn apart by rusty, jagged pieces of metal?"

"No."

"When is my husband exchanged?"

General Meigs straightened.

"There was a massacre at Fort Pillow. Union troops—colored ... Negro troops—already having surrendered, were murdered in cold blood. Several hundred men killed, many more colored than white troops. When this was brought to General Grant's attention he demanded of the Confederate authorities that Negro prisoners be treated identically to white prisoners."

"As they should," Sally interjected, her face reddening.

"Indeed. This demand was refused. Something to the effect that exchanging our—Confederate—troops for Negros would not be tolerated."

Silence lengthened in the room.

"So ...?" Sally looked ready to hit something.

Cora stared at the general.

"When is my husband exchanged?"

"I regret to inform you, Mrs. Norton," General Meigs looked Cora in the eye, "that because of the Confederate position, General Grant has ordered all exchanges canceled for the duration of the war."

Chapter One Hundred Six

The Columbus, Mississippi steamboat landing hadn't changed, other than that the Tombigbee River ran swiftly from spring rains.

"Can't say the same of myself," Jubal observed, limping on the hickory crutch Jordon Hatcher had made for him. Jordon held him under his opposite arm, cautious because Jubal had only learned to walk with a crutch several days earlier and was still weak. Charity carried a satchel and her baby, walking a few steps behind.

"Say what, Masta—Mr.—Jubal?"

"That's right," Jubal declared. "Don't you ever call me 'master' again, ever. 'Jubal' is just fine. You neither, Charity!"

"Yes, suh, Mr. Jubal," the black man replied. Charity just nodded.

"Did he take lessons in being contrary from Sally?" Jubal asked her, though he doubted she would respond, having spoken no more than ten words on the journey south. Not yet eighteen and married hardly a year, Charity shouldered her husband's death with unspoken pride. Outwardly, her only change had been in her reserve in the presence of strangers. Now, Charity looked people directly in the eye, as if she could endure anything.

"Don't be givin' her ideas," Jordon tone belied his smile. 'We's got to be careful."

A month had passed since the apocalypse at Fort Pillow but the slow ride south gave the men long hours to talk. Jubal rode prone in the wagon bed next to the half-barrel of ashes while Jordon drove the mule with Charity and her baby beside him.

Jordon had recovered his sons' bodies and taken Jubal to the field hospital where a medic removed several pieces of grapeshot from his face and legs, but General Forrest had already ordered his troops southward to raid Memphis and the battle surgeons had gone with the army. The only doctor of any experience was drunk when they arrived, and after one glance, the black man carried Jubal away. The four of them set out south for Corinth shortly after.

"You gettin' the gait of it," Jordon observed, as they boarded the steamboat for Mobile.

"If I ever get to walking again," Jubal grunted, relieved that he wouldn't have to endure the agony of the wagon bed, "I ain't going to complain about nary a thing." He could put no weight on his leg without blinding pain.

"Your chest done hurtin'?"

"Doesn't feel like that mule kicked me anymore," Jubal agreed, again marveling that the gold coins had undoubtedly saved his life. His vest had been riddled with grapeshot, and one gold coin still had a spent minié ball embedded in it that had left a purple bruise on Jubal's chest the size of a grapefruit.

Jordon helped Jubal settle in the steamboat cabin and then returned to the landing for Charity and his granddaughter, and to bring the barrel holding his sons' ashes. The grief-stricken resolution to bring their bodies to Gee's Bend had been abandoned after two days on the road. The corpses had bloated, bursting open their uniform buttons and smelling so bad Jubal finally threw up, though he said not a word.

Charity finally directed Jordon to pull into a clearing by a small stream, where he built a bonfire, and then sat with Jubal against a tree watching while Charity lay down by the stream and held her daughter. They spent as mournful an afternoon as any had ever experienced until the flames consumed Isaiah and Daniel's earthly remains. The next morning, when the fire had cooled, Charity nursed the baby and watched in silence as her father-in-law collected her husband's and his sons' ashes. The irony was too painful; when the child was born she had insisted naming the baby for her father, even when Daniel protested. Though Charity didn't know why then, she did now.

Little Daniella was a quiet, observant baby, .

Later that morning Jordon bought a barrel at a farm they passed along the road, the better to store the ashes.

"You notice that warehouse full of cotton, north side of the landing?" Jubal remarked, accepting from Jordon a plate Charity had prepared. Jordon had returned from town with smoked ham, fresh bread, and several bottles of whiskey.

"Gonna buy it?" Jordon asked, still marveling at the ease with which he could purchase any manner of things. A gold coin and the note from Jubal instructing "My man, Jordon Hatcher, shall be afforded every courtesy to provide for my wounds" got immediate attention, enabling him to buy the wagon and mule, food, ammunition, and steamboat accommodations without incident.

"No, not right off," Jubal replied. "But this war is going to end, inside a year I'd wager. A dog fighting a bull, and the bull is angry."

"It's a mad dog," Jordon noted, with an edge of bitterness. Charity watched the conversation, rocking her baby in a small hammock she'd set up in the steamboat cabin.

"Don't matter. Every time they fight the bull gets bit, but the dog's getting stomped. Just a matter of time before it just won't be able to get back up. Then," Jubal pointed a finger at Jordon, "we buy that cotton."

"Can't say as I care no mo', Mr. Jubal."

"I understand. But I give you my word, Jordon. You're family forevermore. Always were, but Lord knows, you are now, hear? Wherever I'm going, you're coming too, 'less you don't want.

"I got to mind my daughter, now. 'Sides, Miss Sally be having something to say about that."

"Crack that whiskey, will you? Suppose she's still in Philadelphia with Cora? Maybe I'll send a telegram, though Forrest's men said every line was wrecked."

"Can't be sayin'. You get that leg fixed, you goin'?"

"Somehow." Jubal lapsed into silence for a time, passing the whiskey back and forth with Jordon. A shine came into the black man's eyes.

"I hope there's a doctor in Mobile can deal with this," Jubal said. "Can't hardly move." He looked at Jordon Hatcher, feeling a mellow glow regardless of the dull ache in his hip. He could tolerate the pain if he kept his weight off the leg.

"You know," Jubal continued, "I got my arm broke, ten years back, thereabouts. I swore to myself if I lost that arm I'd put a gun to my head. That was before I really knew Lester well, and he took me to see Sally, and I brought him here ... it all started with a busted arm. So now I got a bad leg. But by Jesus—that's how Lester would put it!—I declare something right's gonna come of this."

Jordon Hatcher took a pull from the bottle. "I never drank with a white man before." The black man chuckled. "Tha's a gud way to look at 'er."

"Though, might take us some time."

"Yes, suh," Jubal replied, suddenly feeling very tired. His mind wandered. "Comin' onto the doldrums. Always made it 'cross, but ... could take awhile. We is a long way from land." Jubal let himself go, and in a moment was drifting off to sleep. Gentle hands lifted him and though he winced, moments later he lay safe in the cabin bed. Nestling in, a vision of Sally and the boys came to him ... amidst the soft sprinkle of warm spring rain ... rough, calloused hands caressed the raindrops free from his face ...

"Coming boys," Jubal murmured, "Daddy's comin' ..."

Minutes later the steamboat's whistle blew and the crew cast off. Neither the white man lying in his cabin bed nor the black man curled up on the floor beside him stirred as the thrashing paddle wheel pushed into the Tombigbee current flowing to Mobile Bay.

Only Charity stay awake, staring through the cabin window at the setting sun, one hand gently rocking Daniella.

Chapter One Hundred Seven

Florence, Tennessee, June 1864

"Truette, hold Emma's hand and stay close," Cora ordered, stuffing the last of their clothes in the carpetbag. "When we land you never get out of our sight, you hear me?"

Emma opened her mouth to say something, but Sally cut the child off. "I don't want to hear it. You're five now, big enough to take some responsibility. And Truette, don't give her any guff, there's no time for any of that!"

Truette looked as if he had swallowed an earthworm. Emma grabbed his hand and yanked him. "You'll do what I say, hear me?"

Truette slugged her in the shoulder.

"Goddamn it!" Sally snarled, startling the children. She took a deep breath, trying to calm herself. "Listen to me. We have to start being very careful. The steamboat can't go any further. There's rapids ahead, bad, rocky water. So we are taking a stagecoach for several days until we get to another river and can get back on a boat. Understand?"

"Why do we have to be careful?" Emma asked.

"We're going through the lines."

"What lines?"

"North and South, Union and Rebel. Two armies are fighting."

"Will they shoot at us?"

Truette watched the conversation like a game of catch, his eyes bulging.

"No. Cora has a pass."

"What's that?" Emma demanded.

Cora had to chuckle. "You sure are your mother's daughter." She waved a document at the children. "Daddy's general wrote this for us; it's permission to travel between the armies. We don't know exactly what will happen, but don't go worrin' about nothing."

"*Anything*," Emma corrected, a perfect imitation of Lucretia Mott.

"You're right, 'lil miss. But I'm right about this: *stay close!*"

A sudden bump silenced them. Outside, men shouted orders as the gunboat bumped the Florence wharf again, a half-mile below the last whitewater of Muscle Shoals.

Sally glanced at Cora. "Lucretia Mott was right, we are crazy to bring them along."

"You weren't going to leave yours," Cora retorted. "We had to—no telling when or how we'll get back. Let's go, children!"

Cora led the way, a rucksack on her back and lugging a large carpetbag, Emma and Truette following, both with smaller rucksacks. Sally took up the rear, holding Buck on her hip and lugging another carpetbag, smaller than Cora's, holding the gold coins and Union dollar bills.

The column made their way toward the gangplank, where the gunboat captain waited.

"Please sign this, Mrs. Calhoun," the captain said, indicating an order. "General Meigs requires notice that you have arrived safely."

"Why doesn't she sign it?" Sally snapped, motioning to Cora. "General Meigs gave the pass to her."

The captain shifted uncomfortably. "Of course. Mrs. ... Norton?"

"Go 'head," Cora nodded to Sally. "We're here, that's all I care about."

"Begging your pardon, ladies, are you sure you want to travel? With children? Last report was there's a Rebel army due south of here, a day's march, you can't help but contact it directly. They may honor General Meigs' pass, or ..." The captain shrugged, his attitude bordering on disbelief.

Sally scrawled her signature. "Good day, Captain. Thank you for the transport." Cora had ignored him and was halfway down the gangplank. "Emma, Truette, follow Aunt Cora."

Cora walked directly to the stagecoach station without slowing. Emma and Truette tried to keep up but couldn't.

"Aunt Cora," Emma whined.

Cora wheeled in the street, seething. "You chillen move! Or walk with Aunt Sally!"

"Cora, go on ahead, get us tickets," Sally called.

"Why's she so mad?" Emma asked.

"'Cause one more time she was ignored because of her color."

"Why do people do that?"

"If you ever find a good answer to that, dearest, please tell me. I surely don't know."

⁓

For 120 miles, they traveled up and over the ridges, south toward

Tuscaloosa, a town founded on the fall line of the Black Warrior River where the Appalachian plateau met the long coastal plain. The stage traveled only during daylight, as the countryside was dangerous. Roving armies, deserters, outlaws, and highwaymen could be encountered, so Sally had spent what the Florence stationmaster considered a small fortune to hire a coach and three stagehands—an armed driver and two riders with shotguns sitting front and back—to take them all the way to Tuscaloosa. Sally was none too impressed with what money bought: the driver frequently pulled from a hip bottle shared with his men, one of whom was obviously a simpleton that could barely hold a gun and the other missing a leg from fighting with Hood at Sharpsburg, a battle that also seemed to have shattered the man's nerves.

The first evening at a stagecoach inn on the outskirts of a tiny town Sally learned they had missed General Forrest by two days. His army had turned back westward.

"Sherman's burning everything," the stable blacksmith explained, limping from wounds at Lookout Mountain a year earlier that had nearly killed him. "Forrest's been tearing into his supply lines, but word is there's another ten thousand Yankees comin' out of Memphis. So he's got to go back and whip 'em. Will, too."

"Is the road ahead clear?"

"How far y'all goin'?"

"Tuscaloosa, then Mobile."

"You Yankee? That your nigger?"

"Clear or not?" Sally asked, cold as ice.

"Get to one, y'all get to the other. Might want to bring some whiskey."

Sally didn't know what to make of the enigmatic reply but wanted nothing more to do with the blacksmith.

"What the hell would we want whiskey for?" she asked Cora later, as they sat in their room after dinner. Cora shrugged and didn't answer, but she bought a jug of corn liquor at the general store first thing in the morning as the teamsters harnessed the four-mule team.

The second day, intermittent thundershowers brought cloying humidity and turned the rutted roadway into a muddy, bone-crunching slog that sapped the tempers of stagehands and passengers alike. The children complained and whined until both Cora and Sally had to control their urge to spank them into silence. By late afternoon, when the stagecoach pulled into an isolated farmhouse deep in the piney woods, the women wanted nothing more than to find clean water and a decent bed for the night.

Water wasn't a problem; the farmhouse had been located years earlier at a spring that bubbled crystal-clear all year long. Clean beds were another matter.

"No niggers inside," the farmer declared. He was toothless and stooped, with a straggly, greasy beard stained from chewing tobacco. Regarding the women as they approached the ramshackle porch, he stood implacable and spit a stream of rust-colored juice at Cora's feet.

"I paid considerably more than full freight!" Sally stammered, shocked and so furious she wanted to kick the man.

"Not to me."

Behind them, the stagehands chortled. Sally wheeled to the driver. "I demand a decent bed for all of us! We have children!"

Emma and Truette had gone mum, clutching their mother's skirts and watching, wide-eyed and alert. Buck had fallen asleep in Cora's arms.

"Been a hard go," the driver replied. "Another hundred dollars gold if you want to make Tuscaloosa. Otherwise, we're headed back to the river." He turned to his men. "Settle them mules for the night."

"That's extortion!" Sally cried.

"That's business. Don't like it, walk. Them mules is all tuckered out, and us too. Hundred dollars or suit yerself." The driver ambled past, up the stairs and into the farmhouse. With a huck, the farmer sent another squirt of juice into the red mud. "Niggers sleep in the barn," he motioned, before turning into the house.

Sally and Cora stared at each other, then glanced at the dilapidated barn standing at the edge of the farm clearing where the stagecoach headed. The women watched as one stagehand scattered hay in a small, attached corral for the mules while the other released the team from its traces.

"Those sons-of-bitches!" Sally fumed.

"C'mon," Cora said, her voice even, as if not at all surprised. "Don't go arguin', won't do a lick of good."

The barn was dusty but dry, and they arranged bedding in clean straw as twilight gathered. Emma asked once why they couldn't sleep in the farmhouse but Sally snarled a reply and the children seemed to understand it was best not to squabble.

"Take that jug," Cora said, "'n get us some of whatever's cooking."

"I'm not giving them that whiskey!" Sally barked. "Bastards!"

"No. Go give it to 'em, and be nice. I'd do it but no tellin' what would happen I show my face in there. Go on. And tell 'em you'll pay the extra in the morning. I mean it."

Cora's tone was so matter-of-fact Sally bit off a retort and looked her over quizzically, but Cora had turned her attention to settling the children in their makeshift beds.

Ten minutes later, Sally came back with a pot of beans and pork. "I was nice," she reported. "Now what?"

"Feed the children and get us some sleep," Cora replied. Sally was too tired to argue, though she swore to fight this injustice in the morning.

By the time they'd finished eating, darkness had fallen and the children were curled up asleep. From the farmhouse, laughter turned to howls as men passed the whiskey.

"Wake up." Sally woke with a start but Cora had a hand over her mouth.

"Shhh," Cora hushed. "Moon's risin'. Let's go."

"What time is it?"

"Middle of the night. Wake the children," Cora whispered, "but keep 'em quiet. Mules is ready."

Sally clutched at Cora's arm. "What are we doing?"

"Leavin'."

"You're gonna steal the mules?"

"No stealin'. You said yourself they charged enough to buy the whole team."

"I don't know a thing about mules!"

"I do. Been around them all my life. You plowed a horse, didn't you? Mules ain't much different. Just be gentle, and don't come up behind 'em. Let's go."

"They'll come after us!" Sally hissed.

"You think? The driver drunk, and the slow one can't hardly find his buttons? That soldier gonna run after us? On what? We're taking the whole team. Now, let's go!"

Cora had already packed their belongings and loaded two of the mules, tethering them together. Murmuring to the animals, she tied Buck to Sally's back like a papoose and helped her onto a tall hinney, then passed Emma up, before pulling another hinney to the corral fence. Cora lifted Truette onto the mule's back, then stepped onto the fence rail and swung aboard behind her son. Taking hold of the tether line, she led the pack mules out of the farmyard, their hoofbeats muffled by the moist earth, and onto the road, shrouded by the piney woods but barely visible in the moonlight.

***

In the misty light of dawn before many people were up and about, a woman and two children walked next to a second woman leading a pack mule down the main street of Tuscaloosa to the steamboat landing. A few stevedores were starting the workday and a crew aboard one of boats had begun stoking the boiler fires. The men paused, watching the ladies unload several bags at the landing. Before long, the black woman mounted the mule and rode away, though she was back within an hour, on foot. By then the men had forgotten their puzzlement and gone back to work.

In midmorning, the steamboat *Demopolis* was long gone by the time a farm couple drove their produce wagon down Main Street, mentioning to customers that they had seen several mules grazing peacefully in a field on the outskirts of town, though there was no sign of the owners.

The townspeople agreed that was unusual.

Chapter One Hundred Eight

Mobile, June 1864

The steamboat eased into the wharf in late afternoon on a day so hot and humid Sally warned the children not to touch anything metal or their skin would blister. The children were antsy to get ashore and fascinated by the city, but their mothers were exhausted and short-tempered. Neither woman had slept much on the interminable trip downriver. The Black Warrior was so low and serpentine the steamboat sometimes reversed its paddlewheel to shimmy around tight corners. Each evening at sunset they stopped at small-town wharves that became hothouses in the short June nights.

"I want to get to Lester fast as you do, Cora," Sally mused, watching the dockmen secure the steamer to the Mobile pilings. "But I've got no idea what condition Sandy Hill's going to be in. Ezekiel said he'd be here in Mobile; we ought stock up before heading upriver."

Cora had grunted agreement. She hadn't talked much since Tuscaloosa unless she was reading to Truette.

"Does 'Zekiel know we're coming?" Emma asked, as they loaded onto a hackney cab.

Cora smiled, coming out of her shell. People on the wharf—black and white alike—eyed her. She knew it and knew why. Manumission papers, gold, the children, education, her new skills at medicine—Cora was not the illiterate slave that had left this port six years earlier; she carried herself differently and it showed.

Plus, anyone questioning them would have to deal with Sally, who came down the gangway with a shotgun strapped to her back.

"You like Ezekiel?" Cora asked.

"He was kind of like a ghost," Emma explained. The girl turned to Truette. "You'll like him, too. He doesn't say anything!"

"But he knows everything," Sally laughed. "Just like you, right True?"

The boy bobbed his head.

Fifteen minutes later, their open coach pulled into the courtyard at Truette Stubbs' house and stopped before the front porch. The yard was well tended, full of blooming azaleas and bougainvillea; the building looked freshly painted with porch furniture tidy and in place.

The women glanced at each other.

"Mommy," Emma gushed, "it's so beautiful. Where's 'Zekiel?"

"I don't know," Sally answered. "Call him."

Emma called several times as Sally mounted the steps. Not quite sure what to do, she knocked the clapper a few times and looked at Cora, who had directed the cab driver to bring their bags inside.

"It's your house," Cora said.

Sally turned the doorknob; it was unlocked. Stepping into the entry hall, she immediately felt its welcome coolness. The children followed behind, Truette peering around, tiptoeing to look into the parlor. Cora joined them, carrying Buck on her hip.

"Ezekiel?" Sally called, her voice echoing through the house.

"I'm going upstairs to my room," Emma declared, breaking for the staircase.

"Wait," Sally said, but the little girl was flying up the steps and ran along the top railing.

Sally glanced at Cora, who shrugged. "That's your girl."

"*Mommy!*" Emma's scream pierced the coolness and a moment later the child came streaking across the upstairs landing and down the staircase so fast she slipped and slid the last dozen steps on her bottom. Sally already had her thigh pistol pointed upstairs and the cab driver watched in shock as Cora shoved him out of the way, dropped little Lester, tore into one of the large bags and had a shotgun leveled faster than the man could have imagined possible. The ominous *click* of a shotgun hammer rang through the entry hall.

Tap ... tap ...tap ... A sound like rapping wood came from the upstairs hallway. Sally raised her pistol. Cora aimed the shotgun. *Tap ... tap ... tap ...*

A rumpled, bearded man slowly hobbled onto the upstairs landing. His clothes hung on an emaciated frame and a long, vivid scar, healing but still red, splotched his forehead. The man took two more hobbles, for he dragged one leg, and stopped, staring across the stair rail.

The front door shut behind them. Cora and Sally wheeled as one.

Jordon Hatcher smiled, raising his hands. "I give up."

Sally gasped. Cora stood, open-mouthed, looking to a young woman behind him she recognized but couldn't name, who held a wide-eyed infant.

"Jordon?" Emma exclaimed.

Jordon Hatcher looked to the second floor; the women turned, all eyes followed his.

"About time you got here," Jubal said.

Chapter One Hundred Nine

Cahaba, July 1864

Lester sat in the shade of the stockade and dozed, trying not to touch any of the men next to him. Concentrating on his dream, he carefully prepared the suckling pig, ready for the spit. About to peel potatoes, he snorted as a louse crawled up his nostril. Awake again, he brushed off a dozen more lice from his arms and thick beard and rubbed another handful out of his tangled hair. He closed his eyes, searching for the potatoes.

Four months earlier in spring, nearly seven hundred men fought for space in the crowded prison. Now fifteen hundred prisoners occupied the same area, equivalent to an open church sanctuary, with three or four rats per man and every single prisoner infested by lice, eating starvation rations, drinking polluted water, sleeping, shitting, pissing, and dying. If the prisoners were called to attention and spaced evenly apart, every man could extend their arms and touch another prisoner in any direction.

The only thing that kept most of them from going crazy was it took too much energy.

"Fuckin' Grant," someone griped. The news that General Grant had halted all prisoner exchanges was a literal death sentence for some men, who simply gave up hope and soon died. Men died from dysentery, wounds, fights, insanity, loneliness, and despair ...

Every day, Lester watched sunrise knowing another man wouldn't see sunset.

The potatoes wouldn't return. Disgusted, Lester concentrated on squishing the lice that had returned but resorted to flicking them off, figuring the motion took less energy than a squeeze. Little things add up, he reminded himself.

"I don't blame him," Lester said to the afternoon.

"Grant?"

"A prisoner is a prisoner. Black, white, red, yellow, or green."

"You mean I should sit here 'cause the Rebs won't change a soldier for a nigger?"

"You ever serve with a Negro, ready to die right next to you?"

"Ain't got nothin' to do with it!"

"You're an idiot," Lester sighed. "Shut up so the rest of us don't have to listen."

The man did, primarily because Richard sat nearby, and he listened.

A young—not yet nineteen—generally mild-mannered farm boy from northern Tennessee, Richard was both illiterate and literally a giant, seven feet tall with shoulders that wouldn't fit through a doorway and fists the size of small buckets. Lester had befriended the young man, showed him how to survive in camp, and taught him the rudiments of writing and numbers by tracing a finger in the dirt.

Though Richard had probably lost a quarter of his weight, so had everyone else except the most recent arrivals, and when the muggers tried to rob Lester of his meager meal, Richard got upset.

Muggers were predators, a small group of prisoners that formed as the camp population overwhelmed available space until everyone felt like apples in a barrel, literally having to step over men in any direction to do anything.

Four Muggers—troopers only recently captured and imprisoned—had snatched Lester's corncob a week earlier, ready for an easy fistfight. Ordinarily, it would be no contest, four against one, strength versus weakness. But the muggers had not yet realized the struggle was really strength versus survival—regardless of numbers. The man who had swiped the corncob was unluckiest; Lester went right for his eyes, clawing like a bobcat as the others pounced, oblivious of Richard, twenty feet away.

Lester had popped one of the howling man's eyeballs into the dirt and gouged at the other, his teeth sunk in the thief's cheek though almost unconscious from blows raining on his head and back. Abruptly the beating stopped as Richard picked up two of the assailants by the hair and rapped their heads together like coconuts, a sickening *clunk* heard throughout the yard. The fourth man tried to run but Richard looped a long arm out, collaring him, and with two punches broke most of the bones in the mugger's face.

There was very little mugging after that.

Chapter One Hundred Ten

Jordon Hatcher made it into Cahaba Prison two weeks later.

A day after arriving in Mobile, Cora had been anxious to go directly on to Gee's Bend, but after an evening's discussion with all the adults, she had listened to Jordon and Jubal. The men agreed Jordon should return to Gee's Bend alone, quietly, and make inquiries around the prison, see if he could learn about Lester, but not contact him or let on in any way of his interest.

After an initial burst of elation, everyone's behavior—children's and adults', black and white folks', men's and women's—reminded Jubal of experiences he'd had and witnessed many times of a crew taking their first steps on dry land after months at sea. The children were emotional, crying easily, and he and Sally circled each other warily, both defensive and uncertain, though trying to be gentle.

Lester's absence, proximity, and situation loomed large. Cora wasn't the least interested in small talk. "When we're going to Gee's Bend?" she demanded.

"Don't be in a rush," Jubal cautioned. "We need time to figure. Got to get in and learn the lay of the place."

"Jordon you built it! How are you going to get into that prison?"

"We'll think of something," Jubal replied, though he'd already asked himself the same question.

"I'm asking Jordon!" Cora snapped, bringing Jubal up short. He glanced at her, taking stock of a different woman then he'd left on the deck of *Mastiff* four years earlier.

"Miss Amanda," Jordon said, flatly. "I worked for her off 'n on ten years or more. That house I wuz working when Lester first come south, 'member Jubal? Her front door looks at that prison. You can bet she'll know the man runs things. I'll be lookin' for work. They sure to be using it hard, that stockade. Somethin' will need fixin'."

"What does she do?" Jubal asked. "Is the woman alone?"

"Whatever she can, now, 'guess. Her son rode north three years ago; fell in Virginia I heard. Young daughter lives with her last we wuz here."

Amanda Gardner answered her door in midafternoon. Now in her mid-forties, she had come to live in Cahaba a decade earlier, moving into a house that Jordon Hatcher and his boys had renovated.

"Why, Jordon!" she exclaimed. "I'd heard you'd gone."

"I been gone, m'am. Had to take my missus north. But I'm home."

"Missed it here?"

"Buried my sons."

Mrs. Gardner gasped. "Isaiah, Daniel? Both of them … are gone?"

"Fort Pillow, m'am."

"Oh, Jordon," she replied, ashen. By her expression, Jordon knew she had heard of the battle. "I know it an unbearable loss; we have no choice but prayer." Mrs. Gardner did not add that her remaining son rode with General Forrest. For the moment, she was glad she didn't know what he had seen or done.

"Beggin' yore pardon, Miss Amanda," Jordon stood tall, "wuz wonderin' if y'all had any chores needed doin'? Or if you're knowin' who runs the prison, maybe they got's a need or two. I could use a few days' work."

"I'm sorry Jordon, I have the need but not the means to hire you. But I can send you over with books. My father-in-law left me his library—a good one it is—and I've loaned books to the prisoners. The conditions inside are pitiful, a disgrace to any civilized society. Colonel Henderson does what he can; he is a fine gentleman—but times as they are …"

Jordon remembered the woman ten years earlier, young, full of life and delighted to be in her new home. Standing before him now she looked as if a lifetime had passed in that decade. Wisdom and compassion shown through, but not a hint of gaiety remained.

"I'll take them books over, yes m'am. Give 'em to the colonel."

"No, you can go direct to the Yankees. Colonel Henderson approves. There's a sergeant, give it to him. Sergeant Hawes, from Illinois, he's in charge of the books. But be careful of Jones," Mrs. Gardner's jaw tightened, "a new commandant. He commands when the colonel is away at other prisons, in Selma, and another in Georgia for which he is responsible. Lieutenant Colonel Jones is recently arrived. I have only met him once and never have I encountered a more foul man. Now wait while I go to my library."

Armed with a note from Mrs. Gardner and an armload of books, Jordon went directly to the prison and was shown in by the entry guard.

Sitting in a sliver of shade, Lester noticed the black man entering the gate, blinked twice and recognized Jordon immediately from ninety paces. Honed in the skills of surviving captivity, he showed no more notice but watched like a hawk as the guard pointed to Sergeant Hawes, a tall, balding, bearded man, indistinguishable from the other prisoners.

Jordon approached the sergeant, stunned at the sight of emaciated men by the hundreds packed in the open yard, many with only a shred of cloth covering their heads against the sun.

"Books, suh, from Miss Amanda," Jordon said, as men gathered, hopeful for a book. Evidently, the prisoners had some system of distributing Mrs. Gardner's loans, but Jordon paid little mind, unobtrusively scanning the crowd.

Sergeant Hawes looked Jordon over as he accepted the books. "Give my kindest regards to her, along with these requests from other prisoners. Mrs. Gardner will understand." The sergeant handed Jordon a sheaf of torn notepapers.

"I'll pass them to Miss Amanda, suh." Jordon bowed, turned away and bumped into Lester. The men locked eyes for a split second before Jordon dropped the passel of notes. Lester went to his knees to help retrieve them.

'I's sorry, suh," Jordon exclaimed, joining Lester on his knees. "All us in Mobile," he whispered.

"Tell her I love her," Lester replied in a normal voice. In the midst of men lining up for a book that might take their thoughts away from this hellhole, no one took notice of another random, nonsensical thought from a malnourished mind.

Chapter One Hundred Eleven

Mobile, August 1864

Emma walked into the living room and came directly to the couch, wedging herself between Sally and Jubal.

"Don't you touch my mommy," Emma declared, glaring at Jubal.

Jubal checked his temper. "Sally's already told me that."

Emma's eyes narrowed. She wasn't quite sure what to make of this.

"Go on, now," Sally said to their daughter, "go push Truette in the swing."

"He keeps kicking me."

"That's because he knows you'll push him so high and fast he'll get scared."

"So ...?"

Cora came in from the kitchen and motioned to Emma. "Help me bake some bread. C'mon, everybody's got to do their share, we've got eight mouths to feed."

Emma stomped into the kitchen. Cora turned without a word to follow.

"She's got to control everything," Jubal complained, his voice a bit slurred. "When did that start to happen? Emma used to be so sweet."

"Since you took off," Sally replied. "She's still sweet, when she feels safe."

"What am I doing to threaten her?"

"Being present."

Jubal struggled to sit up but winced. He took another pull from a flask of whiskey. "What the hell did you come back here for?"

"Lester!"

"Keep this up, Sally, you can go one way, I'll go the other."

"Like a boxing match?" Sally spit. "Round two? Besides, you can't walk."

Jubal leaned back, determined not to say any more. He could barely move, the only feeling in his leg was the lightning shafts of pain when he tried to walk. The constant tension with Sally had become unbearable. She was just ... so mad.

"Now you're going silent again?"

Sally couldn't help herself. She knew he drank to dull the incessant pain but she had never bargained for a husband usually half-drunk. The initial elation, running up the stairs and nearly tackling her Jubal, everyone hugging and crying, talking at once, the children wailing with fear or yelling from excitement, the radiant smiles of Jordon and later Ezekiel on his return from the market, seemed a distance far longer and greater than three weeks.

Sally breathed deeply a few times, willing herself to settle. "I don't want you to leave, ever again. But …"

"Forget the first part, dear. Just give me the 'but'."

Sally took another big breath, ready to start again. Suddenly, she laughed.

"Goddamn, you're ornery!"

Jubal glanced at his wife, a twinkle in his eye. "Don't forget I love you, Sally. Mostly did from the moment I laid eyes on you."

"What do you mean, mostly!"

"But …"

"Now *I* get the 'but'!"

Jubal started to laugh and took her hand. "I can touch you on the fingers?"

She dissolved and gave him a quick kiss. "I'm getting there. Do you expect me be to be romantic with a man I haven't seen for years who comes back crippled? Regardless whether there is some divine retribution at work, I'll try not to needle you about your stupid political views." Sally put a forefinger to his mouth. "I know: 'Every government, everywhere, derives its power from the consent of the people.' And you didn't consent. And I'll forever disagree. The power of the people supersedes the power of the individual. Our Union of states trumps any single state. Especially when a state claims the right to enslave because of color, or for that matter, any reason. Period, end of story."

Jubal looked at her and released her hands. Raising his eyebrows in mock severity he gave an exaggerated sigh and stuck out his right hand.

They shook on it.

"Cora!" Jubal waited until she came in from the kitchen. "All right. We settled."

Cora stared. "You sure?"

"Hell, no. But I can't live like this, and who knows when or how we could get to New York. I'll take my chances …"

Cora's hands went to her hips. "Then if you two promise to stop arguing, dinner is ready in twenty minutes. Your last good meal."

Jubal looked at Sally. "What'd you do to her?"

The next morning, Sally took the children into the library, where Charity waited.

"Cora and I are going upstairs for several hours to work on Daddy. You do what Charity says. If I hear so much as a peep out of either of you," she pointed to Emma and Truette, "believe you me, there will be hell to pay. If Lester starts squalin', mind to him."

The baby burbled agreement.

"He don't understand nothing," Emma grumped.

"He *doesn't* understand *anything*," Cora corrected, entering the room. "Now pay attention to your mother and mind Charity. Jordon will be nearby, and Ezekiel will take you to the market and get something nice."

"Ice cream?" Emma brightened.

"Nope. No ice here now; that came from home," Sally replied. "But Ezekiel will find you something."

Sally and Cora went upstairs where Jordon and Ezekiel had laid Jubal out on a long table covered with cloth, moving him close to the southern window through which unhindered sunlight would stream for several hours. Cora fished in her carpetbag, brought out a smaller, black leather medical kit, and laid out on a separate table magnifying glasses, tweezers, pliers, scalpels, and a small hand-held drill with several bits. Several swabs of cotton, a strip of linen bandage, and three bottles completed the array.

"I had no idea you had all that stuff," Sally marveled.

"It's what I'm doing while you do the tradin'," Cora replied. "All right. Jubal, did you finish that drink?"

Jubal mumbled something unintelligible and tossed a newspaper he'd been reading on the floor.

"Whiskey and morphine," Cora said, glancing at the *Mobile Evening Telegraph*. "They call it 'soldier's delight.' Now we've got to wash our hands for five minutes, then take some of that ether in the green bottle, wet a cotton swab and hold it over Jubal's nose until he's out. Jordon," the black man waited by the door, "put Jubal on his left side and tie him down so that leg can't move."

Cora directed Sally to spread the newspaper on the floor and donned a sparkling clean apron, washed her hands one last time with iodine, and scrubbed the new scar on Jubal's hip.

After speaking with the two most experienced surgeons in Mobile, both had told Jubal and Sally that a piece of shrapnel was likely lodged between the hip bone and one of several nerves leading to his leg. Only a few specialists in the country—likely in New York or Boston—would attempt surgery. A bungled operation would mean amputation at the hip in the best instance, and more likely, a lingering death.

Cora had come along and listened, though neither of the surgeons paid the least bit of attention to her, even when Sally mentioned that she studied at the Medical College and worked at Satterlee Hospital. Though both doctors were polite, neither asked a thing about Cora's knowledge. Nor would they, she knew, have given it any credence whatsoever.

"I'll go in and find whatever it is," she told Jubal on the way back to Truette Stubbs' house. "If I can't take it out without crippling you, then you'll have to wait. And hope."

"You think you know what you're doing?" Jubal asked.

Cora didn't even bother to answer; Sally looked at him, shaking her head.

"You ought to know better, Jubal. Did they teach you how to ask stupid questions in England?"

"It's my leg!"

"Would you offer to carve into someone if you didn't know how?"

"Jeezus," Jubal muttered.

The pain decided.

As Cora opened the wound, she cauterized blood vessels with a glowing knife tip kept red hot in a small coal brazier Ezekiel had fired. Momentarily, she stopped and looked up at Jordon Hatcher, still watching from the doorway.

"Tell me again, Jordon."

Jordon straightened, as proud of this woman as he had ever been of his children, of Beulah, of anyone he had ever known.

"He say, 'Tell her I love her.' Them exact words."

Standing in the sunlight, Cora listened, as she had every day since Jordon had returned. Savoring the warm deep rumble and its lifegiving message, she smiled and nodded to him and took a deep breath, steadying herself to begin. Just as she about to make an incision, a knock sounded on the door. Charity peeked around Jordon.

"I want to help. Miss Sally said I could ask."

Cora eyed the young woman. "Go wash, Sally'll show how."

Seven hours later, Cora collapsed in a chair, sipping whiskey. Jubal breathed quietly, asleep, as Sally bathed his face. Charity, so tired she stumbled, gathered the bloody sheet, swabs, and bandages for Ezekiel to haul away. The old man also picked up the torn newspaper, briefly glancing at a photograph and the accompanying article reporting the sinking of the CSS *Alabama* off Cherbourg, France, six weeks earlier, before he crumpled it to burn with the stained rags.

In a small glass on the window sill, a white sliver of bone, the size and shape of a button needle, lay unobtrusive and silent, its point no longer lodged behind Jubal's pelvis, wedged between muscle and sciatic nerve.

"A month, more or less." Cora took a sip of whiskey and blew away strands of hair fallen over her eyes. "Not much muscle to a leg that can't get used. He'll want a cane probably, 'till end of summer."

She looked at Sally, sitting at Jubal's bedside. She was crying.

Cora smiled, satisfied. "Then he goin' be chasin' you round a'gin."

Three weeks later, the extended family had all moved back to Sandy Hill, save for Ezekiel, who stayed to mind Truette Stubbs' house in Mobile, though Jubal directed the old man to come forthwith if significant war news arrived in Mobile.

"We've got to be close to Cahaba," Jubal explained, a week after his operation, "and I want us to stay together. It's just safer." The sentiment hid Jubal's greater apprehension that Cora would go upriver anyway to find some way of helping her husband.

"Then let's go," Cora said. "You can travel."

"You sure it's not too soon?" Sally worried. As usual, the conversation took place over dinner, a large assembly that included all the children, Charity, Ezekiel, and Jordon. Dinners had become times of communion that comforted everyone except the children, who were oblivious to their parents' anxiety.

Cora pursed her lips, annoyed at Sally for pinning her dead to rights. "No."

"Doctor Cora?" Sally pressed.

"Well, yes, it would be better to wait. Two more weeks. Then we're going."

"Maybe Sally and I should go first," Jordon said, getting their immediate attention. Jordon usually said little at dinner, though he clearly relished the company. "Then you and Jubie come along, Charity kin help nurse him."

"Why?" Sally and Cora spoke simultaneously.

"Miss Sally, you and Jubal own Sandy Hill. Ain't nobody know about Cora being Lester's wife; ain't no one should. Gonna take us time to move 'round Cahaba easy, raise no fuss, and Mr. Jubal, he needs to move. How long 'fore he can run?"

Cora shrugged. "Depends on him. Two, three months."

"So let's us use that time." Jordon turned to Sally. "Be good for you to meet Miss Amanda, maybe even that colonel runs the prison. I need to be going in easy, like usual."

"How?" Sally asked.

"Dunno. That's what you got to figure with Miss Amanda."

Sally absent-mindedly tapped her teeth for a few moments before her face broke in a conspiratorial smile.

"I have an idea," she said.

Evening had begun to cool as a setting sun eased onto the treeline on the far side of the field from Sandy Hill. Sally stood waiting, her arm entwined in Jubal's as he leaned on his cane watching the buggy pull into the dooryard. Jordon Hatcher climbed down, as did Colonel Henderson; the men reached for the hands of Amanda Gardner and her daughter, Belle.

Sally came down the porch steps to greet them. "Welcome to Sandy Hill," she said, making no effort to hide her Maine accent. "I am Sally; come meet my husband, Jubal Calhoun. You will pardon him, please; stairs are still difficult."

"Your wife's invitation mentioned you are recovering from wounds, sir." Colonel Henderson trotted up the steps to shake Jubal's hand. "Howard Henderson, at your service." Mustachioed and short, he had an open face and firm handshake.

"Yes," Jubal replied, "on the field at Fort Pillow."

Amanda Gardner stopped in midstep, sucking a breath. "Did you per chance know a Private Gardner?"

"No m'am. I was new to Forrest's unit."

"But you were there?"

"Yes, m'am, though I remember very little. I fell early in the assault."

Sally gritted her teeth. She had hoped to steer the conversation in a polite direction, but the war intruded before her guests had even made it up the front porch stairs. When Charity came out of the house with a tray of mint juleps Sally could have kissed her.

"Please," Sally urged, "let's sit and watch the evening come in."

The guests settled and drinks were passed around when Emma strode out of the house and up to Belle.

"I'm Emma. I'm eight."

"Emma!" Sally rolled her eyes. "Will you greet our guests, please?"

Emma curtsied, and turned back to Belle. "How old are you?"

"Ten," Belle replied.

"Good." Emma reached for her hand. "You can come to my room."

Amanda Gardner nodded, looking amused. The tension eased away on the slight breeze.

"Children remind us of the Lord's goodness, don't they?" the colonel remarked.

"Have your duties made you more religious?" Sally asked. "Jordon has told me of your compassionate efforts for the prisoners, and those of Mrs. Gardner."

"Before the war I was ordained in the Methodist Church," Henderson replied, "and I intend to resume my ministry upon the conclusion of this conflict."

"In Alabama?" Jubal asked.

"The Lord will guide me," Henderson shrugged. "I never thought to be here, but this is my path and I strive to do my duties as compassion and decency provide."

"Indeed," Sally said. "May this accursed conflict end, soon. Jordon informed me, Mrs. Gardner, of your literary generosity. I cannot imagine the joy a simple book must hold for prisoners. I wanted to thank you, and add our efforts to yours."

"Mr. Hatcher belongs to you now?"

"Mr. Hatcher belongs to himself. We freed him."

"I see," Mrs. Gardner replied coolly. "I must tell you we are Southern born and raised; I believe our cause is righteous and just. I have given a son to the Lord on the battlefield for our Confederacy."

"I'm sorry for your loss," Sally replied. To hell with the pleasantries, she thought. "My husband agrees with you. I don't. Nonetheless, like the Colonel, we are here. The war is with us, my husband must convalesce for several more months here, and there are how many prisoners, Colonel Henderson, down the track who require care?"

"More than two thousand."

"We wish to follow Mrs. Gardner's example," Sally said. "With your permission, sir."

"Of course," Colonel Henderson smiled. "I'm sure more books would be welcomed. Mrs. Gardner's volumes come back dog-eared and tattered from so many readers."

"Our library may not suffice," Sally observed. "We had something else in mind."

In the momentary silence, Jubal raised his arms and pointed to the fields out front. "Food."

"Corns, beans, vegetables," Sally continued. "I've instructed our people to increase our pig and chicken stock. But," her voice hardened, "may we have your word? As an officer, *and* a man of God."

"I don't understand," Colonel Henderson shifted in his seat, the smile gone.

"Notwithstanding Mrs. Gardner's and your sympathies, I have mine. We willingly will provide and have Jordon deliver what food we can to your prisoners—so long as I have your solemn promise that it will go *inside*, and not be confiscated nor directed to active troops."

Colonel Henderson breathed a sigh of relief. "Most assuredly, Mrs. Calhoun, I promise you. However, I am frequently away; if your provisioning would include the guards also, I do believe the efforts to be more efficacious. Mr. Calhoun is welcome at any time to evaluate our efforts ... as are you, m'am, though I caution the prison is no place for a lady."

"Where were you educated, Colonel?" Sally asked, intrigued. The man had no accent.

"Ohio Wesleyan, and Cincinnati School of Law."

"A lawyer, minister, and commandant of a prison ... in southern Alabama?" Sally smiled.

"The Lord works in mysterious ways," Colonel Henderson replied.

"Doesn't she?" Sally rose. "As my husband would say, and do," she extended her hand, "it's a deal."

"I believe it time for dinner," Jubal said, reaching for his cane.

Chapter One Hundred Twelve

Cahaba Prison, September 1864

Lieutenant Colonel Sam Jones stood on the parapet in front of the assembled prisoners, surrounded by several guards and a few townsmen. Rumors had flown through the yard on his arrival a month earlier; several of the prison guards, many of whom were poor and uneducated but diligently doing an unpleasant, boring duty, reported that Lt. Colonel Jones had been captured and paroled twice, then assigned to the prison after being passed over for command of his unit.

Lester could see by the way the man carried himself he loathed the prisoners.

"You goddamn Yankees goin' obey my rules! This man here," he pointed to Richard, "been eating more than a man's share."

"He's the size of two men!" A prisoner yelled from the yard.

"You, there, back-talkin'!" The colonel turned to his guards. "Get him, too! Bring 'em outside!"

An hour later, Richard and the other man were dragged back into the yard. Neither could stand.

"Get away from them!" Lester ordered, as men gathered round. "Give 'em room!" Lester slowly poured a gourd of filthy water over Richard and did the same for the other man. The day was stifling hot and humid; a cloudless, hazy sky offered no respite from the withering sun directly overhead. "What'd he do?" Lester asked.

"Ladder out there, 'gainst the stockade," Richard gasped. "Had to hang off the rung for ten minutes, toes barely touchin'. Other one kept droppin'; he got five minutes. Took us this long." Richard collapsed, unable to talk. The other prisoner lay unconscious.

Lester looked up at the stockade parapet, searching for Jones. The colonel briefly reappeared, looked the yard over with contempt, and disappeared down the stairway. Several guards resumed their pacing around the parapet perimeter, one accompanied by a man walking with the aid of a cane.

Lester had noticed him earlier, standing to the outside of Lt. Colonel Jones' entourage on the parapet as the commandant addressed his prisoners. Bearded, sandy-haired, and thin, the bearded man with a cane looked about the yard. Lester paid him no more attention.

As the prisoners dispersed, Lester and a few others helped Richard and his fellow inmate to their feet and walked them slowly under the covered roof and onto a pallet to rest. The effort exhausted Lester and he sat down against a post, waiting for a little shade.

Glancing up, he noticed the bearded man had moved halfway around the stockade and was standing still, staring. Lester looked around, wondering who had the man's attention. Seeing no one in particular, he glanced back. His mouth opened; he blinked several times, increasingly certain.

Finally, a trace of a smile ruffled Jubal's beard, indiscernible unless looking directly at him. Slow and deliberate, he moved his cane as if it were a pointer, idly tapped it a few times, then turned and slowly made his way around the parapet to the stairs and disappeared without looking back.

Lester eyes followed until Jubal was out of sight. Stunned, it took a full five minutes for Lester to absorb what had happened. Willing his mind to concentrate, he closed his eyes and imagined the cane tapping. Three times. Why the number, why the tapping? Lester gave up.

A flash caught his eye, the ripple of water. Someone had flushed out the latrines again, sending sewage out the trench under the stockade where it flowed down the embankment and into the river. The width of a man, maybe a foot deep, the latrine trench was as disgusting as four thousand runny shits a day would make it.

Lester stared again. On the parapet, Jubal had tapped his cane, standing directly above the latrine trench.

Chapter One Hundred Thirteen

Gee's Bend, September 1864

"Daddy!" Emma tore into the house, "Ezekiel's here!"

The old black man rode into the dooryard on a mule he had rented further upriver at Cahaba after disembarking from the Mobile steamboat. After a dry summer, the river was low, though boiling thunderheads on the southern horizon promised a wet night.

From the way Ezekiel eyed him, Jubal knew enough to bring the man directly into the library and shut the door. An hour later, as the entire family gathered at dinner, Jubal asked everyone to join hands. Buck had to have his wiped clean; he was already squishing cheese curd through his fingers.

"Lord," Jubal intoned, "bless this food, Charity and Daniella now of our family; Sally and Cora, our beautiful women; Emma, True, and Buck, our lovely children; faithful friends Jordon and Ezekiel; we ask also that you protect Lester in the midst of his severity, and thank you for ending this cursed war between the states, soon. Amen."

Cora and Sally stared at him. Buck plunged his hands back in the cheese curd.

"Atlanta fell." Jubal served Buck a tiny slice of pork. "That's the 'two' of a one-two punch. Mobile Bay fell, now Atlanta. From there, I doubt Sherman will turn around. No, he'll drive to the coast. It's done." Jubal made to serve himself, but stopped and reached for his cane. "Will you ladies excuse me, please?"

"When will it be done?" Sally asked.

"Not tomorrow, or next week, or next month," Jubal replied. "But this will reelect Lincoln, and by now, we know the man. He'll see it through."

"When?" It was Cora.

"Later this year, I'd guess, or early next. You've never seen a sinking ship, but there's a moment when it just … gives up. Crew stream from below, leaving the pumps, jumping overboard … one of the saddest things a man can see, a ship going down." Jubal hobbled out the door. His leg was much stronger, but by sunset the small hole that Cora had drilled in his bone to get at the sliver began to ache enough for him to often reach for a whiskey, though Sally had made clear she wouldn't tolerate him drunk.

Cora's tone stopped Jubal midstep. "I'm not talking about the war."

"As soon as it rains hard for several days," he said. "The river has to come way up. It will—I know it will. But we have to wait. Ask Jordon. We can't see any other way."

Cora put down her napkin. "Excuse me, please." She left the dining room; moments later her steps led upstairs. Jubal pulled his bulldog out and went onto the porch.

"Cheery crowd here," Sally mused to the children. "Ezekiel, show Truette how to talk. What did you hear?"

Chapter One Hundred Fourteen

Cahaba, November 1864

Sally spooned into Jubal, biting his shoulder as the thunder crashed overhead and rain lashed the windows. The house shuddered.

Jubal reached around and pulled Sally close, his fingers between her legs. She pushed against his hand. Roused, Jubal rolled over. "Late season hurricane," he murmured, nuzzling her neck.

"The house is already shaking," Sally's breath quickened and she squirmed under him, squeezing as she felt his hardening, pulling him deep. She kicked the covers off and wrapped her legs high around his hips. Jubal felt her teeth in his shoulder, fingernails buried in his back as they thrust and rolled, one on top then the other. Laughing at peals of thunder and mimicking the thrashing storm, with another crash of thunder that stifled their nearly simultaneous, muted guttural howls they collapsed in a pile of spent giggles and lay back, listening to the unrelenting rain.

"We're getting better," Sally whispered after a time. "Do you think I'm fat?"

Jubal laughed like he hadn't in years. "Huge," he said, then bellowed from a punch in the ribs. "You're the most delicious hunk of horseflesh I've ever known."

"How romantic," Sally burrowed close, then neighed in his ear. She rolled on top and buried her tongue in his mouth as deep as she could until she had to take a breath. "Giddy-up," she growled, pulling at his hair, plunging onto him.

Later, in the middle of the night, she awoke and listened for Jubal's breathing. The windows still rattled, the storm unabated.

"You awake?" she whispered.

"Yeah."

"Is this enough rain?"

"Might be. If it moves slow, hits the mountains hard ... we'll know in a few days. The moon will be right."

"There's almost no moon."

"I don't want 'almost'. *No* moon. Black as Jordon—that's what we want."

"Can I tell Cora?"

"No. But you'll tell her anyway."

"Home by Thanksgiving ... Oh God, Jubal, be careful."

"I'm not bringing him here. Can't, Sandy Hill won't be safe. They'll surely be looking. Maybe, after a month ..."

"Christmas?"

"Could be."

Sally sat up in the darkness. "Tell me!"

Jubal pulled her back down. "Shush, you'll wake the children." He pulled the covers up around them and held her tight. "Let me get him out first, and hidden, without getting either of us, or both, killed. I am *not* telling you or anyone where, so don't ask. Any questions, you don't know and won't even look like you know."

"I can lie."

"You cannot. You'd be a terrible smuggler. Now go to sleep."

"Is that an order?"

"Yes, m'am, it is."

Sally put a hand between his legs, grasping him, and maneuvered her leg between his. Relishing the tangle, Jubal could feel tears on his back.

"Aye, aye, Captain."

Chapter One Hundred Fifteen

Cahaba Prison, December 2, 1864

Four days of torrential rain had made the prison yard a sea of mud. As two prisoners squabbled over their soup ration, one of the young guards patrolling the parapet, a man named Hawkins, casually raised his rifle and put a bullet through the heart of the taller man. Lester saw the entire incident, as did Jordon Hatcher, standing six feet away, lading cold vegetable stew from a large barrel he had brought from Sandy Hill.

"That's the third man that murdering little bastard has shot this week," Lester seethed. Men started shouting at Hawkins as other guards raced to his side, raising their rifles.

"What about me, gonna shoot me over soup?"

"You murderin' bastards!!"

"Slimy Rebel cunts!!"

The prisoner chorus became a roar, heading toward a full-scale riot. The frightened guards cocked their rifles, on the edge of panic, when several pistol shots cut the air. Colonel Jones had run up the stairs and stared down, lowering his smoking pistols to point them at the melee.

"The next man that shouts will be shot!" he shouted.

"Then shoot yourself!"

The colonel searched for the voice but faced a sea of men; his most recent census had counted more than 2,100 prisoners, though several were now dead, including the three Hawkins had shot.

"Who started this?" the colonel shouted.

Lester started to raise his hand but felt a flash of liquid on his arm; Jordon Hatcher had hurled a ladle of soup at him. The black man made one abrupt shake of his head, plain as if he had screamed *No!*

A prisoner, one of the most senior of the captured officers, raised an arm. "Your guard is summarily executing prisoners. Unless you kill us all, I guarantee this conduct will be found a war crime, punishable by hanging!"

The stockade erupted.

Jordon Hatcher was at Lester's side. "Stay close," the black man hissed.

Colonel Jones fired his pistol in the air, quieting the crowd. "You!" he yelled, pointing at the Union officer, "identify that body and come to the gate! Someone get the body out of there!"

Jordon raised his voice. "I be doing that, suh. Take 'im to the cemetery. I need a man to lend hisself!" He looked to the prisoner nearest him. "Gimme hand, if you will."

Lester took the dead prisoner by the feet as Jordon hoisted the warm torso, and they carried him beyond the gate, carting the corpse to Jordon's wagon. Several guards covered Lester from the parapet walls but nobody came near the dead man, his face speckled with disturbed lice. As they arranged the corpse Jordon murmured, his lips barely moving.

"Jubie say tomorrow night, back post by the privy, outbound. Zuby at ten o'clock."

Lester grunted.

—⁓—

Jubal heard the shots and commotion from the carpenter's shop along the Cahaba River, a few hundred yards upstream from where it entered the Alabama.

"Some ruckus at Castle Morgan," the carpenter waved off the distant noise. Nice lookin' skiff, this." He examined his handiwork, custom built from plans Jubal had lofted. "This what you had in mind? You must be a waterman, way she's laid her out. Ain't ya?"

"For a time," Jubal drawled, pointing with the cane he no longer needed around Sandy Hill but used in town with the pronounced limp he affected there. "Blue water. This here's kind of a bastard bateau, a mongrel sort of mix, ends of a Grand Banks dory, belly of a peapod, stretched some like a dugout. I like it. She'll handle upstream all right, 'specially this high water."

"'N you can pole or row it, either," the carpenter agreed. "Made it out of cypress; it'll last you a good long time. Oars are hickory. A hundred dollars will do 'er."

"How about a piglet? Just got us a passel."

"Make it two! Them pigs surely be more useful! When you back for the boat?"

"Two, then. I want to launch her right now. Gonna row upstream aways, do some hunting soon as the water comes down a mite. Coons will be treed, gators out—this water will flush 'em."

The carpenter looked at Jubal skeptically. "Think you can handle it all 'lone? Current's running, gonna get worse. Water'll rise the next couple of days; that was a helluva rain. The big river's comin' on fast. Must have been Noah's flood up to the mountains."

Jubal nodded. The Alabama River, muddy and churning, had risen fifteen feet in two days, which likely meant another ten as the mountains emptied. He needed at least that for the river to climb the embankment and come level with the privy channel.

As the carpenter dragged the bateau over rollers, Jubal belayed it with rope down into the Cahaba, already high with backflow from the Alabama. He tied the boat off as Jordon Hatcher drove the wagon into the yard.

"What was all the shootin' about?" Jubal asked. Jordon hitched a thumb behind him. A body lay sprawled in the wagon bed.

"'Nother dead Yankee?" the carpenter asked. "Good riddance."

Jubal looked at Jordon straight-faced though utterly perplexed.

"How about I meet you up to the cemetery?" Jordon pointed. "You take the wagon."

"Where's that fellow from?" the carpenter asked.

"Iowa, they said," Jordon replied, handing the reins to Jubal.

"Long way from home," Jubal mused, trying to fathom why Jordon would bring a corpse.

"Serves him right," the carpenter turned away. "I'd never go to Iowa, tellin' 'em how to live. Sum'bitch just couldn't leave us alone. Thanks for the business!"

"Jes' a minute, sir," Jordon stopped him. "Any scraps you got? Need us some firewood for to render fat. I'll stow it 'long side the Yank, he ain't gonna mind. You take the wagon, Mr. Jubal, I'll be along."

The carpenter pointed to a pile of scrap lumber. "Your pick."

"Don't need much," Jordon went to the pile.

"You seen Sally?" Jubal muttered, throwing scrap aboard the wagon because Jordon did. She had accompanied them into town earlier, tying a horse to the tail of the wagon so she could do some errands.

"That's 'nough. She said she'd be back to Sandy Hill by sundown." Jordon headed for the bateau.

An hour later and a mile upriver, Jordon tied the bateau to a tree and came up the riverbank, joining Jubal who waited in the wagon at the pauper cemetery a quarter-mile outside Cahaba.

"Mind tellin' me ..." Jubal began.

"Lord provides," Jordon Hatcher said. "We need a body. That Jones man be lookin' long and hard—Lester never be safe. So we'll give him something to stop lookin'."

"This poor wretch don't look like Lester any more than I do."

"A few weeks in da swamp, ain't anybody gonna look like nobody. Just what we need. Yes, suh, Lord done provide."

"I don't know that this fella agrees." Jubal still didn't understand fully, but together they dug into the earth a few feet and then stopped for a rest. At Jordon's direction, and making sure no one could see them in either direction, Jubal helped sling the body over Jordon's shoulder. The black man hurried back to the river, while Jubal chucked the scrap wood he'd bought from the carpenter's shop into the empty grave, mounding the dirt and pounding a cross in at one end. He had to admit no one would ever look at the grave and not think it occupied.

Jubal brought the wagon another half mile up the road to where it bowed close to the river and waited. Jordon Hatcher appeared after a time, soaked from the chest down. Jubal gave him his coat, turned the mules, and they all headed back toward Cahaba, skirting the town on outlying streets behind the Gardner place, past the stockade, and onto the track leading to Sandy Hill.

From a distance, Sally waved, but her men looked ahead and didn't see her. She reined in her horse and dismounted in the dooryard of the house at the edge of town.

―

Amanda Gardner, formal and reserved, welcomed Sally into her home, which stood across a muddy road from Cahaba Prison. Sally immediately noticed the knotted wood floors were no longer covered in carpet and a large bookcase on one wall stood mostly empty.

"I was in town and thought to stop," Sally explained. "Jordon told me you are just about out of books."

"I don't mind," Mrs. Gardner replied, "I've read them all, and Belle, too." She watched Sally carefully; she respected the Northern woman but doubted they would ever become friends.

"May I send several boxes of books from our library here with Jordon?"

"You can take them directly to the prison."

"Perhaps," Sally replied, "though I heard many inquiries come to you."

Amanda Gardner relaxed and smiled. She went to a desk and brought back a handful of notes, passing them to Sally.

Mrs. Amanda Gardner:

Will you please send some books to the subscribers to while away the hours of prison life.

Respectfully,

J. R. Bowen, Chas. Reynolds, James Farrell

Mrs. Amanda Gardner:

If you please to send me some nice interesting book to read and I will return it with care.

B. F. Daughtery Private, Co. 8 37th Reg't. Ills. Inft. Vol.

Madam:

Will you be so kind as to send me—a prisoner—one or two books to pass away the time. Having heard from our men how kind you have been in sending reading matter to them, I make so bold in addressing you in my behalf. I have the honor to be, very respectfully, your obedient servant.

Thos McElroy, Capt. U.S. Navy

Sally fingered the remaining notes, more than a dozen. "How often do these come?"

"Every few days."

"And Jordon told me you used your carpets for blankets? For the prisoners to share?"

"I have no more carpet. Belle and I cut them into pieces. The men are freezing. It will get worse." Mrs. Gardner gestured Sally in. "Will you have some tea?"

"I would love some tea," Sally replied, doffing her coat. "This rain has chilled me to the bone. We need more blankets, then?" She stopped abruptly and tapped her teeth, thinking.

"All the carpets in Cahaba wouldn't be enough. At Colonel Henderson's last count there are two thousand one hundred and sixty-four prisoners. I can't stand the mistreatment these men suffer, even if they should never have invaded us."

Sally held her tongue, aided by a sharp rap at the door.

Mrs. Gardner looked through the adjacent window, recognized the visitor, and set her face before opening the front door.

"What do you want, Colonel?" Mrs. Gardner made no attempt to hide her hostility.

"May I come in, m'am?"

"No."

The Lt. Colonel Jones stood stiff, his distemper plain. "I have been informed of your complaints, m'am." Belle appeared, ignoring Sally to stand beside her mother.

"I will not tolerate your cruelty, Colonel! Forcing men to hang from a ladder in sight of my doorway!"

"Is it the punishment they so richly deserve," the colonel sneered, "or the sight?"

"These poor prisoners suffer inhumane conditions!"

"Your sympathy for the damned Yankees is odious to me," Jones snapped. "Now bear yourself with the utmost care in the future or you shall be an exile!"

"I am a damned Yankee," Sally said. She had come up from behind and stared at Jones as if he were an unfamiliar animal.

Jones shifted, suddenly uncertain.

"Colonel," Sally continued. "I have a proposal that will reflect substantially on your leadership, I believe, particularly in light of recent incidents in the prison. If you won't act on it I will address Colonel Henderson."

Colonel Jones regarded her with suspicion bordering on paranoia. "Just what can a Yankee offer to help us here, feeding the very scoundrels who have fought to enslave us?"

Sally stiffened. "Enslave? Interesting you should use that verb, Colonel. Nonetheless, I propose to telegram Quartermaster General Meigs, of the United States Army, and ask that a Union gunboat, under a flag of truce, steam upriver—now that Mobile Bay is *free*—with clothing, uniforms, and blankets for the incarcerated men."

"Absolutely not!"

"Colonel," objected Mrs. Gardner, "you well know my sympathies. But these prisoners will perish in winter. There are three times as many men as last year! You were not here to witness the suffering. I was!"

"I will not consider it! Do you have any idea how Confederate prisoners are treated? I have been," he paused, flustered, "imprisoned twice!"

"Luck or competence?" Sally scoffed, disgust getting the better of her. "I will go to Mobile and see that one way or another my proposal reaches Washington, and am confident I will prevail. I know General Meigs personally, a man of the utmost integrity and compassion."

"Then why does he invade us?" shouted Colonel Jones. He straightened, chagrined. "Excuse my outburst. Our cause is right and just. This discussion is over." He turned on his heel.

"It is over *if you win*," Sally declared. "'Right,' and history, are determined by the winner. Mrs. Gardner tells me the most recent prisoner census numbers over two thousand. If a substantial number of men in your charge die this winter because you refuse to provide adequate clothing and shelter, I swear by the Lord above you will hang, Colonel Jones."

Sally gathered her cloak. "Should you wish to live," she said, walking directly at Colonel Jones, her voice dripping with contempt, "I suggest you pray for victory."

The colonel moved aside.

Chapter One Hundred Sixteen

"I got another idea," Sally reported the next afternoon. "But I made him mad."

Jubal helped her into the wagon, scanning the sky. "Don't take much effort for you, does it, either one?"

"Have you ever met the man?" Sally retorted. "A mental midget, which is doing a disservice to small people."

"I'm sure you scared him and I'm glad you did," Jubal replied, nodding to Jordon, who snapped the traces. The mules set out from Sandy Hill. "We'll want him preoccupied beyond the disappearance of one prisoner."

"I detest that man."

"Let's hope you put his mind on something besides making examples and letting his guards shoot men down in cold blood. What's your idea?"

"Lester's boss," Sally replied. "General Montgomery Meigs." They rode on for another hour, Sally explaining her plan to contact the general, until Jordon pulled the mule team to a stop.

Jubal pointed to a narrow road that circled the town.

"Here, darling, follow this to the west road out and tell us when you come to the big live oak, about two miles past the cemetery, maybe fifteen, twenty minutes. I don't want anyone seeing us, so keep your bearings. You'll be coming back this same way. Come on, Jordon."

Jordon handed Sally the reins and the two men swung into the wagon bed, lay down and pulled a tarp over them.

A half hour later, under the boughs of an enormous live oak, Sally hugged Jordon Hatcher before she seized her husband. "Be careful Jubal; I'm getting used to you again."

"Decide you'd keep me?"

"I 'spect so." She kissed him. "I mean it—get back." Sally wagged a finger. "Both of you. And tell Lester, from Cora, she loves him."

"She hasn't said much lately," Jubal said, as Jordon hauled a long coil of thin rope and a rucksack out of the wagon bed.

"To hide her feelings," Sally replied. "Cora's nearly out of her mind with worry. And hope."

"She's not alone." Jubal kissed her quick. "Get going, now. One of us will come in tomorrow. That's a good idea you got." He hoisted Sally onto the wagon seat, kissed her hand, and hustled after Jordon, waving one last time before disappearing into the underbrush.

Sally turned the team, looked to the sky and said a prayer, then snapped the mules into a brisk walk home.

~

Waiting for darkness, Jubal shared cigars and a small flask of whiskey with Jordon. "Not too much," Jubal grinned, "just loosen us up some. Here's to you, my poor man." He raised his flask to the soggy body of the trooper gunned down the day before, which Jordon had tied into the bateaux. Overturning the craft, he had weighted the flat bottom with stones to keep it barely awash, snug in the riverbank mud.

"Sky's breakin' some, Mr. Jubal," Jordon whispered. A thin line of red sunset showed through the trees as the frog chorus began. "Couple more hours. Got to be dark as a pocket."

"You told him the time?"

"Zuby at ten o'clock, jes' like you say. What's that mean? I seen clocks before but they don't tell me nuthin'."

"Zuben Elgenubi is a navigation star in Libra. It will rise through the night to about eleven o'clock above the horizon and set again long before daylight." Jubal demonstrated with a stiff arm. "When Zuby is at ten o'clock above the horizon, Lester will know. At sea, we do it all the time, like a way of telling time when there's not enough moonlight to see."

Jordon grunted. "Gonna be dead dark, so don't be lettin' loose that rope, I'll never find yew a'gin. River'll swaller us."

"I won't. You yourself said this were the only way we'd make her."

"We will. That shitstream's the only way out. Jes' don't let go the rope."

Jubal nodded, pulled a piece of jerky from the rucksack, bit it in two and passed a piece. "Our friend still in one piece?" he motioned to the body they'd stuffed in the bateau.

"Is now. In two weeks, no tellin'."

"You've got a diabolical cast of mind, Jordon."

"What's that?"

"Brilliant. Very smart. Got to admit, givin' Jones a body he can't recognize will take him off the scent."

Jordon Hatcher snorted. "Oh, that fellow gonna have smell to him."

"Poor bastard," Jubal sighed.

The night sounds enveloped them until finally, after Jordon had smeared Jubal's face with black mud, they curled the dead trooper astern, piled into the bateau and shoved off. In darkness blacker than the men, Jubal pulled the oars while Jordon sat in the bow keeping watch.

The current flowed swift as Jubal aimed in the middle of a barely discernible corridor through the trees. In the distance, lights from Cahaba flickered on the right bank and Jubal steered further into the river, giving the warehouses as much berth as he dared, knowing the roiling Alabama could seize and shoot the bateau into midstream, making for a hard pull back to the riverbank just downstream of the stockade.

Jubal let the current take them, steering in an arc at the confluence of the Cahaba and Alabama. Burying the oars deep, using the current to orient, he cut across the flow to keep them close. Spotting the corner stockade lantern, Jubal held the oars still to float with the river. Pulling a hood up and lowering his face while Jordon averted his eyes from the prison, their bateau floated past almost invisible, a fleeting shadow of log against the two meager lantern lights at either end of the stockade.

The hurricane had stumbled into the high watershed of the Coosa and Tallapoosa rivers, dumping immense quantities of rainwater that flowed into the Alabama, raising the river level to a few feet below the stockade. As the bateau floated past, they heard footfalls on the parapet forty feet away, heading upriver. With the footfalls receding, Jubal glanced back, but the night was so black he could only catch the darker silhouette of a sentry's tattered hat above the line of stockade logs.

Jordon reached back and poked his finger at Jubal's ankle, signaling to move closer. The downriver end of the stockade loomed above them. Jordon eased over the side, rocking the bateau. Jubal heart clutched as the black man went into the water but Jordon found his footing and dragged the boat to the embankment, tying it to a tree fifty feet downriver, beyond the shadows of the stockade lantern. Jubal carefully shipped the oars, making sure the slipknots tying them to the thwarts were tight but could be released quickly. Then he slipped overboard in knee-deep water and reached for the rope coil. Feeling for Jordon's hand, he pointed it in the direction of Libra, low in the southern sky. Through breaks in the clouds, Jubal could see "Zuby" at about nine o'clock in the night sky. The star's arc would rise to ten in less than an hour, before sinking back below the horizon long before dawn.

Jordon tied one end of the rope around his waist. Jubal's hand clamped his shoulder. Silently, the men hugged and Jubal pressed his forehead against the black man's. He could only see the whites of Jordon's eyes and teeth.

Jordon set off, only his head above the knee-deep water, pulling himself along prone by the freshly flooded grass as Jubal played the rope out behind him. Jubal tied the rope end around his own waist and waited, playing out slack as it passed through his hands. Jordon had insisted on the rope and now Jubal understood why, for beyond a tiny circle from the lantern's glow they could stand an arm's length apart and barely sense each other in the pitch darkness.

Footfalls sounded at the far end of the parapet and began slowly marching toward them. A knot passed through Jubal's hand, sending his heart racing. The rope wasn't long enough; Jordon was still moving and Jubal had tied the knot at twenty feet from the bitter end as a marker.

Jubal waded forward, gathering the rope to keep it taut, until he passed the corner lantern above. Jordon was over a hundred feet upriver when Jubal felt two sharp tugs. He waded forward another twenty feet, grabbed hold of the grassy bottom and settled in the cold river up to his nostrils. The footfalls were near now, then directly above him before continuing on. Jubal gave one tug. The rope played out.

Jubal could smell it now, the privy stream emptying into the river.

Two tugs.

Jordon had been in the fort a dozen times and twice used the privy, a platform held three feet off the ground by corner posts, with six privy holes emptying into the stream that flowed through the prison, past the end of the platform and under the stockade wall, to run down the embankment into the Alabama River. Jordon thought the distance between the back upriver corner post and the stockade wall to be about ten feet, the stream in between now a full, foul sludge of shit, piss, vomit, refuse, and whatever other debris men had dumped.

From outside the stockade, estimating he needed about twenty feet of line, Jordon soundlessly extended his arm seven times, coiling the slack, and yanked twice. The rope grew taut.

The privy stream stunk to high heaven but Jordon didn't mind; it was warmer than the river. Already thoroughly chilled, he breathed through his mouth.

The footfalls started back. He waited, knee deep in the sewage as the sentry passed on the parapet eight feet directly above, pacing upriver.

As the footfalls receded, Jordon took two deep breaths, scrunched his eyes shut and, pinching his nose, lay on his back at the stockade base, reached a long arm to the other side, and pulled himself underneath and through the narrow sewer channel, feeling the stockade logs scrape his belly. Getting clear, he used both hands to pull through, turned over, and wiped the shit from his face.

Jordon Hatcher was inside Cahaba prison, lying in the open sewage channel. He had a momentary thought that with another three-day rain the flow would reverse, the river surging through the sewage channel and into the fort.

Only his head rose above the filthy sludge.

Quickly he scuttled forward, using his hands to approximate ten feet. He reached out and found the end post supporting the privy platform floor.

No one was there.

What to do? Jordon's heart sank and he almost whimpered in frustration. The sentry would make the turn at the far upriver end of the parapet walk and loop back on his ceaseless patrol. Sentries on watch looked *inside* the stockade, and though it was dark, a few lanterns inside the prison cast enough light to see shadows. Jordon no longer had the parapet shielding him. He couldn't stay.

Suddenly, feet scraped above. A man was finishing his business. Jordon waited, motionless, rounding his mouth into an O to breath silently.

Lester came down the steps and sidled to the end of the platform, one of the few places in the prison not covered in sleeping bodies. The dark lumps of men lying in the gloomy shadows reminded him of logjams he had worked in Maine. He came to the end post, stood for a moment, saw nothing and turned away.

A greasy hand grabbed his leg. Lester nearly shrieked.

Jordon Hatcher smelled like shit as he put his arms around Lester and tied the rope across his chest. Soundlessly, urgently, he gave Lester instructions: a tug of the rope, pulling his shirt—*come*—two tugs of the rope, a hand on his chest—*wait*. Jordon gently turned Lester, poked him in the back, turned his shoulders around again and pinched his nose.

A moment later, Jordon sank into the shit stream and was gone.

Lester waited, trembling. All day long he'd thought about that short sentence, even counted the words: "Tomorrow night, back post by the privy, outbound, Zuby, ten o'clock." Thousands of nights at sea came back to him. He knew *exactly* what Jubal meant, and the awareness—that despite everything, they were still a pair—stunned him. Jordon must have set it up, Lester had realized, for this was the only possible way out of Castle Morgan short of mass insurrection.

Lester took a breath and nearly gagged at the smell, struggling to control his breathing, hoping his heart wouldn't explode. A feeling of immense sadness overcame him—for the men he was leaving without explanation or notice who would awake in the morning and look for him, for young Richard, much too big to fit under the stockade wall.

The rope tugged. Without hesitation, Lester waded into the night soil, rolled over, and pinched his nose. He could feel himself pulled along by the rope and held his free arm out, finding the stockade wall. Ducking under, he was out moments later. Lester rinsed his face in the river before savoring the first lungful of freedom in eighteen months.

Footfalls sounded from the far end of the parapet.

Jordon felt a tug and urgently yanked the rope. Immediately, the twenty feet of slack whizzed through his hands.

With one arm securely around Lester—he felt light as a boy—Jordon clawed the bottom as Jubal hauled them downriver toward him. Footfalls came closer.

Jordon, holding Lester behind him, never saw Jubal kneeling on the river bottom until he felt his hand stop him. With a start, he realized Jubal had run out of rope and they were upstream of the bateau. More footfalls sounded, faint at first, then growing louder, and Jordon's heart sank. A sentry was approaching from the opposite direction, walking upstream on the parapet.

Jubal took Jordon's hand and pulled them along as Jordon kept an arm under Lester. Jubal stopped; they were closing the distance with the second sentry. Soundlessly, he turned and took Jordon by the shoulders, pushed him down at the base of the stockade, then lay Lester on top and sandwiched him. The three men lay together silently, half in the river. From three feet away, in the darkness their bulk was no more than a dark lump of logs beached by the hurricane.

Footfalls from either direction came on but stopped, almost directly overhead.

"All quiet, ain't it?" Hawkins said.

"Yeah. You hear?"

"Sherman? Fucker burnin' his way to the sea? Yeah, I heard. Think I ought shoot me a couple more these Yanks, right in the balls. Next one, that's what I'm gonna do."

"You'll answer to Jones."

Hawkins snorted. "You think he cares about one less mouth?"

Feet shuffled on the parapet. A warm stream landed two feet from Jubal's face as one of the men pissed.

"Man, the privy's awful tonight," Hawkins complained. "Smells like shit out here. You take this side."

"No, suh. I got my duty, you got yorn. But Jesus, 'nough of this. I'm movin' 'long."

The second sentry turned and his footfalls receded. Hawkins stood a few moments longer fumbling with his crotch buttons. Jubal calculated how fast he could get to the knife in his boot but stayed still. Hawkins finished, spit into the river, and grumbling about the smell, resumed his patrol. Footfalls faded in the night.

Jubal put his lips next to Lester's ear.

"I do believe, Lester," his voice barely a whisper, "for the rest of my life every time I take a shit, I'll think of you."

The lump of logs lay motionless for another minute, before it suddenly broke apart and vanished.

Two hours later and several miles downriver, Jordon spied the deep-bellied hurricane lantern he had left in a root pocket a foot above the waterline twelve hours earlier. There was barely a spoonful of whale oil left, but it provided enough light for them to pole the bateau a quarter of a mile up the narrowing stream until it grounded in reeds below a rise where a gurgling stream of clear, spring water flowed from further inland.

Jordon carried Lester another hundred yards into the woods, along a game trail marked by a thin, waist-high rigging line, to where the spring emerged from a rocky outcrop. Nearby, an old three-sided shelter had been falling into the soil a month earlier. Now it was solid again, new logs supporting a nearly watertight roof, woven, like the sides, from woodland branches, the whole being so well camouflaged in the dense foliage that it was all but invisible to anyone further than thirty feet away, even at midday.

Lester, nearly delirious, tasted the delicious cool spring water and accepted the sweet, nourishing slurry of stewed peaches and softened grits that Jordon spoon-fed him, finally coming to his senses long enough to recognize Jubal's old woodland shelter he had first visited more than a decade earlier. Soundlessly, the men watched him by the light of the hurricane lantern, refilled from a cache of oil left in the shelter.

Then they gently carried Lester to a deerskin in the corner where a quilt lay open. Rolling him like a cigar, Jubal touched his lips as Jordon looked on with shining eyes.

"Don't be goin' anywhere," Jubal breathed. "We'll be back."

In the sudden quiet, Lester's last thought came as he breathed. Instantly recognizing the scent, he inhaled deeply several times, snuggling in the quilt Cora had deliberately slept in for several days, her beckoning musk a promise of home.

On the river, in utter darkness, a shadow floated downstream. Finally, in the first hint of dawn, a dark figure rose to kneel in the bateau, angling off the river and poling into Ten-Mile Swamp.

Chapter One Hundred Seventeen

Gee's Bend, December 5, 1864

She came to him before dawn two days later, led to the forest shelter by Jordon, who pulled aside the hanging buckskin that passed for a door, hung his small lantern from a rafter, and stoked embers back to life in the tiny fire pit. Admonishing her to keep the fire low and infrequent, he stashed the food supplies in an earthen hole, accepted a tearful hug from Cora, and left them alone.

By the flicking light Cora watched Lester sleep, shocked at his unkempt hair and beard. Jordon had warned her the shelter was rough, nothing more than a bark and thatched-roof wigwam, but it was dry and camouflaged. Regardless, it would have to do, for both Jordon and Jubal agreed that Lester must remain hidden for at least a month. The weekly prisoner muster would make Lester's escape obvious—if an informant hadn't already squealed—and an outraged Colonel Jones was sure to mount an immediate search party.

Finally, as early light filtered through the thatch, Cora undressed and save for a smooth stone hanging between her breasts, kneeled naked beside her husband, stroking his face. Lester slowly awoke, uncertain if he were dreaming, until he realized her tears were real, and that she really did blow out the lantern. With a moan, he opened the quilt and she came to him, weeping in joy and agony at Lester's shivering, emaciated body, choking at the sight of his mangled finger.

"You ain't never leaving me again," Cora whispered, as he burrowed his face in her chest. Pulling the quilt over their heads, she stroked his hair, murmuring and cooing until her heat, ever so slowly and gently, surrounded them in a sublime, loving cocoon.

For five days, they left the wigwam only to use the forest.

A raucous birdcall pierced the morning silence. Lester whipped the quilt off them and bolted for the buckskin door, grabbing a rifle Jordon had left with the supplies. Cora threw a shift on, grabbed her pistol, and peeked out from the opening.

Jubal walked toward them through thick forest. He stopped before Lester, who stood stark naked, the rifle ready.

"You're gaining weight," Jubal observed. "Good."

"Trouble?" Lester asked.

"Nope. Jones has got posses out, but they're mostly searching north, like I figured. The dogs don't have a scent so they're just running in circles."

"I don't imagine he's happy."

"That's a way to put it. No rations for the entire camp for two days. He'd have kept that up but Jordon told Amanda Gardner."

Cora pushed the buckskin aside. "Truette's all right?" she asked. "Behaving?"

"Still fighting with Emma half the day, and refusing to talk." Jubal glanced at Lester and grinned. "Get something on, then come along. You too, Cora. We're going to the riverbank. Hear it?" Far off, a steam whistle sounded, downriver.

Twenty minutes later, the three of them lay atop a rise looking over the broad Alabama, considerably lower than its level after the hurricane but still muddy and turbulent from late autumn rains. Jubal had brought along his telescope and he examined the scene before passing it Lester.

Midstream, spewing black smoke, a low-slung gunboat thrashed upriver flying the Stars and Stripes and a white flag of truce, both snapping straight at its flagpole. Jubal quickly explained Sally's recent machinations.

"That sister of yours!" Jubal shook his head. "Went to Henderson, then to Mobile, got the mayor to contact the Union blockade commander under a flag of truce. In two days, word came back from your general friend. A couple thousand uniforms, four thousand socks, fifteen hundred blankets, and medicine are on that gunboat."

"You don't know Meigs," Lester replied, not the least bit surprised. "He's a combination of the McKay brothers, Josiah Creesy, Truette Stubbs, and James Baines, rolled into one. The most all-round competent man I've ever encountered. Any food aboard?"

"Didn't say."

"They land that stuff and it will be gone in a month. Blankets are fine—last winter was hell—but what the men will want most is food. They'll trade with the guards, eat better for awhile, and then have nothing left."

"Sherman's outside Savannah," Jubal said, getting to his feet. "Then he'll break north and press Lee's rear while Grant keeps coming."

Cora listened to their conversation as the Union gunboat steamed by and continued upriver. Neither showed a trace of anger as the gunboat chugged around a corner, leaving silence and a smudge of black smoke marking its progress.

The echo of a rifle shot punctuated the stillness, though it was far way.

"That's Sally and Jordon," Jubal said. "She'll be bringing a horse for you, Cora. Thought you'd want to go back to Sandy Hill for a few days. We're riding to Cahaba to meet that gunboat and watch Colonel Jones try and act gracious with a bone in his throat."

"Let me know if you see Hawkins," Lester said. Cora and Jubal exchanged a quick glance at the trace of menace in his voice. "A guard, short, bad teeth …"

"I know who he is," Jubal replied. "What do you want with him?"

"Nothing."

"Don't go doing something stupid." Jubal held up a hand at Lester's cold stare. "Just lie low for a time, will you?" he continued. "Jordon's found a piece of osage—thought you'd want make a bow, do some hunting. Be best if you wait this out another few weeks. The less anyone is around here, the better."

"I'm coming right back," Cora declared.

Jubal knew it was useless to argue. "Just be careful," he implored.

"We'll be quiet," Cora replied, the huskiness of her voice settling Lester as surely as if she'd hugged him.

Chapter One Hundred Eighteen

Gee's Bend, Christmas Eve, 1864

Whistling drifted through the forest canopy, a spiritual melody in timbre far deeper than any bird song.

"Tell Jordon to wait," Lester mumbled, his face buried against Curtis' stone in the luscious warmth of Cora's breasts. He recognized the distinctive cadence from the black man's brief periodic visits, bringing news and supplies.

"No," she laughed, her throaty chuckle like a cavalry bugle to Lester's loins. "Gotta get up," she urged, throwing off the quilt. The charcoal fire had cooled through the night, though the shelter was still warm enough to dress without shivering.

Cora had never experienced a need like Lester's and marveled at his seemingly insatiable desire, as if he wanted to devour all of her every day. She had little doubt that if she weren't pregnant yet she soon would be, since Lester wanted her day and night. Two weeks after she had found him, thin as a scarecrow, they managed to make love five times in six hours, though he slept for the next eighteen.

"You're gonna git tired of me," she'd say, and he'd answer by pulling her back down.

Cora stretched into the morning despite his comical pleas for her to return. "No, get up, Lester, Jordon be here any second!"

Grunting, Lester bounded up. After several weeks in the woods, his physical strength and caution—he moved silent as a panther—had increased as he became familiar with the surroundings.

In seconds, Lester had strung his bow. Stark naked but for his arrow quiver, he vanished into the forest. Cora pulled on a shift and waited, stock still. Though she spent several days each week in the wigwam, no one else save Jubal and Jordon Hatcher had any idea the hideout existed.

Lester returned, handing her the bow. "Yep, it's him."

By the time Jordon came through the forest, Lester was back outside, dressed head to foot in deerskin.

"Mornin', Miss Cora," Jordon smiled, leading a horse. He came through the woods in a different direction each visit so as not to create a discernible trail.

"I'm staying," she declared.

"No, ma'm, you don't want to be here. Lester be home by 'n by."

"You think it's safe?" Cora's eyes narrowed. "How you gonna manage that?"

"Got a Christmas present for that Jones fellow—Jubal thought a good time to give him somethin'. Mr. Lester can tell you later, but we needs to get to it."

"Go home, darling," Lester agreed. "Take the venison. Jordon'll bring word."

Cora usually returned to Sandy Hill with surplus game meat Lester had killed in the forest. She admired his bow, marveling at her husband's skill with wood. Made from a stick of osage and the carpentry tools—drawknife, chisels, and a saw—Jordon had brought, Lester spent his second week crafting both the bow, and with straight-grained pine branches, pheasant feathers, and arrowheads Jordon forged, a dozen beautifully crafted arrows.

When he wasn't hunting, Lester used half the arrows for target practice until he could hit a mule deer's heart—the size of girl's fist—at fifty yards. Soon, Jordon tanned the deerskins and Cora had sewn leggings and a tunic; from any distance Lester looked an Indian.

Cora gave her husband a look that made him laugh. "Don't," Lester protested, his loins singing. "I hope to be along shortly."

Satisfied, she allowed Jordon to help her mount, and let him lead her out of the forest, not without a last, lustful glance at Lester.

Jordon returned a few minutes later, carrying a rolled up canvas stretcher he'd made and left in woods so Cora wouldn't ask questions. "This ain't gonna be pretty," he said, his expression somber.

Lester nodded and set out, weaving through the undergrowth for several miles, until the ground became soggy at the edge of swampland. The men stripped and left their clothes on dry land before wading forward, Jordon with the stretcher and Lester carrying a forked stick to ward off snakes. Through the reeds they caught glimpses of the distant chocolate river and made for the tallest landmark in the swamp. A giant cypress, six feet thick at head height, rose from the swamp muck on a root shoulder larger than a stagecoach, its multiple tentacles anchoring the behemoth through a century of storms. Wedged and tied into the root mass, the overturned bateau lay barely awash.

Tugging it loose, the men worked to right and bail the bateau. Pulling the woven saplings that had held the murdered trooper in place and protected him from being totally consumed by alligators, Jordon paused and said a short prayer for the rotting corpse, now chalky and half eaten from nearly a month submerged. Hauling the bateau to the edge of the swamp, they debated how best to get the body out in one piece. Finally, they laid out the stretcher and overturned the bateau, throwing aside the saplings that had held the body and dumping his poor remains onto the canvas. A leg partially tore loose, as a chicken leg would in a stewpot, and one eyelid quivered before a small freshwater crab emerged. Both men turned away to control their stomachs.

A half hour later, Jordon Hatcher snapped the reins and headed a wagon for Colonel Jones' office outside the Cahaba stockade.

Jubal was already in town, reporting that the body of the escaped prisoner had been found. The escape had become widely known; twice, armed men had come to the plantation at Sandy Hill, once completely searching the house, dismissive of Sally's outrage until she brandished a shotgun. As time passed and the Union gunboat's resupply mission commanded Colonel Jones' attentions, he relegated the search to Rebel troopers unfit or too inept for guard duty, though he refused to call off the hunt.

By late that afternoon, Jubal had joined Jordon at the pauper graveyard outside of town. Colonel Jones had taken one look at the decomposed, unrecognizable body—it had quickly begun to smell in the open air—and nearly retched. Stomping from the wagon, he mounted the stockade stairs and made the triumphant announcement to the prison yard that the "damn Yankee bastard" had gotten his just reward. To the suddenly silent yard, he snarled that by his order, whatever the alligators had left would be buried in an unmarked grave.

Jubal and Jordon dutifully carried out Colonel Jones' order, though since they were alone, no one saw them dig into a recent grave, dispose of some rotting wood, and lay the murdered trooper to rest, marked by the cross made in his honor a month earlier.

Chapter One Hundred Nineteen

Mobile, January 1, 1865

On New Year's Day, Lester slipped back into the city disguised in a suit Sally had borrowed from Gustavas Horton that made him look heavier and older. Jubal had few clothes and Lester none, and she didn't want to bring attention by shopping for young men's fashion. Sally trusted Mr. Horton to help and keep his mouth shut; Lester could pass for a rumpled journalist or professor from Great Britain.

Speaking as little as possible aboard the steamboat, and then only in his imitation of a clipped Welsh accent, Lester carried Jubal's forged British passport and deliberately traveled alone, keeping to his cabin on the trip downriver.

Sally, Cora, and the children had arrived several days earlier after Christmas dinner at Sandy Hill, which also celebrated the first time Lester had left the safety of the forest wigwam. Both Jubal and Jordon thought an Englishman in Mobile would occasion less comment than a white man in Indian buckskin living off the land, if he were seen. Already, as winter deepened, the woods were sparser and offered less camouflage.

Jordon still made runs to Castle Morgan with food but they were fewer and less bountiful as the autumn harvest was depleted. Farm animals would not bear young until spring, so the former slaves at Gee's Bend had few farm chores until planting. Jordon reported no further mention of the escaped Yankee. Another five hundred prisoners had arrived at the prison and the entire yard suffered through a wet and dismal December. Since Lester was no longer "missing," Jubal figured the best tactic was to hide in plain sight.

The morning after Christmas, as the women prepared to leave Sandy Hill, Sally took her brother aside. "Jordon will get you across to Camden on New Year's morning so you can catch the regular mail steamboat. Don't do anything foolish." Her admonishment was intended to be playful, but Lester returned a stare as if looking right through her. Taken aback, Sally nearly reacted, but her brother didn't wait, simply kissing Cora and their son goodbye before heading upstairs.

Jubal and Jordon brought the women and children by wagon from Sandy

Hill to the small wharf at Gee's Bend, unused since the last cotton harvest, before rowing them across the river to the Camden steamboat landing.

No one saw the buckskin-clad figure slip out Sandy Hill's back door and into the woods.

Returning from Camden, Jubal had seen the cryptic note:"Back in a few days. John Norton." He told Jordon to saddle horses, intending to search for Lester, but Jordon would have none of it. "Man knows hisself. Leave him be."

Three days later, Jordon returned from his last trip to Castle Morgan until spring harvest, reporting that the Rebel guard Hawkins had "deserted" the night before. "Done up and gone," Jordon remarked. "Ran off in the middle of the night on guard duty. Dogs tracked 'im to the river, then lost 'im."

Long after dark the next night Lester returned, striding through the back door stark naked except for his bow and quiver. "I need a warm bath," he said to the startled men as they sat near the kitchen woodstove. Lester casually pulled the large water pot off the stove and washed in the yard, then bid the others goodnight and went to bed.

Jubal looked at Jordon, baffled. "I ain't a bettin' man," Jordon remarked softly. "You is—not me. But if'n I was, I'd bet that Hawkins fella's got an arrow stickin' out his chest, 'n them buckskins with him." Jordon thought of the cypress tree, the first place he would have searched.

In fact, Jordon Hatcher got one location right and one wrong, though he never checked. Hawkins had stopped on the parapet and in the middle of pissing, peered into the moonlit night at a blacker shadow. The arrow, fired from ten feet below, didn't strike the guard's chest, but higher, dead center through his throat.

The bateau floated downriver to a lowland swamp, stopping briefly by an enormous old cypress where the young killer took up residence in its root tangle, the arrow still embedded, soon to meet the local alligators.

Chapter One Hundred Twenty

Mobile, February 15, 1865

Cora splayed between Lester's legs, tracing various routes north on his torso. "We're here," poking his belly button, "and Philadelphia's here." She scratched the nipple over his heart. "Could go up this side—didn't Jubie say that Savannah had fallen? We could go up the coast."

"That tickles," Lester grinned. "I'd get shot between here and Savannah."

"Better not go that way. Or, go straight up, the way Sally and I did, over to Paducah," she scratched his other nipple, "then up the Ohio to Pittsburgh and over."

"Forrest is still up there; he'd shoot me, too."

"You getting bored?" Lester hadn't been out of the yard in nearly a month.

"No. Truette Stubbs built a wonderful library."

"You must have some slave in you."

"How so?"

"No hair on your chest. White men, most of 'em are all hairy."

Lester's eyes narrowed. "How many have you seen?"

"Hundreds ... at Satterlee."

"Oh. I forgot that."

"Guess we'll have to go down ... to New Orleans ..."

Lester groaned.

"Well, look what we have here," Cora marveled. "Ain't very interesting when it's soft, but ... Lester ... you know ... well, *I* never did 'fore ... you are *delicious.*"

Lester clutched her hair, gasping, until she pulled herself onto his chest and kissed him, smearing his face and licking him. "You is salty," Cora said, in that throaty rasp that turned him to jelly.

She made to wipe his chin with the pillow but he stopped her, grasping her thighs and pulling her up as he wiggled lower. "My feast," he mumbled, his face beginning to glisten.

Later, after Lester had blown out the candle and they'd spooned under the thick quilt, Cora wasn't quite ready to sleep.

"Think we're safe?"

"I'm safer here. In Mobile, a British accent and Jubal's forged passport gives me as good a story as any other foreigner."

"I miss Philadelphia."

"What most?"

"School. Working. My people coming through. William and Letitia Still. Edmonia and Rufus. It's home."

"Then we'll stay there, at least until you finish school. Doctor Cora." He reached around and pulled her closer. "You are an inspiration, you know that?"

"Don't be silly. Think Sally will come back, too?"

Lester shrugged. "I don't know …" he murmured.

—

The fire burned low in the Stubbs library. Lester poured another brandy for Gustavas Horton as Jubal smoked his pipe. The older man, invited by Sally for dinner, had stayed afterward, and the men retired to the library when the women and children went upstairs to bed.

Jubal knew Sally had something in mind. She would never have tolerated being shooed away from a discussion, so voluntarily taking her leave was a signal loud as a shout.

Mr. Horton stared into the fire. Middle aged, with gray sideburns as bushy as his head was bald, he had the look of a gentle undertaker. Lester thought he had aged considerably in the seven years since Truette Stubbs had asked him to bring Cora north.

"You gentlemen have aged considerably," Horton remarked.

Jubal and Lester exchanged glances.

"My son rides with Forrest," he continued.

"I know," Jubal replied. "I met him before Fort Pillow."

"Really! How extraordinary, I didn't know!" Horton suddenly looked stricken. "You were there? Did you see…? Do you know if he …?"

"Was one to 'massacre'?" Jubal asked, his voice even. "By the laws of war, I cannot say if it was … 'legal,' if that be the word. The Union troops refused to surrender; their flag never lowered that I saw. Legal or not, it was slaughter. I can't speak to the conduct of your son."

The man looked back to the fire. "My sons fight for the Confederacy, as my daughter feels required by honor. Eliza thinks this an abomination.

Are we a family any longer? Do we abandon our children? Forsake my sons when they return? I pray to God they *will* return when this war ends, as it must soon."

Silence filled the room, save for snaps of burning pine. Lester added a few more logs to the fire.

"What happened to your finger?" Mr. Horton asked. Jubal went quite still.

"A bullet," Lester replied.

"Hmmm …" Horton looked sad as a bloodhound. "Lincoln met with Southern representatives last week. Jefferson Davis offered to end hostilities if the South's independence was recognized. Lincoln refused. In his view there is, and has always been, one nation."

"The war won't last much longer," Jubal said, "though I can't see how the peace could be reached."

"Will you stay?" Lester asked Gustavas, his voice barely audible.

"In Mobile?" The older man nodded ruefully. "Unless driven out, which is possible. A Yankee sympathizer is an object of hatred here, though I am hardly alone. I must avail myself of your hospitality tonight. Eliza forbids I travel the streets after dark lest she deals with my body in the morning. But we have been here nearly twenty-five years. Yes, we will stay. You?"

"No," Jubal replied, surprising the other two. "The war is lost, but Southerners will never admit defeat. Sally has no tolerance for bitterness."

"Mobile was one of the most cosmopolitan cities in the country," Horton pointed out. "It surely will be again. However the cotton crop may be," he waved his hands, "appropriated, it will again be a primary source of income and of trade."

"I have no intention of being a planter," Jubal replied.

"Will you sell Sandy Hill?" Lester asked.

"No one has any money."

"Northerners will be coming," Horton interjected.

"Which will make it much worse," Jubal said. "The victors claiming spoils over the vanquished. No, I want no part of it. I'm sure my opinion is mild compared to Sally's."

"So what shall you do?" Horton repeated.

Jubal and Lester stared at each other, each understanding now why Sally had orchestrated the evening.

"We're going to Philadelphia," Lester said. "Cora and I."

"I do believe we will as well," Jubal agreed. "Though I haven't asked your sister."

"How much money do you have now?" Horton asked.

Jubal straightened, and glanced at Lester, uncertain how much of the ledger numbers to share. Two weeks earlier, Lester and Cora, Jubal and Sally, had spent the evening after the children went to bed, tallying their savings. Cora thought they had about $40,000 in Northern banks plus the house in Philadelphia. Jubal figured his vest still contained $1,000 in gold coins, two accounts in Liverpool contained another $8000, and they still owned Sandy Hill. By common agreement—no one seemed to have the stomach to discuss it further—they decided to wait until the war was over before deciding how to divide the money.

"We're very fortunate," Jubal mused, "and don't lack for ..."

Gustavas Horton waved him off and pointed a finger at one and then the other, his avuncular mien having vanished.

"I brought your sister, and your wife, from this place. I expected nothing in return then, nor do I now. However, Truette Stubbs, before he left for the last time, asked of me a pledge. Which I gave for reasons I need not reveal since they are decades old. To the extent I can, if you should ever be in need and I am able, I will aid you. As with Cora, it's my duty."

Horton held his empty brandy glass for Lester to refill.

"I am a father. You are not my sons but you are Truette Stubbs' sons, in life if not in blood, and he would ask of you this. A father would require of his sons a biblical dispensation, that you shall forgive our trespasses, and those who trespass against us, that you care for your families and think of them first. My sons are not yet married with children. You are."

Gustavas Horton stood.

"The hour is late. Permit me to retire, asking of you to consider: what example shall you give your families when this conflict ends? As it will. Soon." The older man bowed, his creased face weary with sadness. "Thank you for helping me to contemplate what I must do with my own sons. Goodnight, gentlemen."

Chapter One Hundred Twenty--One

Mobile, March 1, 1865

Jordon Hatcher and Sally came into the library, drenched from driving rain that had been with them from Sandy Hill. Lester looked up from his book, as Jubal did from the diagram he'd been sketching.

"That bastard has them standing in water!" Sally fumed, throwing off a sodden cloak and standing so close to the fireplace her dress started steaming.

"Rivers higher 'n I ever seen," Jordon reported. "Cahaba and Alabama, both over their banks, three feet deep inside the prison." The latter half of February had seen unrelenting rain.

"Where are they going?" Lester asked. "There's no place in the prison—the bunks and privies are the only things off the ground."

"They're going nowhere!" Sally bellowed. "I mean it; three thousand men, standing in water up to their waists. Jones won't let them out—thinks they'll escape."

"They probably would," Lester agreed.

"Can't," Jordon replied. "Whole country is flooded, ain't nowhere to go. Mules bogged comin' up from Sandy Hill."

Cora appeared in the doorway. "Did you get everyone?" she asked Sally.

"One hundred and six. Those older than twelve, we've got their marks, though it's hard to tell them apart."

"The slaves are going to be free soon, anyway." Jubal tried to hide his exasperation.

"They already is!" snapped Cora. "*Are!*"

"I don't care." Sally was unperturbed. "We owned them and we're going to register their manumission papers and pay the bonds. With Lincoln's emancipation and these releases, there is no one on God's earth who can question their status."

"Then what?" Jubal asked.

"Then they're free!"

"To do what? Sally, all this is fine. So they're free, now what? These people are uneducated and possess few skills this society values other than farming. Are we going to ship them all to Philadelphia? What will they do there?"

"We're going to divide up Sandy Hill," Sally replied, matter-of-factly.

"What?"

She had everyone's full attention now.

"Jordon and I talked about it. We'll split the land according to families. Thirty-three families. Evenly. Jordon gets the house."

"Jordon," Jubal looked at the black man, "we're leaving here; we've talked about that."

"*Y'all* talked about that."

Lester watched, not at all surprised. Over the last week, the families had spent dinnertime conversing about what to do when the war ended. Mobile newspapers were filled with dire news: in the Carolinas, the cities of Columbia, Charleston, and Wilmington had surrendered, and Grant besieged Petersburg, downriver from Richmond, Virginia. When Petersburg fell, the Rebel capital was doomed. While no one could predict the war's course, Lester likened it to the tightening of a vise. Jubal was more explicit: "an anaconda strangling *and* crushing a wounded, starving mule."

"Jordon, you're coming with us?" Jubal's question was almost a plea.

The big black man shook his head. "I gonna be buried next to Beulah and my boys. I been to Philadelphia, all respect to Miss Cora," he nodded to her, "it don't hold nuthin' fer me. My life's been in them fields, 'long the river. I be dyin' there."

"I'm coming," Charity declared, coming into the library still wearing an apron. She'd been listening from the kitchen doorway. "Me and Daniella. I'm sorry, Grampa."

Jordon took the news stoically; he'd expected it.

"We can buy any cotton they grow," Sally said, sadness overcoming her. "It's their land. That's how I feel."

Jubal just shrugged. Slowly, he stood, feeling old beyond his years. Nothing made sense anymore.

A sudden sharp rap at the front door snapped everyone to attention.

⁓

Two men in Confederate cavalry uniforms pushed past Ezekiel into the entry parlor. Immediately, Jubal recognized Major Horton and Lieutenant Carter, but before he could acknowledge the soldiers, Sally blew by him.

"Get out!" Sally was livid. "You've no right to barge into my house uninvited!"

"Beg your pardon, m'am," Horton removed his hat but didn't budge. "I thought Mr. Calhoun might be here."

"I am healing from the slaughter," Jubal said.

"Fort Pillow was a *battle*, sir!"

"Tell that to your father."

"I have."

"Good. Did you look him in the eye and describe how surrendering Negroes soldiers, *on their knees*, were put to the bayonet?" On the wagon ride back, lying wounded, Jubal had heard Jordon's account—he had witnessed the entire battle—and believed every word of it.

"They refused to surrender!"

"'No quarter!' Is that the sound of victory?"

"I did not come here to discuss this!"

"What did you tell your mother?" Jubal asked, his voice cold as ice.

"She is ill, that is why I am here. Now, we need every man. I expect you will come with us."

"Expect anything you want, Major. I am a naval attaché; you have no authority over me here."

"A naval attaché for whom?" Lieutenant Carter demanded. "Union or Confederate?"

"American."

"I know your mother and father," Sally interrupted, fearful where this was headed. "They would never countenance such impertinence!"

"I ... overheard my father speak of Mr. Calhoun. And a Mr. Norton?"

"You speak of me?" An English accent sounded from the library. Lester emerged, a robe pulled about him and puffing on Jubal's pipe. "Quite a spot of rain, isn't it? Weather here is as dreadful as London, what? Who are these chaps, Jubal?"

"Confederate cavalry officers, Major Horton, Lieutenant Carter. Where's Chalmers?"

"Dead," Horton replied. "Memphis."

"Fallen on the field?" Lester laid it on a bit thick. "Bloody good I say; no better way to die!"

"Do you have identification?"

"Do you?" Lester snorted, in high dudgeon. Sally had to work at keeping a straight face.

In a flash, Carter drew his pistol. "You heard the major."

Lester puffed his pipe, bemused, then drew the passport and tossed it at Major Horton. "John Norton, at your service."

"What are you doing here?"

"Nothing Her Majesty would care to share with a major."

"You'll come with us."

Click.

Cora stepped from the library, the shotgun leveled at Horton. "You betray your father," she said, her voice quiet and deadly. "Jubal will deal with the authorities presently, and you will leave now ... while your mother can still recognize you."

Lester stepped forward and pushed Carter's gun barrel down. "Run along now, laddies."

Jubal turned to Ezekiel. "Fetch my slicker, will you? I shall accompany these men to the mayor's office."

Sally went to the door and swung it open. She stared at the Confederate officers and stamped her foot. "Get out!"

—

Jubal returned at dusk, whistling as he hung his dripping slicker on the coat rack. Lester, Cora, and Sally waited in the library.

"Where are the kids?" Jubal asked.

"In the kitchen," Sally replied, "baking muffins with Jordon and Ezekiel."

Lester never ceased to be amazed by the rapport both men had with the children. As her reading quickly improved, Emma read Jordon books she already knew and Truette followed Ezekiel around like a puppy. The old man constantly talked to the boy in his quiet whisper, as if they were co-conspirators hatching a plot to bake bread.

"What happened?" Cora asked.

"I was hoping we could stay quietly here, but that's no longer viable," Jubal began. He poured himself a brandy and carefully lit his pipe.

"For chrissakes, Jubal!" Sally snapped. "What the hell happened?"

"They're emptying the prison at Cahaba."

Lester straightened in his chair.

"You were right, Sally," Jubal continued, "that murdering Jones had them standing in water for three days before he let them fetch some driftwood to pile, so they'd have a place to sit. And they have no food to speak of. Grant relented on paroles and Colonel Henderson arranged a transfer—he's been managing several prisons—and they're all going to a neutral camp on the Mississippi." He pointed at Lester, "It's your way out."

"How?"

"There'll be Yankee gunboats going upriver under a flag of truce to transfer the men. A hundred men a trip, maybe more; that means several gunboats for probably a month. We've got to get you on one."

"Why?" Sally demanded.

Jubal puffed his pipe. "Horton—the young one—is suspicious. He'll be back if he doesn't get killed. So when the Union Navy starts to run prisoners out, along the coast and up the Mississippi to this neutral fort outside of Memphis—Camp Fisk I think they're calling it—we'll intercept one and then you're out."

"You're not going without us, Lester!" Cora shook her head, arms folded.

"He's got to," Jubal declared. "It could get prickly."

"How?" Sally demanded.

"I'll have a boat," Jubal replied, simply. "Union troops are moving on Spanish Fort, the other side of Mobile Bay. They'll take it and move on to Fort Blakely ten miles north. Look at the map, it's inevitable." Jubal went to the wall map. "Those forts are on the east side of the bay, they defend the back door into Mobile. All the city's defenses are pointed to the water. Take Spanish Fort and Fort Blakeley, Union troops will land above Mobile and attack from land, coordinated with a naval bombardment. It's not complicated."

"You are driving me to distraction, Jubal!" Sally stamped her foot again. "How are you getting a boat?"

"I'm a naval officer. They'll need to move troops between Spanish Fort and Fort Blakely, *by boat*. I bought a steam tug and a barge."

"You bought?"

"Pledged this house."

Lester nodded. "I get it."

"Get what?" Sally and Cora asked in unison.

"In Memphis," Lester replied, "I'll keep going and get back to Philadelphia." He looked at Jubal. "Buy every bale of cotton or futures contract you can—Sally, go upriver and buy—then use the tug to transport by barge or whatever else you can contract. We've got funds and credit up north and in Liverpool. Cotton will be just as valuable as before the war, even more when it ends. The Union will open trade immediately for cotton taxes to pay down the war debt." Lester shook his head. "It *isn't* complicated."

"Britain is gasping for cotton," Jubal nodded.

Lester turned to Jordon. "Anyone on the plantation can come north to Philadelphia; we'll make sure they are settled. But Cora will tell you northerners have little to no more regard for Negros than people do here. If you work the land, particularly if you plant cotton ..." Lester shrugged, "I can't say life will be any better there than here. And maybe worse."

"How can you say that? After all that's happened?" Sally looked at her brother as if he had gone crazy.

"Cotton was dependent on slavery," Lester said, his voice hard, "and slavery dependent on cotton. Ask Cora what it's like to be an uneducated Negro in Philadelphia with no skills but farming. You saw it!"

Everyone turned to Cora but Jordon. She looked at the black man; he returned the stare. "You want to run a plantation?" she asked him. "Lester's right."

Jordon nodded. "I been there."

"Anybody wants to come," Cora said, "we'll care for them until they find something ... but, Lord knows they better bring that thick skin. Black ain't welcome in Philadelphia."

Charity appeared at the library door. She'd been eavesdropping again. "I'm coming!"

"What you do you want, girl?" Cora voice was even, level.

"I'm goin' where you go, that doctors' school. I'm gonna do what Beulah did."

"Babies?"

"Yes, m'am. Been enough death. I'm gonna see life."

Cora considered and her voice hardened. "Ten years."

Charity didn't flinch. No one spoke for a few moments.

"Come along, then."

Jubal breathed like a walrus come up from sounding. "Yankees will be coming at Selma to destroy the cannon factories. That's where Horton and his man Carter are riding now. He demanded I join them and I told him to go to hell. The mayor was fine with that, much more interested in saving Mobile than Selma." He gave a mirthless smile, glancing at Sally. "The sinking ship?"

"The end is coming fast," Lester said to Sally. "Go to Sandy Hill if you have to, but we ought to buy as much cotton now as possible. I'll be back."

"When? How?" Cora asked, frightened but relieved to see a glimpse of her old Lester.

"A month, two at most. With a ship. I'll either buy it or lease. We'll load the cotton and head for either New England or old England, wherever the price points."

"I want to be in Philadelphia," Cora protested. "I'm goin' back to school!"

"Sell the cotton," Lester nodded, "and then we go home. And stay."

Chapter One Hundred Twenty-Two

Mobile, April 1, 1865

Union steamboats emptied Cahaba Prison in one month, all prisoners bound on a thousand-mile trip for Camp Fisk, near Vicksburg, on the Mississippi River.

Early in the evacuation, at dusk on a rainy night in mid-March along the Mobile roads, a steamboat flying a flag of truce and carrying several hundred Union prisoners was nearly rammed by a small tug crossing the shipping lanes. The steamboat didn't slow but a grappling hook flew across as the tug—flying a similar white flag—turned parallel, and moments later a man clambered aboard the steamboat to explain himself to several Union troopers leveling their pistols.

As the tug, manned by one white man and two black, turned away, a chorus of cheers suddenly erupted from the prisoners, the sound muffled by rain and distance. Lester had been recognized.

Further out, as the steamboat passed into the Gulf of Mexico, another sound echoed across the water: the first blasts of cannon fire bombarding the approaches to Spanish Fort. A Union army of forty-five thousand men converged from north and south on the eastern defenses of Mobile Bay.

Jubal heard the faint cannon fire as he steered his tug back to Mobile. "There's not more than a few thousand troops over in Spanish Fort, and the same at Fort Blakeley," he observed, "with half the guns trained at the water. But Jordon, Ezekiel, there's great news. You can now join the Confederate Army! A new law just passed in Richmond."

The two men looked at him blankly.

"That's right. Negroes can now fight. Everybody's been terrified for two hundred years by the thought of an insurrection. No need to bother with that now, they'll give you arms and you can fight for your right to be slaves!"

Jubal snorted, the hypocrisy too much for him.

A week later, Gustavas Horton rapped at the Stubbs house front door late at night. Earlier in the evening, news had arrived in Mobile that Spanish Fort had fallen.

"May I speak with Miss Cora?" he asked Ezekiel. The house had gone to bed, but Cora overheard from upstairs and came bustling down in her robe, Sally on her heels.

"My son," Horton twisted his hat. "He was wounded at Selma three days ago. Forrest was routed, twenty-seven hundred men captured, hundreds killed and wounded. The hospital is full. Can you come? His leg ..." The old man shivered, holding his head with a trembling hand. "A piece of shell ... fever ... I have a coach. We brought him home. I know, he is Confederate, but he is ..."

The women were already racing upstairs.

An hour later, Cora finished amputating the man's left leg six inches below his hip. Sally gathered the mangled remains, the boot still muddy from the Alabama River shoreline, and went into the anteroom where Mr. Horton waited. "What shall I do with ..."

Gustavas Horton broke down, quietly pounding a fist into his open palm. "Almost ... almost ..." he whispered. Gathering himself, he stood, nodding. Sally held out the bloody bundle, wondering if the man would collapse, but Horton steeled himself, took his son's leg with a shudder and went directly to bury it in the garden.

Cora washed her hands as Sally returned. "Laudanum will wear off in the morning. If he makes it a week, he should survive. Now we'll see how strong his will is."

"You're brutally efficient, Cora."

"Weren't nothing left of that leg. Must have been the size of a plate, that piece of shell. A man can't walk missing four inches of bone."

"It's late to go home," Sally said.

"I've got to stay, watch for fever. Charity will mind the children."

"Did you ..."

Cora frowned. "Did I *what?*"

"Nothing." Sally turned away.

"Enjoy chopping a leg off of somebody wants to own me?"

"Not that!"

"What?"

"Sometimes I struggle ... wondering how I would feel ... if ..."

"If you wuz black?" The drawl thickened. "Well, you ain't! So you'll never know." Cora turned down the lantern. "And don't you never come stupid like that to me agin, hear?"

Sally bit her lip and went to the door.

Chapter One Hundred Twenty-Three

Mobile, April 15, 1865

On Palm Sunday, after two days and a dozen trips under cover of Confederate gunboats, Jubal landed the last surviving defenders from Spanish Fort at Fort Blakeley as it came under attack. By sunset, Blakeley fell. The next day, faced with an unobstructed Union Army and Navy, the example of Selma—almost completely wrecked and burnt in battle—and news that General Lee had surrendered at Appomattox, Mobile's mayor decided to surrender and spare the city.

Hundreds of citizens watched the Confederate flag lowering at the harbor fort. A white cloth took its place, flapping in the midafternoon onshore breeze. The short ceremony had the feel of a funeral and throughout the city Mobile's white population drew inward, alternately dazed, despondent, and sullen.

"One of the most heavily defended places on the earth surrenders without a shot," Jubal observed, as the Stars and Bars disappeared. He had brought the families to witness history.

"So much for Southern courage," Sally growled.

Jubal wheeled on her. "You can go north by yourself, you want! Take the kids! I'll manage!"

Startled, she looked to see if he was joking. He wasn't. "Well ..." she stammered.

"The issue is decided," Jubal spoke through his teeth in a deep drawl. "I made my choices—we all did—and lived the consequences. There's not a person alive here that won't be thinking of these days the rest of their lives. You want to gloat and put on that cloak of self-righteousness, I'll have none of it! I'm not living with that! Do you understand?"

"Jubal ..."

"Three thousand men fell across the river, not two days ago," Jubal seethed. "How many grieving mothers, wives, brothers, children? For just wanting to be left alone!"

"To own slaves!"

Jubal took a deep breath. "One last time. We saw it, see it, and forever will view this conflict differently. But the issue is decided! Either we live for the future, together, or I'm staying and you can go. But I am *not* living with the constant, brittle snarl of sanctimonious virtue—the *Gospel According to Sally!*"

Emma whimpered, trying hard not to cry. "Daddy, Mommy, please don't fight!" Truette held Cora's hand, looking wide-eyed at the adults. Buck reached for his father.

"It's done," Cora declared. "If you two are dumb enough to repeat this fight, y'all will end up bitter and alone. Jubal's right, we've got a future. Just had to go through this hell to get there. But we're through it."

She turned from the somber crowd. "We're packing. Lester will be here shortly."

"When's Daddy coming?" Truette asked in a dry, squeaky voice.

In midstep, Cora stopped dead and looked at the boy. These were the first words she'd heard from him in twenty-two months, each of which she had counted. Tears washed her eyes.

"Why ..." she swallowed hard, "real soon."

"Then are we going home?" the boy brightened, his voice still a rasp from unuse.

"Yes, son," Cora replied, her own voice cracking, "we're all going home."

"Ezekiel, too?"

"Why don't you ask him? I'd bet he'll like it if you do."

Four days later, Jubal arrived home to dinner after a day on the wharves spent buying demurrage for stockpiled cotton that would be coming down the Alabama River over the next two weeks. Three days earlier, the day after Mobile's surrender, Lester had used military lines to telegraph an authorization from General Meigs authorizing procurement of five thousand bales of cotton from any source, including warehoused bales seized by Union forces. Directed to General Canby, the Union general investing Mobile with ten thousand troops, the document named Jubal Calhoun as procurement agent.

Within twenty-four hours, Jubal had made the Mobile market in cotton as buyers competed for contracts that would now pay in currency actually worth something.

Sally greeted him as he came in, enveloping her husband in an unabashed hug, mindful of a conversation she had with Cora the day before.

"You go so hard on him, Sally," Cora warned, "you'll lose him. That man is proud to the bone. Everything we been through—you, me, Lester, Jubal—there's three of us can hold our head high, we made something of this madness. Jubal, he's got to live with it forevermore. Sally, he is *southern*. These people will be bitter; you got no idea. Live's been ripped apart. Great-grandchildren will be fighting this fight. Let your man heal. And be grateful if he can."

Buck came tottering in and Emma tackled her father by the legs. Jubal picked up his children, smothering them with hugs, tickling Emma. Despite his behavior, Sally could sense something wrong.

"You heard?" Jubal asked.

"Heard what?" Emma demanded.

"Heard that I bought some very scarce chocolate that I'll share with y'all while I read a story. Go get Truette and I'll meet you in the study. Go on, now, take Buck with you."

Emma squealed toward the kitchen where Truette was making a mess with Ezekiel.

"What?" Sally asked, dreading Jubal's response.

"Lincoln was assassinated last night."

"My God!"

"Who?" Cora said, hurrying down the stairs. She had come back from the Horton's after checking on the major, who had survived his amputation and now lived with the knowledge that a black woman had saved his life, as satisfying to Cora as the successful operation.

Jubal shrugged, looking weary. "Not too much known yet. But the president was shot in the head last night, died sometime before morning."

Cora shuddered, twisting as though she had been stabbed, her face a mask of anguish. Staggering to a chair, she folded in grief.

Jubal went to her, pulling a telegram from his coat.

"Lester leaves tomorrow from New York," he said, quietly. "You best stay near the house until he gets here. I'm going upriver."

"I don't want you to go," Sally objected, her stomach twisting.

"Jordon's in Selma, loading what hasn't been burned. We'll make up a tow. I'll be all right."

"Put your thick skin on, Jubie," Cora stared at him. "And keep your arguin' to yoreself. There's not a white man in the South safe now."

Chapter One Hundred Twenty-Four

Mobile, May 1, 1865

*M*astiff lay at anchor in the Mobile roads, nearly a thousand bales of cotton jammed in her hold. Jubal tallied the last of the cargo before conferring with Captain Pingree, who ordered the ship's hatches secured. Cub had stayed aboard *Mastiff* for the duration of the war, outliving his childhood nickname and taking command when his captain died of a heart attack onboard while resupplying Sherman's troops at Wilmington three months earlier.

Jubal had supervised the loading after hiring Gustavas Horton to finalize legalities and financial arrangements for shipment of four thousand bales, most bound for New York on four other American merchant ships in the harbor, two now loading at the wharf. Several Union gunboats also lay at anchor. Further upstream, a dozen Confederate gunboats stood idle, manned by skeleton crews of Union naval officers.

The setting sun cast a long, glowing light across the city, shining off the Stars and Stripes that fluttered at the old waterfront fort in the last fitful breaths of an onshore breeze. Streetlights twinkled, and the sounds of city life filtered across the water. "Did this war ever happen?" Sally marveled from the *Mastiff* quarterdeck.

A working tug's smokestack huffed and puffed, steaming in their direction. She could make out several black men and knew Jordon and Ezekiel were coming out for dinner before *Mastiff* set sail.

"Doesn't look much different from a dozen years ago," Lester observed. "Are you settled in your cabin?"

"Like we never left. I still can't believe it."

"I'm glad to be leaving. Things will settle, but Mobile won't be a happy place this summer."

"And you have your ship!" Sally clapped. In Washington, Lester had repurchased *Mastiff*'s lease and then joined it in Baltimore.

"That man is brilliant," Lester replied. The repurchase was General Meigs' idea. "If he went into business, I think he'd be one of the richest men in the world. But his life is the Army—making the Army work. And this is just a tiny piece of it. He doesn't need a cargo ship now. We've got a real Navy."

Cora came up from below with Truette.

"How you feeling?" Lester smiled. She had taken him aside that morning, put his hand on her belly and kissed him, saying she had a present due around Christmas.

Cora hauled the boy, squalling about something, up the quarterdeck stairs. "I'll tell you in the morning. Meanwhile, this child needs a good talkin'-to," she wagged her finger at Truette, "'fore you fall overboard. A ship isn't no place to play. That's what your daddy said to me, first time I was aboard. You weren't even born yet."

A call interrupted them as Jordon Hatcher steered the steam tug alongside. He had quickly learned to operate the rudimentary engine and plied the river between Sandy Hill and Mobile with a few of the plantation's field hands, loading cotton tows and bringing them downriver. Ezekiel was with him and tossed up a line to waiting crewmen. Two young men stayed aboard the tug, tending the boiler.

Captain Pingree came aft with the black men. "I've sent for Mr. Calhoun. Dinner is served in my cabin. Please," he gestured below.

Pingree's mess steward had prepared a sumptuous meal and removed panels separating two officers' cabins to accommodate a table for ten. As the families sat, Jordon Hatcher examined the cutlery, wondering why so many knives, forks, and glasses were needed to eat a meal. Cora deliberately seated herself between him and Ezekiel to help them navigate their dining tools.

To the assembled, Captain Pingree raised a glass of French wine. "Ladies, gentlemen, Mr. Calhoun, Colonel Norton, welcome back aboard your ship."

"Colonel?" Sally gaped.

Lester savored his first sip of Bordeaux in several years. "General Meigs promoted me, effective the date of my capture. With a thousand dollars accumulated back pay."

"Are we supposed to salute?" Emma asked.

"Yes!" Lester laughed. "Your mother, particularly."

"And this load of cotton is ours," Lester added. "The other four ships are government contracts."

Jubal listened, simultaneously intrigued and offended. Lester had said nothing of this to him.

"I'm proposing we go to Liverpool," Lester continued. "Then to

Philadelphia," he quickly added, seeing Cora's reaction.

"When were you going to tell us?" she asked, indignant.

"Now. I received word this afternoon from General Meigs, instructing me to Liverpool. If you want to go directly to Philadelphia, we can, but I'm still an officer, and my orders are to proceed to Liverpool."

"You just got back!" Sally protested. She looked at Cora. "Men never change."

"That's why I propose we all go to Liverpool. Rabbit Lane is in good hands with Rufus and Edmonia. Cora's school doesn't resume until September—we'll be back by then—and the weather is fine to sail the Atlantic. Why not go directly?"

"We can?" Emma asked, looking at her father.

"It's our ship," Jubal replied. Lester eyed him, his expression plain: *Liverpool?* "I'd like to go," Jubal said to Sally.

"Where's Liverpool?" Truette asked. The boy turned to Ezekiel. "You're coming, aren't you?"

"We talk about that after dinner," the old man whispered.

～

Truette cried himself to sleep when Ezekiel explained he was staying in Mobile at Stubbs House.

"You come and see me," the old man whispered to the boy. "Jordon too. He be up at Sandy Hill—we got lot of work to do. Both still y'all's houses. Yore daddy says in winter, when it gets cold up north, you can come down here. Aunt Sally and Uncle Jubie, they be coming too. You come sometimes with them."

No explanation mattered; the boy was disconsolate and had to be pried from Ezekiel's trousers when the black men went overboard onto the tug. Jordon Hatcher hugged the families, unable to talk. Tears glistened in the moonlight as the tug pulled away.

"Stand by to cat the anchor!" Captain Pingree called. "Hands aloft!"

Mastiff's crew scrambled to the ratlines, and sails snapped full in the gathering night breeze as it shifted offshore. The ship retrieved her anchor and moved with the outgoing tide down the deepwater channel, marked with buoys lit for the first time in four years.

A few hours later, the children were asleep as the ship passed between Fort Morgan and Fort Gaines into the Gulf of Mexico. *Mastiff* rose to the ocean groundswell flying all sails in the moonlit night. As if by silent agreement, the couples drifted in opposite directions, Cora and Lester to the bow, while Jubal and Sally stayed on the quarterdeck astern.

"Don't be mad at me," Lester said, holding his wife's hand.

"Then don't be surprising me like that! At dinner! You could have told me beforehand."

"I was still thinking about it. We could go to Philadelphia—we still can—it's only a few days out of the way, up the Chesapeake."

"Long as I get to school …"

"I thought to just lay it out on the table. Jubal's got unfinished business in Liverpool."

"What business?"

"I don't know and don't want to know, but I just know. It's the easiest way to get him there. And I have my orders."

"What's the general want?"

"Other men are heading to London now on the packets to address Britain's conduct during the war. Now's the time—with a huge, experienced army and world-class navy—to confront them with the cost of their … 'cynicism' is the best way to put it. The general told me they captured thousands of British rifles at Fredericksburg—just one battle—and Confederate ships built in Britain destroyed several hundred million dollars of American property."

"You're going to negotiate that?"

"No. Just come to an agreement on cotton contracts to retire war bonds sold to England. That's my job."

"Then we'll go home?"

"For awhile."

"What 'while'?"

Lester pointed at a shooting star. "God, it's wonderful to be at sea again."

Cora elbowed him.

Aft, on the quarterdeck, Sally leaned into her husband and held his arms around her. Suddenly, she broke free, scooted to the rail and threw up overboard.

"Getting your sea legs?" Jubal exclaimed, offering a handkerchief. *Mastiff* sailed a gentle, rolling course over the glittering sea.

"No!" Sally spit.

Jubal waited, baffled.

"Don't be thick, dear husband."

"Huh?"

"Christmas. Give or take."

Jubal grunted as if struck, then stroked his wife's face. "Got a name yet?"

"Ezekiel, Jordon, or Cora. Though you get a vote."

"That's good of you." Jubal drummed his fingers on the ship's rail. "Where do you want to live, Sal? We're going to need some room."

"Not in Alabama. I don't mind going down to visit—I think we'll have to help Ezekiel and Jordon some. Lester says he can probably manage the cotton procurement if we do it right."

"Ezekiel was Truette Stubbs' right hand for twenty years," Jubal replied. "He doesn't say much but he doesn't miss nothin'. Smarter than most any white man I've known, and that includes me and Lester."

"Such exalted company."

"Can't help yourself, can you?"

Sally laughed. "Nope."

"In Philadelphia, then?"

"Outside," Sally held him close. "Near the new college. Let's buy a farm, maybe ten, fifteen miles from the city. At Sandy Hill I got to like going barefoot again. In the city, you've got to be ladylike and I'm not all that interested. But I want to be close enough, and Philadelphia is important for women."

"Now what?"

"Women are going to vote. In my lifetime."

"Still stubborn."

"*You* are telling *me*?"

Footfalls sounded on the steps up from amidships; the shadows of Cora and Lester materialized against the starlit sky.

"Solve the world's problems?" Sally asked.

"If we could just put you in charge," Lester replied.

"Mommy," Emma's tiny voice came from the companionway. "Truette's in my bed and I can't sleep, he won't stay still."

"Ask Charity," Sally called.

"Daniella threw up."

Sally threw up her hands. "Coming." She hugged her brother; Cora did the same to hers.

"I wish one of you were captain," Sally whispered. "Do you think Cub is ...?"

"Go to bed, dear," Jubal replied. "I'll be in shortly."

"Keep us safe," Cora whispered to Lester, before she tugged at Sally and the women disappeared down the companionway.

"I don't want to be captain," Jubal remarked. "Not this trip."

"You going back to sea?" Lester asked.

Jubal looked at him. "I hadn't thought that far. Sally says she wants to live on a farm."

They were quiet for a time.

"Zuby's rising," Lester said, looking between the shrouds to the constellation of Libra, hanging low in the southern sky.

Jubal handed him a cigar, filled his own bulldog, struck a match, and lit both. "Nice night."

Captain Pingree came aft, checked with the helmsman, and approached the men at the rail.

"What's your course, Captain?" Lester asked.

"Sou' by southeast, sir, make for the Florida Straits, turn the corner and run down the wind, ride the Stream to the Lizard. Unless you have other instructions, sir." Captain Pingree smiled, his teeth flashing by the faint light of an aft lantern. "She's your ship."

Lester pulled a pocket flask from his coat and offered it to the Captain. Pingree took a pull and handed it back. Lester did the same and passed it to Jubal.

"Very well, Captain." Jubal savored a swallow of brandy. "Steady as she goes."

THE END

Historical Figures and Events

Josiah and Eleanor Creesy—The Creesys married in 1841, and Eleanor navigated every ship her husband sailed until the Civil War. Retiring from the sea in 1864, the couple moved to Salem, Massachusetts, where Captain Creesy died in 1871 and Eleanor in 1900. *Flying Cloud*'s record for the run from New York to San Francisco lasted 136 years.

Harriet Beecher Stowe—Daughter of a Congregationalist minister, Stowe wrote *Uncle Tom's Cabin* in Brunswick, Maine, after the passage of the Fugitive Slave Act in 1850. The book, published in 1851, sold millions, was celebrated in the North and reviled in the South, purportedly prompting President Lincoln to greet her with "So you're the little woman who wrote the book that started this great war." She died in Hartford, Connecticut, in 1896, after living next door for many years to Samuel Clemens (Mark Twain).

Donald McKay—Canadian born, McKay built over forty ships, including several of the fastest and most successful clippers that ever sailed. He retired in 1874 to farm in Massachusetts, where he lived until 1880.

Lauchlan McKay—Younger brother to Donald, Lauchlan had been a carpenter aboard USS *Constitution*, apprenticed with his brother, and commanded several ships built at the McKay yard in East Boston.

James Baines—Owner of the Black Ball Line, Baines owned eighty-six ships at the height of his success, but due to the advent of steam, the declining performance and maintenance costs of his aging clippers, and an investment in a bank that failed, he lost everything and died a pauper in 1889.

Mary Patten—One of the most extraordinary maritime heroines of the nineteenth century, her story in the book is faithful to actual events.

Lucretia Mott—Quaker, abolitionist, women's rights activist, and social reformer, among the founders of Swarthmore College, she was one of the major reform figures of the nineteenth century.

William Oates—A colonel in the Confederate army, Oates lost an arm at Petersburg, Virginia. After the Civil War he practiced law, served as the twenty-ninth governor of Alabama, became a brigadier general in the Spanish-American war, and died in 1910 after numerous, unsuccessful attempts to raise a monument to Alabama troops at Little Round Top, in Gettysburg.

Gustavas Horton—born in Syracuse, New York, he resided in Mobile for twenty-five years before the Civil War and was jailed for refusing conscription. His two sons fought for the Confederacy. After the war he became the mayor of Mobile and a probate judge for Mobile County.

William Still—A successful businessman in Philadelphia, he is often called the Father of the Underground Railroad. He personally helped more than sixty slaves a month escape to freedom. His interviews with escaping slaves were published, and he founded an orphanage for children of African-America soldiers and sailors. Still died in 1902.

Henry Highland Garnet—Abolitionist, activist, educator, minister, and orator, he advocated armed rebellion to end slavery. Garnet became president of Avery College and later was named U.S. minister to Liberia, where he died in 1882. The sermon delivered at the United Presybeterian Church in Philadelphia is quoted verbatim.

Mary Brown—The second wife of abolitionist John Brown, after his hanging she immigrated to California, where she died in 1884.

Robert Purvis—Of three-quarters European ancestry, he identified with black society, helped organize the American Anti-Slavery Society, used his house as a station on the Underground Railway, and helped over nine thousand escaped slaves to freedom.

James Pennington—Born a slave, he escaped and became the first black person to attend Yale University. He was subsequently ordained and became a minister, orator, and teacher.

Charles Piroleau—As agent for Fraser and Trenholm, he was indispensable in securing European weapons, ammunition, and supplies for the Confederacy while helping build and arm blockade runners and Confederate raiders. Later to disappear into history, his grave was recently discovered in England.

Montgomery Meigs—Efficient, ruthless, and of unblemished integrity, he masterminded the logistical supply of the Union Army, established Arlington National Cemetery, and served as quartermaster general until 1882. His son John, a Union army lieutenant, was killed in action October 1864, in Virginia.

George Trenholm—Senior partner in Fraser and Trenholm, he was one of the wealthiest men in the United States in 1860 and became the Confederacy's treasury secretary in 1864. He declared bankruptcy after the war.

Hornet's Nest—A wooded area at Shiloh, where Union troops held off the Confederate advance for six hours before being surrounded on three sides and surrendering two thousand troops. The delay afforded Generals Grant and Sherman vital time to reassemble Union troops.

James Bulloch—The Confederacy's most audacious secret agent, his orders were simple, the execution incredibly complex. He built a Confederate Navy in England and remained there after the war, fearing he would be hanged for piracy. His half-sister was President Theodore Roosevelt's mother.

Raphael Semmes—Captain, rear admiral of the Confederate navy, and brigadier general of the Confederate army (the only North American to hold both titles simultaneously), Semmes secured sixty-five prizes at sea. After the war he became a philosophy professor and practiced law, settling in Mobile, which gave him a magnificent house for his wartime service.

Lt. Arthur Sinclair—Third officer aboard the CSS *Alabama*, he wrote a memoir of his service and died in 1925.

Alexander McQueen—A hard-drinking Scot, he captained *Agrippina*, an English resupply ship for Confederate raiders.

Cahaba Prison—Nine thousand prisoners passed through "Castle Morgan" from 1862 to April 1865. In 1864 and 1865, three thousand men had an average living space of six square feet, by far the most crowded of any prison, North or South. After Appomattox, Union prisoners recently transferred to Camp Fisk on the Mississippi River were aboard the *Sultana*, a steamboat that caught fire in mid-river on the night April 27, 1865, in the greatest maritime disaster in US history. Of 2400 passengers on the grossly overloaded boat, 1600 died, hundreds of them soldiers who had survived years in Cahaba prison and were finally on their way home. In 1865, a flood inundated Cahaba town, and the next year Dallas County seat was removed to nearby Selma. Businesses and families followed. Within ten years, the prison and the town's houses were being dismantled and shipped away.

New York Draft Riots—From July 13 to 16, 1863, the largest civil insurrection in American history convulsed New York City, when largely poor Irish immigrants violently protested new draft laws, turning on the local black population in murderous rage. Order was restored by Union troops ordered to the city by President Lincoln.

Nathan Bedford Forrest—Land speculator, slave-trader, and later first grand wizard of the Ku Klux Klan, Forrest enlisted as a private in the Confederate Army and was lieutenant general by 1865. General Sherman described him as "the most remarkable man our Civil War produced on either side."

Richard Pierce—Standing nearly seven feet tall, with chest and shoulders "enormous for a man of his gigantic dimensions", the young private from the 3rd Tennessee Union Cavalry was so mild-mannered that his fellow inmates regarded him as an overgrown boy—until four muggers robbed his best friend. "Big Tennessee," as the prisoners called Pierce, tracked down the thugs and knocked all four of them senseless, putting an end to the muggers.

Amanda and Belle Gardner—Though "thorough Rebels," this mother and daughter lived near Cahaba Prison, smuggling food inside, providing books, and cutting up their home carpet for blankets to "relieve the suffering of these poor prisoners." (Quotes taken from letters of Union prisoners)

Jesse Hawes—Held captive at Cahaba Prison, Hawes escaped with two other men through the latrine trench but was captured after two days. He wrote a book about his experiences, *Cahaba—A Story of the Captive Boys in Blue,* published in 1888. Hawes died in 1901.

The rumor still persists that one Union soldier did make good his escape from Cahaba Prison, likely through the latrine trench, though exactly how remains a mystery.

Colonel Howard Henderson—A humane lawyer and Methodist minister, Henderson administered Cahaba prison and supervised numerous prisoner exchanges. In 1883, Ulysses Grant asked Reverend Henderson to preside at his mother's funeral.

Lt. Colonel Samuel Jones—subordinate to Colonel Henderson at Cahaba

Prison, he hated the Union, made prisoners stand in waist-deep flood waters for nine days in February 1865, and was suspected of murdering Yankee prisoners in the final days of the war.

Hawkins—a prison guard who shot three Union prisoners in one week from the walkway atop the stockade wall, "without the least shadow of reason or excuse for the murders," vanished after the war, perhaps into the swamp.